Easter, 1977, the date of

THE END OF THE WORLD

In an isolated French chateau, a group of friends have gathered. While they taste the wine in the deep cellar, a nuclear explosion incinerates the earth. They are survivors, Robinson Crusoes of a dead world, condemned to go back to man's roots and reinvent the means of existence, the ancient forgotten skills of primeval man.

Follow these loving, hating, hoping, fearing human beings as they try to build a new and better world—and as necessity diverts them from defense to aggression in a hauntingly familiar pattern . . .

MALEVIL

"a stunningly true, strong, intelligent book. Through its landscapes and its characters, we truly witness and participate in the horrible destruction of humankind and its slow, difficult, triumphant resurrection."   —Joseph Kessel

MALEVIL

by Robert Merle

Translated from the French by Derek Coltman

WARNER BOOKS

A Warner Communications Company

WARNER BOOKS EDITION

Copyright © 1972 by Editions Gallimard
Translation copyright © 1973 by Simon & Schuster, Inc.

ISBN 0-446-81658-2

Library of Congress Catalog Card Number: 73-11463

This Warner Books Edition is published by arrangement with Simon & Schuster, Inc.

Cover art by S. Fernandez

Warner Books, Inc., 75 Rockefeller Plaza, New York, N.Y. 10019

A Warner Communications Company

Printed in the United States of America

Not associated with Warner Press, Inc., of Anderson, Indiana

First Printing: May, 1975

Reissued: April, 1978

10 9 8 7 6 5 4

TO FERNAND MERLE

I

AT teachers college we had a professor who was insane about Proust and his *madeleine*. I studied that famous passage myself, under his guidance, as an admiring student. But time has dimmed my admiration, and now I find it very literary, that little cake. Oh, I know a taste or a tune can bring back some past moment and make it vivid in your memory again. But it never works for more than a few seconds. There is a brief illumination, then the curtain falls again and the present is back, tyrannical as ever. It's a very nice idea, recovering your whole past from just a little sponge cake dipped in weak tea, if only it were true.

What put me in mind of Proust's *madeleine* was the discovery, just the other day, at the back of a drawer, of an old, an extremely old, packet of pipe tobacco that must have belonged to my uncle. I gave it to Colin. Crazy with delight at the thought of a whiff of his favorite poison after so long, he promptly filled his pipe and lit it. I stayed watching him, and the moment I breathed in the aroma of those first few puffs, my uncle and the world of "before" came welling back up inside me. So clearly that it took my breath away. Though, as I say, it was only for a moment.

And Colin threw up. Either he had become unused to smoking or the tobacco was too old.

I envy Proust. At least he had a solid foundation under him while he explored his past: a certain present, an indubitable future. But for us the past is doubly past, our "time past" is doubly inaccessible, because included in it is the whole universe in which that time flowed. There

7

has been a complete break. The forward march of the ages has been interrupted. We no longer know where or when we are. Or whether there is to be any future at all.

Needless to say, we do what we can to conceal our anxiety beneath the mask of words. When we refer to that break in time we use periphrases. To begin with, following Meyssonnier, who was always one for official jargon, we used to say "Zero Day." But that was somehow still a little too military for our taste. And eventually we adopted a somewhat more veiled euphemism, first hit upon by La Menou with her peasant circumspection: "the day it happened." You couldn't find anything much easier to swallow than that, could you?

And so, still using words, we restored order into chaos and even managed to re-establish a linear progression in time. We now say, "before" or "the day it happened" or "after." Such are the little linguistic devices we've invented for ourselves. And the feeling of security they give us is exactly proportionate to their hypocrisy. Because "after" really means both our uncertain present and also our hypothetical future.

Even without *madeleines* or pipe smoke, we think about it a lot, that world "before." Each in his little corner. In general conversation we all exercise a kind of censorship on one another; such journeys into the past are scarcely helpful to our survival. We avoid allowing them to proliferate.

But once alone, things are otherwise. Although I am barely in my forties, ever since "the day it happened" I have a tendency toward insomnia, like an old man. And it is at night that I do my remembering. Though what I actually remember varies from one night to the next. In order to exculpate myself in my own eyes for this self-indulgence, I tell myself that since the world "before" no longer exists except inside my own head, that means it would cease to exist altogether if I didn't think about it.

Recently I have begun to make a distinction between random memories and habitual memories. Because I have finally grasped the difference between them. The habitual memories are the ones I am using to convince myself of my own identity, a conviction I stand very much in need of in this "after" in which almost all recognizable landmarks have disappeared. And that, really, is what I spend my sleepless nights doing: constantly tacking to and fro across that desert, across those shifting sands, across that past now doubly past, creating landmarks to stop me losing myself. And when I say "losing myself," I also mean losing my identity.

The year 1948 was one of those landmarks. I was twelve. I had just been placed top for our district—ineffable glory—in the national exams. And in the kitchen of La Grange Forte, our little farm, I was trying to persuade my parents over the midday meal that we should clear more land, a course of action that seemed to me the merest common sense. Like everyone else in those parts, we had no more than twenty-five acres of good quality grazing and arable land. The rest was all woods, and useless woods too, since we no longer gathered the chestnuts or used the leaves for fodder.

My father and mother were scarcely listening to me. I might as well have been talking to clods of earth. Which in fact they somewhat resembled, both being brown-haired and brown-eyed. I was brown-haired but had blue eyes like my uncle.

Looking back at that scene over the years, with adult eyes, I understand it better now, I think, and I find it very unpleasant.

My mother, for example. A self-righteous nagger and a whiner. She suffered from the besetting sin of the mediocre. She was a chronic complainer, because it gave her an excuse for her totally hidebound attitude to life. Given that everything in the world was a mess, why move even so much as a little finger to change it? My suggestion that they clear some of the woods caused her immediate umbrage.

"And who's going to find the money?" She sneered. "Are you going to pay for the bulldozer?"

Apart from the scorn in her tone, there was the irritation of knowing perfectly well that the sums entered in their savings bank book were being devalued all the time by inflation. I knew they were being devalued, because my uncle explained it to me. So I explained it to her in my turn, without mentioning my uncle. Wasted caution.

My father listened, but kept quiet. My arguments annoyed my mother even more. Even though they simply slid off that hard red scalp with its thin covering of hair. She wouldn't even look at me.

She addressed herself to my father over my head. "That boy is getting more like your brother Samuel every day," she remarked. "Always full of himself. Giving lessons. And ever since he passed his exam, a head like a pumpkin."

My two little sisters, Paulette and Pélagie, began giggling, so I lashed out with one foot under the table. Pélagie shrieked.

"And completely without feelings as well," my mother said.

And we continued to hear about my lack of feelings at length. The whole of the time it took to eat two platefuls of soup, pour wine into the remains of the second, and then drink that. My mother had a bookkeeper's mind, so my defects were reitemized and retotaled every time a new error was added to the list. The fact that they had already been punished and paid for made no difference. Never forgotten, never forgiven, my past crimes never weighed any less.

This litany of past sins was poured out, moreover, in the plaintive tones I loathed so much: vindictiveness coated with a whining slime. Pélagie was shrieking, Paulette—whom I hadn't so much as touched—was whimpering. Then a climax: Pélagie pulled up her skirt and showed a bright red mark on her shin.

My mother's whine rose an octave to a piercing wail. "And you, Simon, what you are waiting for? Why don't you teach him a lesson, that son of yours?"

Because, of course, I was my father's son, not hers. But my father remained silent. That was his role in that household of ours. Because my mother, impervious to argument, a stranger to logic, never paid even the slightest attention when he did speak. She had reduced him to silence, and almost to slavery, by the simple expedient of her own verbal flux.

"Do you hear me, Simon?"

I laid down my knife and fork and eased my buttocks off my chair, preparing to dodge my father's slap. But still he made no move. It occurred to me that it must have been taking some courage on his part, since he was thereby laying up for himself a curtain lecture, in the conjugal bed last thing at night, during which all his own sins would be interminably reiterated in their turn.

But it was a cowardly courage. I once saw my uncle—a wondrous sight!—rise up in thunder and blast his wife, who was a woman very much resembling my own mother, for the two brothers had married two sisters. I couldn't help wondering what it was about her family that made them all so mean, so ugly, so whining, so greasy-haired.

Only my aunt hadn't been able to stand the pace. She'd died at the age of forty, out of sheer hatred for life. And my uncle started making up for lost time, running after pretty school leavers. I didn't blame him. I did the same when I came of man's estate.

As no clout arrived from my father's direction, my anxiety waned. No slap from my mother's side either. Not that the desire to impart one was lacking, but I had just recently devised a very effective parry with one elbow that succeeded in simultaneously avoiding any obvious lack of respect and also causing acute pain to her attacking forearm. Not exactly a passive parry either, since my own arm was energetically advanced to meet hers.

"As a punishment," my mother announced after a short pause for reflection, "you shan't have any tart. That will teach you to torment your poor little sisters."

My father went tch tch with his tongue. But that was as far as he would go. I maintained a proud silence. And then, taking advantage of a moment when my father's sad nose was lowered over his plate and my mother was away from the table fetching the delicious concoction that had been simmering on the kitchen range since the evening before, I pulled my most hideous face at Pélagie in retaliation for her shrieking. She immediately set up

11

a fresh hullabaloo and whimpered to her mother, in her limited vocabulary, that I had "looked" at her.

"Good heavens," I said, gazing round the table with eyes all innocence (an innocence made doubly effective by their blueness), "aren't I even allowed to look at you now?"

Silence. I made a show of having difficulty in forcing down my mother's excellent ratatouille. I even pushed this display of indifference to the point of refusing the second helping that duty forced her to offer me. And while the rest of them sat enjoying every savory mouthful, I kept my eyes fixed on a flyblown engraving hanging on the wall above the sideboard. It depicted "The Return of the Prodigal Son."

The well-behaved son sat in one corner of the frame looking very glum indeed. I didn't blame him either. Because there he was, he'd spent his whole time slogging away to help his father, and he wasn't even allowed a skinny lamb to give his friends a blowout. Whereas that other little runt, no sooner did he turn up again at the farm gate, after wasting all his substance on his fancy pieces, than they just couldn't wait to slaughter the fatted calf.

Gritting my teeth, I thought, It's just the same with my sisters and me. Soft as dough and silly as sheep the both of them. And yet there's my mother always coddling them, flooding them with eau de Cologne, combing their horrible hair, curling it into those silly curls with her curling iron. I snickered to myself. Last Sunday, stealthy as a fox, I had crept up behind them and thrown dusty spiders' webs all over those pretty curls.

That happy memory was just enough to hold me back from the brink of despair as my eyes crept down from the engraving of the Prodigal Son to the apricot tart, whose aroma I could scent and whose golden curving side I could just make out on top of the sideboard. At that moment my mother rose from her chair, not without a certain ceremonial air, and placed it on the table—right in front of my nose.

I immediately got up, pushed my hands into my pockets, and made for the door.

"What's this?" my father said in the slightly husky voice of someone who doesn't use it much. "Don't you want your share of tart?"

I felt no gratitude for his belated counterorder. I swiveled around without taking my hands out of my pockets, and said curtly over my shoulder, "I'm not hungry."

"Now then!" my mother immediately broke in. "That's your father you're speaking to, my lad!"

I didn't stay for the rest. The interminable rest. I knew she was intent on ruining my father's tart for him now, just as she'd deprived me of mine.

I emerged into the farmyard and began wandering up and down, fists clenched tight in my pockets. Down in Malejac people said that my father was "as goodhearted as good white bread." And that was just the trouble. Too much soft white and not enough crust.

I wandered on in angry, bitter meditation. It was impossible to hold any kind of reasonable conversation with that stupid bitch (that was the term I used). She treated me like a fool, made me a laughingstock in front of those bleating sisters of mine, and to cap it all she dared to punish me. I was not about to forget that tart. Not for its own sake. But because of the humiliation. Fists still clenched in my pockets, I stalked to and fro across the yard, squaring my already broad shoulders. The nerve of it, depriving the district's champion scholar of his dessert!

It was the proverbial last straw. I was boiling with icy rage, I'd had enough. And thirty years later I can still recapture the taste of that rage. With hindsight, I have the impression I was a pretty lousy Oedipus. My Jocasta was in no danger at all, even in thought. Not that I didn't work it out, my regulation complex, but not on my mother, on Adelaide, who kept our local grocery shop in Malejac. Not only was she always generous with her merry laughter and her candies, she was also an abundantly built blonde with breasts that could answer up to any daydream. And as to my regulation "male identification"—what terrible jargon—that was made not with my own father but with my uncle. Who in fact—although I didn't know it then— resided in the very heart of Adelaide's good graces. So

13

without knowing it, I did in fact possess a real family side by side with the one I was rejecting.

And a third one too, a family which is still dear to me and which I created myself: the Club. A supersecret society with seven members that I founded during my primary days in Malejac (population 401, twelfth-century church), and of which I was in my turn the father, constantly displaying in all my fearless feats that spirit of enterprise so lacking in my father, and firm, ah yes, a hand as firm as iron beneath my velvet glove.

My decision had been taken. Perpetually insulted here, I would take refuge in the bosom of that other family. I waited till my father had gone upstairs for his siesta and my mother was busy washing the dishes with her two ringleted milksop daughters clinging to her skirts. I slipped up to my garret room, hurriedly filled my haversack (a present from my uncle), and having buckled it up, threw it out onto the woodpile outside my window. Before making my escape I left a note on my table. It was addressed, very formally, to Monsieur Simon Comte, farmer, La Grange Forte, Malejac.

Dear Father,
   I am leaving. I am not treated in this house the way I deserve.
   Lots of love,

Emmanuel.

And while my poor father dozed behind his closed shutters, unaware as yet that his farm was already without a successor, I was pedaling through the warm sunlight, haversack on my back, toward Malevil.

Malevil was a big thirteenth-century castle, half in ruins, perched halfway up a steep cliff looking out across the little valley of the two Rhunes. Its owner had abandoned it to its own devices, and ever since a block of stone had fallen from the battlements of the keep and killed a tourist it had been made illegal to enter it. The Ministry of Works had put up two large notices to this effect, and the mayor of Malejac had closed the sole access road along the side of the hill with four strands of barbed wire. Reinforcing this barbed wire, though owing nothing to

14

the local council, there were also fifty yards of impenetrable brambles, growing steadily thicker every year, all along the old track that ran up the side of the cliff toward Malevil on its dizzy height and separated it from the hill on which my uncle's farm, Les Sept Fayards, then stood.

There lay my goal. Under my inspired leadership, the Club had violated all the taboos. We had devised an invisible gate in the barbed wire, then hollowed out a tunnel through the gigantic brambles, concealed from the track by a cunningly placed bend. On the second floor of the castle keep, from which the actual boards had long since disappeared, we made a catwalk by nailing old planks from my uncle's junk shed across from joist to joist. In this way we were able to make our way across the vast main room to a small room at the far side, and Meyssonnier, already very much the handyman thanks to having the run of his father's workshop, had put in a window frame and a door with a padlock.

The keep stood too high to be damp. The ribbed vaulting of its roof had resisted the ravages of time. And our den contained a fireplace, an old mattress covered with sacks, a table, and stools.

Our secret had remained undiscovered. It was twelve months now since we had first fitted out these premises, unsuspected by any adult. On my way there I had passed word of my intentions to Colin, who would pass it in his turn to Meyssonnier, who would pass it to Peyssou, who would then tell the others. I was not going into exile unprepared.

I spent that afternoon in my cell, then the night and all the next day. It was less delightful than I'd expected. It was July, the other Club members were all working on various farms, so I wouldn't be seeing them till the evening. And I didn't dare stick my nose out of Malevil. They must have already set the police on my tail down at La Grange Forte.

At seven o'clock there was a knock on the clubroom door. I was expecting big Peyssou, who was due to bring me food supplies. I had already unlocked the padlock on the door, and without getting up from the mattress on which I was uncomfortably stretched with a book of

15

bloody adventure stories in one hand, I yelled out, "Come in, you great nit!"

It was my Uncle Samuel. He was a Protestant, hence the Biblical first name. He stood there, life-size, dressed in an old checked shirt, open to show his muscled neck, and a pair of old Army issue riding breeches (he had served in the cavalry), taller than the open doorway, his forehead touching the stone lintel, and gazing in at me with a deep frown above his smiling eyes.

I freeze on that frame. Because the boy lying on the mattress is me. But the man, my uncle standing in the doorway, he is me too. Uncle Samuel was then more or less the same age as I am now, and everyone agrees that I am very much like him to look at. So that in this scene, during which very few words were exchanged, I have the impression of seeing the boy I once was confronting the man I have become.

In describing Uncle Samuel I shall also be describing myself. He was of above average height, very thickset, yet with slim hips, a square face, tanned complexion, eyebrows black as soot, and blue eyes. Most people in Malejac surrounded themselves from morning till night with a constant murmur of comforting, meaningless words. But my uncle never spoke when he had nothing to say. And when he did speak, he did so briefly, always straight to the point. And he was equally thrifty with his gestures.

It was this decisiveness of his that most attracted me to him. Because at home, my father, my mother, my sisters, everything was always so messy somehow. Their thoughts so muddled. Their speech like cobwebs everywhere.

I also admired my uncle's spirit of enterprise. He had cleared the maximum possible acreage on his farm for cultivation. He had divided up one arm of the river that ran through it into tanks, and now bred trout in them. He had set up a score or so of beehives. He had even bought a secondhand Geiger counter to prospect for uranium in the volcanic rocks that pushed up here and there through the soil on one side of his hill. And when "ranches" and riding stables began appearing everywhere, he promptly sold all his cows and replaced them with horses.

"Knew I'd find you here," my uncle said.

I stared up at him, dumfounded. But we understood each other, Uncle Samuel and me. After a moment he replied to my tongue-tied gaze. "The planks. The planks you used last summer from my junk shed. They were too heavy for you to carry. You dragged them. I followed the trail."

So he'd known for a whole year! And he'd never breathed a word to anyone, not even to me.

"I had a look around," my uncle went on. "The keep battlements are safe enough. There won't be any more falls."

I was flooded with gratitude. Uncle Samuel had been keeping watch over me, but from a distance, without telling me, without bothering me. I looked at him, but he avoided my gaze. He didn't want to get sentimental. He grabbed one of the stools, checked that it was strong enough to bear his weight, and sat down, straddling it as though it were a horse. Then he came straight to the point, at a gallop.

"Now listen, Emmanuel, they haven't said anything about it yet to anyone. And they haven't told the police." A tiny smile. "You know what *she* is like. Terrified what people will say. So here's what I suggest. I'll have you over to live with me till the vacation's over. When school begins again, there's no problem. You'll be going to La Roque as a boarder."

A pause.

"What about the weekends?" I said.

My uncle's eyes sparkled. Like him, I knew how to say things without speaking them. If I was already back at school in my mind, that meant I had agreed to finish my vacation with him.

"Spend them at my place, if you like," he said, the brisk words accompanied by a leisurely gesture.

A short pause.

"Though you must go over and eat now and then at La Grange Forte."

Just often enough, sweet mother, to keep up appearances. I saw immediately that everyone stood to gain by this arrangement.

"Right then," my uncle said as he rose abruptly to his feet. "If you agree, pack up your things and come down after me to the river meadow. I'm just bringing in some hay for the horses."

He was already gone, and I was already filling my haversack.

Once out of the bramble tunnel and through the gate in the barbed wire, I hurtled at full speed down the bed of the dried-up stream that ran between the sheer cliff of Malevile and the dome of my uncle's hill. Overjoyed at being out of my gloomy lair. The trees that had taken root everywhere in the cracks of the ruined walls made it dark with their overhanging branches, and I took in a great breath of relief as I emerged into the bright valley of the Rhunes.

It lay in late sunlight, the sunlight between six and seven, the most beautiful time of all. That was something I'd learned, since my uncle had pointed it out. There was something gentle in the air. The meadows were greener, the shadows longer, the light golden. I pedaled on toward my uncle's red tractor. Behind it was the wagon with its great yellowish mound of hay. And beyond, two parallel lines, the poplars along the banks of the Rhune, with their perpetually dancing silver-gray leaves. I loved the sound they made: like a gentle summer shower.

Without speaking, my uncle took hold of my bike and tied it with a length of rope on top of the hay. He got up onto the tractor seat while I clambered up beside him and settled myself against the mudguard. Not a word was spoken. Not even an exchange of glances. But from the slight quiver of his hands I could sense how happy he was—never having had a child by my scrawny aunt—to be driving a son of his own back home to Les Sept Fayards at last.

La Menou stood waiting for me at the front door, her emaciated arms folded over an absent bosom, her little death's-head face wrinkled into a smile. Her weakness for me was in inverse proportion to the strength of her antagonism toward my mother. And the antagonism she had

18

also entertained against my aunt, while she was still alive. But don't get any ideas. La Menou didn't sleep with my uncle. Nor was she his servant. She had land of her own. He brought in her hay for her, she ran his house, he fed her.

La Menou was thin too, like my aunt, but merry with it. She never whined, she trounced you with relish. Eighty pounds, black clothes included. But at the bottom of those hollow eye sockets her little black button eyes sparkled with a love of life. Though virtuous, virtuous in every way, except when she was a young girl. And in particular, thrifty. So thrifty, in fact, my uncle claimed, that she had starved herself to the point where she had no bottom left to sit on.

And a tiger when it came to work. Arms like matchsticks, but when she was out hoeing her vines, the rows she could do in an hour! And while she hoed, her only son, Momo, then about to turn eighteen, would be out there pulling along a toy train on a length of string and going choo-choo.

To add spice to her life, La Menou kept up a perpetual squabble with my uncle. But he was her god. And his divinity overflowed onto me. So to welcome me to Les Sept Fayards she had cooked a dinner fit to burst your belt. And as its culmination, with deliberate malice, she produced an enormous tart.

If I were making a film I would move in to a close-up of that tart. Followed by a fade and mix into a flashback: 1947, summer the year before. Another "milestone."

I was eleven. I was falling in love with Adelaide, organizing the new premises for the Club in Malevil, and arriving at a new attitude toward religion.

I have already mentioned the role played by the owner of Malejac's grocery store in my awakening. She was thirty, and her very maturity hypnotized me. I might also add that even today, despite so many experiences to the contrary, I still, thanks to her, associate kindness with abundant curves, and thinness, thanks to you-know-who, with lack of feelings. A pity that's not my theme. I should like to tell you about all the fevers excited by all those luscious curves. When the Abbé Lebas, beginning to show concern

19

over the use to which we were putting our attributes, talked to us in our catechism class about "sins of the flesh," I was unable to conceive that the flesh he was talking about was my own, since I was all muscles and sinews, so I immediately applied the expression to Adelaide, and the idea of sin began to seem delightful.

Nor was I even put out by the fact that my idol, although so generously proportioned, had the reputation of being inclined to lightness. On the contrary, that seemed only to augur well for my own future. Though the years that were to make a rooster out of the cockerel I was at eleven seemed to stretch unendingly ahead.

Meanwhile, that summer at least, I had plenty to occupy me. The "war" was at its height. The valiant heretic captain Emmanuel Comte, besieged inside Malevil with his co-religionists, was defending the castle against the sinister Meyssonnier, head of the Catholic League. I say sinister because his aim was to sack the castle and put all the heretics inside it—male and female alike—to the sword. The women were represented by bundles of kindling, the children by somewhat smaller bundles.

Victory was not a foregone conclusion, it depended upon the fortunes of battle. Anyone who was struck or even grazed by a spear, an arrow, a stone, or, in hand-to-hand fighting, by the point of a sword, had to exclaim, "I am slain!" and fall to the ground. It was permissible, once the battle had been won, to cut the throats of the wounded and kill the women, but not, as big Peyssou did on one occasion, to hurl oneself upon one of the more sizable bundles of wood with the intention of raping it. We were hard and pure, like our ancestors. In public anyway. Lechery was a private matter.

One afternoon, when fortune sat on my helm, I sent an arrow winging down from the ramparts straight into Meyssonnier's chest. He fell. I pushed my head through my arrow slit, brandished my fist, and yelled in a voice of thunder, "Death to you, Catholic swine!"

This terrible cry froze the assailants in their tracks. In their stupor they forgot to cover themselves, and our arrows laid them all low forthwith.

At that I emerged with slow stride from the main

gate, dispatched my lieutenants Colin and Giraud to finish off Dumont and Condat, then thrust my sword through Meyssonnier's throat.

As for Peyssou, first I cut off those organs of which he was so proud, then I thrust my sword into his breast and worked it in and out of the wound, asking him "in a voice like cold steel" if it gave him pleasure to be raped. I always kept Peyssou till last, his death throes were always magnificent.

The heat of the day and its battle over, we were once more gathered around the table in our den inside the keep for a last cigarette and the piece of chewing gum that would remove its taint from our breath.

And I could see immediately, just from the way he was chewing, that Meyssonnier was put out. Beneath the narrow forehead, topped by its austere fence of brushcut hair, his gray eyes were flickering nonstop.

"What's up, Meyssonnier?" I asked in a friendly tone. "Is something wrong? Are you mad about something?"

The eyelids flickered even more rapidly. He was hesitant to criticize me, because he usually got the worst of it in the end. But the duty to do so was there all the same, pressing in on his narrow skull from all sides.

"What's wrong," he burst out finally, "is that you shouldn't have called me a Catholic swine!"

There was a murmur of agreement from Dumont and Condat, and though Colin and Giraud kept silent out of loyalty, their very silence held a hint of disapproval that did not escape me. Only Peyssou, his great dumpling face split by a wide grin, remained wholly serene.

"What?" I cried with a brazen show of surprise. "But that was part of the game! In the game I have to be the Protestant; you can't expect me to start saying nice things about the Catholic who's coming to murder me."

"The game doesn't excuse everything," Meyssonnier replied firmly. "There are limits, even in a game. For example, you pretend to cut off Peyssou's you-know-what, but you don't really cut them off."

Peyssou's smile grew wider.

"And besides, it was never in the rules to insult one

another," Meyssonnier added with his eyes glued on the tabletop.

"And especially about religion," Dumont put in.

I looked across at Dumont. I knew him and his touchy spots only too well. "I didn't insult you," I said, hoping to drive a wedge between him and Meyssonnier. "I was talking to Meyssonnier."

"It comes to the same thing," Dumont said, "since I'm a Catholic too."

I protested indignantly, "But so am I!"

"Exactly," Meyssonnier cut in. "You oughtn't to speak ill of your own religion."

Whereupon Peyssou lumbered into the argument with the dismissive comment that "the whole thing is a fuss about nothing, because being a Catholic or a Protestant comes to the same thing really."

He was immediately jumped on from all sides. His specialities were brute strength and filthy-mindedness! Let him stick to them and keep out of religion, since he didn't understand it!

"I'll bet you don't even know your ten commandments," Meyssonnier said scornfully.

"I bet I do then," Peyssou retorted.

He stood up, as though he were at catechism class, and began reciting them full tilt, but he came to a dead stop after the fourth. He was hooted down and collapsed onto his stool again covered in shame.

Peyssou's diversion had given me time to think.

"Right," I said with a guileless straight-from-the-shoulder air. "I agree I was wrong. Because I'm not like some people; when I am in the wrong I admit it right away. So there you are, I was wrong. Does that make you feel better?"

"It's not enough just to say you were wrong," Meyssonnier said peevishly.

"What do you mean?" I exclaimed indignantly. "You don't expect me to start getting down on my knees to you just because I called you a swine?"

"I don't give a damn about you calling me a swine," Meyssonnier said. "I'm quite prepared to call you the

22

same thing. But what you actually called me was a *Catholic swine*."

"Exactly," I came back. "It wasn't you I was insulting, it was the Catholic religion."

"Yes, that's true," Dumont said.

I glanced across at him. Meyssonnier had just lost his strongest ally.

"Oh, for heaven's sake," little Colin burst out suddenly, turning to Meyssonnier, "this whole thing's getting to be a big bore. Comte has admitted he's in the wrong. What more do you want?"

Meyssonnier was about to open his mouth when Peyssou, delighted at a chance for revenge, threw out both arms in a wild gesture and exclaimed, "The whole thing is a load of manure!"

"Listen, Meyssonnier," I said with the air of a person being scrupulously fair. "I've called you a swine, you've called me a swine, so there you are. We're quits."

Meyssonnier went red. "I didn't call you a swine," he said indignantly.

I looked around at the other members of the Club, shook my head sadly, and said nothing.

"You said, 'I'm quite prepared to call you the same thing,' though," Giraud reminded him.

"But that's not the same thing at all," Meyssonnier protested, fully aware of the vast difference between a contingent insult and an insult that has actually been delivered, but powerless to express it.

"You're quibbling, Meyssonnier," I said sadly.

"I don't care," Meyssonnier cried in a last desperate bid at defiance. "You insulted the Catholic religion, and you can't say you didn't!"

"But I haven't said I didn't!" I replied, spreading my hands in a gesture of wounded sincerity. "In fact I explicitly admitted that I did, only a moment ago. Didn't I?"

"Yes, yes, you did," the other Club members cried.

"Very well," I continued in intrepid tones, "since I have insulted the Catholic religion, I shall go and make a clean breast of it to the proper authority." ("The proper authority" was a phrase I'd picked up from my uncle.)

The Club members gazed at me in consternation.

"You don't mean you're going to drag the curé into our private quarrels!" Dumont cried.

Because it was a generally held opinion in the Club that the Abbé Lebas had a twisted mind. At confession he had what was for us a very humiliating way of treating all our sins as the merest trifles—with one exception.

The dialogue always went as follows: "Father, I confess to committing the sin of pride."

"Yes, yes. What else?"

"Father, I confess to having spoken ill of my neighbor."

"Yes, yes. What else?"

"Father, I confess to having lied to my teacher."

"Yes, Yes. What else?"

"Father, I confess to having stolen ten francs from my mother's purse."

"Yes, yes. What else?"

"Father, I confess to having done dirty things."

"Ah ha!" the Abbé Lebas would cry. "Now we come to it!"

And the interrogation began: "With a girl? With a boy? With an animal? Alone? Naked or with your clothes on? Standing up or lying down? On your bed? In the privy? In the woods? In the classroom? How many times? And what did you think about while you were doing it?" ("Well, I just think that I'm doing it" is Peyssou's stock answer.) "Whom do you think about? A girl? Another boy? A grown-up woman? A female relative?"

When the Club was founded, one of the first things we swore was to keep the curé in total ignorance of our activities, since it was clearly impossible for him ever to believe in the innocence of a secret society that held clandestine meetings in a place whose existence was unknown to any adult. And yet, in the sense the abbé gave that word, "innocent" the Club most certainly was.

I shrugged my shoulders. "Of course I'm not going running to tell the curé about it. And let him in on the whole thing? What do you think? I said I'm going to make a clean breast of it to the proper authority. And that's what I'm going to do."

I got up and said in a curt, lofty tone, "Are you coming, Colin?"

24

"Yes," Colin answered, proud at having been singled out.

And taking his cue from me, he strode out with a purposeful air while the Club members gazed after us in amazement.

Our bikes were hidden in the undergrowth down the hill from Malevil.

"Malejac, pronto," I ordered laconically.

We rode two abreast, but without speaking, even on the flat. I was very fond of little Colin, still am, and during his first term or so at school I stood up for him a lot, because among all those great tough lads, already driving their family tractors at twelve years old, he was so slender and slight, like a dragonfly, with his bright, mischievous eyes, his sharply peaked eyebrows, and a sly mouth with corners tilted up toward his temples.

I had counted on finding the church deserted, but we had scarcely settled ourselves in the special catechism class pew before the Abbé Lebas emerged with shuffling steps and bent back from the vestry. With deep distaste, I watched his long drooping nose and bootlike chin emerge from behind a pillar into the growing dimness of the nave.

As soon as he caught sight of us, at such an unusual hour and in such an unlikely place, he swooped down the aisle like a vulture after carrion and fixed his piercing eyes on ours.

"And what are you two doing here?" he demanded abruptly.

"I've come to say a little prayer," I answered, looking up at him with my bluest eyes, hands modestly folded over my crotch. Then, in the most pious of tones, I added, "As you said we should."

"And what about you?" he asked sharply, looking at Colin.

"Me too," Colin said, though his mischievous mouth and sparkling eyes robbed his words of their intended solemnity.

His black eyes even further darkened by suspicion, the abbé scrutinized us one after the other. "You're sure you didn't really come for confession?" he asked, turning to me.

25

"Quite sure, Father," I told him firmly. And added, "I only confessed on Saturday."

He straightened up angrily and said with a darkly meaningful look, "And are you going to tell me that you haven't sinned since Saturday?"

That flustered me. Because unfortunately the abbé was not unaware of my incestuous passion for Adelaide. Incestuous, that is, in my own mind, ever since the day the abbé had said to me, "Aren't you ashamed of yourself! A woman old enough to be your mother!" And then, for some unfathomable reason: "And twice as heavy as you are!" Because love, after all, is never a question of weights and measures. Particularly when nothing is actually happening apart from "evil thoughts."

"Oh, of course. But nothing important," I said.

"Nothing important!" he said, clasping his hands in shock. "What, for instance?"

"Well," I said, casting about at random, "I've lied to my father."

"Yes, yes," the abbé said. "And what else?"

I stared at him. Surely he didn't intend to make me make confession right off like this, without my consent, in the middle of the nave! And what was more, in front of Colin!

"Nothing else," I said firmly.

The abbé threw me a piercing glance, but I parried it with the shining surface of my limpid eyes and it sank harmlessly down either side of his long nose.

"What about you?" he asked, turning to Colin.

"The same thing," Colin said.

"The same thing!" The abbé sneered. "So you too lied to your father! And you consider that's not important!"

"No, Father," Colin answered. "It was actually to my mother I told my lie." And the folds at the corners of his mouth curved up toward his temples.

I was afraid the abbé was going to explode and drive us out of the temple. But he managed to control himself. "I see," he said, still addressing himself to Colin but in an almost menacing tone. "So the idea came into your head, just like that, to come to church and say a little prayer?"

I opened my mouth to answer him, but the abbé cut me short. "Keep quiet, Comte, do you hear? I know you! Always ready with an answer! Just let Colin speak!"

"No, Father," Colin said. "It wasn't me that had the idea. It was Comte."

"Oh, so it was Comte, eh? Excellent! Excellent! Even more likely, I must say," the abbé said with heavy irony. "And where were you when this idea of his occurred?"

"On our bikes," Colin said. "We were just riding along, not doing anything wrong, when suddenly Comte said to me, 'Hey, who don't we go to church and say a little prayer.' 'Good idea,' I said. And that was that," Colin concluded, the corners of his mouth twinkling upward quite unconsciously.

"'Hey, why don't we go to church and say a little prayer!'" the abbé parodied in a voice of suppressed fury.

Then quick as a sword thrust: "And where were you coming from on your bikes?"

"From Les Sept Fayards," Colin said without a moment's hesitation.

Which was a stroke of genius on his part, because if there was one person in Malejac the Abbé Lebas absolutely couldn't go to in order to check how we spent our time, it was my uncle.

The abbé's black glance flicked from my transparent eyes to Colin's gondola smile. He was in the position of a musketeer in the middle of a duel watching his sword sent spinning out of his hand. Or that at any rate was the image I thought up later when giving an account of our conversation to the Club.

"Very well, then, say your little prayer!" the abbé finally shot at us sourly. "Heaven knows you need to, the both of you!"

Whereupon he turned his back on us, as though abandoning us to the Evil One. And shuffling away once more, back bowed, pushing his ponderous profile in front of him, he regained the vestry and slammed the door behind him.

When all was once more silent, I folded my arms on my chest, fixed my eyes on the little lamp over the altar,

27

and said very quietly, but so that Colin could hear me, "God, I'm sorry I insulted Your religion."

If the door of the tabernacle had opened at that moment, bathing us with light, and if a deep, resonant voice like a radio announcer's had addressed me, saying, My child, I forgive you, and as a punishment you must recite me ten Paternosters, I wouldn't have been in the slightest surprised. But nothing happened whatever, and I was obliged to imagine Him speaking in my voice and impose the ten Paternosters on myself. I was just on the point of adding ten Ave Marias, just for symmetry's sake, when I decided I'd better not, on the grounds that if God were by any chance Protestant after all, then He wouldn't be exactly delighted with me for giving the Virgin Mary equal rights.

I hadn't finished my third Paternoster before Colin gave me a dig in the ribs. "What's up with you? Aren't we going now?"

I turned my head and eyed him sternly. "Wait! I have to do the penance He's given me, don't I?"

Colin was silent. And continued silent thereafter. Forever mute on the subject. No surprise. No questions.

And the question that comes into my own mind after all these years is nothing to do with my sincerity then. At eleven everything is a game, so the problem doesn't even arise. What strikes me now, what I remember most is the audacity I displayed in conceiving the idea that it was possible to pass over the Abbé Lebas's head and establish relations directly with God.

April 1970: the next milestone. A jump of more than twenty years. It takes a slight effort to abandon my short pants and put on the long trousers of my man's estate. I am thirty-four, headmaster of Malejac school, and my uncle is sitting opposite me in his kitchen smoking his pipe. His changeover to horses has proved a success, perhaps too big a success even. In order to expand he needs to buy more land, and any land he sets his sights on—he is thought to be rich—doubles in price the moment he appears on the scene.

"Take Berthaud. You know Berthaud. Two years he

28

kept me on the hook. And then asked me a fortune! Though it didn't matter that much. I never gave a pile of horse dung for Berthaud's farm really. It was never anything but a last resort. No, Emmanuel, what I really wanted, I'll tell you straight, what I wanted was Malevil."

"Malevil!"

"Yes," my uncle said. "Malevil."

"But why?" I said, dumfounded. "It's nothing but woods and ruins."

"Ah ha," my uncle said, "I can see I'd better set you straight about what Malevil is. Malevil is a hundred and seventy acres of first-grade agricultural land that has been grown over for less than fifty years with undergrowth. Malevil is a vineyard that in my grandpa's day was producing the best wine in the whole district. It all has to be replanted, that I grant, but the land is there. Malevil is a cellar without a rival in all Malejac: stone vaulting, cool, and as big as the school playground. Malevil is an outer wall against which you can build any number of stables and stalls with almost no trouble, with stone already quarried, already there; all you need do is bend down and pick it up. And on top of that, Malevil is just next door. It borders on Les Sept Fayards. Almost a continuation of it, you might say," he added with unconscious humor, as though the castle had once belonged to the farm.

It was after our evening meal. My uncle was sitting sideways to the kitchen table, pumping away at his pipe, his belt let out one hole over his lean belly.

I looked across at him and he saw that I had guessed what came next.

"Yes, you're right!" he said. "I bungled the deal." Another suck at his pipe. "I told Grimaud what I thought of him."

"Grimaud?"

"The count's business agent. Since he had the count's ear, and since the count (a) never left Paris and (b) wouldn't do a thing without Grimaud, Grimaud wanted a handout for himself. He called it 'negotiation fees.' "

"He obviously has a smooth turn of phrase."

"I'm glad you think so too," my uncle said. He sucked at his pipe.

"Big?"

"Two million francs."

"Wow!"

"Not little anyway. But there was room for discussion. And instead of discussing it I wrote to the count, and the count, idiot that he is, sent my letter on to Grimaud. And Grimaud came to see me to complain." A sigh emerged in a gust of smoke.

"Mistake number two. And this one irreparable; as I say, I told Grimaud what I thought of him. Which proves that you can still make stupid errors even at sixty. In business you must never tell people what you think of them, Emmanuel. Just remember that. Not even when they're crooks. Because even a crook, crook though he is, always has his vanity. From that day on there was no hope. Grimaud blocked every attempt I made. I wrote twice to the count again. He never replied."

There was a silence. I knew my uncle too well to associate myself in words with his inner regrets. He didn't like commiseration. And anyway, before long he shrugged his shoulders, put up his feet on a chair, hooked his left thumb inside his belt and went on.

"Well, what's botched is botched. After all, I can live without Malevil. And I don't do so badly. I'm making enough money, and above all I do as I please. There's no one over me, or even beside me, to muck me about. I find life interesting. And since my health is good, there's no reason why I shouldn't go on for another twenty years or so like this. I couldn't ask for anything more."

Even that, however, was apparently asking too much. That conversation took place one Sunday evening. And the Sunday after, coming back from a football match in La Roque, Uncle Samuel was killed with both my parents in an automobile accident.

It was no more than nine miles from Malejac to La Roque, but the journey was still long enough for a long-distance bus to smash his little Renault against a tree. Normally, Uncle Samuel would have gone to the match with his two apprentices in his Peugeot station wagon, but that was being serviced at the time, and the little Citroën pickup he used for the horse van was out on a delivery job because one of his customers had insisted on a Sunday delivery. And ordinarily, I too should have been in the little Renault, but that very morning one of my older pupils had injured himself very badly on his motor scooter, and I had gone into the nearby town that afternoon to make inquiries about him at the hospital.

If the Abbé Lebas had still been alive he would have said, It was providence that saved you, Emmanuel. Yes, but why me? The frightening thing about explanations of that sort is that they never do anything but postpone the problem. It would be better just to say nothing. Yet that's just what you can't do. The longing to comprehend is so strong, no matter how stupid and meaningless you know what has happened to be.

They brought the three mangled bodies back to Les Sept Fayards, and La Menou and I sat with them waiting for my sisters to arrive. The vigil was spent without a tear, in total silence, with Momo sitting on the floor the entire time in one corner of the bedroom and answering no to everything that was said to him. As the evening drew on, the horses began to whinny. He had forgotten their feed. La Menou looked across at him, but he shook his head with a stubborn, wild look, still saying no. I got up and went out to see to them myself.

I had scarcely returned to the room when my sisters arrived from the city in an automobile. Their promptness surprised me, though less so than their clothes. They were both dressed entirely in black from head to toe, as though the death of their progenitors was an event they had predicted and prepared themselves for down to the minutest detail long since. And no sooner were they over the threshold, even before their hats and veils had been removed, than the cascade of talk and tears began. It was like being trapped with two wasps inside a jam jar.

They shared a particular eccentricity that I at any rate found exceedingly irritating. They both took turns in echoing each other. Whatever Paulette said, Pélagie would immediately repeat, or vice versa. Pélagie had only to ask a question for Paulette to ask it again. It was totally maddening. Not only was everything they said idiotic, but you always had to listen to it twice.

31

They looked alike too: flabby bodies, tightly curled wishy-washy pale hair, always exuding a phony sweetness. And phony it certainly was, because behind those silly sheep faces they were both as ruthless as wolves.

"But why are Papa and Mama not in their beds at La Grange Forte?" Paulette bleated.

"Yes why?" asked Pélagie. "Instead of being here, at Uncle Samuel's, as though they didn't have a home of their own."

"Oh, poor Papa," Paulette went on, "how put out he would be if he were still alive. How he would hate not having died in his own home."

"As it happens, he didn't die at anyone's home," I said, "because he was killed outright in the Renault. And I couldn't split myself in two in order to keep vigil in two places at once, one half at La Grange Forte and the other here."

"All the same," Paulette said.

"All the same," Pélagie went on, "poor Papa wouldn't have been at all happy to find himself here. Or Mama either."

"Mama especially," Paulette said, "feeling as you know she did toward poor Uncle Samuel."

They were picking their way carefully. But that "poor" made me angry, because they were no more fond of my uncle than their mother had been.

"And to think," Pélagie said, "that all this time there's been no one at La Grange Forte to see to the animals."

"That Papa's cows are less important than the horses," Paulette said.

She couldn't say "than Uncle Samuel's horses," because her uncle was there in the room, under her nose, horribly mangled.

"Peyssou is seeing to them," I said.

They exchanged glances.

"Peyssou!" Paulette cried.

"Peysssou!" Pélagie exclaimed. "Well really, Peyssou!"

I broke in almost savagely. "What's all this Peyssou! Peyssou!? What have you to say against Peyssou?" Then I added slyly, "You weren't always so averse to the idea of Peyssou."

They neither of them took up that challenge. They were too busy opening the sluices for another flood of sobs. When that was over there was a dramatic pause for the mopping of eyes and blowing of noses. Then Pélagie returned to the attack. "While we're all here," she said, giving her sister a meaningful glance, "Peyssou is doing just as he pleases at La Grange Forte."

"You can just imagine what scruples Peyssou is going to feel about going through all the drawers," Paulette said.

I shrugged my shoulders. I said nothing. The sobs, the nose blowings, and the lamentations started up again. It was quite a while before they resumed their duet. But resume it they inevitably did.

"I'm horribly worried about all those poor animals," Pélagie said. "I wonder whether I oughtn't to drive on as far as the house to set my mind at rest."

"Because you can be quite sure," Paulette chimed in, "that Peyssou won't have given them even a moment's thought."

"Of course he won't, not that Peyssou!" Pélagie said.

If you had cut open my sisters' hearts at that moment, engraved on both, life-size, you would have found the key to La Grange Forte. They were both more or less certain that I had it. But on what pretext could they ask me for it? Not in order to feed the stock, that was for sure.

And suddenly I'd had enough of their contrapuntal whinings. Without raising my voice, I said, "You know Father. He wouldn't have gone to a football match without locking up behind him. When they brought his body here I found the key on him." Then, articulating very clearly, I went on: "I took it. And I haven't budged from here since your father and mother were brought in. Everyone will tell you that. As for going to La Grange Forte, we'll all three go together the day after tomorrow, after the funeral."

There was a great flutter of protest and black veils. "But we trust you absolutely, Emmanuel! We know you! You can't possibly think such thoughts had even entered our heads! Especially at a moment like this!"

The morning of the funeral La Menou asked me to help her get Momo into a fit state of cleanliness. I had already been present at more than one of these ablutions, and they were not matters of a moment. You had to capture Momo by surprise, skin his clothes off him like the fur off a rabbit, deposit him in a tub to soak, and hold him there, because he fought like a crazed creature yelling at the top of his voice, *"Lebeeoh, fahodsake ahehorter!"* (Let me go, for God's sake! I hate water!)

And that morning he put up an even more savage show of resistance than usual. The tub stood steaming in the April sun, out in the flagged yard. I held Momo under his arms while La Menou pulled off his trousers and underpants at one go. As soon as his feet touched the ground again Momo hooked one leg behind mine and pulled me flat on my back. Then he was off, naked as the day he was born, his thin legs flashing with unbelievable rapidity. He reached one of the big oaks growing below the paddock, jumped, swung, took another grip, then clambered swiftly up from branch to branch till he was wholly out of reach.

I was already in my funeral clothes, and anyway I had no wish to start playing catch-as-catch-can with Momo from oak tree to oak tree. La Menou panted up to join me. I attempted to parley. Although I was six years younger than Momo, he looked upon me as my uncle's double, so my authority over him was almost that of a father.

Even so, my efforts met with no success. I might have been talking to a wall. Momo didn't yell back his usual *"Eevee ahone fahodsake!"* He said nothing. Just looked down at me and kept moaning, his black eyes shining out from among the tiny spring leaves.

The only reply I could get was one *"Hon't ho!"* (I won't go), not yelled but uttered in a low determined voice while his head, torso, and hands all rotated firmly from side to side in a mime of negation.

I renewed my arguments. "Now come on, Momo, do be sensible. You must have a wash before you go to the church."

"Hon't ho! Hon't ho!"

"You don't want to go to church with us?"

"Hon't ho! Hon't ho!"

34

"But why not? You always like going to church."

Sitting perched on a big branch, he waved his hands in front of him in agitated dismissal of the whole idea, all the time peering down at me with those sad eyes through the little shiny oak leaves. And that was that. I could get no further response from him, just that sad gaze.

"We'll have to leave him," La Menou said. She laid the clothes she had remembered to bring with her at the bottom of the tree. "He's not coming down now, no matter what we do, not till we're gone."

She had already turned and was walking back up the paddock. Quick glance at my watch. High time we left. I thought of that long social ceremony before me, almost wholly unrelated to anything I myself felt. Momo was right. Why couldn't I stay there sobbing in a tree, instead of going off to join my tearful sisters in a grotesque simulacrum of filial piety.

I climbed back up the slope of the paddock in my turn. It seemed horribly steep. I looked down at my feet and noticed with surprise that the pasture was dotted with bright green tufts of new grass. In the first few days of sun they had sprung up with incredible exuberance. It occurred to me that in less than a month now my uncle would need me to help on the hay.

It was a thought that ordinarily filled me with joy, and the odd thing was that the joy even then began to well up. And then suddenly it was as though I had been physically struck. I stopped dead in the middle of the sloping field. The tears were running down my cheeks.

II

THINGS begin to move quicker. The next milestone is only a short way on. A year after the accident, Maître Gaillac called me to say he would like me to come and see him at his office in town.

When I arrived at the appointed time, the lawyer himself was not available, and the head clerk showed me into an empty office. Since I had been asked to "make myself comfortable" while I waited, I sat down in one of those great leather armchairs in which so many behinds tensed by the dread of financial loss had rested before mine.

Time became vacant, then stopped. My eyes wandered around the room. I found it extremely depressing. Beyond Maître Gaillac's desk, the entire wall was covered from top to bottom by a multitude of tiny drawers filled with the documents of past cases. They made me think of those pigeon-holes to which people's ashes are consigned in a columbarium. Man's mania for filing everything away.

The curtains were bottle green, the material covering the walls was bottle green, the filing system was dark green, even the leather covering the desktop was dark green. And on it, beside a monumental inkstand made of imitation gold, there stood a macabre knickknack that had always fascinated me: a dead mouse imprisoned inside a block of transparent material that looked like glass. The mouse too had been filed away.

I imagined that it must have been caught red-pawed nibbling at some document or other and had been condemned, by way of punishment, to a life sentence embedded in plastic. I bent forward and picked it up, the mouse and its transparent cell. It was surprisingly heavy.

And then I remembered having seen Maître Gaillac's father, during a visit to the office thirty years before with my uncle, using it as a paperweight. I stared in at it, that tiny rodent condemned to all eternity. When Maître Gaillac, Junior, retired, he would bequeath it in his turn to his son, I supposed, along with the drawers of his columbarium and the graveyard of old files in his attic. I found it all very sad, those generations of lawyers handing on that same little mouse down the line. I don't know why, but it made me very aware of death.

Maître Gaillac, Junior, came in just then. Dark, tall, sallow, and already graying. He greeted me with slightly weary politeness. Then, turning his back on me, he opened one of his little drawers. From it he extracted a file, then from the file a letter sealed with wax, which he pressed between his fingers with a weary, furtive gesture before handing it to me, as though he was amazed by its thinness.

"There you are, Monsieur Comte."

And then in his slightly flaccid voice he began on a long meandering explanation rendered totally pointless by the few words I had already read on the envelope in my uncle's studied handwriting: "To be handed to my nephew Emmanuel Comte one year after my death if, as I suppose, he has taken over the management of Les Sept Fayards."

I had a few errands to run in town before going home, and I carried my uncle's letter around with me in my jacket pocket the whole of that afternoon. I didn't open it till that evening, after dinner, in the seclusion of the little office in the dovecote tower of Les Sept Fayards. My hand shook slightly as I opened the envelope with a daggerlike paperknife my uncle had given me.

Emmanuel,

This evening, for no good reason, since I am in good health, I have been thinking about my death, and I have decided to write this letter. It makes me feel very strange when I think that you will read it when I have gone and that you will be looking after the horses instead of me. As they say, everyone has to die someday. Which simply proves that

37

"they" are stupid, since I can see no necessity for it at all.

Les Sept Fayards is not the whole of what I left you. There is also my Bible and my ten-volume Larousse dictionary.

Of course I know you're no longer a believer (and whose fault is that?), but do read the Bible now and then nevertheless, in memory of me. It's a book in which you have to go deeper than just the way people behave; it's the wisdom there that counts.

While I was alive, no one but myself ever opened my Larousse. When you open it now, you will see why.

And lastly, Emmanuel, I want to tell you that without you my life would have been empty, and that you made me very happy.

Do you remember the day after you ran away from home, the day I came to find you in Malevil. My love to you.

Samuel

I read the letter through twice. My uncle's generosity of spirit made me feel ashamed. He had always given me everything, and yet it was he who was thanking me. That "you made me very happy" was enough to bring a lump into my throat. Just a clumsy enough little phrase in itself, and yet I didn't see how I could ever think myself deserving of the immense affection behind the words.

I read the letter a third time, and that "and whose fault is that?" jumped out at me this time. Once again I recognized my uncle's allusive manner of communication. He was leaving me absolutely free to fill in the name on the dotted line his question left. My father, perhaps, because he had allowed himself to be converted to the "wrong" religion? My mother, with her poverty of heart? The Abbé Lebas, with his sexual inquisitions?

I also wondered why my uncle had alluded to that visit of his to the clubroom in Malevil the day after I ran away. Was it to give me an example of a specific time when I had made him "very happy"? Or was there some other notion lurking at the back of his mind, something he had been unable to make himself express openly? I was too familiar with my uncle's preference for the indirect hint to make up my mind on the point in a hurry.

I pulled my uncle's heavily laden key ring from my pocket and immediately located the key of the big oak armoire. I opened the two massive doors, and there, framed by tier upon tier of shelves crammed with files, I saw the Larousse and the Bible on a shelf of their own, fourteen volumes in all, since the Bible itself was a monumental edition bound in rich brown tooled leather. Four volumes of it. I took them all out, laid them on a table, and slowly leafed through them. The illustrations impressed me immediately. There was an air of genuine grandeur about them.

It had not occurred to the artist for a moment to try to beautify his characters, no matter how holy they were supposed to be. Very much the contrary. He had preserved in them the rugged, wild aspect of savage tribal chieftains. Looking at them, so bony and thin, with such roughly hewn features, all barefooted, you could almost smell the reek of greasy sheep's wool, of camel dung, of desert sand. And a sense of the highly charged and violent life they lived shimmered all around them. Even God himself, as the artist had envisaged Him, was no different in kind from these rough nomads who counted their wealth in terms of children and flocks. He was merely bigger and even more savage of aspect than they, and one glance at Him was enough to make it clear that He had created these men "in His own image." Unless, of course, it was the opposite.

On the very last page of the Bible, written in pencil in my uncle's writing, I noticed a long list of words that immediately intrigued me. Here are the first ten: *actodrome, albergier, aléochare, alpargate, anastome, bactridie, balanobius, baobab, barbacou, barbastelle.*

The arbitrary and artificial nature of this list was evident at a glance. I pulled over the first volume of the Larousse and opened it at *actodrome.* And there between the two pages secured by two tiny strips of Scotch tape to the center of the left-hand one, was a ten-thousand-franc Treasury bond. More bonds, varying in value, were distributed throughout the ten volumes, always facing one of the outlandish words my uncle had listed in the Bible.

Though not staggering, the total was nevertheless something of a shock: 315,000 francs. It is worth noting that this posthumous gift did not at any point fill me with a sense of ownership. My feeling was more that of having been made the trustee of this capital, as I had already been of Les Sept Fayards, and that I was in duty bound to give my uncle an account of the use to which I put it.

My decision was taken so quickly that I even wondered whether it had not in fact already existed even before my discovery. I put it into effect immediately. I remember I glanced at my wristwatch. It was half past nine, and I experienced a moment of childish delight at discovering that it was still not too late for a telephone call. I looked up Grimaud's number in my uncle's address book and dialed it there and then.

"Monsieur Grimaud?"

"Speaking."

"This is Emmanuel Comte. I used to be headmaster at Malejac school."

"What can I do for you, Headmaster?"

The voice was warm and friendly. Not at all the sort of voice I'd expected.

"May I ask you one question, Monsieur Grimaud? Is Malevil castle still for sale?"

A silence, then the same voice, but guarded, circumspect, a hint curter this time: "As far as I know, yes."

It was my turn to let silence work for me, and Grimaud eventually went on: "May I ask you, Headmaster, if you are any relation to Samuel Comte of Les Sept Fayards?"

I had expected the question and knew what I was going to answer. "I am his nephew, but I didn't know my uncle knew you."

"Oh, indeed," Grimaud said in the same cold and cautious voice. "Was it he who gave you my telephone number?"

"He is deceased."

"Ah. I didn't know," Grimaud said in a different tone. I waited for him to go on, but he didn't. There were

40

no condolences, no regrets. I continued: "Monsieur Grimaud, could we meet, do you think?"

"But of course. Whenever you like, Headmaster." And the voice was once more as affable and warm as at the beginning.

"Tomorrow? Late morning?"

He didn't even pretend to be very busy. "Yes, of course, come when you like. I'm always here."

"At eleven then?"

"Whenever you like, Headmaster. I am entirely at your disposal. But eleven is fine, if that suits you."

And so obliging and courteous had he suddenly become that it took me a good five minutes to wind up a conversation whose essence had been expressed in a few short seconds.

I hung up and sat gazing at the red curtains drawn across the windows of my uncle's office. Two contradictory emotions were doing battle inside me. I was overjoyed at my decision and stupefied at the size of what I was undertaking.

An absentee landlord, a shady agent, a determined purchaser; a week later Malevil changed hands. The six years that followed were crammed to the utmost limit with a myriad activities.

I kept up the pressure on all fronts at the same time: the horses at Les Sept Fayards, the clearing of the Malevil land, and the restoration of the castle. I was thirty-five when I threw myself into the last two tasks, forty-one by the time I had accomplished them.

Early to bed and early to rise, I was only sorry I didn't have several lives so that I could devote them all to my undertakings. And Malevil, throughout all those labors, Malevil was my reward, my one love, my madness. Under the Second Empire the bankers had their ballet dancers. I had Malevil. Though I did have my ballet dancer too, as I shall relate shortly.

Buying Malevil was by no means a folly. It was in fact a necessity if I was to expand my uncle's business, since family discord had forced me to sell La Grange Forte in order to hand over their share of the inheritance to my sisters. And besides, I was by now hard pressed for space at Les Sept Fayards to keep my ever-increasing number of horses: those I bred myself, those I bought for resale, and those I boarded. My intention, when I bought Malevil, was to divide my "stable" in two, so that half could be moved to the castle along with La Menou, Momo, and myself, while the other half could remain at Les Sept Fayards in the care of Germain, my hired hand.

So the restoration of Malevil was not entirely the disinterested preservation of a masterpiece of feudal architecture.

Moreover, impressive though it is, and strongly as I am attached to it, I freely admit that Malevil's main attraction is scarcely its intrinsic beauty. A fact that undoubtedly differentiates it from the other castles of the district, all of which are harmoniously proportioned, contoured in eye-pleasing curves, and merge infinitely more satisfactorily into the landscape.

For the landscape around here is a smiling one, with cool streams, sloping meadows, green hills topped with chestnut woods. And in the midst of all those gentle curves Malevil sticks up like a sore stone thumb, savage and perpendicular.

On one side of the double stream of the Rhunes, which must in the Middle Ages have been one vast river, there rises a sheer cliff. Halfway up it, and overhung to the north by the upper half, stands Malevil. The cliff makes it inaccessible on all sides other than by the one road that slopes up to it from the west. And I am certain that the embankment supporting the road was man-made, constructed for the sole purpose of providing a way up to that rocky platform only after someone had decided that the castle and its little hamlet were to be built there.

On the far side of the Rhunes valley, facing Malevil, stands the Château des Rouzies, also medieval, but elegantly, moderately medieval, also a castle rather than just a great country house, but embellished with low, nicely placed round towers that charm the eye and wear even their crenelations with the air of a well-designed decoration.

One glance at Les Rouzies is enough to tell you that its opposite number, Malevil, is a stranger here. Because although every one of its stones certainly came from local quarries, its architectural style is wholly imported. Malevil is English. It was built by our invaders during the Hundred Years' War, and once served as a center of operations for the Black Prince.

The English, far from the mists of home, must have enjoyed being in this country with its bright sun, its wine, its dark-haired girls. And they tried to make sure they stayed. An intention everywhere manifest in Malevil. It was conceived as an absolutely impregnable fortress from which a mere handful of armed men could hold a vast region in thrall.

No curves, no elegance. Everything has its use. Take the gate tower, for example. The entrance to Les Rouzies is a vaulted arch flanked with two little round towers: a construction as elegant in outline as it is harmonious in its proportions. At Malevil, however, the English simply left a gateway with a semicircular arch in the battlemented wall, then to one side of it put up a two-story rectangular building whose sheer face, naked and forbidding, is pierced with tall arrow slits. It's big, it's square, and militarily speaking, as I know beyond doubt, it is murderously efficient. Beneath the ramparts and the gate tower they then hewed out a moat in the living rock twice as wide as the one around Les Rouzies.

Once through this main gate, you are still not inside the castle proper but in an outer enclosure about fifty yards by thirty that once contained the little village housing the castle's retainers. There is a piece of astute military thinking behind this. The castle was certainly a protection for the village, but it was also using the village as an extra defense. Any enemy who succeeded in overwhelming the gate tower and the outerwall would then face a very risky advance through the narrow village alleys.

And even if the enemy won that battle, his troubles were by no means over. He had simply run up against a second line of ramparts running like the first from the overhanging cliff to the steep bluff below, which defended —and still defends—the castle proper.

This battlemented rampart is much higher than the outside one, and its moat much deeper. Unlike the first moat, moreover, this second one presents the attacker not with a convenient bridge but with the additional obstacle of a drawbridge topped by a low square tower.

This little square tower does have a certain elegance, though in my opinion this was not intentional on the English builders' part. As far as they were concerned they simply needed to build a housing for the drawbridge machinery. And luck was on their side. The requisite proportions also happened to be good ones aesthetically.

As soon as you have crossed the lowered drawbridge —also restored now—you are menaced on your left by the vast mass of a formidable square keep, a hundred and thirty feet high, flanked in its turn by a smaller square tower. This smaller tower is not merely defensive in intention. It also serves as a water tower, since it receives the water from a spring emerging from the cliff face, whose overflow—nothing is wasted—also keeps the moats topped up.

To the right, you find a flight of steps leading down to the immense cellar that had so attracted my uncle, and facing you, in the center, at right angles to the keep, a shock to the eye after so much austerity, stands a very handsome two-story house, its staircase housed in a charming little round tower at one corner. This house had not existed in the Black Prince's time. It was built much later on, during more peaceful Renaissance times, by a French nobleman. But its beams and its heavy stone-tiled roof had stood up to the passage of time much less well than the keep's stone vaulting, and I was obliged to restore them entirely.

Such is Malevil, Anglo-Saxon and angular. And I love it just the way it is. For my uncle, and for me too in the days of our Club, it possessed the additional charm of having been the refuge during the religious wars of a Protestant captain who successfully held at bay the powerful armies of the Catholic League, with the help of a small band of comrades, until the day he died. This captain, so determined a champion of his principles and his independence against the powers of his day, was the first hero with whom I identified myself.

I said earlier that there was nothing left of the village

44

in the outer enclosure but heaps of stones. But those stones—of which I still have vast piles left—were extremely useful to me. Thanks to them I was able to build two sets of lean-to stalls for my horses, one against the southern rampart—defending the top of a bluff that was already defending itself very well without any help—and one against the cliff to the north.

Roughly in the middle of the cliff face that forms one side of the outer enclosure there is a wide and deep natural cleft. There are a few traces of prehistoric occupation to be found inside it—not enough to justify calling it a cave dwelling but enough to prove that many thousands of years before the castle was built Malevil was already being used as a refuge by men.

I decided to make use of this cave. First I installed a wooden floor halfway up it, which I used for storing the bulk of my hay supply. Beneath that I constructed a series of stalls for any animals I needed to house separately: a biting horse, a troublesome bull calf, a sow about to farrow, a cow about to calve, or a mare in foal. Since the majority of these cave stalls—which were cool, airy, and fly-free—were usually occupied by various mothers-to-be, Birgitta—to whom I shall return in a moment and whom I had never believed capable of any kind of humor—christened the whole area the "Maternity Ward."

The keep, a masterpiece of English solidity, cost me no more than the price of its floorboards and replacement leaded window glass for the mullioned windows, inserted fairly late on by some French owner. The floor plan of all three stories—first or ground, second, and third—is identical: a large landing about ten yards by ten opening onto two rooms, each five yards by five. On the ground floor I turned the two "small" rooms into a storeroom and a boilerhouse, on the second floor I built a bathroom and a bedroom, and on the third floor two bedrooms.

Because of the wonderful view to the east over the Rhunes valley, I took one of the third-floor rooms as my own office-cum-bedroom, despite the slight inconvenience of having the bathroom on the second. Colin had assured me that the water collected by the square tower could never be got up to the third floor by gravity alone, and I wanted to spare Malevil the unpleasing racket of a motor pump.

It was in the bedroom next to mine, on the third story of the keep, that I lodged Birgitta during the summer of 1976, a period that constitutes my last milestone but one, and to which I now often return in my sleepless nights.

Birgitta had worked for my uncle at Les Sept Fayards several years earlier, and round about Easter 1976 I received a pressing letter from her offering her services during the following July and August.

I would like to put it on record here, as a preliminary to what follows, that my true inclination, as I see it, was to be a stable husband with an affectionate partner. My attempts in that direction all failed. It is of course possible that the two unhappy marriages I witnessed as a child—my father's and my uncle's—contributed to this failure. But whatever the truth in that respect, three times at least things seemed to be well on the way to marriage with me, then were broken off. On the first two occasions on my initiative, on the third, in 1974, on the initiative of the bride-to-be.

The year 1974, that too was a milestone, but I have deliberately effaced it. For a while that appalling woman even put me off women in general, and I don't wish to remember that time.

In short, I had been living for two years in the desert when Birgitta reappeared at Malevil. Not that I fell in love with her. Oh, no, very far from it! I was forty by then, and too experienced and too emotionally fragile to lay myself open to those kinds of feelings. But it was precisely because this affair with Birgitta was confined to a humbler level that it did me so much good. I can't remember who said that the soul can be cured by means of the senses, but I believe it to be true, having experienced such a cure myself.

But that sort of therapy couldn't have been further from my mind when I accepted Birgitta's offer. During her first stay at Les Sept Fayards I had indeed made one or two advances, which she had rebuffed. But I had never followed up the attack after those preliminary skirmishes, having realized in the meantime that I was poaching on my uncle's territory. However, when she wrote me her letter, just before Easter 1976, I wrote back to say we would be expecting her. Professionally she would be invaluable to me. She was a natural horsewoman, gifted with a certain instinct for the equine mind, and richly endowed with the patience and orderliness that are vital for breaking and training horses.

When she arrived, I must confess I was taken aback. We no sooner sat down to our first meal than she began making an all-out play for me. Her advances were so flagrant that even Momo noticed them. So much so that he even forgot to open the window and give his usual whinny to call over his favorite mare, Bel Amour. And when La Menou, as she removed the soup tureen, muttered in patois, "After the uncle the nephew," he burst out with a great laugh. "*Hookhout, Ehanooel!*" (Look out, Emmanuel!)

Birgitta was from Bavaria. Her golden hair was gathered up into a gleaming helmet above her head, her eyes were small and pale, her face on the homely side with a rather heavy jaw. But her body was beautiful, solid, radiant with health. Sitting facing me, not in the slightest tired after her long journey, she was as pink and fresh as though she had just leapt out of bed. And while she devoured a seemingly endless quantity of sliced ham, so at the same time she devoured me with her eyes. Everything she did was a provocation: her glances, her smiles, her sighs, the way she rolled little pellets of bread between her fingers, the way she stretched her back to the great advantage of her bosom.

Remembering her former rebuffs, I didn't know what to think, or rather I was wary of thinking some exceedingly simple things. But La Menou had no such scruples, and at the end of the meal, without moving a single muscle in that fleshless face of hers, she said in local dialect as she slid a vast slice of tart onto Birgitta's plate, "The cage isn't enough for her, now she wants the bird."

The following day I encountered Birgitta in the Maternity Ward. She was busily pitchforking bales of hay through a trapdoor. I went up to her without a word, took her in my arms (she was as tall as I was), and set about kneading the curves of that monument to Aryan Health and Strength. She responded to my caresses with a fervor that surprised me, since I had assumed that she was motivated solely by self-interest.

Which indeed she was, but in two directions. I intensified my attacks, but they were interrupted by Momo. Surprised to find the bales no longer coming through the trapdoor, he climbed up the ladder, pushed his shaggy head through the opening, and began laughing and shouting "*Hookhout, Ehanooel!*" Then he vanished, and I heard him running over toward the gate tower, presumably to inform his mother of this latest turn of events.

Birgitta, her golden helmet scarcely touched by her tumble among the hay bales, pushed herself into a sitting position, fixed her cold little eyes on mine, and said in her laboriously grammatical French, "I shall never give myself to a man who entertains ideas such as yours on marriage."

"My uncle's ideas were the same," I said when I had recovered from my surprise.

"That is not the same thing at all," Birgitta said, modestly turning away her face. "Your uncle was elderly."

So I was the right age to marry her. I looked at Birgitta and silently chortled at her simplicity. "I have no intention of marrying," I said firmly.

"Nor I any intention of giving myself to you," she rejoined.

I didn't respond to her challenge. But in order to demonstrate what small weight I attached to such abstract speculations I set about caressing her again. Her face immediately softened and she lay back.

During the days that followed I continued to desist from any attempt at persuasion. But every time I was able to lay my hands on her I proceeded to caress her, and I noticed that this procedure must have been to her liking, since such opportunities began to occur more and more frequently. Nevertheless, it took her a further three whole weeks to abandon her plan number one and fall back on plan number two. And even then it was by no means a rout, a collapse into anarchy, but a methodically executed retreat, carried out to a strict timetable, wholly according to plan.

One evening when I had gone to visit her in her room (we had reached that stage) she said to me, "Emmanuel, I shall give myself to you tomorrow."

I immediately asked her, "Why not right away?"

She had not foreseen this request and appeared surprised, even tempted. But fidelity to her plan carried the day. "Tomorrow," she said firmly.

"At what time?" I inquired ironically.

But the irony was lost on Birgitta, and she answered with great seriousness, "During the midday siesta."

It was after that siesta (it was during July 1976, and the weather was extremely hot) that I moved Birgitta into the keep bedroom next to mine.

Birgitta was delighted at this cohabitation. She used to come into my bed every morning at dawn, at two in the afternoon during the siesta, and from bedtime till late into the night. I was glad to have her there, but quite glad also when she was indisposed. I was at last able to sleep my fill on those nights.

It was this simplicity that I found so restful in Birgitta. She demanded pleasure like a child demanding cake. And once she had been given her treat she very nicely thanked me. She was particularly enthusiastic about the pleasure I gave her with my caresses. "Ach! Emmanuel, your hands!" I was somewhat astonished by this gratitude, since there was nothing so extraordinary about what I did with her, and I was unable to see what great merit there could be in my kneading her curves either.

What I found most refreshing of all, however, was that apart from my hands, my sex, and my wallet, I had no existence for her at all. I add wallet to the list because whenever we went into town she would linger in front of store windows displaying "fal-lals," as my uncle used to call them, and with her small, slightly porcine eyes dilated by desire, she would indicate her preferences.

Even simple folk have their complexities. Birgitta was not intelligent, but she understood my character well enough, and though uncultured she did have taste. So I

49

knew exactly when to rein in her demands, and what she bought was never trash.

At first I used to ponder the question of her morality a little. But I quickly realized that the object of that mental effort did not in fact exist. Birgitta was neither good nor bad. She just was. And when all was said and done, that was quite enough. She brought me twofold pleasure—when I held her in my arms, and also when she left them, because I was able to forget her immediately.

The end of August came, and I asked Birgitta to stay on for an extra week. To my surprise she refused. "I must think of my parents," she said.

"You don't give a damn about your parents."

"Oh!" Birgitta exclaimed, very shocked.

"You never write to them."

"That's because I'm so bad about writing letters."

She wasn't in the slightest, as events were to show. But a date is a date. And plans are made to be kept to. Her departure remained fixed for August thirty-first.

During the last days of her stay Birgitta sank into melancholy. She was well looked upon at Malevil. My other helper, no more than a lad, was always making eyes at her. The two permanent hands, Germain especially, admired her build. Momo, hands in pockets, dribbled as he stared at her. And even La Menou, setting aside her not particularly deep hostility to sexual looseness, nursed a definite esteem for her. "A strong lass, that she is," La Menou would admit, "and she's never backward when it comes to work."

And Birgitta, on her side, enjoyed being with us. She liked our sun, our cooking, our wines, our fal-lals, and my caresses. I place myself last on the list. I have no idea what place I really occupied in her hierarchy of delights. Not that it mattered, since none of them had the power to sap her sense of values. Everything in its place: on the one hand her French Eden, on the other her German future. And somewhere or other a *Doktor* of something who would make an offer of marriage.

August twenty-eighth was a Sunday, and Birgitta, who was not one to do her packing at the last moment, began collecting her things together. Then came a moment of panic when she realized that there wasn't going to be enough room in her suitcases to accommodate all my presents. Sunday, Monday—the stores would be closed both days. She would have to wait till Tuesday, which was to say "the very last minute"—an appalling notion—to buy another suitcase.

I rescued her from her torments by giving her one of mine. And at her urgent insistence I produced in written form on a sheet of yellow office paper, the first that came to hand, the description I had given her the previous evening in a restaurant of the caresses I would lavish upon her when she came back to Malevil again. This task accomplished, I took it in to her. Although the literary value of the result was not of the highest, her eyes were bright and her cheeks scarlet as she read it through. She promised me that after her return to Germany she would reread it once a week, in bed. I had not asked her for any such promise. She made it completely on her own, while shedding a tear and tucking my yellow sheet of paper carefully away with her other gifts among the booty she was taking with her.

Birgitta was unable to come to us at Christmas, and I was much more disappointed than I would have expected. But Christmas in general was never a very good time for me. Peyssou, Colin, and Meyssonnier always celebrated it at home with their families. I was always left alone with my horses. And Malevil in winter, despite the comforts I had introduced, was scarcely a cozy place. Except perhaps for some young couple who could have kept each other warm inside its great walls and regarded them as an aid to romance.

I didn't mention my gloom in so many words, but La Menou sensed it, and one cold snowy morning over the breakfast table my unmarried state was made the subject of one of those long grumbling soliloquies of which, since my uncle's death, I had become the beneficiary.

All the chances I had missed! And most of all Agnès. Only this morning she'd met her, Agnès, in Adelaide's, because, of course, she's spending the holiday here in Malejac with her parents, and, of course, she'd asked after me, as you can imagine, Agnès had, married though she may be to her newsagent in La Roque. Agnès now, there was a girl made of the right stuff. She'd have been just what I needed. Ah, well. But we must never say die. There would be other opportunities. In Malejac alone, all those young girls, just think, from among whom I could just take my pick whenever I chose, never mind my age, because now I was rich, and still a fine-looking man. And while I was about it, much better to marry a girl from your own country instead of some German. Oh, it was true that Birgitta was not backward when it came to work, but the Germans, you can't say they're the kind of people who know where they belong. Otherwise would they have kept invading us all the time? And even if my French girl wasn't a match for my Boche, after all, marriage isn't there for the enjoyment so much as the children, and I was going to be left looking a real old fool, wasn't I, if after all my work on Malevil I had no one to leave it to.

In the months that followed I still did not take a wife, but I did at least find a friend. He was twenty-five, and his name was Thomas le Coultre. I met him in one of Les Sept Fayards' copses, wearing jeans, a huge Honda motorbike beside him, his knees stained with mud. He was tapping a stone with a little hammer. It turned out that he was doing a third-year thesis on pebbles. I invited him to Malevil, loaned him Uncle Samuel's Geiger counter on two or three occasions, and finally, when I discovered he wasn't happy with the family who were giving him bed and board at La Roque, I offered him a room in the castle. He accepted. And he's been with me ever since.

What attracts me in Thomas is the rigor of his mind, and although his passion for pebbles remains as opaque to me as ever, I love the transparency of his character. I also like his looks. Thomas is beautiful, and better still, he doesn't know it. He has not just the features but also the serene and serious physiognomy of a Greek statue. And almost the same immobility.

April 1977: the last milestone.
When I think back now to those last weeks of happy

existence remaining to us then, I experience an almost piercing feeling of irony at the memory that for all the former Club members, as for myself, the great business of the moment, the all-engrossing thought, the supreme undertaking, the vast and important project we had then conceived, consisted in the overthrow of the local council in Malejac (population 412) and its replacement in office by ourselves. Oh, how disinterested we were. With nothing in view but the common good!

That April, with the local elections imminent, we lived in feverish activity. On the fifteenth or sixteenth, but at all events a Sunday morning, I had summoned our anti-establishment band to a meeting at Malevil, in the great hall of the Renaissance house, since Monsieur Paulat, the primary school teacher, evidently had some scruple or other, he had informed us, about allowing us to meet in his school.

I had just finished furnishing the hall, and as I waited for my friends I walked proudly up and down it contemplating my handiwork with glee. In the center stood a twenty-five-foot refectory table, around it twelve high-backed chairs upholstered in tooled leather. Between the two mullioned windows the wall bristled with antique sidearms. Against the opposite wall stood a big glass-fronted bookcase, and on either side of it two of the rustic Louis XV commodes from La Grange Forte, their feet and doors recently mended for me by Meyssonnier. Mathilde Meyssonnier had polished them with love, and the dark warmth of the walnut seemed to me perfection, set off by the golden stone of the wall. There was no less of a shine on the great flagstones of the floor, freshly scrubbed by La Menou. And despite the sunlight slanting in obliquely through the tinted glass of the tiny leaded panes, La Menou, affecting to believe that "the air struck cold underneath," but in fact feeling that flames would add to the dignity of the general décor, had lit vast wood fires in the two monumental fireplaces that faced each other across the length of the room.

I had asked La Menou to ring the bell in the gate tower as soon as she heard the Club members drawing up in the parking area outside the outer wall, and Momo had been posted as lookout in the square tower over the drawbridge with orders to lower it over the moat as soon as my friends appeared.

I grant that there was a hint of the theatrical in these arrangements, but after all, this was not just any old castle, nor were my visitors just any old friends.

The moment I heard the bell I ran out of the house and bounded up the steps to the drawbridge tower where Momo was turning the winch. Everything was working to perfection; with a muffled yet dramatic rumble of well-oiled chains the great pivoted beams swung down and out, the bridge hanging below them by two more vast chains. A series of pulleys and counterweights was used to gear down the winding up and brake the weight of the descent, and Momo, solemn-faced, thin body arched with effort, was holding back the capstan arms as I had taught him, so that the lip of the bridge should sink gently into contact with the ground.

Through the square lookout window I could see my three friends approaching across the outer enclosure, walking in line abreast across the fifty yards still separating them from the moat, their eyes raised toward us. They too were moving slowly and in silence, as though they were aware of the role allotted to them in this scene.

There was in fact a sort of solemn expectation hanging in the air, emphasized by the horses in their stalls, the long line of heads emerging from their half doors at the same height, and all those beautiful, sensitive eyes fixed with apprehension upon the drawbridge as they listened to its grating chains.

When the wooden apron was finally at rest, I went down and opened the door for my friends, or to be precise, the small door let into the right-hand side of the large door.

"Some entrance!" Colin remarked, smiling his gondola smile and looking at me with a malicious twinkle in his eyes.

Big Peyssou, great round mug split by a happy smile, admired the vast diameter of the pivoting beams, the size of the chains, the solidity of the iron-studded bridge. Meyssonnier said nothing. There was no place for such

54

childish enthusiasms in his austere card-carrying Communist's heart.

Peyssou insisted immediately on climbing up to the little square tower and winding the drawbridge back up again personally, a task he accomplished with a vast deployment of muscle that was clearly unnecessary, since little Colin, having insisted on taking over halfway through the operation, concluded it without any effort. But of course, once up, the bridge had to be lowered again forthwith, since Monsieur Paulat hadn't arrived yet. But at that point Momo interrupted in no uncertain fashion: "*Heevheeahone, hor Hodhake!*" (Leave me alone, for God's sake!) and insisted on resuming command of his machine. Meyssonnier had followed us up, though still without speaking or taking any part, disgusted by our reactionary delight in feudal architecture.

We had barely seated ourselves around the monumental refectory table when Peyssou asked me what the news was about Birgitta, and when he would be seeing that strapping lass again. "At Easter. At Easter, eh?" Peyssou said. "Well, make sure you don't let her go wandering about in the woods on one of your old hacks. Because if I happen to run into her I shall certainly give her a good how do you do. 'Mademoiselle,' I shall say, very polite of course, 'that horse of yours is dropping a shoe.' 'Oh, that can't be,' she'll come back, all surprised, and down she'll leap. And once down, allez-oop. I don't need to tell you, I shall have her down on the moss in a trice, boots and all."

"Better watch out for her spurs then," Colin put in.

General laughter. And even Meyssonnier raised a smile. Not that the Birgitta-in-the-woods joke was by any means new. In fact, Peyssou came out with it every time we were all together. In reality, of course, Peyssou was by now a middle-aged farmer, sedate and settled, who never deceived his wife. But he still remained faithful to the image of him we had collectively created in the past days of the Club, and we all loved him for that fidelity to our past.

At the arrival of Monsieur Paulat, my successor at the school, the conversation took a more serious turn. Monsieur Paulat was dressed in black, hollow-cheeked, sallow-complexioned, his badge of academic office on his lapel. We greeted him courteously, itself proof that he was not one of us. His acid accent contrasting so sharply with our own broader Southwestern (with a hint of Massif Central) sounds, created an uneasiness in us, heightened even further by his flat insipid phraseology. Besides which we were aware that though he had associated himself in principle with our efforts, he was nevertheless hedged on all sides with reservations and ulterior motives where we were concerned.

When he shook hands with Meyssonnier, for example, it was barely more than a touch with the tips of his fingers. Meyssonnier was a member of the Communist Party, and as such the devil incarnate. There was the constant threat that he was going to inveigle his allies into a Communist cell, steal away their souls (so enamored of formal liberties) while they weren't looking, then keep them there bound hand and foot until the victory of the Party made it feasible to eliminate them physically. Colin, though undoubtedly a man of sound sense, was just a plumber, Peyssou an ignorant and somewhat stupid farmer, and as for myself, giving up a headmastership in order to breed horses, I ask you!

"Gentlemen," Monsieur Paulat began, "permit me to begin by thanking Monsieur Comte, in your name as well as my own, for having been so kind as to extend us this hospitality, since I was of the opinion, as a matter of conscience, that the school, being dependent upon the town hall for its maintenance, was not a suitable place to hold this meeting."

He fell silent, pleased with this beginning. We were considerably less so, since everything in his little speech, tone as well as content, seemed to us ill-considered. Monsieur Paulat was forgetting a great Republican principle: The state school belonged to everyone. Which opened the way to a suspicion that while lending his support to us, the opposition, in secret, Monsieur Paulat was at the same time maintaining the best possible relations with the mayor in public.

I watched my friends while he spoke. Meyssonnier was

leaning forward, his narrow forehead and knifelike profile bent over the table. His close-set eyes were invisible, but I knew exactly what he was thinking of the man opposite him just then.

I could also tell from Peyssou's pleasant, guileless face that he didn't think much of him either. Monsieur Paulat was correct in thinking that Peyssou was not very intelligent. Nor had he ever had much education. But he did possess a quality that I suspect Monsieur Paulat himself had never heard of: a native sensitivity that served him instead of intellectual subtlety. Monsieur Paulat's hare-and-hounds side had not escaped him, and furthermore he was perfectly aware of the teacher's low opinion of him. As for little Colin, his eyes began to sparkle the moment I caught them.

There was a heavy silence, the significance of which evidently escaped Monsieur Paulat, since he immediately made himself spokesman once again.

"We are here to discuss certain recent events in Malejac and to consider what steps should be taken in view of them. But first of all, I think it would be best to set out the facts, since I for my part have heard two versions of the matter, and I should be glad to have some light thrown on the subject."

Having thus placed himself above the crowd and assigned himself the expedient role of arbiter, Monsieur Paulat was silent, leaving the honor of wading into the muck and accusing the mayor to others. "Others" in this case clearly meaning Meyssonnier, whom the teacher had given a meaningful glance at the words "it would be best to set out the facts," as though Meyssonnier's "version," coming from a Communist, must inevitably awaken mistrust a priori in any respectable citizen.

None of which escaped Meyssonnier. But unfortunately Meyssonnier suffers from a certain rigidity of mind that is echoed in his speech by an undoubted lack of flexibility. So the ill feeling he was unable to conceal in his reply seemed almost to prove his adversary in the right.

"There aren't two versions at all," he said in an arrogant tone, "there's just one, and everyone here knows it. The mayor, an entrenched reactionary, openly approached the bishop with a request that he should appoint a parish priest in Malejac. The bishop's reply was 'Yes, on condition that you repair the parish house and put in a water supply.' Whereupon the mayor immediately complied. A trench was dug, water was piped in from a spring, and a large sum of money was sunk in improving the house. And all this, needless to say, at our expense."

Monsieur Paulat half closed his eyes, rested his elbows on the table, and laid his fingertips gently together, including the thumbs. Having erected this symbol of balance and moderation, he swayed back and forth slightly and said with devastating fairness, "So far I see nothing very *damnable* in all this."

He permitted himself a subtle smile on the word "damnable" to convey that he did not himself wholly subscribe to such clerical terminology.

"Monsieur Nardillon is supported by a Catholic majority, albeit a rather small one, which it is our hope to overthrow. It is normal enough that he should try to procure them the satisfaction of having a full-time priest [another smile] at Malejac, instead of having to share a priest with La Roque as they have had to do up till now. Moreover the parish house is a genuine seventeenth-century structure with carved gables and a pediment over the door, and it would have been a pity to let it fall into ruins."

Meyssonnier went red and lowered his razor-sharp profile as though he were about to hurl himself to the attack. I didn't give him time however. I began to answer myself. "Monsieur Paulat," I said politely, "if the majority of Malejac's population wants a resident priest, and if that majority is prepared to repair the parish house in order to achieve that end, then I am certainly of your opinion. I don't find anything very 'damnable' in it [an exchange of subtle smiles]. And I would also agree that any local council has a duty not to let the buildings under its jurisdiction fall into disrepair. But nevertheless there are certain priorities that must be respected. For one thing, the parish house was not about to collapse in ruins. In fact, its roof was in an extremely good state of repair. And it is a pity that its flooring should have been renewed

58

before repairing the school playground, which is open to all the children in Malejac, no matter what their beliefs. And similarly, it is a pity that a water supply should have been provided in the parish house *before* providing running water in all the other houses in Malejac, as should have been done a long time ago. And it is even more regrettable, since the pipeline to the parish house passes directly in front of a house at present occupied by a widow who has neither a well nor a water tank, that it did not occur to the mayor to add a small branch pipe in order to spare that widow, who has five children, the labor of fetching all her water from the town pump."

Monsieur Paulat, eyes lowered and fingertips joined, nodded his head several times, then said, "Of course."

Meyssonnier wanted to say something at that point, but I signaled to him to refrain, wishing to allow Monsieur Paulat all the time he needed to give clear-cut and public expression to his disapproval. But he did no more than nod his head once more and repeat with a saddened expression, "Of course, of course."

"And the worst part of all, Headmaster," little Colin put in, the respect in his tone given the lie by his smile, "is that all the money spent on the parish house might just as well have been saved. Because when the old curé at La Roque left, which was no more than a week ago, the bishop simply appointed another parish priest with one foot there and one in Malejac. There was a recommendation to reside in Malejac, it's true. But the new curé plumped for La Roque all the same."

"Where did you hear that story?" Monsieur Paulat asked Colin with a stern glare.

"Why, from the new curé himself, from the Abbé Raymond," Colin said. "As you know, perhaps, Monsieur Paulat, I live in Malejac, but I run a little plumbing business in La Roque, and the mayor of La Roque commissioned me to do some work for the council in the parish house there."

Monsieur Paulat frowned. "And the new priest is supposed to have told you . . ."

"I don't think there was any supposition in it, Monsieur Paulat. He simply told me."

This rebuff was administered with a sweet smile, and with no raising of the voice. Paulat's thin, sallow face visibly twitched.

"He told me," Colin went smoothly on, " 'In the matter of residence I was given a choice between Malejac and La Roque, with a nod in the direction of Malejac. But Malejac, you will agree, is more dead than alive. At least in La Roque there are some youngsters about. And I feel my place is with the young.' "

There was a silence.

"Of course," Monsieur Paulat said.

And that was all. At which Meyssonnier began talking about the "reply" called for by these events, and I allowed my attention to relax, since I had already prepared our "reply," and it was of a nature to cause Monsieur Paulat some embarrassment. I therefore waited for the discussion to run down before putting it forward, and I needed no more than half an ear to tell me when that moment arrived.

I smiled across at Colin with my eyes. It had given me pleasure to see him score off the headmaster, and to score off him moreover in such an academic tone.

While Meyssonnier talked I played quiet scales on the tabletop with my fingers and allowed myself a moment's nostalgic regret. Before Monsieur Paulat's arrival on the scene things had been so clear-cut: At the next municipal elections the opposition would have put a list of Progressive Union candidates against the mayor's men and won by a narrow majority. Colin, Peyssou, Meyssonnier, and myself, and two other local farmers who shared our views would have become local councilors, and Meyssonnier would have been appointed mayor.

Because, despite his partisan connections, Meyssonnier would make a good mayor: dedicated, disinterested, devoid of all personal vanity, and not half as intolerant as he appeared on the surface. With him in office we would be able to provide Malejac with water in every home, street lighting, a football field for the youngsters, and a pumping station by the Rhunes that would enable all the farmers to irrigate their tobacco and field corn.

Momentarily at least, Monsieur Paulat was threatening

our applecart. He had an urban conception of politics and was secretly pursuing a vision of himself as the fulcrum of a balance of power. He saw himself keeping a foot in each camp in order to get himself elected by the left so that he could rule with the right. But in Malejac we had not progressed to such perversions.

Since Monsieur Paulat was sitting directly across from me, I was able to watch him while the debate continued. He had a caramel complexion, a broad fleshy nose, and there was something soft and rubbery about his face in profile. His tongue seemed to be too big for his mouth; you were constantly glimpsing it appearing between his thick lips, reducing his diction to a bubbling mess and causing him to sputter the whole time. There were deep lines radiating from his mouth that betrayed a bad digestion, and I noticed that the skin of his scrawny neck, just above the white collar, was reddened by a number of tiny boils. I foresaw further crops of such little boils by the time I had finished with him.

Yet at the same time I felt a certain pity for him. I have noticed that men of his sort—sallow, dyspeptic, and boil-prone—are never happy in life. They become the slaves of ambition; in other words they devote themselves to things that other people consider important instead of to those that would really bring them pleasure.

There are times when it is essential to listen to people and times when the ear becomes irrelevant and it is enough to watch them. Colin, I could see at a glance, was all asparkle like a good wine. Monsieur Paulat was looking like a slug. Meyssonnier made me think of one of those efficient by-the-book youngsters who are the backbone of armies and political parties. Peyssou, despite that burly carapace, was reacting to every word with the sensitivity of a young girl. Except that suddenly I realized he was no longer reacting at all. He had sagged down on his Louis XIII chair, and just from the way he was now picking his nose with his thumb I could see that he was suddenly fed up with the whole thing and that the debate had finally died on them.

I caught a few words just then that confirmed this impression.

61

"All the same," I put in, "we have to do something. We can't let this go by without some reaction. I have a proposal I should like to put to the vote."

I paused a moment, then went on: "I propose that we write the mayor a letter. In fact I've already drafted such a letter, and if you have no objection I'll read it out to you now."

Whereupon, without waiting for any such objection to be voiced, I pulled the letter out of my pocket and read it.

"No! No!" Monsieur Paulat cried in a trembling voice, waving his hands in front of his chin. "No letter! No letter! I am totally opposed to that kind of procedure!"

He sputtered, he stammered, he was quite beside himself. Because, of course, a written text, and especially a text reprimanding the mayor, is extremely difficult to repudiate once it's been signed.

Monsieur Paulat thereupon launched a rear-guard action lasting an hour and a half, at the end of which, taking refuge in questions of procedure, he demanded an adjournment of the discussion. I immediately insisted that this particular point be put to a vote. Monsieur Paulat demanded that we first vote on the advisability of my vote. He was defeated on both motions.

"Come now, Monsieur Paulat," I said in a conciliatory tone. "Can you tell us precisely which points in the letter you do not agree with?"

He protested. I was hustling him! I was holding a knife to his throat! It was sheer tyranny!

"And besides," he added, "I can't be expected to answer you point-blank like that! The letter is so long, I would need to look it over!"

"Here is a copy," I said, handing him a carbon of my letter to the mayor across the table. It was on a sheet of yellow paper, and carried away though I was by the debate, I gave a fleeting thought to Birgitta.

Monsieur Paulat then executed an amazing piece of business. "No! No!" he exclaimed, rejecting my offer with his voice, with his head, with his shoulders, yet taking the sheet of paper from me even as he appeared to be thrusting it away from him. Then he went on in a tone of utter exasperation: "And besides, I am not a believer in texts of this sort, prepared in advance. We all know what uses—and what abuses—such methods are put to by political parties, and the Communist Party in particular."

I signaled to Meyssonnier not to react to this piece of provocation. And besides, what Monsieur Paulat had said was in fact no more than the truth.

"This text," I said modestly, "summarizes the ideas we have gone over now a hundred times. It is clear, it is not long, it is moderate in its tone, and it contains nothing new. So I can't understand what there is about it that you don't like."

"But I haven't said I don't like it," Monsieur Paulat burst out in despair. "By and large I am in agreement with it—"

"Well then, vote for it!" Meyssonnier broke in abruptly, still smarting from Monsieur Paulat's dig at the Party.

Monsieur Paulat loftily ignored the interruption.

"Come now, Monsieur Paulat," I said with a friendly smile, "won't you tell us on which precise points our opinions differ?"

"Not at half past one in the afternoon!" Monsieur Paulat said after a glance at his watch. "Gentlemen," he then went on with a shake in his voice, "I can see that you are determined to violate my scruples in this matter. So be it. But that being so, it is my duty to warn you that you will have to dispense with my vote."

There was a silence.

"All right," Colin said, "so let's vote. I'm for."

"For," Meyssonnier said.

"For," Peyssou said.

"For," I said.

We looked at Monsieur Paulat. His face was yellow and set. Finally, through clenched teeth, he said "I abstain."

Peyssou heaved up his great bulk, stared at Paulat open-mouthed, then turned his great rough-hewn face to me, eyes as wide as they would go. "What does that mean, 'I abstain'?"

"It means I refuse to vote on the motion, that's all," Monsieur Paulat said acidly.

"But has he the right to do that?" Peyssou asked me in utter consternation, the reference to Monsieur Paulat as "he" making it seem as though he were no longer in the room.

I nodded. "It is Monsieur Paulat's absolute right."

"If you ask me," Peyssou said after a moment, "refusing to vote and voting against come to exactly the same thing."

"Not at all! Not at all!" Monsieur Paulat cried in great agitation. "They are quite different. I am not against this text. I am abstaining from the vote because it is my opinion that I have been allowed insufficient time to discuss it."

Peyssou turned his head slowly toward Monsieur Paulat and gazed at him silently for a while with an air of deep thought. "All the same," he said, "you're not in favor of it. Otherwise you'd have voted for it."

"I am neither for nor against," Monsieur Paulat said, spluttering even more violently as a result of his agitation. "I am withholding my vote. It's quite different."

Peyssou chewed over this answer, his gray eyes fixed on Monsieur Paulat in stupefaction. Meyssonnier shifted on his chair as though about to speak and get to his feet, but I signaled to him with a glance to stay put. I was listening. Colin too. And Meyssonnier did the same. We were waiting to see what would happen now. And we didn't have long to wait.

"There's something I don't understand," Peyssou said slowly. "And that's why you're going along with us when you're not for or against."

Monsieur Paulat went pale and rose. "If my presence here is distasteful to you I can withdraw," he said, the words almost indistinguishable, as though he were being choked by his own tongue.

I got up too. "Now come, Monsieur Paulat, I can assure you that Peyssou meant nothing of the kind . . ."

And I went on in the same tone for a good five minutes, pouring sufficient oil on his departure for it to be accomplished as painlessly as possible. I noticed, however, that as he was replying to me Monsieur Paulat was at the same time folding up the carbon of my letter to the mayor and tucking it into his pocket. I promptly asked if I might have it back, for my "records." He appeared to hesitate for a moment, then realized his error and handed the sheet of paper over with a sickly smile. And that sickly smile was the last I saw of him.

After Monsieur Paulat's departure I escorted my friends down to the parking area at the foot of the outside wall without a word. Perhaps I was a little weary after our long meeting, because I suddenly felt slightly depressed. The whole thing was, after all, so trivial really. And so were the rest of the local elections, that spring of 1977, all over the country, despite the passions they were arousing in our fellow countrymen. And what about the government, so confident that it was in control of our national destinies? Perhaps the problems confronting it were just as inconsequential.

Outside the castle we were confronted with a technical problem. Colin's Renault refused to start. Colin was in a state of panic. He had arranged to meet his wife and two children that afternoon at the local railroad station, where they were due in on the 2:58 express. But it was Sunday, there was no service station open in Malejac. And in any case, there was already barely time left for him to cover the thirty-five miles into town. There was a brief consultation. Eventually, I got out my own Renault and drove Colin to meet the train myself.

I stop writing, read through that last sentence again, and it's almost a physical blow. Not that there's anything so amazing about it intrinsically, of course. "I got out my own Renault and drove Colin to meet the train myself." What could be simpler? And yet, rereading it, I am gazing into a gaping chasm. My Renault, the train—that's where the rift lies, in those two nouns, slicing our lives in two. In fact, the ravine dividing the two halves of our existence is so irremediable that I can't quite bring myself to believe now that it was actually possible for me—"before"—to accomplish that succession of staggering actions: to reverse my Renault out of its garage, stop at a filling station for gas, drive my friend to meet a train, and be back home again by mid-afternoon, after having taken only two hours to cover seventy miles, and all along an absolutely safe road, without incurring any danger other than that inherent in the speed of the car I was guiding along it. How far away all that seems! And what a brave old world it was that had such wonders in it!

It is something I never think about, God be praised. Except incidentally, when the thoughts occurs on the fringe of some personal memory. Or when I consciously linger, as I am doing at this moment, to describe that world of "before"—so protected, so childlike, so easy.

III

NO, I'm wrong. That short drive to meet the Paris train with Colin isn't my last memory of the "before" world. Another has just surfaced, a moment before the darkness. And I know perfectly well why I almost "forgot" it.

A month before, on a Tuesday, I had received a letter from Birgitta. She was methodical in everything, and it was her unvarying custom to write me every Sunday a sort of love letter couched in very simple, grammatically correct French, stuffed with idiomatic phrases that were occasionally slightly misapplied.

The construction was always the same. First a short sentence inquiring about my life at Malevil, then four pages telling me all about hers, and finally a third section devoted entirely to the erotic vein.

Nor was this third section ever any more varied than the letters as a whole. On Saturday evening, before going to bed, she had reread "the yellow paper," she had slid naked between her sheets, she had thought about me and all the things I had described in "the yellow paper," in particular about my caresses ("Ach, Emmanuel, those hands of yours!"), and she had felt "passionately aroused." And as a result, she would add with great emphasis, she experienced great difficulty in getting to sleep.

Why on Saturday evenings? Presumably because Sunday morning was the only morning in the week when she needn't get up to work, so she could indulge in a modicum of insomnia without detracting from her productivity the following day.

Exactly the conscientious Birgitta I remembered. I read her letter, then reread it, or rather I reread the erotic coda;

and although I knew it would be there and found it amusing, there was no denying that it still worked its intended effect on me. And why not? But it was time for me to start being conscientious too and get to work. I stood up and was on the point of putting the letter back in its envelope when I noticed the P.S.

Birgitta was going into the hospital the following Monday to have her appendix out. She appended the address of the hospital together with the hope that I would write to her.

Birgitta's appendix reminded me that I ought by now to have been disencumbered of my own—gross negligence, my doctor had told me—and I made a mental note that after Easter, work or not, I really must set aside a week of idleness to be rid of it. I also wrote to Birgitta and phoned a pharmacist in the county town to have him send a bottle of Chanel No. 5 to the Munich hospital.

A week went by without news. Worried, and afraid that complications had set in, I wrote again. Two weeks later the answer arrived.

All Birgitta's letters were simple, but the simplicity of this one was a masterpiece. Ten lines in all. Birgitta had met a young man in the hospital who had fallen in love with her. She too was in love with him. She was going to marry him. She would of course miss my caresses, because I had spoiled her so much in that respect, "and thank you for the presents too, Emmanuel. I kiss you very hard, Birgitta. P.S.—I am very happy."

I folded the letter, slid it back into its envelope, and said aloud, "Exit Birgitta." But the attempted flippancy didn't succeed, and sitting there at my table, I went through a very nasty few minutes. My throat was constricted, my hands shook, and I was filled with a distressing sensation of loss, of failure, of diminution. I didn't love Birgitta, but all the same there was a bond between us. I had fallen victim, I think, to that ancient Christian distinction between love and lust. Because I didn't love Birgitta, I had assumed that my attachment to her was negligible.

It wasn't true. My morality had been false, my psychology misguided, and I was now experiencing what I cannot avoid describing as genuine grief. It caught me completely off balance, because this time I had assumed I just couldn't lose. Love for Birgitta, I had told myself, nil; friendship for her, a smidgin; esteem for her, very limited (especially on account of her own lack of feelings). Hence my aloofness, my ironical attitude toward her, as well as the numerous offhand gifts.

Lust, the Abbé Lebas would have said. All right. But lust isn't always what we take it to be. He knew nothing about it, the old Abbé Lebas. And how could he have been expected to, after all, poor repressed old maid that he was? Lust is a very strong moral bond, since it causes such pain when it is broken.

I left my table, lay down on my bed, and let the shock take over. It was a horrible few moments. And when I tried to think I immediately became tangled up again in that distinction between the body and the soul, even though I could see how false it was. The body thinks too! It thinks and feels without any reference at all to the soul. I wasn't in the process of falling in love with Birgitta after the event. Oh, no, not in the slightest! She was a monster of insensitivity, that girl. I despised her violently—as violently as she used to embrace me. But the thought of never holding her yielding body in my arms again did tear at my heart. I say "my heart" because that's how they put it in novels. You could use some other word if you like. But I know what I felt.

When I think back now to my desolation that day, it seems almost comic. A tiny grief exactly to scale with my little life, and ludicrously out of proportion with what was about to follow. For it was in the midst of this minuscule private tragedy that "the day it happened" arrived to drive everything out of our hearts but terror.

In a consumer society the product consumed by man in largest quantities is optimism. Since the days when it became known that the planet was gorged with everything needed to destroy it—and if necessary our neighbor planets as well—somehow we had all learned to sleep peacefully at nights again. And oddly enough, the very excess of those terrifying weapons and the growing number of nations possessing them had actually proved a factor in our gradual reassurance. From the fact that since 1945 none of them had yet been used, it was emotionally deduced that no one would *ever dare to* and that nothing was going to happen. This false security in which we lived had even been found a name and given the semblance of a grand strategy. It was called "the balance of terror."

And another thing needs to be said. Nothing, absolutely nothing, in the weeks preceding Zero Day made it possible to predict it. There were wars, of course, and famines and massacres. And here and there a few atrocities. Some of them flagrant (in the underdeveloped countries), others less obvious (in the Christian countries). But nothing, taken all in all, in any way different from what we had been seeing for the past thirty years. And all of these things had in any case occurred at a convenient distance, among peoples far removed from us. We were distressed by them, of course, we expressed indignation, signed petitions, or even donated small sums of money on occasions. But at the same time, in our heart of hearts, after having dutifully experienced these vicarious sufferings, we returned to our usual feeling of security. Death was something that always happened to others.

The mass media—I still have the last numbers of *Le Monde* and only the other day reread them—were not being particularly alarmist during those weeks. Or if they were it was on a long-range basis. About pollution, for example. They were predicting that in forty years' time the whole planet might be teetering on the edge of the abyss. Forty years! It's like a dream! If only we could count on those forty years still!

It is simply a fact, one I state without any intention of irony, since that would really be too easy. Newspapers, radio, television, none of the great organs of communication that used to keep us so well informed—or at any rate so abundantly informed—foresaw in any way or at any point what was about to happen. And when it did happen they couldn't even cover the story after the event; they had vanished from the face of the earth.

Although it's quite possible that what happened was totally unpredictable anyway. Was it perhaps some terrifying miscalculation on the part of a statesman persuaded by military advisers that he at last held the ultimate weapon? Or was it sudden insanity on the part of someone in a position of responsibility who gave an order that no one was subsequently able to reverse? Perhaps a physical breakdown producing a chain reaction of automatic responses, thereby unleashing identical responses from an opponent, until the moment of terminal annihilation was reached?

One could go on piling up such hypotheses ad infinitum. But all means of verifying them have been forever destroyed.

Darkness begins on that day when History came to an end simultaneously with its object. The civilization whose progress it was there to record had ceased to exist.

At eight o'clock I went to pick up my mail at the gate tower, which was La Menou and Momo's quarters. As on any other morning, I found the postman Boudenot there, a good-looking curly-headed young fellow, already a little red-faced and fuddled by the wine drunk from farm to farm. He was sitting at the kitchen table drinking a glass of mine, and when he saw me come in he lifted half a buttock off his chair as a sign of respect. I told him not to get up, picked my letters up from the table, and as usual refused the glass that La Menou had taken out of the closet and filled for me. And as usual too, "so as it shouldn't go to waste," she drank it herself.

Her strength thus restored, she passed on to serious matters: "Emmanuel, we're going to have to bottle the wine this morning, or there's soon going to be none left."

I shrugged impatiently. "Then let's get down to it right away," I said, "because I'm supposed to be driving over to La Roque at ten with Germain."

"Right, I'm away now then," Boudenot announced as he tactfully rose from his chair. I can still see his curly black hair, his broad smile, and merry eyes as he held out his hand for me to shake a second time. He was solidly planted on sturdy legs, the wine singing in his stomach, delighted at being able to visit so many people every morning and drive around in his little yellow post

71

office van with a cigarette between his lips and his behind comfortably ensconced on his private cushion: a fine profession for a fine young lad with a good education who never made mistakes paying out the pensions and money orders and who would one day "enjoy" retirement on full pension. Then he swung around on his heels and I saw his broad back framed for a moment in the opening of the low doorway.

The little yellow *deux chevaux* was found later, twisted and burned out but still identifiable. Of Boudenot there remained not the slightest trace, nothing, not even a single bone.

I stopped off in my room to put on a sweater before calling Germain at Les Sept Fayards. I let him know that I wouldn't be over before half past ten to collect him on my way to La Roque. As I emerged from the keep into the inner courtyard, I met up with La Menou and advised her to put on something warmer, since the cellar was cold.

"Oh, I don't feel the cold," she said. "It's Momo who needs the warmth." As she spoke I was looking down at her from a great height, on account of her tiny stature, so my eyes were directed down the front of her dress. And at that moment an absurd detail in her appearance struck me. She was dressed, as always, in a sort of black smock, shiny from long use, and just below the low square neckline of the smock against her skin, scarcely visible even to me, I noticed a row of safety pins, and I remember wondering with astonishment, first what they were doing there, and then onto what undergarment they were pinned. Certainly not a brassiere, because what would there be to fit into such a thing?

"But you too, Menou," I said, eyes still fixed on the row of pins, "you ought to put on a sweater. It's chilly down in the cellar. There's no point in catching cold."

"No, no, I don't feel the cold. I never do," La Menou answered, though whether it was just a plain statement of fact or a piece of self-congratulation I couldn't have told you.

In a fairly ugly mood, I inserted my wine-drawing gun into a barrel and sat down on my stool about twenty yards from La Menou, because the cellar was huge, "bigger than the school playground." It was lit by electric light bulbs concealed in niches around the walls; but in case of power cuts there were also a number of large candles on iron wall brackets. Neither too dry nor too damp, the cellar's temperature was invariably the same, summer and winter, just fifty-five degrees on the thermometer on the wall over the water tap. The best refrigerator you could have, according to La Menou, who used it to store all our bottled and preserved food, to say nothing of the bacon, sausages, and hams slung from the vaulted ceiling.

It was around the tap that La Menou had grouped her "tools": a bottle rinser screwed to a big tub filled by the tap, a draining frame, and an automatic corker. She was wholly engrossed in her task, and her mood was in complete contrast with my own. For her, although she drank only with moderation, drawing the wine was a sacred ritual, an ancient festival, the joyful proof of present abundance, and a promise of future merriment. For me, it was a chore. And a chore I couldn't get out of. Two people were sufficient for the entire operation—one to draw the wine into the bottles, the other to cork them—but neither of those two persons could be Momo. If he did the drawing, he barely got the wine running when he felt obliged to satisfy himself that it was running well by inserting the barrel of the dispenser into his mouth before inserting it into the neck of the bottle. And if he was doing the corking, then he took a sample swig from every liter before inserting the cork.

So I always did the drawing, La Menou the corking, and Momo was employed carrying the clean empty bottles from her to me and the full bottles back to his mother. Even so, frequent disruptions still occurred. From time to time I would hear La Menou shout, "Momo, do you want my boot in your bottom?"

I didn't need to look around. I knew that Momo was hastily replacing the bottle he had been sampling into the metal crate. I knew because at the same time, totally refusing to accept the validity of eyewitness evidence, Momo always cried out in an indignant tone, *"Hi hin't hoo hehying!"* (I didn't do anything!)

73

As I pulled the trigger, the wine rose so rapidly in each bottle that the task demanded my constant attention. It always amazed me the way any manual task, even one as mechanical as drawing wine, made all useful cogitation impossible. Though it was true that the irritatingly insistent tunes emerging from the transistor radio slung from Momo's shoulder (a recent and unfortunate gift from La Menou) did nothing to help my concentration.

I was gradually emerging from my initial bad temper, but without succeeding in putting much enthusiasm into what I was doing. Drawing wine is not a particularly intoxicating occupation, except when performed after Momo's fashion. But it had to be done. It was my own wine. I was quite proud of its quality, quite happy to be working with La Menou, and at the same time slightly irritated by Momo's antics and his pop music. In short, I was living through a very ordinary, very average moment of my life, concerned with tiny, fleeting, and only weakly felt contradictory emotions, with ideas or the beginnings of ideas that didn't interest me all that much, and including a very average measure of residual boredom.

There was a violent knocking at the door, as though in some Shakespearean tragedy, and Meyssonnier, followed by Colin and big Peyssou, made a pretty undramatic entrance, even though Meyssonnier was in the grip of extreme anger, as I noticed immediately just from the way he was blinking.

"We've been looking for you everywhere," he said as he strode toward me along the length of the cellar with the other two behind him.

I noted with irritation that they had omitted to close the two doors of the vaulted passage that led into the cellar.

"It's big, this dump of yours. Luckily we ran into Thomas. He told us where to come."

"What," I said as I offered my left hand over my shoulder, eyes still fixed on the wine level in the bottle, "hasn't Thomas gone yet?"

"No, he was sitting in the sun, on the keep steps, studying his maps." Meyssonnier's tone changed slightly as he passed on this information, because a young man who spent so much time studying pebbles inspired him with a certain regard.

"My respects, Monsieur le Comte," Colin said. For some reason he found it amusing to address me by this pseudo title since I had bought Malevil.

"Morning," Peyssou growled.

I didn't look at them. My eyes were still on the rising wine in another bottle. There was a silence in which I sensed a certain embarrassment.

"Well, what about your Boche?" Peyssou asked, sensing the same thing. "Is she on her way?"

Here was one subject at least with no complications attached. Or so he thought.

"She's not coming back after all," I said brightly. "She's getting married."

"You didn't tell me that," La Menou observed in a reproachful tone. "Well, fancy that!" she added scornfully. "Getting married!"

I could see that she was itching to issue a moral condemnation, but she could hardly avoid remembering how she had come to marry her own husband, so she fell silent.

"I don't believe it!" Peyssou said. "Getting married? Well I take that badly, really I do, considering the treat I had in store for her."

"You're going to find yourself short-handed," Colin said.

I couldn't turn around to look at Meyssonnier, the wine rose in the bottles too quickly. But I noted that he was staying very silent. "I have three temporaries coming at the end of the month," I said after a moment.

"Girls or boys?" Peyssou asked.

"One boy, two girls."

"Two girls!" Peyssou said. But he didn't follow it up, and the silence started getting heavy again.

"Menou," I said, "go and find three glasses for these gentlemen."

"Oh, don't bother," Peyssou said as he licked his lips.

"Momo," La Menou said, "you go and get them. You can see how busy I am."

The truth was that she had no intention of leaving the

cellar just when the conversation looked like becoming interesting.

"*Hon't ho!*" (I won't go.)

"Do you want my boot up your backside?" La Menou asked, rising from her stool with a threatening look.

Momo was out of reach in one bound, then stood stamping furiously on the floor and said again, "*Hon't ho!*"

"You will go!" La Menou said, taking a step toward him.

"*Momo hon't ho!*" her son cried defiantly, one fist on the door handle poised for flight.

La Menou gauged the distance between them, then calmly sat down again.

"If you go," she said in a quiet voice pulling down the lever of the corker as she spoke, "I'll cook you fried potatoes tonight."

Greed spread over Momo's badly shaven face and lit up his little dark eyes, the bright and guileless eyes of an animal. "*I ha a homise?*" he asked eagerly, scrabbling with one hand in his tousled black mane of hair and with the other inside his trousers.

"It's a promise," La Menou said.

"*Momo ho!*" Momo said with a delighted smile. And he vanished so quickly that he too omitted to close the doors behind him. The sound of his nailed boots could be heard receding up the stone staircase.

Peyssou turned to La Menou. "It looks as though your boy is something of a trouble to you," he said politely.

"Oh, he likes to have his own way sometimes, there's no denying that," La Menou said with an air of satisfaction.

"Well, you've let yourself in for some cooking this evening, just to get yours," Colin said.

La Menou's death's-head face wrinkled into a grin.

"It so happens," she said in the local dialect, "that this is my day for cooking fried potatoes anyway. But he didn't even think of that, poor booby!"

And why it was in fact so much funnier in patois than in French I couldn't tell you. Perhaps because of the intonation.

"Oh, they're wily, women are," little Colin said with his gondola smile. "They can lead you by the nose anywhere."

"And not only by the nose," Peyssou added.

There was laughter, and we all three looked at Peyssou with sudden affection. There he was, big Peyssou. Still the same. As filthy-minded as ever.

Another silence. In Malejac, people took their time. You didn't just rush headlong to the heart of the matter.

"You don't mind, I hope," I said, "if I go on drawing my wine while you talk?"

I could see Colin signal to Meyssonnier with his eyes, but Meyssonnier still remained silent. His knife-blade face seemed even longer than before, and his eyelids were flickering at full speed.

"All right then," Colin said. "We'd better tell you, since you are, after all, a little off the beaten track, up here in Malevil. The letter to the mayor has worked out really quite well. It's been circulated, and the people generally have reacted well. Where that's concerned, no worries. The wind is beginning to blow our way. It's where Paulat's concerned that things aren't going so well."

"Ah, old Paulat is stirring things up, eh?"

"He is that. Especially when he saw that things were beginning to go against the mayor. He went around telling everyone that he approved of it heartily, that letter. He even managed to suggest that it was his brainchild."

"The devil he did!" I said.

"And if he hadn't actually signed it," Colin went on, "that was simply because he didn't want to sign his name next to that of a Communist."

"Whereas," I put in, "he would be quite willing to appear next to a Communist on a list of candidates, provided, of course, that the Communist didn't head that list."

"That's it!" Colin said. "You've got it exactly."

"And the name at the head of the list, needless to say, has to be mine. I would be elected mayor, Paulat would become my deputy, and since I am far too busy to run the town hall properly, he would take over."

I stopped my wine drawing and turned to face them.

"All right. And so what? What have Paulat's little stratagems got to do with us? We just ignore them, that's all."

"Yes, but you see people are pretty much in agreement with him," Colin said.

"In agreement about what?"

"About your being mayor."

I burst out laughing. *Pretty much* in agreement?"

"That was just my way of putting it," Colin said. "Actually they're wholly in agreement."

I looked at Meyssonnier, then returned to my wine. In 1970, when I had resigned my headmastership of the school to take over my uncle's business, people in Malejac had thought me very unwise indeed. And when I bought Malevil, it was clear as day that Emmanuel, for all his education, was as crazy as his uncle before him. But the 160 acres of impenetrable undergrowth had been transformed into lush meadows. Malevil's vineyards had been replanted and now produced an excellent wine. I was about to start earning "fantastic amounts" by opening the castle to tourists. And above all I had returned to Malejac's fold of orthodoxy: I had begun to keep cows again. With the result that in the space of six years I had received swift promotion in local public opinion. Once a madman, I had now become a shrewd devil. And why shouldn't a shrewd devil who looks after his own interests so well also be entrusted with those of the community?

In short, Malejac had firmly grasped the wrong end of the stick twice: first by taking me for a madman, second by wanting to make me its mayor. Because I wouldn't have made a good mayor at all, since it just didn't interest me enough. And meanwhile, the good mayor was there in front of their noses the whole time. But of course, true to their tradition of blindness, Malejac just couldn't see him.

Leaving the doors open, though admittedly he did have both hands full, Momo returned carrying not three but six glasses. Obviously he had no intention of being left out. He was carrying them one inserted into another in a vertical pile, with his filthy fingers deeply ensconced in the top one.

I stood up. "Give them here," I said, promptly ridding

him of his burden. And I began the distribution with him, making sure he got the soiled glass.

I drew a bottle of '75, the best in my opinion, and went the round of my guests, greeted by the customary refusals and protestations. As I was pouring the last glass, Thomas came in, closing the two doors carefully behind him, needless to say, and walked toward us without the slightest trace of a smile, more than ever like a Greek statue someone had dressed up with a crash helmet and a black raincoat.

"Have a glass with us," I said, offering him mine.

"No, thanks," Thomas said. "I don't drink in the morning."

"Good morning again," Peyssou said with a polite smile.

And since Thomas just looked at him without response, either to his smile or his greeting, he added with an embarrassed air; "We've already met once this morning."

"Yes, twenty minutes ago," Thomas said, his face still expressionless. Clearly he was unable to see any necessity for saying good morning again, since he had already been through that formality once.

"I just came to tell you that I shan't be here for lunch this morning," he said, turning to me.

"Turn off that trashy music, can't you," I yelled at Momo. "You're driving us all crazy with that thing!"

"You hear what Emmanuel says?" La Menou shouted.

Momo moved away a few steps, clutching his radio under his left arm with a sullen look and making no move to turn down the volume even slightly.

"That was a brilliant idea of yours last Christmas!" I said to La Menou.

"Poor Momo," she answered, immediately changing sides. "He has to have something to amuse him while he's mucking out your stables!"

I looked at her, effectively silenced. Then I took the line of smiling while at the same time frowning slightly, a reaction that I hoped would convey my recognition of La Menou's victory while at the same time safeguarding my authority.

"I was saying that I shan't be back for lunch," Thomas said.

"Fine," I said. And as Thomas turned to leave again I said to Meyssonnier in the local dialect, "Come on, don't worry your head about the elections. We'll find a way of neutralizing old Paulat."

In my memory, everything freezes at that exact moment, as though the cellar had become a waxworks in which historic characters were forever frozen into familiar postures. In the center, the group formed by Meyssonnier, Colin, big Peyssou, and myself, glasses in our hands, faces enlivened by the prospect of the discussion ahead, all four very concerned about the future of a village with a population of 412 inhabitants, on a planet with a population of four billion human beings.

Striding away from the group, with his back toward it, Thomas. Between Thomas and us, Momo, still looking at me defiantly, holding an already half-empty glass in one hand and in the other his radio, which was still churning out some imbecilic pop song at full blast. Beside him, as though ready to spring to his defense, yet so much tinier than he, La Menou, wrinkled as a little dried-up apple, eyes still glittering from her recent victory over me. And lastly, all around and above us, the vast cellar with its great ribbed and vaulted ceiling lit from below, softening the light before reflecting it back down onto our heads.

The end of the world, or rather the end of the world in which we had lived until then, began in the simplest and least dramatic of ways. The electricity failed. When the darkness fell there was laughter, someone observed that it must be a power failure, a cigarette lighter crackled twice and a flame appeared, lighting up Thomas's face.

"Will you light the candles?" I asked as I walked over to him. "No, better still, give me the lighter. I'll do it myself. I know where the brackets are."

"I can still find my mouth without candles," Peyssou's voice said.

And someone, perhaps Colin, said in a quiet voice with a little laugh, "It's certainly big enough."

With the lighter flame quivering in front of me, I walked past Momo and realized that his radio had ceased its bellowing, although the dial was still lit up. I lit the four candles in the two nearest brackets, and their light, after the darkness, seemed almost too intense, even though they still left the greater part of the cellar in obscurity. The brackets had been fixed fairly low down on the walls in order not to spoil the lines of the vaulting, and our shadows on the latter looked gigantic and dislocated. I handed the lighter back to Thomas, who replaced it in his raincoat pocket and once more set off toward the door.

"So you've turned that damn thing off at last!" I said to Momo.

"*I'nt hur it hoff!*" he answered, looking at me with deep reproach, as though I had cast a spell on the radio. "*It hon't hurk!*"

"It won't work!" La Menou cried indignantly. "A brand new radio! And the batteries new from yesterday! I bought them in La Roque!"

"It would be extremely surprising," Thomas's voice broke in. His face swam once more into the light as he walked back toward us yet again. "It was working only a moment ago, wasn't it? Are you sure you haven't been messing about with the batteries?"

"No, no," Momo grunted.

"Show me," Thomas said as he laid his maps down on a stool.

I expected to see Momo clutch his radio to him and back away, but he handed it over to Thomas immediately, with the air of a worried mother entrusting her sick baby to a doctor. Thomas switched the radio off, thereby extinguishing the dial light, then switched it on again, turned it up to full volume, and slowly moved the needle across the entire tuning range. There were violent crackling noises, but no recognizable sounds emerged.

"When the lights went out, did you drop it? Did you knock it against anything?"

Momo shook his head. Thomas took a red penknife out of his pocket and, using the smallest blade, unscrewed the back of the radio. Then he held it up close to one of the candle brackets and inspected the insides.

"I can't see anything wrong," he said. "It looks in perfect shape to me."

He replaced the screws one by one, and I thought he was going to hand the radio back to Momo and get on

81

his way, but he did nothing of the sort. He stayed there motionless, a preoccupied expression on his face, moving the needle back and forth across the dial.

We were all standing there, the seven of us, silently listening to the silence, if I can put it that way, of the portable radio, when a noise exploded of which I can convey no idea except by using comparisons that all seem to me ludicrously inadequate: rolls of thunder, pneumatic drills, sirens, airplanes going through the sound barrier, herds of maddened locomotives. But anyway, something hammering, screaming, metallically grinding, and screaming, the highest and lowest frequencies of sound at the same time, screwed up to such a volume that it went beyond human perception. I don't know whether noise when it reaches such paroxysmic proportions is capable of killing. But I believe that it would have done so if it had lasted.

I flattened my hands desperately against my ears, I bent double, I tried to turn myself into a ball, and I realized that I was trembling from head to foot. I am certain that this convulsive trembling was a purely physiological reaction to a noise intensity at the limit of human tolerance. Because at that moment I had not yet begun to be afraid. I was too stupid and shaken to form any idea. I didn't even tell myself that this cacophony had to be incredibly loud in order to be reaching me through walls seven feet thick and a whole story below ground.

I pressed my hands against my temples, I shook, and I had the feeling my head was about to explode. At the same time idiotic notions began shooting through my mind. I wondered indignantly who had knocked over my glass, which I could see lying on its side two yards away. I also wondered why Momo was lying flat on his stomach on the flagged floor, face pressed to the stone, hands pressed against the back of his head, and why La Menou, who was shaking him by the shoulders, had her mouth stretched wide open without emitting the slightest sound.

The words I have used—din, cacophony, thunder— give no idea of the intensity of the noise. It stopped after a period of time I have no way of gauging. A few seconds, I suspect. I realized it had stopped when I myself stopped trembling, and when Colin, who had been sitting on the floor to my right throughout, said something in my ear and I recognized the word "racket." At the same time I became aware of a plaintive yapping sound. It was coming from Momo.

I cautiously unstuck my hands from my tortured ears, and the yapping became shriller, mingled now with La Menou's murmurs of commiseration. Then the yapping ceased, La Menou stopped speaking, and following upon the inhuman noise we had just undergone a silence fell upon the cellar so profound, so abnormal, and so painful that it made me want to cry out. It was as though I had been leaning against the noise, and when it ceased I found myself suspended in a void. I felt incapable of moving an inch, and at the same time my field of vision had shrunk. Apart from La Menou and Momo, who were lying directly in front of me, I could see no one, not even Colin, even though he later assured me that he had not budged from his position beside me.

Linked in some way I could not understand to the silence, a feeling of horror filled me. I realized simultaneously that I was suffocating and streaming with sweat. I removed, or rather ripped off, the turtleneck sweater I had pulled on before coming down into the cellar. But I scarcely noticed any difference without it. The sweat continued to well from my forehead and run down my cheeks, under my armpits, and down the small of my back. I was experiencing an intense thirst, my lips were dry, and my tongue was stuck to the roof of my mouth. After a moment I realized that I was holding my mouth open and panting like a dog, in quick short gasps, yet without being able to overcome the sensation of being slowly choked. At the same time I experienced an extreme lassitude, and sitting there on the floor, back against a barrel, I felt incapable of either speaking or moving.

No one uttered a word. The cellar was now as silent as a tomb, and there was no sound whatever to be heard other than that of seven mouths panting for breath. I could now make out the rest of my companions, but the image was blurred, confused in my mind with a sensation of weakness and nausea, as though I was about to faint. I

83

closed my eyes. The effort to look around me seemed intolerably exhausting. There was no thought in my head, no questions, not even puzzlement as to why I was being slowly suffocated. I slumped in my corner like a dying animal, wholly inert. I panted, I sweated, and I experienced a feeling of appalling dread. I knew only one thing with absolute certainty: I was going to die.

I saw Thomas's face appear in my field of vision and come gradually into focus. He was naked to the waist, pale, streaming with sweat. He said in a whisper, "Take your clothes off." I was staggered at not having thought of it earlier. I removed my shirt and undershirt. Thomas helped me. Very fortunately I wasn't wearing my riding boots, since even with his assistance I would never have succeeded in getting them off. The smallest movement reduced me to exhaustion. It took me three tries to pull my pants off, and even then it was only thanks to Thomas that I succeeded. -

A second time he put his mouth to my ear, and I heard "Thermometer . . . by tap . . . hundred and fifty degrees."

I heard him clearly, but it took me some moments to comprehend that he had discovered from a reading of the thermometer over the water tap that the temperature in the cellar had risen from plus fifty-five degrees to plus a hundred and fifty.

I felt a sense of relief. I was not dying of an incomprehensible disease after all. I was dying of heat. But the expression was still no more than a metaphor in my mind. I did not envisage for a second the possibility that the temperature might continue to rise and become lethal. Limited by past experience, I was wholly unable to conceive the notion that it was possible, quite literally, to die of heat in a cellar.

I succeeded in pulling myself up onto my knees, and at the expense of agonizing effort I managed to crawl over to the tub of rinsing water. I fastened both hands onto the rim of the tub, and with my heart thumping against my ribs, everything swimming in front of my eyes, half choking, I managed to pull myself upright and plunge my arms and head in the water. It gave me a delicious sensation of coolness, which meant, I suppose, that it had not yet had time to heat up to the temperature of the surrounding air. I stayed in that position so long that I would probably have drowned if my hands had not come into contact with the bottom of the tub and began pushing as though of their own accord, so that my head finally emerged. I became aware then that while immersed in the dirty wine-tainted water pumped back into the tub by the rinser I had been drinking it. After that I succeeded in keeping on my feet and seeing my companions clearly. Apart from Colin, who had probably heard what Thomas whispered to me, they were all still fully dressed. Peyssou's eyes were closed, and he seemed to be asleep. Momo, incredibly it seemed to me, still had his sweater on. He was lying on the floor motionless, head on La Menou's lap. La Menou herself was propped up against a barrel, eyes closed, emaciated face absolutely without a trace of life. Meyssonnier was looking at me with eyes in which I could read despair and impotence. I realized that he had seen me drink, that he wanted to do the same, but that he hadn't the strength to drag himself over to the tub.

I said, "Take off your clothes."

I had intended to speak with authority, but the result was a shock. The voice that emerged from my lips was wispy, toneless, a feeble croak. I added with absurd politeness, "If you don't mind."

Peyssou didn't move. La Menou opened her eyes and made an effort to take off Momo's sweater, but she was unable to lift her son's torso and fell back again, streaming with sweat, against the curved staves of the barrel. She kept opening and closing her mouth in the most horrifyingly painful way, like a fish dying on a riverbank. Meyssonnier kept his eyes fixed on me, and his fingers began unbuttoning his shirt, but so slowly that I realized he was never going to manage it.

I myself fell down again into a sitting position beside the tub, panting hard, but with my eyes still fixed on the despair in Meyssonnier's, determined to help him if I could find the strength. Pushing myself up on one elbow, I knocked against one of the two six-compartment metal crates that Momo had been using to carry the bottles back and forth between La Menou and myself. I counted the six bottles in it. And so badly was my mind functioning that I had to start over twice before I succeeded in counting up to six. I took hold of the nearest bottle. It seemed very heavy. I lifted it with a great deal of effort to my lips and drank, puzzled as to why I had been drinking dirty water when there was so much wine all around me. The liquid was warm and acrid. I drank about half a bottle at one go. I was sweating so profusely that my eyebrows, despite their thickness, were unable to dam the stream of perspiration. It trickled down in a constant stream into my eyes and blinded me. Nevertheless I felt my vigor returning slightly, and began moving toward Meyssonnier, not crawling, but dragging myself along on my left side while holding the half-full bottle in my right hand.

I noticed that the flagstones were very hot against my hip. I halted to regain my breath while the drops of sweat streamed down my face and body as though I had just emerged from a bath. I threw my head back in order to keep the sweat out of my eyes and caught sight of the ribbed vaulting above my head. I couldn't see it very clearly, because the light from the candles was too dim, but I had the impression that the ribs were glowing as though heated to white heat.

And as I lay there, stupefied and stifling, watching my sweat dripping ceaselessly onto the burning flagstones, the thought came to me that we were all imprisoned in that cellar like roasting fowl in an oven, our skin already blistered and streaming with melting fat. Yet even then, even at that moment when I had succeeded in formulating what was after all a fairly accurate notion of the situation, I still thought of that notion as a metaphor, and so paralyzed was my logical faculty that I did not for a single second try to picture to myself what was happening outside. On the contrary, if I had had the strength to open the two doors of the little vaulted corridor, to climb the stairs and make my way outside, I would have done so, in the complete conviction that I would find the selfsame coolness outside that I had left only an hour before.

I reached Meyssonnier and held out the bottle, then realized that he was incapable of taking hold of it. So I pushed the neck between his dry lips, which seemed to have stuck to each other. At first most of the wine spilled down his chin, but as soon as his mouth was well moistened, his lips tightened around the glass and his swallow became more rapid. I experienced a vast relief at seeing the bottle emptying itself, because holding it up to his mouth required an enormous effort, and I scarcely had the strength to set it down on the floor when he had finished.

Meyssonnier then turned his head toward me, without speaking, but with a look of gratitude at once so piteous and so childlike that in my state of weakness at that moment I felt near to tears. But at the same time the fact of having come to his aid gave me added strength, and I was able to help him to undress. When it was done I arranged his clothes underneath him and under myself to isolate our bodies from the burning stones, and with my head leaning back beside his against a barrel I must have gone into a faint for several seconds, because suddenly I was wondering where I was and what I was doing there. Everything in front of me was so blurred and vague that I thought my sweat must be blinding me. At the cost of an incredible effort I managed to wipe my hand over my eyes, but the blurring still remained for several more seconds. I hadn't even the strength to focus my eyes.

When my vision did eventually become clearer I saw Colin and Thomas moving around Peyssou, undressing him and helping him drink. Turning my head painfully to the right, I saw Momo and his mother lying side by side completely naked, La Menou with her eyes closed and huddled into a foetal position, like those tiny skeletons unearthed from prehistoric burial mounds. I wondered how she had found the strength to undress herself and even to get Momo's clothes off as well, but the thought vanished again almost immediately.

I had just conceived a plan that would require every ounce of my strength, that of crawling back to the tub and climbing into it. How I succeeded in doing so I have no idea, because the flagstones were by now hotter than ever, but I can see myself still at the foot of the tub making desperate efforts to haul myself up its side, pressing the palm of my left hand against the wall, then pulling it back again immediately as though I had touched a sheet of red-hot metal. I must assume that I succeeded, however, since I remember finding myself sitting in the water, knees pressed against my chin and keeping my head just above the level of the liquid. I am certain, having thought it over later, that it must have been the hottest bath I have ever taken, but at the time I experienced an amazing sensation of coolness. I also remember having drunk my bath water on several occasions. And I imagine that I must also have dozed off, because I suddenly awoke with a terrible start to see the cellar door swinging open to disclose the figure of a man.

I stared at him. He took two steps into the cellar, then stood swaying on his feet. He was naked. His hair and eyebrows had disappeared, his body was as red and swollen as though it had been immersed for several minutes in boiling water. But the thing that seemed to me most horrible and froze me with terror was that there were strips of bloody flesh hanging from his chest, his belly, and his legs. Yet despite all that, I don't know how, he was standing upright, he was looking at me, and although his face was no longer anything but one bloody wound, I recognized him by his eyes. It was Germain, my hired hand from Les Sept Fayards.

I said, "Germain!"

And immediately, as though he had only been waiting for that cry, he collapsed forward, rolled over in a somersault, and came to rest flat on his back, motionless, legs straight, arms spread-eagled on either side. At the same time, a current of air reached me from the still open door so scorching that I decided to climb out of the tub and close it. And quite incredibly I succeeded, either by crawling on all fours or dragging myself, I no longer remember, but there I was pushing with all my weight against the heavy oak panel. It slowly began to budge at last, and with an immense feeling of relief I heard the latch click into its slot.

I was panting and streaming with sweat, the flagstones were scorching me, and I wondered with inexpressible anguish if I was going to succeed in getting back to my tub. I was propped on elbows and knees, totally exhausted, head hanging down, barely a few steps away from Germain, and I hadn't even the strength to crawl over to him. But it would have been pointless. I knew that already. He was dead. And at that point, when I no longer had the strength even to lift my head, elbows and knees being burned by the floor, fighting down a desire to give up and let myself die, I looked across at Germain's corpse and comprehended for the first time, in a flash of illumination, that we were surrounded by an ocean of fire in which all human, animal, and plant life had been consumed.

IV

I HAVE just read through what I have written, and a number of things I had not noticed before immediately sprang to my attention. For example, I wonder how Germain, already dying and stripped of clothing—found the strength to reach us down in the cellar. I imagine that he must have received an urgent message from a customer, realized that he couldn't phone me because he knew I was in the cellar, set out for Malevil on his motorbike, and was caught by the holocaust just as he was entering the castle, in other words at some point where he was already relatively protected from the sheet of fire by the cliff. Given that hypothesis, he must only have been licked by the very fringe, as it were, of the titanic tongue of flame that shot down like a vast lightning flash from north to south. Which would explain, it seems to me, the fact that he was not totally consumed by it, like most of the population of Malejac, of whom nothing remained but a few blackened bones beneath a layer of ash.

If Germain had reached the inner courtyard a few seconds earlier, it is possible that his life would have been saved. Because the castle itself in fact suffered very little damage, presumably because the vast cliff overhanging it to the north acted as a massive shield between it and the worst of the inferno.

Another thing strikes me. From the moment when the train-like thunder (again I have to admit that the phrase is ludicrously inadequate) exploded in the cellar, followed by that terrible baking heat, my companions and myself were all seized by a paralysis not only of our limbs and speech but even of thought. We spoke very little, moved even less, and what was even more surprising, as I noted earlier, was that I had no clear notion of any kind about what was happening outside the cellar, until the sudden appearance of Germain. And even then I continued to think in only the vaguest terms. I completely failed to connect or draw any conclusions from the failure of the electricity supply, the persistent silence of all the radio stations, the inhuman noise that followed, and the terrifying rise in temperature.

And accompanying this loss of reasoning power there was also the loss of any sense of time. Even today I cannot tell how many minutes passed between the moment when the lights went out and the moment when the door opened to reveal Germain. The reason for this, I take it, was that my perception of things was interrupted by several blanks, so it no longer functioned other than intermittently and extremely feebly.

I also lost all moral sense. I didn't lose it immediately, since I began by coming to Meyssonnier's assistance at considerable cost to myself. But that was the last flicker, as it were. It never occurred to me for a moment subsequently that it was an extremely unaltruistic piece of behavior to take sole possession of our only tub of water by climbing into it and remaining immersed there for so long. On the other hand, if I hadn't done so, would I have had the strength to crawl over to the door Germain had left open and close it? I noticed, after I had done it, that not one of my companions had so much as budged, even though all their eyes were fixed upon the opening with an expression of suffering.

I said earlier that as I knelt on my hands and knees, exhausted, head hanging, barely more than a yard away from Germain, I hadn't the strength to move toward him. But I ought really to have said courage rather than strength, since I was able to summon sufficient of the latter to get back to my tub. The truth of the matter was that I was still in the grip of the sudden terror I had experienced when I saw his swollen, bloody body appear in the doorway, the strips of flesh hanging half off his torso like the tatters of a shirt ripped in a brawl. Germain was tall and strongly built, and perhaps because I was huddled in the tub, perhaps too because his shadow on the vaulted ceiling was so disproportionately enlarged by the low candles, he seemed to me an immense and terrible figure, as though it was death itself, not one of its victims, that had suddenly appeared. Also he was standing, whereas our weakness had reduced us all to prostration on the floor. And lastly, he was swaying backward and forward as I watched, fixing me at the same time with his piercing blue eyes, and I somehow construed that swaying as containing a terrifying menace, as though he was about to fall forward upon me to destroy me.

I reached the tub, but to my great surprise I was forced to give up any idea of climbing back into it, because when I put one hand into it I decided that the water was too hot. I ought to have deduced that this sensation was merely an illusion, and meant in fact that the surrounding air was beginning to cool down, but the idea didn't cross my mind for a second, any more than that of consulting the thermometer above the tap. I had only one idea in my head: to escape from contact with the stone floor. I hoisted myself with some difficulty up onto two wine casks lying on their sides and touching each other. I settled myself crosswise, sitting in the hollow between them, legs and torso raised up by the two curves. The wood gave me a sensation that was almost one of coolness and comfort, but that didn't last. I was in too much pain, although the site of it was now different. I was perspiring less and no longer stifling, but the palms of my hands, my knees, my hips and thighs—in short all those parts of my body that had been in contact with the floor—were now hurting. I could hear a low whimpering all around me, I thought fleetingly of my companions with a feeling of concern, until eventually I realized with shame that it was I who was whimpering. Later I came to realize that there is nothing more subjective than pain. And the pain I was feeling at that point was in fact out of all proportion to the very superficial burns that were producing it. As soon as I had regained a little strength and begun to act again, I forgot them.

A further proof of how slight they were was the fact that I went off to sleep and must have slept for some while.

As I awoke I noticed that the big candles in the two brackets had burned out, and that someone had lit two of the others a little farther on. Then I experienced a sensation of icy cold all through my body, but particularly in my back. I shivered. I searched for my clothes with my eyes, failed to locate them, and then without my being aware of it my intentions changed. I had decided to get down from my perch and go over to look at the thermometer. Moving was very painful. My muscles were stiff, almost locked, and the palms of my hands hurt me every time I tried to shift position. The thermometer read plus eighty-six, but however hard I tried to tell myself that it was still hot, that I had no reason to be shaking with cold, my reasoning was unable to stop me shivering. As I turned away from the thermometer I saw Peyssou, standing up, leaning against a cask, and struggling back into his clothes. And oddly enough I could see no one except him, even though the five others were all there. It was as though my eyes were so tired that they simply refused to see more than one thing at a time.

"Are you getting dressed?" I asked stupidly.

"Yes," he said in a weak but perfectly natural voice. "I'm getting dressed. I must go home. Yvette must be worried. "

I stared at him. As soon as Peyssou mentioned his wife the light flooded cruelly into my mind. And in some strange way this illumination had a color, a temperature, and a shape. It was white, icy, and like a knife slashing into my heart. I watched Peyssou dressing, and at that moment, for the first time, I really grasped the event that I was living through.

"What's the matter? Why are you looking at me like that?" Peyssou asked aggressively.

I hung my head. I don't know why, but I felt a horrible sense of guilt on his account. "Nothing, nothing, Peyssou, old friend," I said in a weak voice.

"You were looking at me," he said in the same tone, and his hands were trembling so that he had to abandon the attempt to pull on his pants.

I didn't answer.

"You were looking at me. You can't say you weren't,"

he went on with a look of hatred and a note of anger in his voice that his weakness made piteous.

I said nothing. I wanted to speak, but I could find nothing to say. I glanced around me searching for support. And this time I could see my companions. Or rather I was able to see them one by one, with a series of painful reiterated efforts that made me begin to feel sick.

La Menou, leaden-skinned, was sitting with Momo's head on her lap and stroking his dirty hair with an almost imperceptible movement of her thin fingers. Meyssonnier and Colin were seated side by side, frozen into immobility, haggard-faced, eyes lowered. Thomas was standing, leaning against a cask. In one hand he was holding Momo's transistor radio, with the other he was unceasingly winding the needle very, very slowly from one end of the still lighted dial to the other, vainly scanning the world in search of a human voice. His preoccupied face now had not merely the features of a marble statue but also its coloring, and almost its consistency.

None of them returned my look. And immediately, I remember, I felt a wave of mortal bitterness toward them, the same feeling of impotent hatred that I had seen for me in Peyssou's eyes. Like a newly born child howling with pain as the air penetrates into its lungs, each of us had lived such interminable hours turned in wholly upon himself that it was very difficult to enter once more into contact with others.

The temptation to let Peyssou do as he pleased insinuated itself into my mind. I found myself saying inwardly in a coarse aggressive accent, All right, if that's the way he wants it, let him bloody well go, and good riddance. I was so shocked at the baseness of this reaction that I immediately swung to the very opposite extreme and began thinking with maudlin tearfulness, Peyssou, my poor old friend Peyssou.

I let my head sag forward. I was deep in the utmost confusion. My reactions were all so excessive, and none of them like me at all. With a kind of timidity, as if I were excusing myself for being in the wrong, I said, "It may still be a little dangerous to go out yet."

As soon as it was uttered this remark struck me as

almost comic, so wildly did it underestimate the situation. But even so, it made Peyssou angry, and he said savagely, teeth clenched, but in a voice just as weak as my own, "Dangerous? Why dangerous? How do you know about it, whether it's dangerous?"

Apart from anything else, the tone in which he spoke was obviously artificial. He sounded like a bad actor in a play. But I knew what part he was trying to play and I felt I wanted to cry. I lowered my head, and once again at that point, out of weariness and depression, I almost gave up making any effort to restrain him. What stopped me, when I raised my head again, were Peyssou's eyes. They were filled with fury, but there was supplication in them too. They were begging me to say nothing, to leave him as long as possible in his state of blindness, as though my words in themselves possessed the power to create the terrible misfortune that had struck him.

I was sure now that he had understood—as Colin and Meyssonnier had. But they were attempting to evade their appalling loss by withdrawing into stupor and immobility, whereas Peyssou was trying to escape by running toward the threat, denying everything, ready to rush out, eyes closed, to the ashes that had been his home.

I began several sentences in my head, and almost opted for one of them: Just think, Peyssou, judging from the temperature in here earlier on . . . No, I couldn't say that. It was too direct.

I lowered my head again and said stubbornly, "You can't just leave like this."

"And you're going to stop me, I suppose?" Peyssou answered in a defiant tone. His voice was still very weak, and as he spoke he made a pitiful effort to square his great shoulders.

I didn't attempt to answer. I was aware of a sickly-sweet smell in my nostrils and throat that made me feel slightly nauseated. When the four candles in the first two brackets had guttered out, someone, possibly Thomas, had lit the two in the next bracket, so the area of the cellar I was in, near the water supply, was largely plunged in darkness. It took me a little while to realize that the smell I was finding so unpleasant was emanating from the body

95

of Germain, which was lying scarcely visible to one side of the door.

I realized that I had forgotten its very existence. Peyssou, whose eyes were still fixed resolutely on mine, still with their look of combined hatred and supplication, followed my gaze, and at the sight of the body he seemed for an instant to have been turned to stone. Then he quickly pulled his eyes away with a slightly ashamed air, as though he had decided to deny the existence of what he had just seen. He was now the only one of us fully dressed; but although the way to the door was clear, and I was obviously incapable of preventing him reaching it, he still did not move.

I said again, with a stubbornness lacking any kind of strength, "Come on, Peyssou. You can't just leave like this."

But it had been a mistake to speak. My words seemed to provide him with the motive power he needed, and without turning his back on us, yet not actually walking backward either, he took several hesitant and awkward crablike steps toward the door.

At that moment I received assistance from an unexpected quarter. La Menou opened her eyes and said in patois, as though she were sitting in her kitchen in the gate tower instead of lying pale and naked in a cellar, "Emmanuel's right, farmer. You can't just go like this. You need to eat something first."

"No, no," Peyssou answered, also in patois. "Thanks all the same. I really don't need it. Thank you."

But he had halted his steps, caught in the trap of peasant invitations with their complicated ritual of refusal and acceptance.

"Now come on, come on, Monsieur Peyssou," La Menou said, not to be deflected from the customary course of such courtesies. "It won't do you any harm to stop and have something for a moment. Nor all the rest of us. Monsieur le Coultre," she went on, in French now and turning to look at Thomas, "would you kindly lend me your little knife?"

"But really, I tell you I'm not hungry," Peyssou said, though it was clear that these exchanges were affording

96

him vast relief, for he was looking at La Menou with childlike gratitude, as though she was his only lifeline to the familiar and reassuring world she represented.

"Now come on, come on, Monsieur Peyssou," La Menou said, with a calm confidence that he was going to accept. "Come on, you," she went on, pushing Momo's head off her lap, "move over a bit so I can get up." And then, when Momo clung to her knees and began to whimper, "Now stop that, you big booby," she went on in patois, and gave him a good hard slap on one cheek. Where she found the reserves of strength for all this I have no idea, because when she stood up, naked, tiny, skeletal, I was staggered all over again by her fragile appearance. Yet without any help she untied the nylon cord supporting one of the hams hanging over our heads, lowered it to the ground, and removed it from its hook while Momo, his face white and terrified, watched her and gave tiny yells for help like a baby. As soon as she walked back toward him and laid the ham down on a cask over his head to unwrap it, he stopped his whimpering and began sucking his thumb, as though he had abruptly regressed to babyhood again.

I watched La Menou as with great difficulty she managed to cut off a number of small thickish slices from the ham, holding it propped against the cask, the knife handle gripped firmly in her bony little hand. Or to be more exact, I watched her body. As I had foreseen, she did not wear a brassiere, and where her breasts would have been there were just two very tiny wrinkled pockets of loose skin. Beneath her sterile belly the bones of her pelvic girdle jutted out sharply. Her shoulder blades were clearly visible, and her buttocks, thinner than a little she-monkey's, were no bigger than your fist. Ordinarily, when I said La Menou it was a named charged with all the affection, the esteem, and the irritation that characterized our relationship. But that day, seeing her naked for the first time, I was forcibly reminded that her dialect nickname, La Menou—"Tiny"—referred also to a body, possibly the body of the only woman surviving in the world, and observing its decrepitude I experienced a boundless inward sadness.

97

La Menou collected the slices of ham in her right hand, rather like a pack of cards, and proceeded to deal them out, beginning with me and ending with her son. Momo snatched his share with a savage grunt, thrust it whole in his mouth, and pushed at it with his fingers. He immediately went scarlet, and would probably have choked to death if his mother had not forcibly opened his jaws and pushed her tiny hand down his throat to pull out the obstruction. Having done so, she used Thomas's knife to cut up the saliva-covered slice into small pieces, then put them into Momo's mouth one by one, scolding him and slapping him meanwhile every time he bit her fingers.

I watched this little scene only vaguely, without any feeling of either amusement or distaste. As soon as I had my slice of ham in my hand, the saliva flooded my own mouth, and holding it in both hands, I began ripping at it with my teeth, hardly less gluttonously than Momo had attacked his. It was very salty, and eating all that salt along with the pork in which it had been absorbed gave me an incredible feeling of well-being. I noticed that my companions, Peyssou included, were all eating equally greedily, moving away from one another slightly and casting almost fearful glances around them, as though they were afraid that someone might snatch their share of the meat away from them.

I finished eating long before the others, then looked around for the crate of full bottles and observed that it was empty. So I hadn't been the only one to quench my thirst that way. I felt happy at this discovery, because I was beginning to feel remorse at having monopolized the tub for so long. I picked up two empty bottles and filled them with my drawing gun. Once again I handed around the glasses—this time without paying the slightest attention to which one Momo had been handling—and poured out wine for us all. While they were drinking, with the same silent avidity as they had eaten, my companions all kept their hollow, blinking eyes on the ham that was still lying on the flat top of the cask against which La Menou had leaned while cutting it. La Menou understood what their eyes were saying, but she refused to let herself be softened. As soon as she had finished her wine she wrapped the ham up again with inflexibly precise gestures and hauled it back into place, out of reach above our heads. With the exception of Peyssou, we were all still naked. Standing there in silence, bent forward slightly by fatigue, eyes greedily fixed on the meat hanging from the dim vaulting, we were not so very different from the hominids who had once lived in the mammoth cave beside the Rhunes, not far from Malevil, in the days when man had only just emerged from the primate stage.

My knees and palms were still hurting, but strength and awareness were by now slowly returning, and I realized how very little we were talking and with what care we were avoiding any reference to what had happened. At the same instant, and for the first time, I felt slightly uneasy at being unclothed. La Menou must have shared the feeling, because she murmured just then with a disapproving air, "Whatever do I look like, for heaven's sake!"

She had spoken in French, the language of official and polite sentiments. She promptly began to put her clothes back on, quickly followed by everyone else, and as she did so she continued in a louder voice, but in patois, "Not a tempting sight, that's for sure!"

As I dressed I glanced surreptitiously across at Colin and Meyssonnier, and as little as I could at Peyssou. Meyssonnier's face, hollow and shiny, looked as though it had been stretched lengthwise, and his eyes were blinking nonstop. Colin's still wore a gondola smile, but it was strangely artificial and frozen, totally unrelated to the anguish I could read in his eyes. As for Peyssou, who no longer had any reason to stay in the cellar now that he had eaten and drunk his wine, he was making no move to leave, and I carefully avoided seeming to look at him in case I should force him into movement again. His big kindly mouth was trembling, his broad cheeks kept twitching, and with his arms hanging at his sides, his knees slightly bent, he looked like a man drained of all will and all hope. I noticed that he kept glancing across at La Menou, as though he was expecting her to tell him what to do next.

I went over to Thomas. I couldn't see him very clearly, since that section of the cellar was in near darkness. "In your opinion," I answered in a low voice, "is it dangerous to go outside?"

"If you mean from the point of view of the temperature, no. It's much lower now."

"There's another point of view, you mean?"

"Of course. The fallout."

I stared at him. I hadn't thought of fallout. I took note, however, that Thomas obviously nursed no doubts as to the nature of what had happened.

"So it would be better to wait?" I said.

Thomas shrugged. His face was totally without animation, his voice colorless. "The fallout could keep coming for a month, two months, three months . . ."

"So?"

"If you'll let me go and fetch your uncle's Geiger counter from your closet, we can settle the question here and now. For the moment at least."

"But that means exposing yourself!"

His face remained as unmoving as a block of stone. "You have to realize," he said in the same flat mechanical voice, "that in any case our chances of survival are very limited. Nothing will be able to last long, flora or fauna."

"Not so loud," I told him. I realized that, though they had not dared move closer to us, our companions all seemed to be straining their ears to listen.

Without saying anything more, I took the key to my closet from my pocket and held it out. Thomas immediately began pulling on his raincoat, put on his crash helmet, his big watertight goggles, and his gloves. Thus equipped, he suddenly looked rather frightening, since both raincoat and helmet were black.

"Is that sufficient protection?" I asked in a half-choked voice, touching him with one hand.

His eyes behind the goggles remained expressionless, but his frozen features twitched in what could have been the beginning of a smile. "Let's just say it's better than going out stripped to the waist."

As soon as he had gone, Meyssonnier came over to me. "What is he going to do?" he asked in a low voice.

"Measure the radioactivity."

100

Meyssonnier stared at me with hollow eyes. His lips were quivering. "He thinks it was a bomb?"

"Yes."

"And you?"

"I do too."

"Ah," Meyssonnier said, and that was all.

Just that one "ah," then silence. He wasn't even blinking now, and his eyes were lowered. His long face looked like wax. I glanced over toward Colin and Peyssou. They were watching us, but they didn't come over. Torn between the hunger to know and terror of hearing the worst, they remained as though paralyzed. Their faces seemed quite expressionless.

Thomas returned ten minutes later, the headphones still over his ears, the Geiger counter held at arm's length. He said curtly, "Negative in the inner enclosure. For the moment."

Then he knelt down beside Germain and passed the counter to and fro over the body. "He's negative too."

I turned to the rest and said in an authoritative voice, "Thomas and I are going to climb the keep in order to get some idea of what has happened. Don't move from here. We shall be back in a few minutes."

I was expecting protests from the others, but nothing of the sort happened. They were all in that state of stupor, prostration, and bewilderment in which any order at all given in a commanding tone is promptly accepted. I was sure they wouldn't budge from the cellar.

As soon as we reached the small courtyard formed by the keep, the drawbridge, and the Renaissance house, Thomas signaled me to stop, and he began passing his counter methodically to and fro across the ground. I watched him, dry-mouthed, without emerging from the cellar entrance. Even there I was immediately smothered by the heat, which was in fact still much greater than that in the cellar. Yet, I don't know why, it never occurred to me to check it by glancing at the thermometer I had brought up with me.

The sky was gray and leaden, the light intensity extremely low. I looked at my watch: ten past nine. Stunned, my brain like cotton, I wondered vaguely if this was the dusk of Zero Day or the next morning. An absurd question, I eventually realized after an effort of reflection that seemed painful in the extreme. At Eastertime it would already be dark by nine in the evening. So of course this must be the morning of Zero Day plus one. We had spent a day and a night in the cellar.

Overhead I could see neither blue sky nor clouds, but only a dark gray uniform layer that seemed to be closing us in like a pall. The word pall conveys exactly the impression of half darkness, weight, and suffocation that sky gave me. I looked up. At first glance the castle didn't seem to have been damaged, except that the scorched stone of the upper portion of the keep, which rose above the level of the clifftop, was now a russet color.

The sweat began to run down my face, and I finally thought to consult the thermometer. It was registering plus a hundred and twenty-two. Lying on the centuries-old flagstones over which Thomas was moving his counter there lay the half-charred bodies of a few magpies and pigeons. They had been the keep's habitual occupants, and I had occasionally complained about the pigeons' cooing and the magpies' shrieks. I would not have occasion to complain from now on. All was silence, except in the far distance, perceptible only when I concentrated on it, a continuous sequence of cracklings and hissings.

"Negative," Thomas said as he walked back toward me, face bathed in sweat.

I understood him well enough, but somehow, I don't know why, his brevity of speech irritated me. There was a silence and since he made no further move and remained motionless as though he was listening to something with great concentration, I went on impatiently, "Shall we go on?"

Thomas stared up at the sky without answering.

"Well, come on then," I said with an irritation that I was having difficulty in restraining. It was the product, I think, of extreme fatigue, mental distress, and the heat. Listening to people, talking to them, and even just looking at them, everything was painful. I added, "I have my binoculars. I'll pick them up on the way."

The heat in my room on the keep's third floor was

appalling, but everything was still intact, it seemed to me, except that the lead holding the tiny panes of the mullioned windows had melted and run down the outside of the glass in places. While I went through every drawer in my bureau looking for the binoculars, Thomas picked up the telephone, held it to his ear, and moved the cradle up and down several times. The sweat was pouring down my cheeks by now. I threw him a vicious glance, as though blaming him for having induced a shortlived gleam of hope in me by his actions.

"Dead," he said.

I shrugged my shoulders angrily.

"Well, we have to check," Thomas said with what looked almost like a flash of ill humor.

"Here they are," I said, feeling slightly ashamed.

And yet I was still unable to suppress that feeling: a kind of irritable and impotent hostility toward my fellow men. I hung the binoculars around my neck by their strap and began climbing the last section of spiral staircase, with Thomas at my heels. The heat was stifling. I stumbled several times on the worn stone steps and was forced to clutch at the baluster with my right hand, and the palm of that hand began burning again. The binoculars bumped and swung against my chest. The weight exerted by the strap against the back of my neck seemed unbearable.

When we emerged from the spiral staircase into the open air at the top of the keep, we could still see nothing, since the roof was completely surrounded by a wall about eight feet high. There was a set of stone steps jutting out from the wall and leading up to a parapet about a yard wide, but without any rail. It was this parapet, from which a vast area of the surrounding countryside could be seen, that my uncle thought too dangerous for me at the age of twelve.

I stopped to regain my breath. No sky. The same lid of leaden grayness stretching to the horizon. The air was literally burning, and my knees trembled as I made the effort to climb those last few steps, panting for breath, the sweat dripping from my forehead onto the stone. I didn't climb up onto the parapet. I was too uncertain of my balance. I remained standing on the last step, with Thomas on the one below.

I took a slow look all around and went briefly into a state of shock. I must have swayed as I stood, because I felt Thomas's arm against my back pressing me forcibly against the wall.

The first sight I saw needed no binoculars. Les Sept Fayards was just smoldering embers. There was nothing left of the collapsed roofs, the windows, the doors. Nothing still standing but blackened stretches of wall, standing out against the gray of the sky, with here and there the stump of a tree sticking up out of the ground like a burnt stake. Not a breath of wind. Thick black smoke rose vertically from the ruins, and every so often I could see a line of red flames advancing across the ground, flickering up, then sinking back again like a damped-down campfire.

A little farther away, on my right, I finally managed to make out what had been Malejac. The church steeple had vanished. And the post office too. Ordinarily the latter was easily recognizable, an ugly two-story building standing apart from the rest on the road leading up the side of the hill toward La Roque. The whole village looked as though it had been flattened by a vast fire, then raked into the ground. Not a leaf. Not a single tile roof. Everything the color of ashes, black and gray, except when a tongue of flame shot up briefly, only to die again almost immediately, like all the rest.

I raised the binoculars to my eyes and focused them with shaky hands. Colin's house was the first you came to in the village itself, Meyssonnier's stood a little outside it, on the slope down toward the Rhunes. I could find no trace of the first, but I identified Meyssonnier's from a gable that still remained standing. There was nothing left of Peyssou's farm and the beautiful spruces planted all around it but a little blackened mound.

I lowered the binoculars and said in a low voice, "Nothing left."

Thomas nodded but said nothing.

I ought to have said no one left, since it was quite clear from a single glance that apart from our own tiny group the entire countryside all around was dead—with its entire population. The view from the top of the keep was one I knew well, and from an early age. When Uncle Samuel had loaned me his binoculars for the first time I had spent a wonderful afternoon, along with the rest of the Club, lying on the parapet (I can still feel the pleasant warmth of the stone against my naked thighs) identifying all the farms nestling among the little hills, a process accompanied, needless to say, by a vast expenditure of swear words, yells, and virile challenges. "Hey, you great asshole, take a look there, that's Favelard down there, just between Les Bories and La Volpinière!" "What's the matter with your eyes?" "I bet you a pack of Gauloises that's Favelard!" "Cussac!" "Cussac my ass!" "I bet you both balls it's Cussac!" "Dummy, that's Cussac over there next to Galinat. Anyone can see that because of the tobacco shed!"

And now I looked out to find all those farms I had always seen nestling there—Favelard, Cussac, Galinat, Les Bories, La Volpinière, and many other more distant holdings whose names I knew, even though I didn't always know the owners—and all I could see was blackened ruins amid the still smoldering woods.

Because in our part of the world we had always had plenty of woods. In summer, when you looked down from the keep, what you saw was the cool dark green of the chestnut forests frothing away to infinity, broken here and there by clumps of pines or oaks, and down in the valleys the lines of Lombardy poplars—planted for future profit but meanwhile providing the landscape with elegant vertical features—together with occasional Provence cypresses, more costly trees, planted singly beside the farmhouses for the sake of the pleasure they brought.

But now, poplars, cypresses, oaks, and pines had all vanished. As for the vast chestnut woods that had covered entire hillsides, leaving only a few unwooded areas on the upper slopes, where the houses stood with their gently sloping meadows all around them, of all that there was almost nothing to be seen but flames. And sticking up from the flames was a forest of blackened stakes, dying amid the continual crackling and hissing I had heard as I emerged from the cellar. It was the great side branches that had split away from the trunks and fallen to the forest floor that were flaming still, and the effect was as though the hills themselves were slowly being consumed by fire and burning themselves away to ashes.

On the road that ran beside the Rhunes, just below the now shattered and blackened Château des Rouzies, I caught sight of a dead dog. I could see it in minute detail, since the road was quite close and my binoculars high-powered. A dead dog! you may say, when so many men and women had lost their lives! It's true, but there is a great difference between what you know and what you see. I knew that hundreds of human beings had burned like torches in the villages and farms all around Malevil, but that dog, apart from the birds in the court-yard, was the only corpse I saw, and there was a particular and horrible detail in the circumstances of its death that affected me deeply. The poor beast must have attempted to escape from the paddock or yard where it had been caught and tried to run away along the familiar road; but its paws had been caught fast in the melted tarmacadam, and it died there, stuck fast, roasted where it stood. Through my binoculars I could see the four limbs clearly, caught in the blackish gravelly mixture, which as the dog collapsed had been pulled upward by the paws without cracking, forming a little black cone around each leg, and still imprisoning them.

Without looking at Thomas, without even noticing that he was there, as though after all that had happened any relationship between one human being and another was henceforth impossible, I kept saying over and over again in a quiet murmur, "It's horrible, it's horrible, it's horri-ble." It was an insane litany that I was powerless to break off. My throat was gripped in a vise, my hands were shaking, sweat was pouring into my eyes, and apart from that one overwhelming sensation of horror, my mind was blank. There was a gust of wind. I took a deep breath, and immediately a pestilential odor of decay and burned flesh invaded my body with such force that I felt it was actually coming from me. It was enough to make one vomit. I had the sensation of being my own corpse, yet somehow still alive. It was a sharp, putrescent, sweetish odor that seeped in and took possession of my whole being, something I would live with inside me till the end of time. The whole world was now nothing but a vast common grave, and I alone was left, with my companions, to live on in this charnel ground, to bury the dead and live on forever with their odor.

I was losing my reason, and I think I must have realized it, because I turned around and signaled to Thomas that I wanted to climb down. And once back on the flagstones of the keep roof, the high parapet all around us cutting off that view of a burning world, I squatted on my heels, empty, lifeless. I don't know how long I remained in that state of prostration, which was already like a death. It was a kind of psychic coma in which, though I had not lost consciousness, I was totally deprived of reflexes and will.

I felt Thomas's shoulder against mine, and when I turned my head toward him with a slowness that surprised me even at the time, I saw his eyes staring at me. I had some difficulty in focusing my own, but when I had done so I realized what it was his eyes were saying to me, and saying with all the more intensity because he was in the same state of paralysis as myself and unable to speak in any other way.

I watched his lips. They were bloodless and dry. And when he did speak, to utter only a single word, he had difficulty unsticking them from each other. ". . . Solution . . ."

Eyes blinking, I stared at him again with painful effort, for I felt myself ready to sink back at any moment into my trance-like state. Tearing the words out of my throat, terrified by the extreme feebleness of my voice, I said, "What . . . solution?"

The answer took so long coming that I thought Thomas had lost consciousness. But then I realized from the tensing of his shoulder against mine that he was summoning up his strength to speak. I heard him only with the greatest difficulty. "Up steps . . ."

As he said the words he made a tiny painful gesture

with his bent forefinger toward the parapet. Then in a whisper he went on: "Jump. . . . Done with it."

I looked at him. Then I turned my eyes away. I sank back into my passivity. A series of unconnected thoughts milled confusedly about in my head. But then, in the center of them, a clearer idea suddenly formed and captured my attention. If like Colin, Meyssonnier, and Peyssou I had a wife and children, at this moment they would be alive, the human race would not be doomed to vanish from the earth, I would have something to fight for. And now I had to return to the cellar to tell my companions that they had lost their families, and wait with them for the disappearance of mankind.

"Well?" Thomas said in a scarcely audible voice.

I shook my head. "No."

"Why not?" Thomas's lips mouthed silently.

"The others."

Saying that with a certain clarity of thought did me good. I began coughing violently, and the thought came to me that the stupor fogging my brain was perhaps as much due to the smoke I had breathed in as to the terrible moral shock I had undergone. I heaved myself painfully to my feet. "The cellar."

I tottered back to the entrance of the narrow spiral staircase, without waiting for Thomas, and I climbed, or rather tumbled back down it. Fortunately, in preparation for the tourists I had been expecting, I had fixed an iron handrail on the wall, and even though it burned my palm horribly, I was able to cling to that whenever my foot missed a step. In the little yard between the keep and the house, Thomas caught up to me and said, "Your horses." I shook my head to signify no and hurried on, repressing a sob. The thought of seeing them filled me with horror. I knew for certain they must all be dead. I had only one thought: to hide myself away again as quickly as possible in my underground hole.

I shivered as I entered the cellar, so cold did it seem, and my first gesture was to pick up my sweater, throw it over my shoulders, and knot the sleeves around my neck. Colin was drawing wine while Meyssonnier was carrying the bottles over to La Menou for her to cork. I was certain that this activity had been initiated by La Menou, who must have decided that there was no earthly reason not to finish the task she had begun. But whoever's idea it had been, seeing them busying themselves in that way certainly did me good. I walked over to them, took one of the full bottles, drank, then handed it to Thomas. Despite my shivering, the sweat was still streaming down my face, and I used one of the sleeves of my sweater to wipe it. Then I leaned against a cask, and very gradually I felt my thoughts ordering themselves once more in my mind.

After a few moments I became aware that my companions were frozen into the most complete immobility, staring at me silently with an expression of anguish and even of supplication. They obviously already knew what had happened, but none of them had the courage to ask me any questions. Only La Menou, I could see, really wanted to hear me speak. But she too refrained from questioning me, her eyes fixed on the others, aware what my persistent silence meant for them.

I can't say how long it lasted. In the end I must have felt it was less cruel to speak than to go on saying nothing, and in a quiet voice, looking directly at them, I said, "We didn't go far. Just to the top of the keep."

With my throat dry, I went on: "It's just as you thought. There's nothing left."

They were expecting it, and yet as soon as I spoke, it was as though I had poleaxed them. The only one who reacted was Peyssou. Eyes starting from his head, he staggered three steps toward me, clenched his fists onto the sleeves of my sweater, and shouted very loudly, "It's not true!"

I didn't answer. I hadn't the heart. Instead, taking hold of his clenched fists, I tried to disengage them from the sleeves of the sweater. As I pulled at his fingers, the sleeves parted, revealing the binoculars still hanging around my neck. Peyssou noticed them, recognized them, and his eyes remained glued to them in horror. At that moment, I am certain, the whole of that afternoon we had spent on the keep parapet identifying the farms flashed before his eyes. An expression of despair appeared on his face, his hands released their hold, and leaning his head forward onto my shoulder, he began weeping with huge gulping sobs, like a child.

There was a swift bustle in the cellar immediately, a series of movements performed in unison, even though no signals were exchanged, which produced an emotion that affected me deeply and was, I believe, decisive in restoring my wish to live. I put my arms around big Peyssou (he was almost half a head taller than me), and immediately Colin and Meyssonnier were on either side of him, one with a hand on his shoulder, the other with an arm around his neck, attempting in their simple and manly way to quiet him down. I was staggered to see them, those two who had themselves lost everything, lavishing their consolations on our friend. At the same time, I don't know why, I remembered that the last time Colin and I had held Peyssou so tightly was when we were twelve, to keep him still so that Meyssonnier could "stuff his great trap shut." But this memory, far from diminishing my emotion, in fact increased it. There we were, the three of us, clustered around our great shaggy bear, talking to him, squeezing him, hitting him on the back, muttering friendly insults at him. "Come on, you great ninny, that's enough now."

To which he replied through his tears, and gratefully, "Oh, bugger off, the lot of you. I don't need all this!"

The sobs slowly eased off and we moved away from him slightly.

"We must go and take a look though," Meyssonnier said, face pale, eyes hollow.

"Yes," Colin said with a tremendous effort, "we must go and see."

But neither of them made a move.

"I don't know if you'll be able to get through," Thomas said. "The woods haven't stopped burning yet. And from here to Malejac it's woods all the way, on both sides. Not to mention radioactivity. Because, after all, the courtyard is very protected. The risk exists."

"Risk?" Peyssou said, raising his head from his hands. "What have I got to live for anyway?"

There was a silence.

"What about us?" I said, looking at him hard.

110

Peyssou shrugged his shoulders, opened his mouth, changed his mind, and said nothing. His shoulders were saying something different from his silence. They were telling us, There's just no comparison. But he kept quiet because he knew all the same that we did count for something.

La Menou entered the debate then. Her intervention did not take the habitual form of a monologue delivered in a quiet voice for her own benefit and only secondarily directed at others, or of a swift comment in patois deftly inserted into the conversation. She made what was for her a long speech, and she made it in French—in itself proof of the importance she attached to it—yet without taking her hands off her corker.

"My boy," she said to Peyssou, "it is not for us to say whether we are going to live or die. If we are alive, then that's so we can carry on. Life is like work. It's not worth it unless you do the job properly. It's no good just leaving off when it starts to get difficult."

Having said that, she pulled down the lever of her machine and a cork slid noiselessly into a bottle. Peyssou looked at her, opened his mouth, then again changed his mind and said nothing. I thought La Menou had finished, but she inserted another bottle under the corker and went on: "You're thinking now, La Menou, she can talk, she hasn't lost anything, she has her Momo. Which is true in a way. But even if I had lost Momo [she took her hand off the lever and crossed herself] I would never say what you said just then. You're alive because you're alive, my boy. No good looking further than that. Death is no friend to man, not ever."

"You're right, old mother," Colin said.

And indeed, given her age, she could have been our mother, though no one till then had given it a thought.

"Come on," Meyssonnier said and made a few stiff steps toward the door.

I intercepted him and took him to one side. "The both of you, you and Colin," I said in a very low voice, "try not to leave Peyssou alone. You know why. The best thing would be for you all to stay together all the time."

"That's what I thought too," Meyssonnier said.

Thomas now came over as well, his Geiger counter in his hand. "I'm coming with you," he told Meyssonnier, just as Colin with Peyssou behind him joined the group.

They all three stopped and looked at him.

"There's no reason why you should come, Thomas," Colin said to him, apparently unaware that this was the first time he had ever addressed him by his first name.

"You'll need me though," Thomas said, holding up the counter.

There was a pause, then Meyssonnier said in a throaty voice, "We'll take Germain's body out with us. We'll leave it by the gate of the outer wall until we can find time to bury him."

I scarcely thanked him, but I felt the greatest gratitude toward him for having thought of Germain at a time when he was in such distress on his own account. I watched them leave. Thomas went first, his headphones around his neck ready to be slipped on, the counter held out in front of him. Meyssonnier and Peyssou followed, carrying Germain with evident difficulty. Colin brought up the rear, looking even more tiny and frail than ever.

The door closed behind them and I stood there in front of it without moving, distressed at the thought of their mission and wondering whether I ought not to go with them.

"There are no full bottles left to cork," La Menou said calmly from behind me. "Perhaps you could fill some more for me."

I went back to my stool, sat down, and began drawing the wine again. I was very hungry, but I wasn't going to set an example of undisciplined indulgence by claiming owner's rights on my own hams. La Menou had taken charge of provisions, and she had been right to do so. She would always be fair, that was beyond doubt.

"Come on, Momo," she said, seeing that I would soon have no empty bottles left.

And as Momo got to his feet and began filling a crate she added in the same quiet voice, but in a very firm tone, "And try not to drink any on the way over, because now when you drink more than your share you're taking it from the others."

I imagined that Momo would remain wholly deaf to this exhortation, but I was wrong. He had heard it and he respected it. Or perhaps it was simply his mother's tone of voice he was reacting to.

"You were very sparing earlier on with the ham," I said to La Menou after a moment. "I wasn't exactly happy to see them leave with empty bellies." Then with a gesture toward the ceiling I added, "Especially with all the ham and sausages that are here."

"There are seven of us," La Menou answered, following my gesture with her eyes, "and when everything hanging there is finished, there's no saying we shall ever eat pig again. Or drink wine. Or ever bring in another harvest."

I looked across at her. She was seventy-seven, La Menou. She had already envisaged with the utmost clarity the prospect of possible death from hunger, yet her will to live remained unimpaired.

The door of the cellar opened suddenly and Thomas's head appeared around it. With what for him was almost violent emotion, he cried, "Emmanuel! You have some animals still alive!"

He vanished again. I stood up open-mouthed, wondering if I'd heard him correctly. La Menou was on her feet too. She stared at me, then said in patois, as though not sure whether she had understood Thomas's French aright; "Did he say there are animals still alive?"

"*Momo ook!*" her son cried, and he set off at a run toward the door.

"Wait, wait! Wait for me, I tell you!" La Menou shouted as she trotted after him as fast as she could. She looked like a little old mouse with her thin little shanks flickering to and fro. I heard Momo's hobnailed boots clanging up the stone stairs. Then I began running too. I passed La Menou and caught up with Momo just as he was crossing the drawbridge to the outer enclosure. There was no sign of Thomas and the other three. Thomas must have hurried back to bring the news, then sprinted off again to catch up with them on the Malejac road.

As we approached we were greeted by a medley of whinnies, bellows, and grunts, all rather faint. They-were coming from the cave that Birgitta had nicknamed the Maternity Ward.

I sprinted for all I was worth, passed Momo, and reached the cave completely out of breath, streaming with sweat, my heart banging against my ribs. The animals there, in the separate stalls built at the back of the cave, were Bel Amour, Momo's adored fourteen-year-old mare, about to foal at any moment; Princesse, one of La Menou's Dutch cows in the same condition; and my own filly, Amarante, still too young to be serviced, but in temporary confinement in the Maternity Ward because she had been cribbing. And lastly an enormous sow, also on the point of farrowing, whom La Menou—without my permission, though that didn't bother her—had given the name of Adelaide.

All four animals had suffered a great deal. They were lying on their sides, clearly very weak, breathing with difficulty, but nevertheless still alive, thanks to the depth and coolness of the cave. I was unable to get near Bel Amour, because Momo had already hurled himself on her neck, rolling beside her in her droppings and whinnying with love. But Amarante, whose head was lying on the straw, managed to raise it when I came into her stall, and she pushed her nostrils toward my fingers to sniff at them. When La Menou appeared she didn't even stop to scold Momo for dirtying his clothes in the dung. She was far too busy inspecting Princesse, feeling her belly and sympathizing with her. ("There now, poor old thing, poor old thing.") Then she went in to see the sow, though without getting too close to her, on account of her notorious viciousness.

I checked the automatic water troughs. The water was hot, but they were still working.

"*Momo hetch hum harley!*" Momo said, and he began climbing the ladder up to the floor above where I stored my hay.

"No, no!" La Menou cried after him. "No barley! Bran with water and wine for all of them. And look at you, you great ninny," she added. "Look at your pants covered in muck, now you'll be stinking worse than Adelaide herself!"

I stepped away from Amarante and found the courage

to leave the Maternity Ward to inspect the stalls outside. The smell told me all I needed to know before I got there, and I pressed my handkerchief over my nose, so suffocating was the foul smell. All the animals were dead, not burned to death but suffocated by the heat. Being built against the cliff itself, the line of stalls had been protected by it and had not caught fire. But the great flat stones covering them must have been heated to a tremendous temperature, because the beams beneath—all solid oak salvaged from the old buildings, and as hard as iron—had been scorched dark brown, on the surface at least.

La Menou returned with two bottles of wine, mixed it with water and made a bran mash that she divided up into four big bowls. I went back into Amarante's stall, where she was still lying on her side, took a handful of the mash, and held it under her nose. She sniffed at it, blew on it through her nostrils, then curled back her lips with distaste and listlessly attempted to nibble at it. When she had finished I took a second handful and held that out too. She ate very little, and infinitely slowly. It struck me as being rather ironical, since I myself was so hungry I was almost ready to eat the bran that she was turning her nose up at. With one ear I could follow the alternating insults and endearments that Momo was showering on Bel Amour next door in an attempt to make her eat, and in quieter counterpoint the encouragements La Menou was lavishing on Princesse. As for Adelaide, La Menou had contented herself with simply pushing the bowl under her nose, and to judge from the noises she was making, the sow was the only one of the quartet doing full justice to her meal.

"How is it going, Menou?" I asked, raising my voice.

"Not good. What about you?"

"Not so good either. Momo?"

"*Hyupid, hyupid 'el Amour!*" (Stupid, stupid Bel Amour!)

"It's because we can't explain to them," La Menou said. "Talking and common sense, they're useful things when all's said and done. Look at my Princesse now. Hungry, yes she's hungry, but she's so weak the poor thing doesn't even know she's hungry."

Squatting on my heels, feet almost numb by now, I

115

was still waiting for Amarante to finish toying with her second handful of mash. And I found myself murmuring the same tender insults at her as the others. I was under no illusions. These four animals were the condition of our survival. Even the horses, since no plowing was going to be possible without them now that supplies of gas and diesel fuel had dried up forever.

Amarante was by now refusing every mouthful I tried to coax down her. She had let her muzzle sink to the ground again and lay in an attitude of exhausted resignation that didn't augur at all well. I got hold of her forelock and forced her to hold up her head while I held out the mash in the palm of my other hand. Still without attempting to take it, she gazed at me vaguely with her great sad eyes, as though to say, Can't you leave me alone? Why torment me like this?

La Menou, incapable of staying in one place, was trotting to and fro, her feet clacking firm and sharp on the stone, visiting the sow, trotting back to Princesse, and soliloquizing nonstop, for my benefit as well as her own.

"Just look at that great slut Adelaide, already finished her mash, so now I can give her some real feed. Fair play to them, they're tough as old boots, pigs are. When I think of the cows I've lost or nearly lost in calf. And all those horses just from a handful of fresh lucerne or a few yew twigs. It's always their stomachs that are the death of horses, and with cows it's their bellies. But you just try doing away with that great sow! Just from the number of teats on her you can see what a strong beast she is. She's so solid you'd say she was a monument. And she drops those piglets of hers by the dozen, without any help from anyone. Sixteen she gave me once, sixteen!"

I was very worried about Amarante, but listening to La Menou—so everyday, so at ease with these familiar animals and things, chattering on as though nothing had happened—did a great deal for my morale. Momo was having more success with Bel Amour than I was with Amarante. I could tell as much from the way his anger and his threats had gradually given way to endearments and little whinnies.

La Menou poked her head through the stall door. "All right, Emmanuel?"

"No, far from it."

She inspected Amarante. "I'll fetch her some wine and sugar water. You look after Princesse."

I went into Princesse's stall. My uncle had passed on a little of his prejudice against cows to me, but all the same, that great big fat-bellied animal with the square muzzle moved my heart. There she lay, patient and motherly, on one side, revealing her vast belly and the teats that were going to provide us with food. Just looking at her—weak as I was, legs shaky, stomach hollow and gnawed by hunger—filled me with a terrible thirst for milk. I wasn't forgetting that she hadn't calved yet, I just ignored that troublesome fact. In my mind, heated by my fast, I was almost hallucinating now and then, seeing myself as Romulus or Remus being suckled by their wolf, lying under Princesse and sucking with sensual pleasure, squeezing the great swollen teat between my lips, waiting for the moment when it sent its streams of warm liquid spurting against the back of my throat.

I was deep in these fantasies when La Menou returned from the gate tower carrying what from its maroon wrapping was clearly a carton of sugar. Ah, she was not going to stint where the animals were concerned, that was clear. I got up and followed her, hypnotized by her burden. I watched, eyes unmoving, mouth running with saliva, as she took those beautiful shining white lumps of sugar in her thin little hand and dropped them into the bucket of water. She noticed my look.

"Poor Emmanuel, you're hungry!"

"Fairly, yes."

"Only I can't give you anything before the others come back."

"I didn't ask for anything," I said with a pride that rang only too hollow, and which La Menou completely ignored moreover, since she handed me three lumps of sugar, which I accepted. She gave the same number to Momo, who promptly stuffed all three at once into his great maw. Whereas I carefully snapped each oblong tab-

117

let in two so as to make it last longer. I noticed that La Menou hadn't taken any herself.

"What about you, Menou?"

"Oh, me," she said. "I'm so little, I don't need as much as you."

The warm sugary water mixed with wine met with Amarante's approval. She drank it all down greedily, and after that it became possible to make her accept the bran. I experienced an incredible feeling of elation watching her eat the handfuls I held out to her one by one. At that moment, I remember, it occurred to me that even in the country, where people are after all very fond of animals, we don't really value them as much as we ought, as though it were quite natural that they should always be there, to carry us, to feed us, to do our bidding. I looked at Amarante's shining eyes, with the slight margins of white that told me her fear had not yet quite subsided, and I thought, We're not grateful enough. We don't thank them enough.

I got to my feet and looked at my watch. We had been in the Maternity Ward three hours. I emerged from the stall, knees almost giving way under me, remembering that I'd promised myself to bury Germain before the others got back. La Menou and Momo joined me outside.

"They're not doing too badly, that's what I think," La Menou said. Not for anything in the world would she have said that the animals were saved. She would have been too afraid of tempting whichever power it was— God or the devil—that was now keeping watch on the words of men to punish them the moment they expressed too much hope.

V

THE others returned at one that afternoon, hollow-eyed and haggard, covered in ashes, hands and faces black. Peyssou was naked to the waist. He had used his shirt to make a bundle of the bones or fragments of bones they had found in their houses. None of them uttered a word. Except Meyssonnier, very briefly, to ask me for wood and tools. Nor would they eat or wash until he had finished making a small box, about two feet long and a foot wide. I can still see their faces as Meyssonnier, the casket finished, picked up the bones one by one and laid them in it.

It was decided to bury it in the flat area outside the gate, at the place where the rock gave way to soil, and beside the grave where I had just buried Germain. Peyssou dug a hole about two feet deep, throwing the soil into a heap on his left. The little box lay beside him. Its very smallness was a piteous sight. It was hard to imagine that what remained of three families was now enclosed inside that tiny coffin. But presumably my friends had decided not to collect the ashes surrounding the bones, for fear that they were mingled with those of mere objects.

I noticed that after lowering the box into the hole he had dug, Peyssou arranged a number of large stones on top, as though he was afraid it might be dug up by a dog or a fox. A useless precaution, since in all probability the world's entire fauna had been destroyed. Having filled in the hole, Peyssou arranged the soil left over in a small rectangular mound, taking great care to straighten the edges and square off the corners neatly with his spade.

Then he turned to me. "We can't just let them go like this. We must say the prayers."

"But I don't know them," I said, dumfounded.

"You've got a book, though, with them in it?"

I nodded.

"Perhaps you could go and get it."

I said quietly, "You know what I think about all that, Peyssou."

"That's nothing to do with it. It's for them you'll be saying them, not for you."

"Prayers!" Meyssonnier said, also very quietly, looking down his nose.

"What about your Mathilde? She went to Mass, didn't she?" Peyssou asked, turning toward him.

"All the same," Meyssonnier said.

The whole discussion was conducted in low restrained tones, and there were long silences separating our utterances.

"My Yvette," Peyssou said, eyes fixed on the ground, "it was church every Sunday, and every evening Our Father and Ave Maria in her nightgown at the foot of the bed." (While he was expressing it, the memory became too intense. His voice choked and he remained frozen for two or three seconds before going on.) "So there you are," he went on at last. "If she was for her prayers then, now that the moment has come for her to go I'm not going to let her go without them, that's all. And the kids neither."

"He's right," Colin said.

No one knew what La Menou thought, because she didn't open her mouth.

"Anyway, I'll go fetch the missal," I said after a moment.

I discovered later that during my absence Peyssou had asked Meyssonnier to make a cross to mark the grave, and that Meyssonnier had agreed without any protest. When I reappeared, Peyssou said, "It's very kind of you, but if it upsets you that much, then Colin or me can read them."

"No, no," I said. "I don't mind doing it, since you say it's for them."

I was given the benefit of La Menou's opinion when we were alone later. "If you'd refused, Emmanuel, I wouldn't have said anything, because where religion is concerned it's always a delicate subject, but I wouldn't have thought you were right inside. And besides you said them so well, better than the priest. He always stammered through them so fast that no one understood anything, and he looked as though he was somewhere else the whole time. But you, Emmanuel, there was feeling in it."

We had to settle our sleeping arrangements for the night. I offered Thomas the sofa in my room, which left the room next to mine free for Meyssonnier. I gave the one down on the second floor to Colin and Peyssou.

Lying on my bed, exhausted and unable to sleep, I kept my eyes wide open. Not the slightest gleam of light. Ordinarily, the night is a collage of grays. This one was the color of India ink. I could make out nothing, not even the vaguest outline, not even my hand an inch from my eyes. Across from me, lying beneath the window, Thomas tossed and turned on his bed. I could hear him. I couldn't see him.

There was a knock on the door. I jumped, then called out "Come in" automatically. The door squeaked as it opened. Any and every noise in that darkness acquired an abnormal intensity.

"It's me," Meyssonnier said.

I turned toward the voice. "Come on in. We're not asleep."

"Me neither," Meyssonnier said rather unnecessarily.

He stood there in the doorway, unable to make up his mind to come right in. Or so I supposed, since I couldn't make out even his outline. We could have been spirits in some world beyond death and still have been no more invisible to one another.

I could follow his movements from the slight noises he made. He closed the door behind him, moved forward, and bumped against the chair. He must have been barefoot, because he swore. Then I heard the tired springs of the chair squeak beneath his weight. So he wasn't just a shade after all. He had a body still, just like mine, trapped between two dreads: that of dying, and that—no less terrible now—of living.

I thought Meyssonnier was about to speak, but he said nothing. Colin and Peyssou were together in the room downstairs, Thomas and I up on the third floor. Meyssonnier had been alone in Birgitta's room. He had been unable to bear the combination of darkness, sleeplessness, and solitude.

At that moment I suddenly recalled his wife Mathilde and his constant quarrels with her. I felt slightly guilty because I couldn't recall the names of his two boys. How was he managing to go on living at all, that's what I wanted to know. After all, apart from Malevil itself and my work, my life had been a void. But what about him? What effect must it have on a man when everything he has loved is buried under the earth in a tiny wooden box?

I was lying naked on top of my bed and sweating. We had hesitated about the window. The bedroom was so stifling that at first we had opened it as far as it would go. But it had been impossible to go on breathing in the acrid smell of burning for long. Outside, nature was in the final stages of the greatest auto-da-fé of all time. There were no flames by now: at least they would have provided some small light. Nothing came in through the window but the deathly smell of the charred countryside. After a minute or so I had asked Thomas to shut it again.

There was nothing in the absolute darkness of the room but the breathing of three men, and outside, on the other side of the overheated walls, a dead planet. It had been murdered at the height of spring, its buds scarcely formed, the little rabbits scarcely born in their warrens. Not an animal left. Not a single bird. Not a single insect. The earth charred black. Man's habitations nothing but ashes. Here and there, blackened and splintered stumps that had been trees. And in the middle of it all, a tiny handful of men. Perhaps kept alive as guinea-pig observers in some experiment? It was ludicrous. Right in the middle of that charnal house, a few human lungs pumping air in and out. A few hearts pumping blood. A few human brains racing. Racing to what end?

When I spoke, I am fairly certain it was purely for

Meyssonnier's sake. I just couldn't go on any longer bearing what he was thinking to himself over there, all alone, sitting in the blackness in front of my desk.

"Thomas?"

"Yes."

"How do you explain the fact that there hasn't been any radioactivity so far?"

"It may have been a lithium bomb," Thomas said. Then in a weak yet objective tone, apparently devoid of all emotion, he added, "It was a clean bomb."

I heard Meyssonnier shift in his chair. "Clean!" he echoed in a dead voice.

"That means it doesn't produce fallout," Thomas's voice explained.

"Yes, I realized that," Meyssonnier said.

The silence fell again. Breathing, nothing more. I pressed my hands against my temples. If the bomb was clean, that meant that whoever exploded it intended to follow it up with an invasion. But he wouldn't be doing any invading. He had been destroyed in his turn; the total radio silence told us that much. And as for France, it wasn't worth bothering with the possibility that she might have had time to engage in any war. She had been destroyed as part of a global strategy, so the territory could be occupied. Or so the enemy could be prevented from occupying it. A tiny preliminary precaution. A little pawn, sacrificed at the very beginning of the game. In short, "a calculated write-off," as the military jargon had it.

"And would that be enough, Thomas, just one bomb?"

I didn't add "to destroy the whole of France." He knew what I meant.

"Yes," he said, "one large bomb would be enough, exploded twenty-five miles up, above Paris."

He said no more, obviously feeling there was nothing to be gained from further details. He had spoken in a clearly articulated, unemotional voice, as though he was dictating a math problem to a classroom of students.

That's the sort of problem I ought to have used myself, it occurred to me, in the days when I was a teacher with students. A bit more up to date, after all, than the one

123

about the two taps and the plughole. Given that the explosion cannot transmit itself as pressure because of the low air density at high altitudes, but given also that the effect of its heat, for the same reason, will be experienced at a distance that will be proportionally increased by the height of the explosion, at what height above Paris must you explode a bomb of so many megatons in order to burn down Strasbourg, Dunkirk, Brest, Biarritz, Port-Vendres, and Marseilles? And I could have introduced variations too. Have two X factors instead of one; have them calculate the necessary number of megatons as well as the optimum altitude.

"It's not just France," Thomas said suddenly. "It's the whole of Europe. The world. Otherwise we'd have been able to pick up something on the radio."

At that moment I saw Thomas again in the cellar, Momo's transistor radio in his hand, moving the tuning needle endlessly to and fro across the lighted dial. It had saved his life, as it turned out, that inflexible scientific curiosity of his. If it hadn't been for that inexplicable radio silence he would already have left at the crucial moment.

"Hold on though," I said. "What if there were some sort of screen between you and the radiated heat? A mountain, or a cliff, the way it happened here."

"Yes," Thomas said, "locally."

In Thomas's mind that "locally" was a qualification scarcely removed from negation. I took it differently. It confirmed me in the suspicions I had already begun to form. In all probability there had been other spots in France spared the full force of the bomb, and possibly here and there other groups of survivors. Inexplicably, I felt a warm feeling of hope flow through me. I say inexplicably, because man had just signally failed to demonstrate that he deserved to survive, or that any encounter with him was likely to bring unadulterated joy.

"I'm off back to bed," Meyssonnier said.

He had been there for barely twenty minutes and spoken hardly at all. He had come to visit with us in an attempt to drive away his loneliness, but he was carrying the loneliness inside him. It had followed him into our room, and now he was about to take it back with him into his own.

"Good night," I said.

"Good night," Thomas echoed.

Meyssonnier did not answer. I heard the door squeak as it closed behind him. After fifteen minutes or so I got up and knocked on his.

"Thomas is asleep," I said untruthfully. "Am I disturbing you?"

"No, no," he said in a dead voice.

I groped my way over to the little bamboo writing table I'd put in there for Birgitta. To break the silence I said, "Can't see a damned thing."

And Meyssonnier answered strangely, in the same dead voice, "I'm wondering if it's going to get light again tomorrow."

I felt my way to Birgitta's little wicker armchair, and as I touched it a memory came back. The last time I had sat in it Birgitta was standing in front of me, naked between my legs, and I was stroking her. I don't know if it was simply the effect of that memory, but instead of sitting down I remained standing there, arms resting on the back of the little armchair.

"Are you sure it doesn't bother you being alone in here, Meyssonnier? You wouldn't rather I put you in the same room as Colin and Peyssou?"

"No, thanks," he said in the same flat, tenuous voice. "And have to listen to Peyssou talking nonstop about his family? No, thanks. I've enough thoughts like that in my own head."

I waited, but nothing more came. I knew it already. He would never say anything. Not a word. Either about Mathilde or his two boys. And suddenly, just then, their names came back to me: François and Gérard. Six and four.

"It's entirely up to you," I said.

"Thank you, it's very kind of you to take so much trouble, Emmanuel," he said. And so ingrained was the habit of politeness in him that in pronouncing those words, because they were a customary social formula, for a few seconds he regained his normal voice.

"Well," I said, "I'll be off now."

"I'm not throwing you out," he said in the same tone. "You're in your own home here."

"So are you," I rejoined briskly. "Malevil belongs to all of us."

But he refrained from any comment on that.

"Well, see you tomorrow then."

"After all," he said, and his voice had become dead again, "after all, forty, that's not so old."

I stood there in silence, but nothing more came. "Not so old for what?" I asked after a moment.

"Well, if we survive, that means thirty years ahead of us. At least," he said. "And nothing, nothing."

"You mean without a wife?"

"Not just that."

What he meant in fact was "without children," but there was no way he could bring himself to actually say it.

"Well, it's time I went now," I said.

I went over, groped for his hand, and squeezed it. He scarcely responded to the pressure at all.

By some sort of contagion I could feel almost physically what he was going through, and it was so painful that I felt what was almost relief when I was back in my own room. But what was waiting for me there was perhaps worse. Masked, if possible, by an even greater degree of reticence and modesty.

"Is it bad?" Thomas asked in a low voice, and I was grateful to him for his interest in Meyssonnier.

"You can imagine."

"Yes," Thomas said. Then he added, "I had some nephews in Paris."

And also, I happened to know, two sisters and his parents.

"Meyssonnier had two sons. He worshiped them," I said.

"And his wife?"

"Less. She used to have rows with him all the time over his politics. She said they lost him customers."

"Was it true?"

"Yes, it was true. Life in Malejac for poor old Meyssonnier was always a war on two fronts. The mayor and the clerical clan on one side, and at home his wife."

"I can imagine," Thomas said.

But it was said in a slightly curt, irritable tone, as though he had no suffering left over to devote to Meyssonnier. I alone, in fact, had any emotions available for others, and La Menou too, of course, since we had neither of us lost people close to us. I didn't count my sisters as close to me.

While Thomas lay silent in the blackness, I tried to make use of my sleeplessness to revive a little hope in myself. I thought about La Roque. The reason being that La Roque, a tiny town about nine miles away from us, was an old walled town built on a hillside and, like Malevil, protected to the north by a cliff. That morning, up on the keep, I hadn't seen anything in that direction, but then you couldn't see La Roque from Malevil anyway, other than in conditions of exceptional visibility. As for trying to make it to La Roque on foot, to settle the matter once and for all, that wouldn't be possible yet for a long time, at least to judge by the time it had taken Thomas and the others to cover the mere mile or so down to Malejac.

"The métro or the underground parking garages," Thomas said suddenly.

The dominant note in his voice, as in Meyssonnier's, and probably in my own too, was not grief but a gray astonishment. And for my own part, over and above this general mental stupor, I was experiencing a cottony numbness. I was thinking in a vacuum, with infinite slowness. I couldn't manage to link things together. It took me several seconds to work out what Thomas had meant.

"Do you know the Champs Élysées parking garage?" Thomas asked in the same weak but clearly enunciated voice.

"Yes."

"Infinitely long odds," Thomas went on. "But anyone who happened to be in there, or in the métro, could well have survived, for the moment. But what about afterwards?

"What do you mean, afterwards?"

"Trapped like rats, that's what I mean. Running from exit to exit, finding them all blocked by the rubble above."

"Perhaps not all of them," I said.

Again silence, and the longer it lasted the more it gave me the odd sensation that it was making the blackness all around us even blacker. All the same, after a moment I became aware with great clarity that in giving this assessment, apparently so objective, of the possibilities of survival for a handful of the Parisian population, Thomas was actually thinking about his own family.

I said again, "Perhaps not all."

"Let's assume that then," Thomas said. "But it still only puts off the moment. In the country you live so self-sufficiently. You have all you need: salt meat, seed and cereals, preserves of all kinds, jam, honey, barrels of oil. But in Paris what would it be like?"

"They have the big food stores there."

"All smashed to smithereens or burned down," Thomas said with abrupt savagery, as though he had suddenly resolved not to entertain even the slightest hope.

I didn't reply this time. He was quite right. Burned down, smashed into the ground, or looted. Looted by the hordes of survivors killing one another for any food that remained. And suddenly, in a flash of vision, my mind grasped the horror of those vast urban concentrations in their annihilation. Tons of collapsed concrete. Miles of shattered buildings. A chaos in which nothing familiar remained, not even a street. Even walking made impossible by the heaps of rubble. A wilderness of silence and the smell of burning. And underneath those shattered buildings, corpses by the million.

In fact I knew the Champs Élysées parking garage well. I had parked my car there the previous summer when I had taken Birgitta to Paris for a two-day spree. It was a pretty terrifying place to be in at the best of times. And I could imagine it plunged into darkness, the survivors scurrying desperately from floor to floor, finding all the exits blocked.

At that point, I don't know how, presumably from sheer exhaustion, I fell asleep and entered a terrible nightmare world, the underground Champs Élysées parking garage merging into the métro, the métro into the Parisian sewer system, and the bands of survivors into scurrying rats. I was one of the rats myself, and at the same time, standing outside myself, I observed myself with horror.

Momo woke us up next morning by hammering on our doors. La Menou had planned breakfast as a surprise treat. She had spread the long refectory table in the house with a brightly colored, albeit slightly darned, Basque tablecloth (the least new of the dozen tablecloths that my aunt had folded up in her armoire, and that La Menou washed and mended for me with jealous zeal, as though I was sure to live for two hundred years), and on the cloth were wine and glasses, and on each plate a slice of pickled pork belly and a slice of ham—a sign that our domestic economy had relaxed slightly now that La Menou was sure Adelaide would live to farrow—and beside each plate a large slice of bread spread with lard, since it was better to finish a loaf than let it go to waste. The loaf, now three days old, was rock hard. And there was no butter. It had melted in the now defunct refrigerator.

When everyone had appeared I sat down, leaving them all to select their own places. Thomas sat on my right, Peyssou on my lift. Opposite me was Meyssonnier. On his right, Colin; on his left Momo; and on the other side of Momo, at the foot of the table, La Menou. I don't know whether it's true that there is the seed of a habit in every action, but this seating arrangement never varied subsequently—for as long, that is, as there were still only the seven of us to be accommodated.

I experienced a sensation of unreality eating that breakfast—which was not so very different from those that La Menou laid every morning for Boudenot—and eating it what's more with a knife and fork, sitting on a chair, faced with a clean tablecloth, with nothing anywhere in the great hall of the house to remind one of the event we had just lived through, except for the trickles of lead down the tiny colored panes of the windows and a layer of gray dust and ash on the ceiling beams. As for the floor, La Menou had already found time to sweep and wash the flagstones; and she had polished the walnut furniture back to a high shine, as though in her courageous determination to live

and to reaffirm her roots in everyday routine she had resolved to erase even the memory of what had happened.

But she had not been able to erase the expressions engraved on the faces of my friends. They all three ate
without so much as a glance at anyone else, without a
word, and almost without moving, as though looks and
movements might have the power to break the state of
stupor still anesthetizing their suffering. I foresaw that
their awakening was going to be horribly painful and
would result—certainly in Peyssou's case anyway—in
further crises of despair. After my conversation with
Thomas and the nightmares that had followed it, I had
spent the rest of the night thinking things over, and I
had come to the conclusion that the only way to provide
any advance protection against the shock that lay in store
for them was to put them all to work as soon as possible,
and myself with them. I waited till they'd finished eating,
then I said, "Listen, men, I want to ask for your help and
your advice."

They lifted their heads. How dead and sad their eyes
were! And yet I could see all the same that they were
already reacting to my appeal. I had said, "Listen, men,"
a manner of addressing them I hadn't used since the days
of our Club. By using it now I was taking up the same
attitude toward them that I had always taken then, and I
was counting on their doing the same thing. And also,
that "Listen, men" meant that we were about to tackle
something together, something difficult. It was a second
appeal concealed beneath the first.

I went on: "Problem number one. There are twenty-
one very dead animals out in the first enclosure: eleven
horses, six cows, and four pigs. I won't bother to mention
the stink, since my nose isn't the only one aware of it,
but it's quite clear that we can't go on living in these conditions. We'd end up very dead ourselves if we tried. So
that, it seems to me, is our problem number one, the most
urgent one: What are we to do to get rid of those tons
of carrion? [I hit the word "tons" hard.] Luckily my
tractor was garaged in the Maternity Ward, so it wasn't
destroyed. And I have some diesel oil, not a vast quantity,
but some anyway. I also have plenty of rope and even a

130

few hawsers. So my question is How do we dispose of the carcasses?"

They came to life. Peyssou suggested dragging "the poor creatures" out to the public dump near Malejac and depositing them there. But Colin pointed out that the prevailing winds around here were from the west, which meant that they would blow the stench of our dumped carrion back at us almost constantly. Meyssonnier suggested a vast pyre on the road level, so the remains could then be pushed down into the dump below. But I was against such a funeral by fire for twenty-one large animals, since it would require an enormous quantity of wood. And wood was one of the things we were going to need a great deal of next winter, both for cooking and to keep ourselves warm. Indeed that was certainly going to prove one of our most arduous tasks in the near future, prospecting for wood, often at considerable distances, cutting an adequate supply of already half-consumed trunks and branches, then carting it all back to Malevil.

It was Colin who came up with the idea of the sandpit down by the Rhunes. It was quite close. The track was downhill, which meant the actual transporting of the corpses would be easier. And once they had been deposited in the deepest of the pit's bays we could shovel sand down from the pit edge above to cover them.

Someone, I don't remember who now, objected to the length of time the shoveling would take.

Thomas turned to me. "When you and Germain were excavating the trench for the mains cable to Malevil, didn't you once tell me you used dynamite cartridges in the rocky sections?"

"Yes."

"Are there any left?"

"A dozen or so."

"That's more than enough," Thomas said. "No need to shovel at all. I can guarantee to blast enough of the pit bank down to cover them."

Glances were exchanged. The matter was now theoretically solved, but no one was unaware of just how appalling the actual execution was going to be. I didn't want to leave them preoccupied with such a wholly negative prospect.

"There is another decision that will have to be made fairly soon too," I said. "An agricultural matter this time. Here is the problem as I see it: Ought we to risk resowing right away? I have quite a stock of barley in, and hay too. In fact I had enough put by to keep twenty or so animals, feeding them generously, till next harvest. Right, well the 1977 harvest, I don't need to go into that! . . . But if you look at it another way, since I now have only three animals left to feed, what with the hay and the barley together I've certainly enough to hold out till the 1978 harvest. I also have enough for the sow too, and more. The only problem in fact concerns ourselves."

A slight pause, then I went on: "And our problem is bread. I have no wheat, except a small amount of seed grain."

There was a sudden tension in the air and the faces around the table became grave. I looked around at them. It was the age-old fear of not having enough bread to eat that was suddenly griping their guts. An inherited fear. Because they themselves had certainly never experienced that lack, or their parents before them, even during the war. In 1940, in our little neck of the woods, my uncle had often told me, they had reopened the old bakehouses and there had been no lack of clandestine bakings, despite the Vichy government and its bread coupons. "Hard times, yes," La Menou used to say. "But Emmanuel, we never went short of bread."

Proof that though the oral tradition of famines in the old days had been lost, nevertheless that immemorial dread still lived on in the peasant unconscious.

"I reckon you're right about the harvest this year anyway," Peyssou said. "Coming back from Malejac yesterday, I stopped on the way and dug down a little way with a stick into the field I sowed with wheat for this year." (It struck me as a good sign, that reaction, considering what he'd just lived through.) "And I found —nothing," he said, opening both hands palm outward on the table. "Ten times nothing. The dirt was like it had been baked. Nothing but dust, you'd have said."

132

"Your seed wheat, how much do you have?" Colin asked.

"Enough to sow five acres."

"Well, that's something," Meyssonnier said.

La Menou was on her feet, slightly away from the table so as to leave the men free to talk, but all ears, her eyes restless and concerned, her face drawn into lines of profound attention. By no means ready to clear the table, which would have meant going out of earshot. And when Momo began making childish noises and shuffling around the table, she intercepted him with a box on the ears that sent him sulking into a corner.

"In my opinion," Meyssonnier said, "you'd be risking nothing by sowing an acre or two."

"Risking nothing!" Peyssou erupted in his gruffest and most bearlike tone, giving Meyssonnier a look of reproach. "Nothing but losing an acre or two of seed! And you think that's nothing do you, carpenter?" (This habit of addressing people according to their trade was a peculiarity of the Club and denoted as much affection as sarcasm.) "Well I can tell you here and now, with the earth like it is now, it couldn't grow you so much as a single dandelion by the end of summer. Even if you watered it nonstop."

He banged the table with the flat of his hand as he spoke, then followed the gesture through by seizing his glass in the hollow of his great hand and emptying it at a swig to give extra emphasis to his pronouncement. I looked across at him with relief. Argument had resuscitated the Peyssou I knew.

"I think Peyssou is right," Colin said. "In pasture, when you burn a pile of weeds at Easter, it stays bare all summer. For the grass to come again you have to wait till the next spring. And what's a heap of burning weeds when you think what the earth has just been through?"

"But still," Meyssonnier countered, "if you plow well down, if you turn the soil over deeply enough, there's no reason why the soil shouldn't grow something."

I listened and watched them. It wasn't Meyssonnier's argument that decided me but another consideration altogether. I couldn't give them back their families, but I could at least provide them with a purposeful activity and

133

a goal. And without that, once the horses were buried, they would just eat their hearts out in idleness.

"Listen," I said, "I must say I'm pretty well in agreement with what Peyssou and Colin have said in principle. But I don't see why we couldn't give it a try, on an experimental basis." I paused slightly in order to let this weighty phrase make its mark. "And without it costing us too much in the way of seed."

"That's just what I said too," Meyssonnier put in.

I went on: "And it so happens I have just the place for it. A small field down by the Rhunes, an acre and a quarter, no more, down in the valley bottom below the nearest arm of the cliff. Uncle Samuel had it properly drained, and it's perfectly sweet. Last autumn I mucked it well and plowed the muck well in. So it might be worth at least trying there, replowing, sowing again. Just over an acre—that's not going to eat up too much of our seed. And we could even gravity irrigate if the spring turns out too dry, since the main Rhune runs alongside.

"And there's another thing," I said. "I doubt if we have enough diesel oil left to do the plowing, not if we use it to bury the animals. So we're going to have to think about building a single plow"—I looked at Meyssonnier and Colin—"and train Amarante to pull it." I looked at Peyssou, because he'd used a horse to drag-hoe his vines.

"Well, if it's going to be an experiment," Peyssou said with an air of prudent concession, "I must say I'd be interested to see the result. If you can afford to lose a little of your seed."

I looked at him hard. "Don't say 'You,' Peyssou; say 'we.'"

"What do you mean?" Peyssou said. "Malevil belongs to you, doesn't it?"

"No, Peyssou, it doesn't," I said, shaking my head. "All that is finished, in the past. Suppose I die tomorrow from illness or an accident, what would happen? Where's our lawyer? Or our laws of inheritance? Or even our heir? Malevil belongs to those who work in it, and that's all there is to it."

"I'm absolutely in agreement with you," Meyssonnier

said, delighted at finding my pronouncements coinciding for once with his principles.

"All the same though," Peyssou said, unable to believe what he'd heard.

Colin said nothing, but he looked across at me with a shadow of his old smile. He looked as though he was saying, Yes, yes, I quite agree, but what difference does it make really?

"All right," I said, "then that's agreed is it? Once we've buried the animals we start to work making that plow, and then we sow down by the Rhunes?"

There was a murmur of approval. I stood up, and La Menou began clearing the breakfast things off the table, every gesture expressing her disapproval. By saying that Malevil belonged to everyone I had reduced her to a lowest common denominator and stripped her of the power and glory of her position as sole mistress of our ship after me. However, during the days that followed she obviously decided that this collectivization of Malevil didn't mean much, that it could only have been a polite manner of speaking on my part, intended to put my guests at their ease, and eventually she ceased to worry about it.

I have no wish to describe the burial of the animals, it was too horrible. The worst part perhaps was getting the horses out of their stalls, because they had already swelled up and couldn't be got through the doors. We had to knock down the walls.

We also had to start thinking about clothing, because Colin, Meyssonnier, and Peyssou had nothing but the work clothes they'd been wearing when they came to visit me the day it happened. Luckily I had kept a great many of my uncle's clothes, so I was able to provide Meyssonnier with a reasonable wardrobe. But Colin presented a problem. I had to persuade La Menou to hand over her husband's suits, which she had been keeping in mothballs for twenty years without the slightest hope of ever seeing Momo benefit from them, since he was far too big. Which was certainly no reason to give them away! "No, Emmanuel, no! Not even to Colin!" So in the end we all had to set on her, bawl her out, and even threaten to take them from her by main force, those 1950s suits, before she finally gave way. But when she did, it wasn't by halves. She insisted on altering them all to fit him, poor Colin, who was a good two inches shorter than her man had been. A fact that softened her heart. Because small men and little women, as she said, have to stick together. "And me, as I stand here, Emmanuel, never an inch over four foot eight, and that's standing up straight too."

As for Peyssou, his case was hopeless. He was a good half head taller than Meyssonnier and myself with shoulders to match which meant he couldn't even get into my jackets. It preyed on his mind rather, our poor giant, the thought that he was going to find himself one of these days walking about naked. Happily, however, his problems were eventually solved, as I shall explain later.

La Menou grumbled from morning to night about all the things that had disappeared from our lives. Ten times a day she would flick electric switches, or out of sheer habit plug in her coffee grinder (she had several pounds of beans still in reserve), and every time the disappointment caused her to swear with a very downcast air. She was very much attached to her washing machine, to her electric iron, to her electric roaster, to her radio, which she had listened to (or rather hadn't listened to) while cooking, to the television, which she had watched every evening right through to the end of the final program, regardless of what was on. She had adored the automobile, and even in my uncle's time had already begun inventing insidious excuses to have herself driven into La Roque during the week, on top of the regulation visit to the Saturday mart. She even began to miss doctors—though she had never consulted one—as soon as there weren't any. Her ambition to beat her mother's record and live to be a hundred now seemed to her gravely threatened, and she lamented the fact daily.

"When I think of all the idiocies the left-wing press used to reel out about the consumer society!" Meyssonnier remarked to me one day. "I mean, just listen to La Menou. What could be worse for her than a society where there's nothing left to consume?"

Or for him than a society in which one could no longer read the Party newspaper. Because it was a terrible loss to

Meyssonnier, his Party newspaper. As was that division of the world into neat camps, socialists and capitalists, that had always given a meaning and a spice to his life, the former fighting staunchly for the truth, the latter plunged into darkest error. Now that both had vanished from the world, Meyssonnier was totally disoriented. An optimist as befits the true militant, he had based his whole life on the vision of a glorious socialist future. And the future wasn't going to be glorious for anyone, that was quite clear.

Eventually Meyssonnier came upon an old bundle of newspapers in the boiler room. They were all copies of *Le Monde* (dating from 1956, the year of the Republican Front!), and he took immediate possession of them, despite the vast scorn with which he commented to me, *"Le Monde!* You know what I think about their so-called objectivity!" But that didn't stop him reading his way through every one of them, copy by copy, from first page to last, totally engrossed. He even tried to read out extracts to us.

But Colin promptly told him, in very sharp tones indeed, "Meyssonnier, we don't give a bugger about your Guy Mollet and his Algerian war! That was twenty years ago, all that! Keep it to yourself!"

"My Guy Mollet!" Meyssonnier exclaimed indignantly, turning to me. "Did you hear that?"

It was from La Menou that I first learned things weren't going too well between Colin and Peyssou in their room; then little by little they brought their complaints to me.

Peyssou was allowing his grief over his family to overflow a little too freely: anecdotes and memories in an unending flow that was beginning to wear down Colin's nerves.

"And Colin, well, you know him," Peyssou said in his turn, "touchy as they come. But these days you should hear him, pure vinegar, always letting me know what a great dumb ox he thinks I am. And on top of it, not being able to smoke his packet of tobacco every day, that has him on edge all the time. He flares up at the slightest thing, and he's forever going on at me because I'm so big. As if I can help it."

I asked Meyssonnier if he would mind very much taking Colin's place in the room with Peyssou. For on one point I was adamant: Peyssou mustn't be left alone.

"Basically, you know," Meyssonnier said, "I am always the can carrier, aren't I? Even back in the Club days I was the one who always got landed with the boring little chores. Peyssou not clever enough, Colin not responsible enough. And you were always too busy giving the orders. The others we needn't go into."

"Ah, now come on," I said with a smile. "As secretary of your cell you were used to boring little chores, weren't you? Did you mind them?"

He didn't take that one up. "I want you to know though," he went on, "that as far as Peyssou's concerned, I rate him a long way above Colin, even though I know Colin's always been your little pet. Colin can be charming all right, but he can also be very difficult. Peyssou is pure gold all through. But all the same, if I'm going to be sharing a room with him, then someone's got to ask him to go easy on all those reminiscences, because I've got a headful of memories too, you know."

He froze and suddenly began blinking, the corners of his mouth sagging, all his features drawn downward. "Yes," he went on, "there's one memory above all, and I'm going to tell it to you. Then after that I'll never mention it again. The one thing I want to avoid is going on about the past. But here it is. The morning of Zero Day my little François wanted to come with me to Malevil. He wanted to see the castle, and I'd already said he could. Then Mathilde said no he couldn't come, that I wasn't to drag him into our filthy politics at his age. I hesitated. I can see myself still—hesitating. Because the kid was looking very disappointed. But it was only the evening before that I'd had a row with Mathilde over politics, and you know what women are, they yak on and on and on, then they sulk, and there's no end to it. Right, I thought. Suddenly I'd had it, all that, up to the back teeth. So I said all right, keep him here then, your son, I'll go on my own. In other words I just couldn't face another scene just then, not so soon after the one before. I behaved like a coward. So François stayed. He stood and watched me go with tears running down his cheeks. And if I hadn't been such a coward—you see the point, Emmanuel—he'd be here now, my François."

After that he was unable to speak for a good minute. Me too. But all the same, I think it did him good to share that nagging pain with me. I can't remember now what we talked about afterward, though I remember we did talk. And all the while I was wondering how I was going to set about telling Peyssou not to share his sorrows so much. Because basically he was in the right. Meyssonnier had just proved it.

Almost as soon as our terrible burial rites were over, Adelaide decided it was time she gave birth, and promptly dropped a dozen or so piglets. But, since she was even more unapproachable than ever while farrowing, we were unable to count them exactly until she finally got to her feet. Then we discovered that she had in fact produced fifteen, a pretty respectable figure, though still short of her previous record.

It was Momo who gave the alarm, hurtling into the great hall just as we were about to eat our midday meal, all filth and hair, waving his arms in the air and yelling even more unintelligibly than usual. As soon as his yells had been interpreted, we all left our places around the table and ran full speed down to the Maternity Ward, where Adelaide, lying grunting and groaning on her side, suddenly saw the wall of her stall crowned by a row of seven greedy and chattering human heads. She grunted and grumbled, but since nothing more happened she soon returned to her labors and went on extruding more offspring. While we, chins propped on the top rail of her stall (which was nearly five feet high, because it had been intended for horses, and La Menou had to stand on two blocks in order to get her head to the right height), promptly embarked on a lively discussion as to the most judicious use to which this abundance of new provisions could be put. Because unfortunately we just didn't have enough feed to keep fifteen pigs. Which meant that some of them at least would have to be sacrificed as soon as they had finished suckling, a prospect we fell to envisaging with a totally fake objectivity, pretending it distressed us no end, while all the time our mouths were already watering at the thought of a plump suckling pig roasting on its spit over a great fire in the hall. And I noticed how this gluttony had a kind of feverish intensity about it. It wasn't just part of enjoying the good things in life as it had been once; it sprang from our fears about the future. Accounts of past feasts had begun to play an abnormally large role in many of our conversations, I suddenly realized, which showed that the fear of famine was still always there, lurking at the back of our minds, nagging at our guts.

Two days later Princesse dropped a bull calf, thereby insuring the survival of her race, at the price of future incest. It was by no means an easy birth, however, and La Menou had to take charge. Oddly, when she asked Peyssou to help her he refused point-blank. That was the one thing, he said, that he'd never been able to face at his own place. He was always afraid of hurting the cow, and it was Yvette who always saw to it. Or when it was very difficult and they needed to pull, then he'd go and fetch Colin. "All right then, Colin," La Menou said curtly.

But in fact we all went. It was at night, and so La Menou could see what she was doing I found myself squatting on my heels in the stall holding one of the big candles from the cellar. The wax kept running down over my fingers, and I was sweating profusely, partly because of the excitement and worry, partly because of that overpowering smell of cow which I've never been able to stand. The delivery took four hours, and we were all speechless with concern and worry. After a while, what with the hot wax and the proximity of the cow itself, I couldn't stand the discomfort any longer, so I handed the candle over to Meyssonnier, and from then on it continued to change hands every quarter of an hour, until the time came when I found it was my turn again.

Momo was quite useless, sobbing like a calf himself in Bel Amour's stall at the thought of losing our only cow, and even, who could say, perhaps Bel Amour herself, since she too was very near her term by now. He insisted on expressing all his apprehensions aloud in a sort of whining litany, and once or twice La Menou raised her head to give him a verbal drubbing, though without her customary vigor, since she was in too much distress herself to give her whole attention to the task. Momo sensed this, and consequently paid very little attention to his mother's warnings, his only concession being to replace the litany with a series of little rhythmic moans, as though he was the one giving birth.

When the bull calf finally did emerge into that world so devoid—for the moment at least—of all pasture, La Menou, without putting her imagination to any great strain, named him Prince.

The good recovery made by the mother, together with the sex of her offspring, soon made us forget the agonies we had been put through and there was a fresh burst of optimism all around—unhappily killed in the bud a few days later when Bel Amour also gave birth, without difficulties, but alas to a filly.

Bel Amour was fourteen, Amarante three. And Malice (which was the name chosen by Momo, perhaps because she had been such a disappointment to us) one day. Three mares of different ages and varying distinction, but all three destined to die without progeny.

That evening in the hall was a sad vigil.

After the burial of the dead animals used up our last drop of diesel oil, I had decided to devote my stock of gasoline—apart from one gallon can which I put on one side to meet some possible emergency—entirely to the power saw. And while Meyssonnier and Colin were constructing a horse-drawn plow with parts from the one hitherto drawn by my tractor, I set out with Peyssou and Thomas to begin getting in a stock of wood for the winter, taking great care never to touch any trunks, however splintered, in which the presence of sap could be discerned.

Amarante proved as easy to break in to the shafts as she had been to the saddle, and in no time at all she would allow herself to be harnessed to my trailer—henceforward known as the "cart"—which Meyssonnier had adapted for the purpose before attacking the problem of the plow. The blackened wood that we gathered together into great piles at odd intervals, often at quite a distance from Malevil, was then carted to the castle and piled up in one of the stalls in the outer enclosure. Wood burns so quickly, and it takes nature such an infinite time to make it, but at least we started with the one great advantage of being the only consumers around, and of having a vast territory at our disposal. All the same, as much out of prudence as in order to keep us all busy, I refused to stop until we had filled the entire stall, and even the neighboring one as well, which I calculated represented enough for two winters, provided we never burned more than one fire and used it for cooking as well as keeping ourselves warm.

Ever since the day it had happened, the sky had continued to be a uniform dark gray pall weighing down on our heads. It was cold. The sun had never once appeared. Nor had there been rain. Because of the consistent drought, the ash-covered earth had acquired the look of a vast dust bath, and at the slightest breath of wind blackish clouds of fine ash rose into the air, obscuring the horizon even further. In Malevil itself, protected from the outside world by its age-old walls, huddled together around the table, we could still feel a breath of life. But as soon as we emerged from the ramparts to collect our wood, the world was a desolation. The charred landscape, the blackened skeletons of the trees, the leaden pall pressing down on us, the silence of the annihilated valleys, everything combined to crush us into nonexistence. I noticed that we all spoke in whispers, and even then very rarely, as though we were in a graveyard. Whenever the gray light became less dark we began to hope for a sight of the sun; but then the gray blanket would darken again, surrounding us from morning till night in a wan twilight.

Thomas thought that the reason for this twilight was that the dust from the atomic explosions had formed a thick layer up in the stratosphere and was cutting off the rays of the sun. But he also said that in his opinion we ought to hope that it wouldn't rain for a long time. Because if *dirty* bombs had been used, even a long way away from France itself, the drops could well bring radioactive

142

dust down with them to earth. Every time we went any distance from Malevil he insisted that we take raincoats, gloves, and head coverings with us on the cart, while at the same time stressing how inadequate this protection would be.

In the evenings in the great hall the cold was so intense for the time of year that after supper we kept a small fire going as we sat in a circle around one of the room's two vast fireplaces and talked for a little while, simply in order "not to just go and lie in our stalls like animals" (La Menou).

I took part in these evening conversations, but sometimes I read instead, sitting on a small stool, back against the side of the fireplace, with the book tilted toward the fire so that its flames lit up the pages. La Menou's customary position was on one of the two facing hearth seats, and when the flames died down too low she would feed the fire with logs or one of the bundles of twigs she had laid ready under her seat.

In the letter I had received after his death, which I now knew by heart, my uncle had recommended me to read the Bible, adding the comment "It's a book in which you have to go deeper than just the way people behave; it's the wisdom there that counts." But I had been so busy with restoring Malevil since his death, and then with the worries of running it, that I had never found the time to do as he recommended. And now I was almost more overworked than before, but somehow time itself, strange to say, had subtly changed; it had become more malleable, and I noticed that I was now able to "find" it quite easily when I wanted to.

When Bel Amour gave birth to Malice—I don't like to suggest that it was the influence of the name she was given, but never was filly from so gentle a dam more difficult—the evening sank, as I have said, into a morass of gloom. For a start, during our evening meal, you could have cut the silence with a knife. And even when we had settled around the fire, La Menou and Momo facing each other on the hearth seats, me reading with my back against the side of the fireplace, the silence went on so long that we were almost grateful to Colin for remarking that in

143

twenty-five years' time there wouldn't be a single horse left.

"Twenty-five years? That's being a bit gloomy," Peyssou said. "I remember myself, at the Girauds' place—not the Volpinière Girauds but the ones at Cussac—I remember seeing a gelding they had that was nearly twenty-eight then, going a little blind, I admit, and so rheumaticky you could hear its joints grating when it walked, but it was still cleaning old Giraud's vines for him even then."

"All right then, let's say thirty years," Colin said. "What's another five years here or there? In thirty years, Malice will be dead. And Amarante too. And it will be many a long day since Bel Amour breathed her last."

"Now stop that," La Menou said to Momo. Sitting, or rather half lying on the hearth seat opposite her, he had promptly burst into great sobs at this threat of Bel Amour's future demise. "We're not talking about to-morrow; we're talking about thirty years from now. And where will you be yourself in thirty years' time, you great booby?"

"I don't know," Meyssonnier put in. "Momo is forty-seven now. So in thirty years he'll be seventy-seven. That's not so very old."

"Yes, but I'll tell you something," La Menou said. "My mother now, she died at ninety-seven, but I'm not expecting to live that long now, not when I think that there are no doctors, and just the slightest touch of flu, phut, away you go."

"You can't be certain of that," Peyssou said, "because even in the days when you didn't see much medicine and such around here, there were still people who lived a long while. My old granddad for example."

"All right, so let's say fifty years," Colin said with a note of exasperation in his voice. "In fifty years we shall all be gone, the whole lot of us, except perhaps Thomas, who'll be seventy-five. Think of that," he added, turning to look at Thomas. "You're going to have a high old time, aren't you lad, all alone here in Malevil?"

At that, the silence became so heavy that I lifted my head from my book. Though as a matter of fact I had been unable to read a single line of it that evening, so worried was I by the low state of our morale since the

144

birth of Malice. I couldn't see La Menou, because she was perched on the hearth seat behind me, and Momo only indistinctly, because although he was in my line of vision the flames and smoke of the fire made it impossible to distinguish anything but his slouched form. But I could observe the other four on their chairs facing me, and without embarrassing them, since the fire behind me kept my face in shadow. The only drawback to this position was that only my right side got any warmth and light, and eventually my left side would become numb with cold. So before long I got into the habit of shifting myself over to the other pillar of the fireplace halfway through the evening, taking my book and stool with me, in order to warm up my cold side.

Thomas, as usual, was quite expressionless. On Peysou's good-natured round face, with its wide mouth, its big nose, its large and slightly protruding eyes, and a forehead so narrow that he seemed to have difficulty keeping his hairline away from his eyebrows, I could read despair, as though in a book. But little Colin's bitterness was almost more disturbing. Because although it hadn't been able to erase his gondola smile, it had leached him of every trace of gaiety. Meyssonnier had the faded look of an old photograph in a drawer. But still that same knife-blade face, the two very close-set eyes, the high narrow forehead, the brush of short hair. And yet the flame had gone.

"You can't be sure," Peyssou said, turning his head to look at Colin. "How can you be sure Thomas will be the last one here? Even though he is young. At that rate there wouldn't be anyone buried in Malejac graveyard but old people, which you know is not so. Though I don't mean to offend Thomas by saying so," he added with his usual peasant courtesy, bowing slightly in Thomas's direction.

"It doesn't matter to me," Thomas said in even tones. "If I'm left alone it's no problem. Up on the keep and over, right away."

I was angry with him for saying that, with everyone else in such a depressed state.

"Well, my boy, we see things very differently, that I

145

can tell you," La Menou said. "Me, if I was left alone in Malevil, I wouldn't say goodbye so quickly, not while there were the animals to look after."

"That's true," Peyssou said. "There are the animals."

I was grateful to him for having said that, so spontaneously and so resolutely.

"Oh, the animals," Colin said with a kind of bitter violence so different from the almost chirruping, fluttering gaiety that always lay behind everything he said before, "they'd manage all right without you. Not at the moment, I don't mean, now that everything is burned and destroyed, but when the grass starts growing again, then you could just let Adelaide and Princesse go if you wanted. They'd always find enough to live on."

"Yes, but animals can be company for a body too," La Menou said. "Why, I remember La Pauline, when she was left alone on that farm of hers, after her husband fell off the trailer with a stroke and they'd killed her son in the Algerian war. She told me herself, you'd never believe it, 'Menou,' she said, 'but I talk to them all day long, these animals of mine.'"

"La Pauline was old though," Peyssou said, "and the older people are, the more they want to go on living. I really can't see why."

"You'll see right enough when you get there," La Menou told him.

"Oh, I didn't mean that for you," Peyssou said hastily, anxious as always not to hurt anyone. "And anyway there's no comparison. La Pauline was a big woman. She hardly ever moved from that chair. And you, you're always trotting here, trotting there."

"Oh, yes!" La Menou said. "I'm always trotting, all right! I trot so much that one day I shall trot myself right into the graveyard. Oh, do be quiet, you great booby," she was immediately forced to add for Momo's benefit. "I've told you we're not talking about tomorrow, so stop that noise."

"There's one thing I can't get out of my head though," Meyssonnier said. "It's been on my mind ever since Adelaide and Princesse had Prince and the piglets. Fifty years from now, not a man left on earth; but the pigs and the cows, they'll be teeming all over by then."

"It's true," Peyssou said, resting his massive forearms on his spread thighs and leaning toward the fire. "I've thought about that too. And I can tell you, Meyssonnier, it's a thought I can't stand: Malejac with its woods and its pasture again, cows all over, and not a man anywhere."

Silence fell and spread. All their faces were turned toward the flames in a gloomy daze, as though they could make out in their flickering the future Peyssou had described: Malejac with its woods and its pastures again, cows all over, and not a man anywhere. I looked at my friends and saw myself in them. Man is the only animal species capable of conceiving the notion of his own disappearance, and the only one capable of the despair that notion brings. What a strange race: so savagely determined to destroy itself, so savagely intent on preserving itself.

"So what it means," Peyssou said, as though finally reaching the end of a long train of thought, "what it means is that surviving isn't enough. If you want to be interested in it, then you've got to know it will go on when you're gone."

He must have thought of Yvette and his two children as he spoke, because his face suddenly froze and he stayed there without moving, forearms resting on his thighs, mouth still open, staring into the fire with lost eyes.

"There's no proof that we're the only survivors though," I put in after a moment. "It was the cliff shielding us to the north that saved Malevil. It's possible that there are other spots, and maybe not so far away either, where the same conditions saved other people."

But I refrained from mentioning La Roque by name. I didn't want to arouse too much hope in them for fear of the possible disappointment.

"I don't know," Meyssonnier said. "A cellar like Malevil's, that's not something you come across often."

I shook my head. "It wasn't the cellar so much as the cliff. Look at the animals in the Maternity Ward. They survived all right without being in the cellar."

"Ah, but it's very deep as caves go, your Maternity Ward," Colin said. "And just think of the thickness of the stone, above and on both sides. And besides, who's to say that animals haven't got greater powers of resistance than us."

"As a matter of fact," I said, "I'm inclined to believe the opposite. That mentally our power of resistance is greater than theirs."

"I would say that they suffered less physically," Thomas said. "The sudden heat must have been more violent in the cave, but it would have been shorter. The air cooled down quicker out there. There wasn't that oven effect that we had in the cellar." Then with a look at me he added, "But I agree with you. There must have been other survivors here and there all over the place. Even in the cities." Then he stopped abruptly and pressed his lips together as though to prevent himself saying any more.

"Well, all I can say is I don't believe it, that's all," Meyssonnier said with a shake of the head.

Colin raised his eyebrows again and Peyssou shrugged. The fact was that they were almost comfortable now in their unhappiness and didn't want to hear about anything that might disturb it, as though there was a kind of security down there, in the thick mud of their despair, and they didn't want to risk losing it.

There was a very long silence. I looked at my watch: barely nine o'clock. The fire was still a long way from having consumed its nightly wood ration. A pity to waste all that warmth and go up to bed so soon in our icy rooms. I went back to my reading, but not for long.

"And what is it you're reading there then, my poor Emmanuel?" La Menou asked.

"Poor" was simply a term of endearment, it didn't mean she felt sorry for me.

"The Old Testament." Then I added, "The Scriptures, if you prefer."

Because I was pretty sure that La Menou's knowledge of the Bible went no further than the potted and bowdlerized version that she had been given during her catechism classes.

"Yes, of course," she said. "I recognize it now. Your uncle too, he was always there reading at it."

148

"What!" Meyssonnier exclaimed. "You're reading the Bible? You?"

"I promised Uncle Samuel I would," I answered curtly. "And I must say I find it interesting."

"Come on now, Meyssonnier," Colin said with something like his old smile, "are you forgetting that you were always first in Scriptural Knowledge?"

"Oh, what a grind he was, eh, old Meyssonnier!" Peyssou exclaimed with a brief flash of merriment. "He could reel it all off like a talking book. The bit I always remember best is the youngest son and his brothers who sold him into slavery. And isn't it the truth," he went on after a moment's reflection, "that it's always someone in the family who'll do the dirt on you worst?"

Another silence.

"And why don't you read it to us out loud?" La Menou said.

"Out loud?" I echoed.

"And why not?" Peyssou said. "I know I'd like hearing them all again, those stories in there, because I can't remember a one of them now."

"Emmanuel's uncle," La Menou said, "the poor man was always ready to please, and sometimes he used to read me pieces out of his book of an evening."

"Come on, Emmanuel, don't make us twist your arm," Colin said.

"But it may bore you all," I said, taking care not to look directly at Thomas.

"It never would. What nonsense," La Menou said. "And it's a better thing listening to your book than sitting saying nothing worth listening to, or all staying shut up in our own heads thinking." And she added, "Especially now there's no TV."

"I think you're quite right, Menou," Peyssou said.

I looked across at Meyssonnier, then at Thomas, but neither returned my glance. "I certainly don't mind, if everyone wants it," I said after a moment. Then since Meyssonnier and Thomas just went on staring into the fire and refusing to speak, I said "Meyssonnier?"

He wasn't expecting a direct attack like that. He straightened up and leaned back in his chair. "You know

I'm a materialist," he said with dignity, "but as long as no one is trying to force me to believe in God, I have no objection to listening to the early history of the Jewish people."

"Thomas?"

Quite relaxed, hands in pockets, legs stretched out in front of him, Thomas fixed his eyes on the tips of his boots. "Given that you are already reading the Bible to yourself," he said in a totally noncommittal tone, "why shouldn't you read it out loud?"

An equivocal reply to say the least, but I decided to make do with it. I also had the feeling that a reading would do my friends good. During the day they kept busy, but the evening was a bad time for them; that was when they missed the warmth of their homes. There were scarcely bearable silences sometimes, and then I could almost see their minds whirring around, endlessly, pointlessly, in the void of their present existence. And besides, the life of the primitive tribes described in the Bible was not without a certain resemblance now to what our own had become. I was certain that they would find it interesting. I also hoped they might be fired by the example of the Jews' stubborn determination to survive.

I moved over to the other side of the fireplace, carrying my closed book and my stool, in order to warm up my left side. La Menou threw a bundle of twigs onto the fire to provide me with a little more light, I opened the Bible at the first page, and began reading the book of Genesis.

As I read, I felt deep emotions stir in me, mingled with a feeling of bitter irony. It was, beyond any doubt, a magnificent poem. A great song telling of the creation of the world, and there I was reciting it in a world destroyed, to men who had lost everything they ever had.

NOTE ADDED BY THOMAS

While certain details are still fresh in the reader's mind I should like to point out two errors in Emmanuel's account.

1. I think that Emmanuel must have lost consciousness several times while we were in the cellar, because there was no point at which I was not there beside him, and yet for most of the time he couldn't see me and didn't answer when I spoke to him. One thing I can state categorically however: At no point did I see him sitting in the rinsing tub. And no one else did either. This illusion on his part must have been the result of delirium, and similarly his later remorse for his "selfishness."

2. It wasn't Emmanuel who closed the cellar door again after Germain's "terrifying" entrance. It was Meyssonnier. In his semiconscious state at that time, Emmanuel must have substituted himself for Meyssonnier, whose movements, strangely enough, he has described very accurately apart from attributing them to himself: in particular the way Meyssonnier dragged himself over to the door on all fours, but without going over to Germain's body.

I should also like to add an observation:

Although an atheist, I am not anticlerical, and although I did display a certain reticence when Emmanuel began his Bible readings in the evenings, it was purely because this ceremony—that may not be quite the right word but I can't think of a better—seemed to me to reinforce rather too strongly something that already existed: the almost religious nature of the influence that Emmanuel exercised over his friends. Especially when Emmanuel read the chosen passages the way he did, with his beautiful deep voice so vibrant with emotion. I willingly concede that Emmanuel was a man of brilliant imagination, and that his emotion was mainly a literary one. But that's precisely what I found dangerous: the confusion.

Because to say, as Emmanuel does, that Genesis is a "magnificent poem" is to ignore rather too easily the scientific errors with which it teems.

VI

THOSE first weeks after the day it happened leave me with a sensation of grayness—outside as well as in our lives—of dull grief, of marching on the spot, of dead end, of futile striving. Because we worked very hard, at tasks that were often totally uninteresting but that we took on as a matter of discipline, and also because we were trying, despite everything, and without feeling any great love for life, to organize ourselves for survival.

Meyssonnier and Colin continued to perfect a plow to which we could harness Amarante, while Thomas, Peyssou, and I harnessed ourselves to a chore that was less urgent perhaps but in the long run just as useful: collecting, listing, and storing away all the metallic objects we could find—including those that at first glance might perhaps seem of no value but which, from the very fact that they could no longer be made, were from then on literally priceless.

We began, of course, with all our farm and construction tools and equipment. I myself had not always been very thrifty about such things in the past, because if you left a pair of pincers to rust in the grass, or simply lost it, you could always replace it so easily. From now on we had to get it firmly through our heads that such acts of negligence were practically crimes.

The store was set up on the ground floor of the keep, where there was already a quantity of shelving, built to store the apples from an orchard that had now ceased to exist. I placed the most precious of the tools into locked boxes, and with his assent we elected Thomas unanimously for the office of storekeeper. Which meant that from then on no tool could be borrowed without a written record of the borrower and the time of issue being made.

The task completed, I recalled that in one of the unoccupied stalls in the outer enclosure I had stored a number of old planks bristling with nails, my intention at that time, during the restoration of Malevil, being to use them for kindling for the fireplaces during the winter. An unthinkable idea now! The days of such thoughtless waste were over with a vengeance. Nothing could be thrown away any more: not the smallest sheet of paper or cardboard box or empty food can, not a plastic bottle or length of string or cord, not a single bent or rusty nail. The word trash can had ceased to have a meaning.

We retrieved the old planks from the stall. We pulled out all the nails with hammers and pincers, taking infinite pains not to break the heads. And after straightening them all individually on a flat stone, we stored them away, neatly arranged according to size, in a compartmented box in the storeroom. Using a hand saw rather than the power saw, in order to save gasoline, we cut away any rotted or badly splintered sections (the only pieces now destined for the fire), cleaned away the plaster or cement on the two sides, and arranged the planks in piles in the stall, arranged according to size and kept strictly horizontal by means of blocks, in order to make sure they did not warp during cold weather.

In preparation for the expected tourists, I had got in a stock of giant candles. I still had two dozen of them not yet unpacked, plus another four still almost intact in their brackets down in the cellar, and two half burned.

We decided to make use of them with the utmost parsimony, and since I still had two barrels of walnut oil, Colin made us a series of little lamps out of cylindrical food cans. He pinched the edges of them together on one side so as to form a beak to hold the wick, which was just a strand of hemp from an untwisted rope, then he cut little handles from the lids of the cans and used my soldering iron to fix them to the lamps on the side opposite the wicks. He made as many of these lamps as there were bedrooms in Malevil at the time, which is to say four. When our evening session around the fire was over, we all lit our lamps with a twig from the fire so that we could find our way easily to our beds through the darkness and could see to undress. La Menou was given the job of distributing the oil, because she was already responsible in any case for the second barrel, which had been earmarked for cooking purposes but had not yet been broached.

Using an old roofing lath that he scoured and planed, Meyssonier made us a graduated dipstick that enabled us to check on the rate of consumption. At the end of two weeks it was clear that it was very small. According to Thomas's calculations, continuing at our present rate it would take six years to empty the first barrel. After which time we should have to find some other source of light, since it was unlikely that any walnut trees had survived the general destruction of our flora.

I still had two flashlights with almost new batteries in them. I handed one over to La Menou for the gate tower and kept the other in the keep, it being clearly understood that neither was to be used except in the case of an emergency.

Thomas suggested that we could make washing less unpleasant by piling the fresh droppings from our three mares on the flagstones of the keep roof beneath the water tower. Our cold water supply ran in a zigzag course beneath the stones, and Thomas was fairly sure that the fermenting droppings would produce enough calories to warm it. We were all skeptical at the outset, but his experiment succeeded. And apart from the added comfort it contributed, it was also, in the primitive state into which we had fallen, a first step upward, a first victory. Little Colin swore that if only he had the use of his workshop in La Roque he could have made the central heating work again on the same principle.

Peyssou was delighted to have Meyssonnier in his room, but it took a certain amount of diplomacy to persuade Colin to sleep alone in Birgitta's room. What he would have liked, I think, is to replace Thomas in mine. I turned a deaf ear to his hints. The others had always accused me of making a pet of Colin, of "letting him get away with anything." But that didn't mean I was blind to his faults.

154

I was certain that I would have been making a very bad bargain if I had exchanged a roommate like Thomas, so calm, so discreet, so reticent, for little Colin.

And besides, Thomas was already quite isolated enough as it was: by his youth, by his city origins, by his cast of thought, by his character, and by his ignorance of our patois. I had to ask La Menou and Peyssou not to overdo the use of their first language—since neither of them had learned much French till they went to school—because at mealtimes, if they began a conversation in patois, then everyone else, little by little, would begin to drop into patois too, and after a while Thomas was made to feel a stranger in our life.

It must also be admitted that my friends found Thomas disconcerting. The rigor of his mind was matched by an equual stiffness in his manner, which was always cold. He always spoke briefly and to the point. He couldn't reach out to people. And above all, since he lacked all sense of humor, and even a sense of the comic, to an unimaginable degree, he never laughed. This imperturbable air of seriousness, such an oddity in our world, could well be taken for arrogance.

Even Thomas's most visible virtue did not win him appreciation. I noticed that La Menou had very little admiration for him, even though I knew she had a soft spot for handsome men, such as Boudenot the postman, for example. But the trouble was that despite Thomas's undeniable good looks, they were again not the sort of good looks appreciated around here. The Greek statue look and the perfect profile were not part of our canon. In Malejac a great beak and a heavy chin didn't matter, so long as there was vitality behind them. We liked great thickset lads, always ready for a laugh and a joke, and a bit on the boastful side.

And besides, Thomas was a "new boy." He had never belonged to the Club. He had no part in our memories. And because I spent a fair amount of time with him, in order to compensate for his isolation at Malevil, the others were a little jealous of him, especially Colin, who was always needling him. But Thomas was totally incapable of engaging in any kind of verbal ping-pong. His thought processes were so slow and so inflexibly serious that he never even attempted to reply to Colin's sallies. And this silence was construed as contempt, so after having made fun of him, Colin then felt an even greater grudge against him. There too I had to play the diplomat, bear down on Colin a little, and keep the wheels oiled.

The Bible readings had become a nightly occurrence, much less monotonous in practice than I had feared, since they were frequently interrupted by lively observations and exchanges. Peyssou, for example, was very much put out by the discrimination Cain was obliged to suffer at the hands of the Lord.

"Do you think that's fair then? Do you?" he asked me. "You have this boy who's slaved away to make all the vegetables grow, all that digging and watering and hoeing —that takes it out of you a bit more than taking a few sheep for a walk every day—and the Lord doesn't even bother to look at his offerings? And the other young whippersnapper, what's he done, I ask you, except follow his sheep's bottoms over the hills? So why does he get all the favors, eh?"

"The Lord, He must already have had this suspicion, thinking Cain was going to kill Abel perhaps," La Menou said.

"All the more reason not to make trouble between them with unfairness like that," Colin said.

Meyssonnier leaned closer to the fire, elbows on knees, and said with secret satisfaction. "Given that He was omniscient, He must have foreseen the murder. But if He foresaw it, why didn't He prevent it?"

But this insidious argument missed fire with the others. It was too abstract.

The more Peyssou thought about it, the more he identified himself with Cain. "The fact is," he said, "it doesn't matter where you go, there's always a pet. Look at Monsieur le Coutellier in school. Colin always in the front row next to the stove. And me always at the back with my face to the wall and my hands on my head. And what had I done? Nothing!"

"Oh, come on, that's not true!" Colin said with his gondola smile. "We all know why Le Coutellier made you

156

stand at the back. Because you couldn't keep your hands off you-know-what through the hole in your pocket."

There was laughter at this engaging memory.

"And that's why he made you put your hands on your head too," Colin added.

"All the same," Peyssou said, "if someone is making sure you always get the rough end of the stick, how can you help it? You're bound to turn nasty. You've got that good lad Cain, a hard worker who grows his carrots and takes them to give them to the Lord. So what then? He doesn't even look at them. Which just goes to show," he added bitterly, "that even in those days the Authorities didn't give a damn about agriculture."

Although the Authorities were now a thing of the past, this observation met with general approval. Then silence fell, and I was able to continue my reading. But when I got to the place where Cain knew his wife and she conceived and bore Enoch, La Menou interrupted me. "And where did she spring from, I'd like to know," she said sharply. She was sitting on the hearth seat behind me, with Momo opposite her, already half asleep.

I turned to look at her over my shoulder. "Where did who spring from?"

"Cain's wife!"

We all looked at one another, puzzled.

"Perhaps the Lord had made another Adam and Eve somewhere else," Colin suggested.

"No, no, of course He hadn't," Meyssonnier said, as ever a stickler for orthodoxy. "If He had, then the book would say so."

"So she was his sister then?" Colin said.

"Whose sister?" Peyssou asked, leaning forward and staring into Colin's face.

"Cain's sister."

Peyssou continued to stare at him but said nothing.

"Bound to be," La Menou said.

"Still, it seems . . ." Peyssou said, then stopped.

A short silence. It was odd, considering their fondness for a bawdy joke, how uncomfortable the idea of incest made them. Perhaps for the very reason that in the depth of the country . . .

I went on with my reading, but I didn't get far.

"Enoch," Peyssou said suddenly, "That's a Jewish name." Then he added with a slightly self-important and knowledgeable air, "I knew a fellow in the Army named Enoch. He was a Jew."

"Well, it's hardly surprising he had a Jewish name, is it?" Colin said.

"Oh, and why is it hardly surprising?" Peyssou asked, once more leaning forward to stare into his face.

"Because Enoch's parents were Jewish, weren't they?"

"His parents were Jewish?" Peyssou said, opening his eyes very wide and clutching his knees with outspread fingers.

"And his grandparents too."

"What!" Peyssou said. "You mean Adam and Eve were Jews?"

"What of it?"

Peyssou's mouth gaped, he sat for a moment without moving, eyes fixed on Colin. "But Adam And Eve, we're descended from them too," he said at last.

"Right."

"So we're Jews too then?"

"So?" Colin said stolidly.

Peyssou collapsed against the back of his chair. "Well, you know, I'd never have thought it."

He chewed over this revelation for a while and must have eventually construed it as proof of yet another flagrant piece of favoritism, because after a moment he asked indignantly, "Then why do the Jews think they're so much more Jewish than us?"

Everyone laughed, except Thomas. To look at him, lips firmly sealed, arms folded, chin sunk on chest, legs stretched out straight in front of him, it was clear that he was finding little interest in these exchanges, and even less in the readings that provoked them. It occurred to me that, he would probably have gone to bed directly after the evening meal if it weren't for the need, shared by us all, of soaking in a little human warmth after his hard day's work.

The fact that we even laughed on occasion during the course of those evening sessions was something that I found amazing at first. But then I remembered what my uncle had told me about his evenings as a prisoner of war in Germany. "Don't you go thinking we just sat there around the stove wailing our heads off, Emmanuel, out there in East Prussia. Quite the opposite. We amazed the Boches with our merriment. We told jokes, we sang, we laughed. But underneath, Emmanuel, it didn't mean much, you realize. It was a monastery sort of merriment. There was an emptiness behind it. Even good friends around you, it's not really a substitute."

Monastery merriment, yes, that was it, the exact phrase, and I really became aware of its accuracy only then, as I listened to my friends as they argued, with Volume I of Uncle Samuel's Bible on my knees. And since my left side was frozen by that time (what icy weather for May!), I got up and shifted over, stool and book as well, to the other side of the fireplace, though I wasn't going to stay there long, because I was too close to Momo, and the heat of the fire was making his smell even more distressing than usual. I made a note to speak to La Menou and suggest a wash for Momo as one of tomorrow's chores.

Beyond my companions (and it took a conscious effort to include Thomas among them, he is so different) I could see their shadows dancing up the wall as far as the great ceiling beams. I couldn't make out the far end of the hall, it was too big, but between two flickers of flame I could make out on my left, between the two mullioned windows, the stretch of unplastered stone wall bristling with steel-bladed weapons. Behind Peyssou there was the long refectory table, gleaming from La Menou's ever-active duster, and on the right, the two swag-fronted commodes from La Grange Forte. Beneath my feet were the great stone flags covering the vaulting of the cellar below.

An austere setting: stone floor, stone walls, neither curtains nor carpets, nothing warm, nothing to suggest the presence of a woman. A world of men alone, without heirs, waiting for death. An abbey or monastery. Everything was there, the work, the "merriment," the readings from the Scriptures.

I don't know how, but somehow from the Jews who "think they're so much more Jewish than us" the conversation had moved on to the problem of finding out whether or not there were any survivors in La Roque. It was a subject that cropped up every evening. There was a standing plan to go there before long, but it wasn't that easy. After a great struggle we had finally cleared the road from Malevil to Malejac of the trees brought down by the fire, but the nine miles from Malejac to La Roque was a very hilly, twisty road mostly through chestnut woods. From the little we had seen of it, it seemed certain that it must be equally obstructed by the remains of the great fires, and we had no fuel left to clear it. On foot, before, it used to take a good three hours on average to reach La Roque. If we had to negotiate fallen trees all the way, it would take a whole day now, then another day to get back to Malevil: forty-eight hours that for the time being—until our sowing was over and done with—we could ill afford to waste.

Or at least that was my usual argument. Now, with the big book heavy on my knees, I listened to my companions and kept mum. Because I was the one it had first occurred to, I was responsible for raising this hope in them of finding life at La Roque. And now, by dint of talking about it every evening, they had given my abstract conjecture a shape and body. Yet the larger it loomed for them, the more it shrank in my own mind. I made no effort whatever to urge on the projected expedition. Quite the contrary. While Meyssonnier and Colin went on patching together that plow of theirs I was quite happy to stay at Malevil with the other two, pulling nails out of the old planks and organizing our storeroom.

I could see that there was an element of withdrawal and resignation in my attitude. I was shrinking into myself day by day; I was already more than half the compleat monk. And sitting there listening with half an ear—faithful to my strategy of intermittent attention—neck pressed against the stone upright of the fireplace, I wondered whether it would make any difference if I really believed in God. Of course I knew it would land me with a new set of problems, among them: Why has God allowed His creature to destroy His creation? But leaving the field of ideas out of it, would religious faith at least bring a little warmth into my heart? I didn't know. But I didn't think it would. It was so far away, all that. So abstract. When I dreamed, it wasn't about God.

I had two sorts of dreams, the waking, consciously evoked sort with which I furnished my sleepless hours, and then the other, involuntary sort while I was asleep. In my waking hours, with my chest, my belly, my thighs pressed hard against the mattress, I conjured up Birgitta again. And when she was really there, alive, warm, satin-smooth in my arms, then I hurled myself upon her, I kneaded her, I bit her. No, to say I bit her isn't enough. I engulfed her, I drank her, I ate her. And that, I suppose, is why she vanished so soon. And why it was growing more difficult every time to bring her back to life.

The dream I dreamed in my sleep—almost always the same—was far less frustrating. I was walking down some stairs in Cimiez, above Nice, on a bright summer morning. The stairs were familiar, even though I have only walked down them once in real life. They were wide and full of light in my dream, because the sun was streaming in through tall windows. And as I walked down them, a girl was running up to meet me, her hair floating loose, her arms hanging gracefully at her sides. She had lovely breasts, alive with the eagerness of her ascent. And as she moved to meet me across the half-way landing, the sun lit up her hair floating behind her. She climbed the last stairs, face lifted to greet me. I didn't know her, and yet with all her eyes, with all her mouth, she was smiling at me in friendship. And that was all. It stopped there. And yet I felt—how can I express it?—as refreshed by that vision as if I had been breathing in the scent of armfuls of lilac.

The night before, immediately after this dream, I had woken up, and the reaction as it faded had been very painful. I experienced simultaneously an appalling sense of grief and acute physical distress. I could feel my rib cage shrinking tight around my heart, and as though the two things were connected I also had an abominable impression of solitude. Or rather, this loneliness made itself apparent to me in the form of a pain centered in my chest. I sat up in bed and concentrated on trying to breathe. And to my great surprise I succeeded without the slightest difficulty. Heart, lungs, they were performing their functions, there was no specific place where it hurt, just a tremendous tightness in my throat and that curious sensation of tension mounting and mounting while you wait for it to explode—and that does finally burst as the tears start to flow.

As they streamed down my cheeks, without a sob, the same wearisome refrain repeated itself over and over in my head: I didn't marry, I have no children. The death of the human race was at hand. I was going to see it. Because suddenly I was obsessed with the absurd conviction that all my companions, even Thomas, who was fifteen years my junior, would die before me, leaving me alone. And I could see myself, old and bent, walking endlessly through Malevil's enormous rooms, listening to my own footsteps reverberating in the cellar, under the arched ceiling, in the great hall of the house, in my own room up in the keep.

It was the first light night since the day it happened, or perhaps it was already morning. On the sofa across from me, and much lower than the level of my own rustic double bed which stood so high on its wooden legs, I could make out Thomas's face, eyes closed, cheek pressed on his pillow in defenseless sleep, the bedclothes pulled up to his chin and around the back of his neck as a protection from the draft from the window. Once again I admired his features, his Grecian nose, the firm outline of his lips, the molding of his cheeks. I noticed that in sleep he had lost the stern expression always seen on his face during his waking hours. In fact he looked somehow childlike and vulnerable. His beard was fair and grew slowly, so he only had to shave every other day. And since he had shaved that morning, there was not the slightest shadow on his cheek. It looked quite smooth, with a velvety bloom, and the hint of a dimple that I had never noticed before just by the corner of his mouth. His curly blond hair, cut short when I met him that day in the undergrowth, had grown since he had come to live at Malevil, and now gave him an almost feminine air.

I rolled over abruptly in my bed, turning my back to him, and it occurred to me that one day I must revise our sleeping arrangements, have a rota system in fact, so that I wouldn't always have Thomas in my bedroom, since mine is really the most comfortable. And at the same time I became aware of an odd feeling of anxiety and guilt for which I could discern no particular cause but which kept me awake, my muddled thoughts broken only by the briefest dozes now and then. And even these were broken into by nightmares so painful and humiliating that I eventually got up. I picked my clothes up in a bundle from my chair, left the room, and went down to the bathroom on the floor below. But even there, until I had finished shaving, the hateful and shameful fantasies pursued me. I took a shower and stayed under it a long time. I felt that I was washing off the filth of my dreams.

It was five o'clock by my watch when I emerged from the keep into the small courtyard. As on every other day since the day it happened, the weather was cold and gray. I was the only person up in Malevil. My steps echoed on the cobbles. The vast keep, the ramparts, and the house were massive weights bearing down on me. I had two long hours of solitude stretching ahead before breakfast.

I walked out across the drawbridge, then through the outer enclosure to the Maternity Ward. Bel Amour was asleep on her feet, her foal as well, leaning against her flank, but as soon as I put my chin over the partition of her stall, Bel Amour's little ears pricked up, she opened her eyes, saw me, and puffed the air out through her nostrils in a tiny muffled neigh of greeting. She took a step toward me, and the half-wakened foal staggered, then moved forward in its turn, wobbling on its long, slender legs until it had regained the support of its mother's still swollen belly. Bel Amour reached her head over the partition and laid it without any ado on my shoulder, so I could stroke the top of her cheek as I looked over at the foal.

It's something that always melts the heart, a young animal, young human animals included. Malice had the same white blaze on her forehead and the same dark chestnut coat as her mother, and she was returning my scrutiny

163

with an astonished look in her beautiful, innocent eyes. I would have liked to go into the stall and stroke her too, but I wasn't sure that Bel Amour would be very pleased about that, so I deprived myself of the pleasure. Bel Amour laid her mouth, then her soft damp nostrils against my neck and gave another friendly snort. Everything indicated that she was perfectly happy. She was looked after, even spoiled by us, she was well fed, and she had her foal. She didn't know that Malice was her last offspring, and that her kind, like ours, was doomed to extinction.

The day was spent on our customary monotonous tasks. And in the evening I lived once more through the same fireside scene, elbows on my Bible, head in hands, listening intermittently to the conversation about La Roque. The fire had sunk low by now, and La Menou, dozing on her hearth seat, suddenly shook herself and rose, thereby giving the signal that it was time for bed. Immediately there was a great noise of feet on stone and chairs being banged back into place around the table. Tongs in hand, La Menou arranged the dying logs skillfully in the fireplace so as to ensure that there would still be embers left next day, and as I lingered for a moment on my feet, my closed Bible under one arm, joking and laughing with my companions, I was afraid of the moment when I would be back once more in bed, trapped in the same old circle of thoughts like a prisoner in his exercise yard.

I remember that evening well, and the dread I felt at the thought of another sleepless night. It is vivid in my memory because it was the following day that everything changed and things began to move.

As in a classical tragedy, the event was heralded by signs, portents, premonitions. It was just as cold as on all the previous days, the sky opaque, and the horizon still invisible. At breakfast, ever since Prince was born, we all had a little milk to drink, a little less than a bowl each, and even then Thomas had been forced to insist at length that everyone drank it, for dietetic reasons, since neither Meyssonnier, Colin, nor Peyssou liked milk. Momo, on the other hand, guzzled his down with gluttonous delight. Clasping the bowl in both filthy hands and emitting little anticipatory grunts of pleasure, he would fix his shining black eyes on the liquid in it, and gloat over the sight of its snowy surface for a few seconds before gulping it down, so quickly and so avidly that two thin white trickles would run down each side of his chin and then down his grimy neck, through the bristles of his two-week beard.

"You know, Menou," I said when he'd put his bowl down again, "it's time we faced up to it. Your offspring is due for ablution."

My words had been chosen with the intention of leaving the potential protagonist in ignorance as long as possible of the intended operation, which depended for its success on total surprise.

"I've been thinking the same thing a while now," La Menou answered, keeping her language equally allusive and without looking at Momo. "But on my own, as you know . . ." Then she added, "But whenever you like."

"Fine, then right after breakfast, I suggest. While Peyssou is out plowing the plot by the Rhunes with Amarante. After all, four of us should be enough."

I am quite certain that Momo hadn't grasped either the word "offspring" or the word "ablution," which was after all why I had used them. And I had also taken care, like La Menou, not to look at him during our exchange. But despite our precautions, his infallible instinct warned him. His glance flashed from his mother to me, he jumped to his feet, knocking over his chair, and shouted in a furious voice, "*Eave ee ahone, ham hyoo! Momo hate horter!*" (Leave me alone, damn you! Momo hates water!) Whereupon, snatching up the slice of ham from his plate, he took to his heels and was out through the door in a flash.

"He had you nicely there," Peyssou cried with a laugh. "And now you won't get near him for the rest of the day."

"There you're wrong," La Menou told him. "You just don't know Momo. He will just forget. Any idea at all, no sooner does he get it in one ear than it's flown out the other. That's how he never worries about things. He can't remember anything to worry for."

"Well, he's a lucky lad then," Colin said with a shadow of his old smile. "Because my trouble is the opposite, my

165

head's too full of ideas. All going around and around all the time. So that sometimes I'd rather I was an idiot and have none."

"Momo is not an idiot," La Menou told him sharply. "Emmanuel's uncle always said it: 'That Momo, he's intelligent, you know. It's just the language he can't learn. And that's why nothing sticks with him.' "

"No offense intended," Colin said politely.

"Oh, I didn't take it the wrong way, don't worry," La Menou said, flashing him a smile, her bright eyes momentarily lighting up that tiny death's head perched on its thin little neck. "And where do we look for him, my Momo, right after breakfast? I'll tell you where: in Bel Amour's stall, where he'll be fussing over her as usual. You wait for him to come out, and there you are. With four of you to one it will be child's play."

"Child's play!" I said. "It's a game I'd be glad to get out of, I can tell you. And whatever you do, look out for his feet. Meyssonnier and I will take an arm each and get him down. Then you take the right foot, Colin, and Thomas the left. But be careful, because he'll kick. And he has very strong legs on him."

"Just the way you used to dunk me in the river, damn you," Peyssou said, his great peasant's face split by a broad smile. "Rotten mob of bastards," he added fondly.

The laughter this caused was cut off abruptly. The door of the great hall flew open with a crash and Momo reappeared, mad with excitement and joy, yelling and jumping up and down where he stood, arms waving. "*Hehaho! Hehaho!*" he shouted.

Although I was by now at least as expert as his mother in decoding Momo's speech, I had no idea what he was saying. I looked at La Menou, and clearly she hadn't understood either. In Momo language "I'm hurt" came out as "*Haihuh*," and anyway his evident jubilation excluded any idea of a fall or wound.

"*Haho?*" La Menou asked at last as she stood up. "What's that? *Haho?*"

"*Haho! Hawhosake!*" Momo yelled, hopping with fury, as though beside himself with indignation that we weren't able to interpret his words.

166

"Now then, Momo," I said as I too got up and went over to him, "calm down and explain! What exactly is that *haho?*"

"*Haho!*" he screamed again. Then suddenly stretching his arms out on either side of him, he waved them up and down as though he was flying.

"A crow?" I said without thinking.

"*Hess! Hess!*" Momo said, and his face alight with gratitude, he cried, "*Hood oh Ehanooel! Hood oh Ehanooel!*" (Good old Emmanuel!), and would certainly have hugged me if I hadn't held him as far away from me as the length of my arm would allow.

"Now, Momo, are you sure? A crow here at Malevil?"

"*Hess! Hess!*"

We exchanged totally incredulous glances. We had all accepted, ever since the day it happened, that the race of birds was silenced forever.

"*Hum anh! Hum anh!*" Momo cried, tugging at the arm with which I was fending him off. I released my grip, and immediately he was off and out of the door again, his feet scarcely touching the ground. I ran after him, preceded by the clattering of his hobnailed boots across the cobbles and followed in turn by our companions, La Menou included, and not left as far behind as one might have expected, I noticed, looking back.

Ahead, I saw Momo halt and freeze on the drawbridge. I stopped too. And there it was, barely twenty yards away across the outer enclosure, opposite the entrance to the Maternity Ward. Not noticeably thin, obviously not injured, its blue-black feathers gleaming with health, it was hopping heavily to and fro across the cobbles, pecking up a barley grain here and a seed there with its big beak. Once aware of our presence, it froze and turned sideways in order to scrutinize us with one vigilant bead of an eye. It straightened its neck, though without managing to eliminate the bend of its back, so it looked like a hunched old man, hands clasped behind his back, head cocked slightly to one side, peering at us with a very wise and circumspect air. No one in the group moved, and our very immobility must have alarmed it, because it suddenly spread its great blue-black wings and skimmed

167

away from us with a single loud "caw." Then it flapped slowly upward, alighted on the roof of the gate tower, and hid behind the chimney stack, from behind which, after a moment or so, its big drooping beak reappeared, followed by one sagacious eye still fixed on our motionless figures.

We walked out into the enclosure then, heads in the air, eyes fixed on what it was allowing us to see of it.

"Well now," Peyssou said, "if you'd said to me, 'The day will come when you'll be glad to clap eyes on a crow,' I'd never have believed it."

"And seeing it so close," La Menou said. "Because the Lord knows what suspicious beasts your crows are. And so cunning with it that they'll never let you come closer than a hundred yards without they flap away."

"Unless you're in an automobile," Colin said.

The remark cast a chill, because it belonged to the world of before, but the chill was quickly thawed by the general euphoria that had gripped us all, a euphoria masked by a sudden gush of words, but none the less sharply felt for all that. Agreement was reached that on the day it happened, whether by chance or instinct, the crow must have been in one of the many caves with which the cliffs all around are riddled (and in which Protestant fugitives used to hide during the religious wars). It had been wily enough to get well inside one of them and stay there for as long as the holocaust lasted. And when it grew cold again, it had fed on carrion, perhaps even on the corpses of our horses, who could say? But on the reasons that were driving it to seek our company disagreement was strong.

"I know why he's pleased to have found some men still alive," Peyssou announced. "It's simply because where there are men he knows there'll always be something around for him to eat. It's as simple as that, believe me."

But this materialistic theory did not wholly satisfy, and oddly enough it was Meyssonnier who contested it.

"I admit he was here looking for the barley," he said with an air of authority, legs apart, hands in pockets, and nose in the air, "but that doesn't explain why he's so tame. Because there's all the barley that gets wasted in the Maternity Ward—Amarante, for example, is so greedy

168

she always manages to knock a good quarter of her feed onto the floor—and he could come and get that during the night."

"I think you're right there," Colin said. "Crows in a flock, they're always suspicious because they know we're always out to get them. But on their own, you can tame them quite easily. Do you remember the cobbler, over at La Roque, for example?"

"*Hess! Hess!*" Momo crowed excitedly, very pleased with himself because he did remember the cobbler.

"Ah, they're clever birds, and that's a fact," La Menou said. "I remember Emmanuel's uncle one year, he put down his scarers in a field of corn they were spoiling for him. Bang, bang, they went all day. And believe it or not, by the end, those crows didn't care a fig for his fire-works. They didn't even fly away when they went off. Calm as judges they stood there, pecking away at the corn."

Peyssou burst into laughter. "Oh, they're cunning buggers all right," he said with respect in his voice. "When I think how they've made my blood boil! And once, just once, that's all, I managed to kill one. With Emmanuel's .22."

There then followed a long and detailed descant of praise to the crow, his intelligence, his longevity, his willingness to be tamed by man, his linguistic aptitude. And when Thomas, somewhat surprised, pointed out that the crow was after all a pest, no one even bothered to contest so ill-judged an observation. First, because although in the old days one might well have waged war on a pest, it was without hatred, with something even approaching amused respect for its tricks, and with the underlying knowledge, when all was said and done, that everyone needed to eat. And also because this particular crow, who had come there expressly in order to fan our hopes that other survivors still existed elsewhere, was now a sacred animal. From that day on it was to be given its own small daily share of barley; it was already part of Malevil.

It was Peyssou who brought the conversation to an end. The evening before, we had carried the plow that Meyssonnier and Colin had constructed down to the small field beside the Rhunes, and Peyssou was anxious to take Amarante down there and begin plowing. As he set off toward her stall with his slow swinging stride, I gave Meyssonnier a wink; and before he could even yell out, Momo was already powerless, both arms and legs held immovable, then lifted bodily into the air and carried at a trot like a bale of hay toward the keep, with La Menou's tiny legs flashing to and fro to keep up with us as she kept repeating with a happy little laugh every time her son yelled at us to let him go, "Oh, but you must be washed. It's good for you, you dirty big thing!" Because for her, washing Momo, something she had been doing now for almost half a century, ever since she put his first diaper on, was by no means a chore, however much she affected to complain of the task, but a maternal rite that still warmed the cockles of her heart, despite her little boy's age.

At my suggestion, no one had taken a shower that morning, so we were able to fill the tub with tepid water and dump Momo in it to soak while Meyssonnier attacked his beard. Poor Momo, overwhelmed by sheer numbers and by now demoralized, had ceased all resistance, and after a moment or two I was able to withdraw from the scene, taking care to remind Colin that the door must be bolted after me as a precaution against a surprise escape. I went up to my room to collect my binoculars, then made my way up to the top of the keep.

During our discussion about the crow in the outer enclosure I thought I had seen a slightly less gray patch in the gray sky and I was hoping I would be able to make out La Roque. But it had been an illusion, as I realized at my very first glance. The binoculars merely confirmed my disappointment. Leaden sky, visibility minimal, color nonexistent. The meadows in which not a blade of grass remained, and the fields in which not a single sprouting spike could be seen, seemed to be covered in a uniform gray dust. In the old days, when people came out from the town to visit me and admire the view from the top of the keep, they used to marvel at Malevil's *silence*. But that silence was no such thing, thank God, except to city

170

dwellers. A distant automobile on the road by the Rhunes, a tractor plowing, the cry of a bird, an obstinately crowing cock, a guard dog determined to earn his keep, and in summer, needless to say, the grasshoppers, the cicadas, the bees in the Virginia creeper. Now, yes, there was silence indeed. Sky and land, nothing but lead, anthracite, blackness. And then the immobility. The corpse of a landscape. A dead planet.

Eyes glued to my binoculars, I probed at the spot where La Roque ought to be, unable to make out anything but grayness, unable even to say whether the grayness I was looking at was part of the land or of the gray lid pressing down on us. I lowered the glasses gradually till I was looking at the field in the valley where Peyssou should by now have harnessed Amarante and begun plowing. At least there would be something alive to look at there. I looked for the mare, she being the larger and therefore the more easily locatable, then becoming slightly irritable because I couldn't find her, I removed the binoculars from my eyes. At once I could see the plow, stationary in the center of the field, and beside it, stretched motionless on the ground, Peyssou, his arms flung out on either side of him. Amarante was nowhere to be seen.

I hurtled down the two flights of the spiral staircase like a madman, flung myself at the bathroom door and tried to open it, forgetting that it was bolted, then hammering with both fists like a lunatic on the massive wood panels, I yelled, "Come quickly. Something's happened to Peyssou!"

Without waiting for the others, I set off again at a run. In order to reach the field we were plowing I had to run down the road along the side of the cliff to the flat beneath, then turn left around a hairpin bend, cross back under the castle, and keep on down the bed of the dried-up stream till I reached the nearer branch of the Rhunes. I was running as hard as I possibly could, the blood thudding in my temples, completely at a loss for an explanation. Amarante was so gentle and quiet that I simply couldn't believe she'd attacked her driver in order to escape. And anyway, escape to where? Since there wasn't a single blade of grass to be had anywhere and at Malevil she was being fed all the hay and barley she needed.

After a while I could hear the others' boots on the rocky track behind me as they struggled to catch up to me. A hundred yards before I reached the field I was overhauled and passed by Thomas, who was running with long, very rapid strides and was soon a good way ahead of me. I watched him as he stopped, knelt down beside Peyssou, turned him over very carefully, and put a hand under his head. "He's alive!" he shouted to me as I approached.

I squatted down in my turn, exhausted, completely out of breath. Peyssou opened his eyes, but they were still vague. He couldn't focus them. His nose and left cheek were covered with earth and there was a great deal of blood flowing from the back of his head, staining Thomas's shirt where it was resting. Colin, Meyssonnier, and a completely naked Momo still streaming with water arrived as I was examining the wound, which was certainly wide but appeared at first glance to be only superficial. Finally La Menou appeared. She had stopped off to pick up a bottle of brandy from the gate tower, and she was also carrying my bathrobe, in which she proceeded to swaddle the naked Momo before even glancing at Peyssou.

I poured a little brandy onto the wound and Peyssou groaned. Then I poured a generous mouthful between his lips and cleaned the earth from his face with a brandy-soaked handkerchief.

"It couldn't have been Amarante who did that," Colin said "He was lying all wrong for that."

"Peyssou," I said, rubbing his temples with a little of the brandy, "can you hear me? What happened?" Then, to the others, "In any case, Amarante never shies."

"It's something I've always noticed in her," La Menou said, "even when she's playing. That one, she can't bring herself to get her bottom in the air."

Peyssou's eyes began to focus, and he said in a low but distinct voice, "Emmanuel."

I gave him a second mouthful of brandy and began rubbing his temples again. "What happened?" I asked, patting his cheeks and trying to hold his gaze, which kept tending to swim away into vagueness again.

"He's had a pretty nasty shock," Colin said as he stood up. "But he's coming around. He already looks better."

"Peyssou! Do you hear me? Peyssou!"

I looked up. "Menou, pass me the belt of my robe."

As soon as she handed it to me I laid it across one knee, folded my handkerchief in four, soaked it in the brandy, then pressed it carefully over the wound, which was still bleeding copiously. I asked La Menou to hold the dressing in place and tied the belt around his head and forehead to hold it in place. La Menou did as I said without a word, her gaze fixed the whole time on Momo, who had certainly "caught his death" running around outside in the cold like that.

"I don't know," Peyssou said suddenly.

"You don't know how it happened?"

"No." He closed his eyes again, and I promptly slapped his cheeks.

"Come and look at this, Emmanuel!" Colin called. He was standing over by the plow, back toward us but looking over his shoulder, an expression of distress on his face, staring into my eyes.

I got up and went over to him.

"Look at that," he said quietly.

The first time we'd tried Amarante in the plow we had realized that the buckle and strap fastening the shaft to her harness was inadequate. We had replaced it with a length of nylon cord, made secure to the pole by a series of loops and knots. The cord had been cut.

"A man did that," Colin said. He was pale and dry-lipped. "With a knife."

I took the two ends of cord from him so that I could inspect them more closely. The cut was clean, without a trace of raggedness or pulling. I bowed my head without a word. I was incapable of speech.

"The fellow who unharnessed Amarante," Colin said, "undid the breeching buckles and the left-hand buckle of the girth, but when he found the knots on the right side, he lost his nerve and pulled out his knife."

"And before all that," I said in a shaky voice, "he hit Peyssou on the head, from the back."

I realized that La Menou, Meyssonnier, and Momo had gathered around us. They all had their eyes on my face. Thomas was looking up at me too from his position on the ground, one knee on the earth, the other supporting Peyssou's back.

"Lord, Lord, what a thing!" La Menou said, casting a frightened glance all around her and seizing Momo by one arm in order to pull him to her side.

There was a silence. Along with a stirring of fear I experienced a feeling of mocking irony. God knew with what ardor, with what love in our hearts, with what almost despairing eagerness we had prayed in our hearts that there would turn out to be other members of the human race than ourselves who had survived. Well, now we could be certain of it. There were.

VII

I CHOSE the .22 rifle (given me by my uncle on my fifteenth birthday) and Thomas took the over-and-under shotgun. It was agreed that the others would stay inside Malevil with the other shotgun. Not much in the way of armaments, but then Malevil had its ramparts, its battlements, its moats.

As we reached the hairpin bend that led from the Malevil entrance road to the little track down to the Rhunes, I cast a long look back at the castle perched on its cliff. I noticed that Thomas was looking up at it too. No point in trying to tell each other what we were feeling. With every step, we both felt more naked, more vulnerable. Malevil was our refuge, our stronghold, our eyrie. Till now it had protected us from everything, including the utmost refinements of human technology. What a nightmare, leaving its shelter, and what a nightmare too that long walk, one behind the other. The gray sky, the gray earth, the stumps of the blackened trees, the silence and immobility of death. And at our goal the only human beings still alive in that lifeless landscape were waiting in ambush to strike us down.

I was quite certain about that. The theft of the mare, given that it was utterly impossible to cover up the tracks of her hoofs in the burned and dusty earth, could only mean that the thieves had expected us to pursue them, and that somewhere, at some point in that denuded landscape, a surprise attack awaited us. Yet we had no choice. We could not just allow someone to get away with knocking one of us over the head and stealing a horse

175

from us. And unless we wished to remain passive, then we had to begin by playing the aggressor's game.

Between the moment when I had first seen Peyssou lying motionless in the field beside the Rhunes and the moment when we left Malevil, no more than a half hour had elapsed. It was evident that the thief had lost a great deal of his lead in his struggles with Amarante. I could see the places where she dug in her heels then stabbed the earth with her hoofs as she wheeled this way and that. Although so docile, she was also attached to her stable, to Malevil, and to Bel Amour, whose stall was next to hers and whom she could always see through the barred opening between them. Moreover she was a young animal and still easily frightened by the slightest thing—a puddle, a hosepipe, a stone catching her hoof, a newspaper flapping in the wind. The human footsteps running alongside the hoofprints showed clearly that the man had not dared mount her bareback. Proof that Amarante's Anglo-Arab spirit had alarmed him and that he was not a very good rider. The miracle was that Amarante, despite her occasional shows of resistance, had nevertheless consented to let him lead her away.

The Rhunes valley was a plain scarcely a hundred yards wide running between two lines of once wooded hills, with the twin rivers running from north to south and the small local road running parallel to them along the flank of the hills to the east. The thief had not followed the road, which was quite straight and on which he would have been clearly visible from a great distance, but made his way instead just under the line of hills to the west, a much more winding path but one that offered much better cover. It seemed to me that we were in fact in very little danger until he had regained his hideout. Neither he nor any possible companions were going to engage in any action before Amarante was safely out of the way in stable or paddock.

I nevertheless remained on the alert, my rifle no longer slung over my shoulder but held in my hand, eyes constantly on either the ground or the way ahead. Neither Thomas nor I spoke. Despite the cold air, the tension was making me perspire, the palms of my hands especially, and although Thomas was outwardly just as calm as my-self, I noticed that when he removed his gun from his shoulder, where he had been resting it in order to give his arm a rest, there was a damp patch where it had been.

We had been walking for an hour and a half when Amarante's tracks left the Rhunes and turned off at a right angle to the west, between a hill and a cliff. The topography and orientation of the place were the same as those at Malevil: cliff to the north, and running along the foot of the cliff a water course, in Malevil's case now dried up of course, but here a small stream, very full and fast flowing, with the water at the same level as the surrounding land. Obviously nothing had been done to dredge or widen its bed, and its continual flooding had turned the little plain between hill and cliff, an expanse of barely forty yards, into something little better than a bog. I remembered that for this reason my Uncle Samuel had declared it strictly out of bounds for the Sept Fayards horses. And certainly none of us, even in our daredevil Club days, had ever dared set foot in that swamp, onto which no tractor's wheels had ever ventured.

Which didn't mean I was ignorant of who its inhabitants were. They were people generally said to be brutish, dour, immoral, and worse still, poachers. Furthermore, they lived in a cave, a deep recess in the cliff that had been turned into a dwelling by the simple expedient of building a wall with windows in it across the mouth. It was on account of the nature of this dwelling that Monsieur le Coutellier, the schoolmaster, always referred to them as the "troglodytes," a name that delighted us in our Club days. But for Malejac generally they were simply the "foreigners," or worse still—for the fact that the father came from the north caused confusion in local minds—as the "Gips." They were all the more disconcerting in that you never saw hide nor hair of them in Malejac, since they did all their buying in Saint-Sauveur. And all the more terrible, needless to say, because no one knew anything about them to speak of, not even how many members there were in the tribe. Though it was rumored that the father—who in both gait and facial structure,

177

my uncle had once assured me, bore a close resemblance to Cro-Magnon man—had "done time" in prison on two occasions, once for assault and battery, once for having raped his daughter. The latter, the only member of the family I knew, at least by name, was named Catie and was in service with the mayor of La Roque. She was a very good-looking girl, so rumor had it, with extremely bold eyes and a way of carrying on that set many tongues wagging. If rape there had been, then it had certainly not put her off men as a result.

The name of the troglodytes' farm was another thing that used to intrigue us in Club days: L'Étang, the tarn. It intrigued us because, needless to say, there was no tarn any more, just a patch of swampy land between a cliff and hill, itself pretty steep. Neither electricity nor a track to it. A sort of damp gorge into which no one ever ventured, not even the postman, who left their mail, which meant about a letter a month in fact, at Cussac, a beautiful old farmhouse up on the hill. We at least knew through Boudenot the postman what their name was: Wahrwoorde. No name for Christians, it was generally agreed. Boudenot used to say that the father was a "savage," but not poor, far from it. He had stock and some good acreage up on the hillside.

I caught up to Thomas, brought him to a halt with a hand on his arm, and putting my mouth close to his ear, whispered, "It's in there. My turn to lead."

He glanced around him, looked at his watch, then answered equally quietly, "My quarter hour's not up."

"Forget that. I know the terrain. Follow me ten yards behind."

I walked on past him till I was a little way ahead, then waved him to a stop again with my hand at hip level and stopped myself. I took the binoculars out of their case, raised them to my eyes, and inspected the terrain. The narrow meadow sloped up gently between hillside and cliff, divided transversely by earth banks and dry-stone walls. The hillside presented exactly the same naked and blackened appearance as all the others we had seen. But the meadow itself, being well protected by the cliff to the north and also by its sunken situation generally, had suffered, well, let's say one degree less during the holocaust. It presented the appearance of a place whose vegetation had been burned, certainly, but without being totally charred, and without the earth—perhaps because it was so sodden with water the day it happened— assuming that gray, dusty look that was apparent everywhere else. Here and there, in fact, you could even make out yellowish tufts that must have been rank grass, and two or three stripped and blackened trees still upright and recognizable.

I slid the binoculars back into their case and moved warily forward. But another surprise awaited me. The ground was firm and resistant under my feet. The day it happened, drawn up by the intense heat, the water in the ground must have sizzled up into the air like steam rushing from the spout of a boiling kettle. And as there had been no rain since, the marsh was now dry.

While my mind remained perfectly cool, recording all these details with absolute clarity, my body on the other hand was playing nasty tricks on me—sweat pouring from my palms, heart beating far too fast, temples thumping— and as I put away the binoculars I was even aware of a slight trembling of the hands, which didn't augur too well for my aim if it came to shooting. I concentrated on taking slow deep breaths, timing them to coincide with my steps, while I kept my eyes alternately on Amarante's tracks on the ground just ahead and on the meadow sloping up in front of me. Not a breath of wind, not a sound, even in the distance. Ahead, ten yards away now, a low drystone wall.

It all happened very quickly. I noticed a pile of droppings that looked quite fresh. I halted and bent down to examine them. To be more precise, I was intending to touch the back of my hand to the heap to feel whether it was still warm. At the same moment something hissed over my head. A second later Thomas appeared beside me, also squatting, and holding an arrow in one hand. Its black and extremely sharp tip was covered in earth.

At the same instant there was another hiss, just as loud as the first. I dropped flat and began leopard-crawling to the dry-stone wall. I thought I had left Thomas behind, so quickly had I acted, but to my great surprise, when I laid my gun down beside me and turned onto my left side, I found him lying on the ground next to me, already busy building a peephole on top of the wall with dislodged stones. Strangely, it seemed to me, he had thought to bring the arrow with him. It lay beside him on the ground, its yellow and green flight feathers the only spots of color in the landscape. I stared at it. I couldn't believe my eyes! The troglodytes were fighting us with bow and arrows!

I threw a quick glance over the wall. Fifty yards ahead, cutting right across the narrow valley, there ran another dry-stone wall. In the middle of it there was a big walnut tree, burned but still standing. A well-chosen position, but they had made an error nevertheless. They should have let us cross our little wall and then attacked when we had no possible cover. They had fired too soon, presumably encouraged by my immobility as I noticed the heap of droppings.

I heard a fresh hiss, and I don't know why but I drew in my legs. It was a fortunate reflex, because the arrow, which seemed to come straight down out of the sky, embedded itself deeply in the earth about two feet away from my feet. It must have been shot into the air at a very nicely calculated angle to achieve that accuracy in its trajectory. And the bowman's guide mark, I realized immediately, was Thomas's improvised peephole. I signaled to him to follow me and crawled away a few yards along the wall to the left.

Another arrow hissed through the air, perfectly aligned on the peephole we had just left, but a yard away from the previous one. As soon as it embedded itself in the earth I began counting the seconds; one, two, three, four, five. On five, another hiss. So it took the archer five seconds to pull out an arrow, fit it, draw, aim, and let fly. And there weren't two bows either, there was only one. The arrows always came in strict sequence, never two together.

I pulled the telescopic sight off my gun. The very fact of its magnification made sighting a slow business. Then I whispered, "Thomas, crawl back beyond the peephole to the other side. As soon as I've fired twice put your head up above the wall, fire both your barrels at random, then move again immediately."

He crawled off. I watched him. As soon as he was in position I thumbed off my safety catch, drew myself up into a crouched kneeling position, and raised the gun with both hands until it was almost parallel with the top of the wall. I straightened up abruptly, shouldering the gun as I did so, swung around from the waist, thought I glimpsed one tip of the bow behind the walnut tree, fired two shots, and dropped again. At once, while I was still crawling away from my firing position, I heard the boom! boom! of Thomas's two barrels, much louder than the tiny curt cracks of my own bullets.

I waited for the response. It didn't come. Suddenly, to my utter stupefaction, I saw Thomas, about ten yards or so from me, get to his feet. He was standing there quite relaxed, one hip leaning against the little wall, gun resting along his forearm. If it is possible to yell in a whisper, that's what I did: "Get down!"

"They're waving a white flag," he said calmly, turning his head in my direction with infuriating slowness.

"Get down!" I shouted in a furious voice.

He did as I said. I crawled back to the peephole and took a look at the wall opposite. The bow, now almost completely visible, was being waved to and fro, though it was impossible to see the hand doing the waving, and from its upper extremity there hung a white handkerchief. I took out the binoculars and examined the top of the wall very carefully along its entire length. I could see nothing. I lowered the binoculars, made a megaphone of my hands, and said in patois, "What do you want, you over there with your white rag?"

No reply. I repeated the question in French.

"Give myself up!" a young-sounding voice answered.

I shouted, "Hold up your bow with both hands behind your head, and walk toward us."

There was a silence. I raised the binoculars again. The bow and its white flag were in exactly the same position. Thomas rubbed one foot against the ground as he shifted position. I signaled to him to stay still and listened as hard as I could. I couldn't hear even the slightest sound.

181

I waited a full minute, then without lowering the binoculars I shouted, "All right, what are you waiting for?"

"You won't shoot at me?" the voice answered.

"Of course not."

Another few seconds went by, then I saw the man stand up on the other side of his wall, very big in the binoculars, bow behind his head, held in both hands as I had ordered. I lowered the binoculars and snatched up my gun.

"Thomas?"

"Yes."

"When he gets here, move to the peephole and keep watch. Don't take your eyes off that wall."

"Right."

The man grew steadily larger. He was walking very quickly, almost running. To my great surprise he was young, with a great mane of reddish blond hair. Unshaven. He stopped on the other side of our wall.

I said, "Throw your bow over here, then climb over yourself, clasp your hands behind your head, and get down on your knees. I have eight shots left in my magazine. Remember that."

He did as I said. He was a big, thickset lad, dressed in very faded jeans, a mended checked shirt, and an old brown jacket coming apart at one shoulder and with one pocket half torn off. Face pale, eyes lowered.

"Look at me."

He raised his eyelids and the look in his eyes was a shock. Not at all what I was expecting. Nothing cunning or malevolent there. On the contrary. Limpid golden-brown eyes, almost childlike in their innocence, and all of a piece with his rounded features, his good-natured nose, his wide full-lipped mouth. Nothing shifty about him either. I had told him to look at me. So he was looking at me. Frightened, ashamed, like a little boy expecting to be told off. I squatted down two yards from him, gun pointed in his direction. Without raising my voice, I said, "Are you alone?"

"Yes." It had come far too quickly.

"Listen carefully. I'll ask that again. Are you alone?"

"Yes." This time an almost imperceptible hesitation.

182

I suddenly switched subjects. "How many arrows did you have left?"

"Up there?"

"Yes."

He pondered. "A dozen," he said. But there was uncertainty in his voice. Then he added, "Perhaps a few less."

An odd kind of bowman, if he hadn't bothered to count his arrows! I said, "Let's say ten then."

"Yes, ten. Perhaps ten."

I looked at him, then in a quick, harsh voice I suddenly asked, "So if you had ten more arrows why did you surrender?"

He blushed, opened his mouth, but was unable to find his voice. There was panic in his eyes. He hadn't expected that question. It had caught him on the wrong foot. He just knelt there dumfounded, incapable of thinking up an answer, incapable even of speech.

In an even harsher voice I said, "Turn with your back to me and put your hands on the top of your head."

He lurched clumsily around on his knees.

"Sit back on your heels."

He obeyed.

"Now listen. I'm going to ask you a question. Just one. If you lie, I shall blow your brains out." I pressed the barrel of my gun against the back of his head. "Have you got that?"

"Yes," he said in a scarcely audible voice. I could feel his head quivering against the gun.

"Now listen carefully. I shan't ask you the same question twice. If you lie, I fire." I paused, then in the same quick, harsh voice, I said, "Who was with you behind the wall?"

In a voice I could only just hear, he said, "My father."

"Who else?"

"No one else."

I pushed the gun hard against his head. "Who else?"

He answered without hesitation, "No one else." This time he wasn't lying. I was sure of that.

"Does your father have another bow?"

"No. A gun."

183

I saw Thomas turn to look at us, mouth open in shock. I signaled to him to go back to keeping watch and said, "He has a gun?"

"Yes. A double-barreled shotgun."

"So your father had a gun and you had the bow?"

"No. I didn't have anything."

"Why not?"

"He doesn't let me touch the gun."

"And the bow?"

"Nor the bow neither."

"Why not?"

"He doesn't trust me."

A jolly family they sounded. A certain image of the troglodytes' home life began to take shape in my mind.

"And it was your father who told you to surrender?"

"Yes."

"And to say you were alone?"

"Yes."

Of course. And the battle over, relaxed and confident, we would have stood up, poor fools, set off to collect our Amarante, and walked straight into dear Papa's line of fire, while he waited for us cozily behind his wall with his double-barreled shotgun. One barrel each.

I tightened my lips and said harshly, "Unbuckle your belt."

He did as he was told and then, without waiting to be given the order, placed his hands back on his head. His docility made me feel a little sorry for him—despite his size and his broad shoulders, a kid. A kid terrorized by his father, and now by me. I told him to put his hands behind his back, then fastened them securely with the belt. It was only when I'd finished that I remembered the cord in my pocket. I used it to tie his feet, then removed his handkerchief from the tip of the bow and gagged him with it. I did it all decisively and swiftly, but at the same time I was standing outside myself and watching my own actions as though I was an actor in a film. I went over and knelt beside Thomas. "You heard all that?"

"Yes." He turned to look at me. He was looking pale. In a quiet voice, and with what in him amounted to emotion, he added, "And thanks."

184

"Thanks for what?"

"For making me get down just now."

I didn't answer. I was thinking things over. By now the father must know that his trap had been sprung, but a little thing like that wasn't going to stop him trying again. So we weren't out of the woods yet. We couldn't stay where we were and we couldn't just get up and go.

"Thomas," I whispered.

"Yes."

"You stay and watch the wall, the cliff, and the hill. I'm going to try and get behind him up the hill."

"You'll be in the open."

"Not at first. And as soon as you see anything from down here, even the barrel of his gun, shoot. And go on shooting. At least it will make him keep his head down."

I set off along the wall, crawling toward the hill. After a few yards the hand holding my gun began sweating, and my heart was thumping. But I was pleased with the way I'd spoiled the troglodyte's little trick. I felt confident and clearheaded.

The hillside to the south of the no man's land between the two walls jutted out in a kind of spur, terminating in a rounded buttress falling steeply to the little plain. I was counting on this spur to conceal me from the father until I was high enough to sight down on him. But what I hadn't counted on was the difficulty of the actual climb. The slope was very steep, the ground crumbly and covered with pebbles, and now that there was no vegetation left, every handhold and foothold was insecure. I was forced to sling my gun over my shoulder and use both hands. After ten minutes I was drenched in sweat, my legs were trembling, and I was so out of breath that I had to stop and rest.

I stood there for a moment, holding on with great difficulty, even using both hands, one foot lodged against a small outcrop of rock. A few yards above me I could see the top of the spur, or rather the place at which it merged with the line of the hill. Once I reached that point I would be visible to the man behind his wall below, and I wondered with dread in my heart how I was going to keep cool enough to pull my weapon over my shoulder and take

185

aim without losing my balance. I was clinging there, the sweat dripping over my eyes, my limbs shaking with the tremendous effort I had made, chest heaving in order to get back my breath, and so disheartened that I was on the verge of giving up my plan and climbing down again, when suddenly, I had no idea why, with the blood thundering in my temples, I thought of Germain. Or more precisely, I suddenly saw Germain in my mind's eye, shirtsleeves rolled up, sawing wood in the yard of Les Sept Fayards. He was a tall, heavy man, and because he suffered from emphysema, when he pushed himself too hard physically his breathing took on a very particular note—jerky, choking, and whistling all at the same time.

And as my own breathing quieted down and my temples stopped thudding, I suddenly became conscious of a fact that shook me to my boots. I was actually hearing Germain's breathing. It wasn't my own, as I had at first thought before it calmed down. I could hear it quite distinctly, and it was coming from the other slope of the spur, from a point separated from the spot where I was standing by no more than the thickness of a few feet of scree. The father, on the far side of the spur, was climbing a path that would converge with mine at the top.

Sweat sprang from every pore in my body, and I thought my heart was going to stop. If the father reached the top before me, then he would see me first. I was done for. Whatever happened I was caught; there was certainly no time to get down again. I realized in a flash that my life depended on the next two or three seconds, and that my only chance was to rush headlong forward and attack at once. I began climbing again, with the savage energy of the mad, no longer even noticing the fragments of rock I sent skittering down behind me, certain that the man on the other side, deafened by the noise of his own breathing, would never hear me.

I reached the top. I was in despair, almost certain that I was going to find myself looking into the barrel of his gun, so close did the forge-bellows rasp of his breathing sound. I was up there. Nothing to be seen. It was as though a ton weight had been lifted off my chest. And then, coming right on top of my sudden relief, I had another utterly incredible piece of luck. Only a yard away I saw a fairly large and solid tree stump that enabled me to jam my left knee firmly on the ground in front of it and guarantee my balance on the slope, my right leg stretched straight behind me with my foot against a stone. I pulled the sling of the gun up over my head, thumbed off the safety catch, and held the rifle in front of me, butt under my arm, ready to shoulder it and fire. I listened as the raucous, choking sound drew nearer. I kept my eyes fixed on the precise spot, scarcely ten yards away, where the man's head was going to appear, resisting a sudden temptation to glance back down to the little plain below and Thomas behind his wall. I concentrated my whole being on remaining still, relaxing, and keeping my breathing smooth.

The wait, which I think must have lasted several seconds at the most, seemed interminable. My left knee jammed against the stump was going numb, and I could feel all my muscles, even those in my face, gradually and painfully tensing as though I was slowly turning into stone.

The head appeared, then the shoulders, then the chest. Entirely absorbed by sheer physical effort, or else because he was searching for footholds, the man kept his face lowered and did not see me. I brought the rifle up to my shoulder, nestled the butt firmly into the hollow below my collarbone, lowered my cheek against it, and held my breath. At that moment something happened that I had not intended. I found myself looking along my sights straight at the father's heart. At that distance I couldn't miss. But my finger remained inert around the trigger. I couldn't bring myself to fire.

The father raised his head, our eyes met. Immediately, and with incredible swiftness, he brought his gun up to his shoulder. There was a series of cracks and I actually saw the bullets go through his shirt and tear it. A gush of blood, unbelievably copious and powerful it seemed to me, spurted from the wound, the eyes rolled upward, the mouth gaped in a frantic effort to suck in air, then the whole body swayed backward and fell. I heard him tumbling back down the slope he had just climbed amid a

187

great rattle of stones dislodged by his fall, echoing and re-echoing up the gorge beyond.

As I climbed back down I saw that Thomas had climbed our little wall, crossed diagonally through the little meadow, his gun under his arm, and was about to inspect the corpse. Once down on the flat, I went over to untie the son. When he saw me, his eyes widened with stupefaction and fear. His belief in his father's invincibility had been so deeply anchored in his mind that he just couldn't believe I had come back alive. Nor was he able to believe me when I told him that his father was dead. "All right then," I said, gently pushing him in front of me with the barrel of my gun. "Come and take a look."

As we made our way toward the body we met Thomas on his way back from his inspection. He had removed the father's cartridge pouch and shotgun, which he was carrying slung over his left shoulder, the right one being already occupied by his own. In the heart, he said, looking pale. Several bullets in a tight group. As he spoke I removed the magazine from my rifle. It was empty. So I'd fired five shots. But Thomas shook his head when I said I thought I'd seen them pierce the skin. At the speed with which they left the barrel my eyes couldn't conceivably have followed them. What I had seen were the successive tears in the shirt after the bullets had perforated it, one by one.

"You can rest easy," he said. "He died instantly." Then he added, "I'll leave you here. I must go and pick up the arrows. Don't forget I'm the storekeeper around here." And after making a rather unsuccessful attempt at a smile, he walked off.

He was pretty shaken, and I was too when I saw the body. What a hash the chest was! And that white face, drained of blood, I shall never forget it. Try as I might, I could find not the slightest common denominator between the insignificant pressure of my finger on the trigger and the destruction it had unleashed. I told myself that the swine who had pressed the button to unleash the atomic war must have been feeling the same sort of thing, at least if he had survived in his concrete bunker.

The troglodyte must have been about fifty. Tremendously strong. A big heavy man with reddish blond hair, dressed in a filthy pair of brown corduroy pants and a tattered jacket of the same color. I looked down at that great body, so full of strength and so empty of life. I looked across at the son too. He was clearly not feeling the slightest trace of grief. He looked just stupefied and relieved. Suddenly he turned toward me, gazed at me with frightened respect, then grabbed my right hand and bent down to kiss it. I pushed him away. I didn't want any part in that kind of transference. However, when I saw the fear and bewilderment that appeared in his eyes, I asked his name. His name was Jacquet (the diminutive of Jacques).

"Jacquet," I said in a flat voice, "go and help Thomas collect up the arrows."

It was high time he went away. I thought I was going to faint. My legs were cotton, my eyes swimming. I sat down at the bottom of the slope, three yards away from the troglodyte, then when the dizziness still didn't go away I lay down full length on the rising ground and closed my eyes. I felt very bad. Then suddenly the sweat came. I experienced an incredibly strong and delicious sensation of coolness. I was reborn. Still as weak as ever, but it was the weakness of something just born, not the weakness of death.

After a moment I sat up again and looked at the troglodyte. Uncle Samuel had compared him to Cro-Magnon man. There was some truth in it. Underhung jaw, low forehead, jutting eyebrows. But after all, think of him washed, shaved, manicured, hair cut short, his well-muscled body tightly belted into a new uniform, and he wouldn't have looked any more primitive than many a good commando officer. Or any more stupid. Or any less skilled in that compendium of elementary animal ruses that used to be termed the Art of War: the booby trap, the ambush, the pseudo capitulation, holding an adversary in the center in order to outflank him on the right.

I stood up and walked over to join the others. They hadn't noticed my nausea. They just assumed I'd been getting my breath back. Thomas held out the bow, and I examined it. It was a good six feet high and looked to me much more elaborate in its construction than the one I had once given Birgitta as a present.

Thomas had finished his collection. He was making all the arrows into a little bundle and tying it with the nylon cord.

"Over there," Jacquet said, eyes on the ground, apparently too ashamed to allude to Amarante more directly.

We climbed up the narrow meadow with its tufts of yellowish grass dotted here and there, and ugly though they were, it was still a pleasure to see them. I looked at Jacquet, at his big head with its red-blond mane and his good-natured features. I caught his childlike eyes staring at me. As I said, they were golden brown, but the odd thing about them was that the irises were so big, leaving almost no room at all, as it were, for any white, so with his eyebrows raised, as they were at that moment, he had the humble, sad, pleading look of a dog. A dog that's done something wrong and longs for you to forgive it and talk to it. He was positively brimming with willingness to please, with submission, with affection, if only he could be allowed to show it. He was also brimming with physical strength, a strength that he himself seemed barely conscious of as it radiated from his bull neck, his broad shoulders, and his long, slightly simian arms, knotted with muscles and held with a perpetual slight bend at the elbows. His big hands were the same, always half clenched around an invisible handle, never quite managing to open flat. He walked between Thomas and myself with a slightly rolling, musclebound gait, looking at one, then at the other, but especially at me, because I was more or less the same age as his father.

I indicated the bow in my right hand and asked him in French (since I already knew he couldn't speak our patois), "How come your father could use this so well?"

He was so delighted that I'd spoken to him and so anxious to give me the information I wanted that he stammered slightly when he answered. He spoke a rather flat kind of French in which I could detect none of the underlying rhythm and color of our patois. And his accent was neither quite the local one nor quite that of the north. It was presumably the conflicting influences of his

190

father and his primary school that had produced this odd mixture. In short, as they used to say around here, a "foreigner."

"He learned how up north," he said, running all his words together. "In an archery club. He was the champion." Then he added, "And the arrows, he made the heads himself—for hunting with."

I looked at him in astonishment. "For hunting with! He hunted with this? Why not with a gun?"

"Oh, a gun makes a noise, doesn't it?" Jacquet answered with a smile that was on the verge of being conspiratorial. He obviously knew that I was no hunter myself, and that my woods had always been open to all comers.

I said nothing. I thought I was beginning to get some idea of what the troglodyte family's existence had been like: the blows and the wounds, fireside rape, poaching, and in general, let's say a certain indifference to the law. As for the bow and arrow itself, that certainly struck me as a shrewd idea. Much safer than a snare, because a snare you have to leave around to do its job, and a gamekeeper can find it; whereas an arrow does the job in a second, and above all, it kills almost silently, without scaring the game and without warning the neighbors. Those poor neighbors, they can't have found much left in their woods to hunt themselves, the day the season opened.

Jacquet had obviously assumed that my silence was one of disapproval, because now, with a humility clearly intended to disarm the gentleman from Malevil, the rich landowner who had never known hunger, he added, "If it hadn't been for that, we wouldn't have had meat to eat every day."

And Jacquet had had meat to eat every day, that was for sure. One glance told you that. He hadn't done so badly out of his father's hunting forays. But all the same, I found it pretty hard to swallow: a rabbit on the run nailed to the ground by an arrow?

Jacquet was indignant at my doubts. "My father could shoot down a pheasant in full flight!" he exclaimed proudly.

191

Ah, I thought, so that's where Uncle Samuel's pheasants used to disappear to. Every year he used to free two or three brace in his woods, and he never found them again, or any of their offspring.

Carried away by his enthusiasm, Jacquet then added, "Normally, you see, the first arrow he let go at you ought to have killed you on the spot."

I frowned. And Thomas said curtly, "That's not something to boast about."

I felt that it was time our conversation took a less relaxed turn anyway. I said sternly, "Jacquet, was it you who knocked out our friend and stole Amarante?"

He blushed, hung his great head, and lurched unhappily from side to side as he walked. "It was my father who told me to." Then he went on very quickly, "But he told me to kill your friend and I didn't do it."

"Why not?"

"Because it's a sin."

An unexpected answer, but I kept it in mind. I went on questioning Jacquet. He confirmed what I had already suspected. The father's plan had been to trick us into following him by ones and twos, then kill us in order to make himself master of Malevil. It was terrifying to think of. After Zero Day he could have had the whole of France, but what he wanted was Malevil—even at the price of five murders. Because he wouldn't have killed the "servants," his son informed me. Nor my German woman.

"What German woman?"

"The one who used to ride around in the woods."

I looked at him. Defective information service, but a secondary motive not to be underestimated. The castle and the lady. Savage peasant uprising followed by putting to death of my lord and subsequent rape of my lady. The lord or lords. Because it appeared that Thomas, Colin, Peyssou, Meyssonnier, and myself were known collectively by the father as "the gentlemen of Malevil," and that he often spoke of us, none of whom had ever set eyes on him, with rage and hatred. And he had set his son to spy on us.

I stopped, turned to face Jacquet, and looked him in the eyes. "Didn't you ever think to yourself that you could warn us and stop all those murders happening?"

He stood there in front of me, eyes lowered, hands behind his back, overcome with repentance. I wondered if he might not actually go and hang himself if I suggested the idea. "Oh, yes," he said, "but my father would have known, and he'd have killed me."

Naturally, because of course the father had been not only invincible but omniscient as well. I looked at the son: complicity in premeditated murder, a violent assault on one of our friends, theft of a horse.

"Well, Jacquet, what are we to do with you?"

His lips trembled, he swallowed his saliva, looked at me with those innocent, fearful eyes, and said, already resigned, "I don't know. Kill me perhaps."

"That's all you deserve," Thomas said, jaw clenched in anger. I looked at him. He must have been very afraid for me as I clambered up that hill. And now he felt I was being too indulgent.

"No," I said, "We shan't kill you. First, because killing people is a sin, as you said. But what we are going to do is take you back with us to Malevil and deprive you of your liberty for a certain time."

I avoided looking at Thomas. It went through my mind, not without a slight accompanying tremor of amusement, how disgusted he must be to hear me employing so "clerical" a notion as that of sin. Though in fact I had no choice really. How was I to talk to Jacquet at all if it wasn't in the language he understood?

"Alone?" Jacquet said

"What do you mean, 'alone'?"

"Are you taking only me back to Malevil?" Then, when I just raised my eyebrows and kept looking at him, he added, "Because there is also Granny." I had the impression that he was about to add another name, or names, but he stopped.

"If your grandmother wants to come, then we'll take her too."

But there was something else worrying him. I could see that. And I didn't think it was the idea of being shut up, because his face, which was incapable of hiding anything, had become gloomy, much gloomier in fact than

193

during the moments when he was afraid we were going to kill him. I started walking again and was about to start pressing him with questions when the silence of the desolate and devastated gorge through which we were passing was abruptly rent by the loud sound of a horse neighing only a little way ahead.

And it wasn't just any neigh. It hadn't come from Amarante. It was the triumphant neigh, at once imperious and tender, of a stallion preparing to mount a mare, curvetting around her to excite her, to get the fire going, as Uncle Samuel used to say.

"You have a horse then?"

"Yes," Jacquet said.

"And he hasn't been cut!"

"No. My father would never have that."

I looked at Thomas. I couldn't believe my ears. I was ready to burst with joy! Three cheers, this once at least for the troglodyte father. I broke into a run like an eager child. Finding that the bow hampered my movements, I held it out to Jacquet, who took it without any show of surprise as he ran along beside me, his wide mouth hanging open. Thomas, needless to say, left us behind after only a few strides and continued to increase his lead all the time, especially since I was soon out of breath and had to slow down.

But the goal was in sight. A row of great chestnut posts, blackened but still standing, about ten feet high with two strands of barbed wire running along them, enclosed a paddock of about a quarter of an acre in front of the troglodyte dwelling that was three quarters cave and one quarter house. In the middle of the paddock, tied to the skeleton of a tree, quivering but not restive, stood my Amarante, sudden shivers running along her chestnut flanks, tossing back her blond mane with a series of impatient and coquettish jerks. Who would ever have believed that such a sacrilege—admittedly not yet accomplished—would fill me with such joy! A great thick-bodied carthorse mounting an Anglo-Arab mare!

Not that he was ugly, her proletarian mate. Dark gray, almost black, enormous hindquarters, thickset legs, powerful shoulders, and a neck that I couldn't have encircled with both arms. In build, in fact, he was not unlike his human masters. He continued to circle around Amarante, curvetting and flourishing with monumental agility, all the time giving raucous neighs, eyes sparkling with fire. I hoped he was aware of the incredible honor that had befallen him, and that he could tell the difference between a great lump of a carthorse mare and the graceful Amarante, whom the necessities of equine survival were now obliging to suffer his assault in the very flower of her youth, her third year scarcely over, and behind her a long lineage of distinguished ancestors.

Certainly his courtship, though ardent, was without brutality, as he nibbled at her lips, head glued to hers, then turned so that they were head to rump, licking beneath her tail, appearing suddenly on her other side, then laying his vast head on her neck, withdrawing it, returning to her hindquarters, gradually enmeshing the mare in his ponderous dance of seduction, infecting her with his own maddened excitement, imposing upon her, without rushing or treating her roughly, his authority, his strength, and his smell.

How did he know the exact moment when Amarente was ready to accept him, without kicking or shying away? He rose up, a gigantic figure on his back legs, kicking at the air with his front hoofs to maintain his balance, his long black mane waving. And moving toward her in that posture, reared in the air, clumsy and yet terrible, he let himself fall upon Amarante's back.

She gave a moan, and her legs gave slightly at the impact of that ton of muscle. But she took the shock nevertheless, tail lifted compliantly, and he was able to grip her flanks with his great thick legs. Seeing that the stallion was in difficulty, Jacquet slipped quickly forward, took the enormous member firmly in one hand with the greatest simplicity, and slid it home. Amarante arched herself on her tensed and quivering front legs in order to keep her feet against the violent thrusts of her partner's great body.

At that moment the stallion was in profile from where I stood, and I have never seen the idea of physical power better expressed than by that superb head stretched forward over the mare's back, the black mane shaken by his efforts, the nostrils dilated, the proud eyes sparkling and darting fire as they gazed blindly before them. I noticed that he did not bite Amarante's neck in order to maintain his position, and that he remained gentle with her at the moment of his triumph.

When the coupling was finished, he remained motionless, his hind legs trembling slightly. His head sagged until his lips were touching Amarante's mane. He remained in that position for a full minute with an expression of exhaustion on his face, his mouth sunken as it were, the fire draining from his eyes, leaving a sadness there. At last he withdrew clumsily from the mare, and as his forelegs fell back onto the earth a little of the semen of which he had just relieved himself fell to the ground. Then he shook himself, and raising his head suddenly, himself again, he set off around the paddock at a powerful gallop that brought him back toward us at top speed, as though he was about to crush us into the ground. Scarcely a yard away, he wheeled suddenly to avoid us, glancing at us sideways with a joyful braggadocio eye, almost as though to tease us, as he sped off to the far end of the paddock without slowing his pace.

Long after leaving that place I was to hear the rhythm of those four heavy hoofs in my head as they shook the earth. In that dead mute landscape, that muffled and thunderous beat seemed to me as exalting as the renewal of life itself.

There wasn't just one troglodyte building, in fact, but two, side by side, the first for living in and the second, I supposed, for housing animals and storing hay and fodder. They were skillfully constructed, with a brick wall built out about a yard or so in front of the cave entrance, topped by a sloping roof with a chimney in it. In the case of the second cave, the bricks had been left bare, but the wall of the house had been rendered with some care. On the ground floor a glazed door and a window had been let into the wall, and another two windows on the floor above. The windows still had all their panes intact and were flanked by full shutters still bearing traces of claret paint. The whole thing, though obviously done cheaply, was by no means squalid.

Above the sloping jut of roof the cliff went up for another fifty feet. And its upper part, swelling out in a boss, overhung the house, protecting it from the rain and even giving it a kind of cozy air. But at the same time the overhang was rather frightening. You expected little cracks to appear in it at any moment, then to see it split right off and crash down in front of the dwelling. Though it had probably maintained that perilous-looking state of equilibrium for thousands of years. And Wahrwoorde, when he first came to live there, must have decided that it was going to last at least for another brief human life-span.

The general situation and arrangement was identical to that of our Maternity Ward (except that I had never built out around the edge of our cave), and it was to this that the troglodytes clearly owed their lives on the day it happened.

I could see no other buildings, except something that looked like a bakehouse inside the paddock.

I became aware of a presence and of eyes upon me. Standing in the doorway of the dwelling, a voluminous old woman, dressed in a rather dirty black smock, was inspecting us with a look of superstitious amazement. I wondered if this was my adversary's mother, so I walked forward and said with embarrassment, "You must have guessed what has happened, and that I haven't just come to pass the time of day."

She bowed her head without answering immediately and also, I noticed, without any appearance of grief. She was rather short, with a puffy face, cheeks sagging into jowls, a neck so large and so flabby that it was just a continuation of her chin, leading down to the curve of her enormous breasts, which swung about at her slightest movement like two sacks of oats on the back of a donkey. In the midst of all the fat there sparkled two rather beautiful dark eyes, and above her somewhat low forehead an irrepressible mane of thick hair sprang up in all directions, crinkly, dense, and the whitest white you ever saw.

"It must have all happened the way I'm thinking, since here you are, aren't you?" she said serenely.

Not the slightest trace of emotion, and also, oddly it seemed, a local accent, even down to the turn of phrase.

"Believe me I regret what has happened," I said, "but I had no choice. It was your son or me."

Her reply to this was unexpected to say the least. "Come on in, come on in," she said, standing aside.

"You must at least come in and have something with us." And she added in patois, with a sigh and a shrug, "Thanks be to heaven, he was no son of mine."

I looked at her. "So you can speak patois?"

"I should hope so. I was born here," she said, again in patois. She drew herself up, throwing out her chest in a haughty gesture that caused the oat sacks to sway with ponderous emphasis, seeming to say, I'm not one of your savages, you know. "I was born in La Roque," she went on. "Do you know Falvine in La Roque?"

"The cobbler who tamed the crow?"

"He's my brother," La Falvine said with an air of tremendous respectability. "Come in, come in, son," she went on. "Make yourself at home."

But I wasn't going to give my trust absolutely even to a Falvine, the sister of a respectable cobbler of La Roque. I unslung my rifle, slipped a magazine into it, then closed the breech and worked the first cartridge up into the barrel. That done, instead of walking straight in, I pushed La Falvine ahead of me into the house with a gesture of feigned politeness. I had the feeling, as my hand touched her back, that it was sinking into warm lard.

Nothing suspicious. Cement floor, mended in patches, back and side walls formed by the whitish gray rock of the cave. They had been left as they were, with no attempt to soften or remove their roughness or irregularities. No trace of damp. Overhead, the joists and floorboards of the upper story, and that little door in the corner of the brick projection probably led to the stairs up to it. In the front wall, one window, the glazed door, and the fireplace. Inside, the bricks hadn't been rendered, and the drips of mortar binding were still visible. Slow fire in the hearth. Under the window, shelves for the family's boots. A big

Louis XV rustic style armoire, which I opened with a murmured "Do you mind?" for form's sake. Linen on the right, crockery on the left. In the center of the room a big "farmhouse table," as Parisians used to call it, though they insisted on picturesque benches beside it, whereas we humble country folk preferred the comfort of chairs. I counted seven straw-bottomed chairs, but only four around the table. The others stood against the walls. I didn't know whether it was significant, but I noted it all the same.

I walked over to the far end of the table. It was there, I imagined, that the father had always sat, so I took his chair, gun between my legs, back to the wall of the cave. From that position I could command a view of both doors. I signaled to Thomas to take the chair on my right, so that his body wouldn't come between me and either of the two doors. Jacquet, without being told, sat down humbly at the bottom end of the table, his back to the light.

When I pulled out the little packet of ham that La Menou had handed to me as we set out, La Falvine protested at this offense against her hospitality and began buzzing around me. I couldn't sit there and eat off the table when she had plates! I must have an egg with her, she would fry it now, to go with my ham! And a little wine, that I must have with her too! I accepted all her offers except the wine, which I suspected would be pretty poor stuff, and instead asked for milk, which she poured out for me in copious quantities into a big bowl decorated with flowers, accompanying her largesse with a flood of words. Only the day before it happened, they sold the calf, that's how it was, and now there was so much milk, what could they do with it, almost drowning in it they were, and even when she'd made her butter, still some left over for the pig.

But my eyes nearly jumped out of my head when I saw her come to the table and set down a huge loaf and a block of butter.

"Bread! You have bread!"

"Oh, bread, yes," La Falvine said. "That we've always made ourselves here at L'Étang. Because Wahrwoorde, you know, he always had to be different. Every year he would always sow enough wheat so we had enough for a whole year, and longer even. It didn't matter that we had to make our own flour in the horse mill, not to him, and we've no electricity here. And the butter, just the same, in the hand churn. He wouldn't buy anything, that Wahrwoorde."

As I jammed the loaf unright in the drawer at the end of the table, then cut us off a slice each, as the father must have done while he was alive, I meditated on all this information. Clearly Wahrwoorde, with something of the wild animal in his nature, was determined to live tucked away from the world, self-sufficiently, in an autarchy with himself at its head. Even extra-marital love, apparently, was not allowed to go outside the family.

However, when I alluded to the Catie affair, La Falvine hedged slightly. "As to it happening," she said with modestly lowered eyes, "there's not much doubt about it. But to start with, poor Catie she brought it on herself in a way, the way she carried on. And then, you know, she wasn't his daughter after all. Any more than Miette. They were my daughter Raymonde's daughters not his."

At the name Miette, it seemed to me that Jacquet, at the far end of the table, lifted his head and glanced at La Falvine apprehensively. But it was no more than a glance, and it was all over so quickly that I was almost prepared to doubt whether I had really seen anything.

I was scarcely touching my bread. I wanted to wait till the promised egg arrived. But all the same, the taste of that slice of homemade bread, thickly buttered (and they salted their butter at L'Étang, unlike the very few other farms that still used to make their own around here), seemed delicious, and also a little sad, so strongly did it conjure up our life before.

"And who bakes your bread here?" I asked, to express my gratitude.

"Until only a little while ago," La Falvine said with a sigh, "it was Louis. But since he died it's Jacquet."

She talked on and on, La Falvine, all the while bustling around and around the room, breathless and constantly sighing, taking ten times as many steps as she needed, pouring out ten superfluous words for every one that was really required. To fry three eggs, because ostensibly she was not going to eat one herself (I assumed that she must sneak one for herself occasionally when all the others were out, and a "drop of wine" to go with it), it took her a good half hour, during which time, although I remained unfed, since I was waiting for the egg before eating my ham, I was at least crammed with information.

La Falvine—and it was the only thing in which she resembled La Menou—was an old woman with a considerable family tree. And she found it necessary to explore it back as far as her great-grandparents, simply in order to explain to me that her own daughter, Raymonde, had had two daughters by her first husband, Catie and Miette, and after losing that husband she had remarried Wahrwoorde, who happened to be a widower himself at the time, and with two sons, Louis and Jacquet.

"And what I thought about her marriage, well I don't need to tell you, especially because my poor Gaston was dead too, so I had to come here with her, to live among savages, you might say. No electricity, no water in the sink, and not even so much as a cylinder of butane gas, because Wahrwoorde, naturally, he wouldn't hear of such a thing, so there we were cooking on the fire as you see, like the olden days. Ah, the bread you eat in another's house," she went on in patois, eyes raised to heaven, "it is bitter to the tongue. Even though I've never eaten more of his food than I had to all the years I've been in that Wahrwoorde's house!"

A statement that immediately confirmed my previous suspicions about her secret and solitary feasts, her only compensation for the tyranny of her son-in-law. Needless to say, her daughter Raymonde, like poor Gaston before her, soon died too, partly from the harsh treatment, you can imagine, partly from a bad digestion in her belly, and her absence made the stranger's bread even more bitter in the mouth.

All this saw me through to the end of my ham, my egg, and my milk, without La Falvine having at any point sat down at the table with us or eaten the least morsel of food, intent as she was on bustling quite needlessly here and there, like a hen that's lost its chicks, determined to keep up the fiction of her abstinence even after Wahrwoorde's death. Talkative as she was, however, she had not told me everything. In our part of the world, and I imagine elsewhere too, there are two methods of concealing something: keeping quiet or talking nonstop.

"Jacquet," I said as I wiped my uncle's knife on the soft center of my last piece of bread, "it's time you found yourself a shovel and a pick and went out to bury your father. Thomas will keep an eye on you."

Then as I clicked the blade of the knife back into the handle and slipped it into my pocket I added, "I noticed his shoes were not too worn. You'd better salvage those. You'll need them later."

Jacquet stood up, slightly hunched, head hanging to signify his obedience. I stood up too, gun in hand, went over to Thomas, and quietly told him, "Give me the father's gun. Just keep your own and keep our little lad ahead of you on the way there, and while he's digging keep well away, without taking your eyes off him." As I spoke, I noticed that Jacquet, taking advantage of my aside to Thomas, had gone over to La Falvine and whispered something in her ear too.

"Well, Jacquet!" I said in a stern, authoritative voice.

He started, blushed, then without a word, arms swinging from his great shoulders, walked outside with Thomas at his heels. As soon as they had left, I looked across at La Falvine with my gravest expression. "Jacquet has attacked one of us and stolen one of our horses. No, don't bother to defend him, Falvine. I know he was just doing what he was told. But the fact remains, that sort of thing merits some sort of punishment. We are going to confiscate all his belongings and take him back with us to Malevil as a prisoner."

"But what about me then?" La Falvine cried in panic.

"I leave the choice to you. You can come to Malevil and live with us, or you can stay here. If you stay, I'll see to it that we leave you enough to live on."

"Stay here?" she cried, reduced to a state of terror. "But what would I do here if I stayed?"

Then came a flood of words that I listened to very carefully, and which intrigued me, because the one word missing was the one I would most have expected to hear, the word "alone."

Because it was remaining alone at L'Étang that ought to have been frightening her. And yet she hadn't said that, this blabber-mouth who was apparently so willing to tell all. I lifted my nose and sniffed the air like a hound searching for a scent. Without success. And yet she was hiding something from me, this fat old crone, I was sure. I had known it from the start. Something or someone. I stopped listening to her. And since my nose had told me nothing I began using my eyes. I looked around the room, inspecting every detail. Then opposite me, on the bare brick wall at the front of the cave, about eighteen inches above the floor, I noticed the shelf on which the family's boots stood in a row. I cut La Falvine off in mid sentence and said curtly, "Your daughter Raymonde is dead. Louis too. Jacquet is out burying Wahrwoorde. Catie is in service in La Roque. Right?"

"Yes, yes," La Falvine said, apprehensive but puzzled.

I looked her in the eyes, and making my voice crack like a whip, I said, "And Miette?"

La Falvine opened her mouth like a fish. I didn't give her time to recover. "Yes. Miette. Where is Miette?"

Her eyelids fluttered and she answered in a faint voice, "She was in service in La Roque too. And heaven knows what—"

I cut in: "In service with whom?"

"With the mayor."

"The same as Catie then? The mayor of La Roque had two maids, you mean?"

"No, wait, it wasn't the mayor. She was at the inn."

I didn't pursue the matter. I lowered my eyes and looked at her calves. They were enormous. "Do you have trouble with your legs?"

"Do I have trouble with my legs!" she cried, short of breath now, but reassured, delighted at this diversion. "It's my circulation. And you can see what they're like"—she pulled up her skirts to display them—"varicose veins as well."

"When it's wet, do you wear boots?"

"Oh, never! I couldn't get into boots! You can imagine! Especially since I had my clots."

On the subject of her legs, La Falvine was clearly inexhaustible. This time I didn't even make a pretense of listening. I got up, rifle in hand, turned my back on her, and walked over to the shelf of boots. There were three pairs of men's boots, and large ones at that, made of yellow rubber; then beside them, a much smaller pair, black, with higher heels, clearly a woman's. I switched the rifle to my left hand, picked up the pair of small boots in my right, turned around, and from where I stood, without moving forward, without a word, I lifted them above my head and hurled them straight at La Falvine's feet.

La Falvine took a step backward, looking down at the two black boots on the cement floor as though they were snakes about to bite her. She raised her two fat little hands to her face and squashed them into her cheeks. She was crimson. She didn't dare look at me.

"Go and get her, Falvine."

A short silence. She raised her eyes and looked at me. Her fear subsided. Her expression changed. Her dark eyes peered out from the puffy flesh of her face, glinting with sly effrontery. "Wouldn't you rather go yourself?" she asked suggestively.

And when I didn't answer, her jowls wobbled upward on each side of her mouth, and her teeth, tiny and pointed, were bared in a greedy, sensual smile. I began to wonder if I liked La Falvine very much after all. Oh, I realized that it was quite natural from her point of view. I had conquered and killed the tyrant. So now I was in the tyrant's place myself, surrounded by an almost religious aura, and everything was my property. Including Miette. But what she was insinuating was exactly what I was struggling to renounce. Not out of virtue, but because my reason told me it was necessary, I was determined to renounce all such feudal rights.

"I told you to go and get her."

Her smile faded, she lowered her head and scuttled out, quivering like a jelly. Shoulders, buttocks, thighs, enormous calves, everything shook as she moved.

I returned to my chair at the end of the table facing the door. My hands, as I laid them flat on the oak table-top blackened by scrubbing, were visibly shaking, and I made a desperate effort to control myself. I knew that what was about to appear before me in a moment or so was going to be at the same time a tremendous joy and a tremendous danger. I knew perfectly well that this Miette, who was going to be living alone in a community of six men, not counting Momo, was going to face us with a terrifying problem, and that I myself must take care not to make one false move, one mistake, if I wanted life to continue being possible at Malevil.

"This is Miette," Falvine said, pushing her grand-daughter in front of her into the room.

A hundred eyes would not have been enough to devour her with. Twenty years old perhaps. And how misleading that name Miette was! A crumb, never! The whole loaf! She had her grandmother's dark eyes and luxuriant hair, though in her case it was raven black. A good four inches taller though, with wide, squarely cut shoulders, breasts high and rounded like bossed shields, high buttocks, well-muscled legs. It was possible, I suppose, if I could have found it in my heart to criticize her at all, that I might have found her nose a little too big, her mouth a shade too wide, her chin too fleshy. But such carping was out of the question. I admired everything about her, totally, even her peasant awkwardness.

I couldn't see them, but I knew from the sensations they were transmitting to me that my hands were trembling worse than ever. I hid them under the table. Then, leaning forward, chest and shoulders pressed hard against its edge, cheek against the barrel of my gun, I devoured Miette with my eyes, unable to speak. I understood what Adam had felt when he woke up one fine morning to find an Eve beside him, still damp from the lathe on which she had been created. It would be impossible to be more petrified with wonder or more overwhelmed with mindless tenderness than I was then. In that cave, in whose womb I was crouching with my weapons, fighting for my very survival, Miette radiated light and warmth. Her patched blouse dazzled me, her faded red skirt, worn and moth-eaten in places, hung in folds well above her knees. She had the rather heavy legs of Maillol's female nudes, and her generous bare feet were spread solidly on the earth from which she seemed to draw her strength. She was a magnificent human animal, this future mother of mankind.

I tore myself out of my rapt contemplation, pulled myself upright in my chair, grasped the edge of the table with both hands, thumbs on top, fingers underneath, and I said, "Sit down, Miette."

My voice seemed to me very faint and husky. I made a note to ensure that it sounded stronger next time I spoke. Miette, without a word, sat down in the chair previously occupied by Jacquet, separated from me by the whole length of the table. Her eyes were both lovely and gentle. And she looked into mine without the slightest embarrassment, with that serious look you see on children's faces when they are inspecting a newcomer to their home.

"Miette"—I like that name Miette—"we are going to take Jacquet away with us."

A flicker of anxiety shadowed her dark eyes, and I added straightaway, "You mustn't worry. We shan't do him any harm. And if your grandmother and you don't want to stay on here alone at L'Étang, then you can come with us too and live in Malevil."

"Well, what an idea, staying here alone at L'Étang! That we won't," La Falvine said. "And I for one am very grateful to you, my boy—"

"My name is Emmanuel."

"Yes, well thank you then, Emmanuel."

I turned back to Miette. "And you, Miette? Do you want to come?"

She nodded without speaking. Not a chatterbox, but her eyes spoke for her. They never left my face. She was weighing up this new master who'd appeared. Ah, Miette, have no fear, you will meet with nothing at Malevil but friendship and affection.

"How did you come to be named Miette?"

"Her name is Marie really, you know," La Falvine said, "but when she was born she was so tiny, born before her time, poor thing, at seven months. And Raymonde always called her 'Mauviette' because she was such a little slip of a thing. But our Catie, she was only three then, it always came out with her as 'Miette,' and that's what it's always been ever since."

Miette said nothing, but perhaps because I'd shown an interest in her name she smiled at me. Her features were perhaps a little coarse, at least according to the standards of urban beauty, but when she smiled they were lit up and softened in the most unimaginable way. It was a delicious smile, so brimming with honesty and trust.

The door opened and Jacquet came in, followed by Thomas. At the sight of Miette, Jacquet stopped, went pale, stared at her, then wheeled around toward La Falvine as though about to hurl himself upon her and shouted angrily, "Didn't I tell you——"

"Now then, take it easy!" Thomas warned him. He was still taking his role as prisoner's escort very seriously.

Then as he walked farther into the room to control his prisoner he saw Miette, concealed from him till then by Jacquet, and he stopped as though turned to stone. The hand he had raised to lay on Jacquet's shoulder fell to his side again.

I intervened, without raising my voice. "Jacquet, it wasn't your grandmother who told me that Miette was hiding outside. I guessed without her telling me."

Jacquet stared at me open-mouthed. It didn't occur to him for an instant to doubt what I had said. He believed me instantly. More than that, he was deeply repentant at having tried to hide something from me. I had usurped the father's powers as well as his place. I was now infallible and omniscient.

"You weren't thinking you were cleverer than the Malevil gentlemen, I hope!" La Falvine said derisively.

So now I had become a "the gentlemen." Always the wrong note. I looked at her. I was beginning to suspect a certain baseness in La Falvine's character. But I didn't want to judge her too soon. Who wouldn't have been corrupted by years of slavery to the troglodyte?

"Jacquet, just before you left to bury your father, what did you whisper to your grandmother?"

Hands behind his back, head hanging almost onto his chest, eyes on the floor, he said with deep shame, "I asked her where Miette was. She said in the hayloft. So I told her not to tell the gentlemen."

I eyed him. "So you meant to escape from Malevil then? So that you could come back for her and run away together."

He was scarlet. "Yes," he whispered.

"And where would you have gone? How would you have fed her?"

"I don't know."

"And your grandmother? Would she have stayed at Malevil?"

La Falvine, who had risen to her feet when the two men came in (a reflex acquired during her years with Wahrwoorde?), was still standing beside Miette, though now, obviously beginning to feel tired, she leaned forward and supported herself with her hands on the table.

"I hadn't thought about her," Jacquet said in confusion.

"Ah, I can well believe it!" La Falvine said, and a big tear brimmed out of one eye.

I was fairly certain that she was an easy weeper, but all the same, Jacquet was certainly her favorite. She had the right to be a little upset.

Miette laid her hand on Falvine's, raised her face toward her, and gazed at her with a shake of the head that clearly said, But I'd never have abandoned you, don't worry. I would have liked to hear Miette's voice, but on the other hand I could understand why she didn't bother to speak. Her eyes said everything. Perhaps it was during Wahrwoorde's reign, during the long evenings of silence he must have imposed on them, that she had acquired her talents as a mime.

I went on: "Jacquet, had you asked Miette whether she agreed to your plan?"

Miette shook her head violently, and Jacquet looked at her, completely deflated. "No," he said in a voice I could hardly hear.

A silence.

"Miette is coming to Malevil with us," I said. "Of her own free will. Your grandmother too. And from this moment, as I speak to you now, Jacquet, no one has the

208

right to say, 'Miette is mine.' Not you. Not me. Not Thomas. Nor anyone at Malevil. Do you understand?"

He nodded to signify yes.

I went on: "Why did you try to hide the fact that Miette was here?"

"You know why," he said in a faint voice.

"You were afraid I would sleep with her?"

"Oh, no, not because of that. If she wanted to, I mean, then that's your right."

"Because I might force her to then?"

"Yes," he whispered.

The distinction was wholly to his credit, it seemed to me. It wasn't himself he'd been thinking of, it was Miette. However, I felt it incumbent on me to put on a display of sternness. I was letting him soften me up with those innocent dog's eyes of his. It was a mistake. It was my job to teach him how to behave, since he was coming to live with us.

"Listen, Jacquet. There's something you have to get through your head. It's here, at L'Étang, that people kill other people, commit rape, hit people over the head, and steal their neighbor's horse. At Malevil we don't do things like that."

Oh, the shame with which he took his dressing-down! And obviously I had no gift as a moral tutor. Which simply means, I suppose, that I'm no sadist. Jacquet's shame certainly gave me no pleasure. I cut it short. "Your horse, what's his name?"

"Malabar."

"Right. Get out there now and harness Malabar up to your cart. We won't be able to move more than one load over today. We'll come back again with Malabar tomorrow, and Amarante too, with the Malevil cart. It may take several trips, but we'll have the time."

Jacquet immediately made for the door, relieved at the prospect of physical activity. Thomas, rather unenthusiastically it seemed to me, swiveled on his heels and prepared to follow. I called him back. "There's no point, Thomas. Not much chance of his making a break for it now!"

Thomas retraced his steps, delighted at not having to

deprive himself of the sight of Miette. He sank back into his contemplation of her without further ado. I thought he looked pretty idiotic, gaping at her with that hypnotized stare, quite forgetting that a moment ago I must have looked exactly the same. As for Miette, her magnificent eyes never left my own, or rather my lips, every moment of which she seemed to follow whenever I spoke.

I began to speak again. I wanted everything to be quite clear. "Now, Miette, there's one thing I want you to understand. Once you're at Malevil, no one is going to make you do anything you don't want to do."

Then since she didn't answer, I went on: "Do you understand?"

Silence.

"Of course she understands," La Falvine said.

Impatiently I snapped at her, "Let her speak for herself, Falvine."

La Falvine turned and stared at me. "But she can't. She's dumb."

VIII

THAT return to Malevil in the dusk! I rode at the head, bareback on Amarante, my rifle slung over my shoulder with its barrel across my chest. Miette was behind me with her arms around my waist, because just as we were about to set off she had made me understand, with one of her mimes, that she wanted to ride pillion with me. I kept Amarante down to a walk, because Malabar, who would have followed my mare to the end of the world now, began to trot as soon as she got too far ahead, and that made things uncomfortable on the cart behind, which was loaded to the brim, not only with La Falvine, Jacquet, and Thomas, but also an incredible heap of mattresses and perishables. And above all, tied to the back with a rope, lurching along as best she could, there was a cow, encumbered by a vastly swollen belly, that La Falvine had refused to leave behind at L'Étang, even for one night, because, she said, the poor thing might calve at any moment.

We took the track up the hillside, past the former Cussac farmhouse, now just a pile of ashes, because there was no question, with the cart, of getting past the drystone walls across the little plain leading down to the Rhunes. Moreover Jacquet had assured me that the hill track, though longer, wasn't cluttered with charred tree trunks. He had been along it several times on his way to Malevil, under orders from his father to spy on us.

As soon as we had maneuvered the cart up the slope of the meadow to Cussac, no mean feat, we found ourselves on the tarmacadammed road, and since it was already beginning to get dark I was tempted to ride on ahead

211

in order to reassure the others in Malevil. But when I saw, or rather heard, Malabar breaking into a gallop on the metaled surface behind Amarante, and the cow bellowing as the halter attaching her to the cart began to strangle her, I reined in the mare and kept her down to a walk from then on. The poor cow took a long time to recover from her shock, despite the consolations showered on her by La Falvine, leaning dangerously over the back of the cart. I noted that she was named Marquise, which put her some way below our Princesse in bovine rank. Uncle Samuel had always claimed that it was during the Revolution, when the peasants began throwing out their erstwhile masters, that they had begun lumbering their animals with such titles in a spirit of mockery. "And no wonder," La Menou once said, "after all the terrible things they did to us. Even under Napoleon III, you wouldn't believe it, Emmanuel, but there was a count at La Roque who hanged his coachman just because he hadn't obeyed an order. And what happened to him? Nothing. Not even a day in prison."

I went much further back in time than the Revolution at that moment when I glimpsed Malevil in the distance, its great keep lit with torches. My heart was filled with a warm glow, seeing it again like that. And I knew exactly what a baron felt in the Middle Ages, when he had been waging war in some far place and was riding home again, unharmed and victorious, bringing back the carts piled high with booty and with captives to his castle. Of course it wasn't quite the same. I hadn't raped Miette, and she wasn't a captive. On the contrary, I had freed her from captivity.

But we did have booty, and a goodly amount too, certainly enough and more, far more, to compensate for the three extra mouths to be fed: two cows, one of which, Marquise, was about to calve, the other, in full lactation, temporarily left behind at L'Étang together with a bull, a boar, and two sows (without counting the pigs already processed into edible form), two or three times as many hens as La Menou already had, and above all a large quantity of wheat, thanks to Wahrwoorde's insistence on making his own bread. His farm had always been dismissed as a poor one, because Wahrwoorde never spent anything. But in fact, as I have said, it included a fair amount of good land on the hill toward Cussac. And that evening I wasn't bringing even a tenth of L'Étang's riches back with me to Malevil. I calculated that it would take all next day and the day after that as well, ferrying to and fro with both carts, to bring in everything, tools and stock included.

It was odd how much the disappearance of the internal combustion engine had changed the whole rhythm of our life. On a horse, at a walk, it took a good hour to reach Malevil from Cussac, when in my station wagon I could have done it in ten minutes. And what a wealth of thoughts during that long, slow, swaying progress, bareback on Amarante, whose warmth and sweat filled my nostrils, and behind me Miette, her arms wound around my waist, her face pressed against my neck, and her breasts against my back. What gifts she was showering on me! And how sane, how wise our very slowness was!

For the first time since the day it happened I was happy. Well no, not happy, not entirely. I thought of Wahrwoorde under the ground, mouth and eyes filled with the earth that was also blocking the hole in his chest. A wily fellow that! A rough, tough outlaw! Living according to his own law, refusing to accept any other. A collector of male animals too. Because so many of them on so small a farm represented an altogether exceptional extravagance: a boar, a stallion, a bull. In a part of the world where all the other farms kept none but females—because all our cows were virgins, inseminated artificially—Wahrwoorde had indulged his respect for the male principle. It wasn't just a determination to be sole ruler of his own life. There must also have been an almost religious cult of virility itself, embodied in the dominance of the male animal. And he himself had been the super-male of L'Étang's human livestock, confident that every female in the family was his property, stepdaughters included, once past the age of puberty.

We were approaching Malevil now, and I was having difficulty holding Amarante in. She was constantly trying to break into a trot. But because of our poor Marquise behind the cart, her great belly banging to and fro between her short legs, I kept her firmly reined in, elbows tight to my sides. I wondered what she must think, my mare, of the day she'd just spent. Kidnaped, deflowered, and brought back again to the fold. No mystery now as to why she followed her kidnaper: she had smelled the musk of the stallion on him. And now, Bel Amour in the Maternity Ward must have smelled our approach, because a distant neigh reached our ears, answered immediately by Amarante, and after a brief moment of surprise (What! Another mare!) by the deeper voice of Malabar. The falling dusk was full of animal odors floating, calling, answering one another.

It was only we who could sense nothing. With our noses at least, because I could certainly feel Miette as she hugged herself tight against the whole length of my back, her thighs, her belly, her breasts all flattened against my flesh. Whenever Amarante succeeded in breaking into a trot, Miette would press herself against me even harder, cling even more tightly with her hands clasped around my belly. It was probably the first time she'd ever ridden bareback. And she would never forget it. Nor would I. All those soft curves behind me, keeping me warm, quivering with life. I felt buried in them, padded, softly embedded. If only I could neigh too, like Malabar, instead of thinking. And not fear the future in the womb of that present pleasure.

They had been prodigal with their torches in Malevil. Two up on the keep, two stuck in the arrow slits of the gate tower. My heart thumped as I looked up at my marvelous castle, so strong, so well guarded. And as we climbed the steep slope up to it, I gazed in wonder at the vast vertical keep in the background, lit and shadowed at the same time by the torches, at the gate tower in front of me, and running away from it on either side the ramparts, on which quite soon, craning their necks between the crenelations, shadowy figures appeared, not yet recognizable. One of them brandished a torch above the parapet. A voice cried, "Is that you, Emmanuel?"

I regretted not having stirrups. I could have stood up in

them as I answered, "Yes, it's me! And Thomas! We're bringing visitors!"

Exclamations. A confused medley of voices. I heard the muffled cracking as the two heavy oak doors swung open. Their great hinges were well enough oiled, it was the wood itself protesting at being awakened. I rode over the threshold and recognized the torchbearer. It was Momo.

"Momo, close the gate again when the cow is in!"

"*Ehanooel! Ehanooel!*" Momo shrieked, wild with excitement.

"A cow!" La Menou cried with a laugh of pure pleasure. "So he's brought us home a cow!"

"And a stallion!" Peyssou cried.

What a heroic figure I was! What acclaim all around me! I could see black silhouettes moving and bustling about. I couldn't make out any faces yet. Then Bel Amour, now only a few yards away in her stall, smelled the stallion and began neighing for all she was worth, kicking against her door, carrying on as though possessed by devils, while Malabar and Amarante took turns in answering her. Outside the entrance to the Maternity Ward I halted, hoping Bel Amour might quiet down at the sight of our horses. I don't know whether she could actually see them, but she did stop neighing. I personally couldn't see a thing, because Momo, the torchbearer, was behind us shutting the great oak doors, and La Menou, who was holding the flashlight (the first time she had used it since it had been entrusted to her), was inspecting the cow at the rear of the convoy.

The others had all gathered around Amarante, and now I could make out Peyssou by the white bandage around his head. Someone—Colin I imagined, because he was quite short—had taken hold of the mare's reins, and as she lowered her head I threw my right leg over her neck and leapt off, a practice I don't normally indulge in, since I feel it's rather theatrical, but how was I to do otherwise just then, with Miette still behind me, even though I had managed to unclasp her hands. Scarcely had my feet hit the ground when Peyssou seized me in his arms and without the slightest reticence began kissing me.

"Ugh! That's enough, you great slug! Stop slavering over me will you!" Laughter, joy, punches, insults, tremendous nudges. At last I remembered Miette. I took her by the waist and lifted her down. No lightweight! I said, "This is Miette."

At that point Momo returned, brandishing his torch, and Miette suddenly leapt out of the darkness, every curve highlighted, haloed by her great black mane. Dead silence. All three of them stood like stone. Momo too, though his torch, held out at arm's length, began to shake. All eyes fixed and gleaming. No sound but breathing. And also, a few yards away, that of La Menou soliloquizing at the back of the cart, welcoming the new cow with a string of endearments in patois. "Ah, my lovely, ah, my pretty! Look how big you are, all ready to calve, I see, and sweating like that. Ah, poor thing, have they been making you run, my dear, and you in that state? Look at you, with your calf down already inside!"

Since my friends' silence remained unbroken, and none of them seemed able to stir hand or foot, I took it upon myself to introduce them one after the other. This is Peyssou. This is Colin. This is Meyssonnier. This is Momo. Miette shook them each by the hand as I spoke the names. Not a word was exchanged. Their petrifaction still persisted. Except in the case of Momo. Suddenly he began jumping up and down, shouting Miette's name as nearly as he was able. Then he rushed off, leaving us in darkness, to tell his mother about the new arrival. She soon appeared. And since Momo's torch had vanished with Momo, heaven knew where, perhaps to contemplate the new cow, La Menou directed the beam of her flashlight on Miette and inspected her from top to toe. The well-fleshed shoulders, the high round breasts, the strong buttocks, the strong legs, nothing escaped the descending circle of light.

"Well, well! Well, well!" La Menou said.

Not a cheep from anyone else. Miette, being dumb, was dumb. The men still standing like stone statues. And from the way La Menou let the beam of her light linger over Miette's robust body, I sensed her approval. At least with regard to the girl's physical vigor, her reproductive capacities, her usefulness as a worker. In the moral sphere, La Menou was not going to commit herself. Apart from that first "Well, well! Well, well!" she said nothing. Not a word. I recognized her habitual caution. And her misogyny. I knew perfectly well what she was thinking: Better not let those titties go to your heads, my lads. A woman is always a woman. And where women are concerned, there aren't many you aren't better off without.

I don't know if Miette was troubled by that double silence—the gaping speechlessness of the three men, and the discourteous lack of greeting from La Menou—but Thomas saved the situation just then by jumping down from the cart. I watched him—how things had changed!—turn and take the two guns that our prisoner, still perched on the cart, was handing down to him. And then he was among us, hung about with weapons. He was greeted warmly. Perhaps not as enthusiastically as I had been. Or with the breathless surprise Miette had produced. But he received his share of punches, slaps on the back, and nudges. In fact it was the first time I'd ever seen the other three bang him about like that, a sign that he was really accepted into the group at last. That pleased me a great deal. And Thomas himself, delighted by their effusions, responded to them as best he could, still a little stiff, a little awkward about it, still the townsman, his gestures not quite relaxed enough or spontaneous enough, no friendly insult ready on his lips.

"And you, Emmanuel, how are you?" La Menou asked.

I saw her smiling way down below me, her little skull face turned up to me, her tiny body drawn up to its full height, not an ounce of fat anywhere. But it did me good to see it, that emaciated little body, after La Falvine's monstrous lardy bulk.

"Very pleased to see that you're only interested in the cow!" I said in patois.

Then I took her by her elbows, lifted her into the air as though she were a feather, kissed her on both cheeks, and condescended all the same to give her a brief account of L'Étang, Wahrwoorde, and his family. She wasn't much surprised to hear about the troglodyte. She had heard about his wicked ways already.

"I must be off," she said finally. "While you unload I must get a meal for you."

And she was already off, trotting in the direction of the house, a blacker spot against the blackness, tiny and swift, the circle of her flashlight dancing ahead of her, and her minute figure even tinier than ever by the time she reached the drawbridge and the foot of the inner rampart.

I shouted after her, "Menou! Food for nine! There are two more visitors on the cart!"

With the eight of us, it took no more than half an hour to unload, at least temporarily. We stowed everything away for the time being in the Maternity Ward, except for the mattresses, which we needed up at the house for the three newcomers. Everything went off smoothly, apart from a few fits of restlessness from Malabar that forced Jacquet to stand in front of him and hold his head on both sides, and apart also from the necessity of yelling at Momo occasionally when, instead of holding up his torch so that we could see, he began using it to peer between Malabar's back legs.

"For God's sake, Momo! What the hell are you at?"

The only answer was a series of grunted cries, obviously expressing wonder and admiration.

"Momo, the torch, or you'll have my boot up your arse!"

The excited cries redoubled, and standing upright, he flourished his free arm to convey the vast proportions that had so delighted and amazed him. It was odd that Peyssou didn't add his penny's worth. It must have been Miette's presence that restrained him.

Once the animals had been attended to and shut up for the night—Malabar where I used to keep my own stallion before the day it happened, in a stall with a specially strengthened door so that he couldn't kick it down and get out to join the mares—we made our way through into the inner enclosure, carried the bedding to the upper floor of the house, then came down again to the ground floor, where we found the fire blazing in the great hall, the meal laid, and in the middle of the long refectory table a great surprise, the last word in luxury and domestic illumination it seemed to us all, an old oil lamp of my uncle's that Colin had raked out and mended during our absence.

La Menou, however, was not exactly glowing with welcome. As I walked down the room at the head of our little troop she turned to look at me, black and thin, eyes like daggers, lips pinched into a thin line, teeth grinding with wrath. The group behind me slowed to a stop. The newcomers reduced to terror, the old hands discreetly amused as they awaited her outburst.

"Ah, so where are they, the two others?" she asked in a furious voice. "These people from L'Étang, these foreigners of yours! As if we haven't more than enough mouths to feed already!"

I reassured her. I reeled off a list of all the riches I was bringing back for her, not to mention the wheat with which we could now make our own bread, and clothes for Peyssou, since Wahrwoorde had been just about his size. And hands to help with the work too. At that point I led Jacquet forward and displayed him for her inspection.

He made a good impression. La Menou has a weakness for good-looking young men, and for the stronger sex generally. ("A man, nine times out of ten, you can count on it, Emmanuel, he's made of the right stuff.") And after all, a pair of shoulders and arms like Jacquet's! She didn't offer her hand, any more than she had to Miette, or even give him the time of day ("A foreigner from L'Étang! What an idea! A sow's ear doesn't turn into a silk purse overnight!") But she did allow him one very slight, very distant nod of her head. When it came to class distinctions, La Menou could have given lessons to a duchess.

"And this . . ."

But I wasn't given time to introduce La Falvine, or even utter her name. La Menou had noticed her, and before I could do a thing to stop her she burst out into a stream of patois, convinced that this "foreign woman" couldn't understand her.

"In the name of heaven, Emmanuel, what is that behind you? What have you brought back now? What have you lumbered me with, I ask you! An old hag! She must be seventy! [La Menou herself, if my memory served me right, was seventy-seven.] The young one, I don't say anything about her! I can see how useful she's going to be to you! But that old sow, she's so fat it's a wonder she can get that bottom off the floor. Good for nothing but getting under my feet in my own kitchen. What use will she be except to fill her great belly with everyone else's share! And old," she reiterated with disgust, "so old it makes my stomach turn just looking at her! With all those wrinkles! And so fat she looks like a crock of lard emptied onto a plate!"

La Falvine was scarlet. She was having difficulty drawing breath, and those huge round tears, already too familiar, were cascading down her jowls and dewlaps. A pitiful sight, but one that completely escaped La Menou, since she was affecting not to acknowledge the foreigner's presence and addressing herself exclusively to me.

"And not even from here, what's more, your old lard tub. She's a foreigner, isn't she? A savage just like that son of hers! A man who went with his own daughter! And how do we know he didn't go with his mother too, even!"

This gratuitous accusation was so far beyond the bounds that it gave La Falvine the strength to protest at last. "But the Wahrwoorde was no son of mine! He was my son-in-law!" she cried in patois.

Silence. La Menou, dumfounded, turned toward the newcomer and looked at her for the first time as though she were a human being.

"You can speak our patois then," she said, somewhat embarrassed needless to say.

There was an exchange of looks and muffled laughs from the other residents.

"And is that surprising?" La Falvine said, "when I was born in La Roque! Perhaps you know Le Falvine there. He has his workshop just next to the château. I'm his sister."

"Not Falvine the cobbler?"

"Yes, Falvine the cobbler!"

"And if he isn't my second cousin!" La Menou cried.

General amazement. What remained to be explained, obviously enough, was how La Menou could not have known La Falvine, and indeed had never seen her before. But we would come to that, no doubt, little by little. I knew them both well enough for that.

"I hope," La Menou went on, "that you won't take any offense at what I said just now, since it wasn't said to you."

"Oh, no offense, I'm sure. None at all," La Falvine said.

"What I said about you being fat, that especially," La Menou added. "For one thing, it's no fault of yours. And it doesn't mean that you eat more than anyone else necessarily either." A remark that could be construed, according to taste, as either a piece of politeness or a shot across the bows.

"No offense, no offense," La Falvine murmured again, gentle as a lamb.

Thank goodness. Our two old hens were going to settle down together after all. On a sound hierarchical basis of course. And I didn't need to wonder for a moment who was going to rule the roost, or which of the two was going to do the pecking.

I cried gaily, "Come on, let's eat! Let's eat!"

I took my usual chair in the center and beckoned Miette to the one opposite me. A moment of slight hesitation. Then Thomas took his usual place on my right and Meyssonnier the chair on my left. Momo made as if to sit on Miette's left, but this initiative was nipped in the bud by La Menou, who curtly summoned him over and made him sit on her right. Peyssou was looking at me.

"Come on then," I said. "What are you waiting for, you great booby?"

At which he brought himself, in some confusion, to amble over and take the chair on Miette's right. Colin, seemingly much more at ease, took the place on her left. Since Jacquet was still standing, unsure of what to do, I pointed to the chair next to Meyssonnier, which was certain to please him, since from there he could see Miette without having to lean forward. There was now only one place left, next to Peyssou, and I gestured to La Falvine to take it. Although not premeditated, it was a good arrangement. Peyssou, always polite, was sure to take to her from time to time.

I ate like an ogre, though I drank, as usual, with sobriety, particularly since the day was far from over. There were decisions to be taken, and there would have to be a council after the meal. I noted with satisfaction that the color was back in Peyssou's cheeks again. Because Jacquet was there, already paralyzed with shame as it was and not even daring to look at his victim, I refrained from asking how the wound was. Presumably he had waited for me to remove the dressing, but I decided it would be better to leave it on until the morning, for fear he might start bleeding again if he rubbed his head on his pillow during the night. La Falvine, nose to her plate, didn't say a word, which represented quite an effort on her part, I imagined, and she pecked at her ham like a sparrow in order to make a good impression on La Menou. It was wasted effort, however, since La Menou didn't lift her face from her plate either all through the meal.

The only one of us who seemed perfectly natural and at ease was Miette. Though it's true that she was the center on which the entire attention and warmth of the table was constantly focused. Nor did that embarrass her at all. I would swear that it didn't ever occur to her that it was anything to be vain about either. She just looked at us whenever we spoke, perfectly at ease, her eyes filled with childlike gravity. Every now and then she smiled. She smiled at all of us in turn, without forgetting Momo, whom I was amazed to find so clean, quite forgetting that it was only that morning we had put him to soak in the bathtub.

Although merry enough, the meal was at the same time a little constrained, because I didn't want to recount all the events of the day at L'Étang in front of the newcomers. Silent and modest as their behavior was, they nevertheless made us feel slightly uneasy. There was a feeling that all the things that we might ordinarily come out with, without even thinking, would ring false in front of them. And also we were all aware of a whole tradition of life they had brought with them, a tradition different from ours. For instance, as they took their places at the table they had all crossed themselves. I don't know where the habit originated. Not with Wahrwoorde, that was for certain! It made a good impression on La Menou, who was still

222

prepared to look upon these "foreigners" as heathen savages imported from the pre-Christian era.

Meyssonnier, on my left, had given me a nudge with his elbow, and Thomas had shot me a look expressing extreme annoyance.

They clearly felt themselves suddenly even more in the minority, since they were the only two thoroughgoing atheists among us, the only ones for whom atheism was a second religion. Although Colin and Peyssou had rarely accompanied their wives to Mass before the day it happened—a habit that would have seemed to them somewhat unmanly—both went to communion at Easter. As for myself, neither a Catholic nor a Protestant, brought up between two stools as it were, I was a hybrid product of two different educational systems. And they had rather canceled each other out. Vast areas of the beliefs once instilled in me had long since crumbled, and I told myself that someday or other I must make an inventory to decide once and for all what still remained.

I doubt if I shall ever do it now. But at all events, it was a sphere in which I was very much on my guard, and not just where priests were concerned. For example, I have always had a very keen antipathy for all those people who boast of having done away with God the Father, those who treat religion as something quaint and old-fashioned, then promptly replace it with a set of philosophic fetishes that are just as arbitrary. Never having got down to that inventory I mentioned, I would say that what I feel is an emotional attraction to the religious customs of my forebears. In short, all the threads have not been broken. But on the other hand, I'm well aware that sympathy isn't the same thing as support.

I made no response to Meyssonnier's nudge and ignored Thomas's glance. Did this mean that on top of the possible struggle for possession of Miette we were also on the verge of a religious war in Malevil? Because it clearly had not escaped our two atheists that the three newcomers were going to strengthen the clerical party there. And they were disturbed, naturally, because in that sphere they weren't even sure of my support.

The meal over, I sent Jacquet up to light the fire on the

223

upper floor of the house, and as soon as he came down again I stood up and said to the three newcomers, "For tonight, you will all have to sleep upstairs on your mattresses. Tomorrow we'll work out something better."

La Falvine stood up, clearly rather embarrassed, not really knowing how to take her leave, and La Menou made not the slightest effort to come to her rescue, indeed refused to give her even so much as a glance. Miette seemed much more at ease, perhaps because there was no question of her having to speak, but somewhat surprised all the same, and I knew why.

"Come on then," I said, making a herding gesture with my arms. "I'll show you the way."

To get it over with I almost drove them before me toward the door, and as they disappeared through the doorway no one, either among the newcomers or the established residents, so much as murmured a good night. Upstairs, in order to justify my presence, I made a show of checking that the windows were properly closed and the mattresses not too near to the fire. "Well, sleep well," I said at last, raising my arms again in a sort of shrug, distressed at having to leave Miette in that impersonal, distant way, even avoiding her eyes, which I had the impression were fixed on me with a puzzled, questioning look.

I left them. But that didn't mean Miette had left me. She was still there in my thoughts as I walked back down the staircase tower and into the great hall, where La Menou had by now cleared away and the rest, having pulled their chairs over to the fire, with mine empty in the middle, were waiting. I sat down and was immediately aware, just looking around at them, that Miette's presence was filling every cubic inch of space in the room, that they were unable to think of anything else.

The first to mention her, as I knew he would, was Peyssou. "She's a fine-looking girl," he said in a flattish voice. "But not very talkative."

"She's dumb."

"You can't mean it!" Peyssou said.

"*He's nhumb!*" Momo cried, distressed for her, yet at

224

the same time aware that he no longer occupied the lowest rung of linguistic skill at Malevil.

A short silence. We were all thinking tenderly of poor Miette.

"*Maman! He's nhumb!*" Momo cried again, straightening his back with a certain pride against the back of his bench.

La Menou was knitting in her usual place opposite him. What would she do when she had used all her wool? Unravel it all, like Penelope, and start again? "There's no need to shout your head off," she said without raising her eyes. "I heard. I'm not deaf at any rate."

With a slight curtness in my voice, I said, "Miette isn't deaf. Only dumb."

"Well, it's an ill wind, they say," La Menou answered sharply. "At least there'll be no arguments."

Revolted though we all were by the cynicism of this remark, we were anxious not to put weapons into La Menou's hand. We remained silent. And since the silence continued unbroken, I embarked on an account of our day at L'Étang.

I passed as quickly as possible over our military exploits. Nor did I spend more time than necessary on the family life and relationships of the Wahrwoorde clan. I still felt the same concern not to provide La Menou with ammunition. So my main subject was Jacquet, his attack on Peyssou, his passive complicity, and the terror that his father had inspired in him. I concluded by saying that I felt we ought to punish him in some way, by depriving him of his liberty, I thought, just for principle's sake, in order to make it quite clear to him that he had done wrong and so deter him from doing anything like it again.

"But what exactly do you mean by depriving him of his liberty?" Meyssonnier asked.

I shrugged. "Well, naturally I don't mean we ought to put him in irons. Just a sort of house arrest. He won't be allowed to leave Malevil or the immediate vicinity of Malevil. But otherwise he'll be treated just like all the rest of us."

"Well now, I must say!" La Menou broke in indignantly. "If you ask my opinion——"

"I haven't asked it," I cut in very sharply.

I was pleased at having put her in her place. I hadn't at all liked the way she had let La Falvine leave without so much as a good night. After all, La Falvine was her second cousin. What did she mean by snubbing her like that? And in her attitude to me as well, I felt she was beginning to be too free and easy. The fact that she looked upon me as an employer imbued with some sort of divine right didn't stop her, as it hadn't with my uncle, from constantly pecking at me. Even when she prayed, I didn't doubt it was more than she could do not to nag at God Himself.

"I agree with what you suggest," Meyssonnier said.

They all expressed agreement. And from their eyes I could tell that they were endorsing my rebuff to La Menou as well.

We then discussed how long Jacquet's sentence should run. The range of suggestions was wide. The longest, because he'd been so afraid for me, came from Thomas: ten years. The most indulgent from Peyssou: one year.

"You don't seem to rate your own skull very highly," Colin said with his old smile. Then he proposed five years and the confiscation of all the attacker's possessions. We voted, and his proposal was carried. It was to be my task next day to announce the verdict to Jacquet.

I then went on to raise the matter of security. We couldn't be sure that there weren't other groups of survivors wandering around the countryside with aggressive designs on us similar to those of Wahrwoorde. From now on we had to look to our safety. By day, no one must leave the castle unarmed. At night, there must be two men always in the gate tower as well as La Menou and Momo. And luckily there was in fact an unoccupied room on the upper floor of the tower, with a fireplace. I proposed a rotation system in twos. My companions all accepted this idea in principle, but argued with some animation over the frequency of the rotation and the composition of the watches. After twenty minutes a consensus was arrived at that Colin and Peyssou should keep watch in the gate tower on even dates and Meyssonnier and Thomas on odd dates. Colin proposed, and the others all agreed, that I should remain permanently in the keep so that I could organize the defense of the inner enclosure in the event of the outer one being occupied by a surprise attack.

I pointed out that if two of us were always going to be sleeping in the gate tower, that left one of the bedrooms in the keep free. I suggested putting Miette in the one next to the bathroom on the second floor.

As soon as Miette's name was mentioned all animation died, and silence returned. That particular room, as Thomas alone did not know, was the former Club premises. And in those distant schoolboy days, without ever coming to any practical conclusion, we had constantly discussed how pleasant it would be to have a girl among our number, so that she could cook for us and "satisfy our passions." The last phrase was my contribution—I had come across it in a novel—and it made a deep impression, since none of us knew exactly what "passion" meant.

"And the other two?" Meyssonnier asked finally.

"To my mind, they may as well stay where they are."

Silence. Everyone realized that Miette's status at Malevil could not be the same as that of La Falvine or Jacquet. But as to exactly what that status was to be, nothing was said. No one seemed prepared to come forward and define it.

Since the silence was dragging on, I decided I had better speak myself. "Right," I said, "the moment has come to speak out frankly about Miette. On condition, naturally, that anything we say does not go beyond these four walls."

I looked around. Approval on all their faces. However, since La Menou remained completely impassive, her eyes fixed on her knitting, I added, "You too, Menou. Do you agree to keep what is said secret?"

She stuck her needles into her knitting, rolled it up, and got to her feet. "I shall go to bed," she said through tight lips.

"I haven't asked you to leave."

"It's time I went to bed in any case."

"Now, Menou, don't upset yourself."

"I'm not upset," she said, turning her back on me. Then she crouched down in front of the fire to light her little lamp, muttering to herself the while, and though the words themselves were quite unintelligible I could tell from her tone that they weren't complimentary as far as I was concerned.

I said nothing.

"You can stay, Menou," Peyssou said, soft-hearted as always. "We trust you."

I gave him a sharp glance and continued to remain silent. I was quite pleased that she was going, in fact. Meanwhile the incomprehensible muttering continued. I could just make out the words pride and mistrust. I knew what she was angling for, but I persisted in remaining dumb. I noticed it was taking her a long while to light her lamp this evening. Quite clearly she was waiting for me to ask her to stay. She was going to be disappointed.

She was, and boiling with rage as a result. "Come on, Momo," she said in a very curt voice.

Momo, fascinated by the conversation, protested sullenly. But he had chosen a bad moment, poor Momo, to try and disobey! Shifting her lamp into her left hand, La Menou raised her small bony right hand and slapped him across the face with all her strength. That done, she turned her back on him, and he followed her to the door, totally cowed. I wondered for the umpteenth time how the great ninny could still allow himself, at the age of forty-seven, to be knocked about by his minuscule mother.

"Good night, Peyssou," La Menou said as she left the circle of chairs. "Good night, and sleep well."

"And you, Menou," Peyssou answered, slightly embarrassed by her selective courtesy.

She walked away, Momo in her wake, and he slammed the door behind them with a tremendous crash, turning his mother's aggression on him back against me as best he could. And tomorrow he'd be sulky with me all day, just like his mother. A half century of life had still not severed the umbilical cord.

"Right," I said. "Miette. Let's talk about Miette. When I was at L'Étang, while Jacquet and Thomas were out burying Wahrwoorde, I could perfectly well have had Miette and then come back and said, 'There it is, fellows. Miette's mine, my woman, my wife. Hands off, everyone.'"

228

I looked around. No reaction, at least none that I could see.

"And the reason I didn't do that is so that no one else shall do it. In other words, it is my opinion that Miette must not become anyone's exclusive property. In fact Miette isn't a property at all, of course. Miette is her own mistress. Miette can have whatever relationship she chooses with whomever she likes, whenever she likes. Do you agree?"

A long silence. No one spoke and no one even looked at me. The institution of monogamy was so deeply implanted in them, controlled so many reflexes, memories, emotions in their minds, that they simply could not accept, or even conceive of, a system that excluded it.

"There are two possibilities," Thomas said.

Ah! I thought it would be Thomas!

"Either Miette chooses one of us to the exclusion of all the others—"

I broke in. "I must say right away that I could not accept that situation, even if I were the one to be chosen. And if it was someone else, then I would refuse to acknowledge any exclusive rights on his part."

"Do you mind?" Thomas said. "I haven't finished."

"Yes, yes, finish, Thomas," I said amiably. "I interrupted you, but I'm not preventing you from speaking."

"Well, that's something at least," Thomas said.

I smiled at everyone in turn, without speaking. It was a trick that had always worked in the old Club days, and I noticed that it still seemed to work now. My challenger was discredited by my patience and his own touchiness.

"The alternative possibility then," Thomas went on, but it was clear that I had clipped his wings slightly, "is that Miette sleeps with all of us—and it's totally immoral."

"Immoral?" I said. "How is it immoral?"

"It's obvious why it's immoral," Thomas said.

"It's not obvious in the slightest. I refuse to accept such a piece of clerical dogmatism as a fact."

A dirty trick on my part, attributing a "piece of clerical dogmatism" to Thomas, and I relished it in passing. But on the main question under debate he did seem so certain of himself and yet so immature, our sweet Thomas.

"It's not clerical dogmatism," Thomas snapped in a furious voice that harmed his cause no end. "You can't deny it. A woman who sleeps with everyone is a prostitute."

"Wrong!" I said. "A prostitute is a woman who sleeps with people for money. It's the money that makes it immoral, not the number of sexual partners she has. There are women who sleep with everyone and anyone all over the place. Even in Malejac. And no one thinks the worse of them for it."

Silence. An angel flew over our heads. We were all thinking of Adelaide. Apart from Meyssonnier, who had become engaged to his Mathilde at a very young age, we had all been helped over our adolescence by Adelaide. And we were still grateful to her for it. And I felt sure that Meyssonnier himself, despite all his virtue, sometimes felt regret at what he had missed.

Thomas must have sensed that I was exploiting the strength of some shared memory, because he made no comment.

Almost certain now of carrying my argument, I went on: "It's not a question of morality. It's a matter of adapting ourselves to our situation. In India, for example, Thomas, you find a caste where five brothers will get together to marry a single wife. The brothers and the wife make a permanent family, and they bring up their children without even wondering whose they are. The reason they live like that is because it would be quite impossible for each of them to have a wife of his own. They just don't have the resources. So it's their poverty that forces them into that kind of organization. And it seems to me that we're being forced into it simply by necessity. Because Miette is the only woman here capable of producing children."

Silence. Thomas, who felt he'd lost out by now, I think, had given up arguing, and the others didn't seem anxious to speak. But they were going to have to come down on one side or the other eventually, so I glanced around with a questioning look and said, "Well?"

"I wouldn't like that," Peyssou said.

"What do you mean 'that'?"

"That system of yours, out in India."

"But it's not a question of liking, it's a matter of necessity."

"All the same," Peyssou said, "sharing a woman with a lot of other men, no. I say no."

Silence.

"I agree with him," Colin said.

"So do I," Meyssonnier said.

"So do I," Thomas said with an infuriating smile.

I gazed into the fire. Something quite staggering had happened to me. I had lost a vote! I had been beaten! It was the first time it had happened to me since I was twelve, since the day when I had, as it were, assumed the post of chief executive of the Club, all those years ago. And even though I realized that it was childish of me to feel that way, I was deeply mortified. At the same time, I decided I mustn't show it. I must behave as though nothing had happened, keep on talking, move on to the next subject on the agenda, pass it off as a trifle. But I couldn't. My throat was too tight to speak, my mind a total blank. Not only had I been defeated, but my silence was making me lose face.

It was Thomas who rescued me, though certainly without intending to. "So there you are," he said without any attempt at finesse. "Monogamy wins the day!"

I'd given him a hard time earlier, and clearly that "clerical dogmatism" was still rankling.

Thomas's remark was received very coldly. I looked around at the other three. They were red-faced, uncomfortable, clearly at least as embarrassed as I was myself by my defeat. Especially, as Colin was to tell me later, after a day "when you'd run such risks for us."

Their confusion comforted me. "I'm perfectly prepared to accept your opinions as votes and bow to them," I said. "But we still need to know precisely what that vote means. Does it mean that we are going to force Miette to select one particular partner and stick to her choice from then on?"

"No," Meyssonnier said. "It doesn't mean that at all. We're not going to force her to do anything. But if she

231

restricts herself to a single husband, of her own accord, then we shall do nothing to dissuade her."

So. The situation was quite clear now. And the stylistic difference too. I had said "partner," he had said "husband." I felt very much like pointing out to Meyssonnier that for a Communist he had a very petty bourgeois conception of marriage. Stoically, I refrained. I looked at the other three. "Is that what you want?"

That was what they wanted. Let us respect the laws of marriage. No adultery, even between consenting parties. The old conventional morality was still alive and well and living in Malevil. Though I still held the opinion myself that this respectable social system of theirs was absolutely doomed to break down in a community of six men who had just been issued, as it were, a single woman. But what can you do if you're in a minority of one? The position of the others seemed to me to be not only dogmatic but senseless: to remain celibate to the end of one's days rather than settle for a woman who was not exclusively one's own. Though it's true that they were all probably hoping to be the one who was chosen.

I sat in silence. I was worried about our future. I was afraid of the frustrations and the jealousies ahead. Perhaps even impulses to kill. And also, why not admit it, I was by now experiencing an almost painful regret at not having enjoyed Miette at L'Étang while I had the chance. I had certainly reaped very little reward for having controlled my "passions," as we used to say in the days of the Club.

Next day at dawn, after a very bad night, I was awakened by the sound of the great bell on the gate tower being rung. It was a huge church bell that I bought in a sale and had mounted beside the entrance arch so visitors and tourists could ring to be let in. But it was so big, and the din it made could be heard so far away—even in La Roque, I was told—that I had had a supplementary, and now entirely useless, electric bell installed beside the door as well.

I wondered what could possibly have happened to make anyone ring the bell so loudly and for such a length of time. I leapt out of bed, pulled my pants on over my pajamas, and thrust my feet into my boots without bothering about socks. I snatched up my rifle—followed by Thomas as soon as he'd grabbed his gun as well—half fell down the spiral staircase to the ground floor, then raced out over the drawbridge into the outer enclosure.

Everyone in the castle was gathered there scarcely half dressed, congregated outside the Maternity Ward. The event, it appeared, was a wholly happy one. Marquise, the cow from L'Étang, had just dropped a calf in one corner of her box and was now in the process of producing another in the opposite corner. Having been told by his mother to spread the good news, Momo, wild with excitement, had decided it was an occasion worthy of celebrating with a peal on the bell.

I gave him a severe dressing-down, reminding him of my express and repeated orders to the contrary. Then, turning to La Falvine, I complimented her on her cow's two offspring—both heifers, it was now apparent. La Falvine was more puffed up with pride than if she had produced them herself, and she cackled away nonstop in the stall with La Menou. Both of them waited for a chance to give their assistance, though it was obviously quite unnecessary, since the second tiny heifer was already out—plump, shiny with slime, a sight to melt anyone's heart. Peyssou, Meyssonnier, Colin, and Jacquet were all there adding their comments, dominated mainly by Peyssou's loudly rumbled reminiscences about all the other occasions, rare but memorable, when he had seen or heard about a cow producing twins. We were all lined up along the side partition of Marquise's stall, our chins lodged on the top rail, Miette somewhere in the middle of the line.

She didn't have much on, and she was still warm and rosy-cheeked with sleep, her hair rumpled up. At the sight of her my heart began pounding idiotically. Enough of that. Save your admiration for the calves, Emmanuel. They were both mahogany-colored, and not particularly small, as one might have expected.

"And to think," Peyssou observed at that point, "seeing the mother, you'd never have said she was going to drop the two like that when she was no bigger in the belly than for the one."

"Indeed, and I've seen cows bigger with one calf than ever Marquise was," La Menou confirmed. "And there she goes and drops you two, and two fine ones at that. It makes you wonder where she could be keeping them."

"Fair play to you," Peyssou said to La Falvine. "You've got a good cow there. [I don't know why we were all paying such compliments to La Falvine on account of a cow that in fact belonged to Malevil now, unless perhaps because we were all anxious to make it up to her after La Menou's frigid welcome.] I shouldn't think you'll be wanting to sell her though, Falvine, not a cow that makes you twins like that. Though even without that," he went on, very polite, very thoughtful, "if you went and sold your calves at a week old, that would bring you in something like sixty thousand francs. And that's not counting all the milk she'll be giving you after. Lord, Lord, she's worth her weight in gold, a cow like that. When you think she might bring you another two next time as well."

"And who would you sell them to, the calves, tell me that, you great loon," Colin said.

"Well, it was just a manner of speaking," Peyssou said, more thoughtful than ever, eyes half closed. He was doubtless dreaming of some model dairy farm in a better world, with an electric milking bay and nothing but cows specially bred to give birth to twin. He was even forgetting to look at Miette. Though admittedly, after our vote the evening before, we were all tending to glance at her only occasionally, and surreptitiously. We were all afraid the others would think we were trying to steal a march.

I did a mental inventory of our stock: Princesse, Marquise, and the two new heifer calves, which we had decided by now to name Comtesse and Baronne in order to complete our bovine nobility. Ah, and I'd almost forgotten Noiraude, whom we'd left behind at L'Étang, less aristocratic perhaps, but in full lactation, and without a calf. So Malevil now owned five cows, an adult bull, and a bull calf, Princesse's Prince. However, we would certainly have to keep him too, since we couldn't run the risk of leaving ourselves with only a single male.

On the equine side we had three mares: Amarante, Bel Amour, and her daughter Malice. Plus a stallion: Malabar. I didn't bother to work out the number of pigs, since we now had far more than we could possibly keep. At the thought of all those animals I experienced a warming sense of security, only slightly tempered by the nagging fear that the fields would no longer be able to provide food for them, or for us either.

Odd, the way the disappearance of money had also meant the disappearance of all those artificial needs. As in Biblical times, we thought now solely in terms of food, of land, of flocks, of the preservation of the tribe. Miette, for example. I viewed her quite differently from the way I had Birgitta. With Birgitta, as though it was something that went without saying, I had dissociated the sexual act completely from its original purpose, whereas with Miette my whole conception of her was centered on the idea of her future fecundity.

Even with the two carts, it took us four days to bring everything over from L'Étang. City people complain about moving apartments, they have no idea of the things it's possible to accumulate on a farm during one lifetime, all of them useful and most of them horribly cumbersome. And that, of course, doesn't include the stock, plus fodder, bedding, and grain.

On the fifth day we were at last able to resume plowing our little wheat patch down by the Rhunes, which was also an opportunity to put our new security arrangements into effect. Jacquet was to do the plowing while one of the rest of us kept watch, in rotation, armed with the rifle and concealed on the hillside overlooking the valley to the west. If the lookout saw anyone suspicious approaching, then he was to fire into the air without showing himself. This would give Jacquet time to take refuge inside the castle with the horse and to warn the rest of us, so that we could come to the lookout's aid with the rest of the guns—three now, with Wahrwoorde's shotgun, four counting the rifle.

Not much of an arsenal. A thought that reminded me of Wahrwoorde's bow, which at reasonably close range had proved such a formidable and very accurate weapon. Birgitta had once taught me the rudiments of archery theory—a much more complicated matter than you might think at first sight—and amid general skepticism I began to practice out on the road leading up to the outer enclosure. With a little perseverance I began to achieve fairly satisfactory results, and gradually I increased my distance. On my good days I was eventually able to get one arrow out of three into the target at fifty yards. It wasn't exactly William Tell, or even Wahrwoorde, but basically it was rather better than what you can do at that distance with a shotgun, since after fifty or sixty yards the shot has dispersed so widely as to be almost useless. I was also astonished at the penetration power achieved. The arrows used to embed themselves so deeply in the thick braided target that I sometimes needed both hands to pull them out.

My success, moderate though it was, nevertheless sufficed to fan the dormant flames of competition in my companions, and archery practice soon became our favorite pastime. In fact before long I was not only caught up but completely outclassed by little Colin, who was regularly getting all three arrows into the target at sixty yards, and then began gradually edging them closer and closer to the bull's-eye.

Of the five of us—six counting Jacquet, but he wasn't allowed to handle weapons yet—Colin was far and away the smallest and the least strong. We were so accustomed to this fact that his smallness seemed to us somehow part of his very essence, and we all tended to call him little Colin, even to his face. It never occurred to us that this might irk him at all, since he had never protested at the custom. And now, quite suddenly, seeing the immense happiness it gave him to feel his superiority to us all once he held a bow in his hand, it dawned on me how much he must always have suffered from his delicate build. The bow itself was taller than he was. But as soon as it was in his hands—which was pretty often, since he was by now practicing far more than the rest of us—he was king. At midday, after the meal, I would watch him sitting in the embrasure of one of the big mullioned windows in the great hall, poring studiously over the little archery manual that Birgitta had once made me buy for myself, and which I had never even opened. In short, little Colin became our great bowman. And that was how I began to refer to him, noticing how much pleasure that word "great" gave him, even in that figurative sense.

He persuaded Meyssonnier to collaborate with him in the construction of three more bows. Each of us ought to have his own, he said, and he could frequently be heard lamenting the fact that he no longer had his little forge in La Roque (where he had combined the functions of locksmith and plumber), so that he could make more arrowheads for us. I gave him every encouragement in all these activities, because I was only too well aware that the day would eventually come—since our supply of ammunition was limited and we had no means of making more—when our guns would cease to be of use, in a world where it seemed unlikely that violence was going to die out merely from lack of firearms.

A month had already gone by since Momo had rung the bell at dawn to announce the birth of Marquise's two calves. One evening at about seven o'clock I had just closed the door of my bedroom in the keep and was about to go down to the house. I had the Bible under my arm, and Thomas was already out on the landing telling me I looked every inch the man of God. My right hand was just turning the key in the lock when suddenly the big bell rang out once more, not a wild clanging like the previous time, but just two solemn notes, followed by a third, much fainter one, making the succeeding silence seem heavy and strange. I froze. It couldn't be Momo. He would never ring a bell that way. I went back in my bedroom, laid the Bible down on the table, picked up my rifle, and handed a shotgun to Thomas.

Without speaking, and with Thomas streaking ahead of me as usual once we were on the flat, I ran toward the gate tower. It was deserted. La Menou and Momo were presumably in the house, the one preparing the evening meal, the other hanging around her in the hope of filching a little extra food. As for Colin and Peyssou, who were due to sleep that night in the gate tower, nothing in our

237

arrangements required them to be there during the day. It was brought home to me then, as I ran through the gate tower's empty rooms making a quick inspection while Thomas remained outside keeping watch on the door, how inadequate our security arrangements really were. The walls of the outer enclosure. being much lower than those of the inner, were not too tall to be scaled with a ladder, or even by someone using nothing more than a rope with a good grappling hook on it. As for the moat, that was spanned not by a drawbridge. as in the case of the inner one, but by an ordinary permanent bridge that made it quite a feasible proposition for attackers to approach the walls on foot, while we were all inside eating our evening meal, and simply scale them at their leisure.

I re-emerged from the gate tower and told Thomas in a whisper to climb the steps up to the top of the wall and cover our visitor or visitors with his gun through one of the openings in the battlements overhanging the gate. I waited till he was in place. then stole soundlessly over to the Judas in the gate, gently opened it a fraction, and put my eye very gingerly to the slit.

About a yard away from me, and therefore well this side of the bridge, I saw a man of about forty sitting astride a large gray donkey. the barrel of the gun slung over his back sticking up above his left shoulder. He was bareheaded and had a very dark complexion and black hair. He was wearing a charcoal gray suit, somewhat dusty, and on his chest, suspended by a chain around his neck, there was a large silver crucifix, very like a bishop's pectoral cross. He looked to be both tall and strong. His features were stamped with the greatest calmness, and I noticed that he did not so much as bat an eyelid when he lifted his eyes toward the battlements and perceived Thomas's gun aimed down at him.

I slid the Judas violently open till it hit the stop and I shouted loudly, "What do you want?"

The violence of my tone had no effect on the visitor. He didn't even start. He simply looked toward the Judas and answered in a deep, measured voice, "Why, to visit with you in the first place, and then to sleep tonight in the castle. I have no wish to make my return journey during the hours of darkness."

I noticed that he spoke well, rather deliberately so, perhaps, enunciating his words with care, and in an accent that without being quite the same as ours was very close to it. I spoke again. "Have you any other weapon on you besides your gun?"

"No."

"You would do well to answer truthfully. We shall search you as soon as you're inside."

"I have a small penknife, but I wouldn't call that a weapon."

"A switchblade knife?"

"No."

"What is your name?"

"Fulbert le Naud. I am a priest."

I made no comment on his claim to the priesthood.

"Listen, Fulbert. Remove the bolt from your gun and place it in your jacket pocket."

He complied immediately, commenting in a noncommittal voice, "You are very suspicious."

"We have good cause to be. We have been attacked once." Then I went on: "Listen. I'm going to open the gate. You will ride in without dismounting. Then you will stop ten yards inside and not dismount until I tell you to."

"As you wish."

I raised my head. "Thomas, keep him covered the entire time."

Thomas nodded. I took my rifle in my right hand, thumbed off the safety catch, tugged the two big bolts open, pulled one half of the door inward, and waited. As soon as Fulbert was through I pushed the door to so quickly that I bumped the donkey's hindquarters. It gave a jump forward, then kicked back with both legs and almost had our visitor out of his saddle. The horses in the cave began to neigh. The donkey put up its long ears and stood trembling slightly on its legs when Fulbert reined it to a halt.

"All right, down you get," I said in patois, "and hand me that bolt."

He did as I said, showing that he understood our dialect.

239

I put the bolt into my own pocket. I was more or less convinced that all these precautions were pointless in this particular case; but suspicion has one thing in common with the usual virtues: it is only effective on condition that it allows of no exceptions.

Thomas came down, without being told, to take the gray donkey by the bridle and lead it to one of the stalls in the cave. I saw him take a bucket off one of the hooks to fetch it some water.

I turned to Fulbert. "Where are you from?"

"Cahors."

"Yet you understand our patois."

"Not all of it. There are differences of vocabulary."

It was a subject he seemed to find interesting, because he immediately began comparing certain words in our dialect with those in his own. As he spoke, and he spoke very well, I watched him. He wasn't tall, as I had thought at first, but he was well proportioned and had a certain elegance of bearing that made him seem tall. As for his face, I didn't know what to think of that. I let him finish his philological comparisons, then I said, "Have you just come from Cahors?"

He smiled, and I noticed that he had really a rather attractive smile.

"Goodness no. I've come from La Roque. I happened to be there, you see, when the bomb exploded."

I stared at him open-mouthed. "You mean there are survivors in La Roque?"

"Yes," he said, "certainly there are." Then he added, still as calm as ever, "A score or so."

NOTE ADDED BY THOMAS

The chapter you have just read is notable for an omission so flagrant that I feel I must interrupt Emmanuel's narrative at this late date in order to repair it. Before writing this I went on to read the next chapter, to make sure that Emmanuel had not retraced his steps, as he sometimes did, and gone more fully into the matter later on. But he didn't. Not a word about it. It's almost as though he had just forgotten the whole thing.

But first of all, since she was the person chiefly con-

cerned, I would like to say a word about Miette. After all of Emmanuel's poetic effusions, I don't want to appear as though I'm just trying to deglamorize her. But Miette was really just an ordinary country girl, no different from a great many others. True, she was very healthy and solidly built and she did have, in abundance, all those firm and well-muscled curves that Emmanuel found so attractive. But to imply that Miette was beautiful seems to me to be going much too far. She was no more beautiful, to my eyes at the time, than the Renoir painting of a woman washing herself that Emmanuel had a print of over his bed, or than the photograph of Birgitta drawing her bow that stood on the desk in his room (rather odd, really, that Emmanuel should have kept that picture after the foul letter she wrote telling him about her marriage).

Nor do I share Emmanuel's opinion about Miette's "intelligence" either. Miette was born prematurely, a mute from birth, which meant she had a brain lesion that always prevented her from using her powers of speech, and that also, as a direct consequence, impoverished her apprehension of the world. I am not saying that Miette was an imbecile, or even feeble-minded, because Emmanuel would have had no difficulty at all in reeling off a long list of the occasions when Miette demonstrated great shrewdness in the sphere of human relationships. But from that to claiming that Miette was "very intelligent," as Emmanuel had assured me on numerous occasions (another example of sexual overestimation), is a step that I for my part am unwilling to take. Miette, while being extremely shrewd, was at the same time very simple. Like a child, she only apprehended half of reality. The rest is all fantasy and fiction, without any reference to fact.

You may have begun to think I didn't care much for Miette. On the contrary, I valued her very highly indeed. She was generous, she was goodness itself, and there was not the slightest particle of egotism anywhere in her body. If I believed in such dangerous nonsense, I would say that she was made of the stuff of saints. Except that her goodness showed itself in a field not usually associated with saints.

The day following the council meeting during which

241

Emmanuel was defeated over his polyandrous project, there was a certain air of suspense throughout Malevil, since we were all wondering which "husband" (Meyssonnier) or which "partner" (Emmanuel) Miette was going to choose. So much so that none of us even dared to look at her any more—as Emmanuel has already described—for fear that the others might think we were trying to steal a march on them. What a change from the shameless stares with which we had been transfixing her the evening before!

I have no way of telling what Miette thought of our sudden reserve. Because her eyes were like a child's, "transparent and unfathomable" (I am quoting Emmanuel there, though he doesn't use the phrase until the next chapter). However, it's worth adding that during our second day of carting things from L'Étang, Peyssou, the most naturally frank and open of our group, remarked resignedly that obviously "she" was going to choose Emmanuel. This comment was made in the presence of Colin, Meyssonnier, and myself only, the newcomers all being inside the troglodyte dwelling at the time, busy packing up their belongings. Not without a certain gloom, we all three expressed the opinion that it was, as Peyssou had said, obvious.

Evening came. After the meal there was the usual Bible reading, followed now by three additional and fervent listeners, though rather inattentively, I fear, by us four. Emmanuel was in his usual position propped against one side of the fireplace, and Miette was seated in the center of the half circle of chairs, her face and body lit and reddened by the fire's dancing flames. I remember it well, that evening: my sense of expectation, or rather our sense of expectation, and how Emmanuel's voice, though so warm and rich, infuriated me by its slowness. I don't know whether it was from the fatigue after our hard day, the nervous strain of our uncertainty, or the complicity of the half-darkened room, but the reserve that had been constraining us during the day melted away. We all had our eyes riveted on Miette as she sat there, every curve highlighted, completely relaxed, absorbed in the reading. And yet she made no pretense of being unaware of our

242

gaze. From time to time she allowed her eyes to meet ours, and then she would smile. She smiled at all of us like that, impartially. Emmanuel has already described her smile, and it is true that it was extremely attractive, even though it was identical for all of us.

At the end of the evening, with the most completely natural air, Miette got to her feet, took Peyssou by the hand, and left with him.

Peyssou was extremely glad, I suspect, that the fire had by then been banked over with ashes, so there was very little light in the great hall. He was even happier, I think, at being able to turn his back on us so that we could not see his face. And we, the others, stayed there in front of the fire, silent and dismayed, while La Menou lit our lamps for us, muttering a string of acid comments less than flattering to our little group of slumping rejects.

Our surprises were not at an end. Next evening Miette chose Colin. The day after that, myself. On the fourth day, Meyssonnier. On the fifth, Jacquet. On the sixth, she again chose Peyssou. And she went on like that, always keeping strictly to the same order, without ever choosing Emmanuel.

No one felt like laughing, and yet the situation did verge on the comic. There was not one of us who had not been made to look ridiculous. The advocate of polyandry now found himself the only one excluded from the practice he had championed. And the stiff-necked partisans of monogamy were all sharing Miette without the slightest shame.

On one point there was no mystery whatever. Miette was acting quite spontaneously, without any knowledge of our discussions and without asking advice from anyone else. If she gave herself to us all, that was simply because we all wanted her very much, and because she was kind. Because making love was something Miette could take or leave. Which is hardly surprising when you think of how she was initiated into it.

As for the order in which Miette selected her partners, it dawned on us after a very short while that it was quite simply based on our positions around the meal table. And yet there still remained the one colossal enigma: Why

243

was Emmanuel—whom she adored—excluded from her rota?

There was no doubt that she did worship him, and like a child too, without the least shame about showing it. He had only to enter the room and she had eyes only for him. When he spoke, she hung upon his lips. When he left, she followed him with her eyes. It was quite easy to imagine Miette pouring precious ointment upon Emmanuel's feet, then wiping them with her long hair. This comparison should not be taken as a sign that I was allowing myself to be infected by the religious atmosphere of our fireside evenings. I merely borrow it from little Colin.

When my turn came around for the third time, I resolved to get to the bottom of the matter by asking Miette the reason outright, in the privacy of her room. But although Miette had at her disposal a whole arsenal of gestures and mimes with which she could make herself understood (and she also knew how to write), it was not always easy to carry on a dialogue with her, for the simple reason that without being unmannerly you could never reproach her for her lack of communication, as you would another woman, if you suspected that it was deliberate. As soon as I asked Miette why she still hadn't singled out Emmanuel, her face became as blank as a lump of wood, and she refused to do anything but just shake her head. The same question put in several different forms always produced the same response.

So I changed my approach. Didn't she like Emmanuel? Vigorous and repeated nods, eyelashes lowered over tenderly melting eyes, lips apart, face upturned. I promptly put my first question again: Then why? Her eyes and mouth immediately closed, and once again she refused to do anything but shake her head stubbornly to and fro. We were getting nowhere. I left the bed, went over to my jacket, and took out the little notebook in which I recorded all the withdrawals and returns from the tool store, and on one of the pages, by the faint light of her little lamp, I printed in large capitals: "WHY NOT EMMANUEL?" Then I handed the notebook and pencil to Miette. She drew up her knees, rested the notebook on them, sucked the pencil, then with enormous concentration wrote, "Because." After a moment's reflection, she even added a period mark after the "Because," presumably in order to make it clear that this answer was definitive.

It was only completely by chance, three days later, that I finally came to understand her reasons, or rather her reason, since there was only one.

Constantly obsessed with our security, Emmanuel had decided to keep the three shotguns, the rifle, all our ammunition, and our two bows and the arrows in our bedroom, to lock the door whenever we were neither of us there, and to conceal the key at the back of one of the storeroom drawers, a hiding place known only to the two of us and Meyssonnier.

One afternoon, feeling a need to change my clothes— Emmanuel had just given me my first riding lesson and I was drenched in sweat—I went and collected the key from its hiding place. The spiral staircase in the keep was pretty steep, so, being tired, I climbed it slowly, my left hand resting on the stone column around which the steps twisted. I had just reached the second floor and stopped on the landing for a moment to draw breath when to my amazement, at the far end of the big empty room that acted as a sort of antechamber to the two bedrooms, I saw Miette, her ear glued to the keyhole of our door and apparently listening with all her might and main. Odd, because I of course knew for sure that the room was empty. First because I had just left Emmanuel outside the Maternity Ward, and second because I myself had locked it only an hour and a half earlier when I had come up to put on my boots and get ready for my lesson.

I walked up behind her and said loudly, "Miette, whatever are you doing there?"

She started, straightened up, blushed, and glanced all around her with a hunted look, as though she was preparing for flight.

But by that time I was upon her, seized her by the wrist and said, "Whatever is it, Miette? There's nothing to listen to in there. The room is empty!"

She looked at me with such incredulity in her eyes that I took the key out of my pocket, opened the door, and, still holding her firmly by the wrist, dragged her uncere-

245

moniously inside, despite her very vigorous resistance. But once she had been in the room for the short time it took to realize that it was really empty, she stopped struggling and just stood there, clearly dumfounded. Then, completely ignoring my questions, a frown on her face, she opened the big wardrobe. Presumably she recognized the clothes inside as belonging to Emmanuel and myself, because she completely ignored all mine but began stroking his with the palm of her hand. After that she went over and opened all the drawers of the bureau, one by one, her face slowly lighting up with joy as she did so.

When she had finished, she looked at me questioningly, then, since I was still rather taken aback by her search, she pointed with her right index finger at the sofa under the window, then at my chest. I nodded. Then, casting astonished eyes here and there about the room, she suddenly noticed the photograph of Birgitta drawing her bow on Emmanuel's desk. She snatched it up, then waved it in front of my face, narrowing her eyes and pointing at it with her other hand. I don't quite know how she managed it, but her posture, the position of her body, the inclination of her head, the expression on her face, the gestures she was making with her hands, all combined not exactly to ask me a question, since no sound escaped from her lips, but to mime it, to act it, almost to dance it for me. And the question was so clear that I almost believed I had heard it: Where is the German girl then?

Everything became clear. At L'Étang, you will remember, it was generally believed by all the Wahrwoorde clan that Birgitta was still with us. And this error had never been expunged from Miette's mind. On the contrary, she had interpreted Emmanuel's reserve toward her on that first evening back at Malevil as irrefutable proof that his heart was engaged elsewhere. And since she never saw Birgitta anywhere in the castle, she had imagined that Emmanuel must have shut her away somewhere, safe from covetous eyes. And she had been absolutely confirmed in this idea when she discovered that Emmanuel's bedroom—which she did not know I shared—was the only room ever kept locked. She had not paused for a moment to consider all the physical impossibilities contra-

dicting her theory. And in view of her belief, it was quite certainly out of respect for this supposed jealous passion of Emmanuel's that she had never singled him out.

At all events, that very same evening when it was time for bed Miette repaired her error. Apart from the great relief that we all felt at that moment, I for my part also experienced a mischievous additional pleasure at seeing Emmanuel leaving the great hall with his huge Bible in one hand and Miette, as it were, in the other.

IX

FULBERT brought us two very good pieces of news. Marcel Falvine, La Falvine's brother, had survived, and so had Catie, Miette's elder sister. Second, Colin's workshop in the side street, where he kept all his plumbing and locksmith's equipment, was intact.

Less in order to do him honor than to observe his amazing face at my leisure, I placed our guest opposite me at the dinner table, moving Miette along one and separating her from Peyssou, to the latter's acute displeasure.

He had an abundant head of black hair, our newcomer, wavy, shining with health, and lacking any trace of a tonsure at the crown. There was a fair amount of white at the temples, lending him a dignified, serious look, and the thick locks that curled nobly down over the front of his head produced the effect of a kind of helmet or mane and served as an admirable foil to his vast forehead and magnificent eyes, which gleamed with vitality and cunning. Unfortunately, however, the pupils were just a little off center, which introduced a disturbing shiftiness into his gaze. It was also a pity that the lower half of his face ended in a snout, still further accentuating the air of untrustworthiness inflicted on his eyes by his squint.

But that was not the only physical distinction Fulbert presented. There were his hands, for instance. They were broad and strong, with flattened fingers. A laborer's hands in short, which didn't seem to belong in any way to the same persona as the beautiful unctuous voice and the careful diction.

There was also his thinness and its odd distribution. Below his eyes those twin swellings—so charming to behold in children—that we call cheeks and anatomists refer to as facial fat had in Fulbert's case melted totally away, leaving on each side of his nose a deeply dramatic trench that made one think of a patient in the last stages of tuberculosis and lent him the very misleading appearance of an invalid or an ascetic.

I say misleading, and I will tell you why. Before he left Malevil, Fulbert was to ask me "fraternally" (on the strength of our common bond with Our Father, I presumed) to let him have (not "give," you note, but "let him have") one of my shirts, since his own was worn out. A little taken aback, I must admit, at being expected to bear the cost of our new-found fraternity entirely on my own, I nevertheless acceded to the request. And Fulbert promptly effected the exchange on the spot, revealing such a broad well-muscled, generously fleshed, even plump torso that it seemed almost impossible that it could belong to the same body as that emaciated head.

An ascetic and an invalid, however, was precisely what Fulbert laid claim to being during his first meal at our table. He assured us almost before it began that he had "always lived frugally," that he had no "needs," and that he had "accustomed himself to poverty." A few moments later he took us even further into his confidence. He was suffering from "an insidious and incurable illness," though fortunately a noninfectious one (presumably he did not wish to alarm us). He already had "one foot in the grave," he admitted with simplicity. However, he still managed to eat enough for four, and to talk nonstop in that beautiful baritone voice of his, so vibrant with vitality. From time to time, moreover, between mouthfuls, he found time to cast a few little glances at the young lady on his left. And his interest appeared to redouble when he learned that she was dumb.

Meanwhile, I was beginning to ask myself several little questions about Fulbert. According to what he had told us about his life before the day it happened—and on the surface at least he seemed to be very free with such information, even though it was perhaps all a little vague—he had traveled here and there over the whole of central and

southwestern France, staying sometimes with Monsieur
So and So, the parish priest of X, sometimes with a
Madame Someone Else, sometimes with the Good Fathers
at Z, and always at his various hosts' express invitation.
When Zero Day caught up with him, he had just spent a
week with the good curé of La Roque, who had rendered
his soul to God before his visitor's eyes.

So, does our friend Fulbert have no parish then, or
any home of his own? And what did he live on?

Any references he had made to such matters himself
were concerned solely with charitable ladies who provided
for his "needs" (the needs which of course he didn't
have) and constantly showered him with presents while
vying with one another for his company. There, I felt,
a certain coquetry was apparent, and the handsome Fulbert seemed rather too conscious of his charms.

His dark gray suit was somewhat worn, though very
clean now that it had been given a good dusting. Beneath it he wore a shirt whose collar—completely non-
clerical in cut—was threadbare, plus a dark gray knitted
tie. But above all, hanging on its black cord around his
neck, there was that superb pectoral cross, solid silver by
the look of it, which, it seemed to me, no ecclesiastic beneath the rank of bishop ought conceivably to be wearing.

"If you were brought up in Cahors, Fulbert," I said
(I had decided to keep my tone as familiar as possible,
despite his majestic airs), "you must have trained for the
priesthood at the seminary there?"

"Of course," he answered, the heavy eyelids drooping
over his shifty eyes.

"Ah, and when did you enter it, in what year?"

"The things you ask!" Fulbert said, eyes still covered,
but with a little good-natured chuckle. "It's so long ago
now! I am no longer a young man, you know," he added
coquettishly.

"Oh, come now, I'm sure you can remember. After
all, for a priest, the year he entered his seminary must have
meant something!"

"Indeed," Fulbert said in his beautiful deep voice, "it is
a milestone."

And when I did not speak, maneuvered with his back

250

to the wall by my silence, he said, "Let me see. . . . It must have been in fifty-six . . . Yes," he confirmed after a further mental effort, "in fifty-six."

"Ah, I thought it must be about then," I said immediately with a delighted air. "Then you entered the Cahors seminary at the same time as my friend Serrurier."

"Ah . . . But you know there were a great many of us, I'm afraid," Fulbert said with a little smile. "It was a large college. I didn't know everyone."

"But everyone in your year, surely," I said. "And besides, a fellow like Serrurier, you could scarcely not notice him. Six foot four and flaming red hair."

"Oh, of course, yes, now you describe him." Fulbert said.

He had seemed to be speaking rather unwillingly, and was clearly relieved when I asked him to tell us about La Roque.

"After the bomb," he said sadly, "we were left in a state of most grievous affliction."

I noted that "grievous affliction" in passing. I had rarely heard the phrase other than in the mouths of priests, or of those who were aping them. With them it was almost a professional term. And despite its disagreeable meaning, it always seemed to give them a kind of satisfaction. I have been told that the younger generation of priests didn't use it. In which case, good for them. It is a phrase that revolts me because of the complacency behind it. Affliction—especially that of others—is not after all something to sip at like a connoisseur or to be worn as some kind of spiritual ornament.

Fulbert, however, had obviously reveled in this "grievous affliction." It had consisted largely in the necessity for the survivors of burying what still remained of the dead. We too had been through all that, but we never talked about it.

Since he was obviously not going to spare us the slightest horrific detail, in order to change the subject I asked how the people of La Roque were managing to live.

"Well and badly," he said, shaking his head and looking around the table with his beautiful melancholy eyes. "Well from the spiritual point of view, not so well from the material point of view. From the spiritual point of view," he went on, half closing his eyes as he popped a large piece of ham into his mouth, "I am bound to say that I am extremely satisfied with my flock. Their attendance at divine service is quite remarkably good."

Reading a certain astonishment on the faces of Meyssonnier and myself(because the La Roque council had been wholly dominated by Socialists and Communists), he went on, "It may surprise you perhaps, but in La Roque everyone attends Mass and everyone takes communion."

"And to what do you attribute this?" Meyssonnier asked with a frown, very put out.

Since he was sitting on my left, I turned my head to look at him. I was struck by the severity of that long profile. He was clearly utterly dismayed at what he had just heard. Although all his hopes had gone up in smoke the day it happened, Meyssonnier still thought of the world in terms of councils to be conquered by the united forces of the left. I gave him a little kick under the table. There is a time for being honest and a time for being something less than honest. My reservations with regard to Fulbert were growing stronger every minute. I had no doubt that the hold he claimed to have over the survivors at La Roque was very real, and I found it disturbing.

"After the bomb," Fulbert said in that beautiful deep voice that seemed to take such pleasure in its own mellifluousness, "the people turned their eyes in upon themselves and examined their consciences. Their physical, and above all their moral suffering had been so great that they began to ask themselves if perhaps a curse had not been laid upon them to punish them for their errors, their sins, their indifference toward God, their neglect of their duties —and in particular their religious duties. And also it must be said that all our lives have now become so essentially precarious that to turn to the Lord and ask for His protection is a natural and instinctive reaction."

Listening to this little speech, I suspected Fulbert of having done everything in his power to intensify this sense of guilt on his parishioners' part, since it was precisely the grist he needed for his particular mill. I could sense Thomas growing restless on my right. I was afraid he might explode, so I dealt him a warning kick under the table too. On one point I was determined: no violent confrontation with Fulbert on the religious question. Especially since, with the help of those velvety eyes—despite their shiftiness—that noble ascetic face, and that dark brown voice, the voice of a man with "one foot in the grave" (albeit firmly clinging to life on earth with every toenail of the other), it had taken Fulbert rather less than two hours to win the hearts of all three women and also produce quite an impression on Jacquet, Peyssou, and even Colin.

After the meal, Fulbert joined us around the fire, and without any prompting he returned to the subject of the material difficulties of the survivors in La Roque.

At first they had viewed the future with optimism, since the big grocery and cooked-meat store next to Colin's little workshop had not been touched by the fire that ravaged the lower town. But it soon became clear that when these stocks were used up, which they must be one day, the townspeople would not be able to replace them, since all the surrounding farms had been destroyed, together with all their livestock. In the château, whose owners had been in Paris and were therefore presumed dead, there remained only a few pigs, a bull, and five saddle horses, plus hay and grain to feed them.

At Courcejac, a tiny hamlet between La Roque and Malevil that had also been spared, six people had survived but only one cow, unfortunately, and that one was suckling a calf. The loss of the Courcejac cows was particularly unfortunate because there were two small babies in La Roque, plus a young orphan girl about thirteen years old, in poor health and in need of a special diet. Until now it had been possible to provide for their requirements from the stock of condensed milk in the grocery store, but even that was now almost exhausted.

Fulbert left his speech without a conclusion. We all exchanged looks. And since no one else seemed prepared to speak up, I put a number of questions to our guest. In this way I learned that the people of La Roque had suspected from the first that there might be survivors at Malevil, simply because it was so well protected, like

Courcejac and La Roque itself, by its cliff. And they had been confirmed in this suspicion about a month before when they thought they heard our bell ringing one morning. I also learned that they had at their disposal, for purposes of defense, ten or so shotguns, "a large stock of ammunition," and a number of rifles.

I pricked up my ears when Fulbert mentioned the five horses again but I refrained from inquiries. The fact was, I knew everything I needed to know about them already. Because it was I who had sold them to the Lormiaux in the first place. The Lormiaux were wealthy industrialists from Paris who had paid through the nose for a historic but very dilapidated château, spent staggering sums on restoring it, and then only used it for one month out of every twelve. During that month, however, they were determined to live up to their feudal castle, which entailed, among other things, riding a lot. None of them rode well, but they nevertheless insisted that they must have three Anglo-Arabs, one each, no less, despite all my efforts— my very creditable efforts, I felt—to sell them three somewhat less prestigious mounts. But there it was, in those days "before," I couldn't stop making money out of our invading snobs even when I tried to. And apart from the three Anglo-Arab geldings, the Lormiaux had also bought two white mares from me. But more of those later.

I noticed that despite his great fondness for the sound of his own voice, Fulbert was answering my questions very briefly. I concluded from this that his description of the material conditions of life in La Roque had been intended to lead up to a conclusion, but that despite his considerable aplomb he had either not yet dared to voice it, or else failed to find quite the right words. I fell silent, eyes on the fire.

After a moment Fulbert gave a little cough. This did not express embarrassment, but rather the fact it was only with some pain and cost to himself, having one foot already in the next world, that he was able to return to this one and occupy himself with the affairs of men.

"I am bound to say," he began, "that I am very much concerned as to the fate in store for the two babies and our little orphan. The situation is most grievous, and one from which I can see no way out. Without milk, I simply do not see how we can rear them."

Once again he paused and allowed the ensuing silence to make its effect. All eyes were on him, and no one wanted to speak.

"I know, of course," Fulbert went on in his reverberant voice, "that what I am about to ask you will perhaps seem monstrous, but after all, the circumstances are exceptional, since God's gifts are at the moment unequally distributed, and in order to live, to survive even, we must all remind ourselves, I think, that we are brothers, and that we must all help one another as best we can."

I had listened attentively. Taken in itself, all that he said was quite true. But coming from him it sounded false. I had the feeling that this man, so ready to play upon human emotions, in fact felt none himself.

"It is in the name of our poor little babies at La Roque," he went on, "that I make this request. I have observed that you possess a number of cows. We should be most deeply grateful if you could possibly let us have one of them."

Dead silence.

"Let you have?" I queried. "You did say 'let us have'? May I assume that you are envisaging some form of exchange?"

"As a matter of fact, no," Fulbert replied with a lofty air. "I had not envisaged the affair as a commercial transaction. I had conceived of it more as a charitable act, or rather as a duty, a bounden duty, I might say, to help those in mortal danger."

So we had been warned. If we refused, then as far as Fulbert was concerned we were men without hearts and without morals.

"Ah, so when you asked whether we would let you have a cow," I said, "you meant would we give you one?"

Fulbert bowed his head in assent, and Thomas excepted, we all stared at one another in stupefaction. Asking peasants to *give* them a cow! That was townsfolk for you!

"Would it not be simpler," I said in a soft voice (though still by no means as suave as Fulbert's all the same), "if we were to take in the two babies and the orphan and look after them here?"

Miette was sitting between Fulbert and myself, so when I turned toward Fulbert to put this question to him I also had a view of her gentle face, and I saw at once that the idea of having a nursery at Malevil filled her with delight. In a silent aside from the discussion, I gave her a smile. She gazed at me for a full second with those beautiful childlike eyes of hers, transparent and unfathomable, then suddenly she returned my smile. Returned it a hundredfold, I might almost say, as though she had gathered together all the affection there was inside her in order to offer it to me in that one sudden smile.

"That would be extremely possible in the case of the orphan," Fulbert said, "because she does in fact present us with a grave problem. She is thirteen years old, but so thin and retarded physically that she looks no more than ten. She is subject to asthma attacks, and as if that weren't enough, she has some form of character disorder. It is sad to have to admit it, but it is proving difficult for me to find anyone in La Roque to look after her."

His noble ascetic's face was plunged for a brief instant into deep melancholy as he meditated on the selfishness of mankind, and I could tell that we were not exempted from that meditation. However, he had not lost the thread of his reply, because he eventually went on with a sigh: "As for the babies, it is unfortunately impossible to board them out with you. Their mothers are unwilling to part with them."

Since he could not have known in advance that we did in fact possess any cows, or that we would offer to take the babies in if we had, he could hardly have already put such a question to their mothers. I suspected, consequently, that he was lying, and that it wasn't just the babies in La Roque who would be glad of a little milk.

I decided to push him a little further. "In that case, we would be prepared to take the mothers in as well, with their babies."

He shook his head. "That really isn't possible. They both have husbands, and other children. One can't just rip families apart like that." And he rejected my suggestion forcibly as he spoke with a slicing gesture of his right hand. Then he waited. He had stalked us ruthlessly into a very nasty dilemma: either we gave him a cow or the babies died. He could afford to wait.

The silence dragged on.

"Miette," I said, "would you mind letting Fulbert have your room for tonight?"

"Oh, really, no," Fulbert protested halfheartedly. "I have no wish to disturb anyone. A bale of hay in the barn will suffice for my needs."

I courteously brushed this evangelical project aside. "After your long journey you need a good night's sleep," I said as I rose to my feet. "And while you are taking your well-earned rest, we will debate your request. You shall have our answer in the morning."

He rose likewise at that, drew himself up to his full height, and gazed at us with solemn, slightly inquisitorial eyes. I met his gaze with the utmost calm, then after a moment, taking my time, I turned my head away. "Miette," I said, "you can sleep with La Falvine tonight."

She nodded her assent. Fulbert had given up his attempt to hypnotize me. He surveyed his flock with a beneficent paternal eye, then he spread his hands out on either side of him, palms toward them. "At what hour," he asked, "do you wish me to say Mass tomorrow morning?"

An exchange of inquiring looks. La Menou eventually suggested nine o'clock. Everyone agreed except Thomas and Meyssonnier, who studiously took no part in the discussion at all.

"Nine o'clock," Fulbert said majestically. "Very well, let us say nine o'clock then. From half past seven until nine I shall be in my room [I was interested to note that "my" room] to hear the confessions of all those intending to take communion."

Beautifully done. He had taken us all into his charge, body and soul. Now he could depart and sleep in peace.

"Miette," I said, "show Fulbert up to his room. And change the sheets for him."

Fulbert ceremoniously bade us his good nights, naming us all by our names, one by one, in his beautiful baritone voice. Then he followed Miette as she led the way briskly toward the door of the great hall. Probably the one most mortified to watch her disappearing like that was little Colin, whose turn it was to be Miette's guest that evening* and who would now have to forgo that pleasure for want of available premises. He followed her with his eyes, slightly jealous of Fulbert into the bargain. And I too suddenly wondered, remembering certain glances during the meal, whether I had been wise in assigning Miette to be our guest's guide. I glanced at my watch: twenty past ten. I made a note to look at it again when Miette reappeared.

As the door closed, an expression of relief appeared on everyone's face. The pressure Fulbert had been putting on us had reached an almost intolerable intensity. And now that he was gone we felt a sense of liberation. Though not of complete liberation, because though Fulbert himself had gone he had left his demands behind him.

It was not just relief I could read on the others' faces, however. There was also a great deal of uncertainty, distress, and a variety of other rather mixed emotions. I congratulated myself on having prevented Meyssonnier and Thomas from starting a religious affray, because that would certainly have split Malevil right down the middle and added even further to the general confusion.

I looked at them all in turn. A Gorgon or Medusa, inscrutable, eyes lowered, lips firmly pressed together, La Menou sat knitting on her hearth seat. Momo, with nothing to hold his interest now that Miette had left the room, had begun pushing at a half-burned log with his foot. Whereupon his mother demanded in a savage whisper, though without raising her eyes, whether he wanted her foot in his bottom or whether he was going to stop trying to burn off the toes of his boots.

La Falvine was huffing and puffing amid her drapes and folds of fat, great belly flopping onto her crossed knees, sagging breasts resting on the belly, and dewlaps drooping onto the breasts. Whoever heard of such a thing, who-

---

* It will be noticed how Emmanuel here acquaints the reader, though only by implication and as it were in passing, with Miette's polyandrous activities. [Note added by Thomas.]

ever would have believed it possible, her sighs and moans were clearly saying.

Jacquet, our prisoner, whom Colin had jokingly begun to refer to as the "serf," and who in less than a month had managed to trap me into what was almost a father-son relationship—simply by dint of following me around wherever I went and by watching my every movement with those innocent golden brown doglike eyes—Jacquet, needless to say, was gazing calmly at me, and his thoughts were as transparent as they were clearly untroubled: If Emmanuel gives the priest the cow, he will be right to do so. If he doesn't, on the other hand, then he will certainly not be wrong.

Peyssou's honest rugged round face, with its great nose jutting out of it like a knife jammed into a potato, was a pitiful sight to see, so furrowed was it with agonized indecision. I could see him struggling to reconcile his budding veneration for Fulbert with the scandalous nature of the man's demands.

And Colin was no less perturbed, though he showed it less plainly. In addition, he was very edgy and frustrated for the reasons mentioned earlier, as I could tell from his frequent anxious glances toward the door.

In Thomas's eyes, however, there was not the slightest flicker of doubt. Fulbert was Infamy in person. And he held that opinion, I am absolutely positive, without having even the vaguest idea of the sacrilege that Fulbert had just committed in the rest of our eyes—he had dared to lay hands on the Cow. And the Cow, after God (perhaps even before God, come to that), was the most sacred value in our lives. Because there was no conceivable equivalence between a cow and her market value. If we demanded money when a cow changed hands, that was simply a way of giving concrete form, in cash, to the quasi-religious respect we felt for her.

Meyssonnier, unlike any of the others, was forcefully aware of a double infamy in Fulbert's conduct: his theoretical infamy, as it were, as a representative of "religion, the opium of the people," and his infamy in practice, as a person who had just committed the unbelievably cynical act of demanding the gratuitous surrender of a cow. I

259

looked at him. How little he had changed since we first went to school together! Still that same thin knife blade of a face, the narrow forehead, the black brush of hair, the gray close-set eyes that started to blink at the least emotional stress. And now, because he had been unable to visit the barber in La Roque since the day it happened, his hair, from sheer force of habit, had continued to grow straight upward toward the sky, and his long face had grown even longer.

The door opened. It was Miette. I glanced at my watch: ten twenty-five. Five minutes. Physically impossible in that time, even overestimating (or underestimating) Fulbert's powers. As Miette advanced toward us along the great hall, her torso swaying without any conscious attempt at provocation, she radiated a wave of warmth that spread before her and enveloped us all. Thank you, Miette. I could see from Colin's face, from the glimmer of his returning smile, that he was greatly relieved. If our great bowman was not to enjoy the presence of Miette beside him that night, at least no one else had sneaked in and filched that privilege from him.

Our numbers were now complete, and this was the very first time that we had ever held a plenary assembly of this sort, with the three women, Momo, and the "serf." We were becoming a democracy. I would have to point that out to Thomas later.

La Menou bent down to liven up the fire; because as soon as our meal was over we always thriftily extinguished the monumental old oil lamp, and from then until bedtime the fire was our sole source of light. Without poker or tongs, simply by a skillful rearrangement of the logs, La Menou succeeded in producing a bright flicker of flame.

And as though this was the very signal he had been waiting for to blaze up himself, Meyssonnier burst out: "When I saw him riding in, the *cura*," he said, mixing French and patois together in his fury, "I knew in my bones he hadn't come here just to pass the time of day. But even so, I could never have believed this. A thing like this, I just don't know," he said with profound indignation. And as if no other expression could quite convey the enormity of what had occurred, he repeated it several times: "I just don't know," banging his knee with the palm of his hand as he said it.

Then, quite beside himself, he rushed on: "There he was, sitting calm as you please with his arse on one of our chairs, like God the Father in person, and Give me a cow he says, just like that. Hand me a match to light my pipe, he might have been saying! The cow you've raised and fed and watered twice a day for years, yes, and in the winter when the tap is frozen, and you humping the water out bucket by bucket from the kitchen, and the vet with his bills, the money for the injections, the medicines for the scour, plus the worry of the straw and the hay, wondering if there'll be enough with the winter not ending, and how are you going to pay for more? Not to mention the terrible worry of the calving. And then what?" He rushed on in fury: "A fellow ambles in, gabbles you an Our Father or two, and hoop-la! goodbye, and thank you for the cow! Are we back in the Middle Ages or what? Is that what it's come to? The clergy knocking on the door and 'Pay your tithes or else!'? Why not tallage as well, and forced labor, and all the rest of it while we're at it?"

This speech, impious though it was, made its effect, even on the pious members of our assembly. The folk memory of what it was like to have overlords was still a living thing in these parts, and even those who did attend Mass were always mistrustful of their priest's powers. However, I said nothing. I waited. I had no wish to be outvoted a second time.

"All the same, there are the babies," Colin said.

"But that's just it," Thomas put in. "Why shouldn't they be brought over to Malevil? I find it difficult to believe that their mothers wouldn't agree to part with them for a while, if it means their survival."

Not bad, Thomas. Sober, logical, but perhaps just a little too abstract to carry the right weight.

"But that's what Fulbert told us," Peyssou pointed out, incapable of mistrust as always.

Meyssonnier shrugged, and said virulently, "Fulbert told us anything that suited him!"

There, it seemed to me, he was going a little too far

261

for his audience. Because he had accused Fulbert, however indirectly, of being a liar, and apart from Thomas and myself no one was as yet prepared to accept such a judgment. The result was a long silence. Which I did nothing to break.

"Well, well," La Menou said at last, laying her knitting on her lap and smoothing it with the flat of one hand to stop it rolling up on itself, "there's no saying otherwise, but the world is in a sorry state just now. Twenty of them over there in La Roque, and for all twenty no stock but a bull and their five horses, which a sight of good that's going to do them, I'm sure."

"No one is stopping you from giving them your cow, in that case," Meyssonnier said derisively.

I didn't like the sound of that. A tug of the reins needed. Mine and thine seemed to me very dangerous notions just now. I intervened. "I don't agree with expressions of that sort. There is no Menou's cow here, or any L'Étang cows, or any Emmanuel's horses. There is just the livestock here in Malevil, and the Malevil stock belongs to Malevil, which means to all of us. If anyone thinks differently, then he has only to take back his animal or animals and go elsewhere."

I had spoken with considerable vehemence, and my words were followed by a slightly uncomfortable silence.

"And what exactly were you leading up to with that, Emmanuel?" little Colin asked after a moment.

"To the fact that if we are to part with an animal, then it's up to all of us to decide yes or no."

The distinction between "part with" and "give" had escaped no one.

"You have to put yourself in their place though," La Falvine said. We all looked at her in amazement, because during the month she'd been with us, La Menou had given her such a thorough pecking over that nowadays she hesitated to open her mouth at all. But now, encouraged by our silent attention, she gave a deep sigh in order to drag up sufficient breath through all the folds and sags obstructing it, then went on: "Well, if there are three cows for the ten of us here at Malevil and none at all for the

262

twenty over at La Roque, then one day there are going to be envious looks, isn't it so?"

"There's nothing different in all that from what I said just now," La Menou informed her in a cutting voice intended to put her in her place.

Whereupon, having had quite enough of her petty tyranny, I put La Menou in hers: "Well said, Falvine!"

The dewlaps shook, her whole body expanded, and gazing around the circle, she smiled with pleasure.

"We've already had one of our horses stolen," Peyssou said. "No offense meant to anyone, of course," he added as he noticed poor Jacquet shrinking down into his chair. "So why couldn't someone steal one of our cows while it's our grazing?"

"One?" I said. "Why not all three? They have five horses at La Roque, and five men with good mounts could bring that one off with ease. They appear out of nowhere, they knock out our lookouts, and goodbye cows!" I was pleased at being able to slip the horses in there, and for a good reason.

"We can protect ourselves," Colin said. "We have weapons."

I looked at him. "So have they. And more than us. We have four guns. At La Roque they have ten. Plus, and I quote Fulbert, 'a large stock of ammunition.' We can't say the same."

Silence. We were all thinking with dread of what a war between La Roque and us would mean.

"I can't believe such things of the folk at La Roque," La Menou said with a shake of her head. "They were all born in these parts. They are good honest folk."

I indicated the three newcomers. "Good honest folk? And what about them, aren't they good honest folk? Yet look what happened." And I added in patois, "One rotten apple will spoil a whole basket."

"Ah, that's true, that's very true," La Falvine said, particularly delighted at being able to chime in on my side, because it enabled her to contradict La Menou, without risk, at the same time. But La Menou decided to come around to my opinion too. So did Colin, so did Peyssou.

"Yes, you're quite right, Emmanuel," Meyssonnier said in his turn. And raising his eyes to heaven, finger pointed in the direction of the keep so that everyone should take his meaning, he repeated, still in patois, "One rotten apple will spoil a whole basket."

I saw Thomas lean over, ask Meyssonnier for a translation of the proverb, then nod approvingly. Ah, the power those old saws still have! One good adage and suddenly we were unanimous. Fulbertists and anti-Fulbertists were all agreed. It was only on the identity of the rotten apple that we differed slightly. In the minds of some it was clear beyond a doubt, in those of the others it was still unspecific.

Having had my success, I lapsed into silence. The conversation began to turn in circles. The debate was running down, and I let it run down. In the others' voices, in their postures, in their general edginess, I could sense fatigue creeping in. But if they were tired, so much the better. I would wait.

And I didn't have to wait long, because after one particularly long pause Colin said, "Well, and you, Emmanuel, what do you think?"

"Oh, me," I said. "I'll go along with the majority."

They stared at me, disconcerted by this sudden modesty. All except Thomas, in whose eyes I discerned a look of irony. But he wasn't going to say anything out loud. He was making progress, our Thomas. He had learned caution.

I still said nothing. And as I intended, they insisted.

"All the same, Emmanuel," Peyssou said, "you must have your little notion about it?"

"Ah, well, perhaps I do," I said. "And my first little notion is that someone is trying to put one over on us with those little babies. [My "someone," naturally, being the rotten apple, but still unspecified.] Because imagine, Menou [and here I slipped into patois], when Momo was still a little baby. If you had no milk for him, not a drop, well, tell me, would you stop him going to people who had some, who'd feed him when he cried? And would you have the gall to say to them, 'It's not the milk for my Momo I want from you, just give me your cow!'?"

I had said absolutely nothing different from what Thomas had said a little earlier. But I had said it in wholly concrete terms. The same flowers, but a better arrangement. And I'd hit my bull's-eye. I could read that on their faces.

"Right," I said after a moment, "so when we go over and visit them, in La Roque, we'll get to the bottom of that. We'll ask the mothers just how much truth there is in it. But even so, the fact remains, as you've said, that we have three cows while the La Roque folk haven't even one for twenty of them. And given that fact, just imagine how easy it might be for someone to stir them up against us [still that vague "someone"] and put ideas into their heads. And when there are so many more of them than us, when they're so much better armed, make no mistake, those ideas are bound to be very nasty ones."

Silence.

"Yes. Yes," Peyssou said slowly, more at sea than ever. "So you think then, Emmanuel, that we ought to give them the cow?"

I exploded with indignation. "*Give* it to them! Ah, no! Never! Whatever else we do we mustn't give it to them. We mustn't be put in the position, as Meyssonnier said, of paying tithes! As if it were their due! A tax! As if it were the right of townspeople to eat for nothing at the expense of the people in the country! That would be all we need! How could they ever respect us again, those La Roque folk, if they knew we'd been boobies enough to give them a cow!"

All eyes flashed with shared indignation. Absolute unanimity among Fulbertists and anti-Fulbertists alike. Thousands of generations of peasants were there behind me, beside me, urging me on. I felt the ground solid beneath my feet, and I pressed on.

"In my opinion, we must make them pay for their cow. And pay a good price too! Because we weren't the ones who wanted to take her to market. They're the ones who want to buy."

I paused and gave them a shameless wink, as much as to say, I'm not a horse dealer and the nephew of a horse dealer for nothing. Then speaking slowly and distinctly, I said, "In exchange for our cow, we shall ask them for two horses, three guns, and five hundred cartridges."

I paused again, to stress the exorbitant nature of my demands. Silence, exchange of inquiring looks. My success —as I had expected—was considerably less than total.

"The guns, those I understand," Colin said. "They have ten, so we take three and leave them with seven. Which means that with the four we already have, we then have seven too. We'd be on an equal footing. And the cartridges too, that's a good idea, because we don't have all that many left."

Silence. I looked around. Although no one was willing to come out and say it, it was the first part of the bargain they couldn't understand. Suddenly I was feeling rather tired, but I pulled myself together and went on. "I know what you're thinking: Why the horses? We already have enough of those now: Malabar, Amarante, Bel Amour, not to mention Malice. Two more horses is two more animals to feed, you may be thinking, and we'll not be getting much milk out of them either, those horses. And you'd be right. But. Just stop and take a look at our real situation on the horse front, here at Malevil. Malice, still too young to be of any use. And Bel Amour too, idle while she's suckling Malice. So that leaves us with just two horses for both riding and working: Malabar and Amarante. And I say that two saddle horses among six able-bodied men is just not enough. Because there's one thing you've all got to get through your heads [I leaned forward and spoke as emphatically as I could], every one of you here has to learn to ride one of these days. And I mean everyone! Why? I'll tell you. Because 'before the day it happened,' here in the country, the people who always got the rough end of the stick, men or women, the nobodies, were those who didn't drive a car. And now, the nobodies are going to be all those who don't ride, who don't have a horse. In peace and war both. Because if you're fighting, if you want to make a lightning attack, or even if you want to get away quickly when things go against you, there is no other way now but the horse. The horse replaces everything: motorbike, automobile, tractor, even the machine

266

gun. As of now, without a horse you are nothing. Peasant cattle to be exploited, nothing else."

I wasn't sure whether I'd convinced La Menou and La Falvine, but the men yes, beyond a doubt. It wasn't the appeal to their warlike instincts that had tipped the scales, it was the status argument. The definition of a nobody as a man without a horse. Just as "before," the nobody was by definition the farmer without a tractor. They were all quite crazy around here when it came to tractors. Even the man with no more than twenty acres had to have his tractor, sometimes even two! People would rush into debt to buy the latest umpteen-horsepower monster, then keep the old one "as a standby." Like So and So up the lane! Can't let him get away with that! All for the pitiful twenty acres they were prepared to farm, and the rest just useless woods!

Never mind, even men's follies have their uses. At least this one helped me pull the trick of switching the tractor's glamour and prestige back to the horse.

We voted. Even the women were in favor. I heaved a tired sigh of relief, then got to my feet. Everyone else followed suit, and under cover of the ensuing clatter and chatter I went over to Meyssonnier and Thomas in order to tell them in a low voice that I wanted to speak to them both later up in my room. They agreed.

I asked for silence again and said, "I shall be hearing Mass tomorrow and taking communion—that is if Fulbert does not object, since I don't intend to go to confession."

This announcement caused general amazement. I knew it had aroused anger in some (but they restrained it, knowing that they would soon be talking to me in private) and joy in the others. Especially in La Menou, and for a very particular reason. She had been at daggers drawn with our priest in Malejac, before the day it happened, because he had stuck rigidly to the letter of the law—no confession, no sacred wafer—and in consequence would never let Momo take communion. And now, if Fulbert gave way to me on this point, there was a hope in her heart that her son would be able to follow me through the breach I had made.

I went on: "But those who do confess would do well

to be very cautious if anyone [no one in particular, of course] asks them indiscreet questions about Malevil."

Silence.

"What sort of questions?" Jacquet burst out suddenly, aware of how weak and easily influenced he was and already afraid he was bound to say too much.

"Well, questions about how well armed we are, for instance. Or about our stocks of wine or grain or ham, and so on."

"But what shall I say if he asks me questions like that?" Jacquet asked, desperate to do the right thing.

"Just say, 'Oh, I wouldn't know about that. You must ask Emmanuel.' "

"Now listen to me, lad," big Peyssou said, laying a bear-like arm around Jacquet's neck, his great face split in a broad grin. (That knock on the head seemed to have turned them into the best of friends.) "There's nothing to it. To be quite sure you don't make any mistakes, you just answer like that to everything. For example: Fulbert asks you, 'My son, have you committed the sin of the flesh?' And you answer, 'Oh, I wouldn't know about that. You must ask Emmanuel.' "

Everyone laughed. With Peyssou, because he was so pleased with his joke, and with Jacquet too, as well as at him. Our poor serf reeled under the friendly thumps and guffaws. He was in his seventh heaven. L'Étang had never been like this.

The interview with Thomas and Meyssonnier up in my room shortly afterward was a little strained. They both immediately sailed into me for having played Fulbert's game (and even, ultimate horror, having said I would take communion) instead of throwing him out on his neck for the mountebank he was. I explained my position. I was afraid of an armed conflict with La Roque, that was the heart of the matter. And I didn't want to give Fulbert even the slightest excuse—either material or religious—to foment one. That was why I had suggested surrendering the cow on terms that would weaken his firepower. And also why I was prepared to go along with the religious beliefs of the Malevil majority.

"It's a compromise, in fact," I told them. "And you of

all people ought to be able to understand that, Meysson-nier. Your party was not so averse to them in its day." Meyssonnier blinked. "As for Fulbert, I'm as near certain as it's possible to be that he's no priest. My redheaded friend Serrurier at the seminary was a total fabrication, and yet Fulbert remembered him! In short, he's an impostor, an adventurer, a man totally without scruples. And all the more dangerous on that account. If you were wise, you and Thomas, you would attend his Mass tomorrow too. After all, it's not really a Mass, since Fulbert isn't a priest, and it won't be a real communion, because if he's not a priest there won't have been a real consecration."

I could scarcely go any further than that, I felt, in my attempt to bring them around, and I was secretly rather enjoying the thought of the irony that my success would imply: persuading them to attend a Mass by convincing them that it in fact wasn't a Mass.

Just at that moment we heard someone scratching at the door. Not knocking. Scratching. I froze, looked at my two guests, then at my watch. One in the morning. In the silence we heard the scratching again. I took my rifle from the gun rack Meyssonnier had built on the wall opposite the foot of my bed, gestured to Meyssonnier and Thomas to arm themselves likewise, lifted the latch, and pulled the door very slightly ajar. It was Miette.

After the briefest of pauses in order to smile at Thomas, whom she was expecting to see there, and then Meyssonnier, whose presence surprised her, she immediately began using her hands, her lips, her eyes, her eyebrows, her torso, her legs, and even her hair, in order to speak to me. It was a spontaneously devised method of communication all her own, having no connection with the formal sign language usually called "deaf-and-dumb," which she had never learned and I certainly wouldn't have understood. What she had to convey was pretty startling. When she had gone up with Fulbert to "his" room after the meal, he had asked her to come back and visit him when everyone was asleep (circular motion of pointed finger to indicate "everyone" then two hands palms together under her cheek for "sleeping"). She was certain he wanted her to make love to (the gesture here was indescribably crude). Having seen the light in my room (little finger of right hand raised, the other hand describing a halo around its tip to denote a flame), she had come up to ask if she should go to him.

"I have nothing to say against it," I said when she'd finished. "You are free to do as you wish, Miette. No one is going to put any pressure on you, either one way or the other."

All right then, I'll go, she mimed. Managing to convey, however, that it was purely out of politeness and reluctance to disappoint him, not out of any enthusiasm.

"Don't you like him then, Miette?"

Squint and praying hands (Fulbert), then right hand on heart, and finally the forefinger of the same hand shaken vigorously to and fro in front of her nose. After which she swiftly vanished, leaving us all standing there looking at the door she had just closed behind her.

"Oh, that fellow," Thomas said.

"You could have said something to stop her," Meyssonnier said, scowling and speaking through clenched teeth.

I shrugged. "By what right? You know the principle as well as I do. She must be left to do exactly as she pleases."

I looked at them. They were both furious, outraged, like cuckolded husbands. It was a paradoxical and perhaps even a slightly comic emotion, because after all we weren't jealous of one another. Probably because the sharing of Miette had been kept wholly inside the group, in full view of all, with everyone's knowledge. There was therefore no unfaithfulness involved, or even any moral laxity. In fact our arrangement had already acquired a wholly reassuring quasi-institutional character. Whereas in Fulbert's case, not only did he not belong to the group, he had also acted with the utmost underhandedness.

Thomas and Meyssonnier pointed out that if Miette had not been the honest person she was, we would never even have known about her "adultery." Not that they actually used that term, since they did have some sense of the ridiculous, after all, but the concept was not far from their minds. You only had to see the way they were boiling with rage.

"What a swine!" Meyssonnier said, and then, since it didn't satisfy him sufficiently in French, he said it in patois too.

And Thomas, emerging for once from his usual impassivity, enthusiastically agreed.

"But at all events," Meyssonnier said threateningly, "you can count on one thing. I shall be letting Colin and Peyssou know first thing tomorrow how Master Fulbert spent his night."

I exclaimed in alarm, "You won't tell them, surely!"

"And why not?" Meyssonnier said. "They have a right to know about it too, don't you think?"

It was true. They too had the right to know how they had been deceived. And Colin especially, since he had been doubly deceived.

"And even Jacquet. I shall tell him too," Meyssonnier added with clenched fists. "The serf has the same rights as all of us."

I gave ground a little, still hoping to restrain him. "All right then, tell Colin if you wish," I said, "but not Peyssou. Or at least wait till Fulbert's off the premises before you do. You know what Peyssou's like. He's quite likely to smash his teeth in."

"And he'd be quite right!" Thomas said, his own teeth tightly clenched.

For Miette, not a word or even, I was sure, a single thought of blame; on the contrary, a total certainty that the knavish Fulbert had foully abused the poor girl's sense of duty and hospitality. I was also sure that if I were to suggest rousing Colin, Peyssou, and Jacquet from their slumbers there and then, so that we could all go together and smash down Fulbert's door with a view to booting him out of the castle forthwith, donkey as well, then the proposal would be instantly acclaimed. Not wishing under any circumstances to take part in any such scene, I contented myself with imagining it briefly. And as I pictured those six cuckolded husbands hurling themselves into Miette's room and beating the living daylights out of their wife's lover, I couldn't help bursting into laughter.

"There's nothing to laugh about," Meyssonnier said sternly.

"No, but we really must get to bed now," I said. "What's done is done, you know."

This soothing truism failed to soothe him in the slightest, or soothe them, I should say, since though Thomas was doing less talking, he was raging inwardly just as much.

"What sickens me most," Meyssonnier said, "is the thought that he tried to take advantage of the poor girl's disability. He thought to himself, She's dumb. She can't tell anyone. . . . And how could I possibly attend that Mass of his tomorrow," he went on in a much louder voice, "sitting there and listening to him churning out all that imbecile rubbish about sins, knowing what I know now! But you're right," he added, noticing my impatient expression. "It's time I went off to bed."

And he left us, back bowed. I kept my face firmly expressionless as I undressed, so as to give Thomas no opportunity to talk. Personally I couldn't get worked up about it all. For one thing, Fulbert wasn't a priest. And anyway, why shouldn't a priest have sex if he felt like it? And as for him doing it on the sly, poor devil, that was his misfortune that he felt he had to.

I really bore Fulbert not the slightest grudge for having sneaked Miette away from us for a night. I fully intended to use the incident against him quite shamelessly the next day, but for quite other reasons: because I was quite certain that he was a man without an ounce of human kindness or justice in his heart, who wished Malevil no good, and in whose teeth I was determined to restore Malevil's unity. The unity in which this question of religion had so very nearly succeeded in producing a rift that evening.

The lamp out, I got into bed, though as I fully expected, not to sleep. Thomas couldn't drop off either. I could hear him turning this way and that on his sofa. He did make one attempt to open a conversation, but I fended it off with an irritable outburst. If I was to be denied sleep, at least let me have peace and quiet.

X

AFTER breakfast, while Fulbert was receiving the peni-
tents in "his" room, I set off toward the Maternity Ward
in order to saddle Malabar and continue his training.
Despite all my efforts, I was still a long way from having
transformed our great carthorse into a good mount. His
mouth was not very sensitive, he responded to the signals
of the aids only when he chose, and stopping him was not
easy. I was also hindered by the breadth of his back,
which obliged me to spread my thighs wider than I was
used to and consequently weakened my knee grip. And he
was so heavy, that Malabar, that when I was on him I felt
like a knight in the Middle Ages. All I needed was a suit
of armor. And I felt sure that that wouldn't bother him
either. Vast as he was, he was quite capable of carrying
two or three times my weight. He had incredible reserves
of strength, and when he galloped I always had the feeling
that we were charging. Moreover, though I was staggered
by the sheer width of that back I had no criticism to
make of its comfort. You felt really solid and safe up
there, and if it were a matter of making some long expedition where speed was not of the essence, then I would
certainly have recommended Malabar to anyone with a
sensitive behind.

I found Jacquet and Momo already there mucking out
the stalls, and just as I was about to start saddling Malabar
I noticed that Momo had once again given Bel Amour
twice as much straw as the other two horses. Not that the
others had been stinted; it was just that Bel Amour had
too much. I bawled Momo out and made him take half
the straw out again, making him feel ashamed of his

273

favoritism, because it was also a criminal waste. I promised him that if he did it again he'd get my boot in his bottom.

This threat was a purely routine measure. It had been inherited from my uncle, and like him I had never actually put it into practice. You might have expected that it would by now have become so abstract as to lose all its efficacy. But no, it still continued to produce a certain effect on Momo as representing the ultimate in parental displeasure. Because, although Momo was several years older than myself, he had accepted that in inheriting my uncle's material possessions I had also inherited Uncle Samuel's paternal powers over him.

While I was giving Momo his dressing-down I visited each of the stalls, as I did every morning, to check that the automatic water troughs were working properly. Another of our strokes of luck: if the water system at Malevil hadn't been gravity fed and we had to depend on an electric pump, the bomb would have deprived us of our water supply for good and all.

When I went into Amarante's stall she immediately began her usual morning flirtation, butting into my back with her head, pushing her damp nostrils against the back of my neck, and nibbling at one sleeve. If God had given her hands she would have tickled me. At the same time, out of the corner of one eye, she was watching the progress of a hen that had come pecking its way in through the door I had left ajar. Fortunately I too saw the hen just in time, and before Amarante could slaughter it with one deft blow of a hoof, I distracted her with a resounding slap on her hindquarters and quickly pushed the poor feathered imbecile out of the stall with my foot. I glanced in at Fulbert's big gray donkey, or rather at his water bucket, because he had been put in the only stall not fitted with a trough.

With my tour duly accomplished, I gathered up in my palm—or rather in the palm of my old glove, because I have a healthy respect for that great pointed beak—a few grains of barley. And immediately—How did he know that the moment had come? And where was he hiding the moment before?—our crow sailed down from nowhere and landed at my feet. After walking circumspectly all around

274

me in his favorite pose, imitating an ancient humpbacked miser with his hands clasped behind his back, he flew up onto my left shoulder and began pecking at the grain in my palm, without for an instant ceasing to stare sideways into my face with one glittering eye. His meal over, he still saw no reason to leave my shoulder, even when I went into the stall to saddle up Malabar. Malabar and not Amarante, you notice, because Craa had never been known to venture an inch inside Amarante's box. That too I found amazing. How did he know that my Amarante, so gentle with any human, was a killer when it came to birds?

As I was putting in Malabar's bit (while Craa strutted up and down his broad back), La Menou arrived to milk Noiraude and began lamenting from the next stall, without being able to see me, about the lack of help she received. I pointed out to her that La Falvine and Miette could scarcely do all last night's dishes in the kitchen and milk a cow in the Maternity Ward at the same time, and that in any case, where cows were concerned, always the same hand on the teat was a good rule. This observation was greeted by a short silence, then from La Menou's stall there began to emerge a long stream of indistinct but clearly uncomplimentary mutterings in which I could just make out the words "weakness," "big healthy girl," and "thighs," from which I was able to reconstitute the general tenor of her remarks.

I kept quiet, and La Menou moved on, in a louder voice now, to other subjects of complaint. Take for instance how La Falvine, at table in front of me, played at pecking at her plate like a hen. So how could I know that she stuffed her face when no one was looking. (I wondered how that could be possible, since La Menou kept the keys to everything.) And if she went on stuffing herself like that, a bag of lard with more fat than she could carry now, she'd never make old bones. Then a short parenthesis informing me that we would soon be running out of soap and sugar and that we had to ask for some when we took the cow over to La Roque. Then returning to her favorite subject—the imminent demise of La Falvine—La Menou set out to describe it to me in advance: a slow

275

and appalling suffocation of the life force brought on by her own gluttony.

I led Malabar out of his stall, having finished saddling him, and in order to bring La Menou's necrophiliac recital to an end remarked that as a matter of fact La Falvine was on her way over at that moment. Jacquet, in the next stall, had heard the whole conversation; but he wouldn't repeat it to La Falvine, I knew that. And there La Falvine was, in fact, chugging along toward me at top speed, partly in order to demonstrate her zeal for work, partly so that she could intercept me for a moment's gossip before I climbed onto the stallion. After an exchange of greetings, she launched into a brief lament, in which I joined, on the subject of the weather. Ever since the bomb, always this cold gray sky, not a drop of rain, not a gleam of sun. If things went on like this it would be the end of everything. Superfluous words, to say the least, since they were things scarcely ever far from all our thoughts—that absent sun, the rain that never came. It was an underlying dread we had been living with constantly ever since the day it happened.

At that point La Menou appeared and curtly ordered La Falvine to take over the milking. "I've done Noiraude," she told her as cuttingly as she could manage, "but not Princesse. And remember not to take any more than three or four quarts from her. There's Prince to think of. I'm going up to see Fulbert now." And she stalked scornfully off. I watched her as she trotted indomitably away toward the keep, that thin, oh so thin, little bag of bones, and I wondered what sins she could possibly have to confess, our Menou, apart from a few unkind digs at La Falvine.

La Falvine, still huffing and puffing from her recent turn of speed, followed my eyes and said, "La Menou—when you think about it, there's not much of her. Eighty-five pounds perhaps, and there I'm on the generous side. You might say she doesn't have a body almost. Take now, just for instance. If she fell ill and the doctor [What doctor?] put her on a diet, what would she live on? And you have to remember she's not getting younger. Why she's older than me by six years, and six years at our age, they count, they count. I don't like to say it, Emmanuel, but even in the time I've been here I think she's sunk a little. You take certain moments, she's just not there with you, La Menou. You mark what I say now, it's the head that will go first with her. Take for instance the other day. There I was just chatting to her, and suddenly I realized she just wasn't there. I could tell it from the way she hadn't even answered me."

During this speech, on the pretext of needing to walk Malabar around the enclosure a little, to relax him before his lesson, I drew La Falvine away from the Maternity Ward, because Momo, unlike Jacquet, did repeat things. In fact it was his favorite pastime. He would repeat gossip with embellishments, or rather with exaggerations, while his glittering dark eyes watched for the expression of displeasure to appear on his hearer's face.

"It won't be the head that goes first with me at least." I listened to La Falvine and grunted now and then to let her know I was listening. It wasn't the first time that each of our housekeepers had announced the other's approaching end to me. At first it had amused me. But now I had to admit it saddened me. It seemed to me that man must be a strange animal to desire his fellow being's death so easily.

As I walked up from the gate tower toward the inner enclosure, still leading Malabar, and with La Falvine panting along on my left, determined to keep up with me, I saw Miette crossing the drawbridge, then cutting across in my direction. Those forty yards we had to cross before we met in the middle provided me with a delightful few moments. She was dressed in a faded blue blouse, patched and crumpled, but clean and pleasantly filled out, and beneath it a short skirt of blue woolen material, very much patched likewise, which stopped just above the knee to reveal her bare legs above the black rubber boots. Legs and arms alike were bare, strong, and red. Miette clearly didn't feel the cold, because I was wearing a turtleneck sweater and a pair of old but thick riding breeches, and I was far from feeling warm. Her luxuriant hair, so similar to her grandmother's except for its raven blackness, was tumbling in gleaming waves over her shoulders, and her gentle eyes, shining with animal innocence, gazed at me with affection as she came up to me and kissed me on both cheeks, pressing the whole length of her body against mine, not for her own pleasure but solely for mine. I was grateful to her for this act of generosity, because I knew perfectly well, like all the rest of us, that Miette was a stranger to such sensual pleasures. I was sure that if I could have looked into that simple heart of hers I would have found a certain astonishment there, an uncomprehending amazement at this mania that men have for fingering and squeezing the bodies of her sex.

La Falvine made herself scarce with ponderous discreetness, and it was Malabar's turn to receive his share of caresses from Miette's hands and lips. I noted in passing, not without envy, that she kissed him on the mouth, a thing she never did with men. Then having distributed her ration of affection, she turned, planted herself in front of me, and the miming began. She informed me to begin with that the (squint and praying hands) and she (thumb pointing to heart) had, as she had expected (forefinger to forehead), made love (gesture better left undescribed). She was indignant (grimace of disgust), especially considering that he was a (praying hands), but what made her even more indignant (grimace of utter revulsion) was that the (squint and praying hands) had suggested to her (both palms held out like a tray) that she go with him (legs walking on spot, right hand clasping an imaginary hand) to La Roque (sweeping gesture with one arm toward the horizon) and work for him (polishing and washing gestures). What knavery (fists on hips, scowl, curling lip, feet stamping snake to death)! She had refused (violent shaking of the head) and walked out (she half turned away, back stiff with hostility, buttocks tense with rage). Did she do right?

Then, when I said nothing, so staggered was I by Fulbert's audacity, she began going through the last sequence again.

"Oh, yes, Miette, yes, you did absolutely the right thing," I said, putting my left hand under her beautiful heavy hair and stroking the back of her neck, while with my right I urged Malabar forward again to stop his impatient stamping. Immediately, on the wing as it were, as we both walked along, she began dotting kisses over my cheek, rather randomly because we were moving, and I even thought for a moment that she was going to kiss me on the mouth, as she had Malabar. But no. Suddenly she was off again, going to help in the Maternity Ward, from which I saw La Falvine now re-emerging, moving along like a ball, her vast haunches rolling like a battleship in heavy seas, making for the keep.

It seemed to me that Fulbert had gone too far, and that his visit might well turn out very badly for him before it was over. However, I dismissed all thoughts of that kind from my mind and concentrated on the task in hand. I got up into the saddle and worked Malabar around the enclosure, putting him through his paces, using the leading rein sparingly and concentrating above all on his trot. I wore spurs without rowels, but even so I used them with great moderation; and even when he threatened to stick his heels in, I almost never used the crop, which I knew didn't hurt him in the slightest, but which he seemed to take as a personal insult. After half an hour I was drenched in sweat, so much sheer physical effort did it involve controlling the enormous creature.

Out of the corner of my eye as I circled the yard I had seen Jacquet set out for the keep, arms swinging by his side, hands half open, great shoulders bent forward. I was tired, and so was Malabar. I dismounted and led him back toward the Maternity Ward.

Colin suddenly appeared, grim faced, and walked after me into the stallion's stall. As I unbuckled the saddle and bridle and laid them over the top of the partition, he grabbed up a handful of straw from the floor, twisted it into a ring, and without a word began rubbing down Malabar's sweating flank with suppressed rage. I did likewise, though without the rage, on the other side, glancing at our great bowman now and then over the stallion's withers, waiting for the explosion. And before long it came; everything poured out. He had seen Meyssonnier and Thomas. They were in the storeroom, inventorying the booty from L'Étang, and Meyssonnier had told him how Miette had spent the night.

I listened. That was my principal function at Malevil,

listening. Once the explosion was over, I offered counsels of moderation. I was beginning to be uneasy. Things were going almost too badly for Fulbert. I began to wonder whether I wouldn't be forced to alleviate his defeat to some extent, so that we could get him off the premises without violence. "Have you seen Peyssou?" I asked.

"No."

"Well if you do, don't tell him. You hear, just don't tell him."

He agreed with bad grace, then just as I was leaving the stall to hang up the saddle and bridle in the harness room, Fulbert's big gray donkey began braying fit to split our eardrums. Little Colin pulled himself up on tiptoe and peered over into the donkey's stall. "Well, well," he said with deep scorn, "are we taking ourself for a great big stallion in there? Look at him, the great lover with it all hanging down. Do you think our mares are for you, you stupid donkey? And what's to stop us kicking you into our moat, eh? You and your Mr. Big! Yes, it's mighty cold, our moat. That would cool your balls down for you!"

I laughed at this preposterous displacement onto the poor donkey, then deliberately prolonged my laugh in order to remove any conceivable hint of seriousness from the notion. "But anyway," Colin said, a little calmer now after his little joke, "you can be sure I won't be going to any confession now!" I gave him a friendly thump on the back, then set off toward the keep in order to change.

On the drawbridge I met La Menou, who was looking rather thoughtful, it seemed to me. I stopped. She raised her little skull-like face toward me, fixed me with her small bright eyes, and said, "Ah, Emmanuel. I was looking for you. I wanted to tell you that after my confession Fulbert was telling me he's very worried about our spiritual welfare here. And since we certainly can't get over to La Roque every Sunday, with it being so far, he said he was thinking perhaps he should create an assistant, a vicar, and send him here to live at Malevil."

I stared at her, flabbergasted.

"I thought it wouldn't please you too much," La Menou said.

Not please me too much! Some understatement! I

could see only too clearly what lay behind his solicitude. Like Colin's a little while before, but for a quite different reason, my face was very grim indeed as I climbed the keep's spiral staircase. As I reached the second floor landing, one of the two doors opened and Fulbert appeared, showing Peyssou out. Jacquet was standing outside the door waiting his turn.

"Good morning, Emmanuel," Fulbert said with a certain coldness. (He already knew I didn't intend to make a confession.) "May I see you for a few moments in my room before Mass?"

"I'll wait for you in mine," I said. "Next floor up, on the right."

"As you wish," Fulbert said.

My little rebuff had not succeeded in making him lose one jot of his majesty, and it was with a gesture of the utmost graciousness that he ushered Jacquet into his confessional.

"Peyssou," I said immediately, "would you do something for me?"

"Of course I will," Peyssou said.

"I want you to take all the guns into the room next to mine and give them a good clean. And make a good job of it, soldier! One speck of dirt and it's the guardhouse for you!"

This military language tickled his fancy, and he accepted the chore. At which I was delighted, not because it meant clean guns, since they were all perfectly clean already, but because it meant Peyssou was safely out of circulation until the time came for Mass. Things were complicated enough already without having a berserk Peyssou on my hands as well.

Alone in my room, I pulled off my sweater and undershirt and set about freshening myself up. I was in an extremely anxious, nervous state. I couldn't stop thinking about the interview ahead and offering myself a few of my own counsels of moderation. In order to get my mind off Fulbert I opened the drawers of my bureau and indulged in the pleasure of choosing a clean shirt. My shirts were my one luxury. I had literally dozens and dozens— woolen ones, twill ones, poplin ones. La Menou took care of them, since she would never allow "someone from outside" to stain them in the wash or scorch them with a clumsy iron.

I had scarcely finished buttoning up my clean shirt when there was a knock. It was Fulbert. He must have dealt pretty summarily with our Jacquet. He walked in, his eyes fell on the open drawers, and it was at this point that he made the "fraternal" request I have already mentioned.

And I confess I acceded to it with rather ill grace. We all have our weaknesses, and I set great store by my shirts. Though it was true that his—if it was his only one—was indeed threadbare, and he seemed absolutely delighted at being able to exchange it, there and then, for one of mine. I was amazed, as I have already said, at the sight of Fulbert undressed. Because his torso, in contrast to his emaciated face, was very well fleshed indeed. Not that he was lacking in muscles, but his muscles, like those of black boxers, were generously covered. In short, everything about him was a snare and a delusion, even his physical appearance.

I courteously offered him the big chair at my desk to sit in, but it was a courtesy that paid dividends, since it meant I had to sit on the sofa with my back to the light, thereby making it difficult for him to see my face.

"I thank you for the shirt, Emmanuel," he said with calm dignity.

As he finished buttoning the collar and knotting his gray knitted tie, he fixed me with a deeply serious gaze, albeit tempered with a bland smile. He was clever, Fulbert, subtle even. He must have sensed that something had gone wrong, that his plans were in danger, that I represented some kind of threat to him. His gaze was like a long feeler cautiously probing its way all over and around me.

"Will you permit me to ask you a few questions?" he said eventually.

"Ask away."

"I was informed in La Roque that you were somewhat lukewarm in your attitude toward religion."

"That's true. I was, as you say, somewhat lukewarm."

282

"And that you have led a somewhat unedifying life here." He accompanied the words with a disarming little smile, but I didn't respond to it.

"What exactly do they mean in La Roque by a somewhat unedifying life?"

"Not very edifying where women are concerned."

I pondered that. I certainly didn't want him to get away with the remark. But then neither did I want to provoke an open break between us. I was searching for a compromise reply.

"You must be aware, Fulbert," I said in the end, "how difficult it is for a vigorous man like myself, or you, to do without a woman."

As I spoke I raised my eyes and looked straight into his. He didn't flinch. He remained absolutely impassive. Too impassive even. Because given that "insidious sickness" sapping his strength and that "one foot in the grave," he should have protested at the vigor I had attributed to him. Proof that it was not that aspect of my reply that had caught his attention.

Suddenly he smiled. "It doesn't bother you, I hope, Emmanuel, answering my questions? I wouldn't like it to appear that I was confessing you against your will."

Once again I ignored the smile. I said with slightly chilly gravity, "It doesn't bother me."

He continued. "When did you last partake of the Holy Sacrament?"

"When I was fifteen."

"They say you were very much influenced by your Protestant uncle."

He wasn't going to catch me out with that one. I rejected the suspicion of heresy with vigor. "My uncle was indeed a Protestant. I, however, am a Catholic."

"A somewhat lukewarm one though."

"Yes, I was, it's true."

"You mean you aren't lukewarm any longer?"

"You ought to know that."

It was said pretty ungraciously, and the fine shifty eyes blinked slightly. "Emmanuel," he said in his most resonant voice, "if you are referring to your evening readings from the Old Testament, I am bound to tell you that however much I may admire the purity of your intentions, I don't think those readings are very good for your companions here."

"It was they who asked for them."

"I am aware of that," he said rather snappily.

I said nothing. I didn't even bother to ask how he was aware of it. After all, I knew perfectly well already.

"I am intending to create a vicar at La Roque," Fulbert went on, "and then, with your permission, to appoint him as spiritual adviser here at Malevil."

I stared at him with assumed astonishment. "But Fulbert . . . How can you ordain a priest when you're not a bishop?"

He lowered his eyes with great humility. "In normal times you would be right, of course. But circumstances today are not normal. And the Church must go on, after all. What would happen if I died tomorrow? Without a successor?"

The impudence of this was so flagrant that I decided I couldn't let it pass. I smiled. "Of course," I said, still smiling. "Of course. I realize perfectly that as things are today there can be no question of attending the seminary at Cahors, with or without Serrurier."

Momentarily he gave himself away. Although his face didn't move, his eyes, even though it was for no more than half a second, blazed with fury. Quite frightening, our Fulbert. In that brief glance I sensed a vast reservoir of barely restrained violence and hate. I also sensed that he was no coward. If the challenge had been only slightly more open, he would have been ready to take it up in earnest.

"'You are certainly not unaware," he said with perfect calm, "that in the primitive Church the bishops were elected by the assembled faithful. Taking my authority from that precedent, it would therefore be quite in order for me to present my candidate to the suffrage of the assembled faithful of La Roque."

"Of Malevil," I said curtly. "Of Malevil, since it is at Malevil that he would be officiating."

He didn't take up my objection. He preferred to get back onto solider ground. "I have taken note," he went on gravely, "that you did not come to make your confession. Are you perhaps opposed to the practice of confession in principle?"

The heresy trap again.

"Not in the slightest," I answered energetically. "It's just that confession doesn't help me personally."

"Doesn't help you!" he exclaimed with expertly acted astonishment and shock.

"No."

And when I didn't go on, he continued in a gentler tone. "Would you be good enough to explain what exactly you mean by that?"

"Well, even when I've been absolved of my sins, I still go on blaming myself for them."

Quite true, as it happens. I do in fact have the unfortunate kind of conscience that doesn't wash easily. I can still remember the precise fact, about five years ago, that crystallized the uselessness of confession as far as I personally was concerned: that I was still feeling remorse, scarcely attenuated at all, for a very cruel albeit childish action committed twenty years before.

While I was reminiscing in this way, I could hear Fulbert delivering a series of routine priestly admonishments. But he was delivering them with a great deal of genuine fire, it suddenly struck me. Once a layman starts playing the priest, he can usually leave most real priests standing.

Fulbert must have noticed that I was only half listening, because the flow abruptly stopped. "In short, then," he said, "you do not wish to confess?"

"That's right."

"In that case I don't know that I shall be able to admit you to communion as you say you wish."

"Why not?"

"You must be aware," he said, with a flick of the whip in the smooth voice, "that one must be in a state of grace in order to receive communion."

"Oh, yes, but I feel you're exaggerating a little there, you know," I said. "There were quite a few priests in France, before the day it happened, who didn't link communion and confession directly like that."

"And they were wrong!" Fulbert said in a cutting voice.

His lips were pinched together, his eyes glittering. I was stopped in my tracks. This impostor, strange as it might seem, was also a fanatic. A real fascist-style traditionalist. He misunderstood the reason for my silence and decided to thrust home. "Don't ask the impossible of me, Emmanuel. How can I give you communion if you are not in a state of grace?"

"Very well," I said, looking him in the eyes, "in that case we must pray to God to put us in that state. Me after all those years I have lived without the sacraments, and you after the night you've just spent in Malevil."

It was the hardest I could hit him without bringing about an open breach between us. But Fulbert's poise was obviously colossal, because he didn't twitch a muscle. Nor did he speak. He appeared not to have heard me even. Though in a sense his very silence accused him, since if he wished to appear innocent he ought to have asked me what I meant by his night in Malevil.

"Yes, we shall pray, Emmanuel," he said after a moment in resonant tones. "We always have need of prayer. And I for my part will pray most particularly that you will agree to receive the abbé I shall be sending here to you."

"That is not something that depends on me," I answered very smartly, "but upon all of us. Our decisions are all taken in accordance with the wishes of the majority, and when I am in the minority I accept the fact."

"I know, I know," he said as he got to his feet. Glancing at his watch, he added, "It is time I began thinking about my Mass."

I rose as well, and informed him of the terms upon which we had decided to let La Roque have our cow. When I mentioned the guns, he shot a glance at the rack that Meyssonnier had built in my room, seemed astonished to find it empty, but said nothing. On the other hand he kicked quite hard when I came to the horses.

"Two!" he exclaimed with a start. "Two! That seems to me rather excessive! You mustn't go imagining, Emmanuel, that I have no interest in horses. In fact I have asked Armand to give me lessons."

I knew Armand well. The château handyman. He spent

286

more time holding his hands out for tips than working with them. A shifty, brutal customer too. And I knew what his horsemanship amounted to as well. They had three geldings and two mares at the castle, but the Lormiaux (and Armand when they weren't there) never rode anything but the geldings. They were afraid of the mares, and I knew why.

"The two I have in mind," I said, "are the mares. No one has ever been able to ride them. As a matter of fact I advised the Lormiaux strongly against buying them. As Armand must have told you. However, if you wish to keep them, then do. That's your affair."

"But still," Fulbert said, "both of them? For a single cow? And the guns as well? I find the terms a little exorbitant."

A hint of curtness creeping into my voice, I said, "The terms are not mine, they are those of Malevil. They were arrived at last night by a unanimous vote, and I have no power to change them. If they don't suit you, then let us abandon the whole transaction."

This time-honored horse dealer's tactic had its effect. He was obviously shaken, and from his look I knew already that he was going to accept. He couldn't afford to go back to La Roque empty-handed. He glanced again at his watch, excused himself, and stalked hurriedly out of my room.

Left alone, I decided, as my mother used to say, to "make myself nice" for the Mass. (Ah, those curling-iron sessions with my sisters interminably fussing at their ringlets!) I pulled off my boots and riding breeches and put on —I quote Menou here—"my funeral suit." And it was true that in the country, those past few years, there had always been five funerals for every marriage. Even before the bomb, the countryside around us was dying.

I was pleased, and yet I wasn't, though there was no denying that the balance had ended up very much in my favor. I had sidestepped all Fulbert's pressures and outflanked him on every count. I hadn't made confession, yet I was sure he wouldn't refuse me communion when it came to the point, or any of the others either. Which meant that I had prevented communion being indissolubly linked, here at Malevil anyway, with the inquisitorial questioning I was sure was standard in La Roque. I had undermined what in hands as unscrupulous as Fulbert's could have become a formidable source of power, and I had done so in such a way that he could not present me in La Roque as an unbeliever or a heretic.

The bartering of the cow was another very important item to be entered to my credit. And more on account of the horses than on that of the guns. Because Fulbert was going to let me have those two mares, I was sure of that. Intelligent though he was, he wasn't a countryman, he didn't have peasant instincts. He hadn't grasped the fact that as soon as he handed over those two mares of his, I would be the sole possessor not only of the only stallion available but also of every single mare. He hadn't realized yet that once his three geldings had met their noble end, he would be wholly dependent on me for replacements, and that he had conceded me the monopoly of equine breeding in a day and age when the horse had come to represent a very important labor factor and also a crucial military one. He had therefore weakened his position. And I had greatly strengthened mine.

From that point of view, as I saw it, I had nothing more to fear. Except treachery. And given the man, I didn't dismiss that out of hand. I remembered that blaze of hate in his eyes when I alluded to his night with Miette, and to the fact that he was an impostor. The fact was, I had been forced to put all my cards on the table, to show my hand, to reply to his blackmail with counterblackmail. And I knew that kind of man. He wasn't going to forgive me for it.

As I was knotting my cravat, Thomas burst into the room. His face bore not the slightest trace of his customary calm. It was red and twitching. Without a word he passed behind me, opened his closet, and began taking out his raincoat, his crash helmet, his goggles, his gloves, and the Geiger counter.

"What's all this? Where are you going?"

"The barometer is falling. I think it's going to rain."

"It's not possible!" I cried, glancing automatically over at the window. Then I went over to it and opened it as wide as it would go. The sky, gray earlier in the morning, had become much darker, and above all there was that stillness, that sense of expectancy everywhere that always comes before rain. Although we had all longed so hard for it ever since the day the bomb fell, I couldn't bring myself to believe what I saw. I turned back to Thomas. "And why all the gear?"

"To check whether the rain is radioactive or not."

I stared at him, and when I finally recovered my voice it was unrecognizable, toneless and thin. "Can it be? So long afterward?"

"Of course it can. If there's radioactive dust up in the stratosphere, the rain will bring it down. And that means total disaster. We have to face it. The water in our water tower would be contaminated, as well as the wheat you've sown. And us too, if we expose ourselves to the rain. The only possible outcome would be death, either in a few months or a few years. Death by slow degrees."

I stared at him, lips dry. I had forgotten about the possibility of radioactive dust in the stratosphere. Like everyone at Malevil, I had longed for rain so that it would bring the world back to life. I had suppressed the idea that it might, on the contrary, just finish off the work the bomb had begun.

The slow, delayed death Thomas had described, it was appalling. For those few moments I was unable to stir for sheer dread. I didn't believe in the devil, but if I did, how could I avoid the thought that man was Satan's creature?

"We must all gather somewhere and stay together," Thomas said feverishly. "And above all, tell them not to go outside once the rain starts."

"The others are all together already," I said. "In the great hall, for Mass!"

"Then let's get over there quickly," Thomas said, "before the rain begins!"

It wasn't the moment for irony, and the thought that Thomas was going to be attending the Mass after all scarcely did more than flicker through my mind. I followed him out of the room, but halfway down the stairs to the ground floor I suddenly realized that I had forgotten Peyssou, still cleaning the guns in the next-door room. I went back up alone to fetch him, explained the situation as briefly as possible, and we both ran down again as fast as we could. On the ground floor I called out to Meyssonnier as we passed through the storeroom, but he was nowhere in evidence. Thomas must already have warned him and taken him with him. We hurtled across the courtyard, reached the great hall, found the door open, rushed in, and Peyssou slammed it behind us.

I could see from my first glance around that everyone was there, but in my panic state I began counting to make sure, then recounting, because there were eleven of us, one too many! It wasn't till my second recount that I realized the extra person was Fulbert.

Thomas had already told them. They all looked at me, very pale, without a word. Fulbert was white, at least as far as I could make out his features at all, because he had his back to the two mullioned windows. Our chairs were arranged in two rows facing him, on the other side of the refectory table. I don't know who had thought to fetch up two of the huge candles from their brackets in the cellar and place them one on each side of his little portable altar, but it was certainly a good idea as things turned out, because the sky outside was getting darker every moment, and the only light filtering through the windows was a wan end-of-the-world twilight.

There was a chair empty in the front row, beside Miette, but just as I was about to take it I noticed that I would have Momo next to me on my left, and despite the state of panic anxiety I was in, sheer force of habit was still too strong. I automatically changed direction and took my place in the second row, beside Meyssonnier. Peyssou, who had come in behind me, took the chair I had just avoided.

Never can any Mass have been less attended to, I should think, despite Fulbert's beautiful dark voice and the dutiful responses of Jacquet in his role as acolyte. Because all our eyes were firmly fixed not on the officiant but on the windows behind him, straining to pierce the sky outside with a mixture of hope and anxiety. And suddenly I felt the sweat stream down my back. The animals, I thought, what about the animals? We shall have wine to drink. But what about them? What can they drink if the water tower has been contaminated? And as for the earth, if that is impregnated with radioactive dust, washed down who knows how deep by the rain, then who can say how long it will be before the poison is no longer there in our harvests? I was amazed that Thomas had never discussed his fears with me. In what delusory security his silence had enabled us to live since the day of the bomb! I had always told myself that the only natural disaster that could threaten us now was an interminable drought, drying up the rivers, reducing the soil to an annihilation of dust. I had never for a moment imagined that the rain we had been waiting for every day, day after day, could bring us death.

I glanced at Meyssonnier, aware that he had just turned his head in my direction, and what I read in his eyes was not so much anguish as a vast stupefaction. Oh, how well I understood what he was feeling! Because with us peasants, although we do moan and groan about bad weather, when a wet June is rotting the hay for example, we know in our hearts that the rain is our friend, the source of life, that without it we would have no harvests, no fruit, no pastures, no springs. And now we were being forced to conceive the inconceivable: that the rain might kill what it should feed.

Meyssonnier's eyes returned to the windows, and mine too. It didn't seem possible, but the sky had grown even darker. The hill on the far side of the Rhunes valley, bare, blackened, topped by its three gaunt tree stumps, looked like a Golgotha when the darkness lay over all the land. A wan low-lying light was silhouetting it from behind, separating it from the black sky with a pale glowing line. The hill itself was charcoal gray, but above it the piled up clouds were black as ink, with trails of less dark vapor here and there. The spectacle kept changing from moment to moment, heavy with coiling menace. I was almost hypnotized by it.

And oddly, though I wasn't praying or listening to Fulbert, my mind had established a link between what I was seeing and his chanted words. In those moments I had forgotten who Fulbert was, all his lies and his deceits, and only his voice had any substance. And even though I wasn't listening to him, I was aware that this false priest was saying his Mass extremely well, with gravity and deep feeling. I wasn't listening, yet I was aware what the words were telling, that anguish two thousand years ago, the same that we were all living through again now, our eyes staring at those windows.

The clouds were so black and low that I was sure the rain must begin to fall now. The minutes that preceded it were endless. It was taking its time, all right! And it became such a torture just waiting that I was almost longing for the rain to fall, to make an end of us, so that Thomas's Geiger counter could pronounce its sentence of death. I glanced again at Meyssonnier beside me. I saw his Adam's apple travel up inside his thin neck. He was swallowing the saliva in his mouth. Since his chair was slightly farther back than mine, I could also make out Thomas's profile beyond. I watched as he pulled apart his dry lips, which had become stuck together, then wet them with his tongue. I was not the only one, I was sure, who could feel the sweat running down my sides and oozing from my palms. We were all in the same state. If my nose had been keen enough, I would have been able to pick up the odor of fear and perspiration being given off by our eleven motionless bodies.

I was still aware of Fulbert's chanting in my ears, the sound at least, though not the words, because I was still not even trying to catch them. But now in our guest's beautiful resonant voice I could discern a crack, a quiver. Ah, so we do have something in common, Fulbert and I, I thought. I felt a desire to tell him so. To tell him that all the hatreds and tensions between us were pointless now that the rain was coming, the rain that would reconcile us forever, and we all knew how.

Yet when it finally burst, the storm we had all been expecting, it was like an electric shock. We all gave an involuntary start, then the silence became more intense than ever. Fulbert's voice lost even more of its suavity, it had become hoarse and cracked; yet it did not stop. Fulbert was not without guts, or, it would seem, without faith. Later on the idea crossed my mind that he had turned impostor as the result of a missed vocation. But for the moment my head was void. I just listened. The rain was lashing with such fury against the windowpanes, with a pattering so full of violence and hate that at moments it drowned Fulbert's voice, and yet, however tenuous it now seemed to me, I never lost it altogether, I clung to it; it was a thread I was following through the darkness.

It was really dark now, darker than ever, even though the windows were white with rain. The great hall was no longer lit by any glimmer other than that from the two great candles, whose flames were quivering too in the wind coming in under the doors and around the windows. Fulbert's shadow looked enormous on the wall. There were faint glimmers from the blades of the swords and halberds hanging on it. Everything else in the world was gloom, and I had the feeling that we were crouched there, all eleven of us, in an underground tomb, vainly trying to escape from the death that was above us and all around us.

The rain eased off momentarily, then a first flash of lightning brightened the two windows, thunder rolled over to the east, behind the hill opposite us. I knew the storms in our part of the world only too well, they are terrifying. I've been afraid of them ever since childhood. As I grew up I learned how to conceal the panic they created inside me, but never to conquer it. And now that panic was adding a terrible physical distress to the dread I was already feeling. It was as much as I could do to restrain the trembling in my hands as I watched the zigzags of lightning silhouette the three tree stumps on the hill, and then wait for the rumbling that had to follow.

At the same time, the wind suddenly got up and began to blow as though the sky had gone mad. It was our east wind. I recognized the howling sound it made as it rushed under the half-ruined vaulting where I had planned to make my office, the way it endlessly rattled the doors and windows and whistled in every fissure of the cliff face. The rain returned with redoubled fury, and the wind hurled it against the windows like innumerable spears. You felt the leaded panes were about to burst inward at any moment. Fulbert, standing with his back to them, must have experienced the same sensation, because I noticed that he had pulled his neck down into his shoulders and was hunching them as though he expected the hurricane to leap on him and savage him without warning. And yet, between two terrifying rolls of thunder, I could still hear his voice.

I hid my hands away in my pockets and stiffened my neck. The lightning was crawling methodically, savagely closer. The thunderclaps were now gigantic explosions. It was as though Malevil had become a target that the lightning bolts were bracketing with horrible and conscious precision, according to the dictates of some infernal ordnance manual, before annihilating it with one direct and final hit. There was nothing to be seen now of those former zigzags, broken arrows, insane signatures of pure light against the black of the sky. Only on the windows, every now and then, an icy and blinding glitter, immediately followed by a very loud, very abrupt explosion, like a shell hitting its mark. It was almost beyond the capacity of human ears to endure such a volume of sound. One just wanted to run, to escape, to hide.

Between two great claps, in one of the storm's infinitesimal moments of calm, I heard Fulbert's voice, so thin and shaky now that it seemed to be part of the flickering candle flames. Fulbert's voice was all I had to cling to. I could also hear a muffled moaning, and it took me a moment to realize, as I leaned forward and peered round, that it was Momo making the noise, his great shaggy head pressed against La Menou's bony chest and protected by his mother's frail skeleton arms.

Without transition, the storm moved off. The distant rumblings returned, almost comforting in comparison. They receded and grew less frequent as the rain and wind rose to a paroxysm. The muscles of my neck, my arms, my shoulders were hurting me, so rigidly had I tensed them to overcome my trembling. I tried to relax them. The rain was no longer coming in separate spears, it was one great waterfall. The little windowpanes were completely obscured by the streaming water, like an automobile windshield, or a porthole washed by waves. The noise

294

had ceased to be a hostile drumming and was now just a series of muffled thuds breaking at intervals through Fulbert's far-off voice and Momo's moans.

I felt someone touch my arm. Meyssonnier. I turned toward him. I was fascinated by the painful way his Adam's apple pushed its way up inside his throat as he spoke, but I couldn't actually hear any sound. I bent toward him, I almost pressed my ear against his lips, and I heard "Thomas wants to speak to you." Since I was standing just then—we were quite mechanically copying the others in the front row, sitting when they sat, standing when they stood—I moved across in front of Meyssonnier and put my head close to Thomas's.

He pulled his lips apart with some difficulty, and I noticed that a thick, almost solidified thread of saliva remained unbroken between them as he said, "As soon as the rain stops I'll go out and check." I nodded and went back to my place, amazed that he should have felt it necessary to tell me that, so self-evident did it seem. I certainly hadn't expected him to go out and expose himself to the rain, which I was now quite convinced was loaded with lethal dust. So great was my dread by now that it had killed all hope.

The two windows were covered with an unbroken stream of water, yet oddly enough they seemed lighter than before. It was as though the sheet of rain was itself giving out light. Beyond it there was nothing discernible but a dense, opaque whiteness. I had the absurd impression that the deluge had completely filled the little valley of the Rhunes, submerged the castle, and was even now sapping the whole cliff as it penetrated all its clefts and crannies.

I noticed with surprise, and without at all realizing the meaning of it, that a glass filled with wine and a plate containing several cubes of bread were being passed around. I watched Thomas and Meyssonnier as they drank in turn, and from the shock the sight induced in me I grasped that without knowing it they were both taking communion. Presumably they were only too glad to wet their dry mouths with a sip of wine. But at that point they too must have realized what they were doing, because

295

they suddenly caught themselves up and quickly passed me not only the glass but also the plate, without taking any bread.

I realized then that Jacquet was standing beside me. He noticed my difficulty and took the plate out of my hand. Then as I raised the glass avidly to my lips he bent down and said in my ear, "Leave some for me." And he was quite right. I was going to drink it all. When I had finished drinking he held out the plate, and along with my own cube I also hurriedly removed the two that Thomas and Meyssonnier had left untouched. It was a pure defensive reflex. I didn't want Fulbert to know that two of our number had refused communion. At the same time I was amazed at my own instinctive reaction, and at the fact that I was still thinking about safeguarding our future when I was quite certain in my mind that no one in the room had any future. Jacquet had seen my gesture, though it had been masked from Fulbert by Falvine's vast bulk, and he looked at me with a hint of reproof in those simple doglike eyes, but I knew he wouldn't say anything.

All this had taken place, as far as I was concerned, in a sort of cottony vagueness, as though my brain too were obscured by the rain streaming down the windows. I had a bizarre impression that I knew it all already, as though I had lived through this scene and this spectacle in some former existence: the sickly light, the streaming windows, the trophies of weapons on the wall between the windows, Fulbert, whose outline and hollow face I could scarcely make out, the heavy refectory table, and us, grouped behind it, silent, hunched, devoured by terror. A handful of men lost in an empty world. Jacquet had gone back to his place. Fulbert was reciting again, and Momo, now the storm had passed, had stopped his moaning, although as soon as he had gulped down his bread and wine he had immediately pushed his head back under the protection of La Menou's fierce little arms.

It was strange how it all seemed so familiar to me, and familiar too was that great baronial hall, which in that half darkness, scarcely mitigated at all by the wan windows and the two big candles, made me think of some crypt where we seemed to be keeping vigil over our own future graves. In the gloom, Miette's magnificent hair caught a gleam of light, and suddenly an iron hand closed around my heart as I realized that her coming to live with us had been useless, that Miette would never pass life on.

The Mass drew to its close and the rain still bucketed down. Although the gusts of wind were shaking the windows with tremendous violence, they had not succeeded in opening them, only in driving a little water around their edges, and it had begun to collect in pools on the flagstones at the foot of the wall.

It occurred to me to ask Thomas to run his Geiger counter over these pools. Then I immediately rejected the idea. I had the feeling that if I hurried things, that meant the verdict would go against us. Pure superstition on my part, and I was well aware of it. But I gave way to the instinct all the same. Alone with myself, what petty acts of cowardice I would permit myself, I who prided myself so on my courage! Having thus delayed the moment of truth, I turned to La Menou and asked her in a calm voice to light the fire. Thank goodness I had complete control of my voice still. Appearances were saved; the collapse was all inside. Though the fire was in fact very necessary. I observed out loud that since we had begun to move around, oddly enough, there seemed to be a tomblike chill in the room.

The first flame flickered into life. We all huddled around the fireplace, dumb with dread. After a moment I couldn't stand their silence any longer. I broke away and began pacing up and down the hall, my crepe soles making no sound on the stone floor. The windows were so obscured by the rain they made me feel that the whole of Malevil was under water, about to float away like a new ark. As though the tension of my fear had become too unbearable, forcing me to take refuge from it in absurdity, my head began to fill with other such ideas, all equally idiotic. For example, that of snatching down a sword from between the windows and finishing the whole thing there and then by thrusting it through my body, like a Roman emperor.

At one and the same instant the gusts of wind redoubled and the rain stopped. I must have become accustomed to the sound of the water thundering against the glass, because as soon as it stopped I experienced a sensation of silence, despite the continued howling of the wind and the constant rattling of the windows. I saw the group around the fire turn as one to look at them, as though all those heads belonged to the same body.

Thomas detached himself from the group. Without a word, without a glance in my direction, he went over to the chair where he had left his equipment. With slow, competent gestures he pulled on his raincoat, carefully fastened it, then in due order slipped on the big goggles, the helmet, the gloves. Only then, after taking up the Geiger counter and arranging the headphones at the ready around his neck, did he start toward the door. The motorcyclist's goggles, which left only the lower part of his face visible, gave him the air of an implacable robot carrying out some programmed technical assignment, unaware of man's existence. Raincoat, helmet, boots, all were black.

I rejoined the group around the fire. I melted into it. I needed to become part of it if I was to bear the waiting. The fire flickered meagerly. Ah, La Menou's undying concern for thrift! And we huddled closer around her tiny blaze, backs to the door from which our sentence would be pronounced. La Menou was on her hearth seat as usual, with Momo opposite on the far side of the fire. His eyes moved constantly from her to me and then back again. I have no idea what exactly it might have conjured up in his mind, a phrase like "radioactive dust," but in any case he trusted both his mother and myself to know when there was good cause for fear. His face was drained of color. His bright black eyes were fixed in a stare, and he was trembling in every limb. And we would have been doing the same, all the rest of us, if we had not been taught that grownups are supposed to control themselves.

My companions were no longer just pale, they were gray. I was standing between Meyssonnier and Peyssou, and I noticed that we were all holding ourselves in the same rather stiff pose: shoulders hunched, heads bent forward, hands thrust deep into our pockets. On the other side of Peyssou, Fulbert was the same ashen color.

His eyes were lowered, thereby depriving his fleshless face of any glimmer of life, and he looked more than ever like a corpse. Falvine and Jacquet were both moving their lips. I took it that they were praying. Little Colin seemed agitated and oppressed; he appeared to be having difficulty breathing, and he kept yawning and swallowing all the time. Miette alone appeared almost serene—slightly uneasy, but on our account not hers. She kept looking around at us all in turn, attempting little consoling smiles that no one heeded.

The wind dropped. Not a word was exchanged, and the fire, far from blazing and crackling, was just a faint soundless glow. The room slowly filled with a vast weight of silence. What happened next was so quick that I scarcely remember any passage from one state to the next. It's only in books you find transitions. They don't happen in life. The door of the great hall was flung open with a crash. And there was Thomas, eyes wild, without helmet, without goggles. He shouted in a high-pitched voice, ringing with triumph, "There's nothing! Nothing!"

It wasn't very explicit, but we understood. It was a stampede. We all reached the door together and almost jammed it trying to get through.

Just as we emerged the rain began again. It hurtled down in torrents, but what did we care now. Except for Fulbert, who stayed under the shelter of the little tower doorway, and La Falvine and La Menou, who joined him there, we were all out in the courtyard laughing and shouting under the downpour. It was even warm, or seemed so to us. It ran in rivulets down our bodies and made the timeworn black cobbles shine beneath our feet. From the keep battlements, splashing against the ancient stones in their fall, tiny cascades came tumbling from every crenelation to merge with the general downpour below. The sky was a whitish, almost a pinkish, gray. We hadn't seen it so light for two months.

Suddenly Miette pulled off her blouse and offered that youthful torso, which had never known a brassiere, to the caress of the falling rain. She laughed, she pranced, she swayed from side to side, her arms upstretched, her long hair brandished with one hand to the sky. We too

299

would have danced, I feel sure, if the traditions of primitive man had not been lost. And because we could not dance, we talked.

"You see if our wheat doesn't come up now!" Peyssou cried.

"Just the rain's no good," Meyssonnier said. "It's not because we haven't been watering it there's not a blade to be seen! It's the sun it wants."

"But you're going to have it now, your sun! And more than you want," said Peyssou, whose hope would now admit no limits. "The rain will bring it out. Isn't that true, Jacquet?" he asked giving him a tremendous thump on the back.

Jacquet agreed that it was indeed true, that the sun would come out now, but he did not dare to return the thump.

"And high time!" the great bowman Colin said. "Here we are, June already, and cold as March."

The rain showed no signs of lessening. After the first few minutes of madness we all retired to the shelter of the doorway, all except our Miette, who was still dancing and singing, even though no sound actually emerged from her mouth, and Momo, a few paces away from her, motionless, but with head thrown back and mouth wide open to welcome and absorb the rain. Every so often La Menou shouted at him to come in, that he would catch his death (a constant prediction constantly belied, since Momo had a constitution of iron), and that if he didn't do as she said he was going to get her boot in his behind. But he was a good twenty yards away from her, the drawbridge was down, and at her slightest move he could be away in a flash, so, certain of his impunity, he did not even reply to her. He drank the rain with ecstatic swallows, one eye on Miette's naked breasts.

"Oh, fair play to him. Let him alone, damn it!" Peyssou broke in. "Always after him you are! As though a little water isn't going to do him good too. No offense, Menou, but that son of yours is stinking like a boar. He even put me off hearing Mass just now, poor fellow!"

"Well I can't wash him all on my own, can I now?" La Menou said. "He's too strong, as well you know."

"Good God!" Peyssou exclaimed, then stopped in confusion and glanced across guiltily at Fulbert. However, La Falvine was monopolizing the *cura* with inquiries about her brother the cobbler in La Roque, and her granddaughter Catie. Peyssou continued. "I remember now! Do you know he hasn't washed himself, that little wretch, since the day when I was—" He was about to say "knocked over the head" but caught himself just in time. Unfortunately though, we all knew what he had meant. Including Jacquet, whose good-natured face was painful to see.

"Momo, come in here!" La Menou shouted in impotent rage.

"You won't get him back in until Miette's finished her shower," Meyssonnier remarked with calm good sense. "Look how he's drinking it all in. And not just with his mouth!"

We all laughed, except La Menou, with her peasant's sacred horror of nudity. She clamped her lips into a thin line and said, "A heathen that girl is—you can't say otherwise—showing her titties to everyone like that!"

"Ah, come now," Colin said. "Hasn't everyone here seen them already, except Momo?"

And as he said it he turned and looked defiantly at Fulbert. But Fulbert, engrossed in his conversation with La Falvine, didn't hear him, or pretended he didn't. Nevertheless, when I noticed Peyssou glancing at me with a puzzled expression, my former fears returned, and I decided it was time to hurry things on a little and get our holy man off the premises. I shouted to Miette to come in and told La Menou to make us a big fire: "You hear, Menou, a big fire!" A quite unnecessary exhortation, needless to say, now that it was a matter of drying her son!

Miette walked back to join us, blouse in one hand, still glowing with the innocent joy of her game (without Fulbert daring to reprimand her or even look at her), and Momo promptly followed her inside, delighted at the idea of watching her hold out her blouse to the flickering flames. Which she of course did. And there we all were, our clothes steaming in the heat, clustering around her, roasting ourselves at a fire now blazing as hot as the fires of hell, and our thoughts, from what I could see, not all that far from the devil.

Miette looked at me, arranged her blouse over a low chair, because she needed her hands to speak to me, then drew me to one side, indicating by her manner that she had some sort of reproach to make to me. I followed her. The mime began. She had saved me a chair next to her at Mass and she had noticed (one finger under the corner of her eye) that at the last moment I had sneaked away into the second row (hand becoming a fish, swimming along, then changing direction at the last moment).

I reassured her. It wasn't because of her I'd avoided the chair but because of Momo, and I didn't need to tell her why. She agreed that Momo did smell (thumb and forefinger squeezing nose). She found the fact surprising. I described the difficulties involved in washing him, the necessity of a surprise attack, the large number of assailants required, the energy consumed, the cunning and strength with which he evaded our attempts. She listened with great attention, and even laughed. Then suddenly, planting herself in front of me, hands on hips, she announced with a determined look in her eye and a shake of her black mane that from now on she would wash Momo for us.

Then it was La Menou's turn to take me aside and ask in a low voice whether she should serve "the company" a bite to eat. (It was feeding her son she was concerned about, the hypocrite, to fortify him against that "chill" he was sure to catch.) I answered in the same low tone that I would rather wait till the curé had gone, but that meanwhile she should wrap up a big loaf and two or three pounds of butter for Fulbert to take back to the people of La Roque.

All Malevil was assembled at the gate tower when Fulbert left, taking advantage of a moment when the rain had eased off, modestly mounted on his gray donkey. The farewells varied greatly in their warmth. Meyssonnier and Thomas cold as ice. Colin as impertinent as he dared be. Myself generous with the oil, but distantly familiar. The only truly cordial ones came from the two old women and—for the moment at least—Peyssou and Jacquet.

302

Miette didn't come near, and Fulbert seemed to have forgotten her. She was engaged in an animated discussion with Momo about twenty yards away. Since she had her back to me, I was unable to see exactly what she was miming, but whatever it was, Momo was clearly putting up strong opposition, because I could hear his usual grunting cries of refusal. However, he had not taken to his heels, as he would have done if it had been his mother or myself speaking to him. He stayed there, glued to the ground in front of her, eyes hypnotized, face almost lulled to sleep, and it seemed to me that his refusals were gradually becoming less forceful and less frequent.

With a friendly smile I handed Fulbert back the bolt of his gun. He slid it into the breech, and slung the gun over his shoulder. He had lost none of his calm and dignity. Before mounting his donkey, he signified to me, after a deep sigh that plumbed the depths of man's abysmal want of charity with saddened resignation, that he agreed to the conditions I had stipulated in the matter of Malevil's transfer of a cow to the parish of La Roque, even though he found them much too harsh. I replied that the conditions were not mine, but he received this statement with a skepticism that on reflection wasn't really surprising, since he himself had accepted my conditions without consulting his flock. I can scarcely call them his fellow citizens, since he had spoken very pointedly of a "parish," not of a community or township. One thing was certain. Fulbert did all the deciding in La Roque, without any help, and he had assumed that I exercised an identical power in Malevil.

Fulbert then treated us to a little speech on the clearly providential nature of the rain that had brought us salvation just when we were all expecting our sentence of death. As he spoke, he several times held his arms outstretched in front of him and raised them from waist level to just above his head, a gesture I had never much admired when it was used by Pope Paul VI, but which seemed to me frankly grotesque when Fulbert did it. And he observed each of us in turn with his magnificent squinting eyes. He had taken good note of our various attitudes toward him, and nothing would be forgotten.

Having concluded his speech and invited us all to join him in prayer, he reminded us that he was thinking of sending us an abbé of our own, then he blessed us and rode off.

Colin immediately put all his weight behind the heavy iron studded door and slammed it shut as quickly and insultingly as he could. I clicked my tongue reprovingly but without saying anything.

In fact, I wouldn't have had time to say much, because La Menou suddenly let fly a shriek of distress: "But where is Momo!"

"What's the matter?" Peyssou said. "He can't be lost. Where do you expect him to be?"

"I saw him only a moment ago," I said, "arguing with Miette outside the Maternity Ward."

La Menou was already there, running along the stalls, shouting, "Momo! Momo!" But the Maternity Ward was empty.

"Oh, I remember now," Colin said. "I saw him running off just a moment ago toward the drawbridge. With Miette. They were holding hands. Two children they looked like."

"Ah, God in heaven!" La Menou cried. She too began running toward the drawbridge and we all followed, at once intrigued and amused. But because we're all very fond of him really, our Momo, we divided up into groups in order to search the castle, some taking the cellar, others the woodshed, others the ground floor of the house.

Then suddenly Miette's plans for Momo came back to me, and I shouted, "La Menou! Here, here! I know where he is, that son of yours!"

I led her over toward the keep. The others all trooped after us up to the second floor, where I crossed the vast landing and stopped outside the bathroom door. I tried it. It was bolted. I hammered with my fist on the thick oak paneling. "Momo! Are you there?"

"*Ho ahay! Ho ahay! Heavee he!*" Momo's voice yelled back.

"He's with Miette," I said. "And I don't think he'll be coming out in a hurry."

"But what's she doing to him? What's she doing to him in there?" La Menou wailed in anguish.

"She's not doing him any harm anyway, that's for sure," Peyssou said.

He threw back his head and began to laugh uproariously, accompanying his merriment with great slaps on Jacquet's back and his own thighs. And everyone else began to laugh too. Amazing. Not the slightest hint of jealousy for Momo. Momo was one of us, not the same thing at all as someone from outside. He belonged. Even if he was a bit retarded, he was one of us. There was no comparison.

"She's washing him," I said. "She told me she was going to."

"Then why didn't you warn me," La Menou said with deep reproach. "I'd have kept a closer eye on him."

There was general protest at this. Surely she didn't want to stop Miette washing him! "He stinks like a billy-goat, your Momo!" "A good thing for everyone if Miette manages to scrub him a bit! Not to mention the risk of germs and disease! And the lice!"

"Momo has never had lice!" La Menou snapped very sharply. A lie that convinced no one. She was reduced to trotting to and fro in front of that bolted door, scrawny and whitefaced, like a hen that has lost its chicks. She didn't dare call out to Momo in front of us or knock on the door. Besides, she knew only too well what his answer would be.

"These foreigners!" she burst out in fury. "As if I didn't know it inside me that very first day that there was no good to be expected from people like that! Savages like that, they shouldn't be under the same roof as Christian folk."

Falvine was already bending her back resignedly for the coming onslaught. It would all fall on her, she was sure of that. Jacquet was a man, La Menou wouldn't say anything to him. Miette had too many protectors. But poor Falvine, alas . . .

"Foreigners," I said sharply. "How can you say a thing like that? When La Falvine is your cousin!"

"A nice sort of cousin!" La Menou said from between clenched teeth.

"And you! There's nothing very nice about you when you behave like this," I answered in patois. "You'd be better going for some clean clothes to put on your Momo. And you could give him his third pair of pants too, because the pair he's wearing are a disgrace!"

When the bathroom door did eventually open, Colin came and fetched me from my room, where I was re-assembling the guns and stowing them back on their rack.

Momo was seated on the wickerwork stool, swathed in the bathrobe printed with huge blue and yellow flowers that I had bought myself just before the day it happened. Eyes agleam, grinning from ear to ear, he was radiating self-satisfaction like the sun, while Miette stood behind him proudly surveying the results of her labors. He was unrecognizable, this new Momo. His complexion was several shades lighter, he was clean shaven, his hair had been cut and combed, and he sat there enthroned in perfumed glory like a high-class harlot, because Miette had found a bottle of Chanel left in the closet by Birgitta and emptied the entire contents over him.

A little later I had a fairly important conversation in my room with Peyssou and Colin, then they left me in order to go down and make a tour of inspection down by the river. Peyssou was presumably nursing an irrational hope that the wheat was going to sprout there and then. Or else it was simply the farmer's automatic instinct to go around inspecting his fields after a storm, with no definite purpose in mind, just to set his mind at rest. As for me, I went down to the great hall. The noncontaminated rain and the departure of Fulbert had combined to put me in high good humor, and I was whistling as I wandered over toward La Menou. She was alone, with her back to me, peering into a saucepan.

"Well, Menou, what have you got nice for dinner?"

She answered without looking around. "You'll see soon enough." Then she whirled around with a little gasp, and

306

her eyes filled with tears. "I thought it was your uncle for a moment!"

I looked down at her, very moved.

"Just his way of coming in whistling," she said, "and then saying, 'Well, Menou, what have you got nice for dinner?' And the same voice too. It gave me quite a turn. . . . Ah, he was a merry soul, your uncle was, Emmanuel. A man who loved life. Like you. A little too much perhaps," she added, suddenly remembering that in her old age she had become virtuous and a misogynist.

"Oh, bah, Menou," I said, reading the thoughts well hidden behind her words. "You're not going to hold it against Miette because she's cleaned up your son for you? She hasn't taken him away from you. She's only given him a good scrubbing."

"Maybe," she said, "maybe."

I suddenly felt very happy that she'd talked to me about my uncle, and even compared me to him. And because over the past month or so I had often had to speak to her so sharply about the unnecessarily unkind way she treated La Falvine, I smiled at her now. She was quite overcome by my smile and turned away. The old rhinoceros. She wasn't without feelings really, even if you did have to bore your way through so many layers of tough hide to get at them.

"And you, Emmanuel," she said after a moment, "do you mind if I ask why you wouldn't go to confession? It does you good, you know, confessing yourself. It gets you clean inside."

I would never have believed that I would one day be having a theological discussion with La Menou. I planted myself in front of the fire, hands in my pockets. This had been no ordinary day. I was still wearing my funeral suit. I felt almost as majestic as Fulbert himself.

"While we're on the subject of confession, may I ask you a question, Menou?"

"Ask away," she said. "You know you need never stand on ceremony with me." She looked me up and down, bright eyes all attention in the little skull head, ladle poised in one bony little hand. She really was incredibly tiny, whittled away to almost nothing but bone. But what eyes! Shrewd, wise, indomitable!

"When you were in there confessing, Menou, did you tell Fulbert that you were sometimes very unpleasant to La Falvine?"

"Me!" she exclaimed in indignation. "Me, unpleasant to La Falvine? Well really, what a thing to say! What will people say next! Ah, that is the limit, the very limit! I who earn my place in heaven every day by putting up with that fat heap!"

She looked at me and paused, as though seized by a sudden scruple. "Unpleasant, yes, I may be that sometimes, but not with La Falvine. With Momo yes, I can be unkind to him! Every minute of the day after him, shouting at him, making his life a misery. And even slapping his face sometimes, at his age, poor boy! That really does make me feel guilty afterward, as I told Fulbert this morning." Then she added austerely, "But that doesn't excuse it."

I burst into laughter.

"What are you laughing at, may I ask?" she said, rather annoyed.

But big Peyssou happened to come in at that moment with Colin, and their arrival prevented me from giving her my answer. A pity. But when the opportunity arose, I resolved, I would have to tell our Menou that her confession had washed her clean hand instead of the dirty one.

That evening, after the usual communal meal, with everyone made considerably merrier by the departure of our guest, there was another plenary assembly around the fire. This led to two major decisions. First, it was decided that we would not under any circumstances accept the vicar that Fulbert had threatened us with. Second, as the result of our vote on a proposal made by Peyssou and Colin, I was unanimously elected Abbé of Malevil.

NOTE ADDED BY THOMAS

I have just read the last chapter and also, just to make quite sure, the next one. Emmanuel makes no further references to the plenary assembly during which, as a result of our vote on a proposal made by Peyssou and Colin, he was unanimously elected Abbé of Malevil.

I imagine the reader finds this somewhat astonishing. I certainly do. And with some justification, when I have just read the results of a meeting that lasted three hours squeezed into a bald three lines.

There might also be some puzzlement as to how the idea of such a proposal occurred to Peyssou and Colin in the first place. And also, above all, how it came about that Meyssonnier and myself voted in favor.

Here are the answers to those two questions:

1. First, there is the evidence provided by Colin the day after the vote, when I interviewed him in the storeroom during Emmanuel's training session with Malabar in the outer enclosure. I give Colin's statement word for word:

"Well yes, of course it was Emmanuel who asked us, Peyssou and me, to propose him as Abbé of Malevil. You don't need me to tell you it wasn't something we'd ever have thought of ourselves! He asked us up in his room, after Momo's bath. And his reasons, well you know them already. We all heard enough of them yesterday evening, heaven knows. First, we mustn't accept the spy Fulbert was trying to hang around our necks. Second, we mustn't deprive anyone in Malevil of their Mass if they wanted it. Otherwise half Malevil would be off every Sunday to La Roque and the other half would stay behind. There'd be no unity here any more. It would create a very unhealthy situation."

"But all the same," I said, "you knew that Emmanuel isn't a believer."

"Ah," Colin said, "now I'm not so sure about that as you seem to be! In fact I'd be inclined to say, if you asked me, that Emmanuel has always been rather attracted to religion. The only trouble with him was that he would have needed to be his own priest." And then, looking at me with that smile we hear so much about, he added, "And there you are. That's just what he is now!"

There are two elements in Colin's evidence between which we must, I think, distinguish: the fact—Emmanuel arranging with Colin and Peyssou secretly to be proposed as abbé—and the personal comment—"Emmanuel has always been rather attracted to religion."

The fact, corroborated by Peyssou, is undeniable. But the comment is open to dispute. I, at all events, would certainly be inclined to dispute it.

2. The election was in fact the result of two votes, not just one. The result of the first vote was For: Peyssou, Colin, Jacquet, La Menou, La Falvine, Miette. Abstentions: Meyssonnier and myself.

Emmanuel took our abstentions extremely badly. We didn't realize what we were doing! We were weakening his position! Fulbert would certainly use those two abstentions to persuade the people of La Roque that we didn't trust him! In short, we were undermining Malevil's unity! As far as he was concerned, if we persisted in our attitude he would certainly not accept the office of Abbé of Malevil, he would leave the field free for Fulbert's creature, he would wash his hands of everything and everybody.

Let us say in short—and it is the least that can be said —that Emmanuel exerted a certain amount of pressure on us. Since the others were all beginning to look upon us as two serpents warmed in Malevil's bosom and now preparing to bite the hand that had fed us, and since it was clear that Emmanuel was genuinely extremely distressed, and might well throw in his hand entirely, as he had threatened, we eventually gave way. We withdrew our abstentions, agreed to a second election, and the second time voted in favor.

That was how Emmanuel obtained the unanimous vote he had set his mind on.

XI

THE night after my election the rain continued to bucket down, so much so that it kept me awake for several hours, not because of the noise but because of the almost personal sense of gratitude I was feeling toward it. I have always loved moving water, but it had been a careless kind of love till now. It is so easy to grow accustomed to the things your life depends on. You end up taking them for granted. And that's an error, because nothing is given for all time; there is nothing that could not disappear one day. And that knowledge, as I listened to the rain, made me feel like a convalescent.

I originally chose this room for my bedroom, the room in which I am writing now, because of the view from its tall mullioned window out to the east over the Rhunes valley and the charming Château des Rouzies on the far side. It was through this window beside me now that the sun shone in that following morning and awakened me. I couldn't believe my eyes. As Peyssou had predicted, everything was being given us at once. I jumped out of bed, shook Thomas violently awake, and together we gazed out at our first sunlight for two months.

I remembered a bicycle ride in the dark with the other members of the Club, followed by a good hour and a half's uphill scramble to the highest point of the province (1,680 feet) just to watch the sun rise. It's the kind of thing one does at fifteen, with the sort of wild excitement that fades as you get older. And that's a pity. We ought to pay more attention to life while we're living it. It's not that long.

"Come on," I said to Thomas. "We'll saddle the horses and go and take a look from up on the Poujade."

And that's what we did, without stopping to wash or eat. The Poujade, up above Malejac, is the highest point for miles around. I took Malabar as usual, leaving Amarante for Thomas, since Malabar still needed a sharp watch kept on him the whole time, whereas Amarante of course was docility itself.

It is something that will always stay with me, that ride up to the Poujade with Thomas in the dawn. Not that anything happened—there was nothing up there but just the sun and us—and not that anything important was said, because neither of us opened his mouth. Nor was what we saw from the Poujade at all beautiful: a charred landscape, ruined farms, blackened fields, skeletons that had been trees. But nevertheless, above it all there stood the sun.

By the time we had reached the top of the hill the sun was already high above the horizon and had turned from red to pink, from pink to rosy white. Although it was giving off a pleasant warmth, we could still look straight into it without blinking, so thick were the veils still masking it. The rainsoaked earth was steaming everywhere beneath us. The land was streaked with trails of rising mist that seemed even whiter because of the charred ink-colored fields between.

With our horses reined in side by side, gazing out to the east from the summit of the Poujade, we waited in silence for the sun to free itself from its vaporous covering. When it finally rose above them—and it happened suddenly—both mare and stallion simultaneously pricked their ears, as though they had been startled by some unexpected phenomenon. Amarante even uttered a little neigh of alarm and turned her head toward Malabar. He immediately nibbled at her mouth, which seemed to reassure her. But as she turned her head I noticed that she was blinking her eyes with amazing rapidity, much more rapidly, it seemed to me, than any human eyelid could ever move. And Thomas had raised one hand to shield his eyes, as though his eyelids were no longer adequate for the task. I did likewise. The dazzle was almost unbearable.

We suddenly realized, from the pain the light was causing us, that we had been living for two whole months in a subterranean half darkness.

However, as soon as my eyes began to adjust, euphoria drove out all discomfort. My chest swelled. It was very odd, I was sucking the air into my lungs in great gasps, just as though light was something you could breathe. I also had the sensation that my eyes were open wider than they had ever been before, and that I myself was somehow opening with them. At the same time, just from being bathed in that light, I experienced an unbelievable sense of liberation, of lightness. I eased Malabar into a turn so that I could feel the sun's warmth on my back and neck. Then, so as to offer every surface of my body to it in turn, I began circling the summit of the hill at a walk, immediately followed by Amarante, who did not wait to ask for Thomas's opinion before setting off in Malabar's wake. I looked down at the earth at our feet. Battered and soaked by the rain, it had already ceased to be just dust. There was even a look of life in it again. In my impatience I even began looking around for new shoots and staring at the less badly burned trees as though I expected to see buds on them.

The next day we decided to sacrifice Prince, our bull calf. We already had Hercule, the bull from L'Étang, and La Roque also had a bull. So keeping Prince no longer made any sense; and since we were going to give Noiraude to La Roque, and Marquise had her twins to feed, we were going to need Princesse's milk.

The slaughtering was a ghastly event. As soon as Prince was taken away from her, Princesse began the most heart-rending bellowing. Then Miette, who had continued cuddling and stroking Prince till the very last moment, sat down on the cobbles and burst into floods of tears. Which did have at least one happy result. This kind of "sacrifice" had always excited Momo to the most horrible degree in the past, causing him to keep up a barrage of savage shrieks the whole time the shameful business was in progress; but seeing Miette in tears, Momo remained silent, then tried to console her, and eventually, having

313

totally failed, threw himself down beside her and began weeping too.

Prince was already over two months old, and when Jacquet had butchered the carcass we decided to give half of it to the people of La Roque and ask for some sugar and washing powder in exchange. We also decided to take two large loaves and some butter with us—purely as gifts—plus three iron bars to lever aside the tree trunks that must certainly have fallen across the road on the day it happened.

We set off at dawn on a Wednesday, in the cart with Malabar between the shafts, myself with a heavy heart at leaving Malevil, even for one day. Colin was happy at the thought of seeing his shop again, and Thomas delighted at the prospect of a change of scene. We all carried guns slung over our backs.

The three ex-troglodytes were delighted at the thought of seeing Catie and their uncle Marcel again. Miette, hair freshly washed the night before, was wearing a little printed cotton dress on which we all complimented her (smacking kisses to thank us). Jacquet had shaved and was couthly combed. And La Falvine was quite beside herself with jubilation, because added to the pleasure of seeing her brother again there was also that of escaping for a few hours from domestic drudgery and La Menou's tyrannical rule.

The joy of it all was more than she could stand, and no sooner were we clear of Malevil than she began talking —as Colin put it—like a cow pissing. We understood the reasons for her euphoric state and no one had the heart to tell her to shut up. It was easier, as soon as we encountered our first tree trunk, for all four of us, including Miette, simply not to get back into the cart when we moved off again, leaving Jacquet to put up with that terrible verbal flux alone, except for the downhill stretches, when we did all climb back in for a while. There was no question of going faster than a walking pace anyway, because Noiraude was tied to the back of the cart and had to keep up as best she could. It took us more than three hours to cover the nine miles to La Roque. And during that whole time, even though no one was listening,

Falvine didn't stop talking once. Every now and then I briefly lent an ear, curious to know what mechanism lay behind the endless flow. But there was nothing mysterious about it. One thing just led on to the next by the simplest association of ideas. La Falvine's conversation was completely automatic, like prayers mechanically muttered over a rosary. Or better still, like lavatory paper. One tug on the end and it just kept spilling out.

We reached the south gate of La Roque at eight and discovered that the small door cut into one side of the main gate was open. I only had to push it in order to walk through, draw the bolts, and pull both sides of the big gate wide open. I was inside the town, and there was no one anywhere in sight. I called. No answer. It was true that the gate led into the lower town, which was just heaps of charred ruins, so it wasn't surprising to find no one living there; but that the gate was neither guarded nor even kept closed betokened staggering irresponsibility on Fulbert's part, it seemed to me.

La Roque was a tiny town perched on top of a hill with its back against a cliff, entirely surrounded by a wall at its base and crowned at its summit by a château. There were a good dozen or so little towns of the same kind in France, all once dear to the hearts of tourists, but La Roque was one of the most homogeneous, since all the houses were very old, and none of them had been in any way messed about with. The ramparts were still unbroken along their whole length, with two fine gates flanked by round towers, one to the south—the one through which we had just entered—and the other to the west, leading out to the main road to the county town.

Entering by the south gate you found yourself immediately caught in a labyrinth of narrow alleys, then beyond these you emerged into the main street. It was in fact scarcely any wider than any of the others but was called that because of the shops that lined it on both sides. This main street was also referred to as the "traverse."

The shops along it were really beautiful, because luckily, just as the age of modernization was dawning, the Ministry of Works slapped a preservation order on the stone arches that formed their fronts. The rest of the town was all built of a golden-toned stone, with beautiful workmanship, the joins scarcely even visible, and the roofs covered in stone slates, with patches of warm, pale new stone zigzagging through the gray-black of the old where repairs had been done. The big uneven cobbles, like the houses a good four hundred years old, had been worn to a magnificent shine by all the men they had seen come and go.

This main street ran extremely steeply uphill till it stopped at the château gate, which was huge and ornate but lacked a gate tower or crenelated battlements or arrow slits. All such defense works had been long out of date by the time it was built. The wooden gate itself had been painted a dark green by the Lormiaux, which was something of a shock when you first caught sight of it, because all the shutters in La Roque were painted the traditional claret red. The château, like the town itself, was entirely protected by ramparts, against which a number of houses of about the same age had been built in lean-to fashion. It was entirely sixteenth century in origin, having been rebuilt on the site of an older castle gutted by fire. In front of the château itself, below the terrace, there extended a small esplanade, about fifty by thirty yards, which commanded a wonderful view—on a clear day you could even see Malevil—and up to which the Lormiaux had had enormous quantities of topsoil carted in order to provide themselves with an English-style lawn. Behind the château rose the cliff that overhung and protected it.

As we emerged from the asphalted alleys, Malabar's hoofs and the cart's wheels combined to create a rare clatter on the traverse's uneven cobbles. Heads began appearing at windows. I told Jacquet to draw up outside Lanouaille the butcher's, so we could unload our side of veal. And we had scarcely stopped before people had begun to emerge onto their doorsteps.

I found them thin-looking and oddly subdued. I had been expecting a more exuberant welcome. Although their eyes began to gleam when Jacquet hoisted their half of Prince onto his back, carried it into the butcher's little shop, and with Lanouaille's help hung it from a hook,

316

the gleam faded again immediately. The same phenomenon occurred when I produced the two great loaves and the butter. I handed these over to Lanouaille as well, and he took them, I noticed, with a certain hesitation, almost as though he was afraid in some way, while the other inhabitants, now gathered around us in a circle, gazed at the bread with eyes strangely sad for all their intensity.

"Is it to all of us you're giving that?" Marcel Falvine demanded in an abrupt, almost violent tone, tearing himself away from the embraces of his sister and grandniece and advancing upon me with his leather apron flapping at each step.

I was very much taken aback by the aggression in his voice and studied him carefully. I had known him for years by sight, but whenever I had seen him before he had been in his shop, last between his knees, working on a pair of boots or shoes. He was a man of about sixty, almost bald, with very dark eyes and a large fleshy nose with a wart on the right nostril. But what struck me most forcibly about him was the contrast between his legs, which were short and twisted, and his Herculean shoulders.

"Yes, of course," I said. "It's for the whole town."

"In that case," Marcel said loudly, turning to Lanouaille, "there's no point in waiting. You can share it out right away. Beginning with the bread."

"I don't know that Monsieur le Curé would agree with that," Fabrelâtre said. "It would be better to wait."

Fabrelâtre ran the hardware and fancy goods store in La Roque. He looked like a long white church taper, with flabby features, a little gray toothbrush mustache, and blinking eyes behind steel-rimmed spectacles.

"We'll keep his share for him," Marcel answered without looking around and with a violent gesture of the arm. "And Armand's, Gazel's, and Josepha's too. We won't do anyone out of anything, don't worry. Come on, Lanouaille, what are you waiting for, in heaven's name!"

"No call for swearing," Fabrelâtre told him in tones of authority. A silence. Lanouaille looked at me as though begging for my advice. He was a young fellow of about twenty-five, as solidly built as our Jacquet, with full cheeks and honest eyes. As far as I could make out, he was in agreement with Marcel but didn't dare ignore Fabrelâtre's opposition.

There were about twenty people clustered around. I looked around at their faces, some familiar, others unknown, and on all I could read hunger, fear, and gloom. I knew already that I was going to intervene, and on whose side. But I was waiting till I had grasped the situation better.

Someone stepped forward. It was Pimont. He ran the little newsstand in La Roque. I knew him well, and his wife Agnès even better. Both were about thirty-five years old. Pimont had played center forward on the team that beat Malejac the day my uncle and parents were killed in their car crash. Short, square, excitable, brushcut hair, always a smile. Except that today he wasn't smiling.

"There's no reason whatever to postpone the distribution," he said in a tense voice. "All of us present can guarantee that it will be fair, and that no one will be forgotten."

"It would be more courteous to wait, all the same," Fabrelâtre said sharply, eyes blinking behind his steel rims.

I noted that like Marcel and Lanouaille, Pimont refused to look at Fabrelâtre when he spoke. And I also noted that Marcel, excitable and quick-tempered though he was, had failed to protest when Fabrelâtre publicly reprimanded him for swearing. It only needed one glance at the crowd's anxious, famished eyes fixed on the two loaves to see that they were all in favor of an immediate distribution. But apart from Marcel and Pimont, no one had dared speak up. The slow-witted, flabby, amorphous Fabrelâtre was holding twenty ravenous people in check!

"Ah, come, son," old Pougès broke in suddenly, addressing himself to Lanouaille in patois, "cut it up there. My mouth is already watering, looking at that fine loaf!"

I'll come back to old Pougès later. He had spoken in a jesting tone, with a little laugh, but no one echoed it. Another silence fell. Lanouaille looked at me, then at the great dark green gate of the château, as though he was afraid of seeing it suddenly flung open.

When the silence had dragged on for a while, I realized that the time had come to intervene. "Well, this is a crazy

318

argument and no mistake!" I said with a jovial chuckle. "I've never heard such a fuss over nothing at all! It seems to me that if you find it so difficult to make up your minds, all you need do is take a vote, then act according to the majority's decision. So let's see," I went on quickly, raising my voice, "who's in favor of immediate distribution?"

There was a moment of stunned surprise. Then Marcel and Pimont raised their hands. Marcel with barely restrained violence, Pimont more soberly, but without any lack of resolution. Lanouaille lowered his eyes and looked embarrassed. After a second, old Pougès took a step forward and raised his right forefinger, giving me a conspiratorial look as he did so but keeping his hand close to his chest so that Fabrelâtre, now slightly back from him, couldn't see the finger. This petty ruse made me feel ashamed for him and I didn't count his vote.

"Two in favor," I said, without Pougès protesting. "And now, those against."

Fabrelâtre alone raised a finger, and Marcel snickered out loud, though still without looking at him. Pimont smiled derisively.

"And who abstains?"

No one stirred. I looked slowly around at the crowd's faces. Incredible. They didn't even dare to abstain.

"The decision is in favor of immediate distribution," I said in an even voice, "by two votes to one. It will be carried out under the supervision of the donors. Thomas and Jacquet will represent us."

Thomas, breaking off the animated conversation he had been having with Catie (I made a note to look her over properly later on, when I had the time), moved forward with Jacquet in his wake, and the crowd parted docilely to let them through into Lanouaille's shop. I glanced at Fabrelâtre. He was looking very sick and put down. He must be even stupider than I'd suspected, I thought, to have not only gone along with my suggestion but also to have voted himself, thereby revealing his isolation. Poor imbecile, he was nothing in himself, I realized now. It was the power behind the green gate that called the tune in La Roque.

Lanouaille set eagerly to work, and while he began cutting up the loaves I noticed Agnès standing a little apart, her baby in her arms, leaving her husband to stand in line for their share. She seemed to me a little thinner, but still as pleasant to look at as ever, with her blond hair shining in the sunlight, and her pale brown eyes that always gave me the impression they were blue. I went over. Seeing her like that, I felt the old weakness I had always had for her stir again in my heart. And she? She looked at me as I came over with a sad, fond look in her eyes, as though to say, Well, Emmanuel my dear, you see how it is? And if you had only made up your mind ten years ago, then it's at Malevil I'd be today, not here like this. It was true, I knew it. It was yet another of those things in life I had left undone. And I had thought about it often.

While we were exchanging thoughts in this way, we also engaged in a conversation using spoken words. I stroked her baby on the cheek, the baby that might have been mine, and Agnès informed me that it was a girl, almost eight months old now.

"From what we've been told, Agnès, if we hadn't agreed to give La Roque a cow, you would have refused to let your little girl come to live with us at Malevil. Is that true?"

She looked at me with indignant eyes. "Who told you that? It was never even mentioned!"

"You know who it was."

"Oh, that one!" she said with muted anger. But I noticed that she too lowered her voice.

At that moment I noticed out of the corner of my eye that Fabrelâtre was stealthily making for the green gate.

"Monsieur Fabrelâtre!" I called out loudly.

He stopped and turned as all eyes converged on him.

"Monsieur Fabrelâtre," I said with a jovial smile as I walked over to him, "it seems very unwise of you to leave just as the distribution is about to start!"

Still smiling, I took him by the arm, without his attempting to resist, and said half in jest half in earnest, "You mustn't go waking Fulbert up, must you? His health, as you know, is very delicate. He needs all the sleep he can get."

I felt his flabby arm trembling in my grip, and without relaxing it, I led him slowly back toward the shop.

"But Monsieur le Curé must be notified of your arrival, you realize," he said in a shaky voice.

"There is no hurry, Monsieur Fabrelâtre. It is scarcely half past eight yet! Now then, why don't you just help Thomas do the sharing out."

And he obeyed, the great soft creature! He did as he was told! He was soft enough and stupid enough to actually help in the distribution he had publicly disapproved of. Marcel, arms folded over his leather apron, permitted himself to laugh out loud at the sight, though without anyone daring to imitate him, apart from Pimont. But I was a little ashamed even to look at Pimont now, after the slightly overaffectionate conversation I had just had with his wife's eyes.

I was about to go over to Catie when old Pougès intercepted me. I knew him well. If my memory serves me correctly, he must have been just over seventy-five then. He was short, had very little fat on him, very little hair, very few teeth, and very, very little enthusiasm when it came to work. The only thing he had a great deal of was mustache. It was yellowish white, drooped down on either side of his mouth, and was, I suspect, his pride and joy, since he was always stroking it with a knowing look in his eye.

"Now, to look at me, Emmanuel," he used to say when I bumped into him in Malejac, "I don't look like anything, do I? But I've put it over on the lot of them all the same. First, my wife dying. Round one to me. A viper, as I don't need to tell you. And then, at sixty-five, my farmer's pension, and straightaway I get a tenant onto my farm. And there you are, me quietly sitting there in La Roque collecting from both sides, living like a king at everyone else's expense. Doing damn-all, my old son. Ten years that's been now! And not over yet. Ninety, that's when I shall be leaving you all, at ninety like my old man. So that's another fifteen years of this lovely little old life I still have in the bottle! And the others paying!"

I used to run into Pougès and his mustache in Malejac quite often, because every day, even when it snowed, he used to bike the nine miles from La Roque to Malejac in order to drink his two glasses of white wine in the bistro that Adelaide had opened next to her grocery store. Two glasses, no more. One he paid for. The second she gave him, goodhearted as ever where her exes were concerned. And even there Pougès took advantage. The free glass he made last.

"And how come then, Emmanuel," Pougès asked me in a low voice, tugging at his mustache and giving me his knowing look, "how come you didn't count my vote in then?"

"I didn't see you," I told him with a little smile. "You can't have put your hand up high enough. Next time you'd better try a bit harder."

"All the same though," he said, drawing me aside, "I did vote for. Remember that, Emmanuel, I voted for. I'm not in favor of what's going on here."

And not in favor of getting your feet wet either, I'll be bound, I thought.

"You must miss your little bike rides," I said politely out loud, "and your two little glasses of white at Adelaide's."

He shook his head. "Ah, no, the bike rides, that's not what I'm missing. Because, believe me or not, Emmanuel, I still take those every day, same as ever, except it has to be along the main road now. It's the not having anything there at the end to set me up again, that's what I miss. Because the château wine—heh!—you could ride your bike from here to doomsday and you wouldn't get a thimbleful out of them up there!" he went on with deep fury.

"Listen then," I said in patois. "Now our road's been cleared, why not come on a little farther from time to time and pay us a visit in Malevil. Our Menou would be glad to draw you a glass of our red for your pains, and it's as good as Adelaide's white any day of the week."

"Well, I'll not say no to that," he said, scarcely able to conceal the almost insolent sense of triumph he was feeling at the thought of being able to drink at our expense. "And what a good, polite man you are, Emmanuel! I shall tell everyone so too, if ever there's any who try to say bad things about you!"

Whereupon, as a down payment on all the wine he intended to soak me for, he gave me a little friendly tap on the forearm and winked as he tugged at his long yellow-stained mustache. We parted from each other both satisfied with what had been achieved, he at having found another source of free wine, myself at having established a regular and discreet line of communication with La Roque.

In Lanouaille's shop the distribution was drawing to an end. As soon as the inhabitants had received their share of butter and bread they all hurried back to their houses, as though they were fearful of being dispossessed again at the last moment.

"And now you'd better butcher the veal right away," I told Lanouaille.

"Yes, but that's going to take a little while, you know," he said.

"Begin anyway."

He looked at me—a nice lad, so strong and yet so timid —then he went over and lifted the side of veal down from its hook, threw it onto his block, and began sharpening his knives. The only others left in the shop by now were Marcel, Thomas, Catie, and a little girl she was holding by one hand. As soon as the sharing out of the butter and bread was over, Jacquet had gone to help Colin, whose shop was only a few yards down the street and who was occupied loading tools and metal into the cart. La Falvine and Miette were presumably visiting friends somewhere, since they were nowhere to be seen. As for Noiraude, whom, strange to say, everyone seemed to have forgotten as soon as the loaves appeared, she was tied to a ring in the wall beside the big green gate, muzzle stuck in a bundle of hay that Jacquet had shown the good sense to bring along.

At last I had time to take a good look at Catie. She was taller and less well padded than Miette, having presumably come under the influence of women's magazines and their cult of the beanpole during her stay in La Roque. Like her sister, she had a slight heaviness about

323

nose and chin, lovely dark eyes, though heavily made up in her case, a mouth bleeding with lipstick, and less abundant but more artfully tended hair. She was wearing a pair of very tight jeans, a multicolored cotton jersey top, a broad belt with a golden buckle, and around her neck and wrists, dangling from her ears and on her fingers, a great deal of costume jewelry. Got up and bedizened as she was, she looked as though she had just stepped off a page of *Young Miss* or some such magazine, and her nonchalant, carefree posture, as she leaned with one arm against the shop wall, pelvis thrust up and out, looked to me as though it had been consciously copied from the photographs of models in a mail-order catalogue.

La Catie, it seemed to me, did not have such sweet eyes as Miette, but they must have been endowed with a very efficient charge of sexual aggression all the same, to judge from the way in which she had managed, in only a few minutes, to hook, reel in, and stun our Thomas, who was now standing in front of her in a trance of fascination. As we climbed down from the cart, Catie must have made her choice in the blink of an eye, and she had battened upon him with such rapidity and such determination that I suspected the poor victim never stood a chance.

"Emmanuel," Marcel said, "you don't know my grand-niece."

I shook hands with his grandniece, I spoke a few words to her, she replied, and while we were going through this social ceremony she treated me to an expert, thorough, and rapid inspection. I had been judged, measured, and weighed up not as a moral being, and even less with regard to my intellect, but as a possible partner in the only activity that seemed to her important in life. And I think I scored quite high, as a matter of fact. After which Catie swung the full force of her attention back to Thomas. What surprised me in this whole business was the extraordinary speed and almost brutality with which the process of appropriating Thomas had been set into motion. It is true that there was nothing normal about the life we had lived since the day it happened. Witness the way in which the problem of sharing out our gifts had arisen just before. Witness too the fact that not one of us had thought fit to remove the guns we had slung over our backs, even Colin, who must have found his weapon a great encumbrance while loading up the cart.

"And what about you?" I asked the little girl that Catie was holding by the hand. Abandoned to her own devices by the intense eye-to-eye infighting going on above her head, she had been amusing herself for the past few minutes by following all my movements. "What is your name?"

"Evelyne," she said, fixing me gravely with her deep-set, darkly smudged blue eyes, which took up almost half of the thin little face framed by long, absolutely straight blond hair that fell down to her elbows. I picked her up with my hands under her arms and lifted her up to my face to give her a kiss, but she immediately wound both legs around my hips and her two thin arms around my neck. Returning my kisses with a look of delight, she clung to me with a strength that surprised me in that frail-looking body.

"Emmanuel," Marcel said, turning toward me, "if you have a moment to spare I'd like to talk to you in my shop before those other swine turn up."

"Glad to," I said. "You two"—turning to Catie and Thomas—"had better go and help Colin with his loading. Down you get, Evelyne, let go of me now," I said, trying to disengage her thin arms from my neck while Catie took Thomas by the hand and led him out into the street.

"No, no," Evelyne said, clinging to me even tighter. "Carry me like this to Marcel's."

"Will you get down if I do?"

"I promise."

"If you give way to her once, that little wretch, you'll never hear the end of it, I warn you," Marcel said. Then he added, "She's been living with me since the bomb. Catie looks after her. And believe me, it can be pretty tiring sometimes, with her having the asthma. The nights we go through, well you wouldn't believe."

So this was the orphan Fulbert had told us about, the little girl that no one in La Roque could be found to look after. What an unpleasant creature, I thought to myself.

He obviously just lies the way he breathes, even when there's nothing to be gained by it.

Marcel led me through his shop and then, since we would have been too visible there, on into a tiny dining room with a window giving out onto a scarcely larger courtyard. I immediately noticed his lilacs. Protected by stone walls on all four sides, they had been scorched but not actually burned.

"You noticed," Marcel said with a gleam of pleasure in his black eyes. "There are buds on them! They're not done for after all, my lilacs. They're coming again. Come on, sit down, Emmanuel."

I did as he said, and Evelyne immediately took up her position between my legs, clasped my thumbs in her fists, and leaning her back against me, crossed them over her chest. That done, she sat good as gold.

As I sat down, I glanced up at the shelves above the walnut buffet on which Marcel kept his books. All paperbacks and book-club editions. Because paperbacks you could buy anywhere, and the book-club editions you didn't have to go into a bookshop in order to acquire. I remembered that the first time I was surprised by Marcel was when I was twelve. Before taking down a book he wanted to show my uncle, I had watched him carefully wash his hands with soap under the kitchen tap. And when he came back I saw that they were no whiter than before. Broad hands with skin tanned like leather, and ingrained with black deep into the pores and cracks.

"Nothing to offer you, my poor Emmanuel," he said as he sat down opposite me. He shook his head sadly. "You saw?"

"Yes, I saw."

"Mark you, we must be fair. In the beginning Fulbert did a lot of good. He was the one who made us bury the dead. And in a sense he was the one who gave us back the courage to go on. It was only gradually, with Armand behind him, that he began putting the screws on."

"And you did nothing to stop him?"

"By the time we wanted to it was too late. The trouble, really, was that we weren't suspicious enough at the start. He has a tongue like honey, that Fulbert. He told us that

326

all the groceries had to be brought up and stored in the château, to prevent looting, now the owners were dead. Fair enough. It seemed rational at the time and we did it. Same argument for the bacon, sausages, and so on. After that he told us, 'You mustn't keep your guns. People will end up killing one another. Better to store those in the château as well.' Fair enough. That too was far from stupid. And what point could there be in keeping our guns anyway, since there's no game left? And then, of course, one fine day it dawned on us that he had everything up there in the château: hay, grain, horses, pigs, meat, groceries, and the guns. Not to mention the cow you've just brought us. So that was it. It's the château that hands out the rations to us all every day. And the rations can vary from one person to the next, you get me? And also from one day to the next, according to the big boss's mood. And that's how Monsieur Fulbert keeps us under his thumb—by controlling the rations."

"And Armand, what's his part in all this?"

"Armand? He is the secular arm. The terror. Fabrelâtre is the information service. Though Fabrelâtre is more just a stupid asshole than anything else, mark you, as you must have noticed yourself."

"And Josepha?"

"Josepha's the cleaning woman up there. About fifty or so. Not much to look at, but she's not there just to do the cleaning all the same, if you see what I mean. She lives in the château with Fulbert, Armand, and Gazel. Gazel is the vicar Fulbert meant to send you when he's put the finishing touches to his training."

"And what's he like, this Gazel?"

"Gazel? He's just an old woman!" Marcel said, bursting into laughter. And it did me good to see him laugh, because that's how I remembered seeing him in the old days, sitting there in his little workshop, dark eyes sparkling, wart quivering, Herculean shoulders shaking with the laughter he was obliged to contain because his mouth was full of nails, which he was removing one by one to hammer into the boot on his last. And how I loved to watch him knock them in, just one blow for each, always dead straight, never a single one botched, and the sheer speed!

"Gazel," he went on, "is a widower in his fifties. And if ever you want a good laugh, then pop in at his house and take a look at him around ten any morning, doing his housework, his hair all wrapped up in a turban so it doesn't get dusty, and rubbing and polishing and dusting like a little old granny. And what for? He doesn't even live there any more, he lives up in the château! And he's delighted, I can tell you! It means his own house never gets dirty!"

"And apart from that?"

"Oh, not a bad little fellow really, but what can you expect. He's swallowed the whole thing, hook, line, and sinker! And as for Fulbert, total veneration for him! All the same, if he goes to live at Malevil, you'd be as well to keep your eye on him."

I looked at Marcel. "He won't be coming to live at Malevil, don't worry. Last Sunday evening my companions elected me Abbè of Malevil myself."

Evelyne let go of my thumbs, twisted around, and stared up into my face with a scared look; but what she saw there must have reassured her, because she immediately resumed her former position. As for Marcel, he opened his eyes and his mouth very wide, then a second later burst into peals of loud laughter.

"Well, Emmanuel, if you're not just like your uncle," he gasped through his merriment. "And oh, what a pity you don't live here in La Roque! You'd have got rid of these vermin for us. Though mark you," he said, becoming serious once more, "as far as that goes, even taking extreme measures, you know, I don't say I haven't thought about it. But there's no one here I can rely on, except Pimont. And Pimont, the thought of laying hands on a priest! Never."

I looked at him without speaking. Fulbert's tyranny must be weighing heavy on them indeed for a man like Marcel to have started thinking in those terms.

"Hey," he said suddenly, "last Sunday, did you give Fulbert any bread when he left Malevil?"

"Yes, and butter as well."

"Yes, and we heard about it from Josepha. She's a talker, luckily for us."

"But it was for all of you, that bread."

"Oh, I knew that, don't worry!"

He spread his tanned black-stained palms in a gesture of despair. "But there you are, you see. That's what it's come to. If Fulbert decides tomorrow to let you starve, then you starve. Say for instance now, you refuse to go and hear Mass or to confess, that's it. Your rations get smaller. Oh, he won't stop them altogether, ah no! He just whittles them away. A little smaller every day. And if you complain, then you find Armand coming to pay you a little home visit one day. Oh, he wouldn't come here!" Marcel said quickly, straightening up on his chair. "He's still a little afraid of me, our Armand. On account of this."

He slipped a hand into the pouch of his leather apron and took out the razor-sharp knife he used for cutting out soles. It flashed once, then it was back in the pouch again.

"Listen, Marcel," I said after a moment, "we've known each other quite a while, you and I. And you knew my uncle. He thought a great deal of you. If you want to come over to Malevil with Catie and Evelyne and live with us, then you'll be made very welcome."

Evelyne didn't turn around, but tightening her fists around my thumbs, she tugged my arms tighter around her chest with astonishing force.

"Thank you for that," Marcel said, tears welling up in his dark eyes. "Really, thank you, Emmanuel. But I can't accept, for two reasons. First, there are Fulbert's decrees."

"Decrees?"

"Oh, yes. So you don't know about that yet? Monsieur le Curé has taken to issuing decrees. All on his own, without consulting anyone else. And he reads them out from the pulpit on Sundays. Decree number one— I know it off by heart: Private property having been abolished in La Roque, all goods, buildings, stores, victuals, and provisions at present within the perimeter of the ramparts henceforward belong to the parish of La Roque."

"It's not possible!"

"Ah, but wait! That's not all. Second decree: No inhabitant of La Roque has the right to leave the town without the express authorization of the parish council. And that council—which he appointed!—consists of Armand, Gazel, Fabrelâtre, and himself!"

I was staggered. My wariness of Fulbert seemed now to have been justified a hundred times over. But on the other hand, I had seen and heard enough during the last three quarters of an hour to be quite sure in my own mind that Fulbert's regime would find precious few defenders if relations with Malevil became strained.

"And I don't need to tell you," Marcel went on, "that his precious parish council is never going to give someone like me permission to leave. A cobbler is far too useful. Especially now."

I burst out violently, "We don't give a damn for Fulbert and his decrees. Come on, Marcel, pack up your things and we'll take you now!"

Marcel shook his head sadly. "No. Because now I'll tell you my real reason. I just don't want to leave the folks here in the lurch. Oh, I know they're a bit gutless. But then if I wasn't here it would be even worse. Having Pimont and me here, it does keep them in check just a little, our friends up there. And I don't want to desert Pimont. That would be a rotten trick. . . . But if you want to take Catie and Evelyne along with you, do by all means. Fulbert has been pestering Catie for quite a while now to go up and do his cleaning for him at the château. I needn't say any more! Not to mention the way Armand is always hanging around her."

I pulled my thumbs free from Evelyne's grip, lifted her around to face me, and took her by the shoulders. "Can you hold your tongue, Evelyne?"

"Yes."

"Then listen. You are to do exactly what Catie tells you, understand? And not a word to anyone."

"Yes," she said, with the solemn look of a bride saying "I do." Those big blue eyes, made even bigger by the dark smudges around them, amused me and moved me at the same time with their tremendous solemnity, and taking good care to grip her arms so that she couldn't wind them around me again, I bent down and kissed her on both cheeks.

"I'm relying on you," I told her as I got up.

At that moment from the street outside we heard the sound of voices being raised, then a sound of running steps on the cobbles. A panting Catie appeared in the doorway of the little room.

"Come quickly!" she cried. "Armand is starting a fight with Colin!"

She vanished again immediately. I hurried over to the door, then paused and turned as I realized that Marcel was following me.

"If you're staying on here," I told him in patois, "it would be better if you didn't get mixed up in this. Stay here and take care of Evelyne; we don't want her under our feet."

By the time I reached the cart Armand was in a very unpleasant situation and protesting loudly. Jacquet and Thomas had immobilized both his arms. (Thomas with a very neat lock.) And Colin, red as an angry bantam cock, was standing in front of him brandishing a length of lead pipe over his head.

"Now then, now then, what is going on here?" I said in my most pacific tones. Ignoring Colin, I inserted myself between him and Armand. "That's enough, you two. Let Armand go now. Let's hear what he has to say for himself."

Thomas and Jacquet did as I asked, rather glad of my intervention in fact, since they had been holding Armand's arms for some little while now, and the longer Colin put off actually hitting him the more tricky their position was becoming.

"It was him," Armand said, also extremely relieved, pointing at Colin. "It was your plumber there. He insulted me."

I looked at him. Armand had put on weight since the last time we met. The only person in La Roque who had, that was for sure. He was a big man, even taller than Peyssou, and strong, as his thick neck and vast shoulders suggested. His strength plus his reputation had always guaranteed, before the bomb, that he had only to walk into a dance for the hall to empty.

But because he had emptied so many dancehalls, he had ended up unable to find a girl to marry him, even though with his job up at the château he had been paid regularly by the month, with free accommodation, heating and lighting thrown in. For lack of a legitimate spouse, he'd always had to make do with La Roque's overdone leftovers and stringiest old hens, which had of course made him more bitter and vicious than ever. And with those pale eyes, white eyelashes and eyebrows, his broken nose, his jutting chin, and his pimples, he was not an attractive sight. But after all, that's not the point. Even the ugliest man can always find someone to marry him. What put prospective parties off in Armand's case, apart from his brutality, was that he didn't like work. He only liked frightening people. And he was disliked because he gave himself airs as a bailiff and gamekeeper when he was in fact neither the one nor the other. He had even gone so far as to rig himself up with a paramilitary uniform, which alienated any sympathy anyone might have had left: an old forage cap, a black velvet jacket with gilt buttons, black riding breeches, and boots. And a gun. Mustn't forget the gun. Even during the closed season.

"He insulted you?" I said. "What did he say?"

"He said, 'Go to hell,'" Armand said in tones of deep affront. "'Go to hell and take your decree with you.'"

"You said that!" I exclaimed, swiveling around and taking advantage of the fact that my back was now to Armand to give Colin a wink.

"Yes," the still scarlet Colin said. "I said it and I—"

I cut him off. "And what kind of loutish behavior do you call that," I said very loudly in patois. "You ought to be ashamed of yourself. We haven't come all this way to be rude to people. Take back what you said here and now, if you don't mind!"

"All right then, if you like, I take it back," Colin said, at last getting the message. "But that's not all there is to it," he added. "He called me a little asshole."

"Did you call him that?" I asked, turning back to Armand and staring at him sternly.

332

"Well, he'd got my back up, hadn't he?" Armand said.

"Maybe, but you were going a bit far there, damn it. 'Little asshole,' that's much worse than 'Go to hell.' And after all, we're all of us guests of the Curé of La Roque here. There are limits, you know, Armand. Here we bring you a cow, a side of veal, two loaves, three pounds of butter, and all you can do is call us 'little assholes'!"

"It was him I called a little asshole," Armand said.

"Us or him, there's no difference. Now then, Armand, do as he's done, take it back."

"If you really want me to," Armand said with utmost ill grace.

"Bravo!" I said, feeling it would perhaps be imprudent to push my demands any further. "So there we are, that's settled! And now that you've made it up, maybe we can talk this over calmly. What's it all about? What is this decree of yours?"

Armand explained, which gave me time to have my answer ready.

"And so you, naturally enough," I said to Armand when he'd finished, "you were trying to enforce your curé's decree by preventing Colin from moving his stock. Because his stock, according to the decree, now belongs to the parish."

"That's it exactly," Armand said.

"Well now," I said, "I certainly don't say you were in the wrong. You were only doing your duty."

Armand eyed me with surprise, and not without suspicion, his white eyelashes fluttering over his pale eyes.

I went on: "Only the thing is, you see, Armand, there's one difficulty. Which is that we at Malevil have also issued a decree. And according to our decree all the property that used to belong to anyone living at Malevil now belongs to the castle of Malevil, wherever that property happens to be. So Colin's shop and stock in La Roque now belongs to Malevil. I hope you're not going to dispute that," I said sternly to Colin.

"No, I don't dispute it," Colin said.

"So, in my opinion," I went on, "this is a special case. Your curé's decree doesn't apply here, because Colin is not a member of the parish of La Roque but from Male-vil."

"That may be so and it may not," Armand said in an unpleasant aggressive tone, "but it's up to Monsieur le Curé to decide, not me."

"Quite right," I said, taking him by the arm and thereby enabling him to make his exit without loss of face. "The best thing is for you to go and explain all this to Fulbert, on my behalf, and at the same time to tell him that we're here and that it is already quite late. The rest of you," I said over my shoulder, "go on with the loading until further orders.

"Without wishing to boast," I went on in a confidential tone when we had gone a few paces, "I can tell you now that I rescued you from a very nasty spot there, Armand. They can be pretty rough, those fellows, and little Colin is the ugliest customer of the lot. It's a miracle he didn't split your head open for you just now. It's not so much that you called him an asshole, you understand, it's the fact that you called him a *little* asshole. 'Little' is some-thing he doesn't forgive. But after all, Armand"—I grip-ped his arm more tightly—"it would be idiotic for La Roque and Malevil to start fighting each other over a heap of old metal that's no use to any of us any more! Say for instance that Fulbert is unwilling to recognize Malevil's rights over Colin's stuff, and that things turn nasty, and that it even came to an exchange of shots, it would really be too stupid to get oneself killed over a thing like that, don't you agree? And as far as you're concerned, if you were to hand out the guns in the château to the people here, there's no guarantee that it would be us they'd use them on."

"I don't see by what right you say that," Armand said, stopping in his tracks and staring at me, white with fear and anger.

"Well, now," I said, "for a start just look around you. You weren't exactly quiet about your scuffle with Colin just now, were you? Well, look! Go on, look! Not a person to be seen!" I smiled. "You can't say that the people of La Roque exactly rushed to your defense, can you, when you had my three men on your neck just then."

I stopped to give him time to swallow this bitter pill. And swallow it he did, in silence, with my veiled ultimatum as a chaser.

"Well, I must leave you now," I said. "I shall rely on you to explain the situation to Fulbert for me."

"I'll go and see what I can do," Armand said, struggling to gather the tattered shreds of his pride around him as best he could.

XII

IT WAS as though Armand's departure had been a signal. The heads all reappeared at their windows once more. An instant later the population of La Roque was all out in the main street again. Partly because the small share of our bread and butter they had just swallowed had restored their vitality somewhat, and partly too because the discomfiture of Armand, watched from behind their little windows, had strengthened their morale. Their attitude had changed. Not that their fear had vanished by any means, as I observed from the furtive glances directed at Fabrelâtre, and also from the fact that no one even mentioned the recent quarrel or dared to go and give Colin a hand or even risked going anywhere near the cart. But they were all talking rather more loudly and gesturing with a little more animation. You could sense a restrained excitement in their glances.

I went up the two steps to Lanouaille's shop, clapped my hands, and said loudly, "I have decided, before taking the two mares away, to put them through their paces and do one or two stunts with them on the château terrace, to warm them up for the journey. In fact, since it's a very long time since they were last ridden, there may well be some sport. If you're interested, would you like me to ask Fulbert if he will allow you to watch?"

Every hand shot up, and there was an explosion of delight that genuinely took me aback. Although my time was now limited, I lingered a little to observe their joy, so pitiful did it strike me as being in its implications. Was the life of these people so empty, so dismal, that the prospect of seeing a man riding about on a horse could put them into such a state of frenzy? I felt a small warm hand insinuate itself into mine. It was Evelyne.

I bent down. "Go down to the cart and tell Catie I want to see her at her uncle's," I said quietly. "And tell her it's urgent."

I waited till Fabrelâtre had his back to me, then went back to the cobbler's house. Marcel followed me a few seconds later. He too was gayer than before.

"You don't know the pleasure you're going to give the folks here with your circus act, Emmanuel! What's really killing us here is not so much the injustice, it's the boredom. Damn-all to do, you see. Well me, of course, I can still work a bit at my trade. While there's still the leather, that is. But what about the others? Pimont, Lanouaille, Fabrelâtre? And the farmers who can't sow before October? And no radio, no TV, not even a phonograph. At first people used to go to the church just to be together and have someone talk to them. Fulbert, those first days, he was what they had instead of the TV. Only with a curé, unfortunately, you've soon had enough of what he has to tell you. It's always the same tune. You won't believe it, but we all used to volunteer every day to go up and clean out the horse droppings up at the château. It's even become a reward, being picked to clean out the horse droppings! If you ask me, Fulbert's tyranny would be much more bearable if only he kept us a bit busy with something. I don't quite know with what. But for example, clearing the lower town, piling up the stones, salvaging nails and such. And doing it all together, you understand, as a team. Because here the tragedy is that there's no community life. Nothing. Everyone crouching in his own corner. And waiting for our dinners like good little dogs! If it goes on, we soon won't be men at all any more."

I didn't have time to answer. Preceded by Evelyne, who promptly came over and pressed herself against my legs, Catie burst into the room.

"Catie," I said, "I haven't much time to spare. And I don't want to waste it in talk. Would it suit you to come with Evelyne and live at Malevil? Your uncle has agreed to it."

She blushed, and an avid look came into her face. But

she immediately caught herself up. "Heavens! Well, I don't know," she said, lowering her eyes and assuming a sweetly modest air.

"You don't seem enchanted at the notion, Catie. You can refuse if you wish. I don't force people to do things they don't want."

"Oh, no!" Catie exclaimed. "No, it's not that. It's just that it makes me sad to think of leaving Uncle Marcel."

"Well, well," Marcel said.

"If it's going to upset you that much," I said, "then perhaps it would be better if you stayed. We won't mention it again."

She realized then that I was making fun of her. She began to smile and said with a peasant forthrightness I found much more attractive than the fancy airs she'd been putting on till then, "You're joking. Yes! I'd love to leave with you!"

I burst out laughing, and so did Marcel. He too must have observed the little chats and the long looks outside the butcher's shop.

"So you'll come then?" I said. "Not too many regrets?"

"Not too heartbroken at leaving your uncle?" Marcel said.

She laughed in her turn, openly, honestly, and her full-throated laugh, rippling its way from one end of her body to the other, set her shoulders, breasts, and hips in luscious motion. It was a sight I enjoyed, and my eye lingered on it gladly. A fact that she, needless to say, perceived at once, and she redoubled her little dance while throwing me knowing glances.

I went on: "Now listen carefully, Catie. I don't need to tell you that if we asked Fulbert's permission we wouldn't get it. You and Evelyne are going to leave on the quiet. In a few minutes from now everyone in the town is probably going up to the château terrace to watch me do an act with the horses. Don't go with them. Stay in your room. If you're asked why, it's because Evelyne is having one of her asthma attacks. As soon as everyone is up at the château, pack your bag and Evelyne's. Then take them out to the cart and hide them carefully under the bags we used to wrap the bread in. After that, leave on

338

foot through the south gate, take the Malejac road, keep going for three miles, then wait for us at the Rigoudie turnoff."

"Yes, I know it," Catie said.

"Don't show yourselves until you have recognized us. And Evelyne, you must do exactly what Catie tells you."

Evelyne nodded her acceptance without a word, just gazing up at me with mute fervor. There was a silence.

"Thank you, Emmanuel," Catie said with great feeling. "Can I tell Thomas?"

"No, you can't tell Thomas anything. You haven't time. Go up to your room right away with Evelyne."

And she did as she was told, though not without a glance back over her shoulder to see whether I was watching her exit.

"Well, Marcel, time I left you. I don't want Fulbert to see me in here. Too compromising for you."

He kissed me on the cheek. I had scarcely gone out through the door when I turned and came back, took a small package out of my pocket, and laid it down on the table.

"Do me the pleasure of accepting that, will you? It will compensate a little for the tightening up on your rations when Fulbert finds out Catie's gone."

Out in the street I was approached by a massive towering female dressed in a blue sweater and an amply cut pair of slacks. She had thick short graying hair, a very strong jaw, and blue eyes.

"Monsieur Comte," she said in a deep and well-articulated voice, "allow me to introduce myself: Judith Médard, mathematics teacher, unmarried. I say unmarried and not spinster in order to avoid any misunderstandings."

I was pleasantly amused by this forthright approach, and since she didn't have the slightest trace of a local accent, I asked her if she was from La Roque.

"No, Normandy," she said, seizing my right arm firmly in one strong hand. "And I live in Paris. Or rather I used to live in Paris, in the days when there was a Paris. But I also had a house here in La Roque, which enabled me to survive."

Another squeeze of my biceps. I made a discreet attempt to free my arm from that Amazonian grip, but without even being aware of the fact, I would swear to it, she tightened her fingers even more around my muscle.

"Which enabled me to survive," she went on, "and to become acquainted with a very curious theocratic dictatorship."

Here was one person at least who wasn't allowing herself to be terrorized by Fabrelâtre's listening ears. Because there they were, flapping away less than five yards behind us, those great flabby lugs, yet our Amazon didn't even deign to give them a glance.

"Don't misunderstand me," she said in her forceful, clearly articulated voice. "I am a Catholic [third squeeze of my arm]. But an ecclesiastic of that ilk is something I haven't come across often. And what is one to think of our fellow citizens and their passivity? They will take anything! It's enough to make you wonder whether someone has relieved them of their manly attributes!"

Attributes of which she, on the other hand, clearly had plenty, despite her sex. Because there she was, firm as a rock in her tweed pants, square jaw jutting out over the turtleneck of her sweater, blue eyes blazing, boldly defying Fulbert's authority in La Roque's main street.

"Except for one," she said. "Marcel. Now Marcel, he's a man!"

Did she squeeze Marcel's biceps too? She might well have. There was plenty there to squeeze. Though past sixty, he was all muscles, Marcel, and there were other women—and not only unmarried ones—who liked to feel them still.

"Monsieur Comte," she continued in that tribune-of-the-people voice, "I say bravo to you. Bravo for the immediate distribution of the food [squeeze], which was our only chance of receiving our fair share. And bravo too for having stood up to the local S.S. [another squeeze]. I wasn't up at the time, otherwise I'd have backed you up."

She suddenly leaned down toward me—I say leaned down because she gave me the impression of topping me in height by a good inch and more—and said in my ear, "If you should decide to make any kind of attempt against

340

this unpleasing specimen one day, Monsieur Comte, I will help you."

She had said "I will help you" in a low voice, but with great force. She straightened up, and becoming aware of Fabrelâtre almost at her back, she released my arm, swung abruptly around, and banged against him violently with one shoulder, which sent that long tallow taper staggering over the cobbles.

"Air! Let me have air!" Judith boomed with a great sweeping motion of her arms. "Heavens, man! There's enough room in La Roque for us all!"

"Pardon, madame," Fabrelâtre said feebly.

She didn't even look at him. She offered a broad strong hand. I shook it and left her, with one biceps feeling rather sore. I was glad to have discovered such an ally.

I went down the hill to the cart. They had got a move on with the loading and it was almost finished. Craa, who had earlier been pecking up crumbs almost under Lanouaille's feet, was strutting with a scholarly air up and down Malabar's broad back. As I approached, he gave a friendly croak, fluttered over to perch on my shoulder, and began pushing at my head with his.

Thomas, red and tense, eyes constantly returning anxiously to the door of the cobbler's shop, drew me aside and said, "What's happening? Why did Catie leave us?"

I enjoyed that "us." "Evelyne is having an asthma attack and Catie is staying with her."

"Is that really necessary?"

"Necessary? Of course it's necessary!" I said in a shocked voice. "It's a terrible thing, an asthma attack! The patient needs to be reassured and comforted."

He lowered his eyes and looked shamefaced. Then he raised them again, seemed to gather his strength for a great effort, and said in a flat voice, "Tell me, would you see any objection to Catie coming over to live at Malevil with her sister and grandmother?"

I looked at him. The "with her sister and grandmother" was even better than his "us," I felt. "Yes, I would see one very serious objection," I said very seriously.

"What is it?"

"That Fulbert has forbidden all emigration from La

341

Roque and would certainly oppose her departure. It would mean kidnaping her."

"And why not?" he said in a vibrant voice.

"What do you mean, 'And why not'? Do you want to risk an open break with Fulbert on account of one girl?"

"Perhaps it wouldn't come to that."

"Ah, but it would! Because Fulbert happens to have his eyes on the girl, I happen to know. He's asked her to go up and work for him in the château."

Thomas went pale. "All the more reason."

"All the more reason for what?"

"For getting her away from that creature."

"Really, Thomas, you are extraordinary. It doesn't seem to have occurred to you to ask what Catie thinks. Perhaps she finds Fulbert attractive."

"That's out of the question."

"And besides," I said, "we don't really know anything about Catie. It's only an hour since we first met her."

"She's a very fine girl."

"You mean in her character?"

"Yes, of course."

"Ah, then if you have formed that opinion it changes everything. Generally speaking, I put great faith in your objectivity." I even underlined "objectivity" with my voice; but I might as well not have bothered. Thomas was impervious to humor at the best of times. Now I would have needed a rock drill.

"You mean it's yes then?" he asked anxiously. "We can take her with us?"

I looked at him very seriously now. "You must promise me one thing, Thomas. That you won't take any initiative yourself in the matter."

He hesitated, but there must have been something in my tone or my eyes that gave him pause, because eventually he said, "I promise."

I turned away from him, dislodged Craa from my shoulder because he was getting heavy by now, and set off back up the street. At the very top, the dark green gate had just opened, and all conversations came to a halt.

The first to emerge was Armand, pimply face screwed into a sullen glower. Then came a very odd little figure I didn't know but whom I recognized as Gazel from Marcel's description. And lastly, Fulbert appeared.

A good actor Fulbert. Because in fact he wasn't content just to appear. He made an entrance. Leaving Gazel to close the door behind him, he came to a halt and let his gaze wander over the crowd with a paternal air. He was wearing his same charcoal gray suit, the shirt I had "let him have," his gray knitted tie, and his pectoral cross, the lower end of which he was holding between the thumb and forefinger of his left hand as though he was drawing inspiration from it. The sunshine brought out the shine on his helmet of black hair and deepened the hollows of the ascetic mask lit up by those magnificent squinting eyes. There was nothing of the strut in his walk or stance. On the contrary, he held his body slightly back from his head, as though to emphasize how little importance he attached to it. Eyes fixed on his flock below, he had a benign, patient air about him, a humble, willing martyr.

As he caught sight of me climbing the hill toward him and making my way through the little crowd, he advanced to meet me, hands and arms outstretched with a joyful and fraternal air.

"Welcome to La Roque, Emmanuel," he said in his beautiful, resonant voice, taking my right hand in his, then laying his left one on top of it as though imprisoning a precious treasure. "What a joy it is to see you again! And of course there is no problem," he went on, regretfully relinquishing my fingers, "it goes without saying, since Colin is not a member of our parish. The decrees of La Roque do not apply to him. He is therefore free to remove his belongings."

This was said very quickly and in the most offhand tone, as though the question had never really arisen.

"And so here is the cow," he went on without a pause in a voice filled with wonder, turning toward the animal and raising his arms for all the world as though he was about to give her his benediction. "Is it not a miracle that the Lord should have created a beast that is able, from nothing but hay and grass, to provide us with milk? What is her name?"

"Noiraude."

"But despite her name, Noiraude will give us white milk no doubt," he said with a little ecclesiastical chuckle that was echoed by no one but Fabrelâtre and Gazel. "But I see you have your friends with you too, Emmanuel. Good day to you, Colin. Good day, Thomas. Good day, Jacquet," he said in a kindly voice, though without moving toward them or shaking their hands, thereby demonstrating that he made a distinction between master and squires. As for Miette and La Falvine, they had to make do with a single nod between them. "I also know that you have made us splendid gifts, Emmanuel," he said, turning those black eyes, glistening, brimming with kindliness back toward me. "Bread! Meat! Butter!" And at each exclamation he raised both arms in the air.

"The two loaves and the butter are gifts, yes," I said in a very businesslike voice. "But the meat, no. Come and look, Fulbert."

I led the way down to the butcher's shop. "As you see, we have not skimped. A whole side of veal. I told Lanouaille not to wait to cut it up, since the day looks like being a hot one and we don't have refrigerators any more. As I have said, the bread and the butter are gifts. But the veal isn't. In exchange for the veal, Malevil is asking La Roque for sugar and detergent."

There were three things at least that displeased Fulbert in this speech. I had called him Fulbert inside his own fief; the division of the veal was now irreversible; and I was asking him to dip into his own provisions. But he took care not to let any hint of his displeasure show.

Suavely, he admired the veal. "It is the first fresh meat we shall have had to eat since the bomb," he said in his deep cellolike voice, allowing his melancholy eyes to wander first to me and my companions, then to the still silent inhabitants of La Roque. "I rejoice for all of us. But as far as I am personally concerned, as you know, Emmanuel, I have very few needs. As you can imagine, a man in my state of health, with one foot in the grave, can no longer eat a great deal. But on the other hand, as long as I am still alive I shall consider myself accountable for La Roque's meager reserves, and you will forgive me

344

for employing them with some parsimony in our dealings."

"Gifts are gifts," I said coldly. "But trading is trading. If such barter between Malevil and La Roque is to continue, then what we are offered in exchange must not be derisory. It seems to me that I am not being exorbitant in asking twenty pounds of sugar and fifteen cartons of detergent in exchange for half a calf."

"We will see, Emmanuel," Fulbert said in gentle tones. "I have no idea how much sugar we have left now [and I noticed him blast Gazel into silence with a look as the little man was about to speak], but we shall do the impossible in order to meet your demands, or at least to meet them as nearly as possible. You will already have noticed that we live here in the most total poverty. There can be no comparison, certainly, with the plenty you enjoy at Malevil. [Here he looked around at his parishioners with a knowing air.] You will have to forgive us, Emmanuel, but we cannot even invite you to share a meal with us."

"I was intending to leave right away in any case," I said, "after I have taken delivery of the horses, the guns, the ammunition, and the detergent and sugar, that is. Or rather, not quite right away. Because before we leave I must spend a little while loosening the two mares up a little." And I explained the performance I had planned on the esplanade.

"But what an excellent notion!" Fulbert exclaimed, immediately attracted by the idea of being able to play the gracious prince at no expense to himself. "We have so few distractions here in our parish, alas. Your performance will be most welcome, Emmanuel, above all if there is no danger in it for you. Well, let us all make our way there now then," he said with a generous sweeping gesture of both arms to indicate to his flock that they might approach. "Let us lose no time, since you are pressed for it. But I don't see our Catie," he went on while Gazel and Armand, obeying his signal, swung the great green gates open and the townspeople made their way up the château drive, a little more animated now, but still not daring to raise their voices.

"Evelyne is having one of her asthma attacks and Catie

is looking after her," I said. "I heard someone say so a moment ago." And to prevent his lingering, I set off briskly up the drive.

I wanted to save the horses till the end, so I asked Fulbert to let us have the guns, the ammunition, and the dry goods first. Fulbert entrusted me to the care of his vicar, having first handed him a bunch of keys and spoken a few words in his ear. Jacquet and Colin followed me with two sacks.

I never know when it comes to Laurel and Hardy which was the fat one and which the thin one, but anyway Gazel made me think of the thin one. He had the same long neck, thin face, pointed chin, astonished eyes, and simpleton expression. Unlike the comedian, however, his graying hair did not stand up in an untidy shock but was very carefully combed and curled, clearly with the help of curlers, so that it looked not unlike my sisters'. He had narrow shoulders, a slender waist, big hips, and was swathed in an immaculate white hospital smock, with the belt tied not at navel level, where most men would have it, but much higher up. His voice was neither masculine nor feminine but neuter.

I walked beside him into the château and along an interminable marble-flagged corridor. "Gazel," I said, "I understand that Fulbert intends to ordain you into the priesthood."

"No, no, not exactly," Gazel answered in his not-quite-anything voice. "Monsieur le Curé intends to present me to the suffrage of the faithful here in La Roque."

"And then to send you to Malevil?"

"That's if you want me there," Gazel said with a humility that oddly enough didn't ring the least bit false.

"We've nothing against you, Gazel. But from your point of view, I imagine it will grieve you somewhat having to leave the château of La Roque and your little house in the town."

"Oh, yes," Gazel said with a frankness that almost took me aback. "Especially my house."

"Well, don't worry, you won't have to," I told him. "Last Sunday I was unanimously elected Abbé of Malevil by the faithful there."

I heard a chuckle behind me and took it that it came from Colin, but I didn't turn around. As for Gazel, he stopped dead in his tracks and stared at me with his eyes popping out of his head. They look permanently astonished anyway, because they protrude, and also because of the abnormal distance there is between his eyebrows and eyelids. It is this facial formation that gives Gazel his simpleton expression, a misleading one in fact, because he is no fool. I also noticed a swelling at the side of his long neck. I was fairly sure it was an incipient goiter, and was surprised, because in these parts it was usually old women who suffered from that particular affliction. But, poor fellow, none of his glands could be functioning exactly normally.

"Have you told Monsieur le Curé?" he asked in his colorless voice.

"I haven't had the opportunity to do so as yet, no."

"Monsieur le Curé is going to be very put out." Gazel said as he set off again beside me along the corridor.

Which meant, I took it, that Gazel himself wasn't put out in the slightest. The prospect of leaving La Roque, of no longer being able to go and spruce up his perfectly clean house every morning, must have been appalling to him. Nothing dislikable in him really, poor Gazel. A gentle eccentric, adoring his curé, dreaming of entering heaven still untouched, with his beautiful curls, his white unspotted smock, his well-scrubbed little soul, and once there, of throwing himself at once into the Virgin Mary's lap. Inoffensive enough. No, perhaps not. Not wholly inoffensive, since he had accepted a master like Fulbert and was closing his eyes to injustice.

The cellar door was double locked. Gazel unlocked it and opened it. It was here that Fulbert had piled up the booty wrested from La Roque by his gentle persuasions. The cellar was divided into two sections. In the one we had entered were all the non-food items. In the second section, separated from the first by a door secured with a vast padlock, were all the groceries, preserved meats, and wine. Gazel didn't allow me into this inner chamber. My view of it was limited to a couple of brief glimpses when he went in and when he came out.

The guns were in the outer cellar, housed in a rack, with the appropriate ammunition for each neatly stowed on shelves running above the rack.

"There you are," Gazel said in his flat voice. "Just choose which you want."

I was flabbergasted by this generosity. Then I immediately realized that it was entirely due to Fulbert's and Gazel's ignorance and took care not to let my astonishment show, with a glance at Colin to make sure he didn't offer any comment. I counted eleven guns, and among those eleven, mostly ordinary shotguns, I saw shining like a thoroughbred in a string of humble nags a superb Springfield that Lormiaux must have bought in order to take part in some posh safari or other. A very expensive weapon, capable of dropping a buffalo at a hundred and fifty yards (with two or three good shots concealed in the bush to cover up for the client's inadequacies).

I didn't take it right away. I checked the ammunition situation first. The right bullets for it were there, and in abundance too. The other two choices didn't take long: a .22 rifle with a telescopic sight that had presumably belonged to Lormiaux Junior, and third, the best of the double-barreled shotguns. For these too there were plenty of shells and cartridges. They were duly deposited at the bottom of the sack in which I placed the three guns, asking Jacquet to make sure he tied a cord around it so that they wouldn't knock against one another in transit.

Gazel then took the second sack, asked us to stay where we were—that was the regulation, he explained apologetically—and went in alone to fetch the sugar and detergent. Before long he was back with the sack duly filled.

A few minutes later, however, Armand was proving a rather more difficult customer when it came to the horses. The two mares, whose special characteristics I shall come to in a moment, couldn't have had much grain given them since the day it happened from the look of their hollow bellies. And they were pretty filthy too. So not wanting to ride a pair of animals crusted with dung, I spent a certain amount of time currying and brushing them beneath Armand's pale gaze. He was equally determined, I could see, not to leave me there alone for a second and not to lift a finger to help. However, he didn't interfere until he saw me return from the harness room with the two saddles I had picked out and place them astride the stall partition.

"And what do you think you're going to do with those saddles then?" he asked in a loutish, aggressive tone.

"Saddle the mares, naturally."

"Oh, no you don't," he said. "I can't have that! My orders are you're to have the mares, but there was nothing said about saddles. There'll be no saddling unless you promise to bring them right back again after your little circus act is over."

"And how do you expect me to get the horses back to Malevil? Riding them bareback? Horses like this?"

"That's your affair not mine. You should have brought your own saddles, shouldn't you?"

"I only have saddles at Malevil for the three horses we have left. I don't have any for these two."

"Bad luck."

"But Armand, be reasonable. I'm not taking anything La Roque needs. You still have three saddles left for your geldings."

"And when they wear out? What do we do for replacements? And another thing. I notice you haven't taken the worst ones! Saddles from Hermès those are. I went to Paris myself with old man Lormiaux to buy them! Twenty thousand francs each! It didn't take you long to pick them out, did it? You've an eye for these things, haven't you? But then so have I!"

I didn't answer that. I went back to currycombing one of the mares. It wasn't like Armand to show such concern for the interests of his employer, whether Lormiaux or Fulbert. What did it mean, this obstructionist attitude? A little revenge for the business with Colin?

"I don't see why you're making such a fuss," I said after a moment. "Fulbert doesn't give a damn about the saddles."

"There I quite agree," Armand said. "Anything you can't eat, our Fulbert doesn't know the first thing about it.

349

But all the same, if I was to say to him. 'Watch out, mustn't give those saddles away. They're worth twenty thousand each,' then you can be sure of one thing: you wouldn't get them. Not for free anyway."

I discerned two things in this little speech. First, that we were leading up to a little bit of blackmail. And second, that Armand was entirely lacking in respect for his curé. Which permitted the supposition of a secret division of power between the two thieves, with Gazel and Fabre-lâtre a long way behind, and without any say at all.

"Oh, come on, Armand," I said, straightening up, brush in one hand, currycomb in the other. "You wouldn't go and tell Fulbert that, would you!"

"I might force myself."

"You wouldn't get anything out of it."

"What would I get out of it if I didn't?"

So I'd been right. I gave him a little smile to signify that I'd taken his meaning and that I was ready to make a sacrifice. But nothing more came. I went back to brushing the mare. Her white coat had profited markedly from the length of our negotiations. It had begun to rival Gazel's gown.

Elbows on the stall wall, Armand stared in at me, white eyelashes blinking over the pale eyes. "That's a nice gold signet ring you've got there," he said at last.

"Would you like to try it on?"

I pulled it off my ring finger and held it out. He took it, pushing out his thick lips in a grimace of greed, and after a little fumbling managed to push it onto his little finger. That done, he rested his hand on the top of the partition and stood absorbed in deep contemplation of the new acquisition. I immediately returned brush and comb to their shelf and began saddling the mares. No further words were exchanged.

I had bought the mares from a stunt man who had been forced to choose between stunts and drink. One was called Morgane, the other Mélusine, names I deplore, but which I concede must have looked effective on a poster. Both were of an immaculate whiteness with long tails and sweeping manes.

Monsieur Lormiaux had seen them at Malevil and

decided he wanted them as well as the three Anglo-Arab geldings. In vain I objected that they were circus or stunt animals, and therefore dangerous for anyone who didn't know their language. He refused to listen, and in his usual pigheaded, arrogant way promptly made me a take-it-or-leave-it offer: either all five or none at all. I let him have them. Though that of course is just a manner of speaking. Unlike Fulbert with the shirt, Monsieur Lormiaux parted with a hefty sum.

I had expected Lormiaux to get tired pretty quickly of having horses in his stable on which he would never dare risk his neck. But not at all. He was as proud as punch of the fact. During the summer of 1976 he asked Birgitta on two occasions to come over and ride them for his guests to see. He paid her two hundred francs per session. It's true that the act entailed a number of falls. But at that price, not being one to despise money, Birgitta would have willingly fallen off horses all day and every day.

The townspeople were all gathered on the château terrace when I emerged onto the esplanade leading Morgane, followed by Armand with Mélusine. I went over to them and urged them not to move or cry out if they saw me fall. But the recommendation was quite superfluous. I was now their TV, and they were already deep in their normal numbed and blissful spectator state. Their childlike happiness combined with their thinness and the furtive glances they never stopped darting at Fulbert—as though they felt almost guilty at enjoying themselves—touched my heart.

The effects of the bomb had scorched but not wholly destroyed the grass on the esplanade, and I led Morgane twice around my "ring" at a walk, gauging with foot and eye the consistency of the earth. It wasn't too bad, since the rain had softened it without actually making it spongy. I mounted Morgane and walked her around again twice, then a third time with a whole series of volts, just to make sure that she had forgotten none of her training. As I began on the fourth circle, I gave Morgane the signal, or rather signals, to begin her act. I gripped her tightly with my legs, gathered the reins into my left hand, then, digging in even harder with my knees, I quickly raised my right hand high in front of me. Morgane promptly went into a series of prodigious bucks that gave the spectators the impression she was intent on throwing me. In fact, she was merely obeying me. And although I received quite a shaking, I was not running the slightest danger, even as I thrashed desperately at the air with my right arm, as though I was clinging for dear life to the back of some wild, unbroken stallion.

I put Morgane through three series of bucks, separated by rather sedater phases, then after one last walk around the "ring" I dismounted.

Fulbert, flanked on either side by Fabrelâtre and Gazel, had taken up his place in the front row, hands resting on the stone balustrade, eyes following my antics with benign condescension. As I dismounted, he called out a brief bravo and gently brought his palms together in an almost soundless suggestion of applause. What happened then was a surprise. Fulbert was all but submerged in the enthusiasm of his flock. They applauded like mad creatures, and persisted in their clapping long after their curé had ceased his polite imitation. I was by this time occupied adjusting Mélusine's stirrups, so I prolonged the operation and observed Fulbert out of the corner of my eye. He was pale, lips pressed together in a hard line, with a look of disquiet in his eyes. The longer the clapping persisted—and it was in fact quite disproportionate to the brief show I had just given—the more he must have felt that this applause for me was in fact an expression of opposition to himself.

I got into the saddle again. With Mélusine the act was different. She had been trained to fall. What a beautiful, docile creature she was! And what amounts of money she must have earned for her stunt-man owner, biting the dust before an adversary's bullets for the benefit of so many moviemakers' cameras.

The preliminaries took quite a while. It was essential that all her muscles be properly warmed up if she was not to hurt herself when she fell. As soon as I felt she was well run in, I removed my feet from the stirrups and crossed the leathers over her back in front of the saddle.

Then I knotted the reins to make them shorter, so Mélusine would not catch her hoofs in them as she fell. That done, I urged her into a gallop.

I had decided that the best place for our fall was on the bend just before the straight stretch in front of the château, so just as we were entering it I gave a sharp pull on the left rein while bending my body to the right, which naturally put her off balance. She dropped like a stone, brought down in full stride by the enemy's fire. I was sent hurtling over her neck and likewise ended up rolling across the battlefield. There was an oh! of shock, then an ah! as I stood up. Mélusine, meanwhile, lay stretched out on her side, stone dead, even her head flat on the ground, eyes closed. I walked over to her, picked up the reins, and clicked my tongue. She immediately got to her feet.

I restricted the act to two falls. After the second, which proved slightly less painless than I would have liked, I decided that I had by now given Catie enough time and the townspeople enough entertainment. I dismounted and, not without malice, offered the reins with an air of challenge to Armand, whose pride forced him to take them. Since he was already holding Morgane, that meant both his hands were now fully occupied.

This time the audience had gone quite berserk. The applause reached an even greater intensity of volume—I might even say of calculated violence—than after the first part of my act. And partly because they could see that Armand was temporarily neutralized, partly too because their sports-crowd enthusiasm provided a convenient excuse, they all came running and jostling down the steps out onto the esplanade and clustered around me still applauding. Fulbert was left alone on the terrace, flanked by Gazel and Fabrelâtre, a ludicrous and isolated little group. Armand, of course, was down on the esplanade with us, but very occupied at that point with his two charges, since the sudden rush of the crowd had made them nervous, and he was having to struggle to hold them in check and had his back to me. Growing bolder as they noticed the difficulties he was in, and no longer content with mere clapping, the townspeople began rhythmically chanting my name, as though they were preparing to vote for me in a plebiscite. And some of them, taking care that Fulbert could not see them—for as he stood silent and motionless on the terrace his flashing eyes were watching every move —shouted out with conscious intent, "Thank you for the distribution, Emmanuel!"

There was something covertly insurrectional in the situation that could not fail to strike the onlooker. The idea occurred to me that I might take advantage of it to topple Fulbert from power there and then. But Armand had his gun. Mine had perforce been handed to Colin while I did my act, and he was now deep in conversation with Agnès Pimont. Thomas was lost in his own thoughts. And Jacquet was nowhere to be seen. And besides, I was of the opinion, and still am, that affairs of that kind are far better when not improvised. I freed myself from the crowd and began walking over toward Fulbert.

He came down the terrace steps to meet me, Gazel and Fabrelâtre in his wake, the cavernous and imperious eyes fixed not upon me but upon the townspeople, who a second before had been pressing around me and acclaiming me, but who had now fallen silent and moved apart at his approach. He proffered chilly congratulations, but still without looking at me, eyes too occupied darting here and there among his flock, herding them back into the straight and narrow. Loathsome though I found him, I must confess that I admired his calm, his natural power of ascendancy. He escorted me in silence as far as the château gate, but no farther. It was as though he was repelled by the idea, if he went beyond, of finding himself alone among his parishioners once I was gone.

No trace of his former unction remained in his farewells. There was no lavishing of compliments, and no invitation to renew my visit. Once the last of the townspeople was out again, and the horses led through by Colin, the green gates swung shut, leaving Fulbert, Gazel, Fabrelâtre, and Armand inside. From which I deduced that a parish council was about to be held posthaste, with a view to getting the parishioners under control again forthwith.

Jacquet had gone on ahead and was waiting for us with Malabar and the cart outside the town. He had been apprehensive of the stallion becoming difficult in the presence of the two mares, especially in those narrow streets and surrounded by a crowd. We left by the south gate. Against the wall of one of the two little round towers on either side of it I suddenly noticed a post office mailbox. It had lost its fine yellow paint, and indeed was now no color at all, all scaly and black, its raised letters quite erased.

"Do you see?" Marcel commented, for he was walking beside me. "The key is still there in the lock. The poor postman was burned to nothing just as he was about to collect the mail inside. As for the box itself, the metal must have got red hot, but it seems to have stood up to it. Look." And he turned the key in the lock. The little door still opened and closed perfectly. I took Marcel by the arm and led him a little way along the Malejac road.

"Take the key with you and keep it. If I have a message for you I'll have it left in the box."

He nodded, and I looked with a feeling of friendship at those intelligent dark eyes, the wart quivering at the end of his nose, and his enormous shoulders, so powerless to protect him from the sadness I could see seeping into him. I talked to him for a few more minutes. I knew how lonely he was going to feel when he got home again, without Catie, without Evelyne, with the not very pleasant prospect of facing Fulbert's anger and the consequent diminution of his rations during the days ahead. But I couldn't wholly concentrate on what I was saying. My thoughts were too much on Malevil. I was in too much of a hurry to be back there again. Without the walls of Malevil around me, I felt as vulnerable as a hermit crab without his shell.

As we talked, my eyes wandered over the people around us, all the survivors of La Roque without exception, including the two babies, carried down to the gate by their mothers, Agnès Pimont and Marie Lanouaille, the young butcher's wife. Miette was in an absolute ecstasy, rushing from one to the other and back again, while Falvine, exhausted by a marathon of gossip all over the town, was already seated in the cart with Jacquet, the latter working very hard to keep a restless and whinnying Malabar in check.

In that bright noon sun the townspeople looked happy at being released for a few short minutes from their suffocating walls. Though I noticed that even in Fabrelâtre's absence they were not permitting themselves to voice any comments, either about their pastor, the distribution of their rations, or Armand's recent discomfiture. I suspected that by adroit use of a few little perfidies and calculated indiscretions Fulbert had succeeded in creating a climate of mistrust and insecurity among them, a constant fear of betrayal. I noticed that none of them dared so much as go near Judith, Marcel, or Pimont, as though the power of the Church had already laid the trio under its interdict. I myself, as though the coldness Fulbert had displayed to me on parting had been sufficient to render proximity to me dangerous, was no longer surrounded as I had been on the esplanade. And a few moments later, when I finally came to throw them a collective "See you again soon!"—the very phrase that Fulbert had so studiously omitted to say to me—they were to reply with their eyes, but from afar, without daring to venture a single gesture, a single word.

It was clear that the job of bringing the parishioners under control again was already half accomplished. They were well aware that Fulbert was going to make them pay dearly for that equitable distribution of our gifts. And with my bread and my butter scarcely digested inside them, they were not far, I felt, from already holding those gifts against me.

Their attitude saddened me, but I didn't altogether blame them. There is a terrible logic in slavery. I went on listening to Marcel, who had stayed on there solely to defend them, and to whom no one in La Roque dared address a word, apart from Pimont and Judith. And Judith was a gift from heaven! The Egeria of the Revolution! Our Joan of Arc!—except that she was no maid, as she had gone out of her way to stress. She must have noticed Marcel's sadness, because she suddenly appeared at his side and promptly took a firm grip on his biceps, which he abandoned to her grasp, it seemed to me, with considerable pleasure, his dark eyes wandering gratefully over his Amazonian ally's vast proportions.

Pimont seemed to me the least ostracized. I could see him in conversation with two men who looked to me to be farmers. I looked around for Agnès. There she was. Colin, who had entrusted Morgane to a mute and nervous Thomas, was only just succeeding in restraining Mélusine but nevertheless managing to carry on a very animated conversation with Agnès at the same time. We had been rivals for her once. He had stood aside of his own accord, and then, as Racine put it, "carried his heart elsewhere." So poor Agnès, when I drifted away from her too, had ended up with no suitors at all, after having had two. Enough to make any girl bitter, except that Agnès was incapable of bitterness. I noted that she was being charming to our Colin while at the same time keeping a very wary eye on Mélusine, even though Miette had by now taken advantage of her preoccupation and succeeded in getting the baby out of her arms and into her own. Oddly enough I felt no twinge of jealousy seeing Colin and Agnès together like that. The emotion I had felt on meeting her again had already faded.

I left Marcel, went over to Thomas, and said in a quiet voice, "You will ride Morgane."

He looked at me, then at Morgane, appalled at the idea. "You're mad! Not after what I saw up there!"

"That was just a circus act. Morgane is as good as gold."

I explained to him very briefly the signals he must *not* give, and since Malabar was by now almost out of control, I took Mélusine from Colin, mounted her, and rode ahead a little, followed immediately by Thomas. As soon as we reached the first bend I dropped to a walk again, for fear that Malabar would start going too fast if he lost sight of the mares. Immediately Thomas drew level with me and turned to look at me, without saying anything but with a face that certainly had nothing impassive about it now.

"Thomas?"

"Yes," he said with barely controlled excitement.

"At the next bend put Morgane into a trot and go on

ahead. Three miles from here there's an intersection with a stone cross. Wait for me there."

"More mysteries," he replied irritably, but he gave Morgane a little touch with his heels, and she was off and away immediately at her beautifully smooth trot.

After a second's thought I caught up with him again. "Thomas?"

"Yes." Again irritably and without looking at me.

"If you see something that surprises you, remember you're on Morgane and don't raise your right arm. You'll only end up on the road."

He looked at me in puzzlement, then he understood. Immediately his face lit up, and forgetting all his anxieties about Morgane, he set off down the road at a full gallop. The madman! On that metaled road! If only he'd thought to ride on the shoulder!

I held Mélusine back. Malabar, fifty yards behind me, was just starting down a slight hill and this was no moment to make him trot too fast. I was quite pleased to be alone at last, so I could think back over our little visit to La Roque. Barely nine miles away from Malevil. Another world. A whole different social organization. The whole of the lower town that was not protected by the cliff, or not protected enough, completely destroyed. Three quarters of the population annihilated. Not the slightest hint of a community life, as Marcel had so clearly seen. Hunger, idleness, tyranny. And also insecurity. A fortified town, but badly defended despite its ramparts. Plenty of weapons, but fear preventing them being used. The richest land in the district, but whatever it eventually produced doomed to be unjustly distributed. An unhappy, hungry, disunited little town, with very poor chances of survival.

I was no longer afraid of the people of La Roque. I knew now that Fulbert would never send them into battle against me. But I was afraid for them. I pitied them. And in that moment, rising to the rhythm of Mélusine's trot, I made the decision to help them in every way within my power during the weeks and months ahead.

As my glance fell onto the reins, I was surprised for an instant at not seeing my signet ring on my finger. The scene in the stables came back to me. What an idiot, that

Armand! I might just as well have given him a pebble! As if gold, two months after the day it happened, had any value! Those days were over, or if you prefer, they were still a long way ahead. We had regressed to a stage far more primitive than that of precious metals: the age of barter. The age of jewels and metal money was still far, far distant in the future. Our grandsons might see it perhaps. But not us.

Mélusine pricked up her ears, then shied slightly. At the next bend, a few yards ahead, a tiny silhouette stood in the middle of the road, hair lighted up from behind by the sun. I reined the mare to a halt.

"I thought I'd meet you," Evelyne said, walking forward without the slightest fear and looking even more tiny and frail beside the powerful mare. "I left those two to it. They're kissing all the time. You ought to see them! As if I just didn't exist!"

I laughed and dismounted. "Come on, we'll go back to them."

I hoisted her up onto the front of the saddle, where she really took up very little room. "Hold on with both hands to the pommel."

I got back up behind her and arranged the reins on either side of her little body. The top of her head came no higher than my chin. "Lean back against my chest."

We set off again at a trot, and I could feel Evelyne trembling. "Are you all right?"

"I'm a bit frightened."

"Lean back harder. Don't stiffen up like that. Let yourself relax!"

"It bounces a lot."

"You can't fall off, you've got my arms for railings!"

I altered my hold so that I could grip her more tightly, then rode on for another two or three hundred yards in silence. "Better now?"

"Oh, yes," she said in a quite different voice, vibrant with excitement. "It's wonderful! I'm the great lord's fiancée and he's taking me back to his castle."

Presumably she'd thought that one up to help her get over her fright. When she spoke she turned her head around toward me, and I could feel her breath on my neck. After a moment she went on: "You ought to conquer La Roque and Courcejac."

"How do you mean, conquer?"

"By force of arms." The phrase must have been a memory from her last history lesson. Her last for always.

"And if I did, what difference would it make?" I said.

"You could put Armand and the curé to the sword, and you'd be king of all the country."

I laughed. "Now there's a plan that suits me down to the ground. Especially that 'putting to the sword' part."

"Shall we do it then?" Evelyne asked, turning around and gazing up at me with solemn eyes.

"I'll think it over."

Mélusine began to neigh. Malabar, trotting staunchly on thirty or forty yards behind us, answered her, and in front of us, revealed suddenly as we came around a bend, stood Morgane, chin propped unconcernedly on top of Thomas's head as he held Catie in a passionate embrace.

"Oh, look how funny they are, the three of them!" Evelyne cried.

"Emmanuel," Thomas said, gazing up at me with slightly vague eyes, "may I take Catie up on Morgane behind me?"

"No, you may not."

"You've got Evelyne on Mélusine."

"There is no comparison. Either between the weights, the sizes, or . . ." I was about to add "the riders," but I stopped myself because of Catie.

At that point Malabar arrived in a state of great excitement, and because Jacquet up on the cart couldn't hold him alone, Colin had to get down and hold his head while Catie clambered up beside her grandmother. All three ex-troglodytes expressed great joy at seeing her, but no surprise. Miette had discovered the hidden suitcases as they were leaving La Roque and had recognized her sister's things inside them.

"Come on, Thomas," I said, "let's ride on ahead. Malabar is going to become unmanageable if we stay too close."

As soon as I felt we were far enough ahead I dropped down to a walk again.

"Emmanuel," Thomas said in a breathless voice, as though he had been running, "Emmanuel, Catie would like you to marry us tomorrow."

I looked over at him. He had never been so handsome. The Greek statue inside which he had lived imprisoned until now had come to life. The fire of life was glowing at last from his eyes, from his nostrils, from his half-open lips. Incredulous, I echoed, "Catie would like me to marry you?"

"Yes."

"And you?"

He gazed at me in bewilderment. "And I would too, naturally."

"I can't see that it's as natural as all that. After all, you're an atheist."

"Well, if you're going to take that attitude," he said in an acid tone, "you're not really a priest."

"There you are wrong," I answered immediately. "Fulbert is not a real priest, because he is lying when he says he is. That is not true of me. I am not an impostor. My ministry is underwritten by the faith of the believers who elected me. I am the emanation of their faith. Which is why I regard the religious acts they expect of me with the utmost seriousness."

Thomas gaped at me. "But you yourself," he said after a moment, "you're not a believer."

I said curtly, "We have never discussed my religious beliefs that I know of. But in any case, what I believe or what I do not believe has nothing whatever to do with the authenticity of my functions."

There was a silence, then he said in a shaky voice, "And are you going to refuse to marry us because I am an atheist?"

That stung me. "No, Thomas, of course I'm not. Don't be ridiculous. Your marriage will be made valid by the very fact that you want it. It is Catie's and your will to enter into it that creates the union."

And after a moment I went on: "So you can put your mind at rest. I'll marry you. It's a folly, but I'll marry you."

He looked at me, deeply shocked. "A folly?"

"Of course it's a folly. You're getting married because Catie, being still faithful to the ideas of the world of before, cannot conceive of herself other than as married, even though she has no intention of remaining faithful."

He started, and jerked so hard on the reins that Morgane came to a stop. Mélusine immediately halted too.

"I'd like to know what makes you say that."

"Nothing in particular. What's the matter? It's just a hypothesis."

I touched my heels to Mélusine's flanks. Thomas followed suit. "So in your opinion then, it's a folly because she's going to be unfaithful to me?" he said with more apprehension than irony.

"I think it's folly anyway. You know my position on the matter. There is no place for monogamy in a community where there are two women to six men."

There was a silence.

"I love her," Thomas said.

If I hadn't been holding reins I would have lifted my arms to heaven. "But so do I love her! So does Colin! So will Meyssonnier and Peyssou as soon as they see her!"

"I don't mean it in that sense," Thomas said.

"Oh, yes you do! You mean it in exactly that sense! What other sense could you mean it in? Since you've only known her for two hours!"

I waited for him to reply. But for once our great debater had no wish to continue the debate. "Well, let's settle it then," he said sullenly at last. "Are you going to marry us or not?"

"I'll marry you."

At which he said a very curt thank you and closed up like an oyster. I glanced across at him. He didn't want to talk any more. All he wanted was to be left alone to think about his Catie, since Malabar was preventing him from being near her. I could see a sort of light in his face, oozing out from every pore. I was deeply impressed by that great inward effusion. I envied him, my young Thomas, and at the same time I felt a little sorry for him. He couldn't have known a great many girls in his life for Catie to make an effect like that. Let him have his moments of bliss. His heart would be paining him soon enough. I urged Mélusine on and cut in front of Thomas on the pretext that I wanted to let my mare trot on the shoulder instead of on the road. Thomas rode behind me from then on, also on the shoulder.

For a good hour there was no other sound but the heavy beat of the mares' hoofs on the earth, and behind us, at a varying distance, the sharper clattering of Malabar's hoofs on the metaled road and the rumbling of the cart.

Why did my heart always begin to beat so wildly whenever I saw Malevil again? About five hundred feet from the gate tower I saw Peyssou standing in the middle of the road, gun slung over his shoulder, great face split in a broad grin.

I stopped. "And what do you think you're doing there? What's happened?"

"Nothing that you won't be glad to hear," he said. The grin broadened still further. Then he said in a tone of triumph, "The wheat is up!"

XIII

IT WAS true, it was up.

I took just enough time to eat a slice of ham, which La Menou was very sour about cutting for me because I'd given my share to Marcel, and then Peyssou led us all down with enormous strides toward the field by the Rhunes: Colin, Jacquet, myself, and of course Evelyne, who refused to stray a step from my side. We all had our guns slung over our shoulders. Just because we no longer feared La Roque was no reason to relax our security regulations.

From a distance, as we walked down the pebbly track at the bottom of the old river bed, there was nothing to be seen but a patch of cultivated land. A patch of good well-tilled dark earth that had certainly lost its dusty dead look of the months before the rain. But we had to get up really close before we could make out the shoots. Oh, they were tiny, so tiny! A few eighths of an inch at the most. And yet those minute pale green points sticking up out of the earth were enough to make you weep for joy. It was true that we had really worked at that patch of ours, and that we hadn't begrudged the muck either. But considering that the rain had come only four days before, and the sun scarcely three, and that in such a short time the seed had germinated and was actually showing, we were just staggered by the speed of its growth. I felt the earth with the back of my hand. It was as warm as human flesh. I was almost ready to believe that I could feel the blood beating under its surface.

"It will be all right now," Peyssou said with an air of jubilation.

The "it," I imagined, referred to the earth, or to the field, or to the harvest.

"Well, maybe, yes," Colin said. "It's growing, there's no saying it isn't, but . . . And even it won't be long getting away now."

"Two weeks," Peyssou interrupted confidently. "Two weeks to a good full leaf."

"Two weeks then, we'll say two weeks. But the thing is, all the same, we're late in the season now. Maybe it won't have the time to ripen, our wheat."

To Peyssou this remark was pure sacrilege. "No fool talk, Colin, please," he said sternly. "When wheat gets off to a start like this, that means it's set on making up that lost time."

"As long as . . ." Jacquet began.

Peyssou turned his great peasant face, hardened by intolerance now, around to look at him. "As long as what?"

"As the sun keeps on with us," the serf spoke up boldly.

"And the rain," Colin added.

This skepticism was a further irritant to Peyssou. He shrugged his massive shoulders. "The least we can be expecting, what with all the rest we've had here, is a little sun and rain." And raising his rough-hewn head, he gazed up at the sky, as though calling upon it to bear witness to the modesty of his demands.

Standing there beside the wheat patch with my companions, Evelyne's tiny paw in my big one, what I felt was the same vague but powerful feeling of gratitude that I had felt before when the rain began to fall. I know that someone will say that this gratitude of mine postulates the presence of some benevolent force hidden in the universe. And it's true, but a little everywhere, so it seemed to me, not all radiating from one point. For example, if I hadn't been afraid of looking foolish I would gladly have knelt down beside our wheat patch and said, Thank you, warm earth. Thank you, hot sun. Thank you, green shoots. And from there to symbolizing the earth and the shoots in the form of beautiful naked girls, like the Greeks, is really only a step. I was very much afraid that the new Abbé of Malevil was not going to be a very orthodox one.

During the course of the day everyone at Malevil took time to go down by the Rhunes to stand and admire the wheat, even Thomas and Catie.

We had found it was just as well not to get in our two lovers' way by now; they just bumped into you without seeing you. Since our arrival Thomas had been showing his fiancée around, and that took a long time, because the castle was so large and there were so many nooks and corners, and so many reasons for lingering in them.

That afternoon I was unsaddling Malabar, with Evelyne with me in the stall. She was leaning with her back against the partition, her straight pale hair over her face, the dark hollows under her blue eyes deeper still. She looked thin and tired, and she kept coughing. It was only a tiny cough, more like a clearing of the throat, but it was worrying me because Catie, returning to earth for a moment, had warned me a few minutes earlier that it was the sign of an approaching asthma attack.

Thomas appeared, flushed and anxious.

"What's this?" I said. "Without Catie?"

"Yes, as you see," he said awkwardly.

Then he fell silent. I emerged from the stall, carrying the saddle, and walked through into the harness room. Thomas followed me, still without saying a word. Ah ha, an embassy. And an embarrassing one too, since he was alone. It was Catie who had sent him, that was for sure.

I closed the stall door, leaned my back against it, thrust my hands into my pockets, and stared down at my boots.

"There's the matter of a room," Thomas said at last in what he intended to be an offhand tone.

"Do you want mine?" I asked, half jesting and half in earnest.

"No, of course not," Thomas said indignantly. "'We're not going to turn you out of your own room."

"A room? How do you mean, a room?"

"A room for Catie and me, when we're married."

"Miette's then?"

"No, no. Miette needs her room."

Well, at least that hadn't slipped his memory. But he

366

had already become slightly aloof from Miette, I could tell from his tone. And from me too, on another plane. How he had changed, our Thomas. I was happy for him, saddened, and jealous. I looked at him. His face was all anxious furrows. The teasing had gone far enough.

"If I understand you rightly," I said with a smile, and his face lit up immediately, "you would like the third-floor room next to mine. Is that it?"

"Yes."

"And you would also like me to ask the others to vacate the premises and move permanently up to the second floor of the gate tower."

He gave a little cough. "Yes . . . But 'vacate the premises' isn't exactly the phrase I would have used."

I laughed at this tiny hypocrisy. "All right then. I'll see what I can do. Is your embassy now concluded?" I asked jovially. "There's nothing else you have to ask me?"

"No."

"Why isn't Catie with you?"

"You intimidate her. She finds you cold."

"With her?"

"Yes."

"Well, it wouldn't do for me to start wooing your future wife, would it? Since wife it has to be!"

"Oh, I'm not jealous," Thomas said with a chuckle.

Well, well, just look at him, how confident he is our young cockerel.

"Off you go," I said. "I'll see to it."

And off he went, leaving me standing, I'm not sure how, with a warm little hand in mine.

"Do you think that my breasts are going to grow?" Evelyne said, anxious face turned up toward me. "Like Catie's. Or like Miette's, because hers are even bigger."

"Don't fret yourself, Evelyne. They'll grow."

"Do you think so? It's just that I'm so thin," she said despairingly, laying her left hand across her chest. "Look, I'm as flat as a boy."

"That's got nothing to do with it, being thin or fat. They'll still grow."

"You're sure?"

"Quite sure."

"Oh, good," she said with a sigh that ended in a cough.

At that moment someone very discreetly rang the gate-tower bell. I started. I was at the gate in a flash and slid the Judas open a fraction. It was Armand, riding one of the La Roque geldings, a glower on his face, a gun slung over his back.

"Oh, it's you, Armand," I said in a friendly voice. "I'm afraid you're going to have to wait a moment. I have to go and fetch the key."

I slid the Judas shut. The key, needless to say, was in the lock, but I wanted a short breathing space. I walked quickly away across the enclosure and said to Evelyne, "Go up to the house and tell La Menou to bring glasses and a bottle of wine to the gate tower."

"Has Armand come to take me back?" Evelyne said through a cough. She was looking very pale.

"Of course not. Anyway you needn't worry. If he wants to take you back we just put him to the sword right away."

I laughed, and she laughed too. But it was a thin little sound, followed by a cough.

"Listen, tell Catie and Thomas not to let him see them. And you stay with them."

She left me and I went on up to the storeroom on the ground floor of the keep. They were all there, Thomas excepted, putting away Colin's tools and stock.

"We have a visitor. Armand. I'd like Peyssou and Meyssonnier down at the gate, both with guns. Only as a precaution. He doesn't look as though he's going to make trouble."

"I'd like to see the look on his ugly face," Colin said.

"No. Not you or Jacquet or Thomas, and you know why."

Colin laughed merrily. It was pleasant seeing him so gay. His little conversation with Agnès Pimont had done him good.

As I was crossing the inner courtyard I saw Thomas hurtle out of the house. "I'm coming with you."

"What do you mean?" I asked curtly. "I sent you a message specifically saying not to come."

"She's my wife, isn't she?" he said, his eyes glittering.

I could tell that I wasn't going to win that one.

368

"You can come on one condition: that you don't open your mouth."

"That's a promise."

"Whatever I say, you don't open your mouth."

"I've already said I promise."

I wasted no more time getting back to the gate. Once there, I moved the key to and fro in the lock before unlocking it, then pulled open the door. Enter Armand. I shook his hand—the hand with my signet ring on the little finger. Enter Armand with his pale eyes, his white eyebrows, his horrible face, his pimples, and his quasi-military uniform. Beside him I recognized my beautiful, my poor Pharaon. I stroked him and talked to him. I say poor Pharaon because any horse is to be pitied when subjected to a rider who ill treats its mouth to that extent. I found a lump of sugar in my pocket for him, despite our strict rules of economy, and his soft lips snapped it up without even a sniff. And since Momo appeared at that moment accompanying La Menou with her glasses and bottle, I handed Pharaon over to him, telling him to remove the poor beast's bit and give him a bowl of barley. A piece of prodigality that set La Menou muttering immediately.

We went and sat in the gate-tower kitchen, where Meyssonnier and Peyssou joined us, very affable and carrying their weapons. As soon as Armand had a full glass in his hand—looking rather ill at ease, though not because of the glass, needless to say, but on account of what he had come to say—I moved in to the attack, determined to get the thing over as quickly as possible.

"I'm very glad to see you, Armand," I said as I touched glasses with him (I had no intention of finishing my glass, I never drank at that hour of the day, but Momo would be only too delighted to gulp down what was left in it later.) "Because I was just about to send someone over to reassure Marcel. Poor Marcel, he must be very worried."

"So they're here then?" Armand said, hesitating between factual inquiry and accusation.

"Well, of course they are. Where else could they be? Oh, they laid their little plan very cleverly, the little

369

minxes! There they were waiting for us at the Rigoudie turnoff with their suitcases. And the big one says, 'Hallo, I'm just coming to spend a week or two with my granny.' Put yourself in my place. How could I have the heart to send them back?"

"They had no right to go," Armand said savagely.

It was the moment to rap him over the knuckles, but lightly, still keeping things jovial. I raised my arms to the heavens. "No right! No right! That's a bit strong, isn't it, Armand? No right to go and spend a week or two with your granny?"

Thomas, Meyssonnier, Peyssou, and La Menou all glared at Armand in silent disapprobation. I did the same. The sacred ties of family were all on our side!

To conceal his embarrassment, Armand pushed his broken nose into his glass and emptied it.

"Another, Armand?"

"I don't mind."

La Menou began grumbling but poured a second glass. Again I touched glasses but did not drink.

"Where they were in the wrong," I said, very fair, very reasonable, "was in not asking Marcel's permission."

"And Fulbert's," Armand said, already halfway through his second glass.

But I wasn't going to concede that. "Marcel's. So that he could have informed Fulbert."

Armand was not so big an idiot that he didn't grasp the distinction. But he couldn't quite bring himself to talk about the decrees of La Roque inside Malevil. He drained his second glass and set it down. Momo wasn't going to get so much as a drop out of that one.

"Right," he said. "So what are you going to do about it?"

"So in two weeks' time," I said, getting to my feet, "we'll bring the pair of them back to La Roque. You can tell Marcel for me."

I didn't dare even glance toward the corner where Thomas was sitting. Armand gazed contemplatively at the bottle, but since I made no move to offer him a third glass he eventually go to his feet and without a word of thanks or goodbye walked out of the kitchen. It was just sheer awkwardness on his part, I felt certain. It was just that if he wasn't actually terrifying people he had no idea what other kind of relation with them was possible.

Momo was just fitting the bit back into the mouth of a very happy horse. The bowl at his feet could not have been emptier or more thoroughly licked. Rider and steed were both departing well ballasted, and the steed at least was full of gratitude. He would not forget Malevil.

"Goodbye, Armand."

"Goodbye," the rider grunted.

I didn't close the door immediately. I watched him ride away. I wanted him to be out of earshot when Thomas exploded. I swung the gates slowly shut, methodically pushed the great bolts home, and turned the enormous key in the lock.

It was even more violent that I'd expected. "What is the meaning of this rotten, filthy trick?" Thomas was almost screaming as he advanced on me with his eyes starting out of his head.

I straightened up, looked at him without a word, then turned my back on him and set off up toward the drawbridge, leaving him standing there.

Behind me I could hear Peyssou putting him straight. "Hey there, lad, not so loud. What's the use of all that education if you're going to act the ass, eh? You don't think Emmanuel's going to let them have the girls back, do you? You just don't know him if you do!"

"Then why all these damn silly games!" Thomas yelled.

"If you asked him quietly I've no doubt he'd tell you," Meyssonnier said very curtly indeed.

I heard the sound of running footsteps. Thomas appeared in my peripheral vision as he fell into step beside me. Not that I noticed him, of course, because my eyes were fixed on the drawbridge. I kept up my pace, hands in pockets, chin up.

"I apologize," he said in a quiet voice.

"I don't give a damn for your apologies. We're not in a drawing room."

Not a very encouraging start. But what else could he do but persist? "Peyssou says you won't give the girls up."

"Ah, well Peyssou's wrong then. I intend to marry you

371

two tomorrow, then in two weeks' time send Catie back to La Roque so that Fulbert can screw her rotten."

Though in doubtful taste, this remark nevertheless succeeded in reassuring him. "But why all this pretense?" he asked in a plaintive tone very untypical of him. "I just don't understand it at all."

"You don't understand it because you are only thinking of yourself."

"I'm only thinking of myself?"

"What about Marcel? Have you thought about him?"

"Marcel? Why should I think about him?"

"Because he's the one who's going to suffer."

"Suffer? What will he suffer?"

"The reprisals, reduction in his rations, and so on."

A short silence.

"I see," Thomas said in some contrition. "I didn't realize that."

I went on: "That's why I shook hands with that great dungheap and tried to persuade him it was just a childish escapade. To clear Marcel."

"And so what happens in two weeks' time?" Still a little uneasy, the idiot.

"Oh, come on, surely it goes without saying! I write to Fulbert telling him that Catie and you have fallen in love, that I've married the two of you, and that Catie must of course remain here with her husband."

"And what's to stop Fulbert from taking reprisals against Marcel then?"

"Nothing, but why should he? The whole incident has been turned into something fortuitous, unpredictable. There has been no collusion, no plot. It has nothing to do with Marcel, so Fulbert can have nothing against him."

Then I added with a slight chill in my voice, "And that is the reason for all these silly games, as you put it."

Long silence. "Are you angry, Emmanuel?"

I shrugged, left him standing there, and walked back toward Peyssou and Meyssonnier. There was still the matter of the bedroom to be got out of the way. They were wonderful about it. Not only did they accept being thrown out on their ears, but they accepted it with joy.

"For those two young things, well of course," Peyssou

said sentimentally, quite forgetting that only a moment ago he'd been calling one of them an ass.

They were all even more emotional next day when I married Catie and Thomas in the great hall of the house. We'd arranged the room in the same way as for Fulbert's Mass. This time I stood with my back to the two windows, the table served as an altar, and on the far side of it, facing me, my companions were seated in two rows. La Menou, in an act of quite incredible prodigality, had set two of the big candles on the table, even though the weather was quite clear and the sun was streaming in through both great mullioned windows, creating two impressive black crosses on the stone floor. Everyone's eyes were glistening, even the men's. And everyone, Meyssonnier included, took communion when the time came. La Menou was weeping copiously, I will explain why later. But Miette's tears were very different. She wept in silence, the great drops rolling down her fresh young cheeks. Yes, poor Miette, you have cause to weep, I thought. I too could discern something unjust in all this pomp and glory falling to the lot of a girl who had not shared herself.

After the ceremony I took Meyssonnier aside and we strolled up and down the outer enclosure together. There was a subtle change in him. He still had the same long, serious face, the two very close-set eyes, and that way of flickering his eyelids all the time when he was upset. No, the change didn't lie there. It was the brushcut hair that was different. For want of a barber, it had at first grown straight upward, as I have already said, as though reaching for the sky. But now, having grown longer still, it was falling back away from his forehead, introducing a curve into his features that they had always lacked before.

"I noticed that you took communion," I said in a noncommittal voice. "May I ask why?"

A slight flush rose into his honest face and the flickering began. "I hesitated," he said after a moment. "But then I thought it might offend the others if I abstained. I didn't want to set myself apart."

"Well, I must say I think you were right," I said. "Why not give communion that meaning? A participation."

He looked at me in astonishment. "You mean that's the meaning you give it?"

"Certainly I do. The social content of communion seems to me very important."

"The most important?"

An insidious question. I had the impression that Meyssonnier was somehow trying to pull me over to his side of the fence. I answered no, but without enlarging on the subject.

"Now it's my turn to put a question to you, if you don't mind," Meyssonnier said. "Was it solely in order to keep Gazel out of Malevil that you had yourself elected abbé?"

If Thomas had asked me that question I would have thought twice before replying. But I knew that Meyssonnier would never jump to conclusions. He would chew over what I was going to say at leisure and draw cautious conclusions from it. Weighing my words, I said, "Let's say, if you like, that in my opinion any civilization needs a soul."

"And that soul is religion?" He pulled a face as he said it. "Soul" and "religion" were two words he found distasteful. For him they were "obsolete." Meyssonnier was a trained militant; he had attended one of the Party's "officer schools."

"In the present state of things, yes."

He meditated on this assertion, which was at the same time a qualification. Meyssonnier is slow, he advances only one step at a time. But there is nothing shallow about his mind. He pinned me down even further. "The soul of our present civilization, here, in Malevil?" He put quote marks around the word "soul" with his voice, as though he were handling it from a distance, with pincers.

"Yes."

"You mean that this soul is constituted by the beliefs of the majority of those living in Malevil?"

"Not only that. It is also the soul corresponding to our present level of civilization."

In fact, things were a little more complicated than that. I was simplifying things in order to avoid shocking him. But I had shocked him nevertheless. He went a little red and began blinking. That meant he was about to counter-attack.

"But this 'soul,' as you call it, it could just as well be a philosophy of some sort. For example Marxism."

I thought that was coming. "Except that Marxism was derived from a study of industrial society and was intended to apply to it. It has no purpose to serve in a primitive agrarian communism."

He halted, and turned to look me in the face. He appeared to be very impressed by what I had just said. And all the more so because I had spoken quite dispassionately, as though simply stating an everyday fact. "Is that how you define our little society here? Primitive agrarian communism?"

"What else can we call it?"

Looking a little unhappy, he went on: "But this primitive agrarian communism, it isn't the real Communism?"

"You don't need me to tell you that."

"It's a regression then?"

"As you well know."

It was odd. Even though I wasn't a Marxist, he seemed to place more confidence in my judgment than in his own. And he looked very relieved suddenly. Although he could no longer aspire to the "real Communism," at least he could keep it enshrined in his mind as an ideal, a touchstone to which reality could be referred.

I went on: "Yes, it's a regression, in the sense that so much of our knowledge and technology has been destroyed. Our existence is therefore more precarious, more threatened. But that doesn't mean that we are any more unhappy. On the contrary."

As soon as I'd spoken the words I regretted them, because the man standing there opposite me, I suddenly remembered, had lost his whole family only two months ago. Yet Meyssonnier didn't look as though he was remembering them at the moment, nor did he look shocked. He simply looked at me, then slowly nodded his head in agreement, without saying a word. So he too had found his love of life intensified since the day it happened, the pleasures of social intercourse more acute.

I didn't speak any more either. I was thinking. Values

had changed, that was all. Take Malevil, for example. Before, Malevil had been that rather artificial thing: a restored castle. I had lived in it alone. I was proud of it, and half out of vanity, half to make money, I had been about to open it as a tourist attraction. But Malevil now was something very different. Malevil was a tribe—with its lands, its flocks, its stocks of hay and grain, its workers and fighters united like the fingers on a hand, and its women who would bear our children. It was also our stronghold, our den, our lair, our eyrie. Its walls were our protection, and within those walls we knew that we would all one day be buried.

At the dinner table that evening, at which she appeared still coughing, Evelyne managed to oust Thomas from his chair on my right. He simply moved along one without comment, while Catie took the chair to the right of him. There were now twelve of us at table, and the rest of the seating remained unchanged, except that Momo had somehow or other—I have no idea why—replaced his mother at the bottom end, and La Menou had moved to Colin's left. This meant that Momo now enjoyed an enviably strategic position. When winter came again he would have his back to the fire. And above all, he had an extremely good view of Catie, next to him on his left, and of Miette on the other side of the table. And he certainly took advantage of this situation, gazing at them alternately the whole time as he stuffed down his food. He didn't look at them both in quite the same way. Catie he looked at in a sort of delighted surprise, like a sultan suddenly perceiving a new face in the seraglio. Miette he gazed at in pure adoration.

Nor did Catie seem at all put out by Momo's proximity. By no means averse to male homage, she might have found one of Thomas's companions too reserved. With Momo there could be no complaint on that score. His gaze managed to combine the innocence of a child with the licentiousness of a satyr. And also he wasn't offensive to the nose any more, now that Miette was washing him. Apart from the fact that he crammed such enormous pieces of food into his mouth, then pushed at them with his fingers, he was very presentable. And Catie now forcefully took his table manners in hand too. She took his plate away from him, cut up his ham into small pieces, broke up his slice of bread, then replaced it in front of him. He watched her spellbound as she did it. Then when she had finished, he put out one of his long, rather simian arms, gave her two or three little taps on the shoulder, and said, "*Nhice, nhice.*" La Menou made no attempt whatever to interfere throughout the scene.

As a matter of fact, I had been rather apprehensive of La Menou's reactions when I brought Evelyne and Catie back to Malevil. Though in the event they were very restrained. "My poor Emmanuel," she said, "I see you've brought us two more barrens and two more mares." In other words, more useless mouths to feed. But La Menou's fear of famine had decreased slightly now that the wheat was up. Above all, with a marriage at Malevil, she was in her seventh heaven. She had always been passionately addicted to marriages. Whenever one took place in Malejac, even when she scarcely knew the people involved, she would drop everything at Les Sept Fayards and rush down on her bike to the church. "Idiotic old goat," my uncle used to say. "Off to have herself a good cry again, I suppose." And he supposed right. La Menou would station herself just outside the porch—she would never go inside on account of the curé's refusal to let Momo take communion and her subsequent quarrel with him—and as soon as the young couple appeared, the tears would start to flow. In someone who was such a realist it was a quirk that never failed to amaze me.

Momo was also fascinated by Evelyne, but Evelyne paid him not the slightest attention. She never once took her eyes off me. Whenever I turned my head I found them on me, and even when I didn't I could still sense their gaze. I had the feeling that the right side of my face was going to start heating up just from being looked at so hard. And whenever I laid down my fork and let my right hand rest on the table, another, much smaller hand would immediately slide under it.

After the meal, as I took a few turns around the great hall to settle my digestion, Catie came over to me. "I'd like to have a word with you."

377

"What's this?" I said, "Don't I intimidate you any more?"

"What do you think?" she said with a smile.

Except that her eyes didn't have the same animal gentleness, she was very like her sister in looks. For her wedding she had divested herself of all her gaudy finery and was wearing a very simple navy blue dress with a small white collar. She looked much better that way. There was a look of triumph and happiness on her face. I'd have preferred to see only the happiness, but all the same she was giving off a sort of radiance that bathed every one of us there in its warmth. There is a certain generosity there, I thought to myself. Oh, nothing to be compared with Miette's, who is nothing but generosity. But after all, she did cut Momo's ham up for him, and she bent around Thomas several times during the meal to feel Evelyne's forehead or speak to her when she coughed.

"Do you still find me as cold?" I asked, putting an arm around her neck and kissing her cheek.

"Oh, what's this?" Peyssou said. "Watch out, Thomas!"

General laughter. Catie returned my kiss, half on the mouth moreover, then disengaged herself without any sign of haste, in a state of high delight because now she could add my scalp to her belt. And I was quite pleased too. The fact that I was never going to sleep with Catie would give our relationship a pleasant freedom.

"First," she said, "thank you for the room."

"It's those who gave it you who deserve the thanks."

"They've already had them," Catie said simply. "But thank you, Emmanuel, for arranging it. Thank you most of all for letting me come to Malevil. And also, well, thanks for everything," she added with a sudden flash of embarrassment.

I realized that she was alluding to the little argument that Thomas must have told her about, and I smiled.

"I wanted to tell you," she went on in a lower voice, "that Evelyne is certainly going to have an attack tonight. She's been coughing for two days now."

"And when she has an attack, what does one have to do?"

"There's not much you can. You stay with her, you

378

comfort her, and if you have some eau de Cologne you rub some on her forehead and her chest."

That "you" did not escape me. I could see from Catie's face that she was finding the rest hard to say. I decided to help her. "And you want me to look after her tonight?"

"Yes," she said with relief. "My grandmother, you see, she'll just get herself in a panic, run round in circles, cackle all the time, all the absolute opposite of what's needed."

A very recognizable description of La Falvine. I nodded.

"So if Evelyne does start an attack," she went on, "my grandmother can come and fetch you?"

I shook my head. "She won't be able to. At night the door of the keep is bolted from inside."

"And you can't just for one evening . . ."

In a stern voice I said, "Absolutely not. The security regulations admit of no exceptions. Ever."

She looked at me, very crestfallen.

"There's another solution," I said. "I can have Evelyne sleep in my room. There's the sofa free now that Thomas has gone."

"Would you do that?" she cried with joy.

"Why not?"

"Only I must warn you," Catie said with commendable honesty, "if you let her sleep in your room once, then it's all over. She won't want to leave again."

I smiled. "Don't worry. She'll clear out willingly enough one day."

Catie smiled back. I could see that she was immensely relieved.

Evelyne, who had slept upstairs with La Falvine and Jacquet in the house on her first night at Malevil, was wild with joy at the news that she was to share my room. But she wasn't given much time to express it. She was scarcely in her bed on the sofa, and Miette—who had helped me make it—scarcely out of the room, when her attack began. She was suffocating, her nose was pinched, the sweat was streaming down her forehead. I had never seen anyone having an asthma attack, and what I saw now was terrifying: a human being unable to breathe any more.

It took me a few moments to control my own distress.

379

But that was the very first thing that had to be done. Evelyne was staring up at me with anguished eyes, and I knew I had to recover my own calm if I was to keep her calm too. I sat her up against her pillows, but they kept slipping because the sofa didn't have a headboard. I picked her up and carried her over to my own bed, a big double one inherited from my uncle. It had a padded headboard I could prop her up against. I avoided looking at her. From the way she was struggling to get her breath, it sounded to me as though she was about to die of suffocation at any moment. Our tiny lamp didn't give much light, but it was a clear night, and I could see the contortions of her face only too clearly. I went over and opened the window as wide as it would go, then I took the last bottle of eau de Cologne from my closet, shook some onto a washrag, and wiped it over her brow and the top of her chest. She was no longer looking at me. Incapable of speech, eyes staring straight in front of her, head tilted back, cheeks streaming with sweat, she just lay coughing and panting. I noticed that her hair kept falling over her face and seemed to be bothering her, so I fetched a piece of string from my desk drawer and tied it back for her.

That was the sum total of my medical equipment: one bottle of eau de Cologne, one length of string. I had no medical dictionary. My knowledge in that field was nil, and I was afraid my uncle's ten-volume Grand Larousse wasn't going to be of much help either. Nevertheless, as best I could by the lamp's dim light, I did struggle through the "asthma" entry. All it told me was the names of now vanished drugs: belladonna, atropine, ephedrine. Well naturally it wasn't going to give me a lot of old wives' remedies. And yet that was precisely what I needed.

I looked down at Evelyne. I was face to face with our impoverishment, our impotence. I remembered briefly that operation I'd neglected to have while the chance was there, and wondered what would happen if my appendix flared up again.

I sat down beside Evelyne. She threw me a look full of such pain and panic that my throat knotted. I talked to her, I told her it would soon be over, and as soon as her eyes were no longer on me, I observed her. I noticed after a little while that she was having more difficulty emptying her lungs than in filling them. I don't know why, but till then I'd assumed the contrary. As far as I could make out, she was being deprived of oxygen on two counts: first because she couldn't reject her used up air quickly enough, and second because she couldn't get fresh air in quickly enough to replace it. But the blockage seemed to act to some extent like a valve, making the breathing-out part even more difficult than the breathing in. And on top of that there was the cough. The purpose of that, I took it, was to expel whatever was blocking her breathing. It was a dry, hacking cough that shook her whole body and exhausted her. And it wasn't expelling anything at all.

Watching her thin chest pumping desperately up and down, I had an idea. What if I helped her breathing by purely mechanical means? Not by stretching her out flat on her back, but just as she was now, in a position that would enable her to continue coughing and also, if the need arose, to spit. I sat myself on the bed, back propped against the headboard. Lifting her in my arms, I placed her between my legs with her back to me. Then I grasped her upper arms with my hands and began accompanying her every attempt to breathe out with a double movement: pushing her shoulders forward and together while at the same time bending her thorax forward and down. When she was trying to breathe in, I did the same thing in reverse, pulling her shoulders and thorax back and up toward me until her back was against my chest.

I had no idea whether I was doing her any good. For all I knew a doctor would have found my efforts ludicrous. But I must have been bringing Evelyne some degree of comfort, even if only morally, because at one point, in an exhausted, scarcely audible voice, she murmured, "Thank you, Emmanuel."

So I went on. Eventually she let herself relax entirely in my hands, and after a while I noticed that despite the extreme lightness of her torso I was now finding it heavier to manipulate. I assumed that tired as I was I must have dozed off at some point, because I saw that the lamp had run out of oil without my having noticed it go out.

In the middle of the night—I think, because I had left my watch on the desk and had by now lost all notion of time— Evelyne was shaken by a long fit of coughing and asked me in a muffled voice for my handkerchief. I heard her spitting and clearing her throat for quite some time. There were several more coughing fits after that, and each time she had to spit into the handkerchief. Then she fell back against my chest, exhausted but having obviously obtained some relief.

When I opened my eyes again it was bright daylight. The sun was streaming into the room and I was lying twisted across the bed in a most uncomfortable position. Evelyne was still lying in my arms fast asleep. I must have slid down into that contorted position during my sleep. When I got up, I found that my left hip was aching and that I had the beginnings of a stiff neck. Since Evelyne's position was no less uncomfortable-looking than my own, I straightened her out and rearranged the bedclothes over her. I was even able to remove the piece of string tying back her hair without waking her. There were dark rings around her eyes, her cheeks were sunken, her skin dead white, and if it hadn't been for her breathing you could have taken her for dead.

I woke her at eleven with a bowl of warm sweetened milk and a slice of buttered bread brought over from the house on a tray. It was a terrible business getting her to eat anything at all. But I did manage to get most of it down her in the end by dint of alternate coaxing and threats. The threat—it was in fact always the same one— was that if she didn't eat she would find herself back sleeping in the house that evening. And it worked for two or three mouthfuls, then in a sudden burst of incredible vivacity she turned my blackmail around and used it against me. She refused point-blank to eat any more unless I promised to let her stay in my room. In the end we arrived at a compromise. For every swallow of milk she would earn a further day's stay in my room. And a day too for every bite of bread and butter. We managed to reach agreement too, after a great deal of haggling, on the definitions of swallow and bite.

By the time Evelyne had finished her breakfast I was owing her twenty-two days of further hospitality. But then, since I was afraid of being totally disarmed in the future, I reserved myself the right to subtract days from the total if she didn't eat her fair share at subsequent meals. She protested at that: "Ah, yes, you cunning thing, and what's to stop you piling heaps and heaps on my plate so that I can't eat it?"

I promised there would be no cheating and that the size of her portions would be fixed in accordance with her age by a consensus of all those present. Evelyne must have had tremendous reserves of vitality stored away somewhere in that frail little body, because despite the night she'd just spent she was lively and gay during the whole of this scene. Though she did begin to betray a little lassitude at the end. She even wanted to get up, but I forbade it. She was to sleep till noon, and then I'd come and fetch her.

"Do you promise you'll come, Emmanuel?" I promised, and as I walked away from her toward the door she followed me with her eyes, the pale head scarcely denting its pillow at all. And the eyes were enormous. No body and almost no face, just two huge eyes.

When I emerged from the keep carrying the empty bowl on its tray, I found a little group gathered outside. Thomas, Peyssou, Colin with his hands in his pockets, and Miette, who looked as though she had been waiting for me. Which indeed she had, for no sooner did I appear than she took the tray from my hands and made off with it back to the house, though not without giving me what I thought a very strange glance as she left.

"Now the thing is, Emmanuel," Peyssou began, "we'd like to speak to you. Because Colin's old iron is all put away now. And well, as I say, the thing is we're fed up. We've nothing to do."

"What about Meyssonnier?"

"Ah, Meyssonnier," Peyssou said, "now he's nicely accounted for. Working on the bow you wanted. Jacquet and Momo too, they're mucking out the animals. But

383

what about us? We can't just spend our time watching the wheat grow, can we now?"

"Mark you," Colin said with his gondola smile, "we could always tell the women to stay in bed in the mornings, then take them up their breakfasts in bed."

General laughter.

"Colin," I said, "do you want my boot behind you?"

"But it's true though," Thomas chimed in. "It's depressing not having anything to do."

I looked at him. Depressed he was not. Sleepy would be more like it. And not as anxious to work as all that, not this particular morning anyway. In fact the only reason he was there, I suspected, taking part in this unemployment demonstration, instead of where he so acutely longed to be really, was because he didn't want to look as though he was tied to his wife's apron strings too much.

"Well, you were quite right to come and tell me," I said, "because I have a whole program just waiting up my sleeve for you. First, riding lessons for everyone. Second, shooting lessons. Third, building up the gate-tower ramparts a little higher so that they're out of ladder reach."

"Shooting lessons?" Colin said. "But we shall just waste ammunition. And we haven't got all that much."

"Not at all. Do you remember that little air gun my uncle gave me once? I've found it again. Up in the loft. And plenty of pellets for it too. It's just the thing for training and practice."

Peyssou was more concerned about the ramparts. His father had been a mason, he himself was quite handy at that sort of thing, and the ramparts, well he wasn't going to say it couldn't be done. For one thing, there was the cement for it now, part of the booty from L'Étang. And sand, there had always been plenty of that; and the stones too, they were there. He'd already thought about it himself. But.

"But," he said, "the thing is you mustn't spoil the look of it, you see. Now say that you make it higher, then you've filled in the up and down of it, haven't you? That's not going to look good at all, not without the up and down bits. The eye is going to miss something that was always up there."

"I'm sure you'll find a way," I said. "There must be some means of reconciling the look of it and our safety."

He pulled his mouth into a grimace of doubt and shook his head rather grimly. But I knew my Peyssou. He was delighted. He was going to be thinking about his ramparts now day and night. He would start making little drawings. He was going to create something. And when it was done, every time he looked up at the gate tower on his way back from the fields, he would think, without ever saying a word to anyone, That was me, Peyssou. I made that.

"Thomas," I said, "go and show them how to saddle up. Take the three mares, not Bel Amour. I'll see you in the Maternity Ward in a moment."

I went into the house, where the four women, the two old and the two young, were bustling about at the far end of the great hall. The Falvine family now held a clear majority: three to one. But La Menou was perfectly capable of holding her own for all that. As I opened the door she was just putting the finishing touches on a verbal onslaught on La Falvine. The two younger women were both silent, Miette because she was dumb anyway, Catie because she was prudent.

"Miette, can you come here a moment?"

She ran over immediately. I led her outside and closed the door behind me. She was wearing the little patched woolen skirt and the faded short-sleeved blouse—both very clean—and nothing on her feet at all. She had just finished scrubbing the stone floor and hadn't yet had time to put her shoes back on. I looked at her bare feet on the courtyard cobbles, then at her magnificent black mane, and finally at her eyes, whose gentleness always made me think of a horse's eyes. Then my gaze returned to her feet. I don't know why, but I found them very moving, even though there was actually nothing moving about Miette's feet at all in themselves: they were broad and very solid. It was more that their bareness somehow completed the picture of the wild, untamed country child that Miette was presenting that morning. A Stone Age Eve, I

385

told myself, returned to me from the depths of time. Idiotic fantasy. Sexual overestimation, Thomas would say. As though he had a right to talk just at the moment!

"Miette, are you cross?"

She shook her head. She wasn't cross.

"What's the matter?"

Another shake. Nothing was the matter.

"Now come on, Miette. You looked at me very oddly just now."

She just stood, docile but completely uncommunicative.

"Miette, come on! Talk to me, tell me what's wrong!"

Her eyes, fixed on me with such gentleness, also held a hint of reproach, or so it seemed to me.

"Miette, explain. What is it?"

She just looked at me, arms hanging at her sides. Not a gesture, not a single mime. She was doubly mute.

"Miette, you ought to tell me if something is wrong, because you know I love you very much."

She nodded. Yes, she knew it.

"What then?"

Impassiveness.

"Miette?"

I took her by the shoulders. I moved closer to her and kissed her on the cheek. Quite suddenly she threw her arms around me and hugged me very hard, though without kissing me. Then she pulled herself away again, equally suddenly, and ran back into the house and left me standing there.

The end of the scene had come so abruptly that I stayed where I was for several seconds, staring at the heavy oak door she had not taken the time to close behind her.

When I think back over the two months that followed that morning, what strikes me above all is the slowness with which they went by. It certainly wasn't that we lacked for activities. Shooting, riding, building up the wall of the outer enclosure (we all took turns working as big Peyssou's laborers), and in my case, in addition, physical education lessons with Evelyne, to say nothing of her three R's.

We were very busy, and yet there was never any hurry. We had vast quantities of leisure time at our disposal. The whole rhythm of life was slow. And odd though it sounds, although the days still had the same number of hours as before, they seemed to us infinitely longer. What it meant, in fact, was that all those machines that were supposed to make tasks easier—automobiles, telephones, tractors, chainsaws, chaff cutters, circular saws—well, they did make them easier, it's true; but they also had the effect of speeding time up. We always wanted to do too many things too quickly. The machines were always there behind us, snapping at our heels to keep us on the move.

For example, before it happened, the journey to La Roque to announce Catie and Thomas's marriage to Fulbert—always supposing that I had decided not to do it by telephone— would have taken me nine and a half minutes by automobile, and that's allowing for the bendy road. Whereas when I actually made that same journey by horse with Colin—who had insisted on going with me, without doubt in order to see Agnès again—it took us more than an hour. What's more, having arrived and handed our message to Fabrelâtre—since Fulbert wasn't up yet—there could be no question of turning around and starting straight back, because after their nine miles the horses needed a little rest. Added to that, because I didn't want to subject them to too much metaled road in one day, on the way back we took the short cut through the forest, which was in fact no short cut at all, on account of all the dead trees across the track. In short, having left really very early in the morning, we got back finally at noon, tired but nevertheless feeling rather happy, Colin because he'd managed to talk to Agnès, myself because I'd seen green shoots emerging from the ground here and there, and even some on trees that earlier had looked quite dead.

I also noticed that our movements had slowed down. They had become attuned to the new pace of life. Because you can't just jump off a horse the way you used to leave the wheel of an automobile. There is no longer any question of screeching to a halt and rushing up the steps to catch the telephone before it stops ringing. Now when

I arrive back at Malevil, I dismount as soon as I'm through the gate, walk Amarante sedately back to her stall, unsaddle her, rub her down, and wait till she's nice and dry before giving her a drink. In all, a good half hour.

It is quite possible, now that the medical profession no longer exists, that lives will become shorter. But if one is living more slowly, if the days and years don't flash past in front of one's nose at such a terrifying pace, if one has the time to live, in short, then I can't help wondering if anything has really been lost.

Even our relationships with other people have been considerably enriched as a result of this slower pace to life. It's unbelievable, when I think back, the change in that respect. Take Germain, my poor Germain, who died in front of our eyes the day it happened. Even though he was my closest co-worker for all those years, it was almost true to say I didn't know him. Or worse still, I knew him just well enough to make the best use of him. "Make use of"—what an appalling phrase to use in relation to another human being! But there it was, like everyone else then I was in a hurry. Always a telephone call to make, mail to answer, automobiles, the annual horse sales in the neighboring towns, the bookkeeping, the forms, the tax inspector. With life being lived at a pace like that, how could human relationships possibly compete?

Early in August we received our first visit from old Pougès, one day when he managed to extend one of his morning bike rides to take in Malevil. And I can only doff my cap in respect to such a performance from a man of seventy-five: eighteen miles there and back, over very hilly roads what's more, and all for two glasses of wine. To my mind he'd certainly earned them. But it cannot be said that La Menou welcomed him with open arms. I took the wine bottle from her and sent her back up to the house. "Now what did I do to offend her?" old Pougès asked plaintively, tugging at the tips of his long, drooping mustache.

"Nothing, take no notice," I said. "Who's to know what ideas old women get into their heads?" Though in fact I knew precisely what La Menou had against him: the fact that he had once taken her late husband, forty-seven years ago now, to visit Adelaide, with what consequences for the peace of her home life and the names of her sows we all know.

Even half a century had not succeeded in turning the edge of La Menou's rancor. "Well, a fine thing, I must say," she said to me later, just before dinner. "I wonder you've the stomach to let a creature like that in here, a loafer, a drunkard, a low skirt chaser."

"Now, now, Menou! I don't think old Pougès is catching many skirts these days, even with a bike! And as for drink, he certainly drinks no more than you do."

Pougès had news for me from La Roque. The Sunday before, in the chapel during the course of his sermon, Fulbert had denounced my duplicity in the matter of Catie's departure. "Duplicity, yes that was the word, and not a polite one by the sound of it. Right away I thought to myself, He's doing this deliberate, it's to get Marcel angry. And it did too. But as luck would have it, Marcel had Judith there next to him. Because those two are very thick, it seems to me. So she saw him getting very red in the face, and right away she clapped one of those great hands of hers on his arm. Then she turns to Fulbert, and out loud, right in the middle of his sermon, she says to him, 'Monsieur le Curé, pardon me, but I come to church to hear about God, not to listen to accounts of your differences with Monsieur Comte over young ladies.' And you know the way she speaks: very sharp, straight to the jaw. Polite always, but a voice like a sergeant-major. Here's to yours."

"And yours."

"Next day she got short rations. So right away she goes all around the town showing her rations to everyone, so they know about it. And she tells Fabrelâtre, 'Monsieur Fabrelâtre, please tell Monsieur le Curé I thank him for helping me to fast. But if I don't receive normal rations tomorrow, I shall be forced to go begging at Malevil.' Well, you know, Emmanuel, you'll never believe it, but next day she had the same as us all."

"Which proves it pays to have a pair of balls between your legs," I said, looking at him hard.

"Yes, yes, maybe you're right there," old Pougès murmured evasively, at the same time extracting a stained handkerchief from his pocket and carefully wiping both sides of his long, yellowish-white mustache.

This gesture was not inspired solely by a concern for hygiene, if I may so put it. No, its main purpose was to indicate to me the fact that his glass was now empty. I filled it a second time, right to the brim. Then I replaced the cork in the bottle and drove it home with a sharp blow of my palm. I didn't want him getting any ideas.

While savoring his first glass, Pougès had dutifully made conversation. When it came to the second, however, he clearly felt I'd had my money's worth already. He remained as silent as the grave. The second glass was the free one, as it were, as in the old days at Adelaide's. Its enjoyment required meditating on. So I took advantage of this silence to write a letter to Marcel. Pougès was to leave it in the tower mailbox on his way back, then inform the addressee of its presence there by discreet word of mouth, thereby avoiding the possibility of becoming involved and compromised. I advised Marcel in my letter to organize two different forms of opposition in La Roque: the first, open and superficially polite, directed against Fulbert with Judith as mouthpiece; the second, insidious and insulting, directed against Fabrelâtre.

As it turned out, it was Peyssou who was right about the wheat after all. It was clearly, as he had said, set on making up for lost time. On August fifteenth, still very late it's true, the kernels were formed, and by about the twenty-fifth they were half ripe. And it was Peyssou again who one afternoon noticed a number of crushed stems, some gnawed kernels, and the marks of paws on the fringe of the field nearest the river.

"Now that's a badger," he announced, "and a big one too. Just look at those paws, how far apart they are."

"Badgers only eat corn," Colin said, "or grapes."

Peyssou shrugged pityingly. "I won't bother to answer that," he said as a prelude to answering it. "You think just because there's no corn he's going to turn up his nasty snout at what there is? The vermin must have been in his

390

burrow the day it happened. They can dig deep, badgers, with those great claws."

"And how has he kept alive all this time then?" Jacquet asked. "What's he been eating?"

Another pitying shrug from Peyssou. "He hasn't been eating, of course! He's been asleep."

Peyssou was quite right, it seemed to me. It was true that around here, where the cold was never really intense and some food was usually available, the badger didn't really hibernate any more. But it must nevertheless have conserved the faculty of dozing off in its hole when food was short, of living thriftily off its own fat until better times returned.

Council of war. In the old days we used to content ourselves with a slow fire on the edge of the field to keep badgers away. But that method somehow lacked the element of revenge we needed. Because we didn't just want to keep the verminous creature away, we wanted its skin. The peasant's hatred for the pest competing with him for his harvest blazed fiercer in our hearts than it had ever done before.

On the slope of the hill beyond the river, about twenty yards from the edge of the wheat, we constructed a small shelter, a dugout covered with a roof of brushwood supported by four posts. This roof was intended not only to provide the hunter with concealment but also to protect him from rain and wind. And Meyssonnier—for it was he who designed the shelter for us— had even added the refinement of a rough wooden grating at the bottom of the trench so that we needn't stand directly on the ground. Because, he said, even through rubber boots, I don't care how thick they are, the damp always seeps up inside you.

We divided up into pairs to keep watch on a rota system every night in our little dugout. We didn't exclude the women, or at least not the two young ones, because during the past two months we'd been teaching them to use a gun, and they were really not at all bad shots by now. Catie, needless to say, paired off with Thomas. And Miette, though I had been expecting her to choose me, in fact chose Jacquet. Which meant that Peyssou, since

Jacquet was already spoken for, was left with Colin, and myself with Meyssonnier. At which point Evelyne—as Miette presumably foresaw—made a scene in order to be included in my watch too, and when I resisted she even began a hunger strike, and in the end I was forced to agree.

A week went by. No badger. Although such smelly creatures, they must have very sensitive noses, because this one had undoubtedly caught wind of us. Though it's true that from his point of view we were probably the ones that stank. Never mind, we continued to lie in wait for him.

So time passed, slow as a river. I was awakened one morning at dawn by the brightness of the light. Since the weather had become so fine I always left the window open. I liked to lie in bed for a moment after waking up and survey the progress of the vegetation on the hillside opposite. It was incredible. Who would have believed only two months ago that we would soon be seeing so much grass and so many leaves, the latter not so much on the trees—very few of those had survived—but on a fantastic number of little bushes that had taken advantage of their great neighbors' destruction to proliferate amazingly over all the hills.

I looked across at Evelyne, asleep on the sofa. The result of our hospitality-by-barter system—one day for every swallow or bite—was that the one night for which she had originally been admitted to my room had now extended itself to two months. But I didn't dare bring the agreement to an end, because it seemed to have done her so much good. She had color in her face, her cheeks had filled out, and she was putting on muscles. And though her chest had remained quite flat, despite my predictions, at least now it was more athletically flat and not just bones. She had learned to ride quicker than anyone. She was totally fearless in the saddle and riding was a joy for her, those little feet beating her mount's flanks to urge it into a gallop, her blond braids flying out behind her. Braids were strict regulation gear for her now when riding, ever since the day when she was on Morgane and raised her right hand to push her hair out of her eyes. The result had

392

been a series of bucks that eventually deposited her on top of a little bush, fortunately unhurt.

Just as Evelyne sensed my gaze on her face and opened her eyes, there came the sound of a gunshot. Then another, and a quarter of a second later, a third. In a flash I had passed from puzzlement to concern. It had been Peyssou and Colin's turn in the little shelter that night, but by this time they should be almost on their way back. No badger was going to venture into the wheat by daylight. And even if he had, it couldn't have taken Colin and Peyssou three shots to settle him. I was on my feet and already pulling on my trousers.

"Evelyne, run down to the gate tower and tell Meyssonnier to open the gate and wait for me there with his gun."

A month before, I had decided that our guns should be considered as personal weapons and that we would all keep our own in our bedrooms. In the event of a surprise night attack this meant that there would be three guns in the gate tower, three in the keep, and one, Jacquet's, in the house, except when it was Jacquet's turn in Miette's room, which was the case now.

Evelyn sped out of the room, barefoot and in her nightgown, and as I followed her, my clothes scarcely buttoned, Thomas's door opened and he appeared, still in pajama trousers, naked to the waist.

"What's happening?"

"Take your guns, both of you, go up on the gate-tower battlements and keep guard. Don't move from there. You must stay and guard Malevil. Quickly, quickly! Don't stop to dress!"

I hurtled down the spiral staircase and found myself face to face with Jacquet, who had just emerged from Miette's room. His reactions had been quicker than Thomas's. He was wearing pants and carrying his gun. We didn't stop to speak. We just ran side by side.

As we reached the middle of the outer enclosure, a fourth shot rang out from down by the Rhunes. I stopped, worked a bullet up into the breech of my gun, and fired into the air. I hoped they would take it as a signal that we were on our way. I set off again. I saw Meyssonnier ahead, gun in hand, just opening the gate. I shouted as I ran, "Go on! Go on! I'll catch up to you!"

Jacquet, who had continued running while I stopped to fire my signal, was now ahead of me. I ran through the gate arch on his heels and was just starting down the slope outside when I became aware of panting behind me. I turned and saw Evelyne, still barefoot and in her night-gown, running at full speed trying to overtake me.

Wild with anger, I stopped, seized her by the arm as she reached me, shook her, and yelled, "In the name of God! What do you think you're doing! Get back inside! Go on!"

"No! No!" she cried, eyes starting out of her head. "I don't want to leave you!"

I bellowed, "Get back inside!"

I passed my gun from right hand to left and slapped her twice, very hard. She obeyed like a whipped animal, backing toward the gate, but with infuriating slowness, staring at me with terrified eyes. I yelled, "Get inside!"

I was losing precious seconds! And Catie and Thomas not at the gate yet! No one to take charge of her! Certainly not La Menou, because I could see her through the open gate, clutching Momo's shirt with both hands, trying to hold him back.

I picked Evelyne up, threw her over my shoulder, ran back through the arch and dumped her inside as though she was a package I had delivered.

At the same moment I saw Momo's shirt give way. Freed from his mother's grip, he stumbled forward a few steps, recovered, and began haring off down the road toward the river.

"Momo! Momo!" La Menou shouted despairingly and began running in her turn.

The other two were still not down! It just wasn't possible! She must have stopped to make herself up! And he's waiting while she does it!

I left Evelyne inside and began running back down the road again. I passed La Menou, her tiny thin ankles flickering beneath her skirts, and I yelled, "Momo! Momo!" But I knew I hadn't a chance of catching him. He had always run like a young child, his feet skimming the ground, but very fast, and I'd never seen him out of breath.

At the hairpin bend leading down into the dry riverbed, where the road ran almost parallel to itself for a short stretch, I could see La Menou running for all she was worth up above me, and behind her, catching up to her, Evelyne! I was totally, but totally, demoralized by this incredible act of disobedience. I don't know why, but I was now convinced that Catie and Thomas were also going to desert their post and follow us. Malevil was going to be wholly without defenders. All our belongings, all our stores, all our animals abandoned to the first comer! I was in despair, and as I ran on, my heart thumping against my ribs, teeth clenched, my throat was so knotted it was hurting me. I was beside myself with fury and apprehension.

As I emerged into the little valley, quite a way ahead, standing motionless with their backs to me, guns in their hands, I saw Peyssou, Colin, Meyssonnier, and Jacquet, side by side in a line. They were absolutely still. They weren't speaking. They looked as though they'd been turned to stone. What had petrified them like that I had no idea, because I could see nothing but their backs. But certainly their attitude was not that of people being threatened, or needing to defend themselves, or in any way afraid. They were dumb, turned to statues, and even the sound of my running behind them didn't make them turn around.

I reached them at last. Not one of them emerged even for a moment from his stupor, or moved aside to acknowledge my arrival. And then I saw in my turn.

About ten yards or so in front of us, lower down the slope, were twenty or so people in rags, reduced to the ultimate degree of physical deterioration, not just pale but really yellow, the skin hanging on their cheekbones, some of them so weak they couldn't even control their eye muscles, so they were squinting horribly. They were all kneeling or lying on our wheat and devouring the half-ripe kernels with little frightened yapping noises. They weren't even attempting to separate the grains from their coverings, they just ate it all. I noticed that there were

395

green stains around their mouths, which indicated that before coming across our wheat they had been trying to eat grass. They looked like emaciated animals. Their squinting eyes gleamed with fear and greed. And they kept shooting us sideways glances as they hurried to cram the spikes of wheat into their mouths. When they gagged, they spat what was in their mouths out into their hands then pushed it back in again immediately. There were some women among them. Though the only way of telling was by the length of their hair, since their terrifying thinness had deprived them of all superficial sexual characteristics. None of them had a firearm. But lying on the crushed wheat beside them I saw a number of pitchforks and clubs.

The sight was so pitiable that it took me a moment to realize that they had already ruined a quarter of our harvest, and were going to spoil the whole lot if we didn't intervene. It wasn't just what they ate. They were ruining a great deal more than they actually consumed by walking and lying on it. And that grain they were trampling or devouring was our life. If others could destroy Malevil's wheat with total impunity, then Malevil too would be reduced to the state of a wandering band of starving animals, like so many others. Because this one in front of us was only the first, I was sure of that. It was the sprouting vegetation that had brought them out into the country in search of food.

Peyssou was next to me. He didn't look as though he was even aware of my presence. But the sweat was streaming down his face.

"We've tried everything," Colin said in a voice choking with grief and anger. "We've talked to them, we've shouted at them. We fired over their heads. We threw stones at them. Stones! They don't give a damn about stones. They put up one arm to shield their heads and just go on eating!"

"Who are these people, just who are they?" Meyssonnier said with a bewildered look that I would have found comic at any other time. "Where have they come from?"

Then he began shouting at them in patois, shaken by impotent rage, "Get away from there. Get away, in the name of God! Can't you see you're spoiling our wheat! What do you think we're going to eat?"

"Wasted breath," Colin said. "Patois or French, they don't even answer! They just go on cramming it in. And to think we got so wild about one badger!"

"What about using our gun butts, driving them off?" Peyssou said at last in a strangled voice.

I shook my head. No good trusting to their weakness. Any creature at bay is capable of anything. And the fight wouldn't be equal, gun butts against forks. No, I was perfectly aware of the only logical decision to take. My companions too. And I was incapable of taking it. Standing there on the edge of that wheatfield, gun in hand, safety catch off, a bullet already there in the breech, finger on the trigger, it would be an understatement to say I hesitated. I was struck by a total inhibition of the will that reduced me to paralysis, despite a crystal clarity of mind and judgment. I too had been turned to stone.

The only one moving was Momo. He had always been very excitable, but I had never seen him a prey to such insane agitation as he was displaying now. He was dancing, stamping, waving his arms over his head, shaking his fists, yelling his head off. He was totally possessed by mindless rage, constantly turning his glittering eyes in my direction, shaking his shaggy mane, adjuring me with gestures and unintelligible cries to put an end to the pillage. And he kept crying in a high, piercing voice, *"Huh heat! Huh heat!"*

The pillagers must have been fighting among themselves, or with some other band, because their clothes were in tatters, and the dirty stained shreds of cloth, the color of earth, revealed their thighs, their torsos, their backs. I saw one unfortunate creature, a female, whose limp wrinkled breasts were sagging down to touch the ground as she dragged herself on all fours farther into the patch. She was wearing shoes, whereas most of them had only rags wrapped around their feet. There were no children among them, no one either very young or old. The weakest had already succumbed. The ones before us were all "in the prime of life." That expression seemed appallingly cruel when applied to such skeletons. My eyes were drawn by their protruding pelvises, by the enormous knee joints, by the shoulder blades and collarbones that seemed almost to be stuck on as additions. When they chewed you could see the muscles of their jaws quite clearly. Their skin was just a thin, more or less wrinkled bag laid over the bones, and the group as a whole was giving off a sickening rancid odor that caught in your throat and made you want to gag.

"*Huh heat! Huh heat!*" Momo cried, and he seized his hair with both hands as though about to tear it all out.

My right hand was tensed around my gun, but it was still hanging down by my side, barrel pointing to the earth. I couldn't even manage to get it up to my shoulder. I was filled with an insane hatred of these foreigners, these plunderers, because they were devouring our lives. And also because they were what we could so quickly become, all of us at Malevil, if this pillage of our resources continued. But at the same time I was filled with abject pity too, exactly canceling out my hate and reducing me to this impotence.

"*Huh heat! Huh heat!*" Momo shrieked, his agitation reaching a paroxysm of fury.

And suddenly he rushed across the ten yards separating us from the band, hurled himself on the nearest looter with a wild shriek, and began hammering at him with his fists and boots.

"Momo! Momo!" La Menou shouted.

Someone laughed, perhaps Peyssou. I too had an impulse to laugh. From affection for Momo, because an act like that, so childish and so futile, was so very typical of him. And also because nothing that Momo did was really of any consequence. Because Momo was excused from the serious side of life, like a smaller child allowed to join in a game but too little to understand the rules. I never imagined that anything could ever happen to Momo. He had always been so protected—by La Menou, by my uncle, by me, by all of us at Malevil.

A half second too late I saw the savage look on the man's face. A quarter second too late I saw the fork. I thought my shot would prevent the blow. It was already on its way. The three prongs were already driving into

Momo's heart as my bullet ripped out his assailant's throat.

They fell at the same time. I heard an animal howl and saw La Menou rush forward and hurl herself on her son's body. Then I was slowly moving forward like an automaton and firing as I moved. On my right and on my left, advancing in a line, my companions were firing too. We just fired into the mass, without taking aim. My mind was a total blank. I thought, Momo is dead. I felt nothing. I advanced and I fired. There was no necessity to advance —we were already so close—and yet advance we did, mechanically, methodically, as though we were scything a field.

All movement had ceased, and yet we kept firing still, until every cartridge and shell was gone.

XIV

EXCEPT for La Menou, we none of us felt Momo's loss immediately, partly because a kind of incredulity prevented us from accepting it, but above all because the incursion of the looters we had killed resulted in a total immersion during the next two weeks, from morning till night, in a series of back-breaking and wholly engrossing tasks.

First there were the dead bodies to be disposed of. It was a horrible task, complicated still further by the fact that I insisted no one go too near them. I was afraid they might be infested with parasites carrying the germs of diseases against which we would have no immunity. I remembered, for instance, that fleas could be carriers of plague, and lice of typhus. Moreover, the terrible physical state the poor wretches had been in, and the fact that to judge from the rags on their feet they had come from some distance away, combined to make me even more wary of contact with them still.

Near the heaps of bodies we dug a great trench, then in the trench we laid layers of brushwood, and on the brushwood layers of sticks, until the last layer of wood was level with the surrounding soil. Then, using a running noose attached to the end of a pole, we secured one foot of each corpse in turn with a rope, dragged it over to the trench, taking good care to keep well clear of it, and maneuvered it onto the pyre. There were eighteen corpses in all, five of them women.

It was eleven at night when we threw the last shovelful of earth onto the still warm ashes. I wouldn't allow anyone to go back into Malevil wearing the clothes we had on. I rang the bell at the gate, and when Catie appeared I told her to get Miette to help her carry out two boilers for us and fill them with water. As soon as they were brought, we put all our clothes into them, underclothes included, walked back into the castle naked, then took turns under the shower in the keep bathroom. We inspected every fold in our bodies with great care, but no parasites were found on anyone. Next day we lit a big fire under the two boilers outside the gate and boiled the clothes for some considerable time before bringing them back into the castle and spreading them in the sun.

That evening we all ate in the great hall, with Catie serving us. Evelyne was there, but I didn't speak to her, and she didn't dare come near me. Miette, Falvine, and La Menou were keeping vigil over Momo in the gate tower. The meal was eaten in silence. I was overwhelmed with tiredness, and emotionally numb. Apart from the dazed animal contentment of eating, drinking, and getting my strength back, I could feel nothing but an immense need for sleep.

There could be no question of that, however. There were decisions to be taken. An assembly had to be held without delay, directly the meal was over. I was against having the women present. I had some very unpleasant things to say to Thomas and I didn't want to have to say them in Catie's presence. And then there was Evelyne. I had not thrown her out of my bedroom, but I still hadn't spoken to her, and I certainly didn't want her to be present during our discussions.

The faces of the men around me bore the marks of fatigue and grief. I began speaking in a neutral voice, picking my way very carefully. We had just been through a very bad experience, I said. Errors had been committed. It was essential that we should discuss things together and decide where we stood. The best thing would be to begin by allowing everyone to give his opinion of the day's events.

There was a long silence, then I said, "Colin, what about you?"

"Well, you know," Colin said in a choking voice, without looking at anyone, "of course I am very upset about Momo. But I'm pretty upset about the people we killed too."

"Meyssonnier?"

"Well, I don't think our organization was very good," Meyssonnier said, "and I'm afraid there were a great many infractions of discipline." He too had refrained from looking at anyone as he spoke.

"Peyssou?"

Peyssou lifted his great shoulders and spread his powerful hands on the tabletop. "Well, the thing is," he said, "poor Momo, you could say he was asking for it, in a way. But all the same, the way Colin said . . ." And there he stopped.

"Jacquet?"

"I think what Colin said too."

"Thomas?"

I had called on him last deliberately, in order to convey a certain aloofness. Though he had already accepted that aloofness in advance, in fact, by not occupying the chair left vacant beside me when Evelyne left. He straightened his shoulders and continued to stare straight ahead, presenting me with just his tensed profile. Although he was sitting up very straight on his chair, even rigidly, he had both hands in his pockets, something very unusual with him. I imagined that he was concealing them not in order to convey a couldn't-care-less attitude but because they were in fact trembling slightly.

In a voice he had difficulty controlling, he said, "Since Meyssonnier has mentioned infractions of discipline, I would like to begin by saying that I personally have two such infractions to blame myself for. First, after the first shots, Emmanuel told me not to dress but to go down to the gate tower as I was, with my weapon. But in fact I did stay to dress and in consequence reached the gate much too late. I was unable to help La Menou keep Momo inside."

He swallowed. "Second, instead of staying and keeping watch on the battlements with Catie, as Emmanuel had ordered me to, I decided on my own initiative to proceed down to the Rhunes as a reinforcement. I realize that I committed a serious error in leaving Malevil undefended.

402

If the band we were facing had been an organized one, it could have split in two, and one group could have drawn us down to the river by pillaging our wheat while the other seized the castle."

If I hadn't known Thomas so well, I'd have said that this speech of his was very cleverly calculated. Because after all, by conducting his own prosecution like that, he had disarmed us. Any prosecuting counsel would have been left without an accusation to stand on. But in fact, as I knew perfectly well, it was entirely the result of his passion for accuracy. His only piece of manipulation, if it was one, was to present the facts in such a way as to exonerate his wife. Which was touching, but also rather dangerous. Because I had my own ideas about Catie's role in the lapses of discipline he had confessed to, and I intended to voice them.

I said in a noncommittal tone, "I am grateful to you for your frankness, Thomas. But I think you are covering up for Catie a little too much. I would like to put it to you: Wasn't it Catie who insisted on taking the time to dress?" I looked at him. I knew he could never bring himself to lie.

"Yes, it was," he said in a slightly shaky voice. "But since I accepted her point of view, I am the one responsible for our delay."

That admission cost him a lot. He was raw now, our Thomas. But I wasn't going to let him off the hook yet all the same. "And up on the battlements, wasn't it Catie who suggested that you come down to the river to see what was happening?"

"It was," Thomas answered, flushing a deep red. "But I was in the wrong in agreeing. The responsibility for the mistake therefore rests solely with me."

I said in a cutting tone, "The responsibility rests with both of you. Catie has the same rights and the same duties as every one of us here."

"Except," Thomas said through tight lips, "that she hasn't the right to attend this assembly at which you are criticizing her."

"I wanted to spare her that. But if you feel that she

403

should be allowed to speak for herself, go and fetch her. We will wait."

A silence. Everyone looked at him. His eyes were lowered, his hand thrust deep in his pockets. His lips quivered. "It's not necessary," he said eventually.

"In that case, I suggest that we discuss Colin's point of view, which is shared, I think I'm right in saying, by Peyssou and Jacquet."

"I haven't finished speaking yet," Thomas said.

"All right then, speak, speak!" I said impatiently. "You pull this one on me every time! No one is stopping you from speaking!"

Thomas said, "I am ready to accept the consequences of the errors I committed and leave Malevil with Catie."

I shrugged, and since he didn't go on, I said, "Have you finished now?"

"No," Thomas said in a muffled voice. "Since until a decision has been taken on what I have just said I am still a member of Malevil, I have the right to give my opinion on the problem we are debating."

"Then give it! Who's stopping you?"

He waited briefly, then went on in a rather firmer voice: "I don't agree with Colin. I don't think that there is any cause for regret at having killed the looters. On the contrary, I think that Emmanuel committed an error in not making up his mind to fire sooner. If he had not waited so long, Momo would still be alive."

There were no gasps or, properly speaking, any "mixed reactions," but disapproval of what had been said was clearly visible on the others' faces. For once, however, I wasn't going to play the cunning politician. I wasn't going to take advantage of popular support. The issue was too serious. I said in an even voice, "Put rather tactlessly, Thomas, but it's not untrue. However, I would like to correct you, if you don't mind. I didn't commit just one error. I committed two."

I looked around at the others and paused. I could afford to pause. I was commanding absolutely total attention now. "Error number one, and it's of a general nature. I have been far too weak with regard to Evelyne. By presenting everyone with the spectacle of a grownup

404

man allowing himself to be led by the nose like that by a little girl, I introduced an element of laxity into the community and contributed to a slackening of discipline. That slackening produced a concrete result. If I hadn't had Evelyne to cope with as I was leaving the gate, I could have helped La Menou restrain Momo, at least until Thomas arrived."

I paused again, then said, "If I am going into all this, Thomas, it is not simply because I enjoy wallowing in the delights of self-criticism. It is in order to make it clear to you that I see my weakness with regard to Evelyne and yours with regard to Catie as weighing equally in the scale."

"Except that Evelyne, after all, is not your wife," Thomas said.

I said coldly, "And you see that as an aggravating circumstance?"

He looked shamefaced and said nothing. What he had meant, I think, was that the fact of his being married to Catie extenuated his error. But he had no desire to spell this notion out in public; it would have been an open confession of his own weakness. Because he had a conventional—and in his case utterly false—idea of the dominant husband.

"Error number two. As Thomas said, I didn't make up my mind quickly enough to fire on the looters."

Meyssonnier threw both hands to the sky. "Let's be fair!" he said loudly. "If that was an error, then you weren't the only one to commit it. None of us was exactly itching to shoot at those poor people. They were so thin! They were so hungry!"

I said, "Thomas, did you feel that way too?"

"Yes," he answered without hesitation. I love that passion for the truth in Thomas. He couldn't lie, even if it meant ruining his own argument.

"In that case," I said, "we are forced to the conclusion that the error was a collective one."

"Yes," Thomas said, "but you were more responsible for it than anyone else, because you are the leader."

I threw my hands in the air and cried vehemently, "But that's just it! That's the point! Am I the leader? Can you say you are a leader when two adult members of the group you are supposed to be leading disobey your orders in the middle of a battle?"

Silence fell, and I let it fall. The heavier the better. Let Thomas stew in his own juice a little longer.

"In my opinion," Colin said, "the situation we have here is not at all clear. We have the Malevil assembly and the decisions we take together. Right. And in that assembly, Emmanuel certainly plays an important part. But we have never said, not in so many words, that in an emergency, whenever there is no time to discuss things, then Emmanuel is the leader. And as I see it, we ought to say that. So that we all know, when a real emergency comes, that Emmanuel's orders must be obeyed."

Meyssonnier raised a hand. "That's it," he said with satisfaction. "That was just what I meant at the beginning when I said the organization wasn't good. In fact I would say it was pitiful, the way we behaved. People running around in all directions, paying no attention to what they were told. Result, at one point the only two left on the ramparts to defend Malevil were La Falvine and Miette. And not only that. Miette, who can shoot perfectly well, didn't even have a gun!"

"Yes, you're right," Peyssou said, shaking his great head. "A brothel, that's what it was! Down by the Rhunes there was poor Momo, who had no business there. There was La Menou, who was in the wrong place too, but came down because of Momo. There was Evelyne, sticking to Emmanuel like a little burr. And there was . . ."

He stopped and blushed to the eyebrows. Carried away by his emotion he had almost included Thomas in his enumeration. There was a silence. Thomas, hands still in pockets, didn't look at anyone. Colin, as though speaking an aside, flashed me one of his little smiles, eyes asparkle.

"It's like your idea just now," Peyssou said suddenly, stretching his great paw toward Thomas at the end of an arm that seemed to extend the whole width of the table. "It's like your idea just now of wanting to leave Malevil with Catie," he went on in a voice of thunder. "Which is the most completely damn fool thing I ever heard!"

"I quite agree," I put in quickly.

"Because in the first place, where would you go, you great asshole?" Peyssou asked, imbuing his insult with untold warmth and affection.

Colin burst out laughing, as always just at the right moment, and managed to sound utterly natural. It was as though we were a chorus and he had given us our note. Everyone else burst out laughing at once, and our laughter defused the atmosphere to such an extent that even Thomas's lips relaxed into the beginning of a smile. And from then on, I noticed, his body gradually lost its rigidity, and in the end he even took his hands out of his pockets.

When the laughter stopped, we proceeded to a vote. And with the exception of one vote—mine, given to Meyssonnier—I was unanimously elected military leader of Malevil "in the event of emergency and danger." With the understanding, needless to say, that at all other times all decisions, even those concerning our security, would be taken by the assembly. I thanked everyone, then asked for Meyssonnier to be appointed as my lieutenant and, in the event of any incapacity resulting from injury, my successor. A second vote followed, which gave me great satisfaction. Then there was a general shuffling and murmuring of relaxation which I allowed to go on for a few minutes undisturbed.

"I'd like to go back to the point of view expressed at the beginning by Colin," I broke in eventually. "Well, it was something we all felt, that it was terrible to shoot at those people. Which was why we all hesitated so. But there's something I'd like to say, all the same. If our hesitation cost Momo his life, then it was because there was something wrong with our reactions. On the day it happened the world we knew before ceased to exist. We've been living in a new era since then, and we haven't faced up to the fact sufficiently. We haven't adapted to it as we should."

"And what do you mean then exactly," Peyssou asked, "when you say we've been living in a new era?"

I turned to him. "I'll give you an example. Before the day it happened, just suppose someone came to your

407

place in the night, and to get revenge on you he burned down your buildings, with your hay and your stock inside."

"I'd like to see anyone try!" Peyssou thundered, quite forgetting that he had already lost all those things long ago.

"Just suppose. It would be a terrible loss, you'll say, but not a loss that put your life in danger. First, because there would be the insurance. And even if they took their time deciding your claim, there would still be the Ministry, which would lend you the money to buy more cows and more hay for them. Whereas now, this is what you must understand, if a person steals your cow or takes your horse or eats your wheat, there's no way out of it. It's all up with you. He has condemned you sooner or later to death. It's not just a 'mere' theft, it's a capital crime. A crime that must be punished by death instantly, without hesitation."

I was aware of Jacquet fidgeting on his seat, but I was too deeply engrossed in getting my point across to realize why at the time. I had gone over everything I had just said so many times in my head since Momo's death that I had the feeling I was laboring my point horribly. Though even so, I was expecting to have to say it all a lot more times before I'd finished, knowing as I did that it was going to take more than a day, for me as well as the others, to change the attitudes of a lifetime. The instinct for self-defense was not going to abolish overnight the respect we had been taught for human life.

"All the same," Colin said sadly. "Killing people!"

"We must accept the idea though," I said without raising my voice. "It is the new age we live in that makes it necessary. The fellow who takes your wheat, I say it again, he is condemning you to death. And can you think of any reason why you should prefer your death to his?"

Colin didn't answer. Nor did any of the others speak. I didn't know whether I'd succeeded in convincing them or not. But the bomb still weighed heavy on our lives. I could count on it to go on sinking into their memories, to help me inculcate in them, and in myself first of all, that incredibly swift and brutal reflex with which an animal rushes to defend its territory.

408

Preoccupied though I was, in the end I couldn't help noticing that Jacquet's face was by now crimson, and that there were huge drops of sweat standing out on his forehead and running down his temples. I burst out laughing. "Jacquet, stop worrying! The decisions we take now won't be retroactive!"

"Ah, and what does that mean, 'retroactive'?" he asked, good-natured brown eyes gazing hopefully into mine.

"It means they don't apply to anything that was done in the past!"

"Oh, good!" he said with relief.

"Bloody Jacquet," Peyssou said.

And with all our eyes on Jacquet, we laughed, as we had at Thomas just before. I wouldn't have believed such merriment possible after the blood we had lost and shed. Except that it wasn't really merriment. It was the social content of the laughter that mattered. It was an affirmation of our solidarity. Thomas, despite his errors, was one of us. Jacquet too. The community, after its ordeal, was reforming, closing ranks, strengthening its unity.

The burial was fixed for noon, and we agreed to include communion in the service. After the morning assembly, I waited up in my room for those who had decided to make confession.

I heard Colin, Jacquet, Peyssou. I knew what was on their three minds before they even opened their mouths. And if they were under the impression that I could relieve them of that burden, why so much the better. After all, a priest was supposed to be able to remit sins or not remit them in God's name. But God forfend that I personally should ever think I held or ever would hold that exorbitant power! Not when I sometimes doubt whether God Himself is capable of washing a man's conscience clean. But that's enough of that. I have no wish to distress anyone with my heresies. Especially since religion is a sphere in which I personally am sure of nothing.

When Colin had finished, he said with a little smile, "According to Peyssou, Fulbert asks a great many questions when you confess. Then afterwards he bawls you out. That doesn't seem to be your method."

I smiled in my turn. "Would you want it to be? If you've come to make a confession, that means you want to relieve your conscience. Why should I complicate things and make it more difficult for you?"

To my great astonishment, Colin's face became very serious. "But I don't make confession just for that. I make confession to make myself better as well." He flushed as he said it, because the words suddenly sounded ridiculous to him.

I made a doubtful face.

"You don't think it's possible?" he asked.

"In your case, perhaps it is. But for the majority, no."

"Why not?"

"Because people generally, you know, are very good at hiding their own defects from themselves. With the result that their confession is valueless. Take Menou, for example. I've never heard her make confession, please note, otherwise I wouldn't be saying this. But La Menou reproaches herself for her 'unkindness' to Momo, yet never for an instant thinks to blame herself for her unpleasantness to La Falvine. In fact, as far as she's concerned, she hasn't been unpleasant at all. She sees her attitude as totally legitimate."

Colin laughed. Then I realized that I had spoken about Momo as though he were still alive, and a terrible sense of loss stabbed through me. I went on, very quickly: "I've written Fulbert a little note to tell him about the risk of looters in the district. I've advised him to keep La Roque better guarded, especially at night. Would you like to act as messenger for me?"

Colin blushed again. "After what I've told you, don't you think it's a little . . ." He didn't finish the sentence.

"I think that you have a childhood friend in La Roque and that it would give you pleasure to see her. What of it? Where is the harm in that?"

After the three men, I received Catie. She was scarcely inside the door of my room before she threw her arms around my neck. Although this embrace was not without its effect on me, I decided it would be best to treat it as a joke. I freed myself with a laugh.

"You go too far. Have you come here to cuddle me or

confess to me? Come on, sit yourself down, and on the other side of the table, if you please. I shall feel a little safer then."

She was delighted by this reception. She had been expecting something much chillier. Without further ado she began rattling off her confession at the double. I was more interested in what would come after the confession, since I knew perfectly well she wasn't there just for that. While she was pouring out her sins, or rather a string of trifling peccadilloes that had never bothered her for a moment, I noticed that she had done her eyes. Discreetly, but extensively: eyebrows, lashes, lids, the lot. She was still living on her little prebomb stock of cosmetics.

When she had finished her meaningless little recital, I remained silent. I was waiting. And in order to make my waiting more noncommittal I didn't look at her. I began doodling on a sheet of blotting paper with my pencil. I wasn't going to spoil a piece of good paper, it had become too precious.

"So in other words," she said finally, "you're still angry with me?"

I doodled on. "Angry? No."

And when I just left it at that, she went on: "You don't look very pleased."

"No. That's because I'm not."

Silence. More doodling.

"And is it me you're not pleased with, Emmanuel?" she said in her most wheedling voice.

She was doubtless also wriggling, pouting, and doing her full act. But she was wasting her time, because my eyes were occupied elsewhere. I was drawing a little angel on my blotting pad.

"I'm not pleased with your confession," I said in a stern voice.

And only then did I raise my head and look at her. She hadn't been expecting that. Presumably she didn't take me very seriously as Abbé of Malevil. "It was a bad confession," I went on in the same stern tone. "You didn't even admit to your principal defect."

"And what is that, according to you?" she asked with only just restrained aggression.

"Your coquetry."

"Oh, that!" she said.

"Oh, yes," I said. "For you it's nothing, I know! You love your husband, you know you're not going to be unfaithful to him"—here she smiled mockingly—"so you say to yourself, Well, Catie my girl, why don't we have a little fun, come on! But unfortunately, in a community of six men and only two women, such little games are very dangerous. And if I don't do something about it and quick, your flirting is going to have Malevil in total chaos. There's Peyssou, he's already looking at you a bit too much, if you ask me."

"Do you think so?" Catie said. She was radiant! Not the slightest attempt to look even a little contrite!

"Yes, I do think so! And I've watched you flirting with the others too. But luckily they don't give a damn."

"You mean you don't give a damn," she said aggressively. "But I knew that already. You only like great fat puddings, like that girl without a stitch on stuck up there by your bed. Honestly, you surprise me! A thing like that in a priest's bedroom. I'd have expected a crucifix!"

Oh ho! So she bites, does she? "That is a Renoir print," I said, rather taken aback at finding myself suddenly put on the defensive. "You know nothing about art."

"And the photo of your Boche on your desk, is that art? What a frightful cow she looks! Nothing but tits everywhere! But anyway, what do you care, you have Evelyne."

What a little viper! With icy anger I said, "What do you mean, I 'have' Evelyne? Do you take me for a Wahrwoorde?" And fixing my eyes on hers, I blasted her with the full force of my fury. She immediately retired from the battle, picking her way very carefully.

"Oh, no, I never said that! You know I didn't," she said. "The thought never entered my mind."

As if I cared the tiniest damn about what had entered her so-called mind! Or her anything else! But gradually I did manage to calm myself down. I picked up my pencil and removed my little angel's wings. Then I gave him two little horns and a long tail. A prehensile monkey tail. And all the while I was aware of Catie opposite, twisting and wriggling in an attempt to see what I was doing. How proud she was of her little sex, the hot-bottomed little she-monkey! And how anxious she was to make everyone succumb to its power.

I lifted my eyes and scrutinized her. "Your dream, really, is to have all the men in Malevil in love with you, and all reduced to despair. And meanwhile, you, you love no one but Thomas."

I'd scored a bull's eye there, or at least I thought I had. Because I saw that little aggressive flame flicker up again in her eyes.

"Well, what do you want me to do?" she said. "Everyone can't play the trollop, like your Miette."

Silence. Without raising my voice I said, "That's a nice way to talk about your sister. Bravo."

But she was not a bad-hearted girl, Catie, not really. Because she blushed, and for the first time since she began her confession she looked truly contrite.

"I love her very much, you know. You mustn't think I don't." A long silence. She added, "You must think I'm not very nice."

I smiled at her. "I think you're young and thoughtless."

And when she said nothing, amazed to hear me take that friendly tone after all the bitchy things she'd just come out with, I went on: "Take Thomas now. He's well and truly caught. And because you're young you have a tendency to take advantage of the fact. You give him orders, and that's a mistake. Because Thomas is no weakling. He's a man, and he's going to bear you a grudge for it one day."

"He does already."

"Because of the stupid things you made him do?"

"Well, yes!"

I stood up and smiled at her again. "Don't worry. That will sort itself out. In the assembly he took it all on himself. He defended you like a lion."

She looked at me with shining eyes. "But you too, you weren't as beastly as you could have been, in the assembly."

413

"All the same, remember what I said. Be careful about how you behave with Peyssou."

"That I just can't promise," she said with a frankness that took me aback. "It's just the way I am. I've never been able to say no to men."

I looked at her, really disconcerted. I pondered for a moment. Had I failed to understand the girl completely then? If what she said was true, then my whole analysis of the situation lay in pieces.

She said, "You know, you really don't make such a bad priest after all, even though you are such a skirt chaser. Well, I want to say I take back all those horrid things I said, and especially what I said . . . Anyway, I take it all back. You're very sweet. The trouble is I can never stop myself saying what comes into my head. Can I give you a kiss?"

And she gave me one. A very different kiss from the one she had given me on her arrival. But no, I mustn't try to exaggerate the purity of that kiss. If it had been as pure as all that, then it wouldn't have had such an effect on me, and she wouldn't have noticed that it had, or let slip the little chuckle of triumph that she did. At that, I opened the door for her and she fled, crossing the landing at a run, then turning, just as she was about to vanish down the spiral staircase, to give me a last little wave.

We buried Momo beside Germain and the tiny grave that had received all that remained of the others' families. We had begun this embryonic graveyard on the day after it happened. It was part of the new "after" world, and we all knew that we too would lie there one day. It was situated in the flat area beyond the outer wall. There was a little esplanade there, created by cutting back into the cliff, which abruptly narrowed about forty yards farther on until it was just the width of the road between the rock above and the steep slope below. At that point the road bent around the cliff at what was almost a right angle.

It was there, in this narrow bottleneck between precipice below and overhanging rockface above, that we decided to erect a palisade that would protect the ramparts of the outer enclosure from nocturnal attack, since they were low enough to be scaled without too much difficulty. This palisade was constructed of strong oak planks, fitted very closely together, and with a gate that also included a smaller sliding opening at ground level. This was made just big enough to allow a man to enter it on all fours. It was through this "cat door" that any visitor would be required to make his entrance, after having been scrutinized through the peephole concealed to one side of the Judas. This latter was not to be used except for a final check, since even an aperture as small as that represented a risk.

We had also considered the possibility of the palisade too being scaled. Its top, which could be removed to allow a loaded cart through, was protected by four strands of barbed wire that could not be touched without unleashing a teriffic jangling from the tin cans attached to them. However, for bona-fide visitors there was also a bell that Colin had produced from the stores brought back from his shop, and had installed beside the Judas.

Meyssonnier christened the little esplanade area between the palisade and the moat of the outer castle wall our "Advanced Defense Zone," or ADZ.

We further decided, on his recommendation, to cover the entire area of our ADZ with traps arranged in a quin-cunx pattern, leaving only one path about three yards wide which ran along the moat to the right, then around the bend of the cliff, past the tiny graveyard, and on to the gate of the palisade. These booby traps, as Meyssonnier always called them, were of the most classic kind: holes about two feet deep with sharpened stakes hardened in the fire and embedded point up at the bottom, or else small planks with large nails hammered through them. The tops of the holes were concealed by sheets of cardboard covered with earth.

Meanwhile, Peyssou was finishing his additions to the outer wall. He had added a good five feet of masonry supported by strong wooden lintels running across the tops of the original crenelations. When he had finished the stonework, he asked Meyssonnier to add thick wooden panels to close all the rectangular openings he had thus created, and to hinge them so they opened outward and upward.

"That way," he said, "you can pepper the foot of your ramparts nicely without any swine farther away picking you off. And in the bottoms of the panels, there you must make a slit like the arrow slits in the old wall."

He was presupposing, of course, without explicitly saying so—and we were all presupposing the same thing—that any assailants would be armed with nothing more than the shotguns that formed the greater part of our arsenal, and whose shot would never be able to pierce the iron-hard old oak planks. It was, as I say, an almost unconscious supposition, and one that proved false in the event.

I was alone one morning in the ADZ—the palisade having by then been completed, though the booby traps were still in the course of construction—when the bell rang. It was Gazel, on Fulbert's big gray donkey. He dismounted as soon as I slid open the Judas and presented a polite but chilly face for my inspection.

He did not wish to "refresh himself," handed me a letter from Fulbert through the Judas, and told me that he would wait where he was for the reply. I didn't try very hard to coax him in, since the ADZ was still a long way from being finished.

Here is the letter:

My dear Emmanuel,

I thank you for your warning against the bands of marauders. We have not yet seen anything of this kind in our vicinity. Though it is true that we are not as rich as Malevil.

Will you pass on my condolences to La Menou on the death of her son and tell her that I do not forget either of them in my prayers.

Next, I have the honor to inform you that I have recently been elected Bishop of La Roque by the assembled faithful of this parish.

I have thus been enabled to ordain Monsieur Gazel and to appoint him Curé of Courcejac and Abbé of Malevil.

Despite my desire to be helpful to you in every way, I would be failing in my duties if I recognized the sacerdotal functions that you have seen fit to assume at Malevil.

Monsieur l'Abbé Gazel will come to say Mass at Malevil next Sunday. I hope that you will receive him fittingly.

Please accept, my dear Emmanuel, my sincere and Christian wishes for your well-being.

Fulbert le Naud,
Bishop of La Roque.

P.S. Since Armand is indisposed and confined to his bed, I entrust Monsieur Gazel with the task of bearing this letter to you and accepting your reply.

When I had finished this missive, I opened the Judas once more. (I had taken good care to close it as soon as the letter had been taken in. I didn't want Gazel gazing in at our half-finished booby traps.) Gazel was still there outside the palisade, with a slightly tense, anxious expression on that sexually undecided clown's face.

"Gazel," I said, "I can't give you an answer immediately. I must consult the Malevil assembly. Colin will bring my reply to Fulbert tomorrow."

"In that case I will return myself tomorrow morning and collect it," Gazel said in his piping voice.

"No, really, Gazel. I can't make you ride eighteen miles on your donkey two days running. Colin can do it."

There was a silence, then Gazel flickered his eyelids and said with some embarrassment, "You must excuse me, but we no longer admit persons not belonging to the parish to enter La Roque."

"What?" I said, quite incredulous. "And these persons not belonging to the parish are us?"

"Not specifically," Gazel said, lowering his eyes.

"Ah! Because of course there are all these other persons everywhere, aren't there?"

"I'm sorry," Gazel said, "but that was the decision of the parish council."

"Bravo for your parish council!" I said in indignation. "And didn't it even occur to your parish council that Malevil might apply the same rule to people from La Roque?"

Gazel, eyes lowered, was as silent as a martyr on a cross. He was going through what Fulbert would have called "a moment of grievous affliction."

I went on: "Because you can hardly be unaware of the fact that Fulbert is intending to send you over here to say Mass next Sunday."

"Yes, I am aware of it," Gazel said.

"So in other words, you are to have the right to enter Malevil while I, for instance, would not have the right to go into La Roque!"

"One might say," Gazel said, "it's a temporary decision."

"Ah, is it indeed? And why is it temporary?"

"I don't know," Gazel said, in such a way that I was immediately certain he knew very well indeed.

"Very well then, until tomorrow," I said in an icy voice.

Gazel wished me goodbye and turned to climb back onto his donkey.

I called him back: "Gazel!"

He returned to the Judas.

"What exactly is wrong with Armand?"

The idea had crossed my mind that possibly there was an epidemic raging in La Roque, and that the town had put itself into voluntary quarantine to prevent the disease spreading. An idiotic notion on reflection, since it credited Fulbert with altruistic sentiments.

Nevertheless, the effect my question had on Gazel was extraordinary. He blushed, his lips quivered, and his eyes seemed to be revolving in their sockets in an attempt to avoid meeting mine. "I don't know," he stammered out.

"How can you not know?"

"It is Monseigneur who is looking after Armand," Gazel said.

It took me a full second to realize that "Monseigneur" referred to Fulbert. But one thing at any rate was certain: If "Monseigneur" was nursing Armand, then whatever was wrong with him wasn't infectious. I allowed Gazel to ride off, and that evening, after the meal, I called an assembly to discuss the letter we had just received.

I explained that what struck me most about it personally was the absurdity of Fulbert's claims. In my

418

opinion, his letter was a reflection of the neurotic, mega-lomaniac element in his character. It was fairly clear that he had decided to have himself elected bishop so that he could claim precedence over me, ordain Gazel, and thereby eliminate me as an ecclesiastical rival. There was something rather childish in this insistence on being king of the castle, as it were. Instead of trying to make La Roque safe against possible marauders, which would be no mean task, he was engaging in a struggle for power with me, the very person who had warned him of the danger. And he was engaging in that struggle, moreover, without being in any position to win it, since his secular arm consisted solely of Armand, and Armand was confined to his bed, struck down by some mysterious ailment.

I was inclined to laugh at the whole thing, but the others didn't think it funny at all. They exploded with indignation. Malevil had been insulted. You might almost have thought that its flag (an object with no more than a potential existence, be it said) had been spat upon. Fulbert had dared attack the Abbé of Malevil, and therefore the assembly that had elected him!

"Who does he think he is, trying to come and interfere with us, that slimy toad turd," cried little Colin, who was by no means a lover of coarse language. Meyssonnier was of the opinion that we should go over and kick the contemptible wretch where it would hurt. And Peyssou announced that next Sunday, if that Gazel had the nerve to appear here, he would push his holy water sprinkler you know where for him. In short, you might have thought you were back in the days of the Club, when Meyssonnier's Catholic League stood at the foot of Malevil's ramparts, with Emmanuel's Protestant outlaws up above, all bombarding one another with the coarsest epithets they could muster (many of them very inventively turned) before engaging in heroic battle. "Handle and all," Peyssou added with a thump on the table. "I'll ram it right up him handle and all if he sets foot here."

Somewhat astonished by this explosion of patriotism, I then read the assembly the reply I had drafted during

419

the afternoon, and which I was now submitting for their approval.

To Fulbert le Naud, Curé of La Roque.

Dear Fulbert,

According to the oldest documents pertaining to Malevil in our possession, which date from the 15th century, there was indeed at that time a Bishop of La Roque, who was enthroned in 1452 in the town church by the Lord of Malevil, Baron of La Roque.

It is also clear, however, from these same documents, that the Abbé of Malevil was in no way subject to the Bishop of La Roque, but was chosen by the Lord of Malevil from among those of his relatives of the male sex resident with him in the castle. In general, a younger son or brother. The sole Lord of Malevil to depart from this rule was Sigismond, Baron of La Roque, who having neither son nor brother, appointed himself Abbé of Malevil in 1476. From that day onward, right up until our own times, the Lord of Malevil has always been as of right Abbé of Malevil, even though the exercise of his ministry has on occasions been delegated to a chaplain.

There can be no doubt that Emmanuel Comte, as present proprietor of the castle of Malevil, has inherited the prerogatives attached to the castellany. Such is the judgment of the assembly of the faithful, which has unanimously confirmed him in the title and the functions of Abbé of Malevil.

On the other hand, it is not possible for Malevil to recognize the legitimacy of a bishop whose nomination it has not requested from His Holiness and who has moreover not been enthroned in a town that falls within the purlieu of its domain.

Malevil intends, in short, to preserve the integrality of its historic rights over its fief of La Roque, even though in its lively desire for peace and friendly relations with its neighbors it does not at present envisage any direct action intended to vindicate them.

We nevertheless consider that any person inhabiting La Roque who considers himself or herself wronged by the de facto authority established within the town may at any time make appeal to us to have any such wrongs redressed.

We think also that the town of La Roque should remain at all times accessible to us, and that no gate of the town may remain unopened to a messenger from Malevil without such action constituting a grave insult to the castellany and its assembly.

Yours with sincerest best wishes for your welfare,
Emmanuel Comte
Abbé of Malevil.

I must emphasize here that in my mind this letter was no more than a sort of practical joke, its intention being to put Fulbert in his place by confronting his megalomania with a grotesque parody of itself. Perhaps I should spell it out even more clearly: At no point did I ever believe myself to be in any way the heir of the former lords of Malevil. Nor was I any more serious about the vassalage of La Roque. However, I read my letter out with a completely deadpan face, assuming that this would only add to the assembly's appreciation of its humor.*

I was wrong. The humor escaped them totally. They admired the tone of the letter ("It's a real knockout," Colin said) and were genuinely wild with enthusiasm about its content. They demanded to see the documents on which it was based, and I was obliged to go and fetch those venerable relics from the glass-fronted shelves behind me, together with the translations into modern French that I had once had made.

They became wild with excitement. The passages establishing La Roque as our fief had to be read over and over, as well as Sigismond's historic decision to appoint himself Abbé of Malevil.

"Well, there's a thing," Peyssou said. "You know, I'd never have thought we had the right to elect you the way we did, not really. You ought to have shown us all this before!"

The antiquity of our rights plunged them into a frenzy. "Five centuries," Colin said, "just think of it! Five centuries we've had the right to be Abbé of Malevil!"

Meyssonnier, honest as ever, albeit against his will, was forced to point out that there had been the French Revolution.

---

*Possibly I am—as Emmanuel claims—"impervious to humor," but I am not at all certain that this letter was entirely "a sort of practical joke" in Emmanuel's mind. [Note added by Thomas.]

"Oh, but that lasted no time at all," Colin said. "There's no comparison!"

The notion that really excited them beyond anything, however, was that of the *enthronement* of the bishop in our fief of La Roque by the Lord of Malevil. At Peyssou's request, I explained what the word entailed as best I could.

"Well then, Emmanuel," Peyssou said, "it's all as clear as could be. If you haven't enthroned Fulbert, then he's no more a bishop than my backside." (Vigorous approbation.) And after that the only thing they were prepared to discuss was how and when we could mount an expedition against La Roque to avenge the insult done to us and to re-establish suzerainty over our rightful fief.

I listened in silence to this maelstrom of nationalistic passion I had unleashed. As I saw it, the moment had passed when it would have been possible to tell the assembly that my letter had been intended as a parody. They were too inflamed by now, and certainly wouldn't have thanked me for it. However, I attempted to quiet the more ardent among them and finally succeeded, with the help of Thomas and Meyssonnier, then of Colin, once it had been formally and solemnly decreed that we would never abandon "our friends in La Roque" (Colin). And that in the event of their being molested or wronged, Malevil would intervene on their behalf, as I had already stated in my letter.

Gazel came again next day. I handed him the letter without a word, and he rode off. Two days later the ADZ was finished and the wheat was ripe for harvest.

It was a long and arduous business, because we had to cut it with sickles, tie it into sheaves by hand, cart the sheaves back up into the castle, set up a threshing ground in the outer enclosure, and thresh it with hand flails. It was an operation that entailed a great deal of sheer physical hard work, and when it was over we had all of us acquired a new understanding of the Biblical phrase about earning your bread by the sweat of your brow.

Despite everything, however, we were able to tell ourselves that it had been well worth the trouble. Even taking into account the quarter ruined by the looters, the harvest worked out at an increase of ten sacks for every one planted. In all, twenty-two hundredweights of grain. Not very much in comparison with our very considerable reserves (mainly derived, where wheat was concerned, from the booty provided by L'Étang), but a very great deal when considered as our first harvest since the day it happened, and as a promise for the future.

The night that followed the harvest I was awakened by a slight sound somewhere to one side of me, or more precisely by my inability at first, in my half-sleeping state, to understand what was causing it. But when my eyes opened, even without being able to see anything, since it was a moonless night, I realized that it was Evelyne, over on the sofa near the window, sobbing quietly into her pillow.

"Are you crying?" I asked in a quiet voice.

"Yes."

"Why?"

A series of muffled sobs and sniffs followed, then: "Because I'm unhappy."

"Come and tell me about it."

She was off the sofa and onto my bed in one bound, and she snuggled into my arms. Although she had filled out a little, she still seemed incredibly light to me. No more than the weight of a kitten on my shoulder. She continued to sob.

"Evelyne, you're soaking me! It's like being under a waterfall! Come on, mop it up!"

I handed her my handkerchief and she was forced to stop her sobbing, even if only for as long as it took to blow her nose.

"Well?"

Silence. Sniffs.

"Blow your nose, for goodness' sake, instead of sniffing like that!"

"I have."

"Blow it again."

She did as she was told, and to judge by the sound, without success. The sniffing began again immediately. Nervous presumably. Like her cough, like her sobs, like the shudders shaking her body. Perhaps like her asthma. Since the scene in the wheat patch and Momo's death she had already had one terrible attack. I wondered whether this meant there was another on the way. I put my arms around her. "Come on now," I said, "tell me what it's all about."

Silence. "All those dead people," she said at last very quietly.

I was surprised. I hadn't been expecting that. "Is that why you're crying?"

"Yes." And when I didn't speak, she went on: "Why? Does that surprise you, Emmanuel?"

"Yes. I thought you were going to say I didn't love you any more."

"Oh, no," she said. "You love me just as much, I can tell that. The only difference is that you're strict with me now. But I like it better really."

"You like it better?"

Silence. She was thinking, concentrating so hard on trying to unravel her exact feelings that she had forgotten to sniff. "Yes," she said at last. "I feel much more sort of safe."

I made a mental note of that but said nothing.

"Those people that were killed—couldn't we have let them come and live at Malevil? There's plenty of room here."

I shook my head in the dark, as though she could see me. "It isn't a question of room but of provisions. There are eleven of us now. If we had to, we might be able to find food for two or three extra people, but not for twenty."

"All right," she said after a moment, "but then we should have let them eat our wheat."

"And what about the others?"

"What others?"

"The others who will come after them. I suppose we'd have to let them kill our pigs, eat up all our cows, and take away our horses. There'd always be plenty of grass left for us to eat."

This sarcasm was wasted on Evelyne, however. "You said yourself that the wheat harvest wasn't all that big."

"No, not compared with our reserve stocks, thank goodness. But all the same, twenty-two hundredweight

424

sacks of grain, that will make quite a few loaves, you know."

"But we could have managed without it if we'd had to! You said so!" she shot back very quickly in an accusing voice.

Every word I ever said was engraved permanently in her memory, it seemed. "If we had to, yes. But how do we know that next year's harvest isn't going to be disastrous? It's always safer to have a little in hand. Even if it's only so that we can help our friends in La Roque if they need it."

"And the people in the wheatfield, why couldn't we help them?"

"Because there were too many of them, I've already told you."

"There are just as many people in La Roque."

"Yes, but after all, we know them."

And since she didn't answer, I began listing them: "Pimont, Agnès Pimont, Lanouaille, Judith, and Marcel, who looked after you."

"Yes," she said, "and old Pougès. We haven't been seeing him lately, old Pougès."

It was true. It was a good ten days since we'd last watched the old reprobate soaking the ends of his mustache in our wine. And that way of ending an argument, without any conclusions drawn, without any admissions being made, was wholly typical of Evelyne. Apart from which, I was very impressed by the grownup way she'd argued. Nothing childish in her remarks. And her French had improved too. Ever since I had been "strict with her," she had stopped taking refuge in childishness.

"Right," I said, "the hearing's over. Back into your bed. I want to go to sleep."

She clung on. "Can't I stay just a little longer, Emmanuel?" she said, slipping back into her baby voice.

"No, you cannot. Off you go."

She went, and she went quietly. In fact, she even obeyed with a sort of zest, as though there lay before her the prospect of a whole life spent beside me in a state of ecstatic obedience.

All the same, there are things about her I don't under-

425

stand. She talked about the people in the wheatfield, but she didn't mention Momo.

But then, neither did La Menou ever talk about Momo. The day he was killed I had made many private predictions to myself about what her reactions might be; but none of them proved accurate. She had not sunk into stupefied despair. She had relinquished not one jot of her status in the community. She still ruled as tyrannically as ever over the female denizens of the castle, preferably pecking the one who was oldest and most given to cackling, but when the need arose, albeit more cautiously, not sparing the two pullets, and Catie more than Miette, since Catie had quite a sharp beak too. Nor had she allowed herself to waste away. Her fork and glass were just as active as before, even though there could be no hope of her ever getting any fatter. And lastly, she was still as scrupulously clean, a tiny well-scoured little skeleton of a figure in which everything, muscles and organs, had been reduced to its minimum, the hair pulled tightly back over the little skull, the black smock well brushed, the rows of safety pins still decorating a low square neckline revealing the flattest of flat chests. And finally, she was still trotting about just as perkily, as nimbly, as quickly as ever, with her thin scraggy neck stretched out ahead of her.

It was always either Catie or Miette who set the table and La Menou who laid the napkins at our various places. For hygienic reasons, so that we wouldn't use one another's, she had made marks on them that only she could decipher. And one morning as I was about to sit down I noticed with some concern that someone had set Momo's place again at the end of the table and that there was a napkin in the plate. I saw that Colin had noticed as well; he was making apprehensive signals at me with his eyes and head. However, having finally sat down, I counted the places and realized that there were in fact only eleven, as usual now, not the twelve I had expected. Besides, it was Catie who had set the table that morning, and I couldn't believe she'd made a mistake. And indeed, when I leaned forward to question her with my eyes, she waved one forefinger in a discreet negative gesture, as though to say, Don't say anything.

Everyone was now seated, with the exception of Jacquet, who was standing at his usual place, arms hanging out from his sides, golden brown eyes misted with anguish, staring down at the awful void where his plate should be. He looked across at me, eyes humbly asking what crime he had committed that I should deprive him of his food like this. His whole attitude was that of a good-natured dog subjected to a cruel master as a puppy, then adopted by a family that has made much of him, constantly trembling at the thought that he might one day find himself suddenly deprived of this new happiness, a happiness of which he feels unworthy and which he is perpetually afraid may turn out to have been a dream. It wasn't that Jacquet found it unjust that I should deprive him of his food. If I had done so, then that meant it must be just. And he was quite prepared, when the meal was over, to go out and work with us as usual, with nothing in his belly. His only fear was that this deprivation might be a prelude to banishment.

I smiled to reassure him, and was about to intervene when La Menou said gruffly, "Are you looking for your place, my lad? It's here." And she indicated with a jab of her chin the place where Momo used to sit.

A great silence fell. Jacquet, totally bewildered, looked at me. I nodded in confirmation, and he set off to walk the length of the table and sit down in Momo's old place, painfully conscious the whole time—poor Jacquet who had a horror of attracting attention—that every eye in the room was fixed on him.

As soon as Jacquet was seated, Colin tactfully began a discussion. The squares of cardboard over the traps in the ADZ were worrying him. If it rained, then the earth over them would hold the water and they would rot. And even before that they would become less rigid when damp and sag under the weight of the earth. So any assailants would immediately see the traps as a regular pattern of hollows. Peyssou suggested that we should pierce holes in the cardboard so the rain could drain straight through into the traps themselves. And Meyssonnier suggested a system of two pieces of plywood supported by a slender central lath which would collapse under an enemy's weight.

427

While giving just enough of my attention to this discussion to put in a word or two now and then, I was listening to what was happening at the lower end of the table. Jacquet, paralyzed with shame, was eating without a word, hunched over his plate, while La Menou bombarded him with an unceasing stream of brusque injunctions in a low voice: "Sit up straight! . . . Don't mess your bread about like that! . . . Can't you make less noise when you chew! . . . What do you think you are! . . . What do you think your napkin's for? . . . Wiping your mouth with your hand, indeed!" And what struck me most was that each of these sharply delivered reprimands was followed by Jacquet's name, as though La Menou wanted to make it quite clear that her mind wasn't rambling and that she knew perfectly well whom she was addressing, whatever anyone might think. There was a further piece of evidence, moreover, indication that La Menou's mind was still perfectly lucid. In none of the objurgations she addressed to Jacquet did a single word of patois occur, since Jacquet, being a foreigner, would of course be unable to understand it.

Forty-eight hours after the ADZ had been completed, just as we had resumed our routine shooting practice (archery included), old Pougès appeared once more on his ancient bike. He wasn't at all pleased at having to get down on all fours in order to get in through the palisade. And even less so when we blindfolded him to lead him through the traps. As soon as he was settled in the gate-tower kitchen, he gave us to understand that all these ordeals would necessitate adequate compensation. I say us, because all Malevil was there, drawn down to the gate by the news of his arrival, standing around the kitchen listening.

"Well, I can tell you, Emmanuel, it's not so easy getting to your place now," he said, smoothing the points of his yellowish white mustache. "Both ends it's not easy!" He looked around him, very flattered by the attention he was getting.

"Because getting out of La Roque, that's something now that Fulbert has clapped a guard on the gates! You'll not believe me, but going for a little ride along the Malevil road, that's out. There's one of their damned decrees forbidding it. They'll only just allow me out on the main road. But luckily it came to my mind, there's a track that cuts across to your road. Through Faujoux's place, if you remember.

"You came through Faujoux's!" I exclaimed in amazement. "With your bike?"

"Yes, even though there were times when I had to carry it," Pougès said. "Like a cross-country champion! At my age! I hope," he went on after a dramatic pause, allowing his eyes to wander around his audience, "that you won't be so hasty about banging the cork back into your bottle, Emmanuel, seeing the trouble I've had."

"Serve yourself," I said, pushing the bottle across to him. "You've certainly earned it."

"Ah, that I have," old Pougès agreed. "Just remember that it means something, coming through Faujoux's with my bike. And all I have to tell you, my head bursting with it. And my legs almost bursting too, I've pedaled that hard."

"You ought to be in training though," La Menou said, "seeing the number of times you've pedaled from La Roque to Malejac to go and drink yourself stupid at your trollop's place."

"Your health, Emmanuel," old Pougès said with dignity, but livid with fury underneath that La Manou should wreck his hour of glory for him.

"Menou," I said in a stern voice, "why don't you give him a bite to eat."

"I wouldn't mind that," old Pougès said. "I've got quite a hole in my stomach, what with that track through Faujoux's."

La Menou opened the closet on the right of the range, dumped a plate down violently in front of him, then cut a thin slice of ham, which she took between thumb and forefinger and flipped onto the plate from a distance.

I gave her a stern look, but she pretended not to see it. She was occupied cutting Pougès a slice of bread, and concentrating on cutting it as thin as she possibly could—no mean task, since the loaf was very new. And while

429

performing this delicate operation she continued to talk to herself the whole time, half mumbling, half out loud. But since old Pougès was silent because he was busy drinking his first glass, eyes fixed on the bottle, and since we were all silent as well, waiting for the news he had promised us, La Menou's soliloquy was perfectly audible to everyone in the kitchen, and my attempts to catch her eye were in vain.

"There are some people," she said, steadfastly refusing to look up from the loaf, "you'd say were like leeches and worse for sucking blood out of others. That Adelaide, for example. Now you'll say that's no great crime when it's Adelaide, and there I'd agree. With her legs always so wide apart, it's a wonder she could ever get through a door. But there are some that took advantage of her all right, both ways too. First of all getting what they fancied when they felt like it, and when they couldn't do that any more, being past it, then getting drink out of her. That poor great fat slut can't have got very rich with customers like that!"

Old Pougès set down his glass, straightened himself on his chair, and wiped his mustache with the back of his left hand. "Emmanuel," he said with dignity, "it's not that I wish to blame you at all, but you ought to stop your servant showing disrespect for me under your roof."

"Well now, who'd have thought it," La Menou said. "So now he wants respect!"

White with anger at having been called a servant, she threw the slice of bread onto the table as hard as she could, folded her bony little arms across her chest, and fixed Pougès with glittering eyes. But Pougès was already savoring his second glass, as well as his little counter-attack, and all in all feeling quite pleased with himself.

"Menou is not my servant," I said firmly. "She has independent means. If she lives here, that is simply because she keeps house for me. But I don't pay her. I am talking about before the bomb, naturally."

"Like it might be Monsieur le Curé's housekeeper," Colin said. At which everyone, except La Menou, began to laugh, and the atmosphere was relaxed again.

I took advantage of this lull to move over to La Menou

430

and whisper into her ear, "If you go on, I shall throw you out of the kitchen in front of everyone." She didn't answer. She was breathing very hard, eyes flashing, lips tight together, nostrils quivering. And in a sense it did my heart good to see her like that again after what had happened.

I went back to my chair. Old Pougès was just finishing his bite and his third glass. And it was taking an infinite time. He drank quickly, but he chewed slowly.

His third glass finished, he sat there pulling at his mustache and looking at the bottle without saying a word. I filled his glass again, then banged the cork into the bottle. He watched me, then looked at his full glass but did not touch it. Not yet. The last glass, that had to be drunk in silence. So the time had come when he must speak. Even so, he took his time about it.

In the end I had to start him off. "So, Armand is ill then?"

Old Pougès shook his head. "He's not ill," he said with the contempt for ignorance of one who knows, and I could see from his repugnance to go on that it was very distressing for him to have to give us anything, even a little news.

"Well," I said rather sharply, to remind him that he had his side of the bargain to fulfill.

"Well, it isn't a pretty business what's been happening back there." He paused, then added, "Bloodshed it's come to." He looked around, shaking his head. "It was Pimont, came home and found Armand trying to serve his Agnès."

"By force?" Colin said, blenching.

"By force or not by force," old Pougès said, with the malice in his voice enough to set your teeth on edge. "Agnès, she says it was by force. But what do I know? You know her better than I do, lad. You tell me."

"And so," I said with irritation.

"And so Pimont, his blood goes right to his head. He picks up a little kitchen knife, and he sticks it right in Armand's back. Well, believe it or not, it doesn't seem to worry Armand a little bit. He just turns around and he says, 'I'll teach you to come punching me in the back, you little sod you.' And there and then, point-blank, he blows his face off with his popgun, and poor Pimont, he didn't have any face left at all hardly. We all came rushing over, and there was Armand on Pimont's doorstep. White, that he was, but straight as a ramrod, and telling us all how he'd been punched in the back. 'And now,' he said, 'clear off the lot of you, or I blast my way through!' And there he is, waving his popgun at us and walking backward up to the château gate. Well, like that, you see, naturally, it was only when he turned around to open the gate we saw the knife sticking out of his back. And we could see it all right, because Armand had his black jacket on, and the knife handle was red. And there he was, just walking away like that, with the knife sticking out of his back!"

"And Agnès?" Colin said.

"Oh, like a madwoman, you can imagine," Pougès said with total lack of feeling. "Her man done in like that, a big hole in his face, and a pool of blood on her floor, which you'd have thought someone had killed a bullock in there. Luckily Judith took her and the baby away to stay with her. But wait, wait," he went on, as though what he had to say next was far more important and interesting. "Armand, he gets back to the château and he tells Fulbert the whole thing, with Gazel and Josepha there. And Josepha, in that funny gibberish of hers, she suddenly says, 'But, Monsieur Armand, you have a knife stuck in your back!' Well he won't believe her. He feels around with his hand and then whumph! flat on the floor! Fainted dead away. It was Josepha who told us it all."

"And afterward?" I asked impatiently.

"Afterward? That's all," Pougès said, beginning to eye his full glass.

"What do you mean, that's all? Is that the kind of people you are in La Roque? Someone kills a man in his own home in broad daylight, in front of everyone, you all know who the murderer is, and no one says anything? Not even Marcel? Not even Judith?"

"Oh, them!" Pougès said dismissively, but without looking me in the eye all the same. "They didn't do much. Called a meeting and voted a whatsit. Saying how Armand had to be tried and punished for murder."

"And that's what you call nothing?" I said indignantly. "You call that nothing?" And I added, very angry, "And you, of course, when it came to voting, you abstained!"

Old Pougès looked at me reproachfully and tugged at his mustache. "Only in your interests, Emmanuel. I mustn't get too mixed up in Marcel's camp, you know. Not if you want me to go on having my little bike rides." And at that he gave me a wink.

"And Fulbert, what did he have to say about this vote?"

"He said no. He came down to tell us through the grille in the gate. He said it was legally self-defense, that there was no call for a trial. The lads booed him a bit. And since then he's got the wind up a bit, Fulbert has, especially with Armand in bed. So he hands the rations out through the grille opening in the gate and never comes out of the château. He's waiting for it all to simmer down. Your good health, Emmanuel!

These last words sounded like a polite prelude, but in fact they were the exact opposite. They meant that now it was time for him to drink his last glass, and would we all bugger off and leave him in peace, since he'd given us our money's worth.

Silence fell. None of us was ready to speak yet. But we didn't need words. We all knew that we were in agreement on the main thing: that we weren't going to leave a murder unpunished. It was high time to go over and set things to rights in La Roque.

NOTE ADDED BY THOMAS

This expedition to La Roque did take place, but much later than we then expected, and not before we ourselves had confronted a mortal danger. Which is why I am taking the liberty of interrupting Emmanuel's narrative here with a number of remarks that would be out of place later on, when things begin to move rather quicker.

I would like to mention Emmanuel's negative sentiments with regard to Catie. They created an uncomfortable atmosphere in Malevil. Catie admired Emmanuel and was hurt by his low valuation of her. She felt that he was constantly comparing her to Miette, and always to her disadvantage. Hence, I believe, her rebellious and un-

433

disciplined attitude. In my opinion, this attitude would have disappeared if Emmanuel had had a higher regard for Catie as a human being.

I now come to the matter of Evelyne. It is a subject on which I wish to be frank without being odious.

I will state my own firm opinion at the outset: I was quite convinced that on the physical level there was nothing, absolutely nothing, between Emmanuel and Evelyne.

Catie was for a long time convinced of the contrary, and we often argued the question.

What gave rise to all these speculations was an extremely surprising incident that occurred between our return to Malevil from La Roque and the killing of the band of looters. Emmanuel does not make any reference to it in his narrative, but it is not the first time that Emmanuel has omitted things that he found embarrassing. I have already commented on the fact earlier.

You will remember the Malevil custom: Every evening, at the end of the evening, Miette went over to the companion she had chosen for that night and took him by the hand. It was a custom, I must admit, that shocked me at first. Then later, in my impatience for my turn to come around again, I grew accustomed to it. After I married Catie and was comfortably settled in my new privileged position—for a time at least—it shocked me again. Yes, I know what you will say. That man has two moralities, according to whether he personally benefits or not from the act that shocks him.

Briefly, this particular evening, a month perhaps after Evelyne's arrival at Malevil, Miette walked over to Emmanuel when the fire was burning low, and smiling at him with a tender look in her eyes, took his hand. Immediately, Evelyne, who was standing on Emmanuel's left, moved around to his right and without a word, though with a force and determination that took us all by surprise, parted the two hands. Amazed and distressed that Emmanuel should have released her hand without a struggle, Miette did nothing. She just stood looking at Emmanuel. But Emmanuel didn't move or speak. He was examining Evelyne with an air of great concentration, as though he was trying to understand what she was doing—even though it was completely obvious to everyone else. And when Evelyne seized the hand she had just pulled free in her own "tiny paw," Emmanuel did nothing to stop her.

I still remember the look that Evelyne gave Miette then. It wasn't the look of a child either, it was the look of a woman. And it said as clearly as any words could have done, He's mine.

What Miette thought of this incident was easy to guess. But she made no comment, as it were. When Emmanuel's turn came around again she left him out, and Emmanuel didn't appear to notice.

All the discussions I had with Catie on the subject of any supposed intimacy between Emmanuel and Evelyne sprang from this scene. Catie argued that Emmanuel was just not the sort of man who could remain chaste, and that since he had allowed himself to be deprived of Miette, what else could one think?

Colin, when I confided our suspicions to him, was of the contrary opinion. "It's just not true that Emmanuel can't stay chaste," he said. "When he was about twenty, for two whole years, I saw it with my own eyes. Emmanuel just wouldn't even look at a woman. Two whole years. A real devil for the girls before that, and again after, a real terror, and yet for those two years, nothing. Why? If you ask me, it was some girl who'd really given him a bad time."

Then he added, "And besides, you just don't know Emmanuel. Scruples up to his eyebrows. He'd never do anything like that. Emmanuel has never done anything rotten to any girl. The other way around, more like. He's just not a man who could take advantage like that. Never."

So then I asked him how he explained the situation in that case. "Well, there it is, he loves her," Colin said, "but how he loves her, that I couldn't say. I have to admit it's a bit puzzling, seeing that Evelyne is nothing but a scrawny little kitten, and up till now the more woman Emmanuel could get his hands on the better he liked it. And it's pretty amazing too when you think that Evelyne's barely fourteen, and not even pretty, eyes apart. But as for him touching her, no. You can scrub that idea here and now. It's just not in him."

I ought to add that Catie also came around to this point of view later on. She had made it her business to "observe" them for some time and had never come up with the slightest hint of anything to justify her suspicions.

The assembly that Emmanuel described in his last chapter was not important solely because it marked the beginning of our transition to a new "stern morality" better suited to our "new era"; it also made Emmanuel into our military leader "in the event of emergency or danger." And since such events were frequent in the months that followed, authority within the community, spiritual as well as temporal, since he was already Abbé of Malevil, became concentrated entirely in Emmanuel's hands.

Did this mean that Emmanuel was gradually becoming Lord of Malevil in good earnest, that we were simply sliding back into pure feudalism? I don't think so. In my opinion, the spirit in which the community of Malevil debated its internal affairs was entirely modern. And equally modern was Emmanuel's constant concern never to undertake anything without first being certain of our support. Without wishing to talk about humility—I have a horror of such masochistic phraseology—I would nevertheless say that there was a certain transcendence of self involved in the way that Emmanuel and all the rest of us accepted that we had to live in perpetual confrontation with all the others.

XV

TWO days after our visit from old Pougès, I mounted a dawn expedition to reconnoiter the walls of La Roque. The results convinced me that Fulbert was guarding the town badly, and that taking it would be an easy enough matter. The two gates had watches on them, but the long wall joining them was completely undefended along its entire length, and was by no means so high that it could not be scaled with the aid of a ladder, or better still with a rope and grappling hook.

I fixed our assault upon La Roque for the following day, and in the face of general opposition ordered that the night watch we were keeping on the Malevil approach road should continue until dawn. Since the harvest, we had nothing to guard any longer in the valley, so the night watch had moved nearer the castle and now occupied a casemated dugout we had constructed on the side of the Sept Fayards hill, a position which gave an excellent view over the approach road and the palisade.

Since there had been a certain reluctance among the companions to undertake this outside watch the night before our expedition against La Roque—the feeling being that we all ought to keep ourselves fresh for the great day—I decided that I ought to set an example, and consequently detailed myself for the job that particular night, taking Meyssonnier with me.

There is nothing more demoralizing than a night watch: routine and discipline in their pure state. You just have to stay there waiting for something to happen, and most of the time nothing ever does. At least Thomas and Catie had the distraction of lovemaking available to them during their nights on duty, even though the dugout wasn't exactly a convenient place for that activity, despite all the care and thought Meyssonnier had put into it. As in our first one across the river, the walls of the trench were held up by bundles of brushwood. And the bottom of it, apart from the rough duckboarding as before, had also been carefully sloped down to a drainage channel, so that any rain would be collected and disposed of through a pipe leading to the slope below. The roof was made of brushwood but covered this time with a sheet of corrugated iron, itself covered in turn by a layer of earth stuck here and there with tufts of grass, like all the surrounding undergrowth since the explosion of our late spring. And around and about we had transplanted small leafy bushes, which without obscuring our view camouflaged the dugout so well from the road up to the castle that it was difficult to distinguish it, even with binoculars, from the surrounding landscape of charred tree trunks and green bushes.

To ensure an unobstructed view and line of fire toward the palisade, the casemate was open from chest height upward toward the north and east. Unfortunately, however, it was also from the north and east that the rain and the prevailing winds came, so despite the overhang of the roof one still got soaked by any storms that blew up. And more unfortunately still, most of them seemed to brew during the hours of darkness.

I had arranged our watches so I would be the one on duty at dawn, the highest risk period, it seemed to me, since the enemy would need to be able to make out its objective to some extent at least in order to approach it.

I heard absolutely no sound. Everything happened as though in a silent film. I thought I saw two figures approaching the palisade along the road. I say "I thought" simply because at first I thought I was probably seeing nothing of the sort. At eighty yards, a man is really quite small to the eye, and when the figure is more or less gray, moving silently against a gray cliff in misty weather, in the half light just before dawn, then you're bound to wonder whether it isn't an illusion. And perhaps I'd been

438

dozing as well? I think I had, because the touch of the binoculars against my eyes made me start, and right away, while I was still trying to focus them—no easy task in all that nebulous grayness—I began to sweat, despite the cool dawn air. The earth must already have begun warming up though, hence all the mist rising from the ground, piling up in the hollows, and curling in tenuous streamers from the rocks of the cliff. I succeeded in locating the palisade, used it to focus on, then moved slowly along the road to the west, following the cliff.

It was their faces that gave them away. I could see two tiny pink circles against the surrounding gray. It was extraordinary how clearly those little pink spots stood out, despite the mist and the half light, whereas the bodies, dressed in neutral colors, were almost indistinguishable from the cliff face. Nevertheless, now that I had the faces to guide me, I was just able to make out their outlines.

They were moving slowly up the road to Malevil, sticking as closely as possible to the rocky wall of the cliff, it seemed to me. I could make out their bodies better now. One seemed to be much taller and better built than the other. Both were carrying guns, and the guns were a surprise. They certainly weren't ordinary shotguns.

I shook Meyssonnier, and as soon as he opened his eyes I clapped a hand over his mouth and said very quietly, "Quiet. There are two men outside the palisade."

He blinked, removed my hand from his mouth, and whispered, "Armed?"

"Yes." I handed him the binoculars. Meyssonnier refocused them, then said something in such a low voice I didn't hear it.

"What did you say?"

"No packs or bundles."

At the time, the significance of his remark didn't impinge. It wasn't till a few moments later that it flashed back into my mind. I refocused the binoculars. Visibility was improving as dawn approached, and I could see the visitors' pink faces better now, not as mere spots but with distinct contours. There was nothing emaciated about them, nothing in common with the looters in the wheat-

439

field. These two men were young, strong, and well fed. I saw the taller of them go up to the palisade, and from the position of his body I could tell what he was doing. He was reading the notice we'd nailed to it for the benefit of visitors. It was a large square of plywood, painted white, on which Colin had printed the following message in black letters:

IF YOUR INTENTIONS ARE FRIENDLY, RING THE BELL. WE SHALL FIRE ON ANY PERSON SEEN CLIMBING THE PALISADE.

MALEVIL

And it was no rough and ready job either. Colin had outlined all the letters in pencil before doing the actual painting and he had trimmed his brush to a perfect point with La Menou's scissors to make absolutely sure he kept each one neat. He had wanted to add a skull and crossbones under the MALEVIL, but I argued against it. I felt that the very soberness of the words themselves was sufficient deterrent.

Both men were searching separately, and searching in vain, for some crack that would permit them to peer through the palisade. One even took a knife out of his pocket and attempted to attack the iron-hard oak planks with it. Meyssonnier had the binoculars at that point, and he held them out to me, saying in a low, pitying voice, "Look at that poor idiot."

I looked, but just as I had him in focus, the man gave up his attempt. He went over to his companion. Heads together, they appeared to be holding a council. I got the impression that there was disagreement between them. From a number of gestures he made toward the road behind them, I gathered that the tall one wanted to withdraw, while the shorter one, on the contrary, intended to carry on. But carry on with what? That's what puzzled me. They surely couldn't be considering the possibility, just the two of them, of trying to attack Malevil?

A decision had clearly been come to, however, because I saw them both sling their guns over their backs. (Once more I was intrigued by the unusual look of their weapons.) Then the tall one set his back against the palisade, clasped his hands in front of his groin, and hoisted the smaller one up so that he could climb onto his shoulders. It was at this moment that Meyssonnier's remark about neither of them having any pack or bundle flashed back into my mind. The answer was suddenly blindingly obvious. The two men weren't on their own. They hadn't the slightest intention of attacking Malevil, or even of trying to get inside it. They belonged to a band, and they were here on a reconnaissance expedition, just like ours the day before outside La Roque, prior to an attack.

I set down my binoculars and said to Meyssonnier in a low, rapid voice, "I'm going to shoot the little one and try to capture the other."

"That's against the orders," Meyssonnier said.

"I'm changing the orders," I said in a cutting tone.

I looked at him, and although it was hardly the moment for merriment, I suddenly felt like laughing. Because the struggle written on Meyssonnier's honest face between respect for orders and obedience to the leader was painful to see. I added in the same tone, "Don't shoot. That's an order."

I shouldered my gun. In the telescopic sight of the Springfield I could see the little fellow's pink face quite distinctly in profile as he crouched on his companion's shoulders, both hands gripping the top of the palisade, and inched his face gradually upward in order to raise his eyes above the cross beam at the top. At that distance, and with a telescopic sight, it was child's play. It came into my mind that the little fellow over there, so young and healthy, had only one or two more seconds of life in front of him. Not because he was trying to get over the palisade, since that clearly wasn't his intention, but because he was now carrying information useful to an assailant inside his head—the head that the bullet from my Springfield was about to crack open like a nut.

While the little fellow was memorizing the terrain carefully, taking his time, without knowing how utterly useless all the notes he was squirreling away had already become, I brought the hairline cross of my sight up to his ear and fired. He seemed to leap upward and make a sort of somersault before crashing to the ground. His companion stood frozen for a full second, then with a push

441

against the palisade he was racing off down the road as fast as he could go.

I shouted out, "Stop!"

He kept going. I yelled with the full strength of my lungs, "Stop, I said!" And I brought up the Springfield again. Just as I had the cross trained on his back, to my great surprise he stopped.

I shouted, "Hands on your head! And walk back to the palisade!"

He slowly retraced his steps. His gun was still slung over his back. And it was the gun I kept my eye on, ready to fire at the slightest suspicious movement.

Nothing happened. I saw that the man had stopped some way short of the palisade, and I realized that he didn't want to look at his companion's shattered skull if he could help it. At that moment the gate-tower bell began to ring the alarm. I waited till it had stopped, then I shouted, "Turn to face the cliff and then don't move."

He did as he was told. I handed Meyssonnier the Springfield, took his little .22, and said quickly, "Keep him in your sights till I'm over there. As soon as I am, follow."

"Do you think they're part of a band?" Meyssonnier said, wetting his lips.

"I'm certain of it."

At that moment someone, I think Peyssou, shouted down from the gate-tower battlements, "Comte? Meyssonnier? Are you all right?"

"Yes, we're all right."

It took me a good minute to get down the Sept Fayards hill and up the other side. The man hadn't moved. He was still standing facing the cliff, hands on his head. I noticed that his legs were trembling slightly.

Peyssou's voice came from the other side of the palisade. "Shall I open up?"

"Not yet. I'm waiting for Meyssonnier."

I looked at the man. Six feet or just under, thick black hair, young neck. Built rather like Jacquet, only slimmer. Strong but graceful. Dressed like any of our younger farmers around here on a weekday: jeans, desert boots, woolen checked shirt. But on him they looked elegant somehow. In fact his appearance generally was one of elegance. And even in the humiliating pose that I was forcing him to maintain, he still retained his dignity.

When Meyssonnier had joined me, I said, "Take his gun."

I placed the barrel of mine against the prisoner's back. Right away, without having to be told, he moved his arm in order to help Meyssonnier lift the sling over his head.

"Army rifle," Meyssonnier said respectfully. "A .36."

I took my handkerchief out of my pocket, folded it, and said, "I'm going to blindfold you. Lower your hands."

He stood still while I tied the handkerchief in place.

"Right. Now you can turn around."

He did as he was told, and I was able to see his face at last, except for the eyes of course. No more than twenty. Cheeks shaved, but a small black beard cut to a point, and the edges neatly defined. A clean-cut earnest look. But of course, without the eyes . . .

"Meyssonnier," I said, "pick up the dead one's gun and collect any ammunition. There must be some on him."

Meyssonnier gave an odd groan. Till then he had been avoiding looking at the corpse with its shattered head. So had I.

"Peyssou, you can open up," I called.

The top bolt slid open, then the lower one, then the two side ones. There was a click—the padlock opening.

"Another .36 rifle," Meyssonnier said as he got to his feet again.

Peyssou appeared, cast a glance at the body, went white under his tan, and relieved Meyssonnier of the two .36s.

"Was it the Springfield that did that to him?" he asked.

Meyssonnier didn't answer.

"Was it you that fired?" Peyssou asked, seeing the Springfield in Meyssonnier's hand.

Meyssonnier shook his head.

"No, it was me," I snapped irritably.

Placing my hand flat on the young man's back I pushed him ahead of me. Peyssou closed up behind us. I took the prisoner by the arm and made him turn around two or three times on the spot before leading him along the

443

path between the traps. I repeated this operation several times before reaching the gate tower. Peyssou and Meyssonnier followed in silence. Meyssonnier because he had no stomach for talking after emptying the dead man's pockets, and Peyssou because I'd snubbed him.

Up on the gate-tower battlements two of the wooden panels set into the openings formed by the erstwhile crenelations were open, and behind them I could just make out faces. I lifted my face and put a finger to my lips.

Colin opened the main gate. I waited still he'd closed it, then I let go of the prisoner's arm, took Meyssonnier to one side, and said in a low voice, "Take the prisoner up to the house. Zigzag on the way, but don't overdo it. I'll follow you in a moment.

When Meyssonnier had left with the prisoner I signaled to Colin and Peyssou to follow them at a distance, but without speaking.

The two older women and Miette, Catie, Evelyne, Thomas, and Jacquet were coming down the stone steps from the battlements. I signaled to them not to speak. I waited till they were down on ground level, then I said quietly, "Thomas, Miette, Catie, you all stay on the walls. Evelyne too. Jacquet, give your gun to Miette. You will come with us. Menou and Falvine too."

"And why not me?" Catie said.

"You can ask your questions later," Thomas told her sharply.

Evelyne was biting her lip, but she looked at me without saying anything.

"It's not fair," Catie said in a low, furious voice. "Everyone else is going to see the prisoner! Except us!"

"Exactly," I said. "Because I don't want the prisoner to see either you or Miette."

"So you'll be letting him go again," Catie said with eager interest.

"If I can, yes."

"How rotten!" Catie said indignantly. "He's going to be let go again, and we won't even have had a look at him!"

"You've got me to look at, haven't you?" I snapped at her angrily. "Isn't that enough for you? Why is it so important for you to give our prisoner the glad eye? And an enemy into the bargain!"

"And who said I was going to give him the glad eye?" Catie raged back at me, tears gathering in her eyes. "I've had enough of having that sort of thing thrown in my face all the time!"

Miette, who was following this scene with a look of intense disapproval, suddenly took us all by surprise. In a single swift movement she had thrown her left arm around Catie's shoulders and clamped her right hand over her sister's mouth. Catie struggled like a wildcat. But Miette held her firmly to her body, powerless and dumb.

I noticed that Evelyne was looking at me. Looking at me with a demure, meritorious air. She was doing what she was told, oh yes. And keeping quiet too. I took the time to flash the little pharisee a smile.

"Are you coming, Jacquet?"

Jacquet was embarrassed. I'd told him to hand his gun to Miette, and Miette didn't have a hand free to take it with.

"Give Thomas your gun," I said over my shoulder as I walked away.

I heard running footsteps behind me. Jacquet caught up with me. "She's always been like that," he said in a low voice. "Even when she was only twelve. Scratching like a little cat. That's how it began with my father, at L'Étang. But she hasn't learned her lesson yet. She's not worth half of Miette! Miette's different!"

I said nothing. I didn't want to express any opinion on the matter that might be repeated. I was also extremely put out by what had happened. Thomas had understood, but not Catie. Not yet. She still had to learn discipline.

In the great hall the prisoner was seated, still blindfolded, in Momo-Jacquet's place at the lower end of the table, his back to the fireplace. It was daylight now, though the sun wasn't yet up. The window nearest the prisoner was open slightly. The air was warm. It was going to be another fine day.

I signaled to the others to sit down. They all took their usual chairs, sitting with their guns between their legs. The two old women remained standing, La Falvine quiet

445

for once. It was our usual breakfast time, and the meal was laid. The milk had already boiled in the hearth, the bowls were on the table, the bread set out, with our home-made butter. My stomach suddenly felt very hollow.

"Colin, take off the handkerchief."

The prisoner's eyes appeared. They blinked violently, then gradually became used to the light. He looked at me, looked at the companions, and then at the bowls, the bread, and the butter. I rather liked his eyes. And his attitude. He was taking it well. Pale, but well in control of himself. Lips dry, but expression outwardly calm.

"Are you thirsty?" I asked in absolutely even tones.

"Yes."

"What would you like? Wine or milk?"

"Milk."

"Do you want something to eat?"

Hesitation. I asked again, "Do you want something to eat?"

"Yes, please."

He spoke quietly. He had chosen milk in preference to wine. So he wasn't a farmer, though I still wouldn't place him too far from the soil.

I signaled to La Menou. She poured him a bowl of milk and cut him a slice of bread. It was appreciably thicker than the one she had thrown at old Pougès. As I have said, she had a weakness for handsome young men. And our prisoner was handsome, with his black eyes, his black hair, and pointed beard. Hefty too, even though he was slender. La Menou also evaluated a man in terms of work.

She spread some butter on his slice of bread and gave it to him. When the bread appeared in front of him, the prisoner half turned to look at La Menou, gave her a little filial smile, and said thank you with evident sincerity. My mind was made up by now, even though I still continued my show of cold suspicion. And from the glance Colin threw me I could see that he agreed, which strengthened me in my decision.

La Menou served the rest of us, and we ate in profound silence. I told myself that if the smaller of the two, the one I'd shot, had given our prisoner the boost up, then he would be the one lying outside now with a shattered skull. An idiotic, futile thought of no use to anyone, and I dismissed it as quickly as I could, because it wasn't exactly cheering me up. But it came back again several times during the course of the meal and ruined it for me totally.

The prisoner had finished. He laid his hands flat on the table and waited. The food had done him good. There was color in his cheeks now. And bizarrely, he seemed to be happy to be there with us. Happy and relieved.

I began to question him. He replied to all my questions without the slightest hesitation, without any attempt to hide anything. Indeed, he seemed actually pleased to be able to give me the information I asked for.

We were much less so at hearing what we had to deal with: a band of seventeen men, commanded by a certain Vilmain, a former officer in a paratroop regiment, or so he claimed. The band was very rigidly structured into two classes, veterans and recruits, the latter being the slaves of the former. Ruthless discipline. Three punishments: flogging, solitary confinement without food or drink, throat cut in front of the troops. Vilmain was in possession of a bazooka and a dozen small shells for it, plus twenty rifles.

Hervé Legrand—that was the prisoner's name—told us how he had been recruited. Vilmain had attacked and taken his village southwest of Fumel. There had been losses during the attack and he needed to make them good.

"So they rounded us up," Hervé said, "René, Maurice, and me. They took us out into the village square. And Vilmain said to René, 'Do you agree to sign on in my army?' René said no. So the Feyrac brothers just threw him down on his knees and Bébelle cut his throat.

"Bébelle? A woman?"

"No. Well . . . no."

"Description?"

"Five feet six, long blond hair, delicate features, slim waist, small hands and feet. Likes dressing up as a woman. You'd take him for one."

"And Vilmain? Does he take him for one?"

"Yes."

"And the others?"

"Oh, no!"

"The men are afraid of Vilmain?"

"They're more afraid of Bébelle." Then he added, "His skill with a knife is fantastic. He can throw better than any of the other veterans."

I looked at him. "When you're a recruit, how do you get to be a veteran?"

"I quote Vilmain: 'Never by length of service.'"

"How then?"

"By volunteering for missions."

I said sharply, "And was that why you volunteered to reconnoiter Malevil?"

"No. Maurice and I wanted to warn you and desert."

"Then why didn't you?"

He answered without the slightest hesitation. "Because it wasn't Maurice who was with me. It happened like this. This morning Vilmain asked for four men for two missions: one to reconnoiter Courcejac, the other Malevil. Maurice and I were the only ones to step forward. Both recruits. So then Vilmain bawled out the veterans and eventually two of them did volunteer. Vilmain detailed me off to go with one and Maurice with the other. At this moment, Maurice is reconnoitering Courcejac."

"There's one thing I don't understand. This morning Vilmain sent scouts to Courcejac and scouts to Malevil. Why didn't he send any to La Roque?"

A pause. Hervé just looked at me. "But La Roque," he said slowly, "that's where we are."

"What!" I said. And at the same time, I don't know why, I half rose from my chair. "You are in La Roque? Since when?"

My question was meaningless. What did it matter when exactly Vilmain had moved in? The only important fact was that he was there. With his army rifles, his gang of killers, his bazooka, and his experience.

I noticed that my companions had all gone pale.

"We occupied La Roque yesterday evening," Hervé said, "at sunset."

I stood up and moved away from the table. I was shattered by what I'd heard. At dawn the day before I had sent out scouts to reconnoiter La Roque's defenses, and that evening at dusk La Roque had been taken, but not by us! And this morning, if I hadn't taken it into my head just now to take a prisoner, against Meyssonnier's advice, because he wanted to observe my idiotic regulations, this morning I would have presented myself outside the walls of La Roque with my companions and the certainty of an easy victory. Unfortunately I have a good imagination. I could see us there, out in the open, mowed down by the devastating fire from seventeen military rifles.

I could feel my legs shaking under me. I put my hands in my pockets, turned away from the table, and went over to the window. I opened both sides as wide as they would go and took several deep breaths. I reminded myself that the prisoner was watching me, and I forced myself to calm down. Our lives had depended on a minute chance, on two chances in fact: one unfortunate, the other fortunate, and canceling out the first. Vilmain took the town the night before the day I was to attack it, and I took one of his men prisoner a few hours before setting out myself for the attack. Realizing that your life depends on such absurd coincidences, that's something that makes for modesty.

Face deliberately expressionless, I went back to the table, sat down, and said curtly, "Go on."

Hervé told us about the taking of La Roque. Bébelle had appeared outside the south gate at dusk disguised as a woman carrying a small bundle. The fellow guarding the tower—we found out later that it was in fact Lanouaille—let him in, and as soon as Bébelle had made sure Lanouaille was alone, he had slit the butcher's throat. Then he opened the gate for the others. The town fell without a shot being fired.

Meyssonnier then asked to be allowed to speak. I nodded.

"How many of these .36 rifles do you have?" he asked the prisoner.

"Twenty."

"And plenty of ammunition for them?"

"Yes, I think so. It's rationed, but not all that strictly. Vilmain's principle is always to have twenty men for his twenty rifles."

At Meyssonnier's request, Hervé then described the bazooka in great detail. When he had finished, I broke in. "There's one thing I want clearing up. Are there twenty of you or just seventeen?"

"In theory there are supposed to be twenty. But we've lost three since Fumel. So that leaves only seventeen. Well no, not seventeen. Now you've killed another it's sixteen! And with me a prisoner fifteen!"

There was no room for doubt. From the tone in which he spoke he was clearly very pleased to be there with us.

After a moment, I said, "The Maurice who was recruited at the same time as you, have you known him long?"

"I should say!" Hervé said, his voice suddenly bright and eager. "Ever since we were children. I was on holiday at his place when the bomb exploded."

"He means a lot to you?"

"Well, yes, of course!" Hervé said.

I looked at him. "In that case, you can't join us here and leave him there. It's not possible. Can you see yourself firing at him if Vilmain attacks?"

Hervé blushed, and I could read two conflicting emotions in his eyes. He was happy because I had entertained the idea of arming him and letting him fight on our side, but he was ashamed at having forgotten Maurice. I gave a little tap on the table with my hollowed palm. "I tell you what we're going to do, Hervé. We're going to let you go."

He started. Never can a prisoner have been less overjoyed at the idea of being freed. I was also aware, on the periphery of my vision, of mixed reactions among the others.

I kept my eyes on Hervé. The blood had left his face again. I said, "Is there something wrong?"

He nodded. "If you let me go without giving me my rifle back," he said in a choking voice, "you might as well be condemning me to death."

"I'd thought of that. We shall give you your rifle back as you leave."

This time the mixed reactions were even more marked. I pretended not to notice them. I went on: "So here's what you do. You don't say you were taken prisoner, obviously. You say that your companion was killed when he put his head above the palisade and that you fled under a hail of bullets. You will also say that you thought the shots were coming from the top of the keep."

I had no wish for Vilmain to suspect the existence, before his attack, of the little dugout on the Sept Fayards hill.

"Remember that, it's important."

"I'll remember," Hervé said.

"Right. And then at the first opportunity, you and Maurice . . ."

"Yes, you don't need to draw me a picture," Hervé said.

"One last question, Hervé. Which way did you come to La Roque?"

"Along the road," he answered, rather puzzled. "Is there another way?"

I didn't answer. It was over. There was nothing more for us to say to each other. Hervé waited. He let his dark, sensitive, honest eyes wander around him. His little pointed beard suited him. It gave him distinction, made him look older. And he sat there looking at us, at La Menou—he had immediately sensed the soft spot she had for him—at the mullioned windows, the weapons on the wall, the vast fireplace. His Adam's apple moved as he swallowed, and although he was putting a good face on it, I knew that this boy, because he was only a boy, was very moved. And that he had only one fear: losing the people who had already adopted him. Losing Malevil.

I stood up. "It's time then, Hervé."

He rose too as I went over to replace his blindfold. We all escorted him back as far as the main gate, but from that point on, only Meyssonnier and I went with him as far as the palisade. We opened the sliding cat door for him to crawl out. Luckily for him, the body of the veteran had fallen out toward the precipice, so Hervé wasn't

451

obliged to pass too near him as he emerged on the other side. I passed his rifle through after him, and as he stood up he gave us a big wave with one arm, accompanied by a broad childlike grin. I watched him through the Judas as he strode off down the hill.

"We may have lost a rifle there," Meyssonnier said in my ear.

I looked around at him. "But we may end up with two more."

And more important still, with two more fighting men. Because with the dead man's, we now had eight guns. Enough to arm Miette and Catie as well as our six men. No, it was men we needed most now. If Hervé and Maurice succeeded, then Vilmain would be reduced to fourteen. And our strength would be increased to ten. An important consideration, since numbers count for a great deal in a battle dependent mainly on fire power.

I explained this at the assembly I called as soon as Hervé had gone. It was held in the gate tower, while Jacquet was digging a grave for the dead veteran outside the palisade, and Peyssou, a hundred yards farther on, hid beside the road, gun at the ready, to cover him as he worked. "And remember, Peyssou," Meyssonnier had said, "keep under cover yourself. See without being seen!"

Meyssonnier was our military expert. He was the know-all in such matters. Communist though he was, he'd done his military training. Presumably he felt that knowledge was always worth coming by, no matter what the source. So he explained to us at the start of the assembly that the .36 rifle was the rifle used by the French Army at the time of the Second World War. Better weapons had certainly been developed since, but the .36 was not to be sniffed at all the same. As for the bazooka, again according to Meyssonnier, that was almost certainly the bazooka brought out by the Americans in 1942 as an anti-tank weapon. Very accurate up to about seventy yards. There was no danger to the walls of Malevil, they were too thick. If Peyssou had been there he would have added, And built with good mortar. A mortar now more than six hundred years old and harder than the stone itself.

"But the palisade, I'm afraid!" Meyssonnier said with

a shake of the head. "And the main gate! And the draw-bridge into the inner enclosure . . ."

We looked at each other. I made haste to display an optimism that I wasn't in fact feeling in the slightest. "No problem," I said firmly. "The palisade, needless to say, we sacrifice. It was never intended as anything more than an early warning system and a piece of camouflage any-way. It will still fulfill its delaying role by forcing the enemy to destroy it and show himself. But the main gate is a different matter. I suggest we construct a protective shield in front of it, a dry-stone wall, say a good three feet thick and nine high, just far enough from the bridge to allow a man on horseback to get around it, and then, well we have sand in the courtyard, we have sacks in the cellar, so we can make sandbags to pile up in front of the wall."

To my great relief, Meyssonnier approved these sug-gestions, and after the technical explanations he had pro-vided earlier his approbation carried great weight.

Before we set about these tasks, I had a few more words to say. I had insisted on the night watch being maintained the previous night against general opposition. It was as well I had. I didn't want to overdo it, but never-theless it had to be stressed: that resistance had in fact constituted a latent threat to discipline. As was also, and to an even more serious extent, Catie's protest when I de-tailed her to keep watch on the walls during the prisoner's interrogation. And there I lashed out a little. "That kind of thing is no longer tolerable from now on! When I give an order I expect it to be obeyed. And I do not expect to have to waste my time discussing it with thoughtless little troublemakers!"

I stood up. The meeting was over, and it had lasted less than ten minutes. The days of our earlier marathon discussions seemed a whole world away.

Catie hadn't spoken, but she had thrown me a very odd look. A look of hate? Of resentment? Not in the slightest. It seemed to be saying something much more like Oh, so I'm a thoughtless little troublemaker, am I? Well just you wait and see! And yet that "just you wait and see!" was in no way a threat. If I had dared, I would have described it as more like a promise.

When the grave had been dug and the body duly buried, I recalled the indispensable Peyssou from his guard duty out beside the La Roque road and replaced him with Colin. Because I had no wish to be caught unprepared by a daylight attack while we were all unarmed and at work, even though I thought such an event highly unlikely. I divided us into two gangs. The first, with Peyssou as foreman, had the job of providing him with the stone he needed to build his wall. This had to be brought out from the first enclosure, where there were considerable piles of already shaped blocks readily available. The second gang, consisting of the four women and Evelyne, were detailed off to fill the sandbags, tie them, then bring them down to the edge of the moat ready to be piled into position later. And our two iron wheelbarrows were kept more or less constantly on the move all the rest of the day.

In order to keep everyone down near the palisade, thus saving precious time, I had decided that for as long as the state of alert lasted we would all take our meals on a rota system in the gate-tower kitchen, and that they would consist simply of cold cuts, since La Menou and La Falvine had plenty to do without cooking.

Before Peyssou began laying his first course, I had our two carts brought out—my adapted trailer and the one from L'Étang—and parked alongside the moat in the part of the old parking area we had left free of traps. They would not restrict our line of fire there, and they would not be imprisoned inside by the new wall: important, because I had decided that it should remain as a permanent feature of our fortifications. Because if we were attacked again in the future, even by a band without a bazooka, the big main gate, being made of wood, was still Malevil's weak point. The enemy could burn it or smash it in. So it would always be in our interest to impede his access to it.

It was soon borne in upon me that medieval masons didn't stint the dimensions of their building stones. The ones we were handling had come from the ruins of the old hamlet built in the outer enclosure (in the days when there was a resident judge in Malevil), and they were of a weight to command respect. It was no small matter lifting them off the heap, then resting them on the front of one's thighs as one straightened up sufficiently to be able to let them fall, with great relief, into the barrow. Some of them took two of us to lift. I had sent Colin out to keep watch outside precisely in order to spare him a task requiring so much brute strength. But Thomas, despite his excellent physical form, seemed to me to be having trouble. Meyssonnier was streaming with sweat. Only Jacquet, with those gorilla's arms of his, seemed to be perfectly at ease, effortlessly lifting blocks for which I would have had to ask his help.

As for myself, I was disappointed by my performance, and as usual in such situations, instead of thinking to myself, as I would have done at thirty, that I was tired and off form, I told myself that I was getting old, and I sank into despondency. Not for long though, because then I suddenly remembered that I'd had very little sleep the night before, and that I'd certainly had my share of tension and anxiety in the past few hours. Though this realization didn't exactly fill me with renewed strength, it certainly improved my morale, and I found I was able to stand the pace, the sweat streaming off me in the hot sun and the heavy close weather, fingernails broken, hands aching, lower back growing steadily stiffer.

At one o'clock Meyssonnier reminded me of the night watch we had shared and disappeared for a short nap. At three, rather pleased with myself at having broken Meyssonnier's endurance record by two hours, I too had reached a total exhaustion point and had to stop. However, by then Peyssou had more than enough stones and was asking Jacquet to start helping him with the actual building. Meyssonnier was just returning—two hours later—from his "short nap," so I handed over the command to him and announced to no one in particular that I too was going to take a rest. As I walked away, I heard Meyssonnier sending a very tired Thomas to replace Colin at the advance post on the La Roque road.

Once in my room, I scarcely had time to take my clothes off. Despite the coolness of the enormously thick walls, it was very hot in there. I fell like a great weight onto my bed, completely inert, legs like lead, arms drained of strength, and just went out like a light. It was a very disturbed siesta though, ending in a series of nightmares. I won't describe them. There are enough horrors in real life as it is. And besides, they were the kind of dreams that everyone has. You are being hunted down by people who want to kill you. When they catch up with you, you lash out at them, but there is no strength in your blows. If only you dreamed it just once it wouldn't be so bad, but no, it comes again and again. What's so wearing is the repetition. And what was particularly horrid on this occasion was that my pursuer was Bébelle, dressed in a skirt, his long blond hair floating out behind him, his knife in his hand.

Just as the edge of the knife touched my throat, I woke up. I opened my eyes. And there was a woman in my room, but not, thank heaven, Bébelle. It was Catie.

She was standing at the foot of my bed, eyes dancing with wicked mischief. She stared down at me without saying anything. Then suddenly she hurled herself on top of me, weighing my body down with the whole weight of hers, and crushing her lips against mine.

I was still half asleep, and Catie could almost have been part of my dream, especially since she took control of matters with a dexterity that amazed me. When I was at last completely awake, it was too late. I was already ensconced. Remorse came at the same moment as pleasure, then faded as the pleasure became more intense. And it became intense to the point of frenzy, given and shared by a partner totally abandoned to her task, attaining the very peaks of participation right away and finding the means to die and be reborn two or three times in the short while I myself took to collapse into satisfied release.

With some difficulty I regained my breath. I looked at her. I hadn't thought she was all that pretty. So presumably it must be my eyes that had changed. I saw her now, in the warm disorder of that bed, as being quite ravishing. At the same time, however, my moral sense resurfaced, and I said with reproach, though without much real sting in the reproach, "Why did you do that, Catie?"

It was a bit feeble. And a bit hypocritical too, since after all, what she had done had not been done alone.

She answered immediately, "First, because I find you attractive, Emmanuel, even though you are old." (Thanks.) "Really, leaving Thomas out of it, if I had to make a list, I'd put you only just after Peyssou." (Thanks again.)

She paused briefly, then lifted her head, and there was a little flame in her eyes. "But mainly, I wanted you to know that Catie is somebody. Catie isn't just a thoughtless little troublemaker, the way you thought. Catie is a woman, a real one!"

I ignored the rather unkind implication there (poor Miette). Squatting cross-legged on the bed, hair in fine disorder, cheeks pink, small breasts still on fire, Catie gazed down at me in triumph, her eyes shining bright with pride. At first glance it might have seemed rather absurd that she should be so proud of sexual attributes for which she could claim no merit, since she had received them at birth. But what about men? Don't we—myself included—pride ourselves just as much on our virility? Don't we strut and preen like peacocks, proud of our prowess? And besides, it's not so stupid after all. Because the fact was that during the past few minutes my consideration for Catie had increased by leaps and bounds. I too found that she was "a woman, a real one." Had it not been for Thomas, and the unfortunate moral sense with which I was afflicted, I might have been inclined to see this end to my siesta as the beginning of a habit.

And who said that Catie wasn't intelligent? The eyes fixed on mine, those eyes in which I had read such pleasure a moment ago—all the pleasure that she took and all the pleasure that she was now so deliriously proud of having given me—were following and penetrating all my thoughts as soon as they appeared in my mind. She could see, or sense—her method of apprehending these things was unimportant—that the low esteem in which I had held her was now a thing of the past, and that the price I placed on her was now quite considerable. She basked in the ecstasy of this promotion. Her head was tilted back, her lips slightly open, her eyes shining. Her triumph was a wine she could feel streaming down inside her throat.

I said in a muffled voice, "All the same, Catie. Thomas will have to know."

The thought was like a bucket of cold water to me, but not to her. She just said with a chuckle, "No need to get in a stew about it. I'll see to it. You don't have to bother about it at all."

I was staggered by such brazenness. "But Catie, you can't. He's going to be furious, hurt . . ."

She shook her head. "No, he isn't. Not in the slightest. He's far too fond of you."

"No fonder than I am of him," I said, then felt rather shamefaced at having said such a thing at that moment.

"Oh, I know!" she said with a slight hint of her former sharpness returning. "You were fond of everyone at Malevil, except me!" Then she gave a chuckle and said, "But that's all over now!"

She got off the bed and began rearranging her clothes. And as she did so she gazed down at me with an air of possession, as though she had just bought me in the big department store in our county town, and was now on her way home, her purchase tucked under her arm, very satisfied with it and herself. And perhaps I was only part of the purchase. Because her acquisitive gaze was now making a tour of my room, lingering on my desk (the photo of my Boche!), then even longer on the sofa below the window. And each of these two halts was accompanied by a little grimace.

"Well, my poor Emmanuel," she said, "it's a good thing I've taken you in hand, I'd say. No one could say you're getting much in the way of satisfaction these days!"

And her eyes were suddenly shining again. She was standing over me, eyes glittering with insolence. "And with Evelyne? You still haven't made up your mind?"

My God, she thinks she can get away with anything now! I was furious. Except that no, why lie, I wasn't furious. Much less than I would have been before anyway. It was amazing how she'd managed to soften me up! And what's more she could see it. She didn't back down. "No answer?"

"What do you expect me to say? She's only thirteen!"

458

"Fourteen. I've seen her papers."

"Either way, she's just a kid."

She threw up her hands. "A kid? Don't you believe it. A woman! And one who knows what she wants!"

"And what does she want?"

"You, of course!" She burst into a triumphant peal of laughter. "And she'll have you too! I just have, haven't I? Abbé of Malevil!"

Her Parthian shot, except that she wasn't fleeing. She threw herself on my neck and began working her way over my face with her lips and tongue.

"I can see you're worried, Emmanuel. You're thinking, The discipline here, finished! With that crazy girl! Well you just think again! It's the opposite. You'll see! Everything you say goes! On the double! A real little soldier, that's me now! Well, I must be off now!"

What a girl! Pure fire! The door slammed behind her. I lay there dumfounded, ashamed, thrilled. I got up, threw my towel around my neck and went downstairs to take a shower and sort my ideas out a little. But after the shower, my thoughts were just as muddled as before. And I didn't really care. One thing was certain. For a whole hour I hadn't thought about Vilmain, and I felt reinflated, confident, bursting with optimism.

When I reached the worksite I was greeted with complete naturalness by the men, but not by the women. They all knew what had been going on. And who knows? Perhaps they even suspected me of having sent Thomas out to keep watch on the road in order to clear the way. Whereas in fact that had nothing to do with me. It had been Meyssonnier who'd given him the detail.

The first look I met was Evelyne's. It was black, despite the blueness of her eyes. Then La Falvine, all excited complicity. La Menou was shaking her head and carrying on one of her sotto voce soliloquies, clearly not complimentary, her annoyance increased by the fact that she couldn't let me actually hear what she was saying because Evelyne would have heard too. The only eyes I didn't meet were those of Miette, and that made me sad.

Catie was holding open the neck of a sack while Miette threw sand into it with a little shovel. Catie was managing to convey an air of nonchalant triumph just by the almost obscene way she was holding the mouth of the sack open while Miette toiled away like a slave, a dumb and even a blind slave now, because I passed within two yards of her without her even raising her eyes, and without my being given my usual delicious smile.

"Did you have a good sleep, Emmanuel?" Catie asked with calm impudence.

She was doing it on purpose! I wanted to answer her sharply. I wanted to let her know that she had better not start parading the fact that she had "had me," as she put it, in front of everyone. I wanted to let her know as well that I still retained my preference, my partial preference anyway, for her sister. But Catie's eyes confused me with their insistent glances. They were doing their work only too well.

In the end I turned my head away and said rather awkwardly, "Hello there, you two."

Catie laughed, but Miette reacted not at all. She was now also deaf, it seemed, as well as dumb and blind. I felt as guilty as though I had betrayed her. It was as though the new value I attached to her sister had been taken away from her.

I went out through the main gate and found myself once more on the men's side. A simpler world at once. They were doing things without thinking about anything else. Their thoughts were all objective. I looked around at them, all deeply engrossed in their work, and I felt a sense of gratitude.

The task in hand was now it its final stage, the longest and most laborious. The wall was by now nine feet high, and the last three feet were in the course of construction. This meant that there were two ladders leaning against it, up which Peyssou and Jacquet, each with a block of stone loaded onto his broad shoulders, were slowly climbing, feeling carefully for each rung with their feet, then depositing their burdens on the summit. Peyssou and Jacquet were the only two of us capable of this exploit. Colin was helping our two Herculeses as they took turns to settle a block of stone securely on the other's shoulders. As for Meyssonnier, who apparently didn't have the same knack for this task as Colin, he had been reduced to idleness, because there were by now plenty of stones on the site to finish the wall.

I suggested he accompany me on a scouting expedition, an offer he was glad to accept. But before we left I went back inside to ask La Menou for a yard or two of thread.

"Ah, the thing is, Emmanuel, I don't have much left now," she said, her deep-set eyes still heavy with reproach. "And when there's none left, how are you going to get me more, I'd like to know."

"Now come on, Menou, I only want a yard or two. And it's not to play games with either!"

She made her way over toward the gate-tower kitchen, her mutters rising steadily in volume, and most imprudently I followed her. Imprudently, because once inside, out of earshot of the others, I was given the rough edge of La Menou's tongue.

"Ah, my poor Emmanuel," she said with an assortment of sighs and sad head shakes, all hypocritical, since she was about to enjoy herself immensely. "So you'll never change then, that's the way it is. Always running after your own tail! Just like your Uncle Samuel before you! I should think you'd be ashamed! A piece like that, and you yourself married her to your friend! Ah, a fine curé you're making us, and no mistake! And to think of you hearing my confession too! Heaven alone knows which of us ought to be hearing the other! But it's as sure as sure that you'd be the one with more to say! And surer still that the good Lord can't be very pleased up there! Notice! I've said nothing about her! Nothing! I know how to behave. But I can think, and think I do. At least there'll be no worry now if the fire goes out. We can always light it again from you-know-what, which heaven knows is hot enough! And young as she is, a tongue like a viper! And another thing you can be sure of—she's not going to stop with you. Oh, no! It will be Peyssou next, you'll see! And after Peyssou, Jacquet. And all the others! She can make her comparisons then!" (Just a hint of envy there, I felt.)

Like my uncle, I listened and said nothing. And while I listened, again like my uncle, I went through all the

461

motions of the role assigned to me in this little comedy. I frowned, I shrugged, shook my head, in short I showed all the external signs of a displeasure I was very far from feeling. Counting the attack on old Pougès, this was the second great outburst since Momo's death. The old strength of mind, the energy, the aggressiveness, they were all still there. The little skeleton scolding me had never been more alive. Besides which, denounce me roundly though she might, La Menou was very far from condemning me in her heart. Virtuously continent, she would have despised me. Her views were simple. A bull is made for serving. The shamelessness is all on the side of the cow. Or at least it is when she goes looking for the bull instead of just submitting to him, as is her duty.

The outburst showed signs of becoming circular. I was being treated to the remark about the fire being relit from you-know-what a second time. When invention gives way to repetition I always intervene. And since it was part of my role that I should always have the last word, in a gruff, bad-tempered voice I said, "Is it coming or not, this thread?"

Those few sharp words were sufficient to make the thread appear, as if from nowhere, on the table. She measured me out a length, as small a length as she could manage, her grumbles gradually subsiding into a more and more inaudible murmur. I left the kitchen with my ears buzzing, and rather astonished, as I thought about it, that life in Malevil could still be so humdrum in its tone at a time when we were under imminent threat of extermination.

"You know what I'm thinking," Peyssou said from the top of his ladder as he manhandled a vast block of stone the way I would handle a brick. "Those sandbags, the thing we must do is pile them up so the wall doesn't show at all. That way Vilmain will think there's nothing but sand for him to get through. Till he rams his head against the stone."

I gave my approval, told Colin to take over the command while Meyssonnier and I were away, and asked him to come down and close the cat door after us. It was a very undignified way to emerge from a castle, crawling on all fours, but I wanted the habit to become second nature, so I had to give a good example. A whole band of attackers could have rushed through our main gate in a trice, but not through this little hole down at ground level, whose sliding cover—I forgot to mention this earlier —had a scythe blade affixed to its lower edge.

We set off down the La Roque road, and Thomas must have been both well concealed and alert, because we soon heard a curt "Where are you going?" and even then we couldn't see where he was hiding. Eventually he rose to his feet, looking even more like a Greek statue than ever with his naked torso and serene watchful air.

"We're going out to reconnoiter the forest track. I'll relieve you on the way back if you like."

"Oh, you needn't bother," Thomas said. "I've only been lying here keeping my eyes open. Much less tiring than what you've been doing."

I blushed, and felt as though I'd been sewn alive into a traitor's skin. "I want to have a talk with you anyway," I said.

I had made my decision without much prior consideration, but I was glad nevertheless. I wasn't about to hide behind Catie. If there was to be an explosion I wanted to take the full force of it myself. I gave Thomas a little wave and hurried on down the hill, Meyssonnier beside me on my left. Although the charred tree trunks were all leafless, the undergrowth on the other hand had taken advantage of the alternating sun and rain of the past two months to break into a tropical exuberance of growth. I had never seen plants so tall, so spreading, so numerous— an amazing proliferation, I noticed bracken fronds nine feet high, and with stalks as big as my forearm, brambles like walls, hawthorns already almost trees, chestnut and elm suckers forming enormous clumps well above my head.

The Malevil end of the short cut to La Roque through the forest is invisible from the road in summer, but all my old markers were still there and I found it without any trouble. I had often used this track to exercise my horses before the day it happened, partly because it was carpeted with rich black leaf mold, kind to hoofs, and partly because it offered a convenient proportion of hills to flat. I even used to give it a little clean-up each year, cutting away the more troublesome branches and brambles, even though the woods didn't belong to me. I also took good care never to mention it to anyone in La Roque, in case the Lormiaux family should take to using it for their geldings. And more recently still I had cleared away all the blackened tree trunks that had made the journey back from La Roque so difficult that day I rode over with Colin to tell Fulbert of Catie's marriage.

No animals could have survived the bomb other than those in holes. And apart from Craa, whom we hadn't seen since the rifle shot that morning, there were no birds left at all. It was a chilling experience, walking through forest undergrowth without hearing a single bird call and without hearing or seeing a single insect.

I walked in front, eyes peeled for the slightest mark on the soft soil, but I saw nothing. Nor did I really think it likely that any of the La Roque survivors could have known about the track and pointed it out to Vilmain, because the La Roque farmers were lords of rich plains and never used to set foot, or tractor tire, on the Malejac hills. Nor did the path appear on the ordnance map for the district, since it was some time since that had been revised and the short cut was relatively recent in origin, having been cut by a forester in order to drag his timber out to the road. It was therefore unlikely that Vilmain ever used it. But I needed to be sure, as I explained in a low voice to Meyssonnier after we had been walking for about an hour through the oppressive silence of the wood.

I had seen nothing suspicious, no footmarks, no crushed plants, no snapped twigs—or at least none apart from those broken by Colin and myself as we rode back from La Roque, and they were all completely withered by now.

On the way back I left a series of markers that would enable us to be sure that no one else had used the track next time we came along it. They consisted of two flexible twigs, one from either side of the track, tied together by a length of the black thread at about hip height. The wind wouldn't be sufficient to break the thread, but a man walking at any speed would be bound to do so without even noticing. When I was lucky enough to find a bramble bush alongside the path, I dispensed with the thread, selected the longest thorny arm I could, and pulled it over to the other side, where it promptly dug its thorns into some frail branchlet.

It was rather like a game back in our Club days, and Meyssonnier commented on the fact. The difference was that this time our lives were really at stake. But neither he nor I had any desire to make so melodramatic an observation. On the contrary, there was an unspoken agreement to stick to strictly everyday conversation. After two hours of walking we sat down for a rest on a few clumps of grass conveniently growing in a spot that looked down on the La Roque road. Anyone on the road would not be able to see us—even had we been on horseback—because of the thick undergrowth all around. See without being seen, as Meyssonnier would have said.

"I think we'll pull through," he said just then.

Except that he was blinking, and that his narrow face seemed even longer than usual because of the tension, he was as calm as could be. When I just nodded without saying anything, he went on: "I'm trying to envisage it, how it will go. Vilmain arrives with his bazooka. With the first shell he demolishes the palisade and comes through. Facing him, he sees the sandbags. He thinks the gate is the other side of them and fires again. He fires one shell, two shells, no result. He only has ten or so. So of course he's not going to use them all. So then he gives the order to retreat."

I nodded and said, "And that's just what I'm afraid of. If he clears off, that doesn't mean we're out of the woods. On the contrary, Vilmain is a trained soldier. As soon as he sees he's bitten off more than he can chew he'll go right back to La Roque and wear us down with ambushes and surprise attacks."

"We can always catch him with counterambushes," Meyssonnier said. "We know the terrain."

"It won't be long before he knows it too. Even this track, he'll soon sniff it out. No, Meyssonnier, if there's a war of that sort, then we have every chance of losing it. Vilmain has more men than us, and they're better armed.

Most of our popguns are no good beyond forty yards, and his rifles will pick off a man at four hundred."

"And more," Meyssonnier said. And since I didn't speak, he went on: "So? What do you suggest?"

"Nothing at the moment. I'm thinking about it."

As we came back onto the road the sun was westering, its light golden and horizontal.

"Thomas?"

"I'm here," he called, raising one arm to disclose his hiding place on the bank above the road.

It was the serenest hour of day, but serene was the last thing I felt as I made my way up to Thomas, turning to give Meyssonnier a little farewell wave as he continued on up to the castle.

Thomas had concealed himself in a very well-chosen spot that gave him a clear view along at least a hundred yards of the road. His gun was beside him on two flat stones he'd covered with earth. I lay down next to him.

"It's a filthy business, war," Thomas said. "I could see you coming a long way off. I even took a bead on you. I could have sliced your heads off like daisies, the two of you."

Thanks for the daisy, I thought. If I were superstitious it might have occurred to me that his remark was hardly a good augury for the conversation ahead.

"Thomas, I have to tell you something."

"Tell away then," he said, sensing my constraint.

I told him the whole thing. Or rather, no, I didn't tell him the whole thing. Because I didn't want to accuse Catie at all. My version ran as follows: Just as I was finishing my siesta, Catie came into my room, probably in order to tell me something. And it just happened. I couldn't help myself.

Thomas gazed attentively at my face as I spoke. Then he said, "You couldn't help yourself?"

I shook my head.

"Well there you are, then," he said in the calmest possible tone. "She can't be as bad as all that, can she? You've always underestimated her."

And him too! I was completely staggered to find him taking it like this. I remained mute, eyes on the ground.

"You look disappointed," Thomas said, scrutinizing my face.

"Disappointed isn't quite the word. Astonished, yes. A little."

"It's just that my point of view has changed," Thomas said. "And I hadn't got around to telling you about it. Do you remember our discussion the evening you brought Miette back? One husband or several? I argued against you and defended monogamy. You were outvoted. And very cut up about it at the time."

He gave a half smile, then went on. "Well, as I say, my point of view has changed. I think you were right after all. No one can claim exclusive rights to a woman, not when there are only two women to six men."

I stared in amazement at his austere profile. I had assumed he was still as staunch a champion as ever of the monogamic cause, and here he was feeding me back my own opinions.

"And apart from that," he said, "I don't own Catie. She does as she likes. She is a free human being. She didn't promise to be faithful to me, and it's no business of mine what she was doing this afternoon." And in a terse voice he concluded. "We won't mention the matter again."

Had it not been for that resolve not to mention it again, I might have believed that he was totally unaffected by what I'd told him. But he wasn't. There was an almost imperceptible quivering around his mouth. Which meant, I was certain, that he had foreseen Catie's infidelities and armed himself against them in advance with iron-clad inner arguments. Arguments borrowed from me. How well I recognized my Thomas now. Implacable logic, but never insensitive. And lying there beside him, eyes fixed like his on the road we were guarding, my feeling of friendship for him was overwhelmingly intense. Not that I regretted what had happened earlier. But there was no possible comparison, it seemed to me, between what I had experienced that afternoon and the emotion I was feeling now.

After a while, feeling the silence had gone on too long, I propped myself up on one elbow. "You can go back in now, if you like. I'll take over."

"Heavens no," Thomas said. "You'll be far more use inside than me. Peyssou will want you to check his wall, for one thing."

"Yes," I said, "you're quite right. But all the same, don't stay out here after dusk. There's no point. We have the dugout for our nightwatch."

"Who's on duty tonight?"

"Peyssou and Colin."

"Right," Thomas said. "I'll be in before dark."

The only sign of tension discernible was the exaggeratedly normal way we were talking, our voices almost too offhand.

"See you then," I said as I walked off with what I felt looked like very fake nonchalance. And anyway, I'd never have said that "See you then" normally. We didn't usually bother with such courtesies at Malevil.

I quickened my pace, rang the bell once, and waited till Peyssou opened the cat door for me.

"Well," he said as soon as I was standing beside him, "it's finished. What do you think? Can you see it's a wall? And look, even if you walk right over by the graves, or over by the cliff, you can't even see the edge. Good camouflage, eh? Not a pebble to be seen, just the bags. A nasty shock he's got in store for him, that Vilmain."

He was panting a little, bare-chested, still sweating slightly despite the cool evening air, and his great arms swollen with muscles were bent slightly, as though they were too stiff for him to straighten out. I noticed that his hands were red and blistered, despite his callused palms. But he was radiant with pleasure and pride.

"Well what a thing!" he went on. "A day! One day it took us! I'd never have believed it. It's true the blocks were there ready cut. And there were six of us. Well, five. Plus the four women."

Apart from La Menou, La Falvine, and Thomas, the whole of Malevil was there clustering around the wall and admiring it in the fading light. Catie, at the top of one of the ladders, was just putting the finishing touches to the top row of sandbags. She had her back to us.

"She's got a fine figure on her," Peyssou said in a low voice.

"Not as fine as her sister."

"All the same," Peyssou said, "that Thomas, you could say he hasn't done too badly. And not standoffish. She doesn't mind who she talks to. And affectionate too. Always kissing you. It even embarrasses me, you know, sometimes."

Even in the half darkness I could see him blushing. He decided it was time to change the subject. "I wanted to ask you, Emmanuel. If we're going to fight tomorrow, and there is a risk we might be killed, then perhaps we should have a communion this evening. It's for me and Colin I say that."

He was turning the cat-door padlock around and around in his great hands. He hadn't thought to lock it back in place.

"I'll think about it."

But I wasn't given time. A shot rang out. I froze.

"Open up," I told Peyssou. "I'll go. It was Thomas."

"And if it wasn't?"

"I said open up!"

He slid up the cat door, and as I crawled through I said curtly, "No one follow!"

I ran, rifle in hand. It was a long way, a hundred yards. I slowed down at the second bend and jumped down into the ditch and advanced more cautiously at a crouch. Then I recognized Thomas. He was standing in the middle of the road, a statue with a gun under its arm. His back was toward me. There was a pale shape lying at his feet.

"Thomas!"

He turned, but it was almost dark now and I couldn't make out his features. I went up to him.

The pale shape lying in the road was a woman. I could make out a skirt, a white blouse, long blond hair. She had a black hole in her chest.

"Bébelle," Thomas said.

XVI

"YOU'RE SURE?"

Despite the growing darkness I saw him shrug.

"I recognized him right away from Hervé's description. And from his walk. He thought no one was watching, he wasn't bothering to walk like a woman." He stopped and swallowed.

"And then?"

"I let him get past, then I stood up, leaned against that tree trunk over there, and I said 'Bébelle,' just like that, not loud at all. He whipped around as though a dog had bitten his leg. Then he clutched the little bundle he was carrying against his stomach and put his right hand into it. I said, 'Hands on head, Bébelle,' and it was then he threw his knife."

"You dodged it?"

"I don't know. I don't know if I dodged it or if the tree drew his aim. Out of habit. Because he must have practiced throwing at trees when he was learning. Anyway, it hit the tree an inch or so away from my chest. And I fired. Here's the knife, so I didn't dream it."

I weighed the knife in my hand and with the tip of one foot pulled Bébelle's skirt up to disclose his undergarment. Then I bent down, and in the last remaining glimmer of daylight I looked at the face. Very pretty features, delicate and regular, framed by long blond hair. Yes, from the face you could well have taken him for a woman. Well, Bébelle, I said to myself, your problems are solved at last. Death has chosen for you. We'll bury you as a woman.

"Vilmain was trying to pull the same trick as he did at La Roque," Thomas said.

I shook my head. "He isn't anywhere near. He'd already have shown up."

Better not to hang about though. Bébelle could wait for her burial. I ran back to Malevil with Thomas beside me. And I posted Jacquet on the ramparts to keep watch.

We were all gathered in the gate-tower kitchen, packed close around the table, our faces brightly lit by the oil lamp that La Falvine had brought down from the house. We looked at one another in silence. Our weapons were all stacked against the walls behind us, the pockets of our jeans and denims bulged with our ammunition. We only possessed two cartridge belts, and those had been issued to Miette and Matie.

Simple meal: bread, butter, ham, and milk or wine.

Thomas told his story again, listened to by all with profound attention and by Catie with an admiration that piqued me. It was the limit, that reaction. I did my best to repress it, but it wasn't easy.

When he had finished, the general opinion was that Vilmain and his band hadn't been waiting anywhere near. Because at the sound of the shot, knowing that Bébelle had no gun, they would have rushed Thomas right away. Bébelle's mission was not to slit the gatekeeper's throat and open the gate, as at La Roque, but just to bring back information. Like the two sent that morning.

The conversation dwindled into a long anxious silence.

At the end of the meal, I announced, "As soon as the table's been cleared, I'll give communion, if everyone agrees."

General approbation. Thomas and Meyssonnier silent. While the women cleared the table, Peyssou led me outside into the enclosure.

"The thing is," he said in a low voice, "the thing is, Emmanuel, I'd like to make confession."

"Now?"

"Well, yes."

I threw up my hands. "But my poor Peyssou, I know them off by heart, all your sins!"

"There's a new one," Peyssou said. "A big one."

Silence. A pity it was too dark to see his face at all well.

"A big one?" I repeated.

"Well," Peyssou said, "quite big."

Silence. We walked slowly over toward the Maternity We were about fifteen yards from the wall and I couldn't even see Jacquet up on the battlements.

Ward in the darkness.

"Catie?"

"Yes."

"In thought?"

"Oh, yes!" Peyssou said with a sigh.

I weighed that sigh. We reached the Maternity Ward, and Amarante, who had scented me even though she could not see me, made a gentle *pfff* with her nostrils. I went over and felt for her big head so that I could stroke her. It was warm and soft beneath my fingers.

"Is she too affectionate?"

"Yes."

"And she kisses you?"

"Yes, often."

"How does she kiss you?"

"Well," Peyssou said.

"Does she throw her arms around your neck and cover your face in little tiny kisses?"

"How do you know that?" Peyssou said in a stunned voice.

"And at the same time press her body against you?"

"Oh, dear," Peyssou said. "She does more than just press it against me. She wriggles it!"

At that moment I suddenly had a very clear notion of what Fulbert would have done in my place. A good criterion that, as a general guide. Think what Fulbert would do in any particular situation and do the opposite. It produced the following:

"You're not the only one, you know."

"What?" Peyssou said. "You mean you as well?"

"Me as well." Come on, a last little effort. Anti-Fulbertism to the nth. "And with me," I went on, "it's much worse."

"It's much worse?" Peyssou echoed.

I told him how I'd spent my siesta. I leaned against the partition wall of the box to tell my story, and Amarante laid her head on my shoulder. As I talked I was stroking her muzzle with my right hand. And without biting—because though she'll kick things to death she never bites—she nibbled at my neck with her soft lips.

"So there you are, you see," I said. "You came out to make confession, and I'm the one who's done the confessing."

"But I can't give you absolution," Peyssou said.

"That's not what matters," I said forcefully. "What matters is saying what's on your mind to a friend and accepting the friend's judgment."

Silence.

"I'm not judging you," Peyssou said. "In your place I'd have done the same."

"Well, there you are, nicely confessed," I said. "And me too."

I omitted to tell him that it wouldn't be very long before he was in fact "in my place," as he put it. The thought made me jealous. Very well then, I would be jealous, that was all, and I would control my jealousy, like Thomas. One day or another we would have to move beyond such possessiveness if we wanted to go on living at Malevil in peace.

"Well, well," Peyssou said. "You know, Catie and you, I'd never have thought it. I thought there was only Evelyne." And since I said nothing, he went on: "Not that I was meaning anything, not like that, of course."

"I'm glad to hear it."

"No, no," Peyssou said, "if you ask me, it's more like father and daughter there."

"Not that either," I said very tersely.

He was silent. Poor Peyssou, always so genuinely gentle with others' feelings, he was horrified at having ventured onto such thin ice. I took him by the arm, which he immediately tensed so that I could feel his biceps. Good old Peyssou. It was a habit he'd never lost from our Club days.

"Let's go in," I said. "They must be waiting."

I knew that Peyssou would have preferred a properly signed and sealed sort of absolution. But I gave those as seldom as I possibly could. Every time La Menou insisted on one, for example, I felt uncomfortable about it. But I've already gone into all that.

The table had been cleared, swept free of crumbs, and given a polish. Its beautiful dark walnut top glowed in the lamplight. In front of me there was a large glass already filled with wine. And on the plate beside it a number of small cubes of bread that La Menou had just finished cutting. Quite automatically, I counted them. There were twelve. She had cut one for Momo.

The table in the gate tower is much smaller than the one in the house. No one said a word. We were packed very tightly, elbows touching. We had all noticed La Menou's mistake, and it had brought the same thought to all our minds: that tomorrow, at the evening meal, maybe our companions would have to remove our plate. The thought weighed on us. It wasn't so much the idea of dying as the idea of no longer being with the others.

Before the communion itself I said a few words, from which I was careful to banish all rhetoric and even more so any hint of unction. I spoke in the most even, natural tone I could. I wasn't trying for eloquence. In fact almost its opposite: to translate into words as plainly as I could exactly what I had in my mind.

"As I see it," I said, "the meaning of what we are doing at Malevil is that we are trying to survive by drawing our nourishment from the land and our animals. People like Vilmain and Bébelle, on the other hand, have an entirely negative conception of existence. They kill, they loot, they burn. To Vilmain, conquering Malevil means simply acquiring a base for his plundering expeditions. If the human race is to continue, then it will owe its future to little groups of people like ourselves, who are trying to reorganize an embryo of society. People like Vilmain and Bébelle are parasites and beasts of prey. They must be eliminated. However, the fact that our cause is a good one doesn't necessarily mean we're going to win. And if I were to say now, 'I pray to God to bring us victory,' that wouldn't be any guarantee of victory either."

This remark, coming from the Abbé of Malevil, caused astonishment in some of those present. But I felt I knew what I was about, and I continued. "In order to win

474

battles, you need an incredible amount of vigilance. And you also need a lot of imagination. I know that you have made me your leader in the event of danger; but that doesn't mean you are excused from using your own powers of invention too. If you think of any tricks or stratagems or tactics or traps that we haven't thought of before, then tell me. And if the enemy gives us time, we'll discuss them."

I would have liked to stick to that objective tone. But suddenly I changed my mind. Standing with my hands pressed on the tabletop, I looked around at my companions seated in the lamplight. They were so close that they seemed almost to have fused together. A single body. Their faces were tense and a little anxious, but the happiness we were all feeling at being together was what struck me most, and I wanted to express it.

"You know the saying we have in these parts: Each will strengthen each." (I said it in patois first, then repeated it in French for Thomas.) "At Malevil it so happens that we are very lucky from that point of view. I don't think I'm wrong when I say that the affection we feel for one another is such that no one here would want to survive if it meant surviving without the others. So this is what I ask of God, that when the victory has been won, we shall all meet here again, safe and sound, in Malevil."

I consecrated the bread and wine. After I had drunk and eaten, the glass and plate were passed around the table. It was done in profound silence. For my own part, I was only too well aware of the vast disparity between the words I had just uttered and the intense emotion I was feeling. Nevertheless, it seemed to me that somehow or other that emotion had succeeded in spreading to all of them. I could tell from the weight in the others' glances, the slowness of their gestures. In my speech I had laid the stress mainly on the future of mankind, so that even atheists as entrenched as Meyssonnier and Thomas could participate in the common hope. After all, it's not necessary to believe in God to have a sense of divinity in the world. In Malevil divinity might also be defined in terms of the bonds between man and man. Meyssonnier blinked furiously as he drank his share of the wine, and when I leaned toward him to ask what he thought of it all, he answered with his usual earnestness, "It's our vigil of arms."

I wouldn't have employed the expression myself. I'd have found it too melodramatic, but it was accurate. A trained priest would have spoken of "recollection." A little tarnished by overuse, but a good word still. You could almost see it happening. After being scattered, fragmented by our usual multifarious concerns, we were all returning into ourselves, collecting ourselves together into a still whole. Catie, for example, usually so lively and irrepressible; for once she wasn't thinking of what she could get out of her body and out of others' bodies. She was thinking, period. And since she wasn't used to it, she was looking rather tired.

There was great seriousness around our table, and concern for others. Courage too. First and foremost the courage to remain silent, and to look our guest that evening in the face. No one had any wish to name him, but he was there.

Thomas, who had looked quite normal while telling his story, had now gone rather pale. Killing Bébelle had shaken him. And perhaps he was also thinking that if the knife had been just that little bit closer, only an inch or so, then he would not have been here now, seated at this table around which we were all gathered, so fragile, so mortal, with no strength other than in our friendship.

As soon as La Menou had taken communion I sent her to fetch Jacquet in from the ramparts. She was surprised, since there could be no question of her relieving him, but she obeyed. As soon as she'd left I asked Thomas, who happened to be holding the plate at that moment, to take an extra piece of bread. I also asked him to go out and replace Jacquet when he appeared.

When communion was finished, we decided that apart from the noncombatants—La Falvine, Evelyne, and La Menou—who would go and sleep upstairs in the house, we would all stay in the gate tower that night. There were five beds, and we needed no more, since Colin and Peyssou were about to leave—in pitch darkness—to take up their post in the dugout, and I had decided there was nothing to be gained by having more than one sentinel up on the wall. Evelyne found it a bitter pill to swallow, being separated from me, but she obeyed without a word.

This double departure—of the two men out to the dugout and the three noncombatants up to the house—was carried out swiftly, efficiently, with a minimum of noise. As soon as there were just the five of us left—Miette, Catie, Jacquet, Meyssonnier, and myself, Thomas being already up on the ramparts—I wrote down the watch roster on a piece of paper and placed it under the base of the lamp, after having turned down the flame. I had put myself down for the four o'clock watch and also requested that the person coming off duty from each watch should wake me up. This obligation was going to be unpleasant for me, but I was counting on it keeping my sentinels awake. I had asked Jacquet to bring me down a mattress, and I lay down in one corner of the kitchen. The four others went up to their various beds on the upper floors, each keeping his or her weapon at the head of the bed and sleeping fully clothed.

As for myself, I slept very little that night, or thought I slept very little, which comes to much the same thing. I had more Bébelle-type dreams. I was defending myself against attackers with the butt of my rifle, but it just passed right through their skulls without hurting them. In the course of my waking moments, during which I had the feeling that I was getting more rest than when I was asleep, at first anyway, sudden serious omissions sprang into my mind. In the event of a general alert, I hadn't assigned the others specific places on the walls and gate-tower battlements. Or defined our objectives.

Another problem I hadn't thought of: some method of communication between the dugout and the ramparts. It was absolutely essential that anyone in the dugout perceiving an enemy approaching the palisade should be able to warn us with a signal that the attackers would not notice. That way we would gain precious seconds in placing our forces.

I nagged away at this problem during the second watch but didn't find any solution. I knew it was the second watch, because Miette had woken me up, according to

477

orders, then Meyssonnier at the end of his stint, and the whole of that time I was constructing absurd contraptions of wire sliding through rings to join the dugout to the ramparts. I must have dozed too, and even dreamed, because the absurdities proliferated. There was one point at which I realized with joyful relief that the answer was a flashlight.

I must have gone off into a deeper sleep eventually though, because I started violently when Catie shook me by the shoulders and told me in a low voice that it was my turn on duty, nibbling a little at my ear as she whispered into it.

Catie had left one of the panels in the battlements propped open, and someone, Meyssonnier perhaps, had brought up one of our little benches. A happy idea, because the opening was too low to keep watch through it comfortably other than seated. I took several deep breaths. The air was deliciously fresh, and after my troubled night I felt a rather amazing sensation of youth and strength. I was certain Vilmain was going to attack. We had killed his Bébelle, he would want to punish us. But I wasn't so sure that he was going to attack without making a last attempt to find out what he would have to face when he did. Since he now knew, from Hervé, of the existence of the palisade, he must be asking himself, and not without anxiety, what lay behind it. If I had grasped the workings of his army-conditioned mind rightly, then his honor was ordering him to avenge Bébelle, while at the same time his professional training would not allow him to attack blind.

The darkness was slow to pale, and I could still only just distinguish the presence of the palisade forty yards in front of me, especially since the ancient planks of which it was made tended to melt into the surroundings. The strain on one's eyes in bad visibility is very tiring, and several times I found myself rubbing my eyelids with my left hand and screwing up my face in an attempt to ease it.

Since I kept tending to doze off, I got to my feet, paced to and fro a little, and recited all the La Fontaine fables I could remember in a low voice. I yawned. I sat down again. A flash of lightning lit up the sky over toward Les Sept Fayards. I was surprised, because there was no hint of thunder in the air, and it took me two or three seconds to realize that Peyssou and Colin had signaled to me from the dugout with their flashlight. At the same instant the palisade bell rang twice.

I stood up, heart battering against my ribs, temples thudding, palms damp. Ought I to go? Was it a trick? One of Vilmain's traps? Was he going to fire his bazooka into the palisade the moment I opened the Judas?

Meyssonnier appeared at the door of the gate tower, gun in hand. He looked at me, and that look, asking me for action, restored all my presence of mind. I said in a quiet voice, "Is everyone awake?"

"Yes."

"Call them out."

But there was no need. I saw that they were all already there, brought down by the bell, guns in hand. I was pleased by their silence, their calm, the swiftness of their reactions. In a very low voice, I said, "Miette and Catie at the two tower slits. Meyssonnier, Thomas, Jacquet, on the wall, behind the merlons. Meyssonnier in command. No fire without his signal. Jacquet, open the gate for me and close it when I'm through."

"You're going alone?" Meyssonnier asked.

"Yes," I said, very curt.

He said nothing more. I helped Jacquet unbolt one side of the gate as quietly as possible. Meyssonnier touched my shoulder. In the half light he handed me something. It was the key to the cat-door padlock. He looked at me. If he had dared, he would have suggested going in my place.

"Gently, Jacquet."

Despite all the oil in the world, the gate hinges always squeaked as soon as either half of the gate was opened more than forty-five degrees. I pulled it open gently until the opening was just wide enough for me to slip through with my belly pulled in.

Although the night air was cool, the sweat was running down my cheeks. I crossed the bridge, made my way between the moat and the new wall, then stopped to pull off my half boots. I crossed the remaining distance to the palisade slowly, treading carefully in my stockinged feet and trying to keep my breathing quieter and quieter as I got nearer to my goal. At the last moment, instead of opening the Judas, I held my breath and glanced through the tiny spyhole that Colin had fitted beside it. It was Hervé, with another, shorter young fellow beside him. No one else. I opened the Judas. "Hervé?"

"Yes, it's me."

"Who's with you?"

"Maurice."

"Right. Listen to me. I'm going to open the little sliding door. Pass your guns through first. Then Hervé will come in alone. I repeat, alone. Maurice will wait there."

"We understand," Hervé said.

I removed the padlock, slid the cat door up, and hooked it in position. The two rifles appeared. I said tersely, "Further in, the rifles. Barrels first. Put them in."

They obeyed, and I let the door slide down again. I opened both breeches. No bullets in either or in the magazines. I leaned them both against the palisade. Then I unslung the Springfield from my shoulder. That done, I let Hervé in, closed the cat door behind him, led him to the main gate, and not until it had closed behind him did I return to fetch his companion.

Before that morning I hadn't envisaged precisely how we ought to use the ADZ. Now I realized that it worked perfectly as a kind of air lock. It enabled us to admit visitors one by one, after making sure they were disarmed. Once back in the gate tower, I took the sheet of paper on which I had made out the watch list for the previous night, and on the back, in pencil, even before questioning Hervé again, I wrote down the new orders that I had worked out in my head.

While I was still writing, La Menou, La Falvine, and Evelyne appeared. The first promptly set about reviving the fire and sharply ordered the second, who looked anxious to stay, to go and do the milking. As for Evelyne, she stood glued against my side, and when I didn't send her away she took my left arm and pulled it around her waist, clutching my hand firmly by the thumb. She stayed there absolutely quiet and still, watching me write, fearing that she would lose her advantage if she tried to push it any further. Hesitating over a word, I lifted my eyes from the paper and noticed our visitors watching Miette and Catie with interest. An interest that was certainly reciprocated, as a glance at Catie made clear. She was standing in a very martial pose, left hand holding the barrel of her gun with its butt on the floor, right thumb hooked into her cartridge belt, pelvis thrown forward and to one side, eyes fixed on Hervé in a brazenly appreciative stare.

We were still by no means all present and correct, since Peyssou and Colin were still on guard in the dugout and Jacquet was up on the ramparts. Thomas, I noticed, was sitting at the far end of the table and not looking at Catie. Meyssonnier, standing behind me, was reading over my shoulder what I wrote, thus making it clear to everyone that he wasn't my second in command for nothing.

As soon as I had finished my writing, La Menou blew out the lamp and I began questioning Hervé.

He had some interesting things to tell us. The previous evening, Bébelle had not come alone to reconnoiter Malevil. There had been another veteran with him. And both had set out from La Roque on bicycles. But Bébelle had hidden his beside the road two hundred yards short of the castle, then ordered the veteran not to intervene whatever happened. The veteran lay low, heard the shot, saw Bébelle fall, and went straight back to La Roque. Vilmain immediately announced that since Malevil had "knocked out" two of his best men he was going "to wipe out" Malevil as a reprisal. But beforehand, "to strengthen his rear" and perhaps also in order to counteract any feeling of failure, he ordered a night attack on Courcejac: six men under the command of the Feyrac brothers. Unfortunately, that morning, the veteran who had reconnoitered Courcejac with Maurice had stolen two hens. The Courcejac men were keeping a watch, and as soon as the group of attackers appeared they opened fire and killed Daniel Feyrac. Jean Feyrac, insane with rage, ordered an all-out onslaught and massacred them all.

"What does that mean, 'all'?"

"The two young brothers, a couple of old men, the wife, and the baby."

A silence. We looked at one another.

After a moment I said, "And what did Vilmain have to say about their exploits?"

" 'Reprisal. Good military practice. They knock out one of your men. You wipe out the village.' "

Another silence. I signaled Hervé to go on. He coughed to make sure his voice didn't crack. "After Courcejac, Vilmain wanted to attack Malevil right away. But the veterans didn't agree. Jean Feyrac was on their side: 'We can't just go attacking Malevil bullheaded like that. It's got to be reconnoitered first.' "

"Jean Feyrac said that?"

"Yes, it was Feyrac."

I was sick with disgust. "Wipe out a village," yes, when it was easy game. But Malevil, that was different. Malevil made these gallant fellows think twice. And the proof was that when Vilmain again asked for volunteers, not one of the veterans came forward. So Hervé and Maurice had little difficulty getting the detail.

"What did Vilmain say?"

" 'If these little assholes succeed, they get promoted to veterans. If they buy it, we go in, is that understood, you men?' "

"And the veterans?"

"Pretty lukewarm."

"All the same, if Vilmain gives the order to go in, they'll go in?"

"Yes. They're still afraid of Vilmain."

"Why 'still'?"

"Well, let's say they're less afraid of him since last night."

"Since Bébelle was killed?"

"Bébelle and Daniel Feyrac as well. That's quite a slice of the hard core gone. At least that's how I see things."

And he saw them clearly, I suspected. I went on: "If Vilmain were killed, would there be anyone to replace him?"

"Jean Feyrac."

"And if Feyrac were killed?"

"No one."

"It would all fall apart?"

"Yes, I think so."

Breakfast was ready. The bowls steamed on the polished walnut. What a peaceful domestic picture, and only a few miles away, lying in a farmyard, those six corpses, one of them very tiny. We were chilled and stupefied by our horror. What a terrible prestige cruelty must have in men's eyes for them to pay it the tribute of such sentiments! Contempt would suffice. And what struck me even more than the sadism of their massacre was its stupidity. Men savagely intent on the annihilation of human life, destroying themselves in destroying their own species.

I drew my bowl toward me. I didn't want to think about Courcejac any more. I needed to concentrate my thoughts on the battle ahead. We ate in silence, a silence disturbed only by the irrepressible chattering of La Falvine, back from her milking. It's true she hadn't heard the story of the butchery at Courcejac, so she could not know what was going on in all our minds. But that morning, in any case, it was worse than ever before. On her good days La Menou compared this Falvinian chatter to a mill, to a waterfall, to a power saw; and on her bad days to diarrhea. After what we had heard, minds full of that little farm we most of us knew well, we ate on in silence. And La Falvine's infinite gush of verbiage, addressed to no one in particular, was multiplied by the silence and doubly unstoppable because no one could or would answer her. It was a noise entirely external to the community, like a trickle of water falling from a roof onto cobbles, or the builder's concrete mixer in Malejac, in the days before, or the ribbon saw of a sawmill. Although this verbal flux was composed of words, some French, some patois, there was ultimately no human content in it. It was the opposite of communication, because it wasn't flowing in answer to some expectation, because all our ears rejected it, and because it kept streaming out for no reason, for nothing, unwanted by any of those present.

In the end, perhaps tired by the night just past, and already tensing at the thought of the one to come, I said, at the risk of putting fresh weapons into La Menou's

483

hands, "For goodness' sake, Falvine, keep quiet! You're stopping me thinking!"

That was all it needed! The tears now! One way or another something had to flow! And if only the tears had flowed in silence. But no! Now all we could hear were sobs, sighs, sniffs, nose blowings! I couldn't see her because I had my back to her. But I could certainly hear her. And the whining and whuffling going on now was even more intolerable than her interminable chatter. On top of which, I was now being treated to a constant muttering from La Menou, and although I couldn't make out the actual words, no doubt La Falvine could, and they were undoubtedly acid in her wound, if I knew La Menou.

If this went on, Catie would intervene. Not that she exactly adored her grandmother. She too pecked at her on occasion. But after all, she was her grandmother. Blood ties had to be respected, she couldn't let her be plucked before her eyes without a few retaliatory blows of claw and beak to rescue her. And she enjoyed it anyway. She was quick and vicious. And she knew where to aim. I must have been mad, throwing my pebble in the hen run like that! The cackling, the flying feathers, the battering wings, the blood spurting! And to think all I wanted was just a little silence! Thank you, Miette, for being dumb. And thank you, too, little Evelyne, for still being enough afraid of me (it won't last long) to hold your tongue when I hurl my thunderbolts.

First things first. I nipped Catie's imminent counterattack in the bud. "Catie, have you finished your breakfast?"

"Yes."

"And you, Falvine?"

"Well, yes, as you see, Emmanuel, I've finished," One word wasn't enough for her, unlike Catie. She had to use eight.

"All right then. You'd both of you better go and clean out the stables. Jacquet won't be able to do it this morning."

Catie obeyed immediately. She was on her feet in a flash. She was keeping her promise: a real little soldier.

"And the dishes?" La Falvine said, very conscientious and determined that all should know it.

"La Menou can do them with Miette."

"And me," Evelyne said.

"It's just that there are such a lot this morning," La Falvine said, feigning hesitation.

"Go, can't you!" La Menou flared. "I can certainly manage to do a few dishes without you!"

"Are you coming, Grandma?" Catie said, equally irritated.

And Catie was out of the door, slim and swift as an arrow, dragging behind her that vast dumpling, rolling and yawing on its gigantic legs.

So at the price of a stint over the sink, La Menou was left mistress of the field. But it was a price she was only too glad to pay. As she let it be known unequivocally in a last bout of furious muttering, gauged carefully both as to duration and volume so that it made her point without actually driving me to some retaliatory remark that would destroy her advantage. And at last, even that sank by degrees into inaudibility, then silence. I could think again.

The battle was no longer so unequal. Vilmain had lost three veterans, and two of his recruits had defected. His seventeen men of two days ago were now reduced to twelve. And on my side, with Hervé and Maurice, I now had ten combatant personnel. Moreover my arsenal had been enriched by the addition of three .36 rifles.

If I was to believe Hervé, Vilmain's authority had been shaken. With the three recent casualties, the morale of his troops was low. It would sink even lower with the defection of Maurice and Hervé, who would also be assumed killed in action.

So I had three problems confronting me:

1. To fix upon a disposition of my forces that would enable me to exploit the advantages of the terrain to the full.

2. To devise some stratagem to accelerate, if possible, the adversary's process of demoralization.

3. To ensure, if he withdrew from the battle, that whatever happened he was prevented from regaining the

safety of La Roque and pursuing a guerrilla war against us.

And of the three, it was the last that seemed to me of paramount importance.

There had been a continual coming and going in the gate-tower kitchen since I had sent La Falvine and Catie off to the stables. Thomas had left to take up his post of yesterday, keeping watch on the La Roque road, and Jacquet had come in to eat. Meyssonnier had gone to check up on Peyssou and Colin, then he came back with them before setting out with Hervé to bury Bébelle.

I was only waiting for Hervé's departure to question Maurice. I wanted him out of the way because I needed to check that his friend's story corroborated his own.

Maurice was Eurasian. Although I would say he wasn't more than an inch taller than Colin, he appeared much taller because he was so slim, with narrow hips and buttocks no bigger than two clenched fists. On the other hand, his shoulders were relatively wide (even though the bones were delicate), which gave him the elegant outline of an Egyptian bas-relief. His skin was amber. His hair deep black, falling in a stiff fringe all around his head in a Joan of Arc style and framing a delicate, serious face, animated every now and then by a smile of unshakable politeness. And polite he was, polite to the tips of his fingernails. You got the impression that even if he were to do his absolute damnedest, he could never succeed in being coarse or rude.

He explained to me that he was the son of a Frenchman married to an Indochinese wife from Sainte-Livrade in the Lot-et-Garonne. His father ran a small business outside Fumel, and Hervé had come to visit with them for a few days at Easter when the bomb exploded. Apart from that, his story corroborated Hervé's on absolutely every point, despite all my efforts to catch him out. The only difference was that Maurice seemed to have a much more vivid memory of his friend René's death and to harbor a more savage hatred of Vilmain. Not that he expressed that hatred in words. But when he described René's murder, his jet-black pupils suddenly hardened, and the slanting eyes narrowed dangerously. Like Hervé he made a good impression on me. Better even. Hervé talked well and easily, he had the natural actor's gifts and verve. Maurice, without being so impressive at first sight, was a man of finer mettle in the end.

I turned to Peyssou. "Peyssou, when you've finished eating I have a job for you."

"I'm listening."

"We have some iron rings in the store. I'd like you to cement them into the cellar wall with Maurice's help. I want to tether the bull, the cows, and Bel Amour down there during the fight. I'd also like you to construct a temporary sty down there for Adelaide."

"Only Bel Amour?" Peyssou said. "What about the other nags?"

"They can stay in the Maternity Ward, we may need them. When you've finished, tell me, and we'll all help to carry a stock of hay from the Maternity Ward up to the cellar."

Nose stuck in his bowl, eyes only just visible above its brim, Peyssou gazed across at me with an anxious look. "You think we're going to lose the outer enclosure?"

"I don't think anything of the kind. I am simply taking precautions." I stood up. "Menou, can you leave your dishes a moment and come with me?"

Pausing only to take the dish towel from Miette and wipe her sinewy little arms, she followed me immediately. I towed her along in my wake (with her taking two steps to every one of mine) as far as the inner wall, then I led the way up to the machinery room above the drawbridge.

"Do you think, in case of emergency, you could manage this alone, Menou? Or would you prefer to have La Falvine help you?"

"I don't need that great tub of lard," Menou said.

I showed her what to do. And after two or three practice runs, arching her thin little body and gritting her teeth, she was able to maneuver the capstan arms perfectly. It was the first time I'd had the winch working since that day just before Easter when we had discussed the 1977 local elections with Monsieur Paulat. The muffled grating of the huge oiled chains took me back with extraordinary vividness to that time past. Forget it. No time for reminiscences and sad thoughts.

I advised La Menou to hold the capstan arms back more when she lowered the drawbridge again. It must sink onto the stone edging of the moat gently in order to avoid any damage. Through the little square window of the machinery room, I saw Peyssou and Colin appear at the gate-tower door and look up in our direction. The sound of the chains must have been reviving memories in their minds too.

"This is your battle station, Menou. As soon as things begin to get hot, you come up here and you wait. If things go badly and we have to withdraw into the inner enclosure, you wind up the bridge. Do you want to try it once more? Will you remember?"

"I'm not an idiot," La Menou said. And suddenly her eyes filled with tears.

I was shaken, because she didn't cry easily. "Come on now, Menou."

"Leave me be," she said through clenched teeth.

She wasn't looking at me, she was staring straight ahead of her, very upright, head held high, not moving. The tears ran down her tanned face (only her forehead was white, because in summer she protected her head with a big straw hat). With her two hands gripping the bars of the capstan, standing so tense, she looked as though she was steering a ship through a sudden squall. It was Momo who had worked the winch that day, the day of Paulat's visit. He had been wild with excitement, dancing with joy. I could see him still, and she could see him too. She wept, jaw clenched, not loosening her grip on the bars. She didn't give way to her grief. She wasn't going to feel sorry for herself. It was just a bad moment, that was all. She would have steered her ship through in a second or two, the squall would be over. I turned away so as to save her embarrassment and looked out the window. But out of the corner of one eye I was still aware of that in-domitable little figure, head high, weeping with wide open eyes in total silence. Then I caught sight of her reflection in the glass of the open window, and what drew my eyes above all were those tiny fists, clenched with

488

such determination around the capstan arms, as though, little by little, she was reaffirming her grip on life.

I left her there. It was what she wanted, I think. I strode quickly over to the keep and up to my room. I sat down at my desk, and there in the drawer, which I hadn't really looked in much for a long while now, I found what I was looking for: two felt-tipped pens, one black and the other red. I also found something I wasn't looking for: the big policeman's whistle that I had given to Peyssou once, in a moment of insane generosity, one day when we had all laid into him to cure him of the idea that he ought to be our Club leader. Why did I still have it then? Because the next day, taking advantage of Peyssou's good nature, I persuaded him to sell it back to me for a good price. Even now it was with pleasure that I sat turning it around in my fingers. It was still as magical as ever in my eyes. Its chrome had stood up to the years, and the piercing scream it emitted could be heard at a really amazing distance. I slipped it into the pocket of my shirt. Then sacrificing a quarter of a large sheet of drawing paper, I got down to work.

I had been at it for barely five minutes when there was a knock at the door. It was Catie.

"Sit down, Catie," I said without raising my head.

My table was set obliquely out from the wall facing the window, and Catie had to walk around it in order to sit opposite me, with her back to the light. As she passed, she let her left hand drag absent-mindedly across the back of my neck. At the same time she glanced down at what I was doing. I tried to conceal the effect her presence was having on me. But she wasn't taken in. She sat down, slumped back in the chair, stomach stuck out, staring at me insistently through half-closed eyes, a half smile on her lips.

"Are the stables finished then, Catie?"

"Yes, and I've even had time for a shower."

Not an idle remark, I felt sure. But I kept my eyes lowered over my paper. The best listener isn't always the most attentive. "Did you want to speak to me?" I asked after a moment.

"Of course," she said with a sigh.

"What about?"

"About Vilmain. I have an idea. You said if we have any ideas we're to come and tell you."

"Quite right."

"Well then. I've had an idea," she said modestly.

"I'm listening," I said, eyes still intent on my task. Silence.

"I don't want to disturb you," she said. "Especially when you seem to be working so hard. And honestly! How nicely you write!" she said, screwing her head around, trying to read the big letters I was printing with my felt pen. "What are you doing, Emmanuel? Is it a poster?"

"A proclamation for Vilmain and his band."

"And what does it say, your proclamation?"

"Some very unpleasant things as far as Vilmain is concerned, and some much less unpleasant things for his men. If you like, I'm trying to exploit the band's low morale and drive a wedge between them and their leader."

"And will it work, do you think?"

"If things go badly for them, yes. Otherwise no. But in any case, it will only have cost me a sheet of paper."

There was a knock on the door behind me. I shouted, "Come in," without turning around and carried on with my printing. I noticed that Catie had pulled her tummy in and was sitting up straight, and since the silence remained unbroken, I swiveled around to look and see who my visitor was. It was Evelyne.

I frowned. "What are you doing up here?"

"Meyssonnier has come back from burying Bébelle, so I've come to tell you."

"Did Meyssonnier ask you to?"

"No."

"Didn't you volunteer to help with the dishes?"

"Yes."

"And are they finished?"

"No."

"Then go back and help till they are. Once you've begun something you don't just drop it to follow the first fancy that comes into your head."

"All right," she said, not budging an inch, her great blue eyes fixed on mine.

Ordinarily, this refusal to move would have earned her a sharp reprimand. But I wasn't going to humiliate her in front of Catie.

"Well?" I said, more with a smile than a frown.

Her determination melted suddenly at that. "I'll go back," she said, on the verge of tears as she closed the door behind her.

"Evelyne!"

She reappeared.

"Tell Meyssonnier I need him up here. Immediately."

She threw me a luminous smile and closed the door again. Three birds with that particular stone: I really needed to talk to Meyssonnier; I had reassured Evelyne; and it meant I could politely get rid of Catie—whose proximity was not without peril. It's true that my dominant emotion, a very urgent one, was certainly not fear; but I needed to keep my head. Some things were still more urgent than others.

Catie had returned to her provocatively slouching pose. Not that I raised my eyes to look at her, or at least not as far as her face. I had returned to my task. Luckily, all I needed to do now was copy my proclamation out, since I had already prepared a draft of the text on a piece of scrap paper. Catie let out a little chuckle.

"You saw how quickly she got here! She's crazy about you!"

"It's reciprocal," I said curtly, glancing up at her.

She gazed at me with an exasperating smile on her face. "In that case," she said, "I don't see what—"

"In that case, why don't you tell me your idea?"

She sighed, she wriggled on her chair, she scratched her calf. In short, she was very disappointed at having to abandon the fascinating subject of my relations with Evelyne.

"All right," she said, "it's just this. Vilmain attacks. As you say, he draws a blank." (God knows why, but there she laughed.) "He goes back to La Roque, he starts guerrilla tactics against us, and you don't fancy that."

491

"Don't fancy it!" I said. "It would be a catastrophe. He can do us a great deal of damage."

"Well, then," she said, "when he goes away, we must stop him getting back to La Roque. We must go after him."

"He'll have a hell of a start though."

She looked at me with an air of triumph. "Yes, but we have our horses!"

I was staggered. It wasn't just an excuse; she had really had an idea! And one that I hadn't had, even though I had spent my whole life with horses. War and horsemanship had just never been connected in my mind. No, that's not quite true. I had linked them once, just once, when I was trying to persuade the assembly to barter our cow for Fulbert's two mares. But that had been an argument thought up to win a debate, nothing more. It was our one enormous advantage over Vilmain: our cavalry. And I hadn't been going to use it!

I straightened up on my chair. "Catie, you're a genius!"

She blushed, and from the sudden joy that flooded through her, making her look like a happy child with half-open lips and shining eyes, I could see how painful it must have been for her to endure my underestimation of her before.

I pondered a moment. I didn't tell her that her idea needed elaborating somewhat, because we couldn't just rush out and follow Vilmain along the road hell for leather. The horses' hoofs would make a terrific noise on the metaled surface. Vilmain and company would certainly hear us. They would wait for us at a bend, and what targets we'd make for them!

"Bravo!" I said. "Bravo for Catie. I'll think that one over. And meanwhile, not a word about it to anyone."

"Of course not," she said with a proud look. And carried away by the unaccustomed weight of her virtues, she even added discretion to them. "Well now," she said, "I must go. I can see you're busy. I'll leave you alone."

I stood up, somewhat incautiously, since once around the corner of the desk she hurled herself on my neck and coiled herself around me. Peyssou was right; she wriggled.

There was a knock on the door, and I called out,

"Come in," without thinking. It was Meyssonnier. Oddly enough, he was the one who blushed and began blinking. Though I was certainly very sad to be the cause of his embarrassment and shock.

The door slammed behind Catie, and Meyssonnier permitted himself not the slightest reaction, neither the "Well, well" that Peyssou would have growled out in similar circumstances nor the wicked smile Colin would certainly have flashed.

"Sit down," I said. "I won't be a moment."

He sat down on the chair, still warm from Catie's behind. But he sat four square on it, upright, in silence, not moving a muscle. It was very restful sometimes, a man's company. And I certainly finished my poster much quicker and much more efficiently than I'd begun it.

"There you are," I said, handing it over to him. "What do you think?"

He read it out loud:

"DOMAIN OF MALEVIL AND LA ROQUE

The criminals whose names appear below have been condemned to death:

VILMAIN, outlaw and ringleader.

JEAN FEYRAC, murderer of Courcejac.

For the rest, if they lay down their arms as soon as they are required to do so, we shall restrict their punishment to banishment from our territories with a week's provision of food.

Emmanuel Comte
Abbé of Malevil"

Having read it out loud, Meyssonnier then read it again to himself. I watched his long face, the long furrows running down his cheeks. The word "conscience" was written in all his features. He had been a good militant for his party, but he would have made an equally good priest or doctor. And with his passion for public service and his attention to detail, an extremely good administrator. What a pity he had never got to be mayor of Malejac! I was sure that even now he sometimes still regretted that.

"What do you think?"

"Psychological warfare," he said soberly.

That was the statement of fact. The evaluation would

come in good time. He fell to pondering again. Ah, well, I knew he was slow. And I was also sure that the result of his ruminations would be worth the wait.

"But in my opinion," he said, "it will only work if Vilmain and Feyrac are killed. In that case, obviously, since they won't have anyone in command any more, the others may prefer saving their skins to going on with the fight."

Earlier, I'd said to Catie, "If things go badly for them." Meyssonnier, typically, was much more precise about it: "If Vilmain and Feyrac are killed." He was quite right too. The distinction was important. I must remember it when I gave my firing orders just before the battle.

I stood up. "That's it then. So can you find me a piece of plywood, stick that onto it for me, and drill two holes in the top corners?"

"No difficulty there," Meyssonnier said as he rose in his turn. He walked around my desk, still holding the proclamation, and stopped as he was about to pass me. "I wanted to ask you. Do you still want us to use only the arrow slits in the merlons?"

"Yes. Why?"

"There are only five. With the two up on the tower itself that makes seven. And there are ten of us now."

I looked at him. "So what do you conclude?"

"That we must have three men outside instead of two. I thought it worth mentioning now because the dugout is too small for three."

First Catie, now Meyssonnier! All Malevil was pondering, searching, inventing. All intent on a single goal. I had the sensation at that moment of being part of a whole that I was commanding and yet to which I was at the same time subordinated, a whole of which I myself was only one part, one cog, and which was thinking and acting of its own volition, like a single being. It was a heady sensation that I had never experienced during my existence "before," in which everything I did was reduced to the paltry dimensions of my own ego.

"You look pleased about something," Meyssonnier said.

"I am. I was just thinking that it's really working quite well, Malevil." The words, even as I spoke them, seemed

494

to me ludicrously inadequate in relation to what I was feeling.

"All the same," Meyssonnier said, "don't you have a few butterflies in your belly now and again?"

I laughed. "You bet I do!"

He laughed as well, then said, "You know what it reminds me of? The night before the state exams!"

I laughed again and walked out with him as far as the spiral staircase, my hand resting on his shoulder. When he had gone, I went back to collect my Springfield and close the door.

In the outer enclosure Colin, Jacquet, and Hervé were waiting for me, the last two still holding their shovels. Colin, empty-handed, was a little apart from them. Standing too near such giants must have been slightly oppressive for someone so small.

"Hang on to your shovels," I said. "I've more work for you. But we must wait for Meyssonnier."

Catie emerged from the Maternity Ward at the sound of my voice, currycomb in one hand, brush in the other. I knew what she was doing: taking advantage of the fact that Amarante's bedding was fresh to clean her off. Because Amarante had a passion for rolling, whether her stall was full of droppings or not. La Falvine was sitting on a big block of wood conveniently placed near the entrance to the cave, and she stood up guiltily when she saw me.

"Don't get up, Falvine," I said. "Go on, sit down again. You've earned a rest."

"No, no," she said in an ostentatiously self-righteous tone that immediately irritated me. "You don't think I've got time to sit around!" So she remained standing, but without doing a jot more work than when she had been sitting. But at least she was keeping quiet. My sharp words earlier were still having an effect.

La Falvine's behavior had irritated Catie too. Particularly, I imagined, since she would undoubtedly have been obliged to do most of the mucking out very much on her own. Sensing that she was about to start a pecking match with her grandmother, I intervened. "Have you finished with Amarante?"

"Yes, and none too soon for my liking! Whoo! the dung dust I've swallowed! A real waste of time it was taking a shower! And do you think it's easy grooming horses with a gun slung around you?" (She called our attention to the gun sling by pushing out her chest and laughing as she did so.) "And that idiot mare, with nothing in her head but killing our hens! Yes, and that reminds me, she's just polished off another! Oh, I gave her a thump on her nose, your precious Amarante, and she'll remember it a long while."

I asked to see the victim. Luckily it was one of the older hens. I handed it to La Falvine. "Here, Falvine," I said. "You'd better pluck and clean it now. Then take it in to La Menou."

La Falvine took it from me, delighted at the task I'd given her. A nice comfortable sitting job, just her line.

So there we were. Waiting for Meyssonnier. Life at Malevil went on. Jacquet, arms hanging by his side, amazed at finding himself idle, gazed at me with his good-natured, pleading eyes, as moist with affection as any dog's. Hervé, elegantly poised with his weight on one foot, rubbed his seductive little pointed beard and looked at Catie, who was not returning the look but nevertheless calling attention to her charms—partly for his benefit, partly for mine—by moving various parts of her anatomy this way and that with no conceivable utilitarian end in view. Colin, leaning against the wall, was observing the scene from a distance, with one of his gondola smiles on his face. And La Falvine was now seated again, the hen on her lap. She hadn't actually begun to pluck it yet, but she would get around to it; she was gathering her strength.

"The fact is," Catie said, without discontinuing her undulations, "your Amarante has every vice under the sun. She kicks, she rolls in her droppings, and she kills chickens."

"It may be a matter of secondary consideration to you, Catie, but Amarante is also a very good horse."

"Oh, I know. You adore her!" she said impudently. "Her too!" She laughed. "All the same, it would be a good idea if you put a little piece of wire netting along the bottom of her door. What's the point of having eight men about the house if we can't find one to do a little thing like that for us!" She laughed again, and shot Hervé a glance out of the corner of her eye.

I left the group, strode quickly up toward the store in the keep, found a roll of wire and a pair of pincers, entered them on Thomas's withdrawal slate, and all the time, as I went through these mechanical gestures, I was thinking back over Catie's suggestion for using our cavalry, over Meyssonnier's invaluable observation about the number of arrow slits, and suddenly I realized something. What we were in the process of doing in Malevil, and quickly, very quickly, since speed was the precondition of our survival now, was learning the art of war. The evidence was blindingly obvious. There was no longer any state to guard us. There was no order but our guns. And not only our guns, our wiles. We who at Easter, not so long ago, had no other concern but to win the Malejac local elections, were now in the process of inculcating in ourselves, one by one, the implacable laws of primitive warrior tribes.

As I emerged from the store I met Meyssonnier carrying my proclamation. I took it from him. It was perfect. A work of art even. He had left a border of plywood all around the sheet of drawing paper. As I walked back down with him into the outer enclosure, I read it through again. I felt those butterflies in my stomach again suddenly. It wasn't important. It would pass.

As we reached the little group, Catie asked me what was on the little board, and I held it up so that they could all read it. Colin too came over.

"What? Are you an abbé . . . father?" Hervé said, amazed and rather embarrassed. His sudden and belated respect raised smiles from the others.

"I have been elected Abbé of Malevil," I said, "but I'd rather you went on calling me Emmanuel."

"Well you were right to put it on your notice anyway," Hervé said, quickly recovering his aplomb, "because there are some of Vilmain's men that will worry badly. And you were right as well to call Vilmain 'outlaw' like that. Because the way he talks, you'd almost think his extortions were somehow legal, just because of his army rank."

I was pleased to hear both these observations. They confirmed what I'd already been thinking, that in the anarchic times we were now living in, brute strength wasn't in fact all that mattered. Contrary to what one might have expected, a rank, a title, a function, they all still counted. In the general chaos, men were clinging to any straw from the vanished order they could find. Even the tiniest semblance of legality hypnotized them. So I had dealt Vilmain an appreciable blow by ripping off his officer's insignia— on paper at least.

"Catie, you will have to let us all out of the cat door. And you will stay down near the gate tower all the time we're outside. You, Falvine, go up and tell Peyssou that all five of us are going outside. He's in the cellar with Maurice."

"Now?" La Falvine said, without getting up, the hen still completely intact on her lap.

"Now, now!" I told her. "Stir your stumps."

Catie laughed, and pivoting her young bust arrogantly around, she watched her grandma trundling off, quivering like a vast jelly.

As soon as we were all outside on the road, I walked briskly on ahead with Meyssonnier and in a low voice gave him his instructions. He was to choose a good spot on the side of the next hill along from the Sept Fayards slope, with a good view of the palisade, and organize the digging of another dugout for our extra man outside.

He nodded. I left him there with Hervé and Jacquet while Colin and I carried on till we found the forest track. Once off the road, I walked on ahead and told Colin to follow exactly in my footsteps. This was because when I came to the branches I had tied across the track I would be walking around them, through the undergrowth, in order not to break them.

They were all still there. Which meant that the enemy had still not found our short cut to La Roque. I had imagined he wouldn't for the reasons given earlier. But I was glad to have it confirmed.

That left the second stage of my mission. The last time

I had ridden over to La Roque along the road I had noticed a very narrow stretch between two hills, with two charred tree stumps exactly opposite each other on either side of the road. My intention now was to stretch the wire I'd brought along between the two stumps, then hang my anti-Vilmain proclamation from it in the middle of the road. Unfortunately, even using the short cut, it was a long way on foot. I could hear Colin laboring and panting behind me, and I suddenly remembered with a stab of remorse that he couldn't have had much sleep the night before out in the dugout. I turned around. "Are you done in?"

"Pretty well."

"Only another half hour. Can you make it? As soon as I've got my notice up we'll take a rest."

"Don't you worry about me," Colin said, screwing his forehead into a determined scowl and sticking out his lower jaw.

Although he was past forty, he still looked like a little boy to me when he pulled that kind of face. Though I took good care not to tell him so. He set great store by his virility, perhaps not in the same flamboyant style as our big Peyssou, but no less all the same, underneath.

It was very hot. I was sweating profusely. I opened my collar and rolled up my shirtsleeves. I paused and half turned from time to time in order to hold a long branch so that it wouldn't whip back into Colin's face. I noticed how pale he was, the eyes a little hollow, lips set in a grim line. I was relieved on his account when we reached our goal.

From the forest track down to the road the slope was quite a gentle one at first, but the last twenty yards or so were steep and rocky. Getting down wouldn't be any problem; if need be I could just slide down on my heels. But getting back up was going to be quite difficult. The terrain on the far side of the road was identical, which incidentally gave the road itself a rather oppressive feel at this spot. You could sense the two rocky bluffs pressing in as though trying to strangle it.

I shot down rather more quickly than I'd intended, and landed with a nasty thump on the road. I threaded the wire through the two holes in the plywood, twisted one end tight around one of the stumps, then stretched it across the road and made it fast to the other. I didn't stay down there a moment longer than necessary. Colin, though I couldn't see him, was lying concealed in the edge of the undergrowth just before the steep part of the incline, gun in front of him, covering me in the direction of La Roque. Which was a fair guarantee of safety if we had to deal with a single individual. But what about a group? I would be extremely vulnerable then, since I had nothing behind me but absolutely open ground, without a ditch or a bush till the nearest bend, or the alternative, if I wanted to regain the shelter of the undergrowth, of climbing sixty feet of very steep embankment in full view of my attackers.

I noted that with my rifle slung on my back—that is, not immediately usable—and using both hands, it was still only with the greatest difficulty, after repeated efforts, much slipping and stumbling, that I managed to get back up at all, and even then with extreme slowness.

When I did reach the top, Colin was so well camouflaged by the undergrowth that I couldn't see hide nor hair of him. He could see me, presumably, but didn't dare call out for fear of being heard by others. I heard an owl wail. I halted in amazement. Because ever since the day it happened the world had been so silent, no buzzing of insects, no cries of birds. The plaintive wail came again, very close. I walked toward it and stumbled over Colin's legs.

"Hey, watch it! That's me!" he said in a low voice.

"Did you hear the owl?"

"That was me," Colin said with a soundless laugh. "I was calling you."

And he pushed his safety catch back into place with a triumphant click.

"You? It was damned good, I must say! It fooled me."

"Don't you remember our imitations in the old days, in the Club? I was the best."

He was still proud of it, even after all that time. But it was true, Colin was always the best at things that didn't require strength: archery, catapult, marbles, conjuring tricks. And also, of course, juggling with three balls, cutting a flute from a reed, making a paper guillotine for flies, opening locks with a piece of wire, and climbing up onto the teacher's dais then simulating a spectacular fall.

I smiled at him. "Ten-minute break. Have a snooze."

"You know what I was thinking as I was covering you then, Emmanuel? That this little stretch of road is a dream of a place for an ambush. With four guns, two each side of the road, you could wipe out a whole battalion almost."

"Now then, I said get some sleep! You can do your strategic command stuff afterward!"

And in order that he might drop off quicker I moved away, though this time, so that I shouldn't lose him again, I left markers in the undergrowth as I went. I looked back at Colin before moving out of sight. He'd barely had time to lie back before he was out, two or three little bracken shoots crushed beneath his back, his gun cradled in his arms like a cherished mistress.

I looked at my watch. I walked to and fro. My half boots made no sound. The slope we were on faced south, and with the rain we'd been having the moss had covered everything. I was struck anew by the tropical luxuriance of the undergrowth. Though it was pretty unvaried. I got the impression that the bracken, with its overwhelming vitality, was in the process of taking over the world. The silence, the absence of life were oppressive. The smallest spider's web, the tiniest shining thread from one twig to another would have given me so much pleasure. But I was very much afraid, unless they began migrating in from less devastated regions, that we were never going to see any insects again. And what about the birds? Even supposing some had survived elsewhere, how could they live without any insects? The forest would be back more or less as before in less than twenty-five years, but nature would remain shorn of half her riches.

Surrounded like that by the stifling silence, in the damp of the undergrowth, without a breath of wind to stir the leaves, I began to feel very alone, and I went through a very nasty moment. It wasn't fear of the battle ahead.

Guts turning to jelly, hollow belly, thumping heart, I'm no stranger to all those, thank you very much. No, what I felt now was much worse. It was a different sort of dread. Colin lay asleep, and without him, without my companions, far from Malevil, I had the sensation that I was no longer anything at all. An empty, flapping garment.

This feeling of emptiness became so intolerable that I woke Colin up again. What selfishness. I woke him up a good five minutes before the time I'd set. He opened his eyes, stretched, spoke, and the first words he uttered were to bawl me out. It didn't matter, as soon as he began talking to me I was myself again. With my ties of affection, my responsibilities, the role my companions had assigned to me, and the character they recognized as mine. I was back in my skin again, and very relieved to have one too.

"You rotten bastard, you could have left me in peace!" Colin said in a low voice. "Oh, the dream I was having!"

He was burning to tell it to me, but I signaled to him to keep quiet. We were still too near to the road where we were. We walked deeper into the undergrowth, and by the time we were at last back on the track he had forgotten his dream, though not the preoccupation underlying it. Odd, that danger can't wholly manage to repress our everyday thoughts.

He looked at me, eyebrows quirked, a half smile on his face. "Is Catie running after you a little?"

"Yes."

"And after Peyssou?"

"Ah, so you've noticed."

"And Hervé?"

"Perhaps."

A silence.

"Well, well, there's a thing. And Thomas?"

"Thomas thinks that there are two women at Malevil for six men."

"And."

"He wonders whether he was very wise to marry Catie."

Another silence. Then Colin went on: "In your opinion, why are there so few women?"

"In the case of the wandering bands, it's obvious

enough. Either the leaders don't want to be lumbered with them, or else they've just been eliminated by a natural process. When there's almost nothing at all to eat, it's the strong who eat it."

"But with people like us?"

"You mean sedentary communities?"

"Yes."

"That's a different phenomenon, I suspect. Before the day it happened, eighty per cent of all those leaving rural districts for the cities were young women."

"And you think all the cities were destroyed?"

"I can't say. But up till now, none of the bands we've encountered has been composed of city people."

Silence.

"It's rotten, isn't it?" Colin said gloomily. "It would be much better for everyone if we all had wives of our own."

An idea that seemed to me—after giving it some thought—a little uncomplimentary to Miette. Poor Miette. Yet another one who'd grown a little weary of institutionalized embraces.

I changed the subject. "Colin, I want you to get all the sleep you can this afternoon."

As I expected, he bridled immediately. "Oh, and why me?" he asked, squaring his shoulders.

And indeed, why him? Don't go thinking just because he's little . . .

I said seriously, "I want to assign you to a very important post in the defense arrangements."

"Ah," he said, reassured.

"I want you to occupy the single hole that Meyssonnier is digging at the moment."

"And who'll be in the dugout?"

"Hervé and Maurice."

"And me in the hole?"

"Yes. That means you won't be getting any sleep tonight. They'll be able to take turns keeping watch, but you won't."

"The thought of a night without sleep doesn't worry me any," Colin said dismissively. Then he asked, "And what kind of gun will I have?"

"One of the .36 rifles."

"Ah!" he said, very pleased.

He lifted his head and looked at me. "And the others?"

"Hervé and Maurice?"

"Yes."

"Their own rifles."

"Why all three .36s outside?"

"So that Vilmain's men, when you start shooting them up the behind won't be able to distinguish your shots from their own by the sound."

He gave me one of his gondola smiles. "Not by the sound, but by the feel they will." And he added, "You have ideas that no one else would ever think of."

"You too."

"Me?"

"I'll tell you later. I haven't finished. Tonight I shall give you my binoculars."

"Ah!"

"I expect Vilmain to attack just before dawn. I'm counting on you to spot him first and signal to me that he's on his way."

"With the flashlight?"

"Absolutely not. You'd give yourself away."

"How then?"

I looked at him. "Your owl."

It was his turn to look at me, face lit up with a radiant smile, and he looked so childishly proud that his reaction made me feel suddenly a little sad, even though I'd predicted it. If it were only possible, I'd gladly split the difference in our heights with him, so that he needn't go on searching for compensations for his size in every tiniest thing.

"You said something about an idea of mine," he said after a moment.

"An idea of Catie's plus an idea of yours."

"An idea of Catie's?" Colin said.

"You see, you'd never have thought it, would you? Perhaps your image of her has been a little too specialized up till now."

I paused long enough for us to enjoy a little laugh "with the boys," as it were, then went on: "If Vilmain

504

retreats, we're going after him on the horses. But not along the road. Along this track here. We shall get to the proclamation place well before him. And that's where we lay our ambush."

"The idea of the ambush, that was me!" Colin said with discreet pride. "What about Catie?"

"It was Catie who thought of the horses. And I thought of the track."

I allowed him to bask in his glory. We walked on for a good five minutes in silence, then in a slightly different voice he said, "And you think we're going to give him a licking, Vilmain?"

"I think so, yes. . . . I'm only afraid of one thing now. That he won't come."

XVII

THAT night, as on the previous one, I kept the last watch for myself. There was one change: Evelyne was allowed to share my mattress on the floor in the gate-tower kitchen, and my dawn watch as well.

She had two tasks assigned her. As soon as I squeezed her shoulder, she was to alert all our combatants in the gate tower, then go directly to the Maternity Ward and saddle Amarante and the two white mares ready for the pursuit, should it occur. I wasn't going to take Malabar. I was afraid that he might be excited by running with the mares and betray us with his neighing.

All stations had been meticulously assigned. La Menou in charge of the drawbridge. La Falvine in the cellar, where her presence was theoretically supposed to be a reassurance to the cows and the bull we had tied up there. It was the best I could think of to ensure we didn't have to listen to her cackling.

I had numbered the arrow slits from one to seven, working from south to north. When summoned by Evelyne, all those with guns were to proceed directly to the one allotted to them as quickly and silently as possible. Jacquet at number one, Peyssou at number two, Thomas at three, myself at four, Meyssonnier at five, Miette and Catie at six and seven. The last two were the slits inside the tower itself. They were very cleverly designed, enabling our two warrior maids to fire at the enemy without any danger of being hit by his return fire. This was a point we were all totally agreed on—under no circumstances could we afford to lose our women, since the future of the community depended upon them.

Outside, Hervé and Maurice had taken up their places in the dugout. Colin was in the single hole. He was to give the other two the signal to fire by firing a single shot himself—at his discretion, but not until Vilmain and his men were thoroughly engaged.

"I'm taking my bow too!" Colin had said earlier that evening.

"Your bow! When you have a rifle!"

"Ah, but this is another of my ideas," Colin said. "Think of the terror it will strike into their hearts! No noise, no smoke, just phffft!—an arrow right through the chest! That will shake them. And then I open up with my .36."

He looked so delighted by his idea that I said nothing. And later we watched him from the ramparts as he set out, .36 slung from one shoulder, huge bow across his back. Meyssonnier just shrugged, but Thomas was furious. "You let him get away with anything," he said reproachfully.

I didn't sleep much, but as on the previous night, my last watch in the paling dark, sitting on Meyssonnier's little bench at battle station four, found me very calm. The barrel of my Springfield rested on the ancient stone of the merlon, its butt on my thigh. How strange it was that I should be there, a twentieth-century man in the very spot where so many English or Protestant archers had kept watch in their coats of mail. If it were not for Evelyne, there beside me, and my companions sleeping in the tower, I knew I would never go to the trouble of surviving in such precarious conditions. This struggle against marauders, this deadly garrison life on perpetual alert, how many years would it have to go on?

Evelyne was sitting beside me on her favorite little stool. Her back was pressed against my left calf, and her head lay on my lap. So light, her head, that I could scarcely feel it there. She wasn't asleep. Every now and then, with my left hand, I stroked her neck and cheek. Immediately, the little hand clasped mine. It had been agreed that no words were to be spoken.

I knew that my relationship with Evelyne shocked my companions, even while they admired my patience in nursing her, teaching her exercises, educating her. If I made her my wife, they would perhaps disapprove, in their hearts. But they would understand better. Though it was true that I myself had given up trying to understand. My relationship with Evelyne was at the same time platonic yet also sensual in part. I wasn't tempted to possess her, and yet that little body was a source of perpetual delight. And her limpid eyes, her long hair. If Evelyne should become a beautiful young woman one day, then it is likely, being the man I am, that I won't be able to resist. And yet, I had the feeling that I would be losing a great deal. I would have preferred it a hundred times if she could remain just as she was, so that our relationship need never change.

That afternoon, as she was tidying the drawer of my desk while I took a short siesta, she had found a small but very sharp and pointed dagger that my uncle had given me as a paper knife. When I woke up, she asked if she could have it.

"What do you want it for?"

"You know that."

It was true. I did know. And I didn't want to hear her say it. I just nodded.

She immediately tied a piece of string through the sheath ring and attached it to her belt. That evening the whole of Malevil complimented her and teased her about her little dagger. I too asked her at one point if she intended to put Vilmain to the sword with it. I pretended to be taken in, like the others, by her childish playacting. But I knew what deadly resolve lay behind it.

The night was cool, and the pitch blackness had only just begun to lighten slightly. I could see very little through my arrow slit. I was more concerned with my "auditory concentration." It was a phrase of Meyssonnier's, presumably remembered from his army days. Withall birds gone, dawn was eerily silent. And even Craa was not coming near me at the moment. I waited. That strutting cretin was bound to attack. Because having said he was going to, he wouldn't know how to set about reversing his decision. And also because he had such blind confidence in

508

his technological superiority, represented by one practically antique bazooka.

The really sickening thing about that sort of man was that you always knew in advance how his mind was going to work: Since I am the one with the bazooka, I am the one who lays down the law. And his "law" consisted in massacring us. We had dropped two of his men. He was going to wipe out Malevil.

Except that he wasn't going to wipe out anything at all. During the day there had been waves of fear every now and then, but that was over now. The road ahead was clear. Apart from, shall we say a certain measure of residual nervousness, I was calm. I was expecting Colin's owl cry at any moment now.

I was expecting it, yet when it came it surprised me to the point of paralysis. Evelyne had to touch my hand before I remembered that I had to squeeze her shoulder. Which I then did, rather absurdly, I felt, since she knew I was going to do it.

Evelyne promptly left, carrying her stool with her as we had arranged, so that no one would stumble into it or me. I found myself kneeling in front of the little bench on which I'd been sitting, left elbow propped on it, cheek against the wood of my rifle butt. Behind me I could hear —and see from the corner of my eye, since the darkness was paling with every second now— that my companions were moving to their stations. It was all accomplished with amazing silence and rapidity.

After which an infinite length of time elapsed. Vilmain apparently couldn't make up his mind to open fire against the palisade, and quite absurdly I experienced great resentment at his reluctance to play the role I had assigned him in my scenario. I wasn't conscious at the time of saying anything at all, but Meyssonnier assured me later that I never stopped muttering to myself, "What the hell does he think he's doing, damn it? What the hell is he up to?"

At last the explosion we were all waiting for came. And in a way we were disappointed, because it was much less loud than expected. It must have been a disappointment to Vilmain as well, because the shell by no means destroyed the whole palisade, and in fact failed even to rip the two halves of the gate off their hinges. All it managed to do was tear a hole about five feet wide in the center, but it left the splintered upper and lower sections still in place.

What happened then? I was supposed to give the signal to open fire with a long blast on my whistle. I didn't give it. And yet we all began firing, me included, each of us doubtless thinking that the others had seen something. In fact, no one could see anything, because there was nothing to see. The enemy hadn't advanced into the breach.

The testimony of our prisoners was to be quite categorical on this point. At the moment we opened fire, Vilmain's men were still ten yards or so down the road, in no possible danger from our fire, since they were protected by the jut of the cliff. They had in fact just begun their advance toward the breach opened by the bazooka when our premature and totally aimless fire stopped them in their tracks. Not because it was doing them the slightest harm, but because it was raking the remains of the palisade, sending splinters of wood flying in all directions, and in the case of the shotguns, creating an incessant crackle of lead shot on the planks. Our attackers hurled themselves to the ground and began firing back. But of course, the same jut of the cliff that was sheltering them also made it impossible for them to see anything of us. So both armies were now safely under cover and both pouring a deafening barrage of fire into nonexistent targets.

I eventually grasped what was happening, and so did Meyssonnier. He said to me, "Better stop this. It's crazy."

I couldn't have agreed more, but to stop it I needed my policeman's whistle, and grope as I might through my pockets, the sweat standing out on my forehead, I was unable to find it. I was clearly aware, even as I was doing it, and despite the acuteness of my anxiety, how ridiculous I was. The commander in chief can't give orders to his troops just now, I'm afraid. He's lost his whistle! I could have yelled, Cease fire! Even Miette and Catie in the tower would have heard me. But no, I don't know why, but it seemed absolutely essential to me just then to do everything exactly according to the rules.

510

At last I found it, my precious relic. There was no mystery about it, it had been in the shirt pocket where I'd put it. I blew three short blasts at intervals of a few seconds, and eventually our guns fell silent.

However, my whistle must have awakened an echo in Vilmain's military soul, because from the ramparts where I was crouching I heard him yell at his men, "What are you firing at, you damned fools?"

At which, on both sides, silence succeeded to the former tempest. Though to say dead silence would be misleading, since no one had been so much as scratched. The first stage of our battle had concluded in farce and stalemate. We on our side felt no necessity to emerge from Malevil in search of our enemy, and he for his part had no desire to invite annihilation by appearing in a breach only five feet across.

The next events I did not witness personally. They were described to me by the three posted outside.

Hervé and Maurice were in despair. An error had been made in the siting of their dugout. Because although it certainly provided a good side view of anyone approaching Malevil along the road, it did so only as long as those approaching remained upright. As soon as they lay down, as was now the case, they disappeared. The raised grass-covered shoulder of the road concealed them completely. So Hervé and Maurice were unable to open fire. Apart from which, even supposing that an enemy did raise his head, they didn't know whether they ought to fire yet in any case, since Colin's rifle still remained silent.

Colin, on the other hand, was admirably placed. He was directly opposite Malevil, he had a view of the road sloping up in front of him right to the palisade. He could see all the attackers perfectly as they lay on their bellies along under the cliff. And when Vilmain, after my whistle blasts, raised himself on one elbow to yell, "What are you firing at, you damned fools?" Colin immediately recognized him from Hervé's description of his close-shaven blond skull.

So Colin decided to kill Vilmain. A good idea in itself. But when Colin told us later, with that mischievous smile, how he had set about putting it into execution, we were all horrified.

For Colin there was no question of using his rifle. In order to strike terror into the attackers' hearts, as he had put it, by killing without noise or smoke, he decided to use the bow so dear to his own heart.

Colin was short, the hole was narrow, the bow was big. He realized he wasn't going to be able to draw it in that "rathole." Never mind! He jumped out of his hole, leaving his rifle behind, crawled three yards, bow in hand, over to a big charred chestnut stump behind which, for greater ease of movement, he stood up. Stood up! And calmly took aim at Vilmain's back.

As luck would have it, however, Vilmain turned to give an order just then, and the arrow, missing him by a fraction, embedded itself in the back of the man beside him, presumably the bazooka loader, since Colin saw two or three small shells fall from his hands and roll several yards down the road before coming to rest. The wounded man let out a horrible scream, stood up to his full height (becoming visible also to the two in the dugout at that point), and zigzagged off down the road, twisting himself around in an attempt to wrench the arrow out of his back. After a few yards he fell onto his stomach and lay there writhing and scrabbling at the earth with his hands.

Terror had certainly been struck into Vilmain's men, but the result was not decisive. Moreover Vilmain had been allowed time to see where the arrow had come from. He barked an order. And twelve rifles, his own included, spat simultaneously at the chestnut stump behind which Colin was now flattened on the ground, unable to strike back, since he couldn't draw his bow lying down and his rifle was three yards away in the hole.

From my position on the wall I could of course hear the sudden intense fire, but I couldn't see a thing. I didn't even know who was firing at whom, since all our outside men were equipped with exactly the same weapons as the enemy. I was mortally concerned, because any gunfight between our own three outside rifles and Vilmain's twelve would be horribly unequal. Vilmain, thanks to his numerical superiority, could easily outflank our men with one maneuver. And there was nothing the rest of us inside could do to help them, except make a sortie, and that would be madness.

The two in the dugout could still not see the enemy. And since they hadn't seen Colin leave his hole either, they were puzzled as to why Vilmain was pouring his fire into the undergrowth like that. Nor could they understand why Colin's rifle still remained silent, because they knew—or Hervé did anyway, since he'd helped Jacquet dig it—that the single hole provided an excellent view of the road up to the palisade.

But the most worried of all, needless to say, was the object of the fire. It was clear to him by now that he was trapped. He was completely isolated behind his charred chestnut stump, seventy yards from the enemy, without a gun, and all retreat was cut off by the gunfire nailing him to the spot. He could hear the bullets from Vilmain's .36s hitting the other side of the tree stump with wicked little thuds, and even knocking off little chunks of bark very near his head. He had taken his decision. He was waiting for a lull to leap into his hole, which he could see, gaping invitingly, only three yards away, his rifle neatly propped against the brushwood lining. But the lull didn't come, and when they didn't actually hit the tree stump the bullets went whining past to his right and his left with terrifying accuracy. "It was the only time in my life," he was to say later, "when I'd have liked to be smaller than I am."

According to our prisoners, Vilmain began by showing great anxiety when Colin's arrow killed his loader and made him aware that he had an enemy in his rear. But when the enemy didn't reply to his fire, he realized that he was weaponless and decided to flush him out from behind his tree. He detailed two veterans to leopard-crawl over to the hill and outflank Colin's stump on his right, while four of the attackers' best shots continued to nail him to the ground with their fire. But the two veterans had scarcely crawled more than a few yards when Vilmain recalled them. "As you were, men," he said. "I'll drop the bastard for us myself." And he stood up. His intention, presumably, was to take advantage of what looked like an easy victory in order to re-establish his ascendancy over the veterans, after the rather shaky start to his attack.

Anyway, he stood up, and because all his men were lying down, his upright figure immediately took on heroic proportions. At a nonchalant, swinging pace he set off down the road in order to pick Colin off from his flank. It didn't require a great deal of daring, since Colin couldn't shoot back and the jut of the cliff was protecting him from the possibility of fire from us.

Until then, Vilmain had been just as invisible to Hervé and Maurice as all the others, but as soon as he stood up and began swinging off down the road, affecting the feline slouch of the old campaigner, he became the perfect target for them. Hervé, who was still waiting for Colin's signal, watched him closely (he was to do an excellent imitation of his walk for us later) but made no move. Maurice, however, impelled by the icy hatred he felt for Vilmain, immediately took a bead on him, kept him carefully in his sights throughout his nonchalant progress along the road, and as soon as he saw him stop and raise his weapon to his shoulder, took careful aim at his temple and fired.

His skull shattered, Vilmain fell, killed by the new recruit whom he had so carefully taught the principles of standing fire with support a month before. The firing at Colin's tree stump ceased, and Colin leapt into his hole. Once there, he snatched up his .36 and from his well-camouflaged, well-protected burrow began to fire back. He was an excellent shot, rapid and accurate, and he killed two men with his first two shots.

In a few seconds the situation had been completely reversed. Jean Feyrac, who, according to our prisoners, hadn't been enthusiastic about the Malevil expedition anyway, now gave the signal for a retreat. And it was indeed a retreat, not a disorderly rout. A fresh salvo of bullets bit into the lip of Colin's hole, forcing him to lower his head, and by the time he raised it again the enemy had vanished. Though not without taking time to collect the bazooka, the shells, and the dead men's rifles.

Colin uttered a triumphant whoooo! Never did the cry of an owl give me greater joy. It was telling me that the

514

enemy had fled, and that Colin at least was unharmed.

I told Thomas to get the main gate open and hurtled down the stone steps from the wall so fast that I almost fell and had to jump the last five. I landed with a jolt and set off at a run toward the Maternity Ward with Meyssonnier behind me.

I shouted to him over my shoulder, "Take Mélusine!"

As I ran, I clicked my safety catch back on and pulled the sling of the Springfield over my head. Evelyne, who had heard my voice, emerged from the Maternity Ward leading Morgane. I went in and took Amarante's reins myself. She was in such a state of excitement that I was obliged to control my own. I took time to talk to her and stroke her. She made no difficulties at first. But when we reached the scattered debris of the palisade she sniffed and stopped dead, arching back against her stiffened forelegs, neck defiantly curved, head up, shaking her pale mane. The sweat poured down my face. I knew Amarante and her refusals!

To my great surprise, however, and even greater relief, this time she yielded to no more than a few gentle tugs and two or three clicks of the tongue. Once Amarante was through, the two other mares followed placidly enough.

I scarcely had time to count the four bodies and note that the enemy had removed their weapons when our three outside men all leapt out of the undergrowth onto the road at the same moment. They came dashing up, flushed, panting, excited. I hugged them all, but there was no time for reports or emotions. I helped Maurice up behind Meyssonnier, then Hervé, who seemed to me much the heavier, up behind Colin, whereupon I noticed that Colin had his bow still slung around him as well as his .36. It looked vast sticking out on either side of his little body and the top of it came way above his head.

"Leave your bow here! It will get caught in the bushes!"

"No, no!" Colin said, scarlet with pride.

Just as I was about to mount in my turn, I realized we'd forgotten the tethers. And all that time lost if we went back for them!

"Evelyne, you're coming with us!"

"Me!"

515

"You can hold the horses."

She was so overjoyed that she turned to stone. I seized her by the hips and practically threw her onto Amarante's back, then leapt up into the saddle after her. As soon as we had reached the forest track, I twisted around in the saddle, supporting myself with one hand on Amarante's rump, and said in a low voice to Colin, "Be careful of your bow. We're going to gallop!"

"You bet I will," he said with an air of tremendous virility and triumph.

At that point I didn't yet know what part he had played in the battle outside, but just from his expression I was sure it had been considerable.

Amarante hadn't been out of her stall for two days. She needed no urging to stretch those long legs. I felt the magnificent surge of her getaway between my legs, then a cooling flow of air on my forehead. Evelyne, tightly gripped between my arms, was in her seventh heaven of delight. She had an excellent seat, so she was barely holding the saddle pommel at all, and when I bent forward to avoid a branch, she simply gave beneath my weight, lifted her hands, and laid them lightly on Amarante's neck. Our mount's mane streamed in the breeze, and Evelyne's long hair, almost the same shade of blond as the mane, streamed back too against my neck. No sound but the muffled rhythm of hoofs in the leaf mold and the lashing of the leaves brushed aside by Amarante's chest and whipping at my legs. Amarante was galloping at full stretch, and behind her, more heavily laden and therefore slightly less swift, came Morgane and Mélusine. They were the perfect equine machines. But Amarante was fire, blood, the ecstasy of space. I had become part of her, I was horse myself now, her movements were mine. I rose and lowered myself to the rhythm of her back, with Evelyne light as a feather keeping time. And I experienced an unbelievable feeling of swiftness, of abundance, of strength. I galloped with the feeling of Evelyne's little body against mine. I was galloping toward the annihilation of our enemies, the safety of Malevil, the conquest of La Roque. At that moment in time where I existed, neither age nor death could reach me. I galloped. I wanted to cry out with joy.

I noticed that I had left the other two mares behind. I was afraid that if they lost their leading horse from view they might betray our presence by starting to neigh, so at the next hill I reined Amarante in to a trot. Not without difficulty, for she wanted nothing more than to go on sending the leaf mold flying with her powerful hoofs. At the top of the incline the track made a right angle bend, and again in order that the mares behind shouldn't lose sight of Amarante, I came to a halt. On my right, giant bracken fronds rose well above my head, but through their lacy green, way below us, I could make out the gray windings of the La Roque road. Then suddenly, as I watched, Vilmain's men began emerging from the farthest bend. They were spaced out slightly now, walking quickly, but already left far behind. Some were carrying two rifles.

Colin and Meyssonnier rode up. I signaled to them to keep quiet and gestured down toward the group of men below. We held our breath, gazing down for a few silent seconds through the green bracken fronds at the men we were going to kill.

Meyssonnier brought Mélusine up beside Amarante, leaned toward me, and said in a barely audible voice. "But there are only seven. What's happened to the eighth?"

I counted. It was true. There were only seven.

"Lagging behind, I expect."

I urged Amarante forward again. Though this time I held her down to a canter. I had noticed when we stopped that the white mares were blowing. Besides, the ecstasy of that first gallop could never be recaptured now. Victory had lost the abstract exaltation that had given it such charm. Now it wore the face of those poor wretches sweating and toiling along the road.

Ah, there was my last marker across the track. I noticed it at the very moment we broke it. We were there.

"Evelyne, you see that little clearing? That's where you're going to keep them."

"All three? Can't we tie them up by their reins?"

I shook my head. The two mares caught up to us, the

four riders dismounted, and I showed Colin and Meyssonnier how to knot the reins over their mounts' neck so they shouldn't catch their feet in them.

"Are you just going to turn them loose?" Meyssonnier said.

"They won't go far. They won't leave Amarante, and Evelyne is going to hold Amarante. Colin you show them where it is."

They left, and I waited behind to give Evelyne her final instructions. In case Amarante became uncontrollable, she was to mount her and walk her in circles.

"Can I give you a kiss, Emmanuel?"

I leaned down, and at the same moment Amarante decided to pull her favorite trick, which was to push me in the back with her head. I fell on top of Evelyne, or rather onto my elbows. We were both in such a state of tension that it didn't even occur to us to laugh. I got up again. Evelyne as well. She hadn't let go of the reins. Her face was old with anguish.

"Don't kill them, Emmanuel," she said in a low voice. "You promised to spare their lives on your poster."

"Listen, Evelyne," I said in a voice that I could scarcely control, "there are eight of them and they have very good guns. When I see them, if I shout, "Surrender yourselves!' they may very well decide they'd rather fight. And if they fight, then there's a good chance that someone from Malevil will be wounded or killed. Do you want me to run that risk?"

She lowered her head and didn't reply. I left her without kissing her, but after I had gone a few yards I turned to wave, and she waved back immediately. She stood there in the clearing, a little patch of sun on her hair, the little "dagger" hanging from her belt, tiny and frail among the enormous animals whose rumps I could see beginning to steam. It was such an idyllic scene, and my heart sank as I looked at it, knowing the slaughter I was about to unleash so short a distance away.

The others were waiting for me above the road. I went over the orders briefly. No shot to be fired before a long blast of the whistle. Cease fire after three short blasts. Then our positions. The wire from which my proclamation was suspended bisected the road more or less halfway along a straight uphill stretch. Colin and I were to take up our positions twenty yards uphill from the notice on the La Roque side, Colin on the far side of the road, myself on this. Meyssonnier and Hervé would be concealed twenty yards downhill from the notice on the Malevil side, Meyssonnier on my side of the road, Hervé on Colin's.

We took up these positions quickly and silently. The trap was set. The two steep banks on either side of the road were completely covered by our cross fire. All retreat was cut off. All escape forward was equally impossible.

I could still communicate visually with Colin, who was scarcely more than the width of the road away from me, and I kept Maurice beside me so that if the need arose I could send him with a message down to Meyssonnier forty yards below, who could then pass it on to Hervé opposite.

We waited. The wire from which I had hung my proclamation was still intact. That morning at dawn Vilmain's men must have just ducked under the obstacle for want of a pair of pincers to remove it. They would be ducking under it again in a few minutes. And that moment was their rendezvous with death. There was no wind. My proclamation hung there motionless and peremptory, barring the way, the square of drawing paper dazzlingly white in the sun. If I had been carrying my binoculars I could have read the letters I had printed on it. I thought of Evelyne. And I was only too conscious of the savage irony in shooting Vilmain's men down like rabbits at the very foot of that bright white square promising them their lives. But Evelyne herself was one of the reasons I had to destroy them. How could I forget what "wiping out" Malevil would have entailed?

The ground was cold under me, the sun already warm on my head, my shoulders, my hands. Maurice lay elbow to elbow beside me. He had a way of keeping quiet and utterly still that I found very pleasant. Nothing about him was heavy, not even his presence. We had snapped off two little bushes that were in our way, and we waited without a word, eyes fixed on those sixty yards of straight road between the two bends. Colin could see farther

519

than us, because the bend at the top curved away from him, and by turning around he had a view of a further thirty yards that were concealed from us by our embankment.

The first sound I heard puzzled me. It was a squeaking noise. It seemed to be moving up the hill toward us very laboriously. It couldn't be made by an animal, a noise like that. It was mechanical. Except that it was intermittent, it made me think of a bucket being wound up from a well on a chain. But its intermittence was regular, with the squeak coming on every other beat.

I looked at Maurice and raised my eyebrows. Maurice leaned over and said in my ear, "A bicycle chain?"

He was right. And I wondered if perhaps it was the bicycle that Bébelle had hidden just outside Malevil, and that we'd neglected to search for. If it was, then we'd committed a serious error, and now we were paying for it.

I didn't even need to ask Maurice who the rider was when he appeared alone around the lower bend. I remembered Hervé's description. I recognized the black eyebrows running straight across his forehead in an unbroken line. It was Jean Feyrac. And as he entered the sixty-yard uphill straight that separated us, I made out the tube of the bazooka between his legs. He had tied it to the frame of the bike. The hill grew steeper; he was having difficulty. He began to zigzag. It looked as though he might even have to get off and walk. We had all the time in the world.

All the time for what? The sweat ran down my face. Feyrac was the new leader. And what was more, according to Hervé a man with considerable powers of leadership and no pity whatever. I ought to kill him. But if I did, then I was giving a clear warning to the body of the group only half a mile or so farther back. As soon as they heard my shot, they would all leave the road, take to the undergrowth, and who knows, perhaps stumble on Evelyne with the horses. But in any case, once they were in the undergrowth I had lost all my advantage. The odds would be equal again, except that they were seven to our five. It would be back to square one.

As I had foreseen, Feyrac dismounted when he reached

the proclamation and bent down to push his bike under it. He was short-legged, thickset, with a scowling, unpleasant face. Looking at him, I thought with horror of the massacre at Courcejac. But I had made my choice; I was going to let him pass, despite his crimes, despite his bazooka. A leader without troops is less dangerous than seven hunted men fighting for their lives.

He was opposite me now. Separated from me by no more than the height of the bank. He got back onto Pougès's bike and the squeaking of the chain began again, regular, maddening. He was nearly at the bend. Another second and he would be out of sight. My hands were clenched around the Springfield, and the sweat fell drop by drop onto the butt.

Feyrac entered the bend. I could no longer see him. What happened then was over so quickly that I could scarcely believe my eyes. On the other side of the road I saw Colin rise to his feet, take up his meticulous training-manual stance, left foot well forward, draw his bow, and take careful aim. A hiss, then a half second later the sound of a fall. It was maddening not to be able to see anything. Then Colin gave me a joyful thumbs-up and vanished among the bushes. I was flabbergasted.

I was almost prepared to hail Colin as a military genius, and to think I was right to "let him get away with anything," as Thomas had complained. At that point I still hadn't heard how Colin had abandoned his dugout and rifle, outside Malevil, in order to entrust his life to his favorite weapon. Let us say, not to be too harsh, that it was a case of misapplication. And even when I did hear of it, it did nothing to modify the estimate of the bow in general arrived at after my expedition to L'Étang: a safe and invaluably silent weapon in an ambush.

I gradually recovered my calm. So the eighth man hadn't been lagging behind as I'd thought. The eighth man had been Feyrac, valiantly preceding his troops in their retreat. And by my calculations, he couldn't have been preceding them by much. There are some very steep hills between Malevil and La Roque, which meant that Feyrac could hardly have built up very much of a lead. So there were only very few minutes left ahead of me. They seemed interminable though, lying there on my belly in the bracken with Maurice beside me.

They appeared, straggled out along the road, flushed, sweating, panting, their boots ringing on the metaled surface. I looked down at their peasant faces, their red hands, their heavy laboring limbs: the cannon fodder of every war the world had ever known, including this one. If my big Peyssou had been there he would have felt he was shooting at himself.

A group of three headed the line, still quite fresh, it seemed to me. Then two more a few yards behind, then two more farther back still, having difficulty keeping up. According to my firing orders, the three leaders and the two stragglers were our victims. The strongest and the weakest.

I put the whistle between my lips and laid my cheek against my rifle butt. It had been agreed that Colin and I should cross our fire so as to avoid trying for the same target. I was to set my sights on the man nearest the far side of the road, Colin on the one nearest my side. With the exception of those two, Maurice was free to choose. Meyssonnier and Hervé, lower down the straight, had the same agreement as ourselves.

I waited until the leading group had passed the wire. When the middle two reached it I gave a long whistle blast and fired. Our shots all rang out simultaneously, and the only one that could be distinguished from the general detonation was Meyssonnier's .22, whose sharper, fainter crack came very slightly after the rest. Five men fell. They didn't fall quickly, the way they used to in war films, but very, very slowly, as though in slow motion. The two survivors didn't even think of throwing themselves onto the ground, they just stood there, every reflex numbed. It was only after two or three seconds that they raised their hands. It was high time. I gave three brief blasts on my whistle. It was all over.

I turned to Maurice and asked in a low voice. "Those two, who are they?"

"The short balding one with the pot is Burg, the cook. The thin one is Jeannet, Vilmain's batman."

"Recruits?"

"Yes, both of them."

In a loud voice, without showing myself, I shouted, "Emmanuel Comte, Abbé of Malevil, here! Burg! Jeannet! pick up your comrades' rifles and place them under the notice."

Haggard and petrified, hands trembling at the ends of their raised arms, they were just two young lads, ashen beneath their tans. They jumped violently when they heard me. They raised their heads. On the two embankments boxing in the road on either side not a leaf stirred. They looked around them, bewildered. They even looked at my proclamation, as though my voice might have actually come out of that, I was here, when they'd just been besieging me in Malevil! And I'd called them by their names!

They obeyed slowly, fumblingly. Some of the rifles were caught under their owners' bodies, so they were forced to manhandle the corpses in order to retrieve them. I noticed that they did so with great gentleness, and also they took care not to step in the dead men's blood.

When they had finished I gave another three blasts on my whistle. I slid down the bank onto the road, followed by Maurice, Colin did the same. Then Hervé and Meyssonnier appeared forty yards lower down.

"Hands on heads," I said curtly, and the prisoners did as they were told. I saw that Meyssonnier was methodically examining the five fallen figures to make sure they were quite dead. I was grateful to him for that. It wasn't a task I'd have liked to take on myself. No one spoke. Although I was sweating profusely, my legs were cold and numb. I took a few paces along the road. I didn't go far. Blood everywhere. I looked down at it and breathed in its strong and insipid odor. The red of it seemed to me very bright on the slate-gray road. But I knew it wouldn't be long before it became dulled and black. Incomprehensible human race. That precious blood that in the world before we had divided into groups, collected, stocked in banks, while elsewhere, at the same time, we were spilling it in profusion over the earth. I looked at the young dead men. On the pools in which they lay, not a fly, not a gnat. Fine red blood poured out onto the ground, useless to everyone—even to insects.

"Monsieur l'Abbé," the thin prisoner said suddenly.

"Never mind Monsieur l'Abbé."

"Can I take my hands down? I'm sorry, I'm going to be sick."

"All right, lad."

He staggered over to the shoulder, fell on his knees, and took his weight on stiffened arms. I watched his back heave as he retched, and I felt somewhat queasy myself. I shook myself.

"Hervé, go and fetch the bicycle and bazooka. And make sure Feyrac is quite dead."

I turned back to the prisoners, told them to lower their hands, and allowed them to sit down. They needed to sit very badly. Now let's think. Yes, the little balding fellow with the pot was Burg, the cook. Very lively dark eyes, shrewd by the look of it. And the gawky lad whose nerves had given way, that was Jeannet. They gazed at me with superstitious awe.

I learned a great deal from them. Armand had died the previous morning from Pimont's knife wound. The first thing Vilmain had done after moving into the château was to eject Josepha. He didn't want to be waited on by a woman. So Burg did the cooking and Jeannet waited at table. When Vilmain moved in, Gazel also moved out of the château, but of his own free will. He was outraged by the murder of Lanouaille.

I couldn't believe my ears. I made them repeat that piece of information. Bravo for our asexual clown! Who would have foreseen he'd display that much courage?

"It wasn't just the butcher," Burg said. "It was also that Gazel didn't approve of the 'excesses.' "

"The excesses?"

"Well, the raping," Burg said. "That's the word he used for it."

Hervé returned, pushing the bike with the bazooka still tied to it. The cheeks above his little black beard were white, his whole face drawn. He leaned the bike against the bank, unburdened himself of one of the two rifles he was carrying, and came over.

"Feyrac isn't dead," he said in a toneless voice. "He's in terrible pain. He asked me for water."

"So?"

"What should I do?"

I stared at him. "It's quite simple. Just take the Renault, drive into Malejac, call the hospital and ask for an ambulance, then next Sunday we'll all go and take him some nice oranges."

Yet strangely enough, shaking with fury though I was, even as I spoke those words from another world, a great sadness engulfed me.

Hervé lowered his head and scraped at the tarred surface of the road with the toe of one shoe.

"I don't like it at all," he said in a muffled voice.

Maurice came over. "I can go, if you like," he said, his black eyes glittering from between narrowed eyelids as he looked at me. Maurice hadn't forgotten. Nothing. Neither his friend René nor Courcejac.

"No, I'll go," Hervé said, as though he had just woken up.

He slid the sling of his rifle off his shoulder and walked back toward the bend with steps growing gradually firmer as he progressed. I realized what had happened. Feyrac had asked him for water. And instantly the reflex particular to the human animal had come into play: Feyrac had become taboo.

I turned back to the prisoners. "Now where were we? Armand dead, Josepha out on her neck, Gazel out from choice. So who was there left, up in the château?"

"Well, Fulbert, of course," Burg said.

"And did Fulbert eat at the same table with Vilmain?"

"Well, yes."

"Despite Lanouaille's murder? Despite the 'excesses'? You, Jeannet, you waited on them."

"Fulbert, he always sat in between Vilmain and Bébelle," Jeannet said. "And all I can say is he didn't do any less drinking or eating or laughing than they did."

"He laughed?"

"With Vilmain mostly. They got to be thick as thieves, those two."

Well here was an entirely new light on the whole situation. And I wasn't the only one who had appreciated

525

the fact. I could see Colin's ears prick up and Meyssonnier's face harden.

"Listen, Jeannet," I said, "I'm going to ask you an important question. Try to answer the absolute truth. And above all, don't try to say more than you really know."

"I'm listening."

"In your opinion, was it Fulbert who urged Vilmain on to attack Malevil?"

"Oh, as far as that's concerned, yes!" Jeannet said without hesitation. "I could see what he was up to all along!"

"How do you mean exactly?"

"Always telling him what a wonderful stronghold Malevil was. And how Malevil was crammed with provisions and everything fit to bust."

And Fulbert had wanted to see us "busted." For two very good reasons: it would get Vilmain off his back in La Roque the whole time, and he would have flushed us out of Malevil for good and all. The only unfortunate thing was that his active complicity with the mass murderer Vilmain was hard to prove, since none of La Roque's inhabitants had been present at the meals during which they had been "thick as thieves."

A shot rang out. It sounded inordinately loud, I thought, and made me feel strangely relieved. I could read the same feeling of relief on the faces of Colin, Meyssonnier, and Maurice. And even on those of the prisoners. Could it be that they felt safer now that the last Feyrac was dead?

Hervé returned. He was carrying a belt with a revolver in a holster attached to it.

"It's Vilmain's," Burg said. "Feyrac took it off him before he gave the signal to retreat."

I took their ex-commander's weapon. But I felt no desire to wear it myself. And when I questioned Meyssonnier with a look, it was clear that he felt the same. However, I knew someone else the pistol would send into ecstasies.

"It's yours by right, Colin," I said. "You killed Feyrac."

With flushed cheeks, Colin buckled belt and pistol martially around his slender waist. I noticed that Maurice was smiling and that there was a mischievous glint in his

526

jet black eyes. At that point I didn't yet know that he had killed Vilmain. And when I found out later, I was grateful to him for his silence and the concern for Colin's feelings that lay behind it.

It was time to be moving.

"The prisoners will go through the dead men's pockets and collect all the unused ammunition. I am returning to Malevil to fetch the cart. Colin comes with me. Meyssonnier take over command here."

Without waiting for Colin, I set off up the embankment, and as soon as I was out of sight of the road, hidden by the undergrowth, I broke into a run. I reached the clearing. Evelyne was there, her head scarcely reaching Amarante's shoulder. Her blue eyes fastened on me with a blaze of joy that overwhelmed me. She threw herself into my arms and I hugged her tight, very tight, against me. We didn't say anything. We both knew that neither of us would be able to go on living without the other.

We heard a crackling of twigs and a swishing of leaves. It was Colin. I pulled away from Evelyne and said, "You take Morgane." I looked at her again and smiled. Our moments of joy were brief but intense when they came.

I climbed into my saddle and left her to do the same without my help, which despite being so small she did very quickly and very neatly, with an agility I watched in admiration, since she even disdained using an old nearby stump to diminish the distance to the stirrup, or making use of the slope as Colin did. Though it's true that he was by now weighted down with a whole arsenal of weapons, his .36 rifle, the bow, a quiver he'd made for himself, Vilmain's pistol around his waist, and on top of everything, slung around his neck, the binoculars that he'd "forgotten" to hand back to me.

Since the undergrowth was pretty dense just there, I kept Amarante down to a walk at first so Colin shouldn't get into difficulties with his bow. Morgane walked directly behind me, her head almost resting on Amarante's rump. Amarante, vicious though she was to hens, never kicked her stable companions. The most she allowed herself was to give them a nip on the shoulder now and then to show who was boss.

I could feel Evelyne's eyes on me. I twisted around in my saddle and read the question in her eyes. I said, "We took two prisoners."

After that I urged Amarante on into a gallop. As we approached Malevil, Peyssou suddenly emerged from cover on the side of the road where he had been on guard, and I saw the anxiety on his face. I shouted to him, "All safe and sound!" And at that he howled with joy and waved his gun above his head. Amarante promptly shied, Morgane followed suit, and Mélusine gave a little jump that bumped Colin up and out of his saddle on her neck, where he clutched with both hands at her mane. Luckily, however, Mélusine stopped when she saw the other two mares being reined in ahead of her, and Colin was able to get back into the saddle, though he looked very comical doing so, feeling his way backward with his buttocks till they felt the pommel and slipped over it. We all laughed.

"You damned great idiot!" Colin said. "Just look what you nearly did!"

"Hey, what's up with you?" Peyssou riposted with a vast grin. "I thought you knew how to ride!"

I was laughing so much that I decided I'd better dismount. It was totally childish laughter that took me back a good thirty years, as did the thumps and punches that Peyssou began showering on me as soon as I was in range, like some vast hound puppy unaware of its own strength. So I began shouting at him too, because he was hurting me, the stupid great bastard, with those huge fists of his. Happily I was spared much more of his affection by the arrival of Catie and Miette, who had run out along the road to meet us.

"I recognized your laugh," Catie said. "Even from the ramparts. I recognized it!" She wrapped herself around me. This was more like it: gentle, like velvet almost. And as for Miette, she melted in my arms.

"My poor Emmanuel," La Menou said a few moments later as she rubbed her dry lips against my cheek. She said "poor" as though I was already dead. Jacquet gazed

528

at me without saying a word, still holding the pick with which he was digging a grave for the four enemy dead.

Thomas, outwardly wholly unmoved, told me, "I collected their shoes. They're still usable. I've started a special footwear section in the store."

La Falvine seemed to be made of water. She was weeping from everywhere, like lard in the sun. She didn't dare come over, remembering my sharp words the day before. So I went over to her instead, and planted a brief but magnanimous kiss on her cheek, so happy did I feel to be back in Malevil, in the bosom of the community, in our family cocoon.

"Six killed, and two prisoners," little Colin announced as he strode along, hand on holster.

"Tell us, Emmanuel!" Peyssou said.

I threw my hands in the air as I walked. "No time! We have to be away again immediately. With you, in fact, and Thomas, and Jacquet. Colin will stay to take over command in Malevil. Have you eaten?" I asked Peyssou.

"Well, we needed to," Peyssou said, as though I was accusing him.

"Quite right, Menou, make us seven sandwiches."

"Seven? Why seven?" she asked, already bristling.

"Colin, me, Hervé, Maurice, Meyssonnier, and the two prisoners."

"The prisoners," La Menou cried. "You're going to feed that band of robbers as well!"

Jacquet blushed, as he always did whenever any allusion was made to a condition that also applied to him.

"Do as I say. Jacquet, harness Malabar up to the cart. No saddle horses this time, just the cart. Evelyne, help Catie unsaddle the mares. I'm going to throw a little water on my face."

I did more than throw a little water on myself. I took a shower. I washed my hair, and I shaved. Albeit extremely quickly. And while I was about it, in view of my imminent entry into La Roque, I decided to dress up a little. I took off my old riding breeches and the somewhat tired-looking boots I'd been wearing ever since the day it happened, and I replaced them with my white gymkhana breeches, new or nearly new boots, and a white turtleneck

529

shirt. I was an immaculate and dazzling sight when I re-appeared in the outer enclosure.

The commotion I caused was such that Evelyne and Catie emerged from the Maternity Ward, currycombs and coils of straw still in their hands. Miette ran up and demonstrated her admiration in joyous mime. First she pinched a lock of her hair and her cheek (how clean my hair, how smooth my skin!). Then she pinched her own blouse with one hand while opening and closing the other several times (what a lovely shirt, how dazzling white!). Then she placed her hands around her waist and squeezed it (my white breeches made me look even slimmer) and made an indescribable gesture conveying virility (did something for me lower down). As for the boots, she opened and closed her hand again several times. This gesture, symbolizing the rays of the sun, meant that my boots were so bright, as indeed (see above) was my shirt. Finally, she gathered the fingers of her right hand against her thumb, put them to her lips several times (how handsome you are, Emmanuel!), then gave me a great kiss.

I was also assailed by a barrage of jibes from the male quarter. I hurried on. But I couldn't escape them all, how-ever much I tried. There was Peyssou in particular, striding after me, the packet of sandwiches under his arm, saying very loudly that got up like that I looked just as though I was off to my first communion.

"Honestly," Catie said, "if I'd seen you like that at La Roque the first time, it wouldn't have been Thomas I'd have married. I'd have picked you!"

"I had a lucky escape then!" I said good-humoredly as I jumped up into the cart and prepared to sit down.

"Wait! Wait!" Jacquet cried as he ran up with an old sack over his arm. He folded it neatly and arranged it where I was about to sit so that I shouldn't soil my clean clothes. The merriment became general at that, and I smiled at Jacquet to put him back in countenance.

Colin, who at first had joined in the laughter, was now standing a little apart with a very miserable expression on his face. And suddenly, as Malabar started off across the ADZ, I remembered that I had been dressed like this that day, a week before the day it happened, when I had taken him for a meal in a restaurant, him and his wife, after a gymkhana we'd been to. Still very close to each other after fifteen years of marriage, they had held hands under the table while I was ordering the meal. It was during the course of that meal, I remembered, that he had confided to me how worried he was about Nicole (ten years old) who was having a sore throat every month, and about Didier (twelve), whose spelling was so terrible. And now all that was ashes, buried in the little box that contained all Peyssou's family and all Meyssonnier's too.

"Colin," I shouted back at him, "don't bother to wait for me. Tell them what happened. Only one order: no one to leave Malevil in our absence. Otherwise, you're in command."

He seemed to wake up suddenly at my shout, and waved at me in acknowledgment. But he still remained standing where he was, even though the others—Evelyne, Catie, Miette—were running beside us, out past the shattered panels of the palisade and onto the road. Through the noise of Malabar's hoofs and the squeaking of the wheels, I shouted to Miette to take good care of Colin because he was feeling sad.

Jacquet stood at the front, reins in his hands. Thomas was seated beside me, Peyssou opposite, his long legs almost touching mine.

"I've got something to tell you that will give you a bit of a shock," Thomas said. "I looked through Vilmain's papers. He wasn't an army officer at all, he was an accountant!"

I laughed, but Thomas remained impassive. He couldn't see anything funny in what he'd told me. The fact that Vilmain had lied about his identity seemed to him to add to his crimes. Not to me. I wasn't even particularly astonished. It had half occurred to me on several occasions, after Hervé's accounts and descriptions, that there was a hint of the caricature about Vilmain, in his language especially. But when one thought about it! A phony priest, a phony army captain. Nothing but impostors! Was this what our new era was going to be like always?

Thomas handed me the professional card. I glanced at it, tucked it away in my wallet, and then told them in my turn about the part Fulbert had played in the dangers we had just been through. Peyssou exclaimed in disgust. Thomas just clenched his teeth without speaking.

We arrived back at the scene of our ambush and took Meyssonnier, Hervé, Maurice, and the prisoners on board, together with the extra rifles, the bazooka, the ammunition, and the bike. Nine grown men was something of a weight, even for our Malabar, so on the steeper hills we all climbed out, apart from Jacquet, to ease things for him somewhat. Meanwhile I explained my plan.

"First of all a question, Burg. Have the people of La Roque got anything to hold against you or Jeannet personally?"

"Why, what could they have to hold against us?" Burg said with a hint of indignation.

"How do I know? Brutalities? 'Excesses' perhaps?"

"I'll tell you," Burg answered, shining with virtue. "Brutality, that's not my line, nor Jeannet's neither. And as for the other, well I'll tell you something else," he added in a sudden explosion of honesty, "I didn't even get a chance. With Vilmain, a recruit had no rights, none at all. So just supposing for a moment I'd tried a bit of 'excessing,' I'd have had the veterans flogging the skin off my back in no time."

With one ear, I heard Peyssou behind me asking Meyssonnier what "excessing" meant.

I went on: "Another question. When we get to La Roque, is the south gate guarded?"

"Yes," Jeannet answered. "Vilmain detailed off a chap from La Roque for that. Name of Fabre . . . Fabre-something."

"Fabrelâtre?"

"Yes."

"What? What?" Peyssou asked, catching up when he heard me laugh.

I told him. He laughed in his turn.

"And did they issue him with a rifle, Fabrelâtre?"

"Yes."

The laughter redoubled. I went on: "No problem there. When we get to La Roque, only Burg and Jeannet will show themselves. They will get themselves let in. We disarm Fabrelâtre, and Jacquet takes care of him as well as Malabar." I paused. "And this is where the farce begins," I said with a smile and a wink at Burg.

He smiled back. He was delighted by this complicity I was establishing between us. It seemed to promise well for the future, no doubt. Especially since I broke off my explanations at that point in order to open Peyssou's package and hand out the sandwiches. Burg and Jeannet were dazzled by the bread, Burg especially, being a cook.

"Did you bake this bread yourselves?" he asked with respect.

"So? Why the surprise?" Peyssou said. "We can do it all at Malevil. We've got the baker, the mason, the carpenter, the plumber. And there's even Emmanuel, who puts on a fine show as our curé. I'm the mason," he added modestly.

Needless to say, he wasn't actually going to mention the addition to the ramparts, but I could see that he was thinking about it, and that it gave him a warm feeling around his heart to be leaving that masterpiece behind him for posterity.

"The trouble is though, there's the yeast," Jacquet said, joining in the conversation from his perch upon the cart. "There's none left almost."

"There's heaps in the La Roque château," Burg said, happy to be of service to us.

He sank his strong white teeth into his sandwich again and was clearly thinking to himself that this wouldn't be a bad firm to work for.

"Here's the plan," I said. "Once Fabrelâtre is disposed of, Burg and Hervé will go up alone into La Roque, with rifles. They will find Fulbert, and they will tell him Vilmain has taken Malevil. He has captured Emmanuel Comte and has sent him here to you. You are to take him up to the chapel, try him before all the assembled inhabitants of La Roque, and pass sentence immediately."

Mixed reactions: Peyssou, Hervé, Maurice, and the two prisoners delighted at the prospect of such high jinks. Meyssonnier looking at me doubtfully. Thomas clearly disapproving. And Jacquet had twisted around and was looking down at me with an anxious look in his eyes. He was quite simply afraid for me.

I went on: "So, you make sure everyone is assembled in the chapel, then you come down to the south gate to fetch me. I enter alone and unarmed, escorted by Burg, Jeannet, Hervé, and Maurice, rifles slung over their shoulders. And the trial begins. Hervé, since you're supposed to be Vilmain's spokesman, you must allow me to defend myself and also make sure any of the townspeople who want to speak are given the chance."

"But what about us?" Peyssou said, bitterly disappointed at being excluded from the fun.

"You will come in at the very end, when Maurice comes to fetch you. All four of you, bringing Fabrelâtre with you. Did you think to bring a tether for Malabar, Jacquet?"

"Yes," Jacquet said, eyes still heavy with apprehension.

"I've chosen Burg because he was the cook and therefore known to Fulbert well by sight, and I've chosen Hervé because of his talent as an actor. Hervé will be the only one to speak. That way you can be sure of not tripping one another up."

A silence. Hervé was stroking his little beard with a professional air. I could sense that he was already rehearsing.

"You can get back in now," Jacquet said, reining Malabar in.

"All right, get in, all of you others," I said with a gesture of the arms that embraced our new members and the prisoners. "I have to talk to my 'veterans.' "

I could see from Thomas's face that there was an abscess in formation in that quarter, and I wanted to lance it before it got any worse. I allowed the cart to get a good thirty feet ahead of us. Then we followed, line abreast, Thomas on my left, Meyssonnier on my right, Peyssou to the right of Meyssonnier.

"What the hell is all this amateur theatricals?" Thomas said in a quiet but furious voice. "What's the point of it? It's totally unnecessary. All we have to do is take Fulbert by the scruff of his neck, stick him against a wall, and shoot him!"

I turned to Meyssonnier. "Would you agree with that analysis of the situation?"

"It depends on what you mean to do in La Roque," Meyssonnier said.

"We're going to do what we said we would: take power."

"That's what I thought," Meyssonier said.

"Oh, not because I want to. I don't particularly. But because we must. La Roque's weakness weakens us, it constitutes a permanent danger to us. Any band that comes along can just seize it and use it as a base to attack us."

"And also," Peyssou said, "they have very good land around La Roque."

That thought had occurred to me too. I hadn't mentioned it though. I didn't want Thomas to accuse me of cupidity. Because nothing could have been further from the truth. For me, the problem was wholly one of security, not of possession. In a few months I had already lost all sense of private property. I no longer even remembered that Malevil had once belonged to me. What I feared was that some ruthless leader would one day seize the town and see to it that the richness of its land was converted into terms of power. I didn't want a neighbor capable of holding us in subjection. Nor did I want to hold La Roque in subjection to us. I wanted a union between twin communities, so that each would aid and guarantee the safety of the other while always retaining its own distinct personality.*

"In that case," Meyssonnier said, "we can't just shoot Fulbert."

"And why not?" Thomas asked belligerently.

"Because we must avoid taking power by shedding blood."

I cut in: "And particularly a priest's blood."

"He's a fake priest," Thomas said.

"That's irrelevant, as long as there are people who think he's a genuine one."

* This passage was to be cited very often in later days, both by the people of La Roque and by ourselves, sometimes in support of diametrically opposed arguments. [Note added by Thomas.]

"All right, I'll accept that," Thomas said. "But I still don't understand why you need to go about it like this. It's ridiculous, it's just playacting!"

"Playacting, yes. But with a precise aim in view: to lead Fulbert on until he reveals to all the townspeople just how far he aided and abetted Vilmain. Which he will do all the more readily if he believes himself to be in an unassailable position of strength."

"And then?"

"We can use his admission against him in his own trial."

"But you're not going to condemn him to death?"

"Nothing would give me greater pleasure, believe me, but we've told you, it's just not possible."

"So what then?"

"I don't know. Perhaps banishment?"

Thomas stopped, and we all stopped with him, allowing the cart to draw even farther ahead.

"So it's just for that," he said in a low voice shaking with indignation. "It's just to banish him that you're going to put your life in the hands of those four fellows we none of us know from Adam? Four of Vilmain's gangsters!"

I looked at him. I had just realized at last the real reason for his hostility to my "amateur theatricals." It was no different from Jacquet's really. He was afraid for my personal safety. I shrugged. To me, it seemed the risk just didn't exist. Hervé and Maurice could scarcely have had more opportunities to betray us during the past twenty-four hours. Yet they hadn't, they had fought beside us. As for the other two, there was only one thought in both their minds; to integrate themselves as quickly as they possibly could into our community.

"After all, they will be armed and you won't."

"Hervé and Maurice will keep their rifles, with full magazines. Burg and Jeannet will be issued with rifles too, but without ammunition. And I have this."

I produced my uncle's little revolver from my pocket. I had snatched it out of my desk drawer while I was changing. It was really no more than a toy. But accustomed as I was, ever since the day in the wheatfield, to have a gun slung from my shoulder almost every waking hour of the day, I would have felt naked with no weapon at all. And the revolver, tiny though it was, at least served to reassure Thomas, I could see that.

"If you ask me," Meyssonnier said, having by now passed the whole problem through all the various digestive chambers of his brain, "if you ask me, the idea is a good one. With Josepha and Gazel out of the château, the people in La Roque can't have any idea just how hand in glove Fulbert and Vilmain were. And just by agreeing to condemn you, he'll be giving himself away. Yes," he concluded with a grave, judicial air, "on the whole, definitely a good thing. Forcing the enemy to reveal his position."

XVIII

THE chapel in which my "trial" was to take place was the chapel of the château, the church in the lower town having been destroyed by fire on the day it happened. The Lormiaux family used to have Mass said there on Sundays by a friend who happened to be a priest, and as a mark of special favor they also invited in the dignitaries of La Roque and the surrounding district. Which in all, women and children included, made a band of about twenty chosen. The Lormiaux didn't like sharing God with just anyone.

The château of La Roque, as I have said, is a Renaissance structure, which is to say modern to anyone from Malevil, but the chapel dates from the twelfth century. It is long and narrow, with a roof of ribbed vaulting supported on round pillars, themselves in turn supported by enormously thick walls pierced with tall, narrow openings scarcely any larger than arrow slits. The chancel is a semicircular apse, with a different kind of vaulting supported by external buttresses plus a series of small round pillars inside. This section, which was half in ruins, had been reconstructed with great tact by an architect from Paris. Which just goes to show that you can buy anything if you have the wherewithal, even taste.

Behind the altar (a plain marble slab resting on two rectangular piers and facing the congregation) the Lormiaux had insisted on reopening a Gothic arch that had been walled up and putting in a very fine stained-glass window. The idea was that the sun should filter through it and light up the priest from behind as he celebrated Mass. Unhappily, however, the Lormiaux had failed to notice that the window faced west, and that it was therefore not possible—short of a miracle—for it to provide the officiant with a halo of glory in the morning. Nevertheless, no one had ever disputed the usefulness of the window, since the infrequent and very narrow openings in the side walls produced no more than a cryptlike gloom in the nave, even on the sunniest of days. In this mysterious semidarkness, in which the faithful moved so wanly, like the future shades they were preparing to become, at least they could now see the altar—and the hope being offered them from it—in a somewhat clearer light.

The entire population of La Roque was in there, at least as far as I could judge. Because coming in from the warm bright afternoon sun, I could see almost nothing in that medieval cave, whose damp cold fell on me like a shroud. As agreed, Vilmain's four armed men ordered me to sit on one of the chancel steps. Then they sat down themselves, two on each side of me, looking very grim and determined, rifles upright between their legs. Behind me was the stark modern altar already described, and behind that again, higher up, the stained-glass window. It ought to have been lit up, since it was now past four, but in fact it wasn't, because the sun had gone behind a cloud at the very moment I walked in. I sat with the small of my back against the upper chancel step, folded my arms, and set myself to making out the faces before me in the gloom.

For a moment I could see no more than shining eyes, with here and there the white patch of a shirt. It was some time before I was gradually able to identify individuals. Some of them, I noted with sadness, were avoiding my gaze. Old Pougès among them. But on my left, lit by the miserly light from one of the narrow side windows, I finally made out the central core of my supporters: Marcel Falvine, Judith Médard, the two widows—Agnès Pimont and Marie Lanouaille—and two farmers whose names I couldn't quite remember at the moment. In the first row I recognized Gazel, limp hands folded on his lap, narrow forehead crowned with those beautiful curls that always reminded me of my sisters'.

When I walked in through the little side door at chancel

level, I had not seen Fulbert. I presumed that he was pacing up and down the central aisle, and that as I entered he had been approaching the great Gothic door at the far end, about to make his turn and walk back. As I sat down, I still couldn't see him, because the far end of the nave was also its darkest area, there being no side windows at all near the door. But in the silence that settled on everyone at my entrance, long before I saw him I heard his footsteps ringing on the great stone flags. The steps came nearer, and Fulbert emerged gradually from darkness into half darkness. Neither his charcoal gray suit nor his gray shirt and black tie caught much of the light. What I perceived first was his white forehead, the white wings of hair at his temples, his eye sockets, and his hollow cheeks. After a second I could also see his silver cross swinging on his breast at the mercy of the indubitably very human passions that were agitating it.

Walking toward me without haste, with firm and measured tread, heels ringing imperiously on the stone floor, head held well out in front of his body and poised like a snake's about to strike, he looked as though he had every intention of devouring me alive there and then. But instead he stopped about three paces short of me, stood with his hands behind his back, swaying backward and forward slightly on his feet, as though before he struck he wanted to hypnotize me, and looked me slowly up and down in silence, shaking his head from side to side. Even at that distance I could only just make out his body, because its dark clerical garb melted into the darkness of the chapel beyond. But his head, apparently floating disembodied above me, his head I could see extremely well, and I was startled by the look in his magnificent squinting eyes. Because they were expressing nothing but kindness, compassion, and sadness, as indeed were the accompanying motions of his head, so that his whole appearance was that of a man caught up in a situation he was finding very painful indeed.

I was disappointed, and even uneasy. Not that I believed in the sincerity of his compassion for a moment; but if he continued to play this evangelical game to the end, then my little comedy would become indefensible,

540

my plan would collapse under me, and it would be difficult for me in the sequel to pass sentence on a man who had just refused to judge me. Because it was in fact a refusal to pass judgment that his pitying attitude seemed to indicate.

The silence lasted for several interminable seconds. All the townspeople looked alternately at Fulbert and myself, astounded that Fulbert wasn't opening his mouth. Meanwhile, my uneasiness faded. This preliminary silence, I realized, was simply a preacher's trick to command attention, and also, I would swear, a sadistic ruse to inspire false hopes in the accused. As I studied Fulbert's shifty gaze fixed upon me, I had just noticed that his squint wasn't solely the result of a divergence of the pupils but also of the fact that his right eye had a totally different expression from the left one. The left one, in harmony with the paternal head-shakings and the melancholy grimace of the lips, was brimming with fathomless pity. The right one, on the other hand, was glittering with malice and completely contradicting the messages being conveyed by its fellow. By concentrating solely on that one eye and ignoring the rest of his features I could perceive the phenomenon quite plainly.

I was very pleased with this discovery, because it seemed to me to complete the whole Janus-like picture I had been forming of Fulbert's personality: the coarse hands with their flattened fingers belying the intellectual brow, the emaciated face giving the lie to the plump torso. His whole body, eyes included, was in itself a series of lies and contradictions without his needing to open his mouth at all.

But at last he did. He began to speak in a deep, resonant voice that sounded like a cello. It was musical, unctuous. And the content, right from the word go, exceeded all my wildest hopes. Fulbert just hadn't the words, he informed us, to deplore the situation in which he now saw me. A situation that was causing him personally grievous affliction (I'd have bet a hundred to one on that!)—especially given the "great warmth" of the friendship he had felt for me, a friendship I had betrayed, and which he had been obliged with great sadness to renounce, as a consequence of the errors into which my pride had led me, errors that were today receiving a punishment in which he saw the hand of God . . .

I will skip the rest of this nauseating preamble. It was followed by an indictment that deviated further and further from the initial suavity of tone. And in fact, at the very first accusation he hurled at me—it was concerned with what he termed Catie's "kidnaping"—there were mumurs in the nave, and these murmurs continued to grow, despite the increasingly threatening looks that Fulbert shot around him and the ever-increasing sharpness and hardness of tone he employed in the enumeration of his grounds for complaint.

These were of three kinds: I had kidnaped a young woman from La Roque, in violation of the parish council's decree, and after abusing her I had abandoned her to one of my men after a simulacrum of marriage. I had profaned the sancity of the Christian religion by having myself elected priest by my servants and by conducting, with them, a parody of the rites and sacraments of the Church. I had moreover taken advantage of this first blasphemy in order to give free rein to my heretical tendencies by discrediting the sacrament of confession by my words and by my practice. Lastly, I had done everything within my power to support and encourage the evil and subversive elements in La Roque, in open revolt against their pastor, and I had made threats in writing to intervene by force of arms if they were punished. I had even laid claim, with the use of fallacious historical arguments, to the suzerainty of La Roque. It was evident, Fulbert concluded, that if Captain Vilmain—that was how he referred to him—had not taken up residence in La Roque (cries of "Lanouaille! Lanouaille!"), then La Roque would one day or another have been the target of my criminal intentions, with all the consequences that could easily be imagined for the liberties and the lives of the town's citizens. (Loud and repeated cries of "Lanouaille! Pimont! Courcejac!")

The situation in the chapel at that moment could hardly have been more tense. Three quarters of those present, eyes lowered, were keeping a hostile silence, but appeared

542

for the moment at least to be sufficiently terrorized by Fulbert's tone and the threatening looks he was flashing at them to make no protest. The remaining quarter—Judith, Agnès Pimont, Marie Lanouaille, Marcel, and the two farmers whose name I was still vainly trying to recall—were in a state of unrestrained fury. They were protesting, yelling, and even waving their fists at Fulbert as they stood leaning forward in their places. The women especially were beside themselves, and if it hadn't been for my four supposed guards, I had the feeling that they would be quite capable of throwing themselves on their curé and ripping him to pieces in the middle of the chapel.

I had the impression that my trial had worked like a detonator. It had finally set off the buried charge of execration the opposition in La Roque felt for their self-appointed leader. And it was now exploding out into the open for the very first time, with a violence that had clearly stunned Fulbert.

A pastmaster at lying, he must have been equally clever at self-deception. Ever since he took over command in La Roque, he must have been convincing himself that the fear he inspired was in fact respect. It was clear, at all events, that he'd had no idea he was so hated by his flock—by all his flock, since the attitude of the majority, though more cautious and expressed in nothing louder than murmurs, was for all that one of hostility. The impact this hatred had on him was frightening. I could see him literally shake on his base, like a statue about to be toppled from its plinth. He flushed, then paled, clenched his fists, began several sentences without managing to finish a single one, his hollow face convulsed, while terror and fury alternated in his flashing eyes.

But he was no coward. He stood up to them. He strode firmly over to the chancel steps, climbed them, and taking up his stance at the top between Jeannet and Maurice, he spread his arms in a request for silence. And staggeringly enough, after a few seconds he got it, so strong was the habit in La Roque of listening to him speak.

"I see that the moment has come," he said in a voice quivering with anger and indignation, "when we must separate the wheat from the tares. There are people here

543

who call themselves Christians and who have not hesitated to plot against their pastor behind his back. Those conspirators should know one thing: I shall do my duty without flinching. If there are those here who besmirch the community's good name and seek to corrupt it, then I shall cast them out from the church. I will cleanse my father's house from its floor to its ceiling! And if I find filth in it, then I shall surely cast it out!"

This address produced further indignant cries and violent protests. I noticed Marie Lanouaille especially, almost breaking from Marcel and Judith's grasp, shouting in a high-pitched voice, "You are the filth! You, eating with my husband's murderers!"

From my seat on the steps I could see my prosecutor's right eye only. It was flaming with mad hatred. In his fury, Fulbert had lost all his usual self-control and cunning. He was no longer maneuvering, he was going for an all-out confrontation. He wanted to beat the opposition down by force. With Vilmain's rifles behind him he felt strong. He was determined to defy the rebels. And smash them. In a few short minutes he had regressed, perhaps as a result of contagion by proximity, to a mentality as primitive and brutish as Vilmain's own. At that moment, standing confronting his fellow citizens, drunk with rage, he had no other thought in his mind, I'm certain, than mowing them down with bullet or blade.

When Fulbert once again stretched out his arms, a relative silence returned, and in a changed, high, almost hysterical voice, which had nothing in common with his usual cellolike tones, he almost howled, "As for the true instigator of all these plots, Emmanuel Comte, your present attitude leaves me no choice! In the name of the parish council I condemn him to death!"

The tumult that broke out then was wilder than I could possibly have imagined. And I could sense that Hervé, on my right, was becoming uneasy. He was afraid that the townspeople might actually attack and disarm him and his fellow "guards," so violent had their demonstrations of anger become. The fact that they didn't make that transition from words to action was due, I think, to lack of prior planning, and above all to their lack of a leader. But also to the fact that Fulbert, simply by his presence, by his courage, by the open hatred blazing on his face, was still exercising a measure of his old power over them.

Gazel had started when his ex-confederate mentioned the parish council, then he had shaken his head and lifted his limp hands up to his face in a gesture of repudiation.

I leaned over to Hervé and said quietly, "Let Gazel speak. I think he has something to say."

Hervé stood up, slinging his rifle over his shoulder as he did so in order to convey his peaceful intentions. He stood there for a good second, elegantly posed with his weight on one foot, hand raised to request attention, an amiable expression on his youthful countenance. As soon as he had obtained silence, he said in a calm and courteous voice, in striking contrast to the furious howling that had preceded his intervention, "I think Monsieur l'Abbé Gazel has something to say. He has the floor."

After which he sat down again. Hervé's youth, elegance, and polite self-confident tone, plus the fact that he had gone over Fulbert's head in order to give Gazel the floor, produced a stunned pause. And the most stunned of all those present was undoubtedly Fulbert, who simply couldn't understand why Vilmain's spokesman was going to let Gazel express his opinions: Gazel, who had criticized Lanouaille's murder and Vilmain's "excesses"!

Gazel for his part was not a bit happy to find himself being offered an opportunity to speak that he had certainly not asked for. He would have been quite content with his original gesture, a much less compromising form of protest. But since cries of "Speak, speak, Monsieur Gazel!" were by now rising from the nave behind him, while Hervé was making encouraging gestures in front, he steeled himself to stand up. Beneath the beautifully arranged graying curls, his long clown's face looked flabby, bewildered, sexless, and when he spoke it was in that neutered, fluting voice that no one could hear without a quiet smile. But all the same, he said what he had to say, in front of us all, in front of Fulbert, and that took some courage.

"I should like to point out," he said, hands clasped

against his chest, "that since I left the Château on account of all the wicked things that were happening in La Roque, the parish council has not met."

"And what has that to do with anything?" Fulbert jumped in immediately with crushing contempt. "What importance do you think it can have, you cretin, whether you've resigned from the parish council or not?"

Something rose inside Gazel's long goitery neck, and his flabby face hardened. If there is one thing that semi-invalids of his kind never forgive it is a wound to their self-esteem.

"I beg your pardon, Monseigneur," he said in a quite different voice, a sharp, vinegary old maid's voice, "but you said that you condemn Monsieur Comte in the name of the parish council. And I was pointing out to you that the parish council has not met, and that I personally do not agree with the sentence you passed on Monsieur Comte, as it happens."

Gazel was applauded, and not only by the five opposition members but also by two or three of the majority, who, I assumed, had been made to feel ashamed by his courage. Gazel sat down again, blushing and trembling.

Fulbert immediately turned all his thunders on him. "I can do without your agreement, believe me! You have betrayed my trust, you little nonentity. I shan't forget this, and I shall see to it you pay for it!"

These words were greeted with a storm of booing, and Judith, suddenly remembering her Christian Radical days, began yelling at the top of her voice, "Nazi! S.S.!" And Marcel, I noticed, was not trying anywhere near as hard to restrain her as he had been earlier. I was afraid that Judith might prove the leader the townspeople needed to lead an attack, and afraid above all for the safety of my escort.

I stood up and said loudly, "I demand the right to speak."

"Granted," Hervé said immediately with relief.

"What?" Fulbert cried, rounding on Hervé in fury, "you are allowing that wretch to speak? That false priest? That enemy of God! You cannot be serious! I've just sentenced him to death!"

"All the more reason," Hervé said, stroking his little pointed beard with great calm. "The least he should be allowed is a few last words."

"But this is intolerable!" Fulbert raged on. "What does this mean? Is it stupidity or treason? Do you think you can do as you please here? It's incredible! I order you to keep the prisoner silent, do you hear?"

"It is not for you to give me orders," Hervé replied with dignity. "You are not my leader. In Vilmain's absence, I am in command here," he added, tapping his rifle butt with the flat of one hand, "and I have decided that the accused shall be allowed to speak. In fact he can speak for as long as he likes."

At that an amazing thing happened. Hervé was applauded by a good half of those present. Though it was true that he was only a recruit in Vilmain's band and had taken no part in the "wicked things" referred to by Gazel, so they had no grievances against him personally. But all the same, to applaud any member of Vilmain's crew! They were obviously in a state of total confusion.

"This is intolerable!" Fulbert shouted, clenching his fists, squinting eyes almost bursting out of their sockets. "You seem to be unaware that by allowing that creature to speak you are making yourself an accomplice of conspirators and rebels. But you are not going to get away with it! I warn you now, I shall report you to your leader and he will punish you!"

"That seems to me very unlikely," Hervé answered, with a serenity so unfeigned that I wondered whether he hadn't gone too far and given the game away. "In any case," he added, "I'm not going back on my word. The prisoner may speak."

"In that case," Fulbert cried, "I shall not stay to listen! I shall leave! I shall return to the château and wait for Vilmain's return!"

He walked down the steps and set off up the aisle, running the gauntlet of the opposition's invective, toward the main door at the far end. This didn't suit my plan at all. Without Fulbert there could be no countertrial. Raising my voice, I shouted at his retreating back, "So you're so

547

terrified of what I'm about to say that you haven't even the courage to stay and listen!"

He stopped, swiveled around on his heels, and faced me. I went on in a clear, firm tone: "It is now a quarter past five. Vilmain said that he would be here at five-thirty. I therefore have another quarter of an hour to live, and you, during that last quarter of an hour, you are still so afraid of me that you are trembling like a leaf and rushing off to hide under your bed to wait for your master! Yes, under your bed! Not even on top of it!"

Hervé's attitude had succeeded in making Fulbert very uneasy. I had reassured him a great deal by announcing that Vilmain was only a quarter of an hour away. And that accusation of cowardice had really made him smart. Because a coward he was not, as I knew. But that strength hid a weakness. Like many courageous people, he was vain of his courage. And as I had expected, that vanity obliged him to take up my challenge.

He stood quite still, pale, stiff, eyes burning above those emaciated cheeks, then he said with vast disdain, "You may deliver yourself of any idiocies you choose. They will not disturb me. Talk if you must. While you can."

I seized the opening he had offered me immediately. "I mean to. And I shall begin with a complete refutation of all your accusations. Catie first. I did not 'abuse' her as you dared to claim, and I did not kidnap her. That was a total fabrication. Of her own free will, and with her uncle's permission"—"that's true!" Marcel immediately cried; and I was glad I need no longer worry about compromising him—"she went to pay a visit to her grandmother at Malevil. And while there she fell in love with Thomas and married him. Which put your nose out of joint, didn't it, Fulbert? Because you wanted to have her up in the château waiting on you."

There were snickers at this, and Fulbert exclaimed, "That is totally untrue!"

"Oh, pardon me!" a small, voluminous woman of about fifty said immediately, without asking permission to speak. She stood up. It was Josepha, the château housekeeper. Though not held in much esteem theoretically on account of her Portuguese origin (the people of La Roque were racists), she was in practice quite well liked because she had a very ready tongue and told you anything straight to your face when she had something on her chest.

Josepha was no beauty. She had one of those skins apparently beyond the aid of soap and water. Apart from which she was stumpy, jowly, and busty. But with her strong white teeth, her strong jaw, her extremely bright eyes and her luxuriant hair she projected a pleasing impression of animal vitality.

"Pardon me!" she went on in a harsh, vulgar accent that seemed to add a great deal of force to what she said. "You oughtn't to say things are untrue when they aren't. Because it's true that Monseigneur didn't want me up there any more, and he did want that girl instead. Even though she wouldn't have served his turn as well," she added, though whether with false or genuine naïveté I couldn't say.

She sat down again amid a barrage of jibes and laughter at Fulbert's expense. And I noticed that Monseigneur avoided taking issue with Josepha over her statement. He clearly knew that tongue of hers too well, and preferred to turn what she'd said back against me.

"I fail to see what you, Comte, have to gain," he observed haughtily, "by inciting low gossip against your bishop!"

"You are not my bishop!" I said. "Very far from it! And I have everything to gain by throwing your lies back in your teeth! And here is another of them, another monstrous one! You said that I had myself elected to the priesthood by my servants. That is untrue in the first place," I said with great vehemence, "because I have no servants, I have only friends and equals. And contrary to what happens in La Roque, nothing important is ever done at Malevil without all of us having discussed the matter together.

"Why was I elected to be their abbé? I'll tell you. You were very anxious to palm Monsieur Gazel off on us in that capacity, and we for our part did not particularly want him at Malevil. I hope I shall not offend him by saying that. That is why my companions elected me to the office of priest. As for being a good or a bad priest, I

549

know nothing about that. I am an elected priest, like Monsieur Gazel. I do my best. When there is no horse for the plow, then the ass must needs serve. I don't think I am any worse a priest than Monsieur Gazel, and I don't have to try very hard to be a better one than you." (Laughter and applause.)

"It is pride that makes you speak thus!" Fulbert cried. "In reality, you are a false priest! A bad priest! An abominable priest! And you know it! I will not even touch on your private life."

"Nor I on yours!"

He didn't take that one up. Afraid I'd mention Miette, presumably. "To cite only one example," he rushed on in his rage, "your conception of confession, and your practice in that respect, are totally heretical!"

"I don't know whether they're heretical or not," I said in a modest voice. "I'm not educated enough in religious matters to decide that. What I do know is that I am a little wary of the practice, because in the hands of a bad priest it can become a method of spying and an instrument of tyranny."

"And you are quite right, Monsieur Comte," Judith shouted in her stentor's voice. "That is precisely what confession has become here in La Roque, in the hands of that Nazi there!"

"Silence, woman!" Fulbert said, turning toward her. "You are a rebel against religion, a madwoman, and a bad Christian!"

"You should be ashamed," Marcel cried at that, leaning forward, his powerful hands clenched around the back of the chair in front of him. "You should be ashamed talking like that to a woman, and to a woman much better educated than you are too. She even corrected you the other day about the stupid mistakes you made about Jesus's brothers and sisters."

"Corrected me!" Fulbert cried, throwing up his arms. "That poor hysteric knows nothing whatever about it! Brothers and sisters is an error of translation. They were his cousins. I've already told you that!"

While this amazing theological dispute got under way in the very middle of what was supposed to be a trial, I said quietly to Maurice, "Go and fetch the others. Tell them to come to the main door of the chapel and wait there. When I announce Vilmain's death they are to come in, not before."

Maurice melted away, supple and silent as a cat, and I permitted myself to interrupt our Judith, who, quite forgetful of time and place, was still conducting her passionate argument with Fulbert on the subject of Christ's kith and kin.

"One moment!" I said. "I should like to finish!"

Silence fell, and Judith—who had quite forgotten me—glanced over with a repentant air. I went on in a calm voice: "I come now to the last crime Fulbert has imputed to me. He claims that I wrote a letter claiming suzerainty in La Roque, and announcing my intention of taking the town by force and then occupying it. It is a great pity that Fulbert did not see fit to read my letter out, since everyone here would then have been in a position to know that it said nothing of the kind. But let us suppose that it did. Let us even suppose that I had in fact announced in that letter my intention to attack La Roque. The only question to be asked is this: Did I in fact do it? Was it I who came at nightfall to occupy La Roque? Was it I who slashed the throat of the guard at the gate? Was it I who plundered your stores, threatened your men, and raped your women? Was it I who slaughtered every human living creature at Courcejac? Yet the man who did all those things, Fulbert treats as his friend! While he has condemned me to death for having, so he claims, the intention of doing them! That is Fulbert's justice: death for the innocent, his friendship for a murderer!"

The sun had certainly chosen the right moment to light up the window behind me, and behind Hervé too, as he spoke the last lines of his commander's role. "Hey there, that's enough, prisoner!" he said. "We can't have you talking about the captain like that!"

I cut him short. "Don't interrupt, Hervé. The joke is over."

Hearing me talk in that tone to my guard, Fulbert started violently, and all the others stared wide-eyed. I drew myself up to my full height. I basked with almost

551

sensual pleasure in the light from the window. I could feel my eyes opening wider and my whole being unfurling in that sudden brightness. It was amazing too how warm the sun felt on my shoulders and back, even filtered through the colored glass. And it was very welcome. I was numb with cold.

I began to speak again, but discarding my previous calm tone, allowing my voice full rein, till it filled the chapel with its volume.

"When Armand killed Pimont after attempting to abuse his wife, you protected him. When Bébelle had slit Lanouaille's throat, you entertained him and Vilmain at your table. When Jean Feyrac had massacred the people at Courcejac, you continued to drink and joke with him. And why did you do all that? To win Vilmain's friendship, because now that Armand was dead you were counting on Vilmain's help to perpetuate your tyranny over La Roque, to rid yourself at one and the same time of Malevil and all internal opposition too."

I had thundered my accusations out in total silence. As I finished, I saw that Fulbert had managed to pull himself together.

"I can only wonder what the point of all this chatter is," he said, the cello tones back again. "It is not going to alter your fate one iota."

"You haven't answered!" Judith stormed, leaning forward, square jaw jutting from the turtleneck of her navy blue sweater, blue eyes shooting sparks of fury in Fulbert's direction.

"I was about to do so, and very briefly," Fulbert said with a furtive glance at his watch. (I supposed that he had by now succeeded in stilling his apprehensions and was expecting Vilmain to arrive at any moment.) "I need hardly say," he went on, "that I do not approve of all the things that Captain Vilmain and his men have done, here and elsewhere. But soldiers have always been soldiers, and there is nothing we can do about it. My role, as Bishop of La Roque, is to consider the good that I can extract from that evil. If I am enabled, thanks to Captain Vilmain's aid, to root out heresy root and branch in La

552

Roque and in Malevil, then I shall consider that I have done my duty."

At that, a paroxysm was reached, the crowd's fury knew no bounds. Not just the opposition either. The whole population had been goaded into rage by this admission. And I wasn't even thinking of turning the fact to my advantage at that moment. I was speechless, because I had just realized, with profound astonishment, that Fulbert had been almost sincere in what he said. Not that I am denying his hunger for personal revenge! But all the same, at that instant, it became quite clear to me that this false priest, this mountebank, this scheming opportunist, had ended up by identifying himself with his role. He more than half believed in his mission as guardian of the true faith!

Without entirely grasping its significance, the docile attitude of my guards toward me must have encouraged and reassured the congregation, because insults and threats were being showered on Fulbert now from all sides, and mingled with them, here and there, albeit enunciated with no less passion, a variety of petty personal grievances. For instance, I caught the voice of old Pougès at one point, filled with hate as he reproached the *cura* for having refused him a glass of wine one day. Fulbert now seemed to me to be almost the only person present who still believed in Vilmain's imminent arrival. He was clinging to that illusion desperately. And I could see that he was strengthened in his hopes when he heard a noise behind him at that moment beyond the great main door. He turned, and as he did so Maurice slipped in through the side door and signaled to me that the others were outside.

Even more furious, the imprecations and insults continued to rain on Fulbert as he stood, stoical and still, in the center of the main aisle. If words, looks, and gestures alone could kill, he would have been already ripped to pieces. And at the very moment when I was about to give him his coup de grâce, knowing quite well what would happen when I did, I hesitated. Needless to say, that hesitation was no more than a little indulgence I was allowing my conscience, at the very last moment, to make

553

my soul as white as my clothes. Because in fact it was too late. I had set the machinery in motion now, and I could no longer stop it. Just as Fulbert had judged my execution necessary on the grounds that I was a heretic and a troublemaker, so I considered his indispensable to any union between Malevil and La Roque, the necessary foundation of our mutual security. The difference was that I was about to kill him for real, and without any sentence of death, any trial, any shot being fired, wtihout even soiling my hands.

Fulbert's voice was drowned by the hate-filled clamor of the congregation, and I admired his courage as he stood there, incapable of making himself heard, but still returning hate for hate, with interest, with his blazing eyes. For a moment, however, there was a sudden lull, and he found the strength to throw them one last challenge. "You will sing a different tune when Captain Vilmain comes!"

He had given me my cue. This was my big scene. At the last moment I had hit upon what I was sure was the right way to play it. So I improvised. I stretched out my arms to ask for silence, as Fulbert himself had done earlier, and as soon as the din faded, I said in my most calm, even voice, "I can't help wondering why you insist on referring to Vilmain as 'Captain.' Because he wasn't a captain." I didn't emphasize that past tense too much in speaking it. "I have here"—removing my wallet from my revolver pocket—"a document that proves it irrefutably. It is a professional card. With a very clear photograph. All those here who knew Vilmain will recognize him easily. And it says on this card, in black and white, that Vilmain was an accountant. Monsieur Gazel, would you like to take this card and show it to Fulbert?"

Silence fell like an ax descending, and the entire congregation turned their heads as one toward the central aisle, necks craning, heads tilting simultaneously to watch Fulbert's reaction. Because after all, however much he might wish to be at that moment, he was not blind. If the document being carried over to him had come into my possession, what was he to conclude from that? Fulbert snatched the card Gazel held out. One glance was enough. His face remained expressionless, his color didn't change. But the hand holding the card began to quiver. It was a very slight movement, but extremely rapid, and one that was apparently impossible for him to stop. From the tension in his features, I sensed that Fulbert was making desperate efforts to immobilze that card quivering like a tiny wing at the end of his fingers.

A long second passed, he still didn't manage to get out a single word. What I was seeing now was simply a man struggling with every ounce of strength he could muster against the terror welling up in him. The sight of that torture made me feel suddenly sickened, and I determined to cut it short.

In a voice I hoped was loud enough to be heard on the other side of the main door, I said, "I see that I owe you an explanation. The four armed guards you see with me are all honest young men whom Vilmain recruited by force. Two of them had come over to my side before the battle, and the two others entered my service immediately after it. These four are the only survivors of the band. Vilmain, at this moment, is occupying two square yards of Malevil territory."

There was a stunned murmur, over which Marcel's voice could easily be heard: "You mean he's dead?"

"That is exactly what I mean. Jean Feyrac is dead. Vilmain is dead. And with the exception of these four, who have become our friends, all the others have been killed too."

At that moment, the great Gothic door at the far end of the chapel swung half open, and one by one, Meyssonnier, Thomas, Peyssou, and Jacquet, moved forward into the nave, guns in hand. I say moved forward, because it was not an irruption. The movement was calm and even slow. Had it not been for their rifles, they could have passed for friendly visitors. They advanced a few paces up the central aisle, then I signaled to them with one hand to stop. My guards, who at another signal had stood up, were now gathered around me and equally motionless. There was a moment of stunned silence, then the congregation began howling threats of death at Fulbert. Only the two armed groups blocking both ends of the central aisle remained silent.

555

It was all over in no time. At the grating sound made by the main door, Fulbert swiveled around to look, and the last shred of his illusions vanished. When he turned back to face me again, face contorted, he saw me with my guards closing the trap on him. His nerves were unable to bear so great a fall after all the hope I had held out to him. His courage snapped. He had no other thought in his head but to escape—escape physically—from his hunters. In his panic he tried to reach the side door by going between two rows of chairs. But in his blindness he ran just in front of the one occupied by Marcel, Judith, and the two widows. Marcel didn't even strike him with his fist. He just pushed him with the flat of his hand, but without counting on the strength of his arm. Fulbert was hurled back violently onto the flagstones of the central aisle. A savage growling and howling went up. The mob closed in on him, scattering their chairs, and Fulbert vanished beneath the furious pack clustering and clinging around him. I heard him cry out twice. At the other end of the aisle I could see Peyssou's sickened and horrified expression, and his eyes fixed on mine asking me if he should intervene. I shook my head.

Mob justice is not pleasant to watch, but in the circumstances it did seem to me genuinely just. And it would have been hypocritical to try to stop it or deplore it when I had done my damnedest to bring it about.

When the cries of the crowd finally ebbed, I knew that they were clutching no more than an inert body in their hands. I waited. And little by little I watched the tight cluster around Fulbert loosen and disperse. They moved away from one another, returned to their places, picked up the chairs they had knocked over, some still flushed and angry, others, it seemed to me, rather ashamed, their eyes on the ground, hangdog expressions on their faces. I looked at the body abandoned in the middle of the aisle. I signaled to my companions to join me. They advanced along the aisle, walking around the body when they reached it, without looking down. Only Thomas stopped to examine Fulbert.

We didn't speak, even though the new recruits had all moved discreetly away. When Thomas got up from his knees and continued up the aisle toward me, I detached myself from the group and took two steps forward to meet him.

"Dead?" I said in a low voice.

He nodded.

"Well," I said in the same quiet tone, "you should be glad. You've got what you wanted."

He looked at me for a while. And in his eyes there was that mixture of love and antipathy that he had always shown toward me. "You too," he said tersely.

I climbed the chancel steps again, turned to the congregation, and asked for silence. Then I said, "Burg and Jeannet will carry Fulbert's body to his room. Monsieur Gazel, will you be good enough to accompany them and keep vigil? As for the rest of us, I suggest that we resume our assembly in ten minutes from now. We have decisions to be made together that involve the interests of both La Roque and Malevil."

The shuffling and murmuring were subdued at first but grew in intensity as soon as Burg and Jeannet had carried Fulbert's body out, as though the collective act that had deprived him of his life had been expunged by its disappearance. I asked my companions to keep away all the people trying to crowd around—though as tactfully as possible of course—since I had two or three urgent interviews ahead of me that required a certain measure of secrecy.

I walked down the steps and went over to the opposition group, the only section of the population that had shown courage in time of misfortune and dignity in triumph, since none of them had taken part in the killing, not even Marcel. After the push that had knocked Fulbert to the floor, he had not budged from his place, nor had Judith, the two widows, or the two farmers, whose names I now discovered were Faujanet and Delpeyrou. It was the ones who had trembled before him who had rounded on Fulbert and killed him.

Agnès Pimont and Marie Lanouaille kissed me. Marcel had little tears running down that shoe-leather face of his. And Judith, more manly than ever, seized my arm as she said, "Monsieur Comte, you were magnificent. Dressed in white like that—mystic, wonderful—you looked just as though you'd jumped out of the window there to slay the dragon." And as she spoke she continued to dig her strong fingers into my right biceps. I was to observe later that she was incapable of talking to any man still of an age to attract her (which given her own age was no narrow category) without massaging his upper limbs. I remembered that she had introduced herself at our first meeting as "unmarried" as opposed to "a spinster," and as I thanked her I couldn't help wondering if, in these months since the day it happened, she had remained insensible to Marcel's Herculean shoulders, or Marcel to her powerful attractions. I thought that without irony, because she is really attractive.

"Listen," I said, lowering my voice and drawing them aside, together with Faujanet and Delpeyrou, whom I shook warmly by the hand, "we haven't much time. You must organize yourselves. You can't let Fulbert's ex-bootlickers run La Roque. You must propose the election of a town council. Put your own six names on a piece of paper and produce your list there and then. No one will dare oppose you."

"Don't put my name," Agnès Pimont said.

"Or mine," Marie Lanouaille said quickly.

"Why not?"

"There would be too many women. That would annoy them. But Madame Médard, yes. Madame Médard is a teacher," Agnès said.

"Call me Judith, my dear," Judith said, placing her hand on Agnès's shoulder. (So she squeezed women too.)

"Oh, I don't think I would ever dare," Agnès said with a blush.

I looked at her. It was a lovely sight, that fine, fair skin with the color rising behind it.

"And what about a mayor?" Marcel said. "The only one of us here that can talk is Judith. I wouldn't want to offend you at all"—he looked at her with tender admiration—"but a lady mayor, that they will never accept. Especially with you not speaking the patois."

"I have a question to put to you," I broke in immediately. "Would you accept someone from Malevil as your mayor?"

"You?" Marcel said hopefully.

"No, not me. I was thinking of someone like Meyssonnier."

I could see out of the corner of my eye that Agnès Pimont was a little disappointed. Perhaps she had been expecting another name.

"Well now," Marcel said, "he is a responsible fellow, and an honest fellow . . ."

I put in, "And he's had military training. Which is going to be very useful in organizing your defense of the town."

"I know him," Faujanet said.

"Me too," Delpeyrou said.

That was all they were going to say. I looked at their frank squarecut tanned faces. That "I know him" implied no reservations.

"Still and all," Marcel said.

"What 'still and all'?"

"Well, he's a Communist."

"Now, Marcel, be serious," Judith said. "What's a Communist without a Communist Party?"

She tended to speak in a very clearly articulated classroom voice that would have got on my nerves slightly if I'd had to be around her day in and day out. But Marcel seemed to find it very impressive.

"That's true," he said with a shake of his bald head. "That's true, but all the same we don't want any dictating here. We've had quite enough dictators for a while."

I said sharply, "Meyssonnier is not that kind of man at all. Absolutely not. In fact it's an insult to suggest it."

"No offense meant," Marcel said.

"And you forget that now we will have the guns," Faujanet said.

I looked at him. Face almost a perfect square, the color of earthenware. Shoulders equally square. And not a fool, clearly. I liked the way he'd brought up the question of the guns by presupposing the solution he intended.

"I take it," I said, "that the council's first decision will be to arm the inhabitants of La Roque."

"In that case, all right," Marcel said.

Looks were exchanged. Agreement had been reached. And Judith, surprisingly I thought, had shown great tact. She had scarcely spoken at all.

"Right," I said with a quick smile. "Now all I have to do is persuade Meyssonnier."

I left them and turned to beckon Marie Lanouaille over to speak to me. She came promptly. She was a brunette, about twenty-five, with a plump, firm body. And as she stood there with her face tilted up, waiting for me to disclose my plans, I was suddenly seized by a powerful, violent desire to clasp her in my arms. Since I had never even flirted with her, never thought about her in that way at all before, I had no idea to what I should attribute this sudden impulse, unless it was an automatic physical desire for relaxation. No, perhaps relaxation wasn't the right word. Because love too is a struggle; but a struggle that must suddenly have appealed to some deeper instinct in me as being more positive than the one I had just been involved in, and even an antidote to it, since it gave life instead of taking it.

Meanwhile, however, I suppressed even my desire—as Judith our great biceps kneader would not have—to fasten my hand on the plump and charming flesh of her upper arm, a temptation made very difficult to resist by the fact that her dress had no sleeves.

"Marie," I said in a slightly muffled voice. "You know Meyssonnier. He's a simple man. He won't want to live up in the château. Your house is quite big. You wouldn't like to take him in, would you?"

She looked up at me open-mouthed. The fact that she hadn't said no immediately was encouraging.

"You won't have to cook for him. He'll almost certainly institute communal meals in La Roque. You could look after his washing and so on, but that's all he'd need."

"Well, now," she said, "I wouldn't say no myself, but then you know what people are like. If Meyssonnier came to live in my house you know what they'd say."

I shrugged. "And even if they did say that, what can it possibly matter? Even if it were true?"

She looked up at me rather sadly, then nodded, and

at the same time, because it had been cold in the chapel, she rubbed the arms I would have so enjoyed squeezing myself.

"Ah, my poor Emmanuel, you're right, you're right," she said with a sigh. "After all we've been through here!"

So finally it was yes. I thanked her and asked after her baby, Nathalie. Then came five minutes of absolutely mechanical conversation of which I heard not a word, not even the things I said myself. However, right at the end, Marie expressed an emotion that awakened and moved me.

"I'm almost afraid to breathe, you know. Because of everything happening, she hasn't had any injections against things. Nor Agnès's little Christine either. So naturally, I'm thinking all the time, My Nathalie, she can catch anything. And we have nothing! No doctor, no antibiotics, and all those horrible diseases in the air, which you never thought about before, because there were the injections. The smallest little pimple, and I'm terrified. And not even any peroxide left now. Do you know all I have to nurse her with? A thermometer!"

"And who's looking after her for you now, poor Marie?"

"An old lady in the town. She's looking after Christine too."

Then I asked her to find Agnès for me. She came over at once. And with Agnès it was different. I could be brief, authoritarian, and secretly tender.

"Agnès, I want you to assign your vote to Judith for the meeting and go back down into the town. Go and see that Christine's all right, then wait for me in your house. I have something to say to you. I won't be long."

She was a little bewildered by this shower of orders, but as I expected, she made no protest. We exchanged a look, just one, then I left her to look for Meyssonnier.

I was taking a lot on myself with Meyssonnier, I knew that. As I approached him I felt a certain remorse at manipulating my fellow beings like this, and especially when it came to him. And yet, it was in the interests of us all, of Malevil as well as La Roque. That is what I always told myself when my own cunning became a little odious even to me, as I knew it did to Thomas sometimes. It was monstrous, what I was going to ask of Meyssonnier. I was slightly ashamed about it. And yet that had not prevented me from busily going around collecting up my trumps, making sure I presented myself for the fray with a winning hand, one that had carefully taken into account all his mayoral ambitions and even his private temptations.

He listened to me without a word, with those narrow features molded by years of conscientious effort and duty, the flickering eyes, the straight fence of hair above (which somehow or other he had contrived to cut or have cut). I was very much aware of what I was doing: I was offering him the keys to both La Roque and Marie Lanouaille on a golden salver. And even both of those together would not easily persuade him to say goodbye to Malevil. It was going to break his heart anyway, I knew. But what choice had I? Who was there in La Roque to replace him? No one.

When I'd had my say, he said neither yes nor no. He needed more information, and he needed to ruminate.

"If I understand you correctly, my task in La Roque will be a double one: to establish a community life and to organize the town's defense."

"The defense first," I said.

He shook his head doubtfully. "The thing is, that won't be easy, you know. The walls are too low. You could climb them with a ladder. And how can I man that length of battlements? I won't have the men. Especially young ones."

"I'll give you Burg and Jeannet."

He replied with an unenthusiastic grimace. "And then weapons. I would need Vilmain's rifles."

"We have twenty. We'll split them."

"I'd need the bazooka too."

I laughed. "You're going too far! What's this sudden nationalism? You're already taking the interests of La Roque a little bit too much to heart, it seems to me!"

"I didn't say I was going to accept," Meyssonnier said coolly.

"And now you're blackmailing me into the bargain!"

But I couldn't get even a smile from him.

"All right then," I said after a moment's thought, "when

562

La Roque's fortifications are completed, I'll let you have the bazooka two weeks out of every four."

"Well, that would be something," Meyssonnier said, still cool, still giving nothing away. "Then there's all the booty Feyrac brought back from Courcejac. Quite a lot. Would you be claiming any of that?"

"What is there? Do you know?"

"Yes. Someone just told me. Poultry, two pigs, two cows, good stocks of hay and beets. The hay is still there in the barn. At least they weren't fool enough to burn that down."

"Two cows! I thought they only had one at Courcejac."

"They'd hidden the other so as not to have to give it to Fulbert."

"Well there's a thing! What people! They didn't give a damn if the La Roque babies died of hunger as long as their own were well fed! A fat lot of good it did them in the end!"

"So," Meyssonnier said curtly, bringing me back to the subject in hand. "What do you say? Do you want a share?"

"Do I want a share! What gall! The whole lot belongs by rights to Malevil, since it was Malevil that conquered Vilmain!"

"Listen," Meyssonnier said without a smile. "This is what I propose. You can take all the poultry——"

"The poultry you can stuff. We've already got more than enough at Malevil. They eat too much grain."

"Wait. You take the poultry, the two pigs, and we keep the rest."

I began to laugh. "Malevil two pigs and La Roque the two cows! And that's your idea of fair shares? But what about the hay? And the beets?"

He said nothing. Not a word. After a moment, I said, "But in any case, I can't make the decision all on my own. I would have to ask the assembly."

Then since he still remained stubbornly silent, eyes grave and stern, I went on with rather bad grace: "Well, since you have only the one at La Roque, we could perhaps stretch a point with the cows."

"Well, that's something," Meyssonnier said dolefully, as though he had just got very much the worst of our bargain.

Then silence. He was ruminating again. I didn't try to hurry him. "If I've understood correctly," he said with an expression of distaste, "I am also going to have to respect all the democratic forms, spend my time arguing the clock around, and listening to petty criticisms about everything from people who'll do nothing else, just sit on their behinds and complain."

"Don't exaggerate. You'll have a town council worth their weight in gold."

"How do I know they won't be just a weight around my neck? What about that woman, for instance?"

"Judith Médard?"

"Yes, Judith. What a tongue she has on her! And what is she exactly, anyway, the woman?" he said suspiciously. "A so-called Socialist?"

"Not at all! She's a Christian Radical."

His face cleared. "Ah, that's not so bad. I've always got on quite well with that kind of Catholic. They are idealists," he added with half-concealed contempt.

As though he wasn't! But at all events he seemed completely reassured. Because Marcel, Faujanet, Delpeyrou —those he knew. It was Judith who had seemed to him, if I may so express it, pregnant with uncertainty.

"I accept," he said at last.

Since he had accepted, it was my turn to state my conditions.

"Listen," I said, "there's one thing I want clearly understood between Malevil and the La Roque town council all the same. The ten rifles, and the two cows from Courcejac, if conceded, will not be gifts to La Roque. They are being put at your personal disposal during the entire duration of your functions in La Roque."

He looked at me critically. "You mean you want them back if La Roque kicks me out again?"

"Yes."

"It might not be so easy."

"In that case," I said, "the rifles and the cows will become elements in a general negotiation."

"More horse trading, you mean," he said with an indefinable air of accusation.

All this, on his side, a little cold. Distant even. I was

564

embarrassed. It was painful for me, taking leave of him like that, without anything to recall the warmth that always marked our relations back in Malevil.

"Well," I said with rather forced bonhomie, "so here you are, mayor of La Roque! Are you happy?" My question wasn't an apt one, as I realized immediately I'd asked it.

"No," he said curtly. "I hope I shall make a good mayor, but I'm not happy."

One blunder always tends to lead to another. Trying to cancel the first I made a second. "Even though you'll be staying with Marie Lanouaille?"

"Even though," he said without a smile, and walked away.

I stood there, his rebuff heavy on my heart. And the fact that I'd deserved it was no consolation at all. Fortunately, however, I wasn't given time to brood too long about the state of my soul. Fabrelâtre touched me on the elbow and asked to talk to me, with a politeness only a hairbreadth away from obsequiousness. I wasn't exactly fond of that long white church taper, with the little toothbrush under his nose and his eyes blinking away behind his steel-rimmed spectacles. And nasty breath into the bargain.

"Monsieur Comte," he said in a quivery voice, "there are people here talking about putting me on trial and hanging me. Do you think that's just?"

I took a good step back, and not solely to discourage familiarity. I said coldly, "I certainly don't think it's just to talk of hanging you, Monsieur Fabrelâtre, not *before* you have been tried."

His lips trembled and his eyes wavered. I felt sorry for the poor flabby creature. But ought I to forget his informer's role over the past months? His complicity in Fulbert's tyranny?

"Who are these people?" I asked.

"What people, Monsieur Comte?" he quavered in a barely audible voice.

"The ones who are talking about putting you on trial."

He gave me two or three names, all of them, needless to say, of people who had remained studiously silent dur-

565

ing Fulbert's reign. And now, Fulbert having been toppled —without their having lifted a little finger—they had begun to play at tough guys.

The amorphous Fabrelâtre was nevertheless no idiot, because he had guessed my line of thought. He said in the same toneless thread of a voice, "And after all, what did I do that they didn't? I just obeyed."

I looked at him. "Perhaps, Monsieur Fabrelâtre, you obeyed just a shade too much."

God, how soft the man was! He shrank into himself like a frightened slug under my accusation. And I've never been able to squash slugs, not even with boots on. I just flick them away as quickly as possible with one toe.

"Listen, Monsieur Fabrelâtre, to begin with, just keep well out of the way. Don't talk to anyone; don't make a fuss. As for your trial, I'll see what I can do."

Then I sent him packing as quickly as I could and turned to meet Burg, who was striding toward me from the far end of the chapel on his short little legs, eyes lively and resourceful, his little cook's pot bobbing in front of him.

"Oh, dear," he said, panting slightly, "if you'd just heard what's been going on with Gazel. Some people have come and told him he's not allowed to say his prayers over Fulbert's grave. Beside himself, poor Gazel is. He asked me to come right out here and tell you."

I couldn't believe my ears. At that moment the stupidity and vileness of the human animal seemed to me to be without limits. Why should anyone go to so much trouble, I wondered, to perpetuate such a nasty little species. I told Burg to wait for me while I went in to see Gazel. On the way I glimpsed Judith and quickly took her to one side.

If I was going to talk to her, she would need something to squeeze. I was used to it by now. I practically offered her my arm.

"Madame Médard," I said, "people are getting impatient, and there's not much time. May I offer you one or two suggestions?"

She bowed her heavy head in assent.

"First, as I see it, Marcel should be the one to present

the list of candidates for your council. And he needs to do it diplomatically. May I be frank?"

"Of course, Monsieur Comte," she said, the broad hand giving my biceps an encouraging squeeze.

"There are two names on that list people are going to shy at a little. Yours, because you're a woman. And Meyssonnier's, because of his former connection with the Communist Party."

"What discrimination!" Judith exclaimed.

I hurried on before she could indulge in an outburst of liberal indignation. "In your case, Marcel ought to emphasize the advantages the council will derive from your education. As for Meyssonnier, he must introduce him as a specialist in military matters, and an indispensable link in the town's relations with Malevil. Not a word about him being mayor for the moment."

"I must say that I admire your tact, Monsieur Comte." Another of her own extremely tactile squeezes.

"If you will allow me, I will go on. There are certain people who want to put Fabrelâtre on trial. What do you think?"

"That the idea is idiotic," Judith said with masculine terseness.

"I am entirely in agreement with you. A public reprimand will be quite sufficient. There are others—or perhaps the same ones—who want to prevent Gazel from giving Fulbert a Christian burial. In short, we have a new Antigone affair on our hands."

Judith smiled shrewdly at my classical allusion. "Thank you for warning me, Monsieur Comte. If we are elected, we will nip all these imbecile ideas in the bud right away."

"And perhaps it would be as well, if I may be permitted to make the suggestion, to begin by revoking at Fulbert's decrees."

"But of course, that goes without saying."

"Right. And meanwhile, since I don't want to look as though I'm pressuring people in any way while they vote, I shall make myself scarce and pay a visit to Monsieur Gazel."

I smiled at her, and after a moment's hesitation she was good enough to hand my arm back to me. Little defects included, she was the salt of the earth, that woman. And I was pretty well certain by now that she and Meyssonnier were going to get on.

Burg led me through a labyrinth of passages to Fulberts bedroom, where I reassured our Antigone—who was as worked up as I'd been told—that I was absolutely determined, come what may, to ensure that the fallen enemy was buried in accordance with the rites of our religion. I glanced at Fulbert's body, then looked away again hurriedly. His face was just one wound. And someone must have stabbed him, for I glimpsed blood on his chest.

Gazel, reassured by the promise of my support, expressed his lively gratitude. He had begun sorting out Fulbert's papers (I suspect him of having an ungovernable old-maidish curiosity), and he offered me back the letter in which, in the name of History, I had laid claim to the suzerainty of La Roque. I accepted. What had been a good move in time of war, to put Fulbert in his place, was no longer apposite in the present state of our relations with La Roque. And there would always be the danger, if the letter was left lying around, that it might one day be used by someone out to make trouble.

As I crossed the château esplanade on my way down to the big green gate, I was enveloped by the late afternoon sunlight and felt myself expand in its warmth. It occurred to me that La Roque's new council would be wise to find a room in the château for the townspeople to hold their meetings in. Possibly it might be less impressive than the chapel, but it could scarcely fail to be lighter and less damp.

Agnès Pimont lived on the main street over the newsstand her husband used to keep, a tiny, very old, very dainty little house in which everything was on the minutest scale, including the very steep spiral staircase that led to the upstairs rooms, which forced me to hold my shoulders sideways in order to get up it at all. Agnès greeted me on the landing and led me into a tiny parlor lit by an equally tiny window. The place had the air of a doll's house, an impression that had always been reinforced in the old days by a windowbox of geraniums on the windowsill overlooking the street. The walls were papered with old gold burlap, there were two dainty little tub armchairs, the tubbiest and tiniest you ever saw, and a large divan, covered like the chairs in blue velvet. One couldn't help wondering how it could possiby have been got into the room in the first place. Certainly not through the window or up that staircase. Perhaps it had always been there, even before the walls were built. It looked old enough for that, even though it was entirely lacking in any discernible style.

On the floor of the little room, between tub chairs and divan, there was a carpet, and on the carpet a Persian rug made in France, and on the rug a white simulated animal fur. I took it that the Pimonts must have inherited the latter two, and that unable to think what to do with them in so tiny a dwelling they had taken the easy way out and just piled them on top of one another. The result was rather cozy. And so was Agnes: fresh, pink, and blond, with those kind, lovely light brown eyes that always gave me the impression, as I said earlier, that they were somehow really blue. She made me sit in one of her little tubs, where I was so low down and so near to the white fur that I felt as though I was actually sitting on the ground at Agnès's feet when she perched herself on the divan.

I always experienced a feeling of intimacy, of warm trust, and also of melancholy in her company. I could have married her, and I didn't. Yet far from bearing me a grudge on that account she still felt this warm friendship for me. I admired her for that. Not one girl in a thousand, I'd say, would have reacted the way she had. And as for me, every time I met her I always thought to myself, and not without regret, There is one of the possible paths my life could have taken. And I would wonder once again what it would have been like. A futile yet tantalizing occupation, because how was it possible to tell? How can any man ever say that he would have been happy with some particular woman without trying the experiment? And if he does try it, why then, however it turns out, however well or badly, the experiment has by then ceased to become an experiment, because it is his life.

One thing was certain anyway. If I had married Agnès

fifteen years before, she would have done me good service. She had aged very little. Or rather, she had aged very well, without fading, without drying up, just becoming slightly—but not excessively—more fleshy. The waist was still charmingly slender, despite Christine, but above and below it everything was generously rounded, and with that complexion of hers, so pink, so fresh, she always had the look of having just stepped out of a bath. She'd done her hair and made herself up while she waited for me, I noticed. And that made things easier for me, because I was well aware that I was going to have the whole weight of a vanished civilization against me in this little interview.

No peasant hemming and hawing, no cobwebby preambles. Although she lived in such a tiny town, Agnès was an urbanite, even though her grammar wasn't muct better than La Menou's. I sank down into my tub chair, I looked her straight in the eyes, trying to still the voice of all emotion, and came straight to the point: "Agnes, would you like to come and live with us at Malevil?"

I had said "with us," not "with me." But I wasn't sure whether at that stage she had quite grasped the distinction, because her clear shin flushed a deep and deeper pink, then a wave seemed to run through her, beginning in her feet and rising till it lifted her breasts. A deep silence. She looked at me, and I tried as hard as I could to stop my eyes saying more than they ought to, so afraid was I that she might misunderstand.

She opened her mouth (a beautiful full-lipped mouth), closed it again, swallowed, then finally brought herself to say, elliptically, "If that would give you pleasure, Emmanuel."

I had feared as much. She was going to turn it into a personal discussion. I would have to make myself more clear. "It's not to me only that you would be giving pleasure, Agnès."

She jumped as though I'd slapped her. All the color ebbed from her face, and with what seemed like a mixture of disappointment and remorse she said, "You mean Colin?"

"I don't mean only Colin."

And when she just stared at me, not daring to under-

570

stand, I explained to her about Miette and Catie, especially about the latter and the failure her marriage with Thomas had been in our community. Again she tried to bring things down to a personal level.

"But, Emmanuel, I could have told you before it happened that with a girl like Catie——"

I cut in on her. "Let's leave Catie out of it, because it's not a question of personalities. At the moment there are eight men at Malevil, and two women. Three if you come too. How can one of those eight claim the sole rights in one of those women? And if he does, what will the others think?"

"But what about people's feelings, then? Where do they come into it?" Agnès said with a vehemence very close to indignation.

People's feelings. Yes, she was in a strong position there. With centuries of courtly and romantic love behind her. I looked at her. "You haven't understood me, Agnès. No one will ever force you to do anything you don't feel like doing. You will be absolutely free in your choices."

"My choices!" Agnès cried. And in that plural she managed to convey a whole world of reproaches. And not only reproaches, because she had never been so near before to a declaration of love. At that moment I was almost ready to let myself be carried away in the tide of her emotion and let her have her way. I took my eyes off her. I remained silent. I needed to summon up my strength. It took me quite a little while to overcome that temptation. But I knew only too well that I must, that any monogamous couple would soon prove incompatible with Malevil's community life. The disproportion between the number of men and the number of women—on which I always based my arguments in our discussions—wasn't really the essential factor. In reality, the choice was one between the nuclear family and the nonpossessive community.

I realized too that I couldn't even tell Agnès what a sacrifice I was making in renouncing her. If I told her, I would only be strengthening her in her "feelings."

"Agnès," I said, leaning toward her, "if only for Colin's sake, it's impossible. If I were to marry you he would feel desperately let down and jealous. And if you married him, I wouldn't be happy about that either. And it isn't just Colin. There are the others too."

Colin was an argument that reached her. And because she could sense my inflexibility in any case, and because she couldn't see herself, even after this, choosing to live in La Roque instead of Malevil, she just didn't know where she was or what to think. So she took a feminine way out that is no worse, after all, than any other. She retreated into silence and tears. I heaved myself up out of my tub, sat down beside her on the divan, and took her hand. She wept on. I understood her well enough. Like me, she was renouncing one of those possible paths her life might have taken, a path she had often dreamed of taking and now never would.

When I saw the tears begin to ebb a little, I held out my handkerchief and waited. She looked up at me, then said quietly, "I was raped. Did you know that?"

"I didn't know. I suspected it."

"All the women here were raped, even the old ones, even Josepha."

When I didn't say anything, she went on: "Is that why you . . ."

I protested. "Agnès, are you insane! There is only one reason, the one I've given you!"

"Because it wouldn't be fair, you know, Emmanuel. Even though I was raped, that doesn't make me a trollop."

"Of course not, of course not," I said vehemently. "It was nothing you could do anything about! It didn't enter my mind!"

I took her in my arms, I stroked her cheek and her hair with a trembling hand. What I ought to have been feeling at that moment was compassion. The only thing I felt in fact was desire. It burst upon me absolutely unexpectedly, and took possession of me wtih a brutality that frightened me. My eyes became vague, my breathing changed. I had just enough clarity of mind left to think that I must at all costs obtain her consent, and quickly, if I didn't want to find myself in the position of having raped her in my turn.

I urged her. I pressed her to answer me. Even though

she lay passive in my arms, she hesitated, she continued to resist, and when she did finally acquiesce, I think it was more because she had been infected by the urgency of my desire than persuaded by my arguments.

We slid down onto the white fur, which thereby proved its usefulness at last, without my affection, my tenderness for her surfacing for even an instant. It was as though I had locked it away, that tenderness, deep in some corner of my consciousness where it couldn't deflate the violence of my physical desire. And I took Agnès roughly, violently, there on her floor.

However, when the first violence of the storm abated, I gave as well as took. And if it is true that one can be happy at different levels, then I was happy at the humblest level of all at that moment. But after all our battles, after all that blood, was there still room for any happiness other than in the survival of the group?

"I no longer belong to myself." That is what I told her as I said goodbye, a little hurt, too, that she could take leave of me with a hint of coldness in her manner, just as Meyssonnier had done a little while before.

When I rejoined Meyssonnier, however, back in the gloom of the chapel, where the meeting had just ended, I found him more relaxed, more friendly suddenly. He came over to me and took me to one side.

"Where have you been? We've been looking for you everywhere. Well, never mind," he added hurriedly, with his usual discretion. "Listen, I've got good news. It went absolutely without a hitch. They elected the whole list. Hardly a murmur. Then Judith proposed Gazel for curé. And he was elected too, by a rather small majority. And finally, carried away by their own enthusiasm, they elected you Bishop of La Roque."

I was flabbergasted. With some cause. To walk out of the little interview I had just had and find myself a bishop! It is true that absence lends added virtues. But if the hand of God was in this, then He was showing an indulgence for the weaknesses of the flesh that belied His reputation.

At the time, however, it wasn't the irony of it that struck me. I protested vehemently. "Me? Bishop of La

Roque! But my place is at Malevil! Didn't you tell them that?"

"Wait, wait! Of course they knew you're not going to leave Malevil. But as I understand it, they want someone over Gazel to keep him in check. They don't want him getting too zealous." He laughed. "It was Judith's idea in the first place. But I backed her to the hilt."

"You backed her to the hilt!"

"Of course. For one thing I agree it's a good thing to have you over Gazel. And for another, I thought it would mean I'd see you more often." And he added very quietly, "Because, you know, leaving Malevil . . ."

I looked at him. Our eyes met. After a moment he turned his head away. I didn't know what to say. I knew what he was feeling. Ever since primary school, Peyssou, Colin, Meyssonnier, myself, we'd always stuck together. Look at Colin, for instance. He'd set up his plumber's business in La Roque, but he'd always gone on living in Malejac. And now that was over. The Club was beginning to break up. I realized it then. For us at Malevil too, it was going to be a wrench, not seeing Meyssonnier.

I gave his right shoulder a squeeze and said rather awkwardly, "You'll see, you'll do damned good work here." That was all I could think of to say. As though doing damned good work ever consoled anybody.

Thomas came over to us and offered me his quiet congratulations. Then it was Jacquet's turn. I couldn't see Peyssou until Meyssonnier pointed him out to me, only a few yards away, firmly and apparently willingly anchored to the spot by one of Judith's strong hands. She was delighted at having at last found a man who topped her by a good head. And while she talked to him she kept letting her eyes wander over his ample proportions. An admiration very much reciprocated, because later, back at Malevil, Peyssou was to say to me, "Did you see that piece? I'll bet you she'd set the feathers flying in the sack, a woman like that!" They hadn't reached that stage yet. For the moment she was just kneading his biceps. And I watched as our big Peyssou, obliging as always, tensed it into a great ball. A turgescence that must have given Judith enormous pleasure.

"Don't pay any attention to how I acted just now," Meyssonnier said. "My morale was a bit low just then."

I was very touched that it had occurred to him to apologize for his coldness, but once I again I could think of nothing to say and remained silent.

"The thing was," he went on, "back there on the road, after the ambush, when you'd left me to go and collect the others from Malevil, I was there quite a while with all those bodies, and my thoughts, well they weren't too gay."

"What thoughts?"

"Well, take for instance now that Feyrac, the one we had to finish off. Well, just suppose one of us came in for a serious wound like that. What could we do? No doctors, no drugs, no operating theater. It would be pretty rotten, watching someone die like that, not being able to help."

I didn't say anything. I'd thought the same thing. So had Thomas, I could tell from his expression.

Meyssonnier went on: "We're right back in the Middle Ages."

I shook my head. "No. Not quite. There's some similarity in our situation, I agree. A day like the one we've lived through today, yes, there must have been days very like it in the Middle Ages. But you're forgetting one thing. Our level of knowledge is infinitely superior. And that's not even counting the considerable body of knowledge represented by my little library at Malevil. All that has survived. And it's very important, surely you see that? Because one day that knowledge is going to enable us to build everything up again."

"But when?" Thomas said disgustedly. "Right now we are just spending our lives struggling to survive. Looters, famine. Tomorrow epidemics. Meyssonnier is right. We're back in the days of Joan of Arc."

"But we're not!" I said vehemently. "How can a trained scientist like you make such a mistake? Mentally we're far better equipped than people in Joan of Arc's day. It won't take us all those centuries to get back to our former technological level."

"You mean just begin all over again?" Meyssonnier said, raising his eyebrows in an expression of doubt.

575

He was looking at me. Eyes flickering. And his question pulled me up short. Mainly because it was he, Meyssonnier —the champion of progress—who had posed it. And because I could see only too clearly what he was envisaging there in the future, at the end of that new beginning.

NOTE ADDED BY THOMAS

It falls to me to finish this story.

A personal note first. After the mob-killing of Fulbert, Emmanuel wrote that he read in my eyes "that mixture of love and antipathy" I had always shown toward him.

"Love" is not exactly the right word. Nor is "antipathy." Admiration and reservations would be nearer the mark.

I would like to explain those reservations. I was twenty-five when the bomb exploded, and for someone of twenty-five I had acquired very little experience of life, and Emmanuel's skill at manipulating people shocked me. I found it cynical.

I am more mature now. I have been called upon to assume responsibilities myself since then. And I no longer think the same way. On the contrary, I now believe that a fair measure of Machiavellism is essential in anyone who wishes to govern his fellow beings, even if he loves them.

As is often clearly apparent in the preceding pages, Emmanuel was always rather pleased with himself and always pretty certain he was in the right. I am no longer irritated by those faults. They were merely the other side of the self-confidence he needed in order to lead us as he did.

And I would like to say this. I do not believe for a moment that a group, on whatever scale, always produces the great man it needs. Quite the contrary. There are moments in history when one senses a terrible void. The necessary leader has not appeared, and everything goes lamentably wrong.

Our problem, despite the smallness of its scale, was no different. At Malevil we were extraordinarily fortunate in having Emmanuel. He maintained our unity and he taught us how to defend ourselves. And Meyssonnier, under his direction, also ensured that La Roque became less vulnerable.

Even though by installing Meyssonnier at La Roque Emmanuel was sacrificing him to the common interest, it must be allowed that Meyssonnier did, in effect, do very good work as mayor. He raised the town walls, and above all he added an extra tower between the two fortified gates. It was a large square structure, the upper story of which was a habitable guardroom, with a fireplace and protected loopholes giving extensive views on all sides. This square tower was linked to the two gates on either side by a wooden gangway running along behind the ramparts. The materials for all this were taken from the ruins of the lower town, and clay was substituted for cement.

Beyond the ramparts, Meyssonnier devised an ADZ with a whole system of traps and obstacles imitated from the one at Malevil. The ground outside, sloping fairly steeply but very open, made the construction of a barricade out of the question; but Meyssonnier found some rolls of barbed wire in the château outhouses, presumably intended for some fencing project, and he used them to close off the two access roads—the metaled road to Malevil and the main road to the county town—with a series of staggered barriers intended to remove the possibility of surprise attacks.

Although Meyssonnier got on well with his council and the townspeople generally—thanks in part to Judith, who thought a great deal of him—he eventually fell out with Gazel on a matter of a religious nature. Meyssonnier, faithful to the promise he had made to Emmanuel, continued to attend Mass and take communion, but he refused absolutely to confess. Gazel, taking up the torch of strict orthodoxy, was determined, like Fulbert, to link communion with confession. Not without courage, he decided to have it out with Meyssonnier in front of the council, and the disagreement became rather bitter, with Meyssonnier refusing any concession whatever. "I don't mind making a public self-examination if I've made mistakes," Meyssonnier said in an ungracious tone, "but I don't see why I should keep my little confession for you alone."

In the end, appeal was made to Emmanuel, in his capacity as Bishop of La Roque. He mediated prudently *and skillfully, listened to both sides, and then instituted a system of community confession, which took place once a week on Sunday mornings. Everyone had to tell the others in turn what he or she felt merited blame in himself and in others, on the understanding, of course, that any person accused had the right to reply, either in order to protest or in order to admit the fault in question. Emmanuel was present, in the capacity of observer, at the first of these sessions in La Roque, and he was so pleased with the result that he persuaded Malevil to adopt the same system.*

Emmanuel called it "washing our dirty linen in public," a very healthy institution, he told me, and quite entertaining too.

He told me how, in La Roque, one of the women had stood up and criticized Judith for being unable to talk to a man without squeezing his arm. That was funny enough, Emmanuel said, but the funniest thing of all was Judith's answer. She was sincerely flabbergasted. "I am not aware of doing such a thing at all," she said in that precise voice of hers. "Are there other persons here who can corroborate this statement?"

"Which just goes to show," Emmanuel added with a laugh, "that it's a good thing to hear how others see us, since we are unable to see ourselves."

At the same time, private confession was abolished totally. And Gazel had to renounce the privilege, one he set great store by, of "remitting" or otherwise the sins of others, a privilege that Emmanuel, it will be remembered, considered "exorbitant" and had never exercised without the greatest unease.

Before hitting upon the ingenious solution that eventually put an end to any possibility of an "inquisition" by the Curé of La Roque, Emmanuel was very concerned for some days over the dispute between Meyssonnier and Gazel. I remember he talked to me about it on several different occasions, and once in particular up in his room, with the two of us sitting on either side of his desk and Evelyne, pale and exhausted, lying on the big bed, recovering from a very acute asthma attack (due, in my opinion, to Agnès Pimont's recent arrival at Malevil).

"You see, Thomas, you can't have two heads to a community: a spiritual head and a temporal head. There must only be one. Otherwise life just becomes an unending series of tensions and conflicts. Any commander in chief of Malevil must also be the Abbé of Malevil. If one day when I'm dead you are elected military leader, then you too must—"

I protested. "You can't mean that! It's against all my opinions!"

He interrupted me vehemently. "No one gives a damn about your personal opinions! They have absolutely no importance! The only important thing is Malevil and the unity of Malevil! You have to get that firmly fixed in your head: no unity, no survival!"

"But all the same, Emmanuel, you can't see me standing up, facing all the others, and beginning to recite prayers!"

"And why not?"

"I'd feel ridiculous!"

"And why should you feel ridiculous?"

The question was articulated with such violence that I was taken aback. Then after a moment Emmanuel went on in a much more relaxed tone, as though he was talking to himself as much as to me. "Is it so idiotic to pray? We are surrounded by the unknown. And because we need to be optimistic in order to survive, we assume that the unknown is kindly disposed toward us, and we ask it to help us."

In any evaluation of Emmanuel's "faith," for lack of any genuinely "committed" texts in his hand, one is free to choose between maximal and minimal hypotheses. I personally feel no need to make any such choice, but I quote the above remarks as tending to confirm the minimal theory.

What follows causes me so much pain to write that I shall say what must be said very quickly and very baldly, with a minimum of details. Magic, unhappily does not exist, for if it did, if by refusing to utter the event I could annul it, then I would remain silent till the end of time.

During the spring and summer months of 1978 and 1979, Malevil and La Roque, by combining their forces, succeeded in destroying two bands of looters. We had established a system of visual and aural telecommunication with our neighbor which enabled us to give each other reciprocal warning in the case of attack, so each could immediately rush to the aid of the other.

It was on March 17, 1979, that the most serious of these alerts occurred. The chapel bell in La Roque suddenly began to ring at dawn, and the exceptional duration of its tolling informed us of the extent of the danger. Emmanuel left Jacquet and the women to defend Malevil, and after three quarters of an hour at full gallop along the forest track the rest of us reached the fringe of the wood a hundred yards from the town walls. What we saw stunned us momentarily. Despite traps, barbed wire, and intense fire from the defenders, five or six ladders were already in place at intervals along the wall. There must have been at least fifty attackers, and we learned later that ten or more had already scaled the ramparts by the time the Malevil forces appeared and took the attackers in the rear, killing many of them with their gun and bazooka fire (it was our turn to have it that particular day) and putting the rest to flight. Emmanuel immediately organized a methodical mopping up of the survivors, who had split up into extremely dangerous small groups and were hiding in the undergrowth. This hunt lasted eight days, during which the entire Malevil forces were almost constantly in the saddle riding up hill and down dale.

On March 25 we knew for sure that the last looter had been killed. Dismounting from Amarante that day, Emmanuel experienced a sharp pain in his abdomen. He was seized with recurrent fits of vomiting and took to his bed with a high fever. At his request, I palpated his belly and pressed the fingers of one hand at the place he indicated. He gave a cry, which he immediately repressed, then gave me a look I shall never forget and said in an absolutely flat voice, "No point going on. It's an appendicitis attack. My third."

During the days that followed he told me that the first two attacks had occurred during 1976, and that he was supposed to have had his appendix out at Christmas. It had all been arranged, his room had even been booked in the hospital, but at the last moment, overwhelmed with work and feeling physically on top of the world anyway, he had postponed the operation till Easter. He added without looking at me, "A piece of stupidity, and now I'm paying for it."

A week after the acute attack on March 25, however, Emmanuel was back on his feet. He began eating again too. However, I noticed that he didn't ride at all and avoided any physical effort. Moreover he only ate very little, was forced to lie down a great deal, and was continually feeling queasy. More than a month went by like that, with him in a state we all hopefully construed as a convalescence but which was in fact merely a remission.

On May 27, during the evening meal, Emmanuel was seized by violent pains. We carried him up to his room. He was shivering, and his temperature had shot up to 106. His abdomen was swollen and hard. This hardness increased during the days that followed. Emmanuel was in appalling pain, and I was horribly struck by the rapidity with which his features changed. In less than three days his eyes had sunk into their sockets, and his face, usually full and on the ruddy side, had turned ashen and lost all its flesh. We had nothing to help him with, not even an aspirin tablet. We prowled around outside his room, weeping with rage and impotence at the thought that Emmanuel was going to die for want of an operation that only a short while before would have lasted a mere ten minutes.

On the sixth day the pain eased off. He was able to drink half the bowl of milk I brought him up that morning, and he said to me, "I'm forty-three. I had a very strong constitution. But do you know what amazes me most? That my body, which has always given me so much joy, should suddenly present me with a reckoning like this before saying goodbye."

And then he looked up at me with his sunken eyes, half smiled with his bloodless lips, and said, "Well, 'saying goodbye' is just a manner of speaking. I'm more inclined to think we shall be leaving together."

That afternoon Meyssonnier came over from La Roque to visit him, as he did every day. Emmanuel, although very weak, questioned him about his relations with Gazel and seemed happy to hear that they were improving. He was entirely lucid. That evening he asked me to gather the whole of Malevil at the foot of his bed. When we were all there, he lay and looked at us, one by one, as though he was trying to engrave our features in his memory. Although he was still capable of speech, he did not utter a single word. Perhaps he was afraid that if he spoke he would be unable to restrain his emotion and we would be forced to watch him crying. Whatever the truth, he contented himself with simply looking at us with a heart-rending expression of affection and regret. Then he signaled to us with one hand to leave him, closed his eyes, opened them again, and as we were leaving asked Evelyne and myself to stay. After that he did not speak at all. At about seven in the evening he clasped Evelyne's hand hard in his and died.

Evelyne asked to be the first to keep watch over him. Since she had made the request in a calm voice, without a tear, I granted it without the slightest suspicion. Two hours later she was found lying on top of Emmanuel. She had stabbed herself in the chest with the little dagger she carried attached to her belt.

Although none of us was an advocate of suicide, no one was surprised, or even shocked. Evelyne's gesture had in any case done no more than hasten slightly an already predictable outcome. All Emmanuel's efforts had succeeded in no more than keeping her alive, and she had always given us the impression that she only clung to life in order not to leave him. We held a meeting, and it was decided unanimously—with the exception of one vote, Colin's—that we would not separate her from Emmanuel and that she should be buried with him. Colin's negative vote—which he justified on religious grounds, although it shocked everyone else—was the occasion of the first dispute that arose among us after Emmanuel's death.

Having thought about it a lot since then, I am no longer surprised by Evelyne and Emmanuel's relationship. Although, before it happened, Emmanuel had decided against monogamy in his life, and although he persisted in that choice after the bomb, for the reasons I have given, I think that the aspiration to a great and exclusive love

582

had never faded in his heart. It was this aspiration that his platonic relationship with Evelyne secretly fulfilled. He had at last found someone he could love with all his might. But she was not quite a woman. And their marriage was not quite a marriage.

Apart from two men posted on the ramparts by Meyssonnier to keep guard, all the inhabitants of La Roque came to attend Emmanuel's funeral, which even along the forest track meant a fifteen-mile walk here and back. It was the first of the annual pilgrimages made by the people of La Roque to the grave of their liberator.

Judith Médard, at the request of the town council, made a rather long speech in which there were certain expressions that went rather over her listeners' heads. Insisting on Emmanuel's humanity, she spoke of "his fanatical love for mankind and his almost animal attachment to the continuation of the species." I remembered that phrase particularly, because it seemed to me very accurate, and also because I had the feeling it hadn't been understood. As she neared the end of her speech, Judith was forced to break off momentarily to wipe away her tears. Everyone was grateful to her for her emotion, and even for her obscurity, since it gave her funeral oration a dignity that seemed suitable to the occasion.

We were not at the end of our griefs. About a week after the funeral, La Menou broke off all communication with her fellow beings, stopped eating, and fell into a state of mute prostration from which nothing and no one could make her emerge. She had no fever, she complained of no pain, she showed no symptom of any kind. She would not even go to bed. All day she stayed sitting on her hearth seat staring into the fire, lips pressed together, eyes empty. At first, when we asked her to get up and come to eat with us, she used to answer, as Momo had so often done when he was alive, "Leave me be, can't you, for God's sake!" Then gradually she stopped answering at all, until one day, as we were all seated at table, she slid off the hearth seat and fell into the fire. We rushed over. She was dead.

Her disappearance left us in a state of shock. We had assumed that the sheer force of her own vitality would carry her over Emmanuel's death just as it had over Momo's. But that was counting without the cumulative effect of two losses one on top of the other. I think too that we hadn't understood the fact that La Menou's energy needed another source of strength to rely on, and that source had been Emmanuel.

After the burial, the Malevil assembly wanted to appoint me military leader and elect Colin Abbé of Malevil. I refused, on the grounds that Emmanuel had always been absolutely opposed to any separation of the spiritual and temporal powers. It was then proposed that I should assume the ecclesiastical functions at Malevil as well as the military ones. Again I refused. Emmanuel's criticism of me before he died had been accurate: I was still pettily attached to my own personal opinions.

It was an appalling error on my part. Because Colin was then chosen to fill both functions in my stead.

While Emmanuel was alive, Colin was shrewd, sweet-natured, helpful, and gay. But he was all those things only as long as he could bask in the affection of Emmanuel, who had always protected him. Emmanuel once dead, Colin took himself for another Emmanuel. And since he had neither Emmanuel's natural authority nor his powers of persuasion, he became tyrannical without becoming any more respected. When I think that I had been half afraid Emmanuel might become Lord of Malevil in good earnest! Emmanuel was the spirit of democracy itself compared with his successor! Colin had scarcely been elected before he stopped convening the assembly and began ruling as an autocrat.

Malevil's new "leader" was soon having serious and almost daily altercations with Peyssou, with me, with Hervé, with Maurice, and even with Jacquet. And Colin succeeded no better with the women. He fell out with Agnès Pimont because he had tried, though without any success, to monopolize her affections. Nor was he any more fortunate in his dealings with La Roque, which, having heard through us of his despotic tendencies, refused to elect him bishop. He was very mortified by this, half quarreled with Meyssonnier, and attempted—unavailingly—to draw us into the quarrel on his side.

It was certainly no easy task to succeed Emmanuel as leader, but Colin's vanity and need for psychological self-aggrandizement verged on the pathological. As soon as he was elected Abbé of Malevil and military leader, he began talking exclusively in the lower register of his voice, became very aloof, shut himself away at table in a haughty silence, and frowned when one of us spoke first. We noticed that little by little he was hedging himself around with a childish system of little privileges and points of protocol which no one could infringe without causing him grave affront. His native shrewdness—which Emmanuel liked to praise—seemed powerless to help him correct the absurdity of his behavior, and served only to make him aware of how much we disapproved of it. He began to think of himself as persecuted. And because he had isolated himself, he felt alone.

Disunity had put down roots in Malevil. There were unpleasant looks, unbearable tensions, and no less unbearable silences. On two occasions Agnès Pimont and Catie both spoke of going back to live in La Roque. These threats of secession did nothing to mollify Colin's attitude. Quite the contrary. He no longer addressed a word to any of the men except to give an order. And eventually there came the moment when he decided to believe that he was in personal physical danger. He began wearing his pistol on his belt all the time, even at the dining table. And as he ate he looked around at us with eyes alternately raging and hunted.

Since everything that was said caused him offense, conversation at table ceased altogether. And that did nothing to lighten the atmosphere. The castle's somber walls began to sweat with boredom and fear.

Colin was terrified of the plots he thought we were hatching, and eventually, of course, we hatched one. We were considering convening the Malevil assembly without his permission and voting his deposition. But we were not given time to put our plan into execution. Before it happened, Colin got himself killed. It was during the course of a battle with a tiny band of looters consisting of no more than six badly armed men. Colin, perhaps counting on regaining some luster in our eyes with a demonstration of his military prowess, exposed himself as insanely as he had done that day in the battle against Vilmain, and he took the discharge of a shotgun in his chest at pointblank range. His face recovered in death the childlike expression and mischievous smile that had led Emmanuel, when they were both alive, to treat him with such indulgence.

After his death I agreed to assume the twin powers in Malevil. I renewed the links of friendship with La Roque that Colin had allowed to lapse, and at the end of another year La Roque elected me bishop.

The harvest in 1978 had been good, that of 1979 even better. I convinced the council of La Roque, with some difficulty, that all future harvests should be considered common property and divided up in proportion to the number of inhabitants. For the moment, two thirds for La Roque and one third for Malevil, since there were ten of us and a score or so of them. In a normal year we gained a great deal from this arrangement, on account of the fertility of La Roque's rich alluvial soil. But I pointed out to them, with justification, I thought, that their flat terrain was much more vulnerable to invasion than our hills. If La Roque's fields were one day ravaged by looters, then they would be only too happy in their resulting state of destitution to receive two thirds of all that we produced.

Meyssonnier, whose allegiance by now had been wholly transferred to La Roque, made no concessions during these negotiations. But I remained resolutely patient and, as Emmanuel would have said, "flexible in my firmness." Back in Malevil, after I had successfully concluded the affair, I was offered warm congratulations by the assembly. "Well, I'll even say this," Peyssou said. "Emmanuel couldn't have done better himself. Do you remember him with Fulbert and the cow?"

Even while Emmanuel was still alive, a veritable cult of the child had developed among us with the introduction to the castle in 1977 of Christine Pimont, then ten months old. We couldn't believe our eyes. She seemed so new among those ancient walls. Although imported, she was our first baby; and adopted by us all with almost insane delights, she spent all her early life in the arms of one or

586

other of us. Constantly carried, coaxed, amused, and played with by everybody, Christine soon began calling all the women in Malevil mama, and all the men papa. When I was elected leader, I decided, with the approval of the assembly, to make this spontaneous practice of hers into a law. For since 1977 other children had been born to us: Gérard, son of Miette; Brigitte, daughter of Catie; Marcel, son of Agnès, who was born four months after Emmanuel's death. Agnès, for obvious reasons, would have liked to call her son by the name of the departed, but I succeeded in dissuading her, and on my suggestion, the assembly of Malevil also forbade that constant search for physical resemblances between the child and its progenitors which I consider an undesirable habit even among couples, and all the more so in a community like ours.

The arrival of Agnès Pimont at Malevil after Fulbert's death upset the balance of power among our womenfolk. Agnès very soon took to the freedom Emmanuel had allowed her like a duck to water, but without ever distributing her favors impartially, as Miette did. Like Catie, she made use of exclusivities, caprices, and coquetry. But she employed them better, with a more accomplished art. In Catie's arms one had the feeling that one was dancing on the brink of a volcano before being drawn into its central fires. Agnès, "gentle and serene as an April stream" (Emmanuel), enchanted you at first by her very freshness, before enveloping you in her flames.

The rivalry between the two women, underground during Emmanuel's lifetime, exploded into an open struggle for power after the death of La Menou. The war of words raged for several weeks before finally degenerating into fisticuffs. At which point Miette intervened, and before the astounded gaze of our sole witness, Peyssou, "beat the living daylights out of the both of them." After which she asked them both for forgiveness, kissed them, and consoled them, thus assuring her future domination as much by her sheer goodness as by her superior strength.

Colin, through his tyranny, made enemies of both the rivals and thus completed their reconciliation. They entered into a league against him and plagued him ceaselessly with their stings. Unhappily, however, they acquired a taste for this sport, extended it to the rest of the companions, and by the time of Colin's death had become quite unmanageable. It required a great deal of firmness and patience on my part to disarm our two Amazons. I think that in their heart of hearts they bore us a grudge for the liberty we allowed them, even though they could not have borne to be deprived of it. I also think that with Emmanuel's death a certain necessary father image had disappeared, and that they felt the loss of it very acutely. I discovered that the three women were given to holding meetings in Miette's room, and I surprised them in there one day. They were all three weeping and praying in front of a table on which they had placed a picture of Emmanuel, as though on an altar. I don't know whether I did right or wrong, but I let them continue. And before long, having first infected the women of La Roque with the same contagion, they had organized that cult of the dead hero that has almost become a second religion here with us.

In 1979, partly thanks to two successive years of good harvest, partly thanks to the agreement I had negotiated with La Roque, Malevil was rich, if you accept an abundance of grain, fodder, and stock as wealth. Moreover, in 1979 we were subjected to only a single incursion by looters, the one during which Colin lost his life. Although still as determined as ever to maintain perpetual vigilance, Malevil and La Roque then held consultations to consider what should be done with this peace, or rather with any interludes of peace that we might possibly be permitted to enjoy.

There was a private discussion first, attended by Meyssonnier, Judith Médard, and myself, followed by a public debate that confirmed the decisions at which we had already arrived.

Fundamentally, the question was that which Meyssonnier and Emmanuel had asked themselves the day we liberated La Roque from Fulbert's tyranny. Apart from the little library in Malevil, we also had the one in the château in La Roque, a collection particularly well provided with scientific works, since Monsieur Lormiaux had been a former student at the Polytechnique, that pinnacle

588

of scientific training in France. So, on the basis of all the knowledge lying there ready to hand—and of our own very modest personal acquisitions—were we going to engage in research aimed at the development of tools to make our lives easier, and weapons to defend them? Or, knowing only too well, from the terrible experience we had just been through, what the dangers of technology were, were we going to outlaw all scientific progress and all production of machines once and for all?

I think that we would have chosen the second of these alternatives if we could have been sure that other surviving human groups, whether in France or farther afield, would not choose the first. For in that case, it seemed incontrovertible to us that those groups, once they held an overwhelming technical superiority over us, would immediately conceive the project of subjugating us.

We therefore made our decision in favor of science, without optimism, without the slightest illusion, all wholly convinced that though good in itself it would always be misused.

At the assembly of La Roque and Malevil during which the problem was discussed, Fabrelâtre, who had been appointed storekeeper for La Roque, called our attention to the fact that our ammunition for the .36 rifles was nearing exhaustion, and that the rifles would be of no further use to us once our last bullet had been fired. Meyssonnier then pointed out that it would doubtless be possible to manufacture simple gunpowder, since there was an old coal mine not far away, there was sulphur available from the sulphur springs, and it would be easy enough to collect saltpeter from our cellars and old walls. As for metal, we had a reasonable abundance of that, with the combined resources of Fabrelâtre's hardware store and Colin's former workshop. There remained only the problems of the casting and crimping, neither of which seemed likely to prove insoluble.

In the end, the general assembly of La Roque and Malevil decided, on August 18, 1980, that practical research into the manufacture of .36 rifle bullets should be instituted immediately and given top priority.

A year has passed since then, and I may say that results

have so far exceeded our expectations that we are at present attacking other projects—still in the realm of defense —considerably more ambitious in their scope. From now on, therefore, we feel increasingly able to put our trust in what the future has to bring. Though "trust," of course, may perhaps not be quite the right word.

The MS READ-a-thon needs young readers!

Boys and girls between 6 and 14 can join the MS READ-a-thon and help find a cure for Multiple Sclerosis by reading books. And they get two rewards—the enjoyment of reading, and the great feeling that comes from helping others.

Parents and educators: For complete information call your local MS chapter, or call toll-free (800) 243-6000. Or mail the coupon below.

Kids can help, too!